W9-BWY-697

Books by Judith & Garfield Reeves-Stevens

Icefire
Quicksilver

Published by POCKET BOOKS

QUICKSILVER

JUDITH & GARFIELD REEVES-STEVENS

POCKET STAR BOOKS
New York   London   Toronto   Sydney   Singapore

A Pocket Star Book published by
POCKET BOOKS, a division of Simon & Schuster Inc.
1230 Avenue of the Americas, New York, NY 10020

ISBN: 0-671-02854-5

First Pocket Books paperback printing June 2000

10 9 8 7 6 5 4 3 2 1

POCKET STAR BOOKS and colophon are registered
trademarks of Simon & Schuster Inc.

Cover design by Tony Greco

Printed in the U.S.A.

For Suzanne Reeves
and
Richard Baldwin.
The only real Americans in the bunch.

There will one day spring from the brain of science a machine or force so fearful in its potentialities, so absolutely terrifying, that even man, the fighter, who will dare torture and death in order to inflict torture and death, will be appalled, and so abandon war forever.

—THOMAS ALVA EDISON

It is a fundamental law of defense that you always have to use the most powerful weapon you can produce.

—MAJOR GENERAL JAMES HENRY BURNS

ORGANIZATIONS

ACLU American Civil Liberties Union
CIA Central Intelligence Agency
CONDEFCOM Continental Defense Command
DELTA FORCE United States Army 1st Special Operations Detachment, counterterrorist response unit
DIA Defense Intelligence Agency
DPS Defense Protective Service
FBI Federal Bureau of Investigation
FEMA Federal Emergency Management Agency
GAI Global Atmospherics, Inc.
GSG-9 *Grenzschutzgruppe 9,* German police counter-terrorist unit
HMX-1 Marine Aviation Squadron 1
KSK *Kommando Spezialkräfte,* German Army Special Forces
MIT Massachusetts Institute of Technology
NASA National Aeronautics and Space Administration
NATO North Atlantic Treaty Organization
NIA National Infrastructure Agency
NIMA National Imagery and Mapping Agency
NOAA National Oceanic & Atmospheric Agency
NRO National Reconnaissance Office
NSA National Security Agency
NSC National Security Council
SAS Special Air Service, British commando force
SEAL U.S. Navy Special Operations Forces (Sea, Air, Land)
USASC United States Army Signal Command
USNA United States Naval Academy
USSPACECOM United States Space Command

TERMS

AFB Air Force Base

AWOL Absent Without Leave

BDA Bomb Damage Assessment

BDU Battle Dress Uniform

C³I Command, Control, Communications, and Intelligence

CINC Commander in Chief

DGZ-1 Desired Ground Zero 1

DSO Defensive Systems Operator

EMP Electromagnetic Pulse

ETA Estimated Time of Arrival

football see Technology under CAT

H&RP Heating and Refrigeration Plant

MARINE ONE Call sign of Marine helicopter carrying the President

mid/mids midshipman/midshipmen

OSO Offensive Systems Operator

RLF Remote Loading Facility

SAM Surface-to-Air Missile

SECDEF Secretary of Defense

SERE Survival, Evasion, Resistance, and Escape

SIOC Strategic Information and Operations Center, FBI

SOP Standard Operating Procedure

THREATCON Threat Condition

TECHNOLOGY

ADEOS-II Advanced Earth Observation Satellite II
CAT Command Authority Terminal
FCG Flux Compression Generator
FORTÉ Fast On-orbit Recording of Transient Events satellite
H&K Heckler & Koch MP5 submachine gun
HARM High-speed Antiradiation Radar Missile
HUMVEE High-Mobility Multipurpose Wheeled Vehicle
JSAMS Joint Service Automated Messaging System
LCD Liquid Crystal Display
MAJIC Multiple Aperture, Joint Imaging Capability
MDF Magnetic Direction Finding
MIR Micro Impulse Radar
NALDN North American Lightning Detection Network
PAVE LOW III Sikorsky MH-53 helicopter
proxcard proximity card
SLAM-II Selectable Lightweight Attack Munition, Mark II
STS-75 Seventy-fifth flight of the Space Transport System (Space Shuttle *Columbia,* February 22 to March 9, 1996)
TSS-R1 Tethered Satellite System Reflight 1
UAV Unmanned Aerial Vehicle
VH-3D Executive transport version of Sikorsky S-61 helicopter

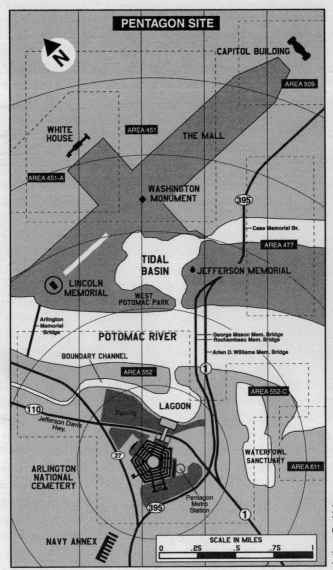

PENTAGON SITE

CAPITOL BUILDING

AREA 509

WHITE HOUSE

AREA 451

THE MALL

AREA 451-A

WASHINGTON MONUMENT

395

Case Memorial Br.

AREA 477

TIDAL BASIN

JEFFERSON MEMORIAL

LINCOLN MEMORIAL

WEST POTOMAC PARK

Arlington Memorial Bridge

POTOMAC RIVER

George Mason Mem. Bridge
Rochambeau Mem. Bridge

BOUNDARY CHANNEL

Arlen D. Williams Mem. Bridge

AREA 552

1

110

LAGOON

AREA 552-C

Jefferson Davis Hwy.

Parking

27

ARLINGTON NATIONAL CEMETERY

WATERFOWL SANCTUARY

AREA 611

395

Pentagon Metro Station

1

NAVY ANNEX

SCALE IN MILES

0   .25   .5   .75   1

Anthony Fredrickson

THE PENTAGON BUILDING

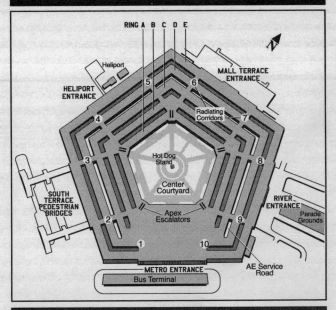

RING A B C D E

Heliport

MALL TERRACE
ENTRANCE

HELIPORT
ENTRANCE

5

6

Radiating
Corridors

7

4

Hot Dog
Stand

3

8

Center
Courtyard

SOUTH
TERRACE
PEDESTRIAN
BRIDGES

RIVER
ENTRANCE

Parade
Grounds

Apex
Escalators

2

9

1

10

AE Service
Road

METRO ENTRANCE

Bus Terminal

Washington Headquarters Services
BUILDING CIRCULAR No. WHS 04-02   **Date:** 10/05/02   **Expiration:** Indefinite
SUBJECT: THREATCON (Threat Condition) Information at Pentagon Entrances.

In order to provide building occupants with timely information regarding the THREATCON level at the Pentagon, the Defense Protective Service (DPS) will be placing THREATCON level information on the police desks at all Pentagon building entrances. THREATCON is a DoD process that sets the level for a terrorist threat condition (as described below) at a given location (in this case, the Pentagon) and is based on existing intelligence and other information.

THREATCON NORMAL
No threat of terrorist activity is present.

THREATCON ALPHA
There is a general threat of possible terrorist activity against installations, building locations, and/or personnel, the nature and extent of which are unpredictable.

THREATCON BRAVO
There is an increased and more predictable threat of terrorist activity even though no particular target has been identified.

THREATCON DELTA
A terrorist attack has occured or intelligence has been received that action against a specific location is likely.

Ref: Operation CLOUDY OFFICE.

THREATCON CHARLIE
An incident has occured or intellignce has been received indicating that some form of terrorist action is imminent.

SCI LEVELS

THREATCON ECHO
A terrorist force occupies a specific location, initiating a series of countermeasures to protect hostages and limit the ability of the terrorist force to resist a counterattack.

THREATCON X-RAY
A terrorist force occupies a specific location which cannot be reclaimed, initiating a series of actions to deny the location and its assets to the terrorist force.

*Ref: Operation CLOUDBURST,
Operation ATLANTIS RISING.*

Anthony Fredrickson

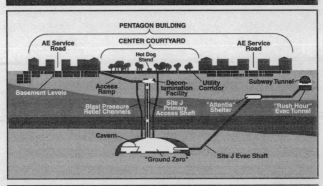

PENTAGON ALTERNATE
NATIONAL MILITARY COMMAND CENTER
SITE-J UNDERGROUND SCHEMATIC

PENTAGON BUILDING

CENTER COURTYARD

AE Service Road

Hot Dog Stand

AE Service Road

Basement Levels

Access Ramp

Decontamination Facility

Utility Corridor

Subway Tunnel

Blast Pressure Relief Channels

Site J Primary Access Shaft

"Atlantis" Shelter

"Rush Hour" Evac Tunnel

Cavern

"Ground Zero"

Site J Evac Shaft

GROUND ZERO

DEPTH
280'
300'
320'
340'
360'
380'

(A) - PRIMARY ACCESS SHAFT
(B) - LEVEL ONE LIVING QUARTERS
(C) - LEVEL TWO COMMAND FLOOR
(D) - LEVEL THREE ACTION FLOOR
(E) - LEVEL FOUR UTILITIES DECK
(F) - COMMAND CENTER
(G) - ATLANTIS SHELTER ACCESS TUBE
(H) - SECURITY ENTRANCE FROM LIFT

(I) - STAINLESS STEEL OUTER SHELL
(J) - 75,000 GAL. POTABLE WATER TANK
(K) - SUPPLY DEPOT
(L) - FREIGHT AND PASSENGER LIFTS
(M) - GENERATORS
(N) - SERVICE RING
(O) - AIR SCRUBBERS / CONDITIONERS
(P) - COMPRESSED OXYGEN TANKS
(Q) - ANTI-SHOCK SPRING PODS
(R) - GRADED BASALT CAVERN FLOOR

Anthony Fredrickson

QUICKSILVER

ARCTIC SHADE
SIX YEARS FROM NOW

**USS _VALLEY FORGE_, THE PACIFIC, 4°18' N, 145°22' E,
FRIDAY, DECEMBER 24**

Five miles from the QUICKSILVER target site, on the starboard observation deck of the USS _Valley Forge,_ United States Army Major Margaret Sinclair took a deep breath of the clean, sea-scented breeze, stared up into brilliant blue sky, and waited for the world to change.

Even as she enjoyed the warmth of the intense equatorial sunshine, she was aware of Air Force Major General Milo Vanovich beside her. Ashen with nausea and thrown off-balance by the slow rise and fall and rhythmic roll of the deck, he was watching her and not the sea.

"Ten more minutes, General. Then we'll have the answer." Though Margaret spoke reassuringly, she knew that after so many years of working together, he'd know exactly what she was really thinking.

But as if to deny he himself felt any trace of apprehension, Vanovich patted the victory cigar he carried in the pocket of his pale blue, long-sleeved service shirt. "Forget about it, Major. It's going to work."

The deck heaved again and Margaret saw Vanovich pull himself close to the gray-metal railing and heard the small moan that escaped him.

She knew how much her old friend hated the ocean, how much he wanted to be back in his office at the Pentagon, the floor solid beneath his feet, away from what he called the creeping stink of diesel fuel and the dying stench of the ocean. And that was on his good days. Only his need to oversee today's test in person had made it possible for him to endure the past three weeks at sea. As it was, he'd been even sicker on this trip than during any of their other naval operations.

In stark contrast, Margaret relished the wild pitch of the waves. In her twelve years in the Army, she'd learned that the wilder the ride, the better she liked it. Which was precisely why, she knew, the general had invited her to join America's newest and most highly classified intelligence agency—the obscurely titled National Infrastructure Agency. As the first director of the NIA, Vanovich made the case to the Secretary of Defense that because his new agency would be involved in activities no one had even contemplated before, he absolutely required operatives experienced in doing what had never been done before. Margaret had been first on his list of operational appointments, and her accelerated promotion to major had quickly followed.

As the deck began to rise again, Margaret discreetly put a hand on the general's elbow to momentarily steady him. She was confident that he would not resent her action. He had never made her feel self-conscious about her gender or her physical appearance.

At thirty-two, Margaret still trained rigorously, running and lifting weights to maintain her compact and athletic build—the habits of her first years in the Army impossible to abandon. She knew her fit appearance was not unappreciated by her male colleagues, but, fortunately, there'd only been a few quickly crushed incidents of attempted fraternization, and only in her first two years of service.

At five foot two, she barely exceeded the minimum height for women in the Army, but she'd been able to turn the possible disadvantage into an asset. Spared the "Amazon" label so frequently applied to taller women in the forces, she'd become convinced over the years that her size, more than any other factor, explained why she was so often underestimated as a potential competitor. Those who were unaware of her background saw her as just another administrator in Army intelligence. And since she was not permitted to wear all the ribbons to which she was entitled, her real history was inaccessible to coworkers without sufficient clearance.

Margaret was comfortable with the subterfuge. She preferred to have the enemy underestimate her abilities and be surprised in defeat than know her strengths and be prepared to deny her victory.

The general, though, knew almost everything about her. Ten years ago, before the NIA, when she'd been a second lieutenant and he a colonel, there'd been a time she worried that his early, admiring encouragement might hide other, more troublesome emotions. But she'd soon realized his interest was that of a mentor, and then, as their working relationship matured, of a friend, even if his friendly attempts at guiding her life hadn't always worked out.

As friends, Margaret was aware that she and the general made an odd pairing, as different in physical makeup as they were in their seaworthiness. Solidly built and balding, Vanovich had a good twenty-five years and half a foot on her, with one of those bullet-shaped heads that rose straight from his shoulders on a neck whose circumference seemed the equal of his skull's. To those who didn't know him, Vanovich's powerful appearance was as deceptive as hers. To those who did, it was obvious that the Air Force hadn't given the gentle general his second star because he was a fierce warrior. They were rewarding his fierce intellect. And they were wise to do so, Margaret thought. A mind like the general's would be priceless on the open market. Perhaps even dangerous.

For a moment, the warm wind lessened and the translucent green swells flattened. As the deck steadied, Margaret saw General Vanovich brighten with relief.

"I'm serious," he insisted. "You're going to be glad you were here. I know it's difficult being away at Christmas . . ."

But Margaret shook her head. She had long ago reconciled herself to the sacrifices an Army career entailed. Fortunately, the few people she remained close to understood. "It's not difficult, sir. I'm proud to be here." She waved a free hand at the other eight officers on the deck, three from the Navy, three Air Force, one each from the Army and Marine Corps, all liaison officers to the NIA. Most were intently peering through their binoculars at the target vessel. "We all are. And," she added, "you should be, too." She knew Vanovich believed that serving one's country was privilege enough. But surely a little bit of pride never hurt anyone.

The ship's public-address system crackled behind her: "At T minus eight minutes, the platform has successfully completed the second stage of its Hohmann transfer and is now on final approach to Alpha Range."

Reflexively, Margaret looked up to the northwest, into a magically peaceful and undisturbed tropical sky, with only a distant front of pure white billowing clouds tracing the horizon. Unseen, 2,400 miles uprange, in silent, inexorable orbit 200 miles above the Earth, General Vanovich's project was approaching, code name: QUICKSILVER. Patiently waiting for the commands that would bring it to life.

Margaret closed her eyes to picture that approach, remembering her first sight of the QUICKSILVER flight model in its hangar at Vandenburg. Excluding its winglike solar panels, the main body was eight feet wide, forty-three feet long. It had a mass of 10,000 pounds, and was completely sheathed in faceted black carbon-fiber panels doped with metal particles to scatter and absorb radar beams as effectively as the skin of a Stealth fighter. A large jagged bell of similar material masked the platform's main thruster to hide its infrared signature during firing maneuvers.

QUICKSILVER wasn't just invisible to the naked eye at its altitude. It was invisible across the entire electromagnetic spectrum. For this initial test, the orbital platform's precise location was known only because it was in constant two-way communication, via the MILSTAR satellite system, with Arctic Shade ground control in Site J, the Pentagon's most secure command-and-control facility.

The PA clicked back to life: "At T minus seven minutes, USS *Shiloh* reports all AEGIS systems are good to go."

Margaret watched as Vanovich gingerly released his grip on the railing to focus his binoculars on the target site. Then, brushing aside a few strands of fair hair that the sea breeze had teased from her tightly knotted chignon, she redirected her own image-stabilized lenses at the horizon. At first, she could see nothing but a glimmering mosaic of sun-topped waves. For a moment, she thought of walking barefoot on a sun-warmed beach, the welcome image one of peaceful relaxation. *Maybe next month,* she thought, *when this is over.*

It had been two years since her last real vacation—an intense Hawaiian interlude with a NATO exchange officer studying NIA counterterrorist strategies. For the first time in her life, she'd allowed herself to be directed by her heart instead of her mind. But even then—she had to be honest with herself—it was because she'd known all along that her suitor's Pentagon tour would last only six months, and then he'd be gone from her life forever. She had complications enough to deal with.

At least, she thought, *I still have one regular guy in my life.* She was confident he'd jump at the chance to accompany her someplace warm in the next month or two. And then Margaret made contact with the target.

The USS *Shiloh* was a gray smear of shadow within the compressed perspective of the binoculars, its hull masts and superstructure dotted with the shimmering points of purpose-built, high-intensity running lights installed for this test. Like the *Valley Forge,* she was a Ticonderoga-class cruiser, one of the most advanced surface combatant ships in the world. She was 567 feet long, 55 feet in the beam, and the top of her mainmast swayed almost 130 feet above the waves.

Both the ship's masts, main and fore, clearly established that the vessel was a product of a new style of warfare, when battles were fought with information as much as with more traditional weapons. To the untrained eye, those dark masts were a confusion of bristling antennae combined with a gray, central spherical radome and two six-foot microwave dishes on an ominous, boxlike, blank-walled forward super-structure. The antennae, in conjunction with others clustered near the bridge, supported the ship's AEGIS combat system, perhaps the most complex and capable integrated threat-assessment-and-response technology in use by the Navy.

Right now, Margaret knew, the *Shiloh* was scanning the sea and the air around it with such high resolution that it could track an incoming missile the size of a football at 500 miles and automatically select an appropriate countermea-sure for it. Against air and sea targets, those available coun-termeasures included 16 Tomahawk cruise missiles, 120 2MR surface-to-air missiles, long-distance naval guns with a range of 14 miles, and the computer-controlled Phalanx Mark 15 gun system capable of firing 3,000 53-caliber rounds out to a mile each minute.

To be certain that the *Shiloh* was operating at the peak of its capabilities, a third naval vessel was also taking part in the Arctic Shade exercise. Twenty miles away, at a depth of one hundred feet, the Los Angeles–class attack submarine *Baton Rouge* was using active sonar to acquire the *Shiloh* as a target. In response, the *Shiloh* was towing its Nixie AN/SLQ-25 torpedo decoy array and standing by to fire its own torpedoes at the closing sub.

Even the *Valley Forge* would add to the information load that the *Shiloh* must contend with, in order to more intensely simulate what was called the fog of battle—that adrenaline-charged environment of fear in which every-thing happened at once, nothing worked as expected, and an instant of indecision could cost hundreds of lives. A *Val-ley Forge* fire-control team stood ready to launch one of the ship's newly fitted land-attack Tomahawk missiles at T minus ten seconds. A second team had already locked a

Harpoon antiship missile on the *Shiloh,* and would fire at T minus five seconds. For safety purposes, both weapons carried dummy warheads filled with sand, and their fuel supplies had been adjusted to ensure that neither could reach their targets. The torpedoes of the *Baton Rouge* and the *Shiloh* had been similarly modified.

At the same time, the *Shiloh* was prepared to launch its own Tomahawk, also with a dummy warhead, at T minus ninety seconds. The locked-in course would take the missile within one mile of the *Valley Forge* before its fuel was exhausted. At T minus zero, all the target ship's phased-array radar sensors would be engaged in active tracking, as would the ship's surface-search and gunfire-control systems.

And, to further ensure that every data-processing and communications system on the *Shiloh* was tasked, one of the ship's two Sikorsky SH-60B Seahawk helicopters was powered up on the *Shiloh*'s rear helipad, rotor turning, though locked safely into its hauldown system.

By T minus zero, the successful implementation of Arctic Shade would mean that every component of the *Shiloh*'s integrated attack and defense systems was fully engaged. Its three generators would be producing a peak of 2,500 kW of power. All 364 of her crew members would be at general quarters, prepared for battle.

And if all went as General Vanovich had explained it would, by T plus ten seconds, one of the most sophisticated fighting ships in the arsenal of the United States would be a useless tub of metal at the mercy of the waves, unable to take any hostile action, yet with every member of her crew unharmed.

"The age of weapons of mass destruction will end today," General Vanovich had declared this morning over breakfast. "We are on the threshold of the era of weapons of mass *disruption.*"

It was Margaret's belief, however, that military history showed that disruption was never an end in itself, only a prelude to more destruction. She had argued, in the debates they'd been having ever since the general had briefed her on his revolutionary project, that QUICKSILVER, though a radical step forward, could only be considered the next logical stage in the evolution of America's defenses. If today's test was successful, the world would change, but not, Margaret believed, because a new era had been reached. It would change because the United States would have successfully fielded a new defensive system that was decades ahead of what any potential enemy could develop, and for those decades, the world would be safer.

In her experience, advances in weaponry never brought lasting peace, they only bought breathing room. Though Margaret understood the general was hoping his gift to the world would be nothing less than an end to war, unfortunately he was not the first to make such a wish. She doubted he'd be the last.

A hatch opened behind her as another officer stepped onto the deck. For a moment, Margaret heard the soft chorus of calm, assured voices from the bridge relating weapons status, system updates, and the closing speed of "the platform." For security, the classified code name QUICKSILVER was not spoken aloud during this exercise. Of the 824 personnel directly participating in today's Arctic Shade exercise, only 26 besides herself and the general knew its true purpose. Everyone else believed the cover story that a new satellite surveillance system was being tested. Even in the Pentagon, except for three assistant directors of the NIA with a critical need to know, only a select few knew what General Vanovich was truly attempting in the Pacific today.

The PA provided another update: "At T minus one minute, fifty seconds, the *Baton Rouge* confirms torpedo launch."

A flush reddened Vanovich's bald spot. Despite her reservations about the true significance of her superior's project, Margaret felt her own pulse quicken. Over the past ten days, she and the general had witnessed the perfect execution of three Arctic Shade rehearsal exercises with this same intricate dance of weapons and warships. Today's test would be the first to add QUICKSILVER's capabilities to the equation.

Through her binoculars, Margaret saw a plume of white smoke and red flame erupt from the gray smudge of the *Shiloh.*

"At T minus ninety seconds, onboard AEGIS confirms the *Shiloh* has launched her Tomahawk."

She let her binoculars drop around her neck. "This is it, sir. You'll be able to follow it better inside on the screens."

But Vanovich shook his head. "I'll watch the tapes later. I'd rather see this with my own eyes."

Margaret understood his decision, to a point. The general had been recruited into the Air Force almost thirty years ago, when short-lived spy satellites still dropped capsules filled with exposed film and the electronics revolution in information acquisition was on a distant horizon. He had been a postdoc at MIT at the time, and the Air Force had courted him for his mind. For all the different ways he said his specialty had changed over the years, from the hand-soldered motherboards of his youth to the nanoengineering and virtual-reality simulations of today, General Vanovich was always extolling the virtues of the hands-on approach.

But in this case, his decision left Margaret with an important question. "Will there be anything to see, sir?"

"Maybe some arcing from the masts. It depends how long the platform maintains contact. The scale was too small for the simulations to be conclusive."

"At T minus one minute, all systems on all ships are good to go. The platform is 300 miles uprange, closing at a speed of 15,600 knots."

Margaret raised her binoculars again. She saw a sudden cloud of debris billow around the *Shiloh*: infrared decoys and chaff to confuse the airborne weapons locked on to the ship.

"At T minus forty-five seconds, platform telemetry reports it has acquired the target. No response from the *Shiloh* AEGIS."

Margaret was impressed. Even in its pre-fire, active targeting mode, QUICKSILVER remained undetectable.

"At T minus thirty seconds, platform has initiated power-up sequencing. . . ."

Margaret glanced away from her binoculars to see Vanovich tensely braced against the deck railing. She knew what he was feeling. Failure in QUICKSILVER's first operational test would threaten his independent control of the project and even, perhaps, of the NIA.

At T minus ten seconds, Margaret's ears rang with the roar of a Tomahawk launch from the *Valley Forge*. Five seconds later, an even louder explosion and thrumming deck vibration accompanied the launch of a Harpoon antiship missile.

". . . four . . . three . . . engagement sequence initialized . . . and platform is engaged at T minus zero."

QUICKSILVER was firing.

Despite her outward appearance of calm, Margaret held her breath, intently peering through her binoculars, though she knew the whole point of the exercise was that there would be nothing dramatic to see.

The Harpoon was above her range of vision but she could track the Tomahawk from the *Valley Forge* as it skimmed the ocean's surface, closing on the *Shiloh*.

Margaret bit her lip. The *Shiloh* herself seemed unaffected. The target ship's high-intensity running lights, which should have winked out the instant QUICKSILVER fired, were still clearly visible, each one blazing away.

Almost unnecessarily, the PA confirmed the bad news. "T plus five seconds, no effects registered. *Shiloh* AEGIS remains fully operational."

Margaret couldn't look at the general. She kept her binoculars focused on the ocean's surface where she saw a fountain of water spray up as the Tomahawk from the *Valley Forge* dropped safely from the air, out of fuel. Just as it had during the rehearsal exercises.

QUICKSILVER was a failure. There was nothing to show for Vanovich's almost eight years of work. Not even one faint spark from the *Shiloh*'s mast.

"General," she said, "I'm sorry. I—"

A blade of silver fire pierced the *Shiloh*.

Margaret stared up at the huge, shimmering sheet of something molten and metallic, hundreds of feet wide, miles high, that suddenly connected the heavens to the sea. In an instant, the *Shiloh* was enveloped in a writhing web of blue-white lightning, the whole scene eerily silent because of the distance.

Margaret looked to Vanovich for some explanation. How could a discharge like this be possible? In all his briefings, the general had stressed that the absolute power output of QUICKSILVER could be measured merely in tens of kilowatts, enough to light a house but little more.

Then the first shock wave of sound rolled over the *Valley Forge*. Its massive, stuttering boom drowned out the unintelligible, shouting protests of the officers on the observation deck.

Margaret turned back in time to see the *Shiloh* wrenched from the sea, its almost nine-and-a-half-thousand-ton mass raised twenty feet above the waves, thirty feet, water streaming from her exposed hull. Suddenly, shockingly, the *Shiloh*'s hull shattered like glass, the edges of each jagged shard flaming with coronal discharges.

Then the target ship vanished in multiple, soundless flashes of chemical explosions, as all her munitions ignited at once.

A cloud of fire replaced the *Shiloh*. At Margaret's side, General Vanovich stood rigid at the railing, stunned into silence with the rest of the incredulous observers on the *Valley Forge*. QUICKSILVER was supposed to disrupt computer circuits and overload transformers—to stop machinery, not destroy it.

Margaret flinched as the fiery cloud shot out blistering tendrils of lightning so intense that black spiderwebs embroidered her vision.

One madly snapping whip of incandescent fire snaked upward to strike the Harpoon missile and hurl it from the sky.

Then another jagged bolt leapt the five-mile gap between the *Shiloh*'s death cloud and the *Valley Forge*.

Margaret heard Vanovich cry out a warning and in the same instant, she was slammed against the observation deck as if the bolt's roll-clap of thunder were a physical blow, crushing her, deafening her, filling her entire body with a sound of such intensity that she could no longer hear it, only feel it.

The rough deck reverberated beneath her outstretched hands. She sensed other explosions, other screams. She lifted her head to locate the general, but a glowing fog of impenetrable light suffused everything around her.

For a disorienting moment, Margaret felt light, not air, physically enter her mouth. Instinctively, she gasped and felt a hot wind scorch her throat. As she struggled to draw breath, the electric scent of ozone stung her nostrils.

Then, as quickly as if a switch had been thrown, QUICKSILVER's attack ended.

Margaret got shakily to her feet, limbs trembling. Her ears still rang with the echo of the thunderbolt. Supporting herself against the deck railing, she stared out to sea. A faint and turbulent sheet of incandescent air now sparkled like evaporating mist above the cloud of smoke and burning streamers of debris that marked the *Shiloh*'s last position. The funeral pyre of her 364 crew.

Vanovich staggered to the railing beside her. Neither he nor she even attempted to speak. As one, they looked up to the brilliant blue sky, once again pure, peaceful, undisturbed.

Unseen, miles downrange, in silent, inexorable orbit high above the Earth, QUICKSILVER flew on. Patiently waiting for the commands that would bring it to life once again.

Not as a defensive system. But as a weapon. And everything Margaret had learned about the history and progress of war told her a weapon of such destructive capability could not remain unused for long.

The world *would* change, but not as General Vanovich had intended.

Whatever happened next was up to the Pentagon.

CLOUDY OFFICE

SUNDAY, JUNE 19
SIX MONTHS LATER

ONE

UNITED STATES NAVAL ACADEMY/ANNAPOLIS, MARYLAND

They had stolen her underwear.

Again.

Amy "Nuke" Bethune cursed like the sailor she hoped one day to become as she charged down the empty corridor on the third floor of Wing Three of Bancroft Hall, the hem of her tightly clutched b-robe flying behind her. Three years at the United States Naval Academy and everything she had done to earn her place as an equal among her classmates had come to nothing. She was still treated this way.

Not by the men. But by the other women.

Amy skidded to a stop on the slickly polished linoleum outside Midshipman Annika Marsh's dorm room. Marsh's name and graduating year were cut into the white plastic ID plate on the door, the color to alert other mids that this was a room for females. Male mids had their names cut into black plates.

Amy had targeted this room for two reasons, the most

important being that Marsh was about her size. She knew that some might think she was about to take a strong initiative that would violate the Academy's honor concept, the solemn vow to never lie, cheat, or steal. But it was the only way she could complete her duty for today. Besides, the honor concept also stated that midshipmen were to ensure that others were able to benefit from the use of their own property. *So it's not stealing,* Amy told herself, *it's emergency borrowing.* The distinction made what she had to do a bit easier to justify. But not by much.

Amy pushed hard against the metal doorplate and the oversized, heavy door swung open as she knew it would. The level of trust among the Academy's 4,000-strong brigade of midshipmen meant that virtually none of the dorm-room doors was ever locked, except during long absences over holiday and vacation breaks. Considering that Marsh was more than likely one of the masterminds behind the disappearing underwear, though, Amy was surprised that her classmate seemed unprepared for retaliation.

Marsh's dorm room was the size of a small and spartan studio apartment, identical to Amy's and typical of the Hall. There were two narrow bunk beds, one to either side, with a built-in desk beneath each, and two closets along the wall. In one corner was a shower and sink—an absolute timesaving necessity when 4,000 midshipmen had to follow identical schedules.

But Amy took no time to study the room. She headed straight for the cupboard unit built in against the end of Marsh's bunk, trying not to think what might happen to 12th Company's status if she were caught in the act.

Twelfth Company was Amy's cadre of 124 fellow mids from plebes to Firsties, one of the 36 companies making up the Academy's brigade of midshipmen. It was also the Academy's current Color Company, an honor it had earned for the past three years. Amy considered it no coincidence that 12th Company's ascendancy had begun when she had joined it. Points in an Academy-wide competition were awarded for academic, athletic, and professional excellence. Her performance in the classroom and on the diving team had added significantly to 12th Company's point score. This past year, she and her cadre had accumulated 320.6 out of a possible 360. Her accomplishments had also, obviously, raised her profile among the company to the point where her textbooks had begun disappearing, her e-mail account was regularly acquiring new passwords, and—as had happened this morning—her alarm clock could no longer be trusted.

For all that the Academy made a point of searching out young men and women who would excel in the Navy and Marine Corps, Amy was painfully learning that it also hewed to a military culture which valued team solidarity over individual achievement. Somewhere, unofficially, there existed an invisible boundary between excellence and independence. Marsh, among others, apparently thought Amy Bethune had crossed it.

But as Amy quickly searched through the stack of drawers in Marsh's cupboard, trying to find the midshipman's underwear, she rebelliously thought again that it was not her obligation to hold herself back in her quest for the controversial career goal that had earned her her nickname. Rather, it was her classmates' obligation to raise themselves to her standards.

Some might call—and had called—her attitude arrogant. To which Amy always replied, Welcome to the real world. If people didn't like her being the best at what she set out to do, then it was their mission to try to do even better. If they weren't prepared for that challenge, they'd soon find out that their only other choice was to get out of her way.

She hit pay dirt in the third drawer down. A sports bra and briefs, both, fortunately, still folded from the laundry. She quickly rifled through the remaining stack to see if she had the luxury of a choice in what she appropriated, but the only other option, crammed out of sight at the bottom of the stack, was a flaming-pink combo: transparent above and little more than a G-string below. Definitely not regulation.

As a calling card, Amy draped Marsh's racy weekend underwear over the green shade of the lamp beside the desktop computer, confident that even such flagrant disorder would be unlikely to cost Marsh a demerit. Commissioning week, when the latest class had graduated and all other classes moved up one year, had come and gone three weeks ago, putting the Academy into summer-leave and summer-training mode. That meant the Yard was noticeably less populated, especially on weekends, when not even the high-school students brought in for one of three introductory summer seminars were present. Room inspections, a frequent fact of life during the other semesters, especially for plebes, were almost nonexistent.

In fact, there were no plebes at the Academy right now. Most mids who had completed their plebe year, and were now officially Youngsters, were off patrolling New England ports on the Academy's unarmed Yard Patrol craft, training on the Academy's forty-four-foot sailing sloops, or taking part in joint maneuvers that simulated SEAL and Marines Corps exercises. The second-class students, those entering their third year, were getting firsthand introductions to naval aviation at Pensacola or to submarine operations off Florida, or fighting war games with Marines in the wilds of Virginia. And most new Firsties, like Amy—those midshipmen who had been raised to their fourth and final year—were serving as junior officers in operational fleet squadrons around the world. Except for the volunteers from 12th Company.

As the Academy's Color Company, they had earned special privileges and duties for the academic year, including the honor of representing the Academy at official government functions. And few events in recent memory were as official or as historic as today's at the Pentagon. Which was why forty-two second-, third-, and fourth-year midshipmen had responded to Commandant Rigby's invitation to give up part of their precious three-week summer leave to volunteer for a special honor detail: attending the President's NATO ceremony.

Every mid knew that even if they were to do little more than seat dignitaries and help set tables, their participation in what was surely to become one of the defining moments of the new century would forever mark their service records apart from others. To say nothing of the opportunity to clock face-time with the top brass.

But it was equally clear that there were those in the company, besides Marsh, who didn't want Amy to be able to share in that distinction and opportunity. Unfortunately for them, they obviously hadn't yet learned that Nuke Bethune was impossible to stop. She'd make it the way she always did— on her own. Determinedly clutching the borrowed underwear, Amy flew out of Marsh's room, bare feet slapping the floor.

Back in her own room, she slammed the door behind her and checked her watch. That action was ingrained in every mid from his and her first day of induction. As many as fourteen times every day, Academy students were subject to accountability—the requirement to establish their presence at a specific place at a specific time, from class attendance to bed checks. Punctuality became instinctive, which was all the more reason Amy pushed herself this morning. Being late was unprofessional, and unacceptable.

The time right now was 6:51. The bus was scheduled to leave from the seaward side of Macdonough Hall at 0700. Reaching it in time was just within the realm of possibility. Just.

She threw off her b-robe, dragged on Marsh's regulation underwear, then grabbed the pristine set of summer whites hanging in her closet. She yanked up her skirt zipper, took a few precious extra seconds to tie her shoes tightly, then crammed her cap onto her unruly chestnut brown hair—disastrously thick but short enough to meet regulations and take care of itself without wasting valuable time. She stuffed her wallet and her Pentagon day pass into an inner pocket of her dress jacket, then burst from her room into the corridor, blouse still undone, but on her way at last.

As she had anticipated, there was no one in Bancroft to see her careen down the wide stairs, holding the metal handrail tightly at each landing in order to whip around at full tilt, open jacket and blouse a double-layered cape behind her.

By the time she exploded from the foyer onto the broad stone steps leading down to Tecumseh Court, she had enough buttons done up for propriety's sake, and brought her speed up to maximum. She gave no thought to pacing herself. This was an all-or-nothing effort. Either she'd make the bus with ample time to catch her breath and straighten herself out on the ride to Arlington, or she would fail and nothing more would matter.

And Nuke Bethune *never* failed. The word was not in her vocabulary.

But a minute later, it was clear her vocabulary was in need of revision.

As she breathlessly rounded the eastern wing of Bancroft Hall, Amy caught sight of the gleaming silver-and-blue Academy VIP bus pulling out from the Macdonough Hall parking lot to turn right on Holloway Road.

Amy flung herself after the bus in futile pursuit. Waving her arms wildly, she leapt from the narrow concrete pathway to the edge of the parking lot, shouting as much in frustration as in any hope of attracting the bus driver's attention. But the bus disappeared behind the hall in seconds, and she reluctantly stumbled to a halt.

One more minute and I'd have been on that bus. The simple recognition of her tactical situation was as close to self-pity as Amy could allow herself to come.

Drenched in sweat, her dress blouse ruined, she leaned over to rest her hands on her knees, gasping deep lungfuls of humid air. It was supposed to reach an unseasonable ninety-five degrees today, and even this early in the morning the June heat was verging on oppressive. But she pushed physical comfort to the side. Her mind churned with alternative scenarios.

She could jog back the way she had come, head for Gate One just past Lejeune Hall. She could use a phone in the guardhouse. But for what?

There was no public transportation between Annapolis and Washington, let alone Arlington, Virginia. She didn't have enough cash to take a cab all that way and she knew her maxed-out Visa card couldn't take the strain, either. This early in the summer, she was still drawing second-class midshipman's pay, which, after deductions for everything from laundry to the payments for the Academy-assigned computer, netted her slightly less than two hundred dollars cash each month.

Which left her with only one solution. The Harley.

Amy had no idea how her summer whites would fare on the thirty-five-mile drive to Arlington. And she doubted the security arrangements at the Pentagon would permit her to take the cycle onto the grounds. But showing up on time in a deficient uniform was better than not showing up at all. Marginally, at least.

Amy made her decision in less than a second—another benefit of Academy training. She'd sprint back to her room, get the key to the Harley, then leave the Yard and run the three blocks to the garage she rented in town. Technically, no midshipman was authorized to operate or even maintain a motorcycle within twenty-two miles of the Academy—the most common cause of death for mids was traffic accidents. But that cycle had been in Amy's life as long as she could remember, and Commandant Rigby had personally signed the special-request chit that had given Amy permission to keep her father's cycle within the town's liberty limit, provided she rode it only during vacation leaves.

But Amy was certain the Dant wouldn't object to her planned use of it today. And regardless of what the Dant might think or do, she wasn't about to let Midshipman Marsh or whoever had set her up this morning win this round. With any luck, Amy decided she might even be able to catch up with the bus and talk her way back on before it reached its destination.

Decision made and strategy outlined, Amy started the run back to Bancroft Hall, filled with new purpose. She had been an attentive student for the past three years. As the Navy would expect of those selected for the Academy, Midshipman Bethune was thoroughly trained to accept no other outcome but victory.

No matter what the cost.

Half a mile away, in the air-conditioned comfort of the Academy's VIP bus, Midshipman Annika Marsh was exceptionally pleased with herself.

As she had known it would, the bus had pulled out of the parking lot at precisely 0700 hours. And, as she had hoped, Nuke Bethune wasn't on it.

It was a sweet plan. Today's honor detail was volunteer duty. No demerits would accrue to the company if one of its members screwed up. So Bethune's failure would be completely her own, not shared.

It would be a particularly fitting punishment, because that was exactly how Bethune had chosen to pursue her naval career—on her own. Now maybe her egotistical classmate would see what the result of not being a team player could be. And far better she learn it here than on a warship where the lives of her fellow sailors could be at stake.

Her objective achieved, Marsh gazed contentedly out the bus window, watching the lofty green elms and quaint antique buildings of the Academy pass by. Few of her classmates spoke, and those who did kept their voices low. Marsh approved of their demeanor. They weren't midshipmen off on an excursion. They were naval officers on a mission. The excitement was real, but suppressed. Marsh knew the unspoken question all shared was who, if any, would be assigned to the President's table.

The guards at the blue-awninged Gate One security post raised the traffic barricade and the bus pulled out onto the peaceful Sunday streets of Annapolis, in bright, early-morning sun. In just a few hours, as day tourists and week-end sailors descended on the small town, the narrow down-town streets, most dating back to pre-Revolutionary times, would become impossibly congested.

It was a glorious morning and Nuke Bethune had been taught a lesson. Already, Marsh knew this was going to be a perfect day, made even better by the certainty that she her-self would be a participant, no matter how minor, in a truly momentous occasion.

The bus quickly left the historic sections of Annapolis behind as it headed northwest to Highway 50, just outside the city limits. The newer streets here were wider and smoother, and few other vehicles were on the road. The only interruption occurred on the approach to the new con-struction on the twisting interchange between 70 and 50. As the bus slowed, Marsh craned her neck to see a portable traffic-advisory sign announcing closed lanes ahead. Behind it, a row of orange plastic traffic cones snaked into the overpass tunnel, shutting down both right lanes. A young highway worker in an orange safety vest and hard hat held up a stop sign as he listened to a hand radio.

The Academy bus downshifted and hissed to a stop. All the midshipmen looked ahead, questioning the delay. Then the curved concrete wall of the overpass tunnel glowed with light and a red pickup truck with its headlights on sped out. Marsh saw the young worker say something into his radio, then he turned his sign around. Now it read SLOW.

The bus rocked to life again, pulled into the oncoming lanes, then entered the tunnel. Marsh half-expected the bus to start splashing through water. Whatever had prompted the highway department to send out a repair crew on a Sunday morning, she knew it would have to be something drastic, like a broken water main.

As the bus crawled through the dark tunnel, Marsh noticed that the lights running along both walls were not working. She peered through the side window, catching the reflection of regular flashes of red light up ahead. That explained it. A traffic accident. Marsh impatiently tapped a finger against the laminated Pentagon security pass she wore on a chain around her neck—every mid on the bus wore one.

Sure enough, at the deepest bend of the tunnel, the bus stopped again. A large, silver tractor-trailer was parked to the right, angled across three of the tunnel's four lanes. The red flashing lights came from two white cars blocking the one free lane remaining.

Marsh pushed herself up from her seat to look over the heads of the midshipmen in front of her. She didn't see any insignia on the cars, and the flashing lights were portable, held on to the roofs by suction cups. Maybe the cars were unmarked police vehicles. Maybe it wasn't an accident. Maybe it was an arrest.

Eight men, all in orange safety vests and hard hats, were grouped by the gleaming silver tractor-trailer, the unmarked white cars, and now, in front of the bus. Still looking ahead through the large front windows, Marsh saw one of the men approach the bus, holding up an open badge case.

At any other time, Marsh would have been interested to know exactly what was going on here. At some level, everyone who joined the Navy looked forward to a life of action, so three years of classrooms and training maneuvers at the Academy could take their toll on a mid's enthusiasm. But today, instead of wondering if there were escaped criminals in the area, Marsh was anxious to move on. Especially since she didn't put it past Bethune to try and catch up with the bus on her Harley.

Of course, Marsh thought smugly, first she'd have to find the key to the Harley, and old Nuke wasn't likely to do that anytime soon. Marsh ran her fingers over the key's outline, where it rested secure in her jacket pocket.

The conversation level in the bus increased as the driver opened the front doors and the man holding up the badge ran up the stairs. He was in his thirties, Marsh estimated, lean, though his broad face was full-featured. He also looked as if he had had a recent sunburn. His reddened cheeks contrasted strongly with his short, almost military-style black hair, though his long, wide sideburns were definitely not regulation. The driver, a civilian assigned to the Academy's transportation department, leaned forward to examine the man's badge. At the same moment, the red-faced man suddenly struck him down with the dark object he held in his other hand. The driver slumped sideways, half out of his seat.

Marsh didn't have time to be startled by the unexpected violence of the action. The man in the vest was facing the bus full of midshipmen, screaming hoarsely as he waved the handgun he had used to fell the driver.

"HANDS ON YOUR HEAD! NOW! NOW! NOW!"

Even as she slowly began to raise her hands, Marsh felt empowered at the sudden charge that crackled through the bus. She was in the company of forty-one of the Navy's finest young men and women on this bus. Everyone had trained in hand-to-hand combat. Everyone knew small arms. Everyone had slogged through Virginia swamps with Marines.

The enemy didn't have a chance.

Marsh knew she and her classmates all shared a single thought: *They* were going to shape this battle space, not one lone, crazed civilian with a gun.

Marsh began thinking tactics. The two mids sitting in the front seats, just an arm's length from the enemy, were Bragonier and Shelton. With them was Lieutenant John Roth, an ethics instructor at the Academy who had volunteered to serve as the company's liaison today. The lieutenant also helped train the Academy's power-lifting team, and he had the broad shoulders and solid physique to prove it.

With those three capable sailors up front, the tactics of the situation were clear. Roth would jump the enemy, one mid would take his gun, and the other would take over the bus and ram it through the cars blocking the fourth lane. It was as simple as that.

And then the man in the vest stopped shouting, swung his gun to the side, and shot Lieutenant Roth in the head.

The abrupt noise of the gun's explosion shocked Marsh as much as the sight of the back of the lieutenant's head exploding outward in a geyser of blood.

When he spoke again, the red-faced man no longer shouted. His words were succinct, crisp, and unhurried. "You have been subdued by a superior force. If one of you resists, you will *all* be killed. Is that understood?" Deep within, Marsh responded to the cadence and sincerity of his speech—the voice of command. This was no civilian. The enemy was an officer.

With no hesitation now, everyone's hands clasped the back of their heads. Marsh's heart was racing. This was the real thing. But she was still prepared for the consequences of action. There was no way the man was getting off this bus, except as the Navy's prisoner. The rest of her company had to be feeling the same way.

A second man now stepped onto the bus. His features were almost chiseled, his tanned skin smooth and unlined, his military-short hair luminously blond. Although he wore faded orange workman's coveralls, the second man had the same intent manner as the first and Marsh concluded he must also be a soldier.

"Put your passes in the case," the blond man ordered as he began walking down the aisle, holding out a well-worn, soft-sided, black leather attaché case that opened from the top. To Marsh, his clipped accent sounded almost British.

At the same time, at the front of the bus, the gunman had placed his weapon two inches from Midshipman Shelton's forehead. "If anyone does not give up his pass," he warned, "this woman will die."

Marsh heard someone in one of the front seats begin to vomit. Her gaze traveled to the side window near Lieutenant Roth's body. Rivulets of blood and bits of tissue were slowly dripping down the glass. Marsh's own stomach tightened. When her time came, she surrendered her laminated Pentagon security day pass and its neck chain without resistance. Like her classmates, she knew, her mind was working furiously, seeking the right time to take action.

His mission accomplished, the blond man walked backward up the aisle to the front of the bus, where the gunman waited with Shelton.

Now! Marsh thought, barely able to keep her seat. This was the moment.

And it was.

Just as the blond man with the case reached the gunman's position, the gunman stepped aside to allow him access to the steps that led out of the bus. For that instant, Marsh knew the gunman's contact with Shelton was momentarily deflected, and he'd lost sight of Bragonier.

The two midshipmen acted at once, leaping forward from their double seat, Bragonier tackling the man with the case, Shelton engaging the gunman.

Then every member of the company was on his and her feet. Marsh couldn't see anything. She heard a cry of pain, a muffled gunshot, shouts of victory, and then a jarring explosion of glass as a fusillade of bullets blew out the middle-right windows of the bus.

Marsh ducked in the aisle as she heard screams. A fine spray of blood rained across her white skirt and jacket. More gunmen outside the bus. With automatic rifles.

Someone up front screamed. "Get him! Get him!"

The gunfire stopped. Marsh lifted her head. The two men were gone. Shelton's body hung limp across a seatback, her dark face a ragged scarlet mass without features. But Bragonier was behind the wheel, the unconscious driver sprawled in the aisle beside him.

The bus engine revved violently, but Marsh felt no motion. Then a wet hand gripped her knee. Midshipman Fisher. In the aisle. His white jacket sodden with blood.

Four weeks ago, Joe Fisher had been only a plebe. Just turned twenty. Fresh blood trickled from the corner of his mouth as he moaned words she couldn't hear. Marsh's body trembled with outrage. To hurt one member of a company was to hurt everyone. The enemy had to pay for what they had done.

The bus engine revved again. This time Marsh heard gears grind. Felt the bus rock with renewed life.

She grabbed Fisher's slippery hand. "We're going to

win . . ." she vowed fiercely. Nothing could stop 12th Company.

She leaned forward, tensely anticipating the forward lurch, but the bus only vibrated as its gears ground more loudly.

Given their helplessness, Marsh didn't understand why the gunfire had stopped. The ambush had been perfect. Why would the enemy let them escape without renewing the attack?

Then she heard more glass breaking at the back of the bus. She twisted around and saw a dark green, hat-sized, disk-shaped object hit the aisle with a thud, then vanish in a sudden swirl of white fog.

In a heartbeat, the mist swept forward with the cutting smell of ethylene oxide.

A terrible understanding possessed her as she remembered the scent from her summer in Virginia. She knew what would happen next.

That's why they're not firing, she thought. *They don't have to.*

Annika Marsh squeezed Joe Fisher's hand tightly, offering the only comfort she could. Then she closed her eyes, took a last breath, and wished she'd missed the bus like Nuke Bethune.

Every intact window in the Academy bus blew out at once, accompanied only by a dull thud and a dim yellow flash.

Ranger, the blond leader of the intercept platoon—four squads of four men each—rubbed his hand over his close-cropped hair and allowed himself a moment to exhale. The first stage of the operation had played out almost perfectly.

The SLAM-II, a fuel-air-explosive version of the U.S.

Army's Selectable Lightweight Attack Munition, had lived up to specs. It had neutralized everyone in the bus's passenger compartment without causing appreciable structural damage to the vehicle or risking a collateral detonation of its fuel system. He'd specifically chosen this variation of the weapon because it had been developed for close-quarters urban combat, when mission objectives deemed it desirable to kill enemy personnel without destroying civilian structures. Instead of projecting its lethal energy from a single ignition point, as with conventional explosives, the SLAM-II first released a volatile gas which expanded to fill a contained space, then detonated the entire volume at once.

For the midshipmen who had been on the bus, Ranger knew, it was as if they had been embedded in the explosive matrix. The SLAM-II pressure wave came from all sides at once, ensuring that there would be no blast-shadow areas of survival. For those who had, in their last second of life, inhaled the gas, even the air in their lungs would have ignited. But despite the blast's lethality, the overall pressure in a confined space would barely be enough to cause cracks in drywall.

Now, even as the last glittering fragments of shattered safety glass bounced along the tunnel roadway beside the motionless bus, Ranger circled his hand in the air.

With rehearsed precision, two figures in highway-worker coveralls swung open the rear doors of the silver tractor-trailer that blocked three of the four lanes in front of the bus. Just as quickly they pulled out the two long tire ramps stowed inside. The harsh metal clatter of the ramps banging on the asphalt joined with the sudden, deep rumble of a diesel engine turning over inside the trailer.

Ranger motioned to a third figure, who immediately

wrested open the front doors of the Academy bus and leapt over the bloody pile of limp bodies to reach the driver's seat. The bus engine was still running—the midshipman who had attempted to drive the bus had not known how to put it in gear.

Ranger's commandos needed no more instructions. Accompanied by Norway, the senior communications member of the first squad, Ranger jogged over to the nearer of the two white LeBarons that blocked the fourth lane of the tunnel.

He placed the attaché case containing the collected security passes on the roof of the car, then quickly shrugged off his faded orange overalls to reveal the spotless summer-white dress uniform of a naval lieutenant. The name on his ID badge read ROTH.

As he expertly straightened his shirt and belt, he saw Norway fingering the gun in the hidden holster in the orange safety vest he wore. During the training simulations, the communications officer had insisted that the midshipmen of 12th Company would not have enough experience to recognize a hopeless situation. Norway's prediction that they would foolishly resist had been correct.

Ranger, in truth, had been surprised by the midshipmen's actions. In the tactics sessions, though he had conceded that their young targets would have little experience in combat situations and so could possibly misjudge the strength of their position, he had not expected them to resist. These days, few in America had any stomach for death—especially their own.

In the end, though, whatever the reaction of the targets had been, Ranger knew it was unimportant to the final outcome of the mission's intercept stage. Holding prisoners, even for the short duration of the full operation, had never been an option. The violence of this encounter had been strictly scripted by necessity. The Pentagon passes had to be recovered undamaged and on schedule. Norway's authorization to shoot one passenger at random at the beginning had actually been useful to hasten the collection process. Ranger regretted the violence—*As would any good officer,* he thought—but accepted that it was unavoidable to serve the greater good.

Three minutes after the SLAM-II's detonation, Ranger heard the chirp of Norway's radio. It was the flagman at the tunnel's west entrance reporting that three civilian cars were waiting to pass. Ranger instructed Norway to radio back his response: The tunnel would be clear within two minutes, exactly on schedule.

The Academy bus was now inside the trailer, its engine switched off. In only a few seconds, his commandos would have the tire ramps stowed and would close and seal the trailer's rear doors. The plan called for the entire tractor-trailer to be abandoned in an industrial park ten miles away where a parking space had already been arranged, and three months' rental paid in cash. If the rear-door seal held as it should, it would be weeks before anyone investigated.

The duplicate bus that had been concealed in the trailer was already on the road. Two technical specialists were almost finished attaching the license plates from the original bus. Ranger could see the duplicate passengers inside, their white uniforms ghostly through the tinted windows. All forty-one were sitting ramrod straight, facing forward, properly focused on the mission's next objective.

As Ranger made the final adjustments to his uniform and the cap he now wore, Norway handed him the black attaché case, then, unexpectedly, snapped to attention and saluted.

Touched, even honored, Ranger made a point of returning the salute with the same passion and precision. Despite their many differences, he and Norway were brothers-in-arms, and together they had just survived their first contact with the enemy. That alone would serve to bind them through the engagements to follow.

Salutes exchanged, Norway spoke a single word, awkwardly. *"Stasglivo."*

Ranger shook his head at Norway's execrable pronunciation. *"Et vous, mon ami. Bonne chance, aussi."* His French was much better than Norway's Russian. But then, given their respective histories, it had to be.

Then Ranger walked away from the LeBaron, over to the duplicate bus. Once on board, he had two replacement midshipmen hand out the passes, matching them according to the list he had prepared. At the same time, the duplicate bus pulled out of the tunnel, passed the flagman and the waiting, unsuspecting civilian cars, and smoothly took the entrance ramp to Highway 50.

In less than a minute, Ranger knew traffic flow would resume through the tunnel, even as the last of his commandos removed the traffic cones, swept up the shattered window glass, and drove off in the two white LeBarons, along with the stolen Department of Highways trucks towing the portable traffic-advisory signs.

Except for a few errant cubes of safety glass, the tunnel and the 70-50 interchange would be back to normal, as if nothing had happened.

Taking his place in the front passenger seat, Ranger switched on a small radio and dialed to the Washington news station, WTOP. Not hearing what he was waiting for, he kept the radio on at low volume, just enough that he would be able to hear the first reports from the National Archives.

Then he cleared his mind and settled back to watch the passing landscape, alive to each subtle nuance of color, light, and shadow. His mind no longer held thoughts of what had happened, nor of what was still to come. Experiencing only the sensations of the moment, he savored the clarity of a warrior in battle, knowing all was as it should be.

The temperature was seventy-eight degrees. The morning sun was rising in a cloudless blue sky. A silver-and-blue United States Naval Academy bus filled with forty-one white-clad midshipmen was rolling westbound on Highway 50, its destination, the Pentagon.

Team Two was on its way to Ground Zero.

And Ranger was confident that even before he heard the news from the Archives, thirty-five miles away, Team One was already in position.

TWO

NORTH AMERICAN LIGHTNING DETECTION NETWORK, TUCSON, ARIZONA

After six months of analysis, at the exact same second Stan Drewniak had his breakthrough about the Grinch, he heard footsteps behind him and reflexively hit the F1 key on his keyboard. Instantly, a half-completed game of solitaire filled his desktop computer screen.

But in this case, instantly wasn't fast enough.

"I saw that," his boss said.

Stan spun around in his squeaking swivel chair to smile winningly at Dr. Helen Shapiro. She was a wiry fifty years old to his waist-thickening thirty, carried a thick black binder, and wore a sagging, brown cardigan over blue jeans, a denim shirt, and a turquoise and silver bolo tie. She didn't smile back. "I don't even have to guess what you're doing, do I?" she said.

Stan thought about brazening it out. Dr. Shapiro, like everyone else at Global Atmospherics, Inc., was overworked this year. The America-based subsidiary of the Japanese company had begun with a localized sensing system developed in the 1970s for the Bureau of Land Management, to aid in the early detection of lightning-caused forest fires in Alaska. Those first crude Magnetic Direction Finding sensors had been able to pinpoint a lightning strike with an accuracy ranging between two to four miles. By the late 1990s, that technology had evolved into a satellite-linked network of more than two hundred sophisticated sensors covering the entire country. As accuracy improved, most ground lightning strikes could be pinpointed within one hundred yards of their actual location. And not only could the system detect air-to-air strikes that never reached the ground, it could now distinguish among the up-to-twenty return strokes that accompanied each flash event.

By the turn of the century, the North American Lightning Detection Network had linked GAI's National Lightning Detection Network for the continental United States to additional networks covering Canada, Mexico, and the Pacific Ocean from the west coast of North America to Hawaii. Stan knew the chief reason he'd been hired by Global Atmospherics was that its management believed the next decade could bring a fully integrated lightning-detection network that would span the world. The amount of research that required was responsible for the incredible workload and most of the new jobs at GAI. One of those new jobs was Stan's.

Ten years from now, he was sure, the latest, ultimate network would probably be able to identify the nature of the Grinch within seconds of the elusive event's next appearance. But he had put a lot of time into solving his latest pet puzzle over the past six months. He didn't feel like waiting ten years before he had the answer.

So Stan chose his strategy, scratched his scraggly black beard, and confessed, more or less, mostly less. "I was . . . on my break."

Shapiro sighed. She was a cloud physicist with twenty-five years of experience who, to Stan and to anyone else who worked with her, only seemed to come to life that one time each spring when she disappeared into the field to fly through Florida's thunderstorms. The rest of the year, locked up in the new and ferociously air-conditioned NALDN monitoring station in the Arizona desert, she was like a storm system of her own, ready to burst at any second. It was a common enough problem in high-technology endeavors, Stan knew. The people with the technical expertise for a task rarely had a matching level of managerial experience for directing support staff. Dr. Shapiro was undeniably intelligent enough to have become one of the country's foremost lightning experts. But she was also incredibly negative and judgmental, and, even worse, she was responsible for his performance reviews.

Right now, the cloud physicist was speaking to him as his manager and not as a fellow scientist. "We're short-handed today, Stan. We don't have breaks."

Swiftly mounting his defense, Stan waved his hand in the general direction of the main event display, twenty feet away on the far wall of the expansive monitoring room. The ten-foot-wide screen showed an outline of North America, including all the states, provinces, and territories of Canada, the United States, and Mexico. The grid map scintillated with red dots, most of them concentrated in a band crossing Louisiana into Florida, and in separate clumps over Portland and the Canadian prairies.

Each flashing dot represented one lightning event, appearing on the display approximately ten seconds after the event took place. That was the length of time the company's computers needed to compare time-of-arrival data transmitted from ground sensors and to calculate each lightning bolt's triangulated position, polarity, and amplitude.

"The system's working perfectly." Stan knew he was on solid ground so far. The grid map showed that every bolt of lightning originating anywhere across an eighth of the Earth's surface was being monitored precisely, efficiently, and automatically.

Dr. Shapiro rubbed her wildly disordered salt-and-pepper hair. The best explanation Stan had heard for her remarkable hairstyle was that it was the direct result of her lightning-hunting airplane taking dozens of direct hits each time it went up. But then, for someone who studied lightning, that was the point.

"Stan, what if a sensor baseline went down? And you're lost on your Grinch hunt?"

Stan glanced over at the handful of other computer specialists sitting at their monitors in low-walled cubicles, struggling through the Saturday-midnight-to-Sunday-morning graveyard shift. Like Shapiro, most of them were swathed in bulky sweaters, despite the fact that the outside temperature in Tucson this morning was well on its way to 115 degrees. Air-conditioning was an all-or-nothing effort in this computerized facility. But unlike the other, freezing staff members, Stan defiantly wore cotton shorts, a Banzai Institute T-shirt, and desert sandals. No matter how cold it got inside the dark, cavelike detection center, his inner thermostat always knew how hot it was outside. "Um . . . one of the Popsicle sticks would tell me and I'd get right on it?"

"Wrong answer, Stan. *You're* the shift manager. *You're* supposed to notice it. That's why this company hires *peo-*

ple, not robots." Shapiro tapped one elegantly manicured finger on the pictures of playing cards on his computer screen. "Why are you the only one who covers up his work by pretending you're playing games and not the other way around like everyone else?"

Stan shrugged.

Shapiro shook her head as if she'd never understand him, which he knew she wouldn't, ever. "I want you to get your Grinch program off the company network."

"But . . ." Stan hesitated, then went for broke. "I think I can catch it in twelve days."

Shapiro's large blue eyes widened, startled. "The Grinch?"

Stan nodded, surprising himself by the depth of the pleasure he took in her reaction of disbelief.

"It's a random, high-altitude, transient event, Stan. Everyone's gone over it. Japan's gone over it. NOAA's gone over it. We have perfect agreement."

"Perfect?" Stan dismissively ticked off the ludicrous possibilities on his fingers. "Your experts' top three theories are meteor, high-altitude aurora—within four degrees of the *equator,* for God's sake—and stratospheric luminous discharge, which has got to be the most meaningless buzzword of the decade in this business."

Shapiro shifted her binder from one hand to the other, making the movement a sign of her growing impatience. "And so now *you* know what it is?"

"Oh, no. Not a clue." He held up a hand to forestall her protest. *"But . . . I do know it's not random." There,* he thought. *Let's see what she does with that.* No matter how ineffectual a manager Shapiro was, she was also a scientist. And there was only one way for a scientist to respond to the claim he had just made.

Shapiro hesitated for a moment, then nodded, almost wary. "All right. What's the pattern?"

Yes. Stan spun back to the computer on his desk and hit the F1 key to toggle the solitaire screen away. Now what appeared was a grid map of the world, centered on the Pacific, crossed by a series of different-colored sine waves.

As he knew she would, Shapiro recognized what she was looking at. "Those are satellite orbits."

"That's right. Polar." He pointed to the different colors one at a time. "That's Landsat IV, Landsat V, ADEOS-II, FORTÉ, the space station, and SPOT II."

"Stan, the Grinch has appeared three times in six months, on a completely irregular basis. These satellites orbit like clockwork. They can't be the cause."

"I didn't say they were," Stan countered. "But look at this." He rapidly typed in a series of commands on his keyboard, and the sine-wave path of the orbits disappeared, then began to be redrawn on the screen from the left. "These are the orbital paths of all those satellites on December 24, last year."

The paths continued to draw themselves for a few seconds, then stopped as a red dot appeared in the Pacific, almost a thousand miles southeast of Hawaii. "And that's the Grinch. An electromagnetic event of unknown origin and awesome power. First appearance. December 24th. Five-seventeen P.M. Mountain time." He glanced sideways at his manager, revelling in her dawning expression of enlightenment as she gradually registered what was on the screen.

"Okay. Show me the second appearance."

Stan suppressed his feeling of triumph. Her tone had been neutral but he had her. He could tell.

He cleared the screen again, then requested orbit-adjustment for February 15. This time, the Grinch's location, plus or minus 150 miles, was approximately 1,200 miles due south of Hawaii.

Shapiro leaned forward, but she only needed to see the screen for a moment. "And the third?"

Stan advanced to the final screen. April 28. Eight hundred miles west of Hawaii. He used his finger to draw a circle on his computer screen, outlining the area around the Grinch location that was completely free of orbiting satellites. "In all three cases," he said, "the Grinch only appears when there are *no* satellites overhead capable of observing a transient discharge event. Now, *that* can't be a coincidence. Not three times."

Shapiro straightened up. "And the next gap in coverage occurs in twelve days?"

Stan nodded. "There's a fifty-five-minute window on July 1st, centered on a point nine hundred and fifty miles southwest of Hawaii."

Shapiro stared at the screen for a few long seconds.

"Okay," she said at last. "This is good science. You analyze the data, detect a pattern, and make a prediction. In twelve days, we'll know if your prediction is right. Assuming it is, what do you think is the causative link?"

Stan was surprised she'd even ask so obvious a question. "Military, of course. It's got to be. I say somebody's testing an EMP bomb. For our network to detect a discharge event at that distance, the electromagnetic pulse being generated has got to be humongous."

Shapiro's eyes lost focus, as if her mind were off working on some other problem. "An EM pulse *there* strong enough for us to pick up *here* would turn off half the power grids in Hawaii and make every plane over the Pacific drop from the sky. I think we might have heard about something like . . ." She stopped as another expression of enlightenment came to her. She looked at him intently.

"Like . . . what?" Stan prompted, curious rather than defensive now that she seemed to be taking his obsessive quest seriously.

"That Navy ship. The one that was sunk in the training mission. That was Christmas, wasn't it?"

Stan knew exactly what was in his manager's mind. "The USS *Shiloh*. That was one of the first things I thought of, too." Everyone knew about the *Shiloh*. Almost four hundred sailors had been killed when a cruise missile, supposedly disarmed for a training exercise, had accidentally slammed into the ship and sunk her within minutes. The hearings in Washington had lasted almost a month. The televised Navy footage of the rescue attempt among the burning debris had been dramatic, and the startling satellite photo showing the cruise missile in flight only seconds before the *Shiloh* was hit had made the cover of every newspaper and news magazine in the world. But the Navy disaster had nothing to do with the Grinch. "That was on the 26th," Stan explained. "The Grinch was two days earlier—on the 24th. And anyway, the two locations are about a thousand miles apart. No connection."

Shapiro nodded, apparently accepting his reasoning. "Okay. So, go write up a formal report."

"Really?" Stan couldn't believe his luck. All he'd been hoping for was her reluctant consent to his continuing work on the Grinch problem in his spare time. But now she was making his investigation part of his official duties.

"Really. We're definitely not seeing an EMP bomb, but the fact that we are picking up something that the Pentagon probably wants to keep secret means someone else could be picking it up, too."

"The Pentagon? I said 'military,' Dr. Shapiro. Not *our* military."

"C'mon, Stan. Who else is there these days?"

"My guess is the French. They're always blowing up islands and things in the . . ." Stan ended his explanation in a mumble. Too late, he remembered that office gossip had it that Shapiro supposedly had had a hot French lover back in prehistoric days.

"These Grinch events are *not* explosions, Stan." Shapiro spoke as if Stan had no clue about how to interpret data logically. "They could be . . . a tryout of a new radar system. Somebody could be measuring ionization effects in the upper atmosphere with sounding rockets. Our picking that up could be good for the company. Help sell our services to the defense industry."

Stan refrained from crossing his eyes at her to let her know what he thought of her reasoning. He knew a good scientist was supposed to consider every possibility, but Shapiro's suggestions were definitely problematic. Still cocky from his unexpected initial success with her, he pressed on. "Doctor, radar and ionization studies aren't exactly cutting-edge technologies. And they don't produce a lot of visual data. So why would anyone bother to hide them from satellites?"

"I don't know," Shapiro said sharply. "Force of habit, maybe. If you're ever unfortunate enough to do defense work, Stan, you'll discover that the military lies. *All* the time. Cover stories, camouflage, deception . . . it's their rule rather than their exception."

Stan stared with new interest at his manager. He'd never

heard such venom in her voice. He wondered if anyone in the office knew about any defense work Shapiro might have done in her past.

But whatever her experience had been, Stan's manager now quickly brushed aside any disturbing memories it might have left. "Look, write your report. Include screen dumps of the orbital tracks you showed me. And. . . ." She glanced at her watch. "Can I get it all before you go this morning?"

Stan wisely decided to stop arguing. "Sure. No problem."

"And one more thing. . . ." Shapiro leaned past Stan to hit the F1 key on his computer. The Grinch map on the screen was once again replaced by a half-completed game of solitaire. "If we *are* straying into a classified area, it might be a good idea to keep it to ourselves for now." She stepped back, then looked out over the detection center. "Is anyone else helping you with this?"

Stan shook his head. He knew better than that. Misuse of company resources was a real offense at GAI. Past experience had taught him how to keep a secret. "Nope. Just me."

"Good. You give me the report. I'll take it to Dr. Green tomorrow. And twelve days from now, maybe you'll be a company hero."

"Works for me," Stan said.

Shapiro nodded in the direction of his screen. "Meanwhile, you'd better keep up appearances, too."

Stan stared at her blankly. He had absolutely no idea what she was talking about.

"The black ten goes on the red jack."

Then Shapiro told him she'd see him at the end of the shift, and walked off, binder under her arm, through the center of the monitoring room, toward her office.

With his mouse, Stan obediently moved the ten of spades onto the Jack of diamonds, then clicked over a few new cards, all the while mentally composing the introduction for his report.

But as he did, something Shapiro had said kept turning over in his mind.

The military lies. All *the time.* She'd spoken with such conviction.

He toggled back to his Grinch maps, running them backward and forward.

He had three more hours left in his shift. He might as well put them to good use.

If the Pentagon was somehow lying about the Grinch, then Stan Drewniak was going to find out why.

THREE

CHASE RESIDENCE, QUANTICO, VIRGINIA

In the supposed safety of the living room of his own home, Tom Chase braced himself for the inevitable attack. Even as his opponent gripped his hand and began to methodically swing it up and down, Tom forced himself to concentrate. He would not pull away, because that was what the enemy wanted. The movement would change his center of gravity. It would allow his attacker to use his own momentum against him. Instead, Tom stood his ground, braced himself, and—

"Hey!"

Completely unexpectedly, a sharp shock of intense pain flashed into Tom's thumb. All his mental preparations vanished as he tried to snatch his hand back from his opponent's grip. He was too late.

Tom's living-room floor and ceiling blurred past him, then stopped with a bang as he slammed onto his back.

He heard the flimsy walls of his townhouse rattle. He heard something on an Ikea bookshelf topple.

He heard his eight-year-old son giggle proudly.

But Tom couldn't say anything. He couldn't even draw a breath. His lungs were paralyzed from the force of his impact. He regretted not having had the money to upgrade the inexpensive gray broadloom. The standard half-inch underpad had done nothing to cushion his fall.

Tyler stopped giggling. A look of concern flickered over him.

Tom forced himself up on one elbow, mouthing the words "I'm fine." He glanced over at the blank, off-white common wall he shared with his next-door neighbors, but didn't detect any protests from that half of the townhouse. It was just after seven in the morning. With luck, the Lufkins had slept through his latest martial-arts encounter with his son.

Tyler gallantly held out a hand to help his decrepit old man to his feet.

Tom took a shallow breath, felt better, made a show of moving his hands out of Tyler's reach. "Forget it, pal. I'm not falling for that twice."

Tyler put one hand on his stomach, one in the small of his back, and took several bows for his invisible audience. "Thank you, thank you."

Tom sat cross-legged on the floor, marveling at his son's capacity to surprise him. "Your mother taught you that?"

Tyler looked defensive. "I'm a yellow belt. I learned that in class."

"Not the flip. I mean the trick with the hand."

Tyler grinned and moved his eyebrows up and down. "The old Vulcan death grip." He made a pinching motion with his thumb and forefinger. That was all it had taken to inflict serious pain in the fleshy muscle between Tom's thumb and forefinger.

Tom's hand still ached. He stood up, trying his best to look stern. "There's no such thing as a Vulcan death grip."

"That's what Mom called it."

Tom studied his son, trying to ignore the somewhat grotesquely illustrated Black Lung T-shirt. He supposed his own preadolescent worship of Kiss had similarly escaped his parents. As a first-time father, Tom was finding himself constantly caught up in an unwinnable war between what he knew was best for his child, and what he remembered best from his own childhood. He was beginning to suspect no one ever struck the right balance.

Tyler Chase was a bit smaller than other boys his age, just edging in under four feet, even with his black custom high-tops. And he was definitely lighter, still less than fifty pounds soaking wet. But judging from the amount of milk the kid could drink, and the number of mini microwave pizzas that disappeared on his weekends at the townhouse, Tom was convinced his son was on the brink of a major growth spurt. He hoped so. The kid was definitely going to inherit his mother's looks. He could use a bit of his father's height to back them up. *And thinking about his mother . . .* Tom shook his still painful hand. "Only true aliens need to know things like that."

Tyler shrugged. His universal gesture for whatever subject he chose not to discuss. "What time is it?"

Tom looked at his watch—that is, he looked at his wrist where his watch used to be.

Tyler was wearing it now. Smirking.

"Missing something, Dad?"

Tom frowned in what he hoped was a good impression of authority-figure disapproval, but he knew it couldn't hide his pride. "That was smooth. First time I didn't feel a thing."

Tyler's smirk blossomed into a full-fledged and honest smile, not a hint of artifice about it. That simple expression was enough to trigger a full-scale wave of fierce parental love in Tom. At once, he saw in his son an echo of the child the boy had been, and a compelling glimpse of the adult he would someday become. That Tom had had a hand in the creation of this small, maddening, yet perfect being was something that astounded him on a daily basis. But whenever he threatened to become awash in maudlin sentimentality, he was also able to see an echo of his wife in Tyler. *Ex-wife.* That cooled things off pretty quickly.

Tyler adjusted his father's large silver-banded watch. Its metal links hung loosely on his young wrist. "Mom says no one needs to know things like *this.*"

"Yeah? Well, trust me, knowing a couple of classic magic tricks is a lot more useful than knowing how to kill someone with a . . . a Gummi Bear and an elastic band."

Tyler's sudden, intensely hopeful expression warned Tom he'd chosen the wrong example. He could almost hear his son's amazed thoughts: *I can get a Gummi Bear . . . I can get an elastic band. . . .*

"That was a joke."

"I know." Tyler's obvious disappointment gave Tom a quick, terrible thought.

"She hasn't taught you how to kill someone with anything else, has she?"

"Daa-ad."

"Just checking. You know, when you get older and go to parties with girls—"

"Yuck."

"Yuck away. They're gonna love the stuff I'm teaching you. Maybe someday you'll even thank me."

•

Tyler smiled brightly. "I'll thank you now. Shake?"

Tom pretended not to notice Tyler's straining-to-look-innocent eyes. "Sure."

This time, as soon as Tyler slapped his other hand to Tom's wrist to begin the karate throw, Tom was ready. With a savage roar of attack, he swiftly lifted his arm up, leaving Tyler's midsection exposed, then swung in with his free arm, grabbed the startled boy around the waist, and spun him into the air so he hung upside down at Tom's side.

Tyler squealed with delighted laughter, kicking wildly, desperately trying to reach around and tickle his father.

That was when Lufkin pounded on the common wall from his side of the townhouse. A muffled roar informed Tom precisely what time it was.

"Sorry!" But Tom's shouted reply only served to plunge himself and his son into even greater whoops of laughter, made all the stronger by their ineffectual attempts to stop.

Tyler's kicking now threw Tom off-balance, made him sidestep to recover, directly into the side of the old gray-cord couch. Tom tossed Tyler dramatically clear onto the couch's well-worn cushions, then collapsed to the floor for the second time, rattling all the metal-shelved bookcases in the tiny, L-shaped combination living and dining room.

By the time they caught their respective breath, Tom was sitting on the floor with his back to the couch. Tyler was on the floor beside him, leaning against Tom as if he were three again and not worried whether hugging his dad was cool or not.

Tom roughed up his son's hair. Where the red came from, neither he nor his wife—ex-wife—had ever been able to figure out. "Your turn to make breakfast."

"Waffles."

Tom frowned. Waffles were merely Tyler's excuse to guzzle maple syrup and inch-thick slabs of butter. "Okay, my turn. Omelettes."

"Waffles."

"Fruit, no syrup."

"I get to have Coke at the game."

"One."

"And candy."

"Don't push it, pal." Tom had noted that Tyler was turning everything into a drawn-out negotiation these days and that, too often, it was resulting in the kid's getting his way. But summer vacation was just starting and this was their day for fun. Anything serious could wait for September and the start of school. He gave his son a poke in the ribs and leapt to his feet before Tyler could physically counterattack. "Let's go. Shower, bed-making, and . . . change the shirt."

"Mom lets me wear this shirt."

Tom didn't want to play that game. Trying one from the self-help books, he changed the direction of the potential argument. "Show some team spirit. Wear your Orioles shirt."

Unfortunately, Tyler hadn't read the same books. "Mom bought me Black Lung's new album. With autographs."

"I bought the tickets to the game."

"Why didn't you buy a ticket for Mom? She's not doing anything today."

Tom felt a familiar wall descending. He knew there was no way he was going to win this particular argument.

"Maybe next time."

"Why not this time?"

Tom spoke slowly, emphasizing each word. "I only have two tickets."

"You could buy—"

"Tyler. This conversation's going nowhere."

Tom knew Tyler understood what that particular code phrase from his father meant, but the kid persisted anyway. "Mom would ask you to a game. She's always asking about you."

That revelation caused Tom to hesitate, but then he caught himself. Tyler had almost outmaneuvered him again. "C'mon. Let's go make omelettes."

"Waffles!"

"Waffles." He got to his feet, held out his hand to Tyler. Tyler grinned at what he obviously thought was the opening to an attack and got up by himself. Then the grin suddenly left his open, freckled face. His thin arm seemed to twitch.

All of Tom's parental senses went on alert. Was his son feeling unwell? Food poisoning? Seizure? All the unlikely, even ridiculous nightmares only a parent could know suddenly alive within him.

Then he realized what had happened.

"Give me the watch."

Reluctantly, Tyler handed it over.

It was a Timex-Motorola, two time zones, timer, day and date, stopwatch, 150 phone numbers, and full 900MHz SkyTel pager functions.

Tom had set the watch to vibrate silently when a page came in so it wouldn't interrupt his classes. That's what Tyler had felt.

Seven o'clock Sunday morning and dad might have to go to work.

Tom read the display: 703 1. So much for the ball game.

Tyler pulled the watch down to his eye level as Tom fastened the metal strap. "Who is it? Mom?"

Tom angled the watch for Tyler, but the boy twisted Tom's

arm around so he could see the display from the opposite direction.

He hesitantly read the letters the upside-down numbers made. ". . . I eol? What's that mean?"

"Nothing. It's just numbers." When Tom had given Tyler his own pager, they had made a game of constructing upside-down code messages they could send to each other. On Tyler's pager display five dash five oh five— 5-505— was an SOS from school, meaning whoever it was who was supposed to pick him up was late. Four dash five oh five— 4-505—was a homework emergency. This past year, Sunday nights had seemed incomplete without an urgent page from Tyler, who had suddenly remembered he had some project or other due first thing Monday morning.

Tyler twisted Tom's arm the other way. "It's not a phone number. So, that makes it a code, right?"

Tom looked for the cordless phone. It was over on the television, on top of last night's pizza box. "Top Secret. They're going to have to send me back to the space station."

"Heyyy!" Tyler didn't let go of Tom's arm as he walked over to the phone. Tom played along, let his son swing like a monkey. "You're not an astronaut!"

Tom switched on the phone. He didn't have to think about the number he was going to dial. "Oh, I don't need a spaceship. They just beam me up."

Tyler pounded rhythmically on the matte black casing of Tom's oversize television set. *"Who* is it?!"

Tom held up a finger calling for instant silence. The number he had called was answered halfway through the first ring. It always was.

"Hey, Tommy. Thanks for getting back so fast." Despite the certain loss of his day with his son, Tom felt a stirring of interest. The man who had answered was more than his part-time employer. He was a friend. A good one. "You're at home, I see." It went without comment that Tom's location was known to his caller. The phone system Tom had made contact with automatically overrode any form of call-blocking that civilian switching systems could provide. The theory, engineering, and programming of such systems was one of the subjects Tom taught at the FBI Academy ten miles from the townhouse.

"It's my day with Tyler," Tom said. He wasn't complaining. He was just making it known that certain arrangements would have to be made.

"Taken care of."

Tyler, meanwhile, stood in front of his father, hands on his hips, slowly and silently mouthing, "Who is it?" over and over. *"Who?"*

"Just a second," Tom said, "there's someone here who wants to say hello."

Tom handed the phone to Tyler.

Tyler held it to his ear and cautiously said, "Hello?" Then he broke into a huge smile and added, "Uncle Milo!"

Tom was pleased by that reaction. Tyler had no grandparents or aunts or uncles, and since the day the boy was born, Milo Vanovich, who had no children, had gladly and enthusiastically taken over the all-purpose-relative role. Tom had met enough people on Vanovich's staff to know this was the general's *modus operandi*. He didn't have staff, he had family. Tom enjoyed being included within that extended group. He was even more pleased that the general's interest extended to Tyler.

Tyler said a few things about the afternoon's ball game and his plans for the summer, then handed the phone back to Tom.

"So, should I pack a bag?" Tom asked.

"I just need you at the office. With any luck, I'll get you back by noon."

Tom heard an odd huskiness in Vanovich's voice. Maybe the old guy was finally getting out on Saturday nights. A little fun could only be good for him given the kind of job the general had.

"Huh. I've heard that before. I saw the news last night. What's it going to be like getting in there today?"

"There's a car on the way. Just bring your pass."

Tom knew better than to ask for additional details. "See you in an hour, then."

He could sense Vanovich's smile form on the other end of the line. "Oh, sooner than that, I'd say."

The line clicked off and the doorbell rang at the same time.

Tom saw the undisguised look of disappointment in Tyler's eyes. "Sorry, pal."

"I know. Uncle Milo told me. It's work." Tyler sighed. They had talked about this often enough that the boy knew, in this matter at least, arguing wasn't an option. Ever since Tom had begun teaching at the FBI Academy, and had regular hours like other fathers, it was rare for him to cancel on Tyler. Now when he did, Tyler was more accepting of the fact that there were still some parts of Tom's work that absolutely had to come first. Even Tyler's mother had helped him understand that. It was one of the few subjects on which she and Tom could agree.

Tom headed down the steep, oak-veneer staircase that led to his minuscule entrance hall. Through the sheers covering the three strips of glass on the white Colonial-style front door, he saw two men in nondescript gray suits—definitely not the clothing of choice on a muggy June day in Virginia. Tom opened the door. "I just got the call."

There was already a sheen of sweat on both men. The larger of the two took off his aviator-style sunglasses. Tom watched the man's hooded eyes efficiently scan the still unfurnished entry hall behind Tom, then lock on to Tyler as the boy noisily jumped down the uncarpeted stairs, two steps at a time. At the same time, the man opened a small, black leather wallet to reveal his Defense Intelligence Agency identification. Tom knew that was the ID of choice carried by agents of the National Infrastructure Agency. Since the agency Vanovich headed was not publicly acknowledged to exist, no one from the NIA could admit working for it.

"Mr. Chase, I'm Captain Lassiter." He nodded at the man beside him. "This is Captain Dorsey. He'll be your driver. The general asked me to . . ." Lassiter nodded at Tyler as the boy took up position at his father's side.

Tom looked down at his son. "Tyler, this is Captain Lassiter. He's going to be your baby-sitter." Tom jammed a hand into the front pocket of his jeans.

Tyler caught the move. "Watch this," the boy warned the captain.

Tom tried some misdirection. "Watch what?"

Tyler poked a finger against Tom's hand in his pocket. "Whenever you put your hand in your pocket like that, you're going to pull something out of my ear."

"This hand?" Tom pulled his hand free, turned it back and forth, nothing in it. "I am not."

Then Tom reached out suddenly with his other hand as if to cup Lassiter's ear. The captain's hand was on Tom's wrist like a whip had been snapped, before Tom had even seen him move.

Tyler voiced Tom's surprise. "Whoa . . . cool . . ."

Tom studied the soldier in civilian garb. He was definitely Special Ops material. As far as Tom was concerned, guys like that shouldn't be let outside without a leash and muzzle. "Captain . . . it's Sunday morning, you're not on base . . . how about taking things a little easier."

Lassiter released his grip and Tom slowly moved his hand back. Held edgewise between his index and middle finger were two tickets for the afternoon's game at Oriole Park in Baltimore, five rows back from the visitors' dugout. He handed them over. "My son is apt to try a few moves like that himself. Think before you defend yourself, okay?"

Lassiter clearly didn't appreciate Tom's unstated warning, but he was under orders.

Tom put a hand on his front door. Despite the heat, no soldier was going to cross his threshold again. Fortunately, like garlic and crosses for vampires, the chain of command would keep Lassiter and Dorsey in their place.

"The general wants you to wait here. I have to get my pass." Tom could see that Lassiter wanted to object. In the army, when a general said *Now* it meant *Now*—a soldier in Tom's position would wear his pass around his neck at all times just in case a call came in at the most inopportune time. Nor was Tom going to change out of his gray Polo shirt and blue jeans. He wasn't in the Army and there was nothing anyone like Lassiter could do about it.

"I'll be right out." Tom closed the front door firmly, then he raced Tyler up the oak-railed stairs to the bedrooms. He let Tyler beat him to the top-floor landing.

As his son grumpily brushed his hair and teeth as directed, Tom closed his own bedroom door, shifted his old pine dresser to one side, and exposed the compact, metallic wall safe hidden behind it. He punched in his assigned code number, then waited until the small red light on the safe turned green. Somewhere, a central computer in Fort Meade, Maryland, had been told over a cellular phone link that Tom Chase was accessing his government-supplied, secure storage unit. Of the four different code sequences Tom could have input, the one he had used indicated he was not under duress.

Tom heard the safe click as an authorization signal was returned by the computer. Then he spun the combination dial to its required settings. There was little the military loved more than redundancy.

Tom opened the safe. It was fifteen inches wide, nine inches tall, but only eight inches deep, specifically designed for installation by the Army Corps of Engineers in the narrow walls of civilian housing. But the metal-alloy unit was also welded to a pair of six-foot-long, diagonally crossed steel beams which would force anyone intending to steal the safe to tear out an entire bedroom wall.

Redundancy and *overkill,* Tom thought. *Emphasis on the kill.*

Of the two objects within the safe, Tom took only one—his security pass. The gun, a compact Beretta M9 semiautomatic pistol, remained behind. He had accepted possession of it only as a condition of his security clearance. So far, he had been successful in avoiding all the training sessions the Army had set up to teach him how to fire the weapon. He was content to let it rot in the safe, unused, unwanted, and no possible threat to his child.

The day Tom had returned home with that gun, he had sealed it in the safe, then promptly thrown away the two boxes of ammunition that came with it, along with the key to the trigger lock. As far as Tom was concerned, he didn't own a gun, and he never intended to fire one.

Tom shoved his pass and its neck chain into the front pocket of his jeans, then closed the safe and entered a new code sequence to let the Fort Meade computer know he hadn't been executed by terrorists when the safe had opened. As he pushed the pine dresser back into place, he heard Tyler turn off the water in the bathroom sink. He met his son in the hall. Tyler was wearing his new Orioles shirt. It hung down to his knees, almost obscuring his black-cotton surfer shorts. "Thanks, pal."

But Tyler didn't want his father to get the wrong idea. "I got toothpaste on the other one. What time's Mom coming tonight?"

"Eight. But I'll be here after the game. We'll phone out for pizza?"

Tyler pumped his arm in the air as he started down the stairs. "Two nights in a row!"

They reached the entrance hall. "Only if you don't tell your mother."

Tyler hung back from the front door. "Dad . . . you're going to be okay, right?"

Tom understood. He crouched down to look his son in the eyes, face-to-face. "I'm just going to Uncle Milo's office. Nothing fancy this time."

"Don't you need your kit?"

Tom patted his back pocket. "This is all I needed to fix the Space Shuttle when those flying saucers attacked."

"Daa-ad!"

"Oops, I forgot. That's still classified. Don't tell anyone I told you or—" Tom pointed knowingly at the hulking silhouettes of the plainclothes NIA agents in the front-door windows. "—they'll have to . . . you know." He drew his finger across his neck with an appropriate reproduction of the sound of flesh being cut.

But Tyler had heard that particular joke too many times. "Seriously."

"Seriously, they have everything I need at the office." Tom reached for the front door's brass doorknob. Through the door's windows, he saw the agents outside shift their positions, as if there were a chance that someone other than Tom Chase would be coming through. "I'll beep you when I'm finished. Promise."

Tyler lifted up his shirt to check the transparent orange pager clipped to his waistband. Then he suddenly lurched at his father and hugged him.

Tom hugged back, accepting what was unsaid. "I love you, too." He mussed his son's freshly brushed hair. "Go get your glove. It's in the backseat."

Tom opened his front door and Tyler charged out past the soldiers, down the concrete patio-stone walk and across the lawn to Tom's five-year-old red Cherokee parked in the driveway he shared with the Lufkins. Tom squeezed his keychain and heard the vehicle beep once as the doors unlocked. There were two other vehicles parked at the curb in front of the gray-shingle townhouse. An innocuous beige Chevy Cavalier with three short and stubby black antennae attached to the trunk, letting careful observers know it wasn't as innocuous as it appeared. Lined up behind the Cavalier was a white Chevy Suburban with impenetrably tinted windows, the ubiquitous unmarked government vehicle of choice in D.C. Tom saw the pronounced tread on the wide tires and recognized the Suburban as a class-four transport. It could drive over a mine and take a direct hit from a

Stinger missile at the same time, and still get all of four miles to the gallon.

"Is that necessary?"

After a brief glance at Tom's casual, weekend attire, Captain Dorsey gave what Tom considered to be a classic military reply. "General's orders." With that mind-set, Tom knew, necessity and logic need play no part in a soldier's thinking. *Assuming a soldier is capable of thought in the first place.*

Tyler slid out from the backseat of the Cherokee with his yellow-leather fielder's glove. As he pounded his fist into the battered glove's pocket, he half-spun and kicked the Cherokee's door closed with what Tom recognized as a well-executed karate side kick, accompanied by an appropriate cry of attack. The kid was a force of nature. Letting him spend the day in the company of someone who had been through Special Forces training was asking for trouble.

Tom pushed down Lassiter's sunglasses so he could see the captain's eyes. Lassiter stiffened but made no outward gesture of response. "He can have two hotdogs, one Coke, one popcorn. Spread them out over the game. No ice cream, no candy bars." Tom stuffed two twenties into Lassiter's jacket pocket. "And consider this general's orders, too: Keep the conversation on baseball. No war stories. No training stories. Even if he asks. And *especially* if he asks how to blow things up. Is that understood?"

Lassiter nodded once, slowly, his cheeks darkening with his effort to maintain control in the face of reckless provocation. He clearly found it as trying to be in Tom's presence as Tom found it to be in his.

"Good. If you make it through the day, I'll tell the general you deserve combat pay." Tom turned to Captain Dorsey. "Let's go."

Meeting Tyler in the driveway, Tom held out his hand so they could exchange a high five. Tyler, predictably, moved his hand away at the last second. Tom, just as predictably, recovered by jabbing Tyler in the ribs. "No karate moves on the captain."

Tyler did that thing with his eyebrows again. "Heh, heh. He'll never know what hit him." Tom grimaced. Definitely too much Nickelodeon.

He got into the front seat of the Suburban before his NIA escort could open the back door. Dorsey hesitated, then walked around to the driver's side.

Tom watched through the Suburban's tinted side window as, in the driveway, Tyler formally shook hands with Captain Lassiter, without apparent incident.

Dorsey pulled an impossibly thin radio from his inside jacket pocket, held it close to his mouth. "Eighty-five." Tom heard no acknowledgment in reply. But, apparently, the code meant all was well since Dorsey put the radio away, then leaned forward and turned the key in the ignition.

Outside, Tyler and Captain Lassiter walked down the driveway toward the innocuous Cavalier at the curb. Tyler was already talking earnestly to his companion. Tom almost rolled his window down to wish the captain luck.

"Quite the young man you have there, sir," Dorsey said as the Suburban pulled away from the curb. "Think he'll be going into your line of work?"

"He'd better not." *And don't let him be a soldier, either,* Tom thought, turning his head to watch Tyler now getting into the backseat of the Cavalier. With approval, he watched as Lassiter leaned in to secure Tyler's seat belt.

Dorsey adjusted a control on the dash. "Are you getting enough air-conditioning, sir?"

Tom was, and he slouched down, making himself comfortable as the Suburban turned the corner, away from the neatly spaced cluster of upright gray townhouses backed by towering stands of elm. Dorsey chose the lane that would take them away from the outskirts of Quantico, toward Interstate 95. This early on a Sunday morning, traffic would be nonexistent. "Just fine. Any idea what the trouble is?"

"I really couldn't say, sir."

No surprise there. "Just thought it might have something to do with the ceremony."

"I'm sure the general will fill you in."

Tom realized he'd have to create his own entertainment. "I guess it's a big day for you guys."

"Sir?"

"Another couple of treaties like this, and you people are pretty much out of a job, right?"

"I wouldn't say that, sir."

"C'mon, Captain. *Russia* joining *NATO?* They're making history today. You're running out of enemies."

Dorsey snapped on the Suburban's blinker with a bit too much force, Tom thought. "You'd be surprised, sir."

Tom waited expectantly, but the captain volunteered no other comment. Restless for stimulation, he turned on the radio.

"—at least twenty dead, including two security guards manning a video surveillance station on the second floor." The announcer sounded flustered, as if she'd been forced to fill airtime, nonstop, for hours. "So far, no one has taken responsibility for the massacre, and we have been unable to determine if police have identified a motive behind the deadly attack. We're going live to Bill Jennings to get the latest on this terrible tragedy. And we remind you to stay with WTOP for continuous updates on this fast-breaking story."

As Dorsey took the entrance ramp to the interstate, the look on his face told Tom the captain knew as little as Tom did about whatever had just happened.

Tom leaned forward and turned up the volume as a new voice came over the radio. The sound quality was different, less clear. "This is Bill Jennings reporting live from outside the National Archives on Constitution Avenue." Tom sat back, frowning. He had taken Tyler to the Archives last October. His son's favorite document at the Archives, like Tom's, had been the $7,200,000 check used to buy Alaska from Russia in 1867. Ornate as it was, it hadn't even been certified.

The reporter's tone was grave. "The death toll for last night's massacre now stands at eight security personnel and twenty-four visitors to the Archives' exhibition hall. We are still waiting for confirmation that some of the most important documents stored here, including—" The voice paused solemnly before continuing. "—America's three great Charters of Freedom, are unharmed. But, as yet, the police have still not set a time for a press conference."

"That's what I meant, sir," Dorsey said grimly. "There's always someone out there who's after us."

Tom slumped down in his seat, sickened. He wondered if any of the twenty-four had been children, innocent civilians slaughtered on the new, urban battlefield. Since becoming a parent, he was no longer able to listen to the ever-increasing stories of random madness sweeping the country and the world without fearing for his child's future, and his own.

But he took some comfort from the fact that for at least today, he had nothing to worry about.

Tyler was being escorted to the ball game by a Special Ops bodyguard.

And as for himself, Tom couldn't think of a building in the world that was more secure than the Pentagon.

FOUR

MARINE ONE, WASHINGTON, D.C.

Seen from Marine One, the stately, gleaming green-and-white Sikorsky VH-3D helicopter operated by Marine aviation squadron HMX-1, the Sunday-morning haze was thicker over the Potomac, so that the river's eastern edge was like an ocean shore. There was a gentle westward curve of land, a narrow brush stroke of calm dark water, then nothing but featureless mist that dissolved into the far horizon.

No, not the edge of the ocean, Hector MacGregor thought, staring out through one of the Sikorsky's thick, blastproof windows. *It might as well be the edge of the world.* At least, that's what the old-timers he worked with would probably think. Their world ended at the Beltway, that ring of I-495 that surrounded Washington, D.C., like an isolating, insulating moat. But Hector didn't hold the insiders' atrophied vision against them. He was pragmatic enough to know that the traditional shortsightedness of the politicos and policymakers was exactly why someone like him was riding up front today with the President of the United States of America.

Just this morning, prior to boarding, the President's pilot had told Hector that the two-mile flight from the south lawn of the White House to the Pentagon seldom took more than seven minutes from takeoff to secured landing. But as a matter of security, different routes were used on a random basis for all the President's air travel over Washington, to lessen the chance of potential assassins lying in wait for the helo with a surface-to-air missile.

If the worst happened, the seventy-two-foot-long helicopter did carry extensive countermeasures against SAM attacks. Though the "V" in its model designation indicated the helicopter was an Executive Transport Configuration, complete with wet bar and galley, a toilet, and several hundred pounds of soundproofing, it was also heavily armed and armored. In addition to missile decoys, radar and laser-ranging jamming devices, infrared suppressors, and smoke generators, it carried three 7.62 Miniguns in concealed gunports. As a final resort, the four-person Marine crew—rigorously selected from the Corps' best pilots—and the Secret Service contingent accompanying the President, riding on all five helicopters of the Presidential formation, also had access to an onboard emergency store of weapons and personnel protection devices in the event Marine One was ever forced down.

Thus, despite the added safety concerns of flying, up to an altitude of 500 feet, the crew assured Hector the President was at least as safe in Marine One as if he were in his armored limousine.

This morning, the flight path of the helicopter formation

would bring them in north of the Pentagon, banking near Arlington National Cemetery before touching down on the helicopter landing pad directly outside the Building's southwest wall.

The helipad, a 100-foot-by-100-foot square of concrete slabs, had been added in 1955. At the time, its purpose was to provide for the rapid evacuation of key military and civilian personnel. However, by the sixties, when the Pentagon's security chiefs had realized that the confirmed alert time for offshore, submarine-launched Soviet missiles fired at the Pentagon was considerably shorter than the time it would take the Pentagon's key personnel to run from their offices to the heliport, other defensive strategies had been pursued. The heliport then had reverted to its secondary role as a landing site for official visits, and as an occasional medical-evacuation facility.

However, Hector knew, the President's arrival this morning was being treated as a routine visit, and he would not be greeted with military honors. The choice of Marine One had been an expedient measure to avoid the traffic delays expected to ensnarl the immediate area for the day. Since Saturday midnight, key highways, roads, and bridges within a mile of the Pentagon had been closed to all but authorized traffic.

Almost directly to the east, the George Mason and Rochambeau Memorial Bridges, and the Arlen D. Williams Memorial Bridge, had been shut down on the Washington side. Directly north, approaches to the Arlington Memorial Bridge had been blocked just past the Lincoln Memorial.

On the Arlington side, the web of north-south highways north of the Pentagon, including the George Washington Memorial Highway and the Jefferson Davis—which ran directly beneath the Pentagon's River Entrance Parade Grounds as if the grounds were an overpass—had been closed by concrete traffic barriers guarded by Virginia state police. Traffic that would normally travel the half-mile route between Washington and Arlington along Interstate 395 now had to face a six-mile detour that forced it north to the Theodore Roosevelt Memorial Bridge, and all the way around Arlington National Cemetery until it could rejoin the interstate a mile southwest of the Pentagon.

Underground, both Metrorail subway lines that served the area were being allowed to keep running, but no trains would be allowed to stop at the Pentagon Metro station until Monday morning. Aboveground, even Ronald Reagan National Airport, less than a mile to the south along the Potomac's shore, would be closed for the day.

For the next twenty-four hours, the only traffic allowed into the area would be military, diplomatic, or news media.

As MSNBC was so fond of reporting, the security arrangements were unprecedented.

But then, so was the event. And Hector MacGregor was going to witness it from a front-row seat because the President felt he needed what modern bizspeak called a contrarian—the fashionable label for a devil's advocate whose job function was to argue the opposite opinion to an organization's common wisdom and provide a change in perspective. Hector, actually, preferred to see his job in more direct terms: He was the President's designated link to the real world. Strangely, given that D.C. housed the people's representatives, who were supposed to be in touch with the country they served, the nation's capital had a decided shortage of those links.

When Hector had begun working as an unpaid consultant

to the President's party, he'd been twenty-six and, incredible even to him, close to making his first million as an Internet marketing consultant. He'd been expecting that after establishing and selling his company, and traveling around the world at least once, he'd move on to some other challenge in advertising and marketing. In a way he'd been right. Hector had since learned there really wasn't much difference between leading consumers to prefer a particular brand of soup, or voters a particular candidate. When it came to American elections, ninety-four percent of the winning candidates were those who had spent the most on their campaigns.

Just turned twenty-eight, Hector now held the vague but multipurpose title of Outreach Advisor to the Presidential Staff. His office address was 1600 Pennsylvania Avenue: a cubicle in the West Wing of the White House to be precise, only thirty-seven steps from the Man himself. Late one night, in the throes of adrenaline-induced insomnia during his first month in his new job, Hector had carefully paced out the distance himself.

Naturally, the old-timers resented his office and his proximity to the President, especially since the President's direct request had literally airlifted Hector into a staff position without their prior knowledge. But the last election had been tight, and Hector had delivered core support among young voters. It didn't hurt, either, that his mixed-up racial and cultural heritage made him the living model of the President's election-year vision of a Brave New World for the Brave New Century—America Without Boundaries. Or, as the media had come to grandly call it, the *Pax Americana*. Thanks to his parents and grandparents, Hector Mac-Gregor could make almost equal claim on Samoan, French, Japanese, and Bahamian ancestry.

So far, the President's handlers had been willing to let the Chief Executive reward his lapdog, at least till next year's midterm elections. By then, Hector knew, they expected his novelty to have worn off and he could be safely and swiftly discarded. While he was still in place, though, the party's election managers were courting him to find out how he had used the Internet so successfully to identify, contact, and woo young voters they'd written off as too apathetic to court.

Hector, however, wouldn't give up all his secrets. He had just as firmly made up his mind to outlast the old guard, and even this President. Not only had he discovered that he loved the work he did as a member of the President's staff, he'd become addicted to the fantastic perks his position had brought him.

Simply by having the President's ear, he'd already experienced, first-hand, the almost visceral thrill of seeing the advice he gave, at times, become policy, guiding some small part of the future of the United States, and even, in rare cases, the world.

Of course, his miserable civil-service salary was no match for what he might be earning in private industry, but he still had more than $700,000 in the bank from the sale of his company. That nest egg had given him a unique perspective from which to learn that success and power could be measured in terms other than dollars.

An old girlfriend, who had somehow faded from his life when he'd been swallowed up by the election, had left him a parting gift, superglued to the middle of his home-computer monitor as it sat on the dining table that dominated his cramped studio apartment in D.C.'s Adams-Morgan district. POWER ENNOBLES, the unremovable sign had read. ABSOLUTE POWER ENNOBLES ABSOLUTELY.

Hector still had that outdated computer and it still sat on his dining table. He'd kept its defaced monitor as a souvenir, not to remind him of his old girlfriend—he had trouble even remembering what she had looked like—but because as far as he was concerned, the aphorism was true. Especially at times like this, when the President looked at him from across the remarkably quiet and spacious, vibration-free passenger cabin of the official Presidential helicopter, and said, "Well, Hec, here we go."

With that, at the edge of nothingness, at the edge of the world, Hector saw the Building resolve from the mist ahead, a glacier, intimidating and inscrutable. And despite the generic nickname used by those who worked inside it, Hector knew the Pentagon was more than any mere building.

It was an icon, a concept recognized and understood by more than half the world, though some nations obviously would choose to understand it differently than others.

Even its name was the sum total of its address. The Pentagon Building. No other name or designation was required.

As Marine One closed on its approach, the radiating bands and rings of the Building's dark- and light-gray roofs became clearer, suggesting to Hector nothing so much as a mechanistic spider's web.

Through his window, Hector watched as that pattern formed against the canvas of mist making clear the Building's near-primitive simplicity: five sides, five rings, five corners, a Platonic ideal made solid. But, as he and nearly everyone else in the world knew, that simplicity backed a statement of power that was direct and unequivocal, a fitting description of the forces shaped within the fortresslike walls.

Hector could see that even the President was affected by

the sight of the Pentagon. Or, at the very least, by his contemplation of the events that would take place there at eleven o'clock this morning. So it was time for Hector to do his job as a contrarian. He held up a hand to the large window beside him, easily blocking the entire Building. "It's actually kind of small, don't you think?" he asked.

The President put down his carefully folded newspaper and placed a pen on top of it. His dark blue eyes, as always, were riveting, and helped distract attention from his rapidly receding hairline. Most Presidents went white during their time in office. This President was growing balder every month. He'd always been a serious guy, Hector thought, but he'd begun to look almost goofy toward the end of his first year in office. Fortunately, he had finally taken the advice of his image consultants and abandoned his pathetic attempts to comb what hair he had left over the growing expanse of his scalp. In the past year, the President's dark-brown hair had been closely shorn at the sides and even his detractors agreed he now had a more appropriate appearance.

The President brought the full weight of his inherent gravity to bear on Hector now. "The Pentagon small? You be sure to tell General Flores that."

For a moment, Hector worried that he'd been rebuked. He glanced at the other passengers in the cabin. The stone-faced Secret Service agents and other members of the President's traveling party gave him no clues, each fixedly staring out the large passenger-compartment windows or reading other sections of the Sunday *Post*.

But a second later, the President's stern expression gave way to a quick wink and playful grin, and Hector realized he was safe. General Jaime Alvarez Flores, United States Army, was the Chairman of the Joint Chiefs of Staff. In this fiscal year, the last thing anyone in the White House wanted to do was encourage the general in his ongoing battle for increased defense funding. Especially since the Building was still in the throes of a billion-dollar-plus renovation marked by unexpected budgetary shortfalls.

The President was just letting Hector know that changes in perspective worked both ways. So Hector filed the lesson away with the others he had been accumulating. He was counting on them to serve him well during the years he would spend in Washington, long after the President, and his hidebound advisors, were gone.

Lesson learned, Hector took his hand away from the window.

In protective formation with four of its kind, Marine One roared across the Potomac. It was on its final approach now.

From Hector's new perspective, the Pentagon expanded until it filled the window, rushing at him like an avalanche.

HIGHWAY 50, MARYLAND

The highway, the sky, the green hills around her, everything was a blur to Midshipman Amy Bethune. She was aware only of the sound and the speed of her motorcycle reverberating in her helmet, and the knowledge that she was still in the game.

When she had raced back to her dorm room and found that the key to the Harley was missing from her key ring, she hadn't wasted energy becoming angry. Nor had she felt surprise. Her key's disappearance had merely been further evidence that all the delays heaped upon her today were not intended as minor inconveniences or pranks. This was war.

Which meant she was free to escalate the conflict as she saw fit. And she *was* in a position to escalate.

First of all, the missing key wasn't even an issue. Three years at the Naval Academy had taught her valuable lessons that were as applicable to everyday life as they were to a Naval career.

One of those lessons was to anticipate possible future threats and take measures to avert them now, when time was an ally, not when they became real and time had become the enemy.

Thus, she had spare keys for her Harley. Her father's Harley, actually. A 55 Panhead, his pride and joy, all chrome and glossy black paint, nurtured since his adolescence, kept in storage during the family's postings to Air Force bases overseas, disassembled every winter, reassembled every spring during their tours Stateside. Their homes had changed, but the Harley had remained a constant.

Some of Amy's earliest memories were of being with her father in a garage, fascinated by her flowing reflection in the mirror finish of the motorcycle's chromed parts. She had learned, almost by osmosis, the power that lay in the precise way her father would arrange the parts, this gasket *here,* that screw *there,* so that when picked up in order they would magically transform themselves into the Harley.

As a child, she'd nestled securely in her father's arms, wearing a helmet that was so big her laughter echoed in it, while she sat on the Harley's fuel tank as her father drove the cycle oh so slowly down the driveway, around the block, and back again.

As a teenager, she had found the calming satisfaction that came from taking the Harley apart herself, cleaning and adjusting each piece, then rebuilding it, the magic flowing through her this time, until the transcendent moment when she would turn the key and it would live again.

And later, all the long nights as her father lay dying in their last home, the small, wooden-frame house in Topeka, Kansas, the cancer taking apart the ordered structure of his body, they would talk about the Harley, how they'd fix it up again that winter, take it out again for the first spring ride.

Amy had taken it out by herself that spring. But when the speed was right and the motor roared and the world flashed by in a blur of sensation, she had not felt alone.

The Harley was in her heart as much as her father had been—and still was—and nothing as small and inconsequential as a missing key was ever going to keep them apart.

Of the three spare keys she kept, the most accessible was the one hidden in a rolled-up pair of bright orange socks in her bottom drawer—a color she felt no other midshipmen would ever be tempted to "borrow."

Seeing that the first key had been taken off the ring that she kept in her desk drawer, though, had served to focus her intentions. It was no longer enough to merely catch up with 12th Company; she had to appear as if it had not been a struggle. Thus, Amy had changed from her uniform into jeans and Reeboks and a gray Navy sweatshirt, then carefully folded her uniform and packed it with a fresh blouse in her sports bag. As a Firstie, she had "civvies"—the right to wear civilian clothes when leaving the Academy for authorized absences—and she knew no one would question her outfit.

The picture she formed of her victory was inspiring: to be seen in a perfectly presentable uniform, waiting to meet the bus at the Pentagon as her company arrived. Then, as soon as the opportunity presented itself, she would see to it that Annika Marsh ended up with something colorful and greasy spilled on her own uniform.

Unfortunately, the more Amy analyzed that scenario, the more she realized its central flaw. Without a vehicle pass, she would not be able to gain entrance to the Pentagon on her own. According to the briefings Lieutenant Roth had given the company, the only way any of the midshipmen could get through the Pentagon's security today was by being on the bus.

But another of the lessons the Academy taught was to be flexible. So Amy set her dream of total victory aside. A simple victory would be enough.

She would have to go back to her original plan of catching up to the bus and getting it to pull over so she could board.

As she twisted the throttle on the Harley and leaned into the long curve heading toward the Anacostia River, Amy prepared herself for the challenge ahead.

She could see the shining silver of the Academy bus about a mile farther on, about to cross the bridge from Maryland to the District of Columbia. The highway here cut through the green, pastoral parkland bordering the Anacostia River. The rush of warm wind and the brilliance of the cloudless blue sky were exhilarating.

Amy rehearsed exactly how she would make her move, pulling beside the bus, waving to get the attention of the driver. Then she realized another flaw. No one would be able to recognize her. She slowed for the few seconds it took her to unfasten her black, full-coverage helmet, tug it off, and wedge it in front of her. Then, leaning forward to keep her helmet in place, she began to accelerate again.

The Academy bus was half a mile ahead now. Amy

squinted against the force of the wind. She could feel grit in her eyes already. But her heartbeat quickened in response to the chase, to the flat-out pursuit. At some level, she did not deny that she was responding to the excitement of the day. She twisted the throttle farther forward, thrilling to the deep roar of the engine.

She glanced at the speedometer. She was at eighty miles an hour now, flying. Without her helmet, it was as if the sound of the rushing air went through her, became part of her.

And then the air filled with the wail of a siren.

Blue light sparkled and twirled in the bright disk of her handlebar mirror.

Amy opened her mouth to swear but the wind stole her protestations.

The white-and-blue county police patrol car flashed its headlights and drew closer behind her. She had no choice. She swung the Harley over to the paved shoulder, wondering if anything was going to go right for her today.

HIGHWAY 50, DISTRICT OF COLUMBIA

A quarter-mile ahead of Amy, the Naval Academy bus disappeared over the curve of the bridge, crossing the Anacostia River into the District of Columbia. In the front passenger seat, Ranger leaned forward, eyes on the slowing police car in the bus's long side mirror until the road rose up to hide it.

The flashing blue lights had attracted more than his attention. Behind him, two weapons specialists held ready the Heckler & Koch MP5 submachine guns that had been stowed under their seats. Ranger's team of infiltrators would not risk taking these weapons through the Pentagon's security checkpoints, but they were prepared should anything unexpected occur on the way there.

Fortunately, the police car had been chasing a speeding motorcyclist, not the bus. Additional, time-costing deaths would not be necessary.

At least until he and Team Two reached their destination.

Ranger turned up the volume on the radio he held to keep track of the latest news bulletins. The police were still unaware who was responsible for the Archives massacre. Ranger had expected no less of Team One.

He checked his watch. It was 0755 hours.

The President was scheduled to speak at 1100.

And that meant Team Two's next attack would begin in precisely two hours, fifty minutes.

INTERSTATE 95, VIRGINIA

The Suburban took forty-five minutes to complete the northbound drive through Virginia on Interstate 95 to the point of land on the Virginia shore of the Potomac where the Pentagon waited.

By the time Captain Dorsey made the turnoffs onto Highway 27, and then Columbia Pike, on his approach to the Building through the checkpoints set up just below the Navy Annex south of the Arlington Cemetery, the WTOP lead news became even worse. Forty-eight people were now confirmed dead, a twelve-person renovation crew assigned to work an evening shift at the Archives was missing, and though it had not been officially confirmed, the press was reporting that the Declaration of Independence, the Bill of Rights, and the first and fourth pages of the Constitution were missing. Speculation was rampant that the shocking event might have some connection to the NATO ceremony for Russia at the Pentagon today, though no one had any clear idea what that connection might be.

They're just objects—what about the people? Tom thought to himself as the Suburban stopped at a Virginia State Police checkpoint and Dorsey held up his ID. The words of the Charters were safe in millions of books and computer files around the world. Realistically, the theft of the physical documents would mean nothing.

A state trooper took only a quick glance at Dorsey's ID through the captain's closed window before he waved the car on. So far, the security arrangements for the NATO ceremony were less than impressive to Tom. Not that his evaluation mattered one way or another, or that he really cared, but MSNBC had reported they would be among the strictest ever enforced during peacetime. The Pentagon and its soldiers could, however, certainly defend the American commander in chief and others like him. It was the civilians, like those at the Archives, who were defenseless these days.

As the Suburban sped up again, Tom told Dorsey what he thought about the theft of the Charters, that in his opinion the act amounted to nothing more meaningful than a protester burning the American flag. That it made no difference to the country if every historical document were stolen, so long as its content was preserved. That once symbols became more important than the ideals they represented, the ideals became meaningless.

Being a soldier, Dorsey predictably did not appreciate Tom's lack of outrage.

"It is a calculated insult," Dorsey insisted. "A deliberate attack on the United States of America. There's no other reason for such an act."

"Sure there is," Tom countered. "They're historical documents. They're worth a fortune."

But the captain's attention had transferred from Tom to their next obstacle. The state trooper roadblock had only been a preliminary screening area. Up ahead, Tom saw soldiers in combat gear waiting by a twisting maze of concrete barricades that blocked Columbia Pike a half mile from the Pentagon.

This time, Dorsey rolled down his window to speak to the soldier who waved the vehicle to a stop. The Suburban had been directed into one of five bays at the side of the road, each bay defined by four-foot-high, white concrete barriers. Tom watched Dorsey remove a proxcard from his jacket—obviously, the captain's DIA badge wasn't enough to get past this blockade. Then a tapping on his own window startled Tom.

He turned to see a second soldier motioning him to roll down his window. Like the others at this station, the soldier wore BDUs—a battle dress uniform of splotched greens and browns, jungle camouflage. Tom felt like asking him how much good a jungle pattern would do against the gray asphalt of an interstate highway, but didn't.

The young soldier scrutinized him; then, as if concluding that Tom's blunt-cut brown hair could only belong to a civilian, his attitude became slightly less threatening. "Good morning, sir. What's the purpose of your visit today?"

But Tom could feel his ACLU card burning a hole in his wallet. The soldier, though polite, was carrying a rifle and blocking a public roadway. Tom couldn't make it that easy for the guy. "I'm the photocopier repair guy."

The soldier's less-threatening attitude vanished as quickly as it had appeared. "Step out of the car, sir." Tom considered the soldier's response proof of his long-held observation that military personnel had no sense of humor.

Tom was reaching for the door handle, looking forward to the altercation to come, when Dorsey suddenly leaned across him, holding up his badge case to intercede. "Soldier—that won't be necessary. I'm escorting my passenger under the direct orders of Major General Vanovich."

Tom's soldier looked questioningly over to Dorsey's soldier on the other side of the Suburban. Dorsey's soldier called out, "His prox is good."

But Tom's soldier wasn't letting the matter go. "No one gets in without an authorized building pass cleared for today. Those are the direct orders of the SECDEF."

Tom liked poker. He liked any game with cards, with numbers, with odds and possibilities that followed the strict rules and probability curves of chance.

Tom's soldier had raised him by invoking the Secretary of Defense. Tom would see him and call. He dug into his jeans and pulled out his royal flush—the security pass that an hour ago had been locked in the secure storage unit in his bedroom.

The soldier had a card reader the size of a paperback book clipped to his green web belt. Without expression, he pulled it up, turned it on, held it out for Tom.

Tom touched his card to a metal square on the reader. Like Dorsey's pass, Tom's was a proxcard—it didn't need to be run through a magnetic-strip reader, the information encoded on its embedded smartchip could be scanned just by being in close proximity to a reader.

Tom felt a justifiable sense of victory as he saw the soldier's expression change in response to the information displayed on the reader's small screen. The soldier stepped back from the car and for a moment Tom wondered if the soldier was going to salute him.

"I'm sorry, Mr. Chase. I have—"

"Orders," Tom said. "I've heard that one before."

Once again, Tom saw his soldier look across the Suburban to Dorsey's soldier. Dorsey's soldier was making hand signals to another pair of soldiers at the end of the barricade maze, maybe one hundred feet away. Two large armored vehicles were parked to either side there, also painted in amoebalike patches of brown and green. Their surfaces were flat, severely angled, cut by narrow window slits. There were no obvious weapons on them, but each had a bulldozer blade beneath the forward cab. Other soldiers stood in positions around the vehicles, all eyes intently focused on the Suburban. From this distance the soldiers looked like department-store mannequins. Identical haircuts, identical uniforms. Tom felt as if he were entering a surreal world of life-size G.I. Joe action figures.

Dorsey carefully thanked his soldier and slowly backed up from the bay and into the beginning of the maze. Tom realized then that there had been a third soldier by the Suburban, carrying something that looked like a mine detector. Obviously, the vehicle had been checked for explosives at the same time its occupants were being assessed. Maybe MSNBC had been right, after all.

Dorsey drove slowly forward between the white concrete barricades as Tom noted the pattern. They'd been laid out in a series of S-shaped curves to prevent potential terrorists from smashing through them in a fast-moving vehicle. At two points along the curve, there were turnoffs. Soldiers at those intersections indicated which route Dorsey should follow. Tom took a look back at the layout of the barricades and saw that in both cases the other routes led to blind alleys. He had no doubt that the soldiers they passed had practiced training their weapons on those dead ends.

Captain Dorsey didn't seem interested in the security arrangements, though. He was still upset about Tom's off-hand reaction to the Charters' theft.

"I can't agree with you, sir. The Charters can't be sold, so they have no monetary value. What could a buyer do? Put them in a museum and charge admission?" Dorsey punched the accelerator as the Suburban cleared the last barrier, leaving the G.I. Joes and the armored bulldozers behind.

"More likely cut them into half-inch squares, stick 'em in Lucite, print up some certificates of authenticity, and sell them on the Home Shopping Network. That's the American way."

Tom enjoyed the way Dorsey clenched his jaw to keep his response to himself. The Suburban proceeded without Dorsey's further comment, passed a small guard booth, then clanged over a closed metal vehicle-barricade flush with the road's surface. In the event of a security incident, the security officer in the booth could cause a serrated metal plate to pop out of the road with enough strength to rip the axles off a tractor-trailer.

As soon as the vehicle was clear of the barricade, Dorsey picked up the argument again. He'd had time to think of a calmer response. "Forty-eight people are dead, sir. The people who are responsible must be punished."

"Of course they should. That's why we have jails."

"They should be executed."

"Oh, so then we become killers, just like them. Who do we punish then?"

Dorsey's voice revealed his bewilderment. "Punishing murderers isn't the same as killing innocent civilians."

"Killing innocent civilians. Isn't that what you guys call 'collateral damage'?"

Tom saw Dorsey's hands tighten on the steering wheel. The Suburban approached the entrance to the short tunnel running beneath Washington Boulevard.

"Mr. Chase, one of the great things about this country is that we're all entitled to our opinion." Dorsey gave Tom a look of profound disapproval. "No matter how ignorant and misinformed it may be."

Tom returned the look pleasantly. "How about that. We finally agree on something."

The shadow of the tunnel vanished in a blast of sunlight as the Suburban emerged onto the Pentagon's grounds. But Tom's attention was not directed toward the Building. The headquarters of America's armed forces held no wonder or meaning for him. Instead, the first thing he noticed was the massed formation of green-and-white helicopters hovering over the southwest lawn.

Five of the gleaming behemoths held positions a hundred feet off the ground, flattening the grass in sweeping spirals of hurricane-force wind, making the trees against the Pentagon's southwest wall lean back as if in fear.

As the combined thunder of the helicopters' engines and rotors made the windows of the Suburban vibrate, Captain Dorsey drove past the helipad, toward the vast South Parking Lot, which took up almost the same amount of square footage as the Pentagon itself. Despite having room for more than four thousand parked cars, the lot was almost empty this Sunday. Only a handful of military vehicles occupied it, most of them squat green HUMVEES, grouped near one end like a herd of robotic creatures gathered around a water hole.

Tom looked back at the tableau behind them. One of the five hovering helicopters carried the President, he knew. The other four, identical to the fifth, were there as decoys, simply to draw fire. Given that fact, how hard could it be for any potential assassin to realize that the President's helicopter was the one in the middle, in the most protected position?

In addition to having no sense of humor, Tom was becoming convinced the standard-issue military mind had no imagination, either.

Which is probably just as well, Tom suddenly thought.

Imagination let loose in the Pentagon could cause a whole lot of trouble.

FIVE

THE PENTAGON

When Marine One's rotors had come to a full stop, the plainclothes Secret Service agents already in position at the helipad's edge gave the all-clear and one of the backup Marine pilots opened the forward hatch from the inside and deployed the fold-down passenger stairs.

From his position behind the President at the hatch, Hector MacGregor recognized the three people who had come to greet their commander in chief—being six inches taller than the six-foot-tall Chief Executive had its advantages. Two of the welcoming party were military: General Jaime Alvarez Flores, Chairman of the Joint Chiefs of Staff, and his chief aide, Major Elena Christou, a reserved, athletic-looking woman somewhere in her early forties, Hector guessed.

Both officers wore crisp blue uniforms. The intricate braid on the visor of Flores's cap and on his jacket sleeves shone in the bright sunlight as if it were real gold. Major

Christou's uniform made a not-so-subtle political statement because she was wearing trousers. Until last year, the Army had remained its usual two to three decades behind the rest of the country and had permitted women to wear trousers only as part of their least formal service uniforms. But General Flores had pushed through the final regulation changes that brought complete parity to male and female soldiers in everything except ground combat duty. Since the general's interest in equality of the sexes had come to him late in his career, it was widely assumed that his change in posture was one of several steps he was undertaking in preparation for his own run at the Presidency in one or two elections. Certainly, the political realities of America in this new century were easing the electorate toward the idea of a Hispanic president more swiftly than toward any other minority. For that reason alone, Hector wanted to get along with the general. Perhaps they'd be working together someday.

The third person waiting at the foot of Marine One's folding metal stairs was Nicholas Guilbert, technically a civilian. He wore a subdued, dark-blue pinstripe suit, a solid dark-blue tie, and a shirt almost painfully white against his deep black skin. But his rigid bearing and focused attitude made that suit as much a uniform as anything Flores and Christou wore. The President had done well to choose a Secretary of Defense who made other soldiers feel comfortable in his presence.

As the President stepped from the hatch, General Flores and Major Christou saluted with machine precision. Flores was the first to speak. "Good morning, Mr. President." He had to shout because of the thunder from the other four VH-3Ds that were holding their positions about fifty feet above the ground now, ringing the helipad. The combined wind from their enormous rotors made everyone's clothes flap, and kept the air full of dust and grass clippings.

Despite the noise and the wind, though, the President returned the salutes without the awkwardness Hector had noted during the Man's first few months in office. The President had turned eighteen after the draft had ended, and had not served in the military. Upon his election, he had not been comfortable with the military honors suddenly due him. In private, he constantly worried that the military leaders he met would feel he was an impostor. During one early staff meeting, Secretary of Defense Guilbert had helpfully pointed out that even if one of the Joint Chiefs of Staff felt the President was a horse's ass, the 88th Article of the Uniform Code of Military Justice meant the officer could be subject to court-martial for saying so. The President's concerns had not been eased by this protection, but he had worked at increasing his rapport with the military. So far, his strategy seemed to be effective, evident by the way General Flores leaned close to speak to the President, as if to a friend. "I still don't consider this the proper way to welcome the commander in chief. Even an honor guard would—"

Hector saw the President stop the general by putting an equally friendly hand on his upper arm and shaking his hand. "Al," he heard the President shout, "this is going to be one heck of a day. The fewer distractions, the better." Once again, Hector marveled that in private, the President treated everyone the same way he did in public. He also doubted any Chief Executive had used the word "heck" for at least fifty years.

"Do I have a choice?" the general asked.

To Hector, the President's smile was clearly his answer.

Then the President reached out to shake hands with the general's aide. "Major Christou, good to see you again."

Hector watched how the major responded to the President. She was still at attention, and looking flushed, as if she were delighted he could remember her name from their last meeting almost two months ago. Hector decided that she had forgotten her uniform included a name badge.

Two plainclothes Secret Service agents now moved into position in front of the President. One was Mike Zibart, a former Army Ranger and head of today's Presidential protection detail. At his side was Jerry Harrap, another top agent who had transferred to the Treasury Department from the FBI. Both men had the lean, intent look Hector had come to associate with frontline soldiers.

The two agents led the way along the path that ran from the south edge of the helipad, past the facility's newly constructed support buildings. The farther building to the north, dwarfed by the Pentagon behind it, was a low, beige-painted structure with a few small windows and a compact yellow fire truck and a white ambulance parked inside its open garage. The closer building was a miniature aircraft control tower. Though the tower was only two stories tall, its top floor was ringed by large, outward-slanting windows. Hector could see the tower personnel inside, headphones on, standing at those windows to catch a glimpse of the President as he walked by. With the President safely on the ground, the other VH-3Ds that had arrived in formation with Marine One had climbed back into the sky for the thirty-mile trip back to Quantico Marine Air Station, home base for HMX-1. As always, two other VH-3Ds would remain on standby at the Anacostia Naval Air Station, two miles across the Potomac.

Behind the President, another plainclothes Secret Service agent joined their formation, accompanied by Air Force Major Ron Fielding, dressed today in a standard uniform that made him appear as just another of the President's military aides. Hector still didn't know all the Secret Service agents who rotated in and out of White House duty for major operations like today's, but he knew Fielding as a low-key, unassuming fellow who was one of six officers to fill his particular position in the White House Military Office on a round-the-clock basis. Major Fielding carried the slim, black, hard-sided briefcase known as the "football"—a holdover from the worst days of the last century when it was considered necessary for the President to have instant access to the codes and communications equipment that could authorize the use of the country's nuclear weapons.

Fielding's briefcase, the latest in an ongoing string of upgrades and redesigned replacements, was currently known as the Command Authority Terminal, though the ability to authorize the use of nuclear weapons did not strictly rest with the President alone. Following a series of Presidential directives, the first originating with Eisenhower in 1957, predelegation launch authority could actually be assumed by more than twenty other individuals in the chain of command, including the Secretary of Defense, nuclear submarine commanders, and even Army and Air Force commanders in the field who believed they faced a nuclear threat.

The CAT carried by the major today was the scaled-down version typically used within the continental United States when access to secure communications was not an issue. Inside, Hector knew, was an always-on, dedicated, encrypted videoconference link to the MILSTAR satellite network and from there to the geographically distributed nodes of the National Command Authority. Though the CAT was intended to give the President instant communication capability in the event of any form of critical national emergency, the case also held a set of envelopes, each contained within brittle, clear-plastic shells. Those envelopes were still replaced every day, and held cards with letter-code sequences matching those in identical envelopes kept in safes in missile silos, Air Force bomber bases, and submarines around the world. When necessary, the codes would be used to authenticate the President's command to prepare nuclear weapons for use.

The last time the CAT had been opened in front of a President, for any reason other than a drill, had been in January 1995, when Russia's deteriorating early-warning system had responded to the launch of a Norwegian science rocket as if it were the forerunner of an American first strike. Then Russian President Boris Yeltsin, in consultation with his Defense Minister and his Chief of General Staff, had come within eight minutes of ordering a retaliatory strike.

The National Security Agency's satellites and covert, ground-based listening stations had long been able to conduct real-time intercepts of all secure transmissions throughout Russia's *Kavkus* nuclear command-and-control communications network. Consequently, the NSA detected the change in Russia's nuclear alert status at once, and recommended an immediate and matching escalation of preparedness for American forces.

Only the absence of any significant political tension between the two countries had led the Russians to delay their decision long enough to confirm that the Norwegian rocket was following a trajectory that did not threaten Russian assets. When the Russian forces stood down from alert, another innocuous Air Force major had closed the President's CAT and resumed his role as a gray man, always in the shadows, but always present.

Behind Major Fielding and the third Secret Service agent, Marine One's hatch remained open, its forward metal stairway flanked by two of its four-man Marine crew, standing at ease, wearing sidearms. Today, the two primary pilots would be staying in their seats, keeping the helo on standby for immediate takeoff should the President's safety require it.

It was precisely this electric atmosphere of expectancy surrounding the President that Hector MacGregor found so intoxicating, the sense that at any moment something of historical import might occur, despite the fact that the function of the Secret Service was to ensure that the President's life would never get that exciting, and the function of the U.S. military was to ensure that the nuclear football would never need to be used.

As the Presidential party walked on, Hector could see Agent Zibart speaking into the small microphone pinned under his collar. Beside him, Agent Harrap was scanning the Pentagon's roofline, five stories overhead, where another figure in a gray suit and aviator sunglasses stood with two riflemen in black fatigues.

The three figures on the Pentagon's roof were looking in every direction except the President's, though Hector was hard-pressed to think where a potential attack might come from out here. Flat green lawn spread out in all directions. Hector savored the strong, bright smell of sun-warmed, freshly cut grass that was quickly overpowering the hot, gassy fumes of the departing helicopters.

He was only able to see, rising here and there across the

lawn, a handful of trees, most growing alongside the Building itself, and all had branches too high and thin to provide useful ground cover—an intentional landscaping choice, he decided. Beyond the helipad, almost parallel to the Pentagon's northwest face, ran a narrow, paved jogging path, then eight lanes of Highway 27, all shut down and empty of traffic. The only place where Hector could envisage a potential attacker concealing himself within half a mile of the Pentagon's northwest wall was in the underpass serving the interchange between Highways 27 and 244, and the remarkably twisted braiding of overpasses and tunnels connecting to Interstate 395, the whole mess affectionately known locally as the "Mixing Bowl."

Clearly, the long-established security of the Pentagon was one of the key reasons it had been selected to host the NATO ceremony.

As Agents Zibart and Harrap reached the pathway at the Pentagon's wall, they turned right, to the south, heading for one of the Building's minor entrances halfway between the helipad and the corner. As much as Hector wanted to keep up with the President, General Flores, and Secretary Guilbert, to listen in on their conversation, sometimes it was best not to look too eager. Carrying the President's small, brown-leather briefcase at his side, he held back to walk with Major Christou.

"So, Major, how's it going?"

Christou's glance at him was noncommittal. "As planned."

Hector thought he understood the reason for her reaction to him. "Is everyone feeling that way?"

"What way?"

"Like you're about to have a going-out-of-business sale?"

Up six stone steps and past the utilitarian, square columns framing the entrance, two Army sergeants in green uniforms saluted as the twin glass doors leading into the Pentagon automatically opened. The Secret Service agents stepped to either side of the doors, allowing the President, the Chairman of the Joint Chiefs of Staff, and the Secretary of Defense to continue without them. Once inside the Building, the President was presumed to be in a controlled environment, as secure as if he were in the White House. Hector knew other Secret Service personnel were stationed inside, but they were there primarily for logistical support during the NATO induction ceremony and luncheon.

Two paces from the steps leading up to the entrance, Hector suddenly froze as a deep pulsating roar engulfed him. He looked up in time to see an enormous black helicopter thunder overhead, definitely not part of the Presidential formation.

"I thought airspace was closed," he said.

"That's a Pave Low III."

Hector looked at her, waiting.

"One of ours, sir. An MH-53J."

He nodded, but they both knew he didn't speak the language.

"Air Force Special Ops. It's a rescue helicopter. Two teams will be in the air at all times today. Two more on standby."

"Are you actually expecting trouble?"

"It's our job."

THE PENTAGON, SOUTH ROTARY ROAD

The Suburban followed the entrance road to the right, merging onto the South Rotary Road that continued along the edge of the sprawling South Parking Lot. Dorsey's determined silence forced Tom to contemplate the Pentagon as it rolled past to the north.

From ground level, at a distance, there was nothing too remarkable about the Building. It was a long, low, exceptionally bland structure. The south façade was less imposing to Tom than the other four exterior walls, even though, like the others, it was almost a thousand feet long. The recent round of renovations had added twin, two-story entrance structures that divided the wall into thirds. They awkwardly reached into the South Parking Lot like landbound piers.

Someone with a completely different outlook on the Pentagon had once told Tom that the Building's architectural style was "Stripped Classicism." But all Tom saw was its heritage of bleak wartime austerity. The Pentagon had been built during World War II and, as far as Tom was concerned, the practices and beliefs of most of its inhabitants still belonged in that long-ago era.

The Suburban turned left, taking a roadway that cut through the South Parking Lot, then along the Building's southeastern side. This view of the Pentagon had always reminded Tom of a bus terminal with its indented parking spaces for at least twenty buses in the stretched-out, open-air Metro station. Most of the bus stands were empty today. But four at the end were taken up by large green army buses marked with prominent red crosses in white circles. Army medical personnel moved among them, including the first uniformed women Tom had seen today. He looked away.

Beyond the bus terminal, on Dorsey's side, Tom noticed a few changes since his last trip to the Building. The segment-by-segment renovation project, under way since 1994, was apparently nearing its end. Construction hoarding and a ten-foot, chain-link fence masked by green plastic sheets now surrounded the Pentagon's far corner, incompletely hiding large waste bins and temporary disposal chutes. This latest segment to be rebuilt had little to do with the defense of the free world, and everything to do with free commerce.

The Pentagon's contract construction crews were renovating the Building's shopping mall.

Years ago, Tom's first visit to the original Concourse had been when he'd realized how much a part—an accepted part—the business of war had become in American life. The Pentagon mall with its florist shop, bookstore, barber shop, and souvenir stores housed in the same structure that held the Department of Defense was, in fact, a telling example of how Americans currently regarded their country's military actions in far-off locales: as a weekend's entertainment with smart bombs and sanitized military briefings on C-SPAN.

Commerce and death, Tom thought. *An inspiring combination.*

The Suburban exited the South Parking Lot, coming up on the Pentagon's northeast side—the only one that could be thought of as being the Building's main entrance. It was called the River Entrance because it faced the Potomac. Technically, though, the body of water directly in front of it was the Boundary Channel and Lagoon that separated the Building from the river. VIPs most often entered the Building here because it was the entrance closest to the offices of the Secretary of Defense and the Joint Chiefs of Staff, as well as the National Military Command Center.

Directly in front of the main steps of the River Entrance was a small, ultra-VIP parking lot. Beyond it stretched a grassy, flat parade ground, the favored site in the past for elaborate military ceremonies. Tom wondered just when it had occurred to Pentagon security that a major six-lane highway ran directly beneath those parade grounds, offering a perfect parking spot for a devastating truck bomb. In the past few years, at least, most official ceremonies were being held in the Pentagon's much more defensible interior courtyard, located in the very center of its five rings.

The Pentagon, Tom noted, obviously considered the press to be more expendable. He could see that the parade grounds today were cluttered with temporary stands erected by the dozens of broadcast news organizations from around the world that would report on today's historic ceremony.

Dorsey drove past the small, River annex parking lot that was down one level from the elevated River Mall. This short access road, too, was similarly packed with power-generator trucks and vans sprouting antennae of all configurations, from the small clipped disks of microwave links, to the tall, twisted helixes of short-range radio, and the large bowls of direct satellite uplinks.

As the Suburban drove toward the entrance to the underground parking structure and the Tricare health facility beneath the upper-level ramp, Tom risked a joke. "Sneaking me in through the back door?" The entrance was guarded by two Marines in dress blue uniforms. A temporary sign on the wall beside the entrance said OFFICIAL VEHICLES.

Dorsey didn't respond as he turned the Suburban to the

right, then headed into a temporary parking space labeled on the wall as DIA2 in freshly painted yellow letters. He shut off the Suburban, pulled out the keys, took off his sunglasses, and then sat quietly for a moment, as if gathering his thoughts. Tom waited in the muffled silence. He could guess what was coming.

It did.

"Why the hell do you work for us?"

"Why do you?"

Dorsey didn't hesitate. "To do my duty for my country."

"Me, too. But here's the difference. You've been programmed to say that. I haven't."

Tom had no doubt that if Dorsey had not been on duty, if this conversation had been held after hours in a bar, he would be flat on his back right now with the imprint of Dorsey's fist on his jaw.

But they were in the Pentagon.

The captain closed his door a touch too forcefully as he got out of the car. Closing his own door gently, Tom paused in surprise at the near-suffocating physical grip of the outdoor heat and humidity. It felt like the worst day in August.

As Dorsey strode ahead of Tom toward the two Marines guarding the garage entrance, a large silver-and-blue bus suddenly appeared and swerved directly into the captain's path. Reacting instantly, with a parent's reflexes, Tom held Dorsey back as the bus squealed to a stop in front of them. He caught the flash of consternation Dorsey was unable to hide. He clearly didn't want to be beholden to Tom for anything.

The silver bus was decorated with a narrow band of dark blue, and a discreet line of type identifying it as belonging to the United States Naval Academy. Inside, Tom could see young white-uniformed men and a few women standing up, filing off in regimented silence, photo-security passes conspicuously hanging around their necks.

Tom started around the bus, but Dorsey gestured to him to wait for the line to pass.

A blond naval officer, carrying a scuffed, black-leather attaché case, stood by the door like a teacher counting students. Tom found himself staring at the officer's uniform. He wasn't expert at identifying military markings, but he recognized the twin stripes on the man's shoulder board. The blond officer was a lieutenant.

Then as if the lieutenant sensed Tom's scrutiny, he turned his head suddenly and met Tom's gaze directly. For a moment, his pale eyes narrowed and the set of his mouth subtly altered, almost as if he recognized Tom.

Unsettled, Tom stared back, trying to recall if he'd ever met the man. But then the officer's face shifted back to blank indifference. He nodded at Tom, then at Dorsey, as if thanking them for their decision to wait.

Dorsey nodded in return.

Tom did his bit to promote world peace. He flashed a V-sign and said cheerily, "Go Navy, beat Army."

The officer hesitated for an instant, puzzled, but then quickly moved off after his charges through the limousine entrance, the scuffed attaché case swinging at his side.

Dorsey's hand on his arm prevented Tom from following. The captain's face was tight with anger.

"Mr. Chase, some advice. You are no longer in your own territory. You are in *ours*. You are entitled to your own opinions about the military, but in here, I'd keep them to myself."

Of all the possible replies Tom could have given the livid captain, by force of habit, he chose the worst possible one.

"Don't hold your breath."

Then Tom stepped into the Pentagon.

Directly behind Team Two and Ranger.

SIX

NORTH AMERICAN LIGHTNING DETECTION NETWORK, TUCSON, ARIZONA

One half hour before his shift was finished, Stan Drewniak took a big gulp from the last can of his evening six-pack of Jolt Cola, and realized everything he had just typed in his report for Dr. Helen Shapiro was invalid.

His data set was not large enough to justify the conclusion he had reached. In layman's terms, he had not covered all his bets.

Of the 972 operational satellites in orbit of Earth, fully one-third of them were military. Yet he had only tracked the orbits of civilian satellites in identifying what he now called "Grinch Gaps"—those irregular times when large areas of the Pacific were not under direct visual observation by satellites capable of detecting a large, lightning-like discharge.

But what about the orbits of military satellites?

In a caffeine-and-sugar-induced flash of insight, several new possibilities suddenly presented themselves to him, and he twitched his toes so that the sole of his sandal tapped against his heel more or less in time to the opening theme from *Buckaroo Banzai.*

One possibility was that he would discover that at the time of the civilian Grinch Gaps there was no military coverage over the same section of the Pacific. That would strongly imply that whoever was responsible for the enormous electromagnetic pulse spotted by the North American Lightning Detection Network was not associated with the United States. Stan was still leaning toward the French. The United States had tens of thousands of square miles of remote desert in which to test new military equipment. The French didn't. So they had to wreak destruction on other people's real estate.

The other possibility, Stan knew, was that he would discover that U.S. military surveillance satellites were, in fact, in position to cover the area missed by civilian satellites. That would imply that the Grinch events were being staged by the U.S. military and timed to avoid public notice. Stan was certain that would be the possibility his paranoid manager would consider more likely.

Stan saved his incomplete report, then accessed the GAI satellite listings. Because the NALDN was dependent on commercial communications satellites to maintain its sensor system, Global Atmospherics kept on file complete ephemeris tables for almost every other satellite known to be in orbit. Occasionally, especially during periods of intense solar winds, some satellite signals could interfere with others. At those times, it was necessary for the company to quickly determine if a communications problem in its network was the result of its own hardware, or someone else's. One of the first troubleshooting methods used during a communications slipup was to see if satellite interference could be possible.

As he selected U.S. surveillance satellites from the list of 274 military space platforms presented by his computer, Stan understood that he might not find anything useful. It was definitely probable that the Pentagon had many more satellites on orbit than GAI would be aware of. But the orbits of the military's largest platforms were laughably easy to determine from publicly announced launch dates, government publications, and actual eyeball sightings. In particular, he knew, visible-light astronomers around the world kept careful note of satellite positions in order to avoid having a satellite trail mar a long photographic exposure of the stars.

For his first attempt at determining what U.S. military assets might have been in position over the Pacific for the first Grinch event, Stan skipped over anything he knew to be a military communication satellite or related to the Global Positioning System. He clicked his mouse to select only surveillance satellites which observed the Earth in visible light. Since the Grinch event on December 24th had taken place in daytime, and in an area where weather photos had shown almost no clouds, Stan also ignored those satellites that observed the Earth at infrared and radar frequencies. At this stage, all he wanted to know was if the Pentagon had anything up there that could snap a picture of the Grinch.

After scrolling through the entire list, he ended up selecting eight military satellites. Publicly, most were known as the Keyhole series. But since that code name dated from the 1960s, he was certain the Pentagon had other names for them by now.

Since eight seemed like a low number, Stan went back through the list and selected three National Security Agency satellites in the Trumpet series that would normally be used to intercept microwave radio transmissions and cellular phone conversations. With that level of sensitivity, they would be able to detect the Grinch event from thousands of miles away, though they wouldn't be able to image it.

His satellites selected, Stan instructed his computer to trace their orbits over the Pacific on December 24th of last year. The grid map of the world appeared, and at once eleven colorful sine waves began to weave across his screen. And by the point at which the time code read 5:17 P.M. Mountain time, it looked to Stan as if five of those satellites had collided directly over the area he'd identified as the most probable location of the Grinch event.

Stan hummed softly to himself as he had the computer put the orbital tracking on pause. "So much for the French." Whatever had caused the Grinch event, it had done so when no civilian satellite was nearby, but when three of the U.S. military's visible-light and two of its radio-frequency surveillance satellites were almost directly overhead. Much as he hated to admit it, Shapiro might be right. The Pentagon appeared to be connected to the Grinch.

Stan tapped the keys that would save the orbital tracks as a graphic file he could print out, then hesitated as he realized he was about to make another mistake.

One of the worst things a scientist could do when he found the results he had hoped for was to stop looking. How did he know that those five satellites didn't achieve the same orbital positions over the Pacific on a regular timetable? It could be a coincidence that they were in orbital alignment when the Grinch event occurred. What about during the two other events?

"What's the pattern?" he muttered to himself. He still had to establish one. He knew Shapiro wouldn't be interested in anything he had to say until he did.

There were only ten minutes left in his shift. Stan looked over to the main event display where he could see his relief, Teej Cluet, schmoozing with one of the system operators. Since Stan was working with his manager's blessing for a change, he decided he shouldn't have any difficulty staying a few minutes later at his desk. Teej could keep an eye on things from one of the terminals that wasn't being used this Sunday morning.

Totally committed now to finishing the report before he left, Stan took the orbital traces off pause. He watched as all eleven sine waves began slowly crossing the map of the world, some diverging, some closing, but all relationships between them apparently random. He waited to see how many orbits it would take for four or five of them to come together as they had over the Grinch.

The time code rolled over to December 25. The satellites were scattered across the globe. He typed in a command to speed up the screen-drawing program. It was time to test his formal prediction that the next time the satellites would cluster together over the Pacific wouldn't be until February 15 of this year, when the Grinch had made its second appearance.

The time code rolled over to December 26. The Pentagon's surveillance satellites showed no sign of converging at all. Their orbits continued to spread apart like oil drops on water. Stan decided to speed the process even more.

But even as he moved his hand to press the F10 acceleration key, he changed his mind.

He pressed F5 to stop the traces.

Then he ran them backward to midnight, December 25, and started them forward again, slowly, this time, paying close attention to the orbital paths followed by the Pentagon's visible-light surveillance satellites.

Stan sat back with a smile. He took another sip of Jolt Cola.

By midnight, December 26, not one of the military satellites had been in position to capture the dramatic shot of the cruise missile that had destroyed the USS *Shiloh.*

He had found the Pentagon's lie.

Thirty minutes later, Stan was in Shapiro's office, thrumming from equal parts caffeine and excitement as he watched her scan through the material he had brought her. At the top of the pile was a copy of the satellite photo that had been the key exhibit at the *Shiloh* hearings. He had downloaded it from the *USA Today* Website.

The photo was in black-and-white, and had been taken from almost directly overhead, though from an altitude of several hundred miles. The Navy had said the surveillance satellite was taking part in the same training exercise as the *Shiloh,* an exercise intended to help military photoanalysts identify different weapons systems in use.

In the upper right-hand corner of the image, the *Shiloh* was a knife-sharp, narrow streak of light gray. The shadow the vessel cast across the mottled surface of the ocean was solid black. In the lower left-hand corner was an even shorter streak of white, the cruise missile's exhaust. The streak was enclosed by a white circle, and an even more extreme blowup of that section of the photo was inset beside the circled area. The enhanced blowup showed the blocky silhouette of a missile with stubby wings toward the back. The edges of it were jagged, like a low-resolution computer graphic. Offset from the missile itself was a matching shadow on the ocean. At the hearings, the Pentagon's photo-analysts had testified that six seconds after this image had been recorded, the cruise missile had struck the *Shiloh* amidships. The resulting explosion had detonated the *Shiloh*'s own missile warheads. She had sunk in less than a minute, with no survivors.

Stan watched as Shapiro briefly glanced at the photo, then skimmed through his five-page report and accompanying printouts of orbital traces. Fighting the irrational urge to blurt out his own conclusions, Stan looked out through the half-glass wall into the main work area. Teej was at the shift manager's desk now. Only four other programmers were at their stations. On the main event screen, thunderstorm activity across North America looked light.

Stan sneaked a quick glance at his manager, but she was still flipping through the pages. He switched his attention to the framed print on the wall behind her, some improbably photorealistic painting of a Hopi Indian on a mountaintop, arms raised to gathering storm clouds arranged in the shape of a soaring eagle and laced by glowing strands of lightning. Beside it was a much smaller framed photo of a flight crew in orange jumpsuits, cradling white helmets, as they stood in front of a silver aircraft with a large NASA logo on the side. Stan recognized Shapiro as one of the two women in the photo. The plane was the *Lightning Chaser*. It was how she spent her summer vacations.

He looked away from the photo and the print to find Shapiro studying him, idly twisting one of the sterling-silver tips of her bolo tie around one lean finger.

"The Grinch sank the *Shiloh,*" she said. She made her pronouncement sound like a statement, but Stan knew it was a question.

So he answered it. "The photo of the cruise missile couldn't have been taken on December 26th when the Navy says the ship was sunk because there were no surveillance satellites overhead."

"None that you know of," his manager corrected.

Stan shook his head. He'd found the pattern. She'd almost pointed him to it. "But, there were at least three visible-light surveillance satellites over the Grinch site on the 24th that *could* have taken that picture. If we get someone in here who knows how to calculate angles and shadows, he could probably tell us which of those three satellites took the shot, and exactly when it was taken."

Shapiro uncoiled a few inches of bolo string from her finger. "And why would we want to do that, Stan?"

Stan had the disconcerting sensation that he had just dropped into a completely different conversation.

"Uh, because this is a cover-up," he said.

"And . . . ?"

"And four hundred people died."

"That wasn't covered up. They held hearings."

"Say what?"

Shapiro continued before Stan could think of any better way to express his confusion. "Stan, all you've got here— no, all you *might* have here, is evidence suggesting the Navy changed the time of the *Shiloh* accident by about forty-eight hours, and changed the location by about a thousand miles. I can imagine all sorts of legitimate security reasons to explain why those measures were necessary."

"But what about the Grinch?"

Shapiro's elegantly shaped fingernail tapped the photo. "If your analysis is correct, it's right here. You found it. Congratulations."

Stan gave his head a shake. It was almost as if Shapiro was being deliberately obtuse. He spoke slowly, in an effort to make her understand. "No, Doctor. That missile's nowhere near big enough to hold an explosive that could generate the electromagnetic pulse we detected."

Shapiro shrugged as she shuffled the pages of his report together. "Then I don't know what you're trying to tell me. Is this the Grinch event or isn't it?"

"No. The Grinch is what sank the *Shiloh*. Not that cruise missile. This picture was taken just before it happened."

"You just told me you couldn't be sure exactly when this picture was taken."

"Not to the exact second. But since the *Shiloh*'s there and undamaged, the photo had to have been taken before the ship . . . blew up or whatever."

Shapiro placed his report in the center of her green desk blotter. Stan felt some slight relief as he realized she wasn't going to give it back to him. That had to mean that she was at least going to pass it on to Dr. Green, the NALDN operations manager. "To tell the truth, Stan, I don't think you've thought this through very well."

"What?"

Shapiro tapped the report. "There's absolutely nothing in here that tells us what the Grinch is. And that was the entire rationale for the assignment I gave you, wasn't it?"

Feeling dizzy, Stan sat down in one of the two hard-backed wooden chairs facing the desk in Shapiro's office. "But I was right the first time. The Grinch *is* a military system. I think it was on the *Shiloh*. I think when that cruise missile was launched at the *Shiloh,* the *Shiloh* was supposed to use some new electromagnetic-pulse generator to knock out the missile's electronics. And instead, it blew up the ship."

"Stan." The cloud physicist walked around her desk, pulled up the second chair, and sat down beside him. "I can tell you're getting upset, but you don't have to be. Even if everything you say is true, what do you want the company to do about it? If the Navy was testing a new defensive system and it didn't work, don't you think it's a good idea to keep those results secret? I mean, we still do have enemies in the world. Why would GAI want to do anything that would let our country's enemies know we have a weakness?"

"Dr. Shapiro, about four hours ago, you told me that the military lies. *This* is a lie."

"And what good comes of exposing it? I mean, if the Navy had said that four hundred men *hadn't* died, if they were covering up something hideous like that, well, then, okay, you'd have a point. But they're not covering that up."

"They used this thing two . . . more . . . times," Stan said. Even to himself, his voice sounded as if he were pleading. "February 15th. April 28th. Both times, Dr. Shapiro, there was *no* civilian satellite coverage, but lots of military coverage. The orbital traces are right there."

"And are any other ships missing?"

"Not . . . that I know of."

"Then what's your point?"

"You're the one who asked me to write this report."

"Because GAI is in the business of detecting, analyzing, and reporting electromagnetic phenomena. When I asked you to bring me your research, I expected that's what would be in it. Not some diatribe against the Navy for understandably keeping classified information classified."

Stan felt shell-shocked. "It's *not* a diatribe. All that I'm saying . . . I mean, what's so obvious . . ." But his mind was becoming jumbled. In his frustration at not being understood, he couldn't find the words he wanted to say.

"I think you should call it a day." Shapiro stood up. "Go home and sleep. We'll talk about this again tomorrow."

"What about Dr. Green?"

"I can't show him this. We'll talk. Maybe we'll find a way to present your material in a more . . . coherent way."

Shapiro was moving to the door. Stan knew he was being herded out. "But it is coherent," he insisted. "The Navy was running a test of something new. Something that wasn't supposed to hurt anyone."

"You have no evidence to support that."

"Yes, I do. If they were testing something that was supposed to blow up, Dr. Shapiro, they would have done it in New Mexico. They would have used it on an unmanned barge. But they wouldn't have used it against a ship full of sailors."

Shapiro put her hand on the doorknob. "They had hearings. The Navy admitted its mistakes."

Impulsively, Stan put his hand on the door to keep her from opening it. "Maybe we don't know what the Grinch is," he said. "But I say the Navy doesn't know, either. I say they built something to do something . . ." Stan felt his exhaustion overwhelming his vocabulary again. ". . . but . . . it did something else they weren't ready for. It blew that ship out of the water. It set off every detector we have on the West Coast. And they're so scared shitless about it, they lied about where and when the *Shiloh* went down because they don't want anyone to know that they've developed a weapon that's out of control!"

Stan's manager just stared at him until he remembered to take his hand from her door.

"Well, I'll say this much, Stan, a scientist needs a good imagination, and you have a beaut. Go home, and don't you dare talk about this with anyone. This company is not in the business of spreading unfounded rumors about a potential client."

Stan felt too rattled to say anything else. Shapiro held open the door to her office. As he walked out, chest tight, face flushed, Stan felt like a first-grader who'd just been lectured by the principal.

Starting back across the main work area, he stopped, finally realizing what he *should* have said. He *should* have told Shapiro that it was obvious the Navy didn't know exactly what it was testing because they ran the test when visible-light surveillance satellites were overhead. And why would anyone need visible-light photos of an electromagnetic weapon, unless the people involved had no idea what was going to happen?

He paused beneath the main event display, fully intending to go back to Shapiro's office. But his manager's door was closed again, and he could see through the observation windows that she was on the phone. No sense in getting in trouble with her twice in the same day, he decided. He turned back to the exit door, and left the building, barely noticing in his self-absorbed state the 120-degree heat that enveloped him the instant he stepped outside.

But all through his drive home in his open-air Jeep, he replayed the conversation he had had with her, thinking of all the other exceptionally concise and inarguable things he should have said.

By the time he arrived home at the tan, Spanish-style stucco bungalow he shared with three other programmers, Stan had fully convinced himself that Shapiro hadn't understood a word he had said because she wasn't capable of understanding him. It was incredible that the company kept someone so thick in her job. There could be no other explanation for her obstinacy.

The small bungalow was dark, its muggy 80-degree interior made bearable only by the gurgling swamp cooler on the red-tile roof. Judging from the number of empty beer bottles in the tiny living room, Stan decided his housemates wouldn't be up for a few more hours, so he went into his pit of a bedroom to listen to some *Best of the Hong Kong Cavaliers* on his headphones. That and a joint of San Francisco's finest helped take the edge off his Jolt Cola jitters and his frustration at being the only person to know how right he was about . . . everything.

Stan smoothed out the tangle of once-white sheets on his floor mattress, and settled back to stare at the few pinpricks of light that spiked in through the tinfoil he had duct-taped to his window to help him sleep through the days. He blew out deeply inhaled marijuana smoke to watch it swirl through the narrow shafts of light, converting them into miniature laser beams.

Stupid Shapiro, he thought drowsily. *Stupid Pentagon, too.*

It was just so obvious that the military had come up with something it didn't understand. And probably nobody else understood what they had yet, either.

Except me, Stan thought, carefully stubbing out his joint in an overflowing ashtray he had lifted from Maria's Restaurant up the street. *I know everything about the Grinch.*

A faint, defiant smile touched his lips.

And I'll tell the first person who asks me.

SEVEN

THIRD FLOOR, E RING

"It *is* the photocopier?"

From behind his huge walnut desk, in his office overlooking the Pentagon's River Entrance and Parade Grounds, Major General Milo Vanovich leaned forward in his ergonomically molded armchair, cradling a gray phone receiver to his ear, one hand over the mouthpiece. "Eh, Tommy . . . photocopier, printer, what can I tell you? That's what the software guys say." Vanovich squinted and his wildly tufted gray eyebrows moved up like feelers. "What's so funny?"

Tom Chase decided the joke would take too long to explain. But he still wasn't convinced his old friend was leveling with him. "Isn't there something called building services? You know, trained technicians who service photocopiers twenty-four hours a day?"

Vanovich waved a broad, thick-fingered hand as if clearing the air of a bad smell. "Tommy, it's Sunday morning . . ."

"So I noticed."

". . . there's an all-day love-in in the Courtyard . . ."

"You never told me you were a hippie."

". . . and I've had two jerks from tech support already take a look at it."

"The verdict?"

"Broken."

"And it's the only photocopier in the Pentagon?"

"It's the only Red Level in my office."

"Ah," Tom said, at last understanding why the general needed him in particular.

Suddenly, Vanovich's mood changed as he focused all his attention on the phone call. Whoever he was speaking with had come back on the line. "Just a sec, Tommy. Yeah, I'm still here, Doctor. Have you locked the files?"

Tom stood with his hands in the back pockets of his blue jeans, waiting for Vanovich to finish the call. He glanced around the office, looking for anything that had changed since his last visit before Christmas.

Like most of the upper-echelon offices in this renovated section of the Pentagon, it was conservatively tasteful in decor: dark wood paneling, neutral beige broadloom, a few subdued though inexpensive prints of classic warplanes as befit the working environment of a two-star Air Force general, various framed certificates, and brass highlights everywhere, from the floor and desk lamps to the light-switch covers. But despite the bland uniformity required to prove that taxpayers' dollars weren't being squandered on frills, Vanovich had managed to introduce a few decorative elements to personalize his domain. The most notable among them were the ergonomic chair and the three model stands on his massive desk.

One rounded triangle of polished dark wood held up a ten-inch-long, blocky blue-and-silver model of a MIL-STAR communications satellite, the backbone of the military's strategic and tactical relay communications system. Even a cursory glance told Tom that the model was missing a number of crucial technical details, making it acceptable for display in an unclassified environment. The second stand bore aloft a matte black version of the old, bizarre Darkstar unmanned aerial vehicle. *Tyler would like this one,* thought Tom. The long wings attached to the flying-saucer-like body made the long-cancelled UAV look more like a prop from the latest *Star Wars* film than an actual aircraft.

Tom paused appreciatively before the third stand. Now, this one was typical of Vanovich's decidedly nonmilitary sense of humor. The brass plaque on the base identified the model only as NEVADA RAIN (OPERATIONAL MODE). But no satellite or cutting-edge aircraft adorned the stand's empty support arm. Whatever the Nevada Rain was, aircraft or satellite, Tom decided it must have impressive Stealth characteristics.

The other stamp of individuality on Vanovich's office was, of course, the not-so-subtle scent of cigars. The Pentagon, like every other U.S. military installation, was a completely no-smoking building. But Vanovich enjoyed keeping a few unlit cigars around, as if threatening to break the rules at any moment.

"No, no," Vanovich said to whoever was on the phone. "He won't cause trouble." The general shrugged at Tom as if to apologize for the length of the call. Tom shrugged back, knowing that with Vanovich's propensity for making all his staff part of one big extended family, the phone call could be about anything from a colonel who might have gone AWOL to a secretary's kid busted for stealing a bike. Vanovich shifted the receiver to his other ear, the movement revealing to Tom, surprisingly, that the general was wearing what appeared to be a small hearing aid in his left ear. Not that it seemed to be slowing him down.

As Vanovich continued his conversation, Tom wandered over to one of the tall windows that looked down onto the parade grounds. There was a limestone pillar almost directly in front of the window, but he saw enough to know that the circus was in full swing below.

Tom counted eight stretch limos, each with a different set of national flags, lined up on the ramp leading to the VIP parking lot directly in front of the River Entrance. Beyond them, he could see enough of the parade grounds to know they had been turned into a city of news broadcast trailers and elevated stages, with clusters of brilliant television lights switched on despite the full sun. Typically, the majority of news teams seemed to be foreign. Today's NATO ceremony for Russia was recognized as a precedent-shattering event everywhere but in the country that had made it possible.

"Okay," Vanovich said, and Tom could hear that the phone call was coming to an end. "I'll send someone out. Say, Tuesday morning? Okay, the afternoon works, too. Just don't spook him. Yeah, that's right. That's my job. Thank you, Doctor. You, too." Vanovich hung up, but stared at the phone a few moments longer, lost in thought. The multiline set was one of three on his desk. With a casual glance, Tom checked the wire coming from it and saw it had been the general's secure phone. Tom had done some consulting work on the Pentagon's three-tiered phone system, back when the first renovations were starting.

Finally, Vanovich looked up at him. "Is Captain Dorsey still hanging around?"

"I think so," Tom said. He went to the office door, opened it to find Dorsey standing outside in the corridor. "The general wants you."

Dorsey entered the office as if Tom weren't there. "Yes, General."

Vanovich tore a sheet of numbered notepaper from a pad, placed it on the glass top of his desk, and scrawled a series of words across it. "Captain, I'd like you and Captain Lassiter to take a trip to Tucson, ASAP." He handed the sheet of paper to Dorsey. "This guy's supervisor is faxing his personnel file into Records right now. Run it through the FBI. And come back as soon as you've put it through."

Dorsey knew when he was being dismissed. "Yes, sir."

After Dorsey closed the door behind him, Vanovich got up from behind his desk.

Tom didn't do a good job of hiding his shock at the general's appearance. Inwardly, he was outraged. *Why hadn't he been told?* Now that he was standing, the general looked almost shrunken to Tom, and even paler than usual.

"Forty pounds," Vanovich said as he shook Tom's hand with both of his.

As usual, Vanovich could read his mind. "Yeah. It's what you think. But not that bad."

"How bad?"

"They caught it fast, Tommy. I had my regular checkup last October. Other than being too fat, I checked out okay. Then I had a bunch more tests in January, and . . . son of a gun, you know. But that means they got it within two months of it starting up. They say it gives me a good shot at beating it."

Tom didn't question the facts, but he wasn't falling for the spin Vanovich was putting on them. "Beating what, Milo?"

"Cancer. Colon."

"Jesus."

"Tommy, look at me, will you." Vanovich patted his considerably deflated chest. His crisply pressed blue shirt was tucked smoothly into his uniform trousers. His dark tie hung almost flat, instead of curving over the bulging belly that was no longer there. "I never felt better. I'm looking great. I'm going to stop wasting my time fixing you up and get some action of my own now."

"You're full of shit."

Vanovich grimaced. "You'd be amazed. I've got to shit through a hose these days."

"Milo . . ."

Vanovich grabbed Tom's arms, gave them a squeeze. "Tommy, I'm fine. I'll be a smelly old fart in the front row when our boy graduates from Yale. But I'm going to be there."

"You'd better be." Tom didn't know what else to say. But if Vanovich was going to tough it out, then so would he. "So . . . the photocopier? I take it it's in your *office* office?" He held up his proxcard.

Vanovich beamed at Tom. "That's my boy." He gave Tom's proxcard a tap. "Now, where was I going to find another one of those on a Sunday morning in this joint with all that crap going on outside?"

Tom sighed, but he knew the general was right. "Show me the patient," he said.

General Vanovich walked—*no, shuffled,* Tom thought angrily—over to a door at the side of his outer office, and

Tom's concern intensified. Last year, despite his weight, Vanovich had moved like a boxer, full of pent-up energy. Tom found himself wondering why it was the general had had medical tests run only a few months after his regular checkup. It was more than likely that Vanovich hadn't told him the whole story.

Tom stood back as the general placed his eye against a small black-rubber cup mounted on a gray metal box beside the door. A moment later, a chime sounded from the box and the door lock clicked, signifying that a computer in the Pentagon's basement was satisfied that the retina pattern it had just scanned was on the authorized list for the facility that lay beyond.

In Pentagon parlance, Vanovich had just opened a "green door," the name given to an entrance to areas whose activities were decidedly sensitive.

As Vanovich pushed the door open, a cool draft of air-conditioning swept out over Tom. The lighting in the room beyond was subdued, most of it coming from four display monitors clearly visible on a sleek, Red Level workstation. Tom knew there were no outside windows in the general's inner office. Where the Pentagon's most secure operations took place, there never were.

But entrance to the restricted room was not as simple as Vanovich's merely opening the green door and allowing Tom to step through. Thermal sensors above the entrance would detect the presence of two people entering when only one had been scanned, and would trigger an instant security alert, followed by the deployment of protective measures. That safeguard was to keep the general from ever being forced, at gunpoint, to give entry to the Red Level room.

Now it was General Vanovich's turn to wait, as Tom

touched his proxcard to the metal square beneath the retina scanner, then placed his eye against the scanner, taking care not to blink. For a brief instant, a pale red disk floated before him in multiple levels of dark glass—a reflected image of the back of his eyeball, the network of blood vessels there as distinct as any fingerprint, but far more accessible to computer interpretation.

The pattern area of fingerprints typically fell into one of three types, with each type possessing further subgroupings of similar ridge structures. No two sets of fingerprints were ever identical, not even those of twins. But the characteristics that distinguished one from another could sometimes be so subtle that even the most sophisticated computer programs could not reliably see the differences between two fingerprints sharing the same pattern family and subgroupings. In those cases, the final decision had to be made by human specialists. Fingerprint identification was an art, not a science.

Retinal patterns of blood vessels, however, appeared to be completely random and, except in the case of certain diseases, did not change over time. Thus, when real-time identification was required, retinal scans were much easier for computers to deal with than fingerprints.

As for hand-geometry scanners, the military's interest in those had cooled after a group of terrorists had come within two locked doors of an anthrax vaccine storage center at Fort Detrick, Maryland, by using the severed hand of a Department of Agriculture researcher who had had the proper clearance.

The scanner chimed again. Tom Chase's retina pattern had been in the Pentagon's computers for years.

Vanovich invited him in. It was a small room, ten feet by

twenty, but it gave the general total access to all the relevant assets of every other organization in the intelligence community. That was the power of the National Infrastructure Agency.

The National Security Agency collected electronic intelligence from around the world, intercepting everything from ordinary phone calls, e-mail, and faxes to the most secure military communications of other countries, and the National Reconnaissance Office collected imagery intelligence. Most often, the NRO intelligence came from satellites that could look down from space in a complete range of wavelengths, allowing detailed photographs to be made not only in daylight but in darkness, and through clouds, fog, and smoke, as well. Above the NSA and the NRO was the Central Intelligence Agency—the coordinating agency for the entire intelligence community, including the separate agencies run by each branch of the military.

But Vanovich's NIA eclipsed *all* agencies, for it functioned not only as a gatherer of intelligence, but as a protector of it as well. The more complex the underlying systems of America had become—with vast power grids, integrated-communications networks, and electronic banking that transferred trillions of dollars as bits of electronic data, as only a few examples of the changes that had come with the twentieth century—the more vulnerable America itself had become to disruption.

To protect that national infrastructure, the NIA had been given broad powers to both integrate with and monitor it. And since that same infrastructure supported the operations of all the other intelligence agencies, the NIA had inevitably become the ultimate watcher, with access to all the secrets held within the entire intelligence community.

The only safeguard that held the NIA in check was that, deliberately, it had been given absolutely no operational authority. In theory, it had no covert operatives; it could take no action based on what it discovered. Its agents could only compile reports and share them with the National Security Council. But in practice, in a world where knowledge, more than ever, was power, the sheer quantity of information the NIA had access to, domestic and foreign, had made it the most influential arm of the U.S. government, though fewer than a thousand people even knew it existed.

"Feels good to be back, doesn't it?" the general said as he stood before the smoothly curved lines of the Red Level workstation that dominated the room. "You don't get to play with these at the FBI Academy."

"Not yet," Tom said.

"I want you to come back to work for me, Tommy."

Caught off guard by Vanovich's sudden change of subject, Tom frowned. *That had been settled years ago.* "I already do."

"Not as a consultant. Full time. Here. In the NIA."

"That's not where I belong, Milo. We both know it."

Vanovich looked directly into Tom's eyes, and in one stomach-wrenching moment, Tom knew exactly what the general was going to say.

"I'm dying, Tommy."

Protests of useless denial sprang up inside Tom. He wanted to tell Vanovich he couldn't die, that he wouldn't let him, that he and Tyler needed him to live for a long, long time. But Tom knew he also had to treat the offer with respect. The general was serious. They would have to discuss it.

"It gets worse." The general paused, choosing his next words carefully. Tom had never seen his old friend look so defeated. "I can't let these fuckers take control of my agency when I'm gone. It's too dangerous. I made a mistake. We've gone offensive."

For a moment, Tom almost felt as he had when Tyler had flipped him in the living room. His chest felt paralyzed. Vanovich's NIA, America's newest intelligence agency, the highly classified department that was to protect the country from one of the most destructive new forms of warfare in the history of humanity, had somehow developed a way to wage that type of war itself.

"Jesus, Milo, what have you done?"

The general seemed too afraid to answer.

EIGHT

THE PENTAGON/ "G" PARKING LOT/CHECKPOINT ROMEO

"I swore at a cop, okay?"

Amy sat astride her Harley, still fuming from her encounter with the county police. Two hundred and forty dollars it was going to cost her—more than she cleared in a month—for twenty-five lousy miles an hour over the speed limit. And no helmet.

She'd fight the ticket. That's what she had told the sanctimonious mother— . . . she wouldn't say the words again. Not even to herself. When she had said them to the cop, that's when he had torn up the ticket for nine miles over the limit and changed it to the full twenty-five.

The Army sergeant at her side swiped her pass through the slot on his card reader. He looked to be about forty, probably from a reserve unit, not overly familiar with the equipment or the attitude. Amy fought down the urge to rev the Harley to relieve her impatience.

The sergeant swiped the card again.

"Oh, man," Amy sighed. Then shrugged at the sergeant's look of annoyance. He was not to be rushed. "Sorry, it's just that cop. . . ."

More than an hour he had kept her at the side of the freeway. A whole, God— . . . no, she wouldn't start. She wouldn't.

The sergeant started to hook his card reader to his belt. "Sorry, ma'am, it's not going through. I'm going to have to ask you to get off the motorcycle and—"

"Come on!" In addition to travel time, it had taken Amy another hour and a half just to get to a military checkpoint near the Pentagon. The first police checkpoint she'd reached, near the Jefferson Memorial, had refused to let her through. She had had to fight traffic all the way up to the Roosevelt Bridge to cross the Potomac, then swing all the way around the Arlington Cemetery, before she'd found a second police checkpoint on Columbia Pike, near the Navy Annex. And those sons of . . . those myopic, hidebound . . . robots . . . hadn't let her through, either.

She had then had to poke her way through Pentagon City on surface streets until she'd come to her last chance—the police checkpoint at Jefferson Davis and the 395. At least those cops had finally succumbed to her nonstop verbal outpouring and waved her through to tell her story to the Army checkpoint up ahead.

After all that, she wasn't about to give up now just because a weekend warrior didn't know how to operate his God— . . . reader.

"I'm sorry, ma'am. But this is not a valid pass."

"Look," Amy pleaded, "sometimes the magnetic strips get screwed up, okay? Type in the bar-code numbers."

"I can't—"

"Yes, you can." Amy swept her hand behind her. The

road was clear. "There's no lineup. You can give me a f— . . ." She bit her lip, swallowed the word she was about to say. "Please, Sergeant, enter the card manually."

The sergeant sighed. He snapped Amy's pass into a clip at the top of his reader so he could see it; then he laboriously typed in the sixteen-digit, five-letter code that ran at the bottom of the pass's bar code.

"Thank you."

The sergeant nodded as he typed on the reader's minuscule keyboard. Twice he hit two tiny keys—raised plastic blisters, actually—at the same time and had to erase his entry and start again.

Amy looked past the checkpoint to the Pentagon's River Entrance, less than half a mile away. She could see the fleet of limos parked bumper-to-bumper beside the parade grounds, dotted with fluttering patches of color from the official flags they flew. A field of brilliant lights blazed with blue-white intensity beside them. Television coverage, she guessed, like for the arrival of stars at the Academy Awards.

Amy's gaze followed the angles of the ramps and intertwining roadways that knotted around this part of the Pentagon. She pictured herself gunning the Harley, speeding forward, then soaring over the barricades and checkpoints like Steve McQueen in *The Great Escape*. That had been her father's all-time favorite movie. It still was hers.

"Bethune, Amy Leanne, midshipman, United States Navy," the sergeant said.

Amy frowned. She didn't know what the sergeant meant by his recitation. That information was printed on the front of the pass along with her photo ID. "That's me."

The sergeant turned the reader around so Amy could see that a second ID photo of her had appeared on its small LCD screen, flanked by several lines of small type. "Says here you were supposed to have arrived almost three hours ago."

Amy forced herself to retain her composure. "And that's what I've been saying."

"It also suggests that for your duty assignment at the luncheon, you're out of uniform."

Amy slapped her dark-blue sports bag, strapped to the back of her cycle. "It's right here, ready to go."

The sergeant seemed close to making up his mind. "You going to get into trouble for this?"

"I can handle it."

The sergeant gave a small chuckle. "I bet you can. Okay. You're in."

Amy stood up to push the Harley off its stand.

"Except," the sergeant continued, "not on that. The pass is good for you, only. No parking privileges."

Amy rocked back on the cycle, knowing another half hour had just been added to her morning. The speeches would be *starting* by then.

Seeing her crestfallen face, the sergeant at least tried to be helpful. "You can lock it up in G lot, right over there. We'll be at this station all day, so it'll be safe."

"Thank you, Sergeant." Amy pulled herself together with an effort and started to walk the cycle backward. "Can you tell me what entrance I have to go to?"

The sergeant checked the screen. "Tricare service entrance under the River Entrance . . . but that's not going to do you any good. It's packed with all the official arrivals by now. Hold on." He switched on a small radio clipped to his camouflaged shirt front. "Gate Control, this is Checkpoint Romeo. I have a late service arrival for the Tricare entrance. Please advise on alternate. Over."

After a moment, a woman's voice replied. "Romeo, this

is Gate Control. Late-arrival entrance is the Corridor Three, South Terrace pedestrian bridge. Over."

"Copy that. Romeo out." The sergeant pointed to the low white bus terminal structure running along the Pentagon's southeast wall. "The South Terrace bridges are right around the corner. The Corridor Three entrance will be the second one you see on the far side."

"Thanks, Sergeant. I really appreciate that." Then Amy hesitated. The sergeant looked as if he hadn't finished speaking. "Yes?"

"Go park the Harley. I'll get you a ride."

HELIPORT ENTRANCE

Hector followed Major Christou into the Pentagon. The morning's heat went with them. In the midst of rebuilding virtually every interior floor, wall, and ceiling, the Pentagon's still-ongoing, fourteen-year, "slab-to-ceiling" renovation program was also replacing every environmental, electrical, and communications system in the Building. There were, however, many details still to be fine-tuned, and the air-conditioning system was one of them.

The Pentagon was one of the largest office buildings under one roof in the world, with an interior volume more than twice that of the Empire State Building. The maintenance and environmental controls it required were more like those for a small city than for a single building. Indeed, in one report Hector had seen cross the President's desk, he'd learned it was not unusual for there to be up to thirty local power outages in a typical day in the Building. Despite the Pentagon's reputation for achieving military perfection, its domestic day-to-day support services, from heating and cooling to plowing the parking lots in winter, were seldom any more efficient than in most civilian buildings.

The first thing Hector encountered in the renovated Heliport Entrance foyer was a digital time-and-date sign, four feet by three feet, placed prominently behind the raised security desk. The desk functioned as visitor control for this entrance, and since use of the heliport was restricted to military staff or dignitaries, no metal detectors or X-ray scanners were in use. Under normal conditions, the two Air Force guards on duty would confirm that each visitor swiped his or her pass through a reader on a security turnstile, but no one seemed eager to ask the President for his ID. He and his party continued through a special, open-access path.

As Hector passed the guards, he saw that the digital sign also displayed the entrance's location on a stylized Pentagon floor plan, and identified the Building's current security condition: THREATCON BRAVO.

Hector caught up to Christou as the Army major strode briskly past the Air Force guards to the left. She was heading for a wide passageway marked by an overhead sign reading CORRIDOR FOUR in a modern, severely unornamented typestyle. "Is that good?" he asked her.

"There're five threat condition levels, Mr. MacGregor. Bravo is level three."

"Alpha, Bravo." Hector held up two fingers. "Shouldn't Bravo be level two?"

Christou held up her hand, showing five fingers. "The sequence starts with Normal, then Alpha, Bravo, Charlie, Delta."

Twenty feet ahead, in Corridor Four, Hector could see the

President, Secretary Guilbert, and General Flores engaged in an intense conversation as they walked along.

"How bad is ThreatCon Delta?"

"A terrorist attack has occurred, or intelligence indicates an action against a specific target is likely."

Christou increased the speed of her stride and Hector easily matched it, not about to be left behind. From past experience, he had no desire to find his own way through the labyrinth of the Building's confusing halls and corridors.

Theoretically, it was supposed to be a simple matter to find any location in the Pentagon. On paper, the system for numbering offices was as logical as a city map laid out in a grid of numbered streets and avenues. A typical room designation consisted of a single digit, a letter, and then a three- or four-digit number. The position of each number and letter signified a different subset of Pentagon coordinates.

But in Hector's introduction to the mapping system of the Pentagon the theory had broken down quickly.

On his first visit to the Building, almost two years ago, a helpful DPS officer at the Mall entrance had given him an explanation of the numbering system. Hector had come at the request of the President's Chief of Staff, who had asked him to attend an Air Force budget briefing in Room 4E225—a number forever burned into his memory.

The officer had told him the number 4 indicated the briefing theater was located on the fourth floor. The letter E meant the room was in the Building's E Ring, the outermost one. The next digit, 2, indicated which of the Building's ten spokelike corridors Hector should take. Then, since the actual room number, 25, was under 50, all Hector had to do was enter the E Ring from Corridor Two to the left.

"Quick and simple," the officer had said, as if he had actually believed it. Then he had added proudly that the Building's arrangement of radial corridors and concentric hallways was so efficient that no two offices along its seventeen and a half miles of hallway were more than seven and a half minutes apart—five minutes if the center courtyard was used as a shortcut. But that day, Hector had managed to more than triple that time, finding the correct theater only when a military guard on the third floor of E Ring had personally escorted him from the corridor checkpoint of a limited-access, high-security area.

By the time he'd reached the briefing theater, unacceptably late, he'd been lucky enough to slip into the dark room, unnoticed. Inside, he'd joined twenty-four others who were struggling to stay awake for an endless chain of overhead-projector slides presented by a soft-spoken major. Hector no longer recalled anything about the projected costs of a proposed new system to give incentive payments to qualified Air Force pilots to entice them to stay in the military rather than leave for the higher-paid civilian sector. But he'd never forget the small theater's room number.

Only later did he learn that getting lost was an honored Pentagon rite of passage and that the common experience had helped inspire one of the Building's alternate names—the Puzzle Palace. Despite what the civilian guard had told him, the theoretical logic of the Pentagon's office-numbering scheme was always breaking down because of the many unmapped half-corridors, the constant rearrangement of modular office space, and the deliberately out-of-sequence numbers assigned to areas with classified functions. Adding to the confusion was the reality that the only freely available floor plans of the Building were deliberately, though subtly, misleading. The layouts on the entrance display signs and map handouts depicted an ideal arrangement of rings and corridors that in reality had little to do with the detail of the actual floor arrangements.

Hector's capitulation to the impossibility of ever truly understanding the Pentagon's layout came several months after the infamous Air Force briefing when, again, at the request of the President's Chief of Staff, he placed an order for topographic maps of the region around the Chief's vacation home on the Oregon coast. The Pentagon room address for the Defense Mapping Agency was BG720, flagrantly violating the theory that all Pentagon office addresses began with a number from one to five, followed by a letter from A to E. Not only did the Pentagon have two additional levels—the Basement and Mezzanine—it clearly had two additional underground rings, F and G. Hector decided he wouldn't put it past the Pentagon to have even more hidden rings and levels. All unofficial, off the maps, and strictly classified.

The only sure way Hector knew to correctly navigate through the official and unofficial Pentagon was to always have a guide. Thus, this Sunday morning, he was determined not to let Christou out of his sight.

Fortunately, the march along Corridor Four seemed quite straightforward, as the President's party continued directly toward the bank of new escalators and elevators at the intersection where the corridor came to an end at the Pentagon's innermost A Ring.

As the President's party reached the escalators, Hector and the major remained a respectful twenty feet behind, out of earshot. Christou took the opportunity to inform Hector that the original Pentagon had been built with only five elevators—one VIP car to serve the River Entrance offices, and four freight elevators. By 2010, the renovation goal was to update the Building with twelve passenger cars and a bank of new escalators at each apex of the innermost ring. In return, Hector told the major that someone at a cabinet meeting he'd attended had joked that, with all the new pedestrian efficiencies, elevator and escalator shutdowns would probably push the famous seven and a half minutes separating any two offices in the Building to fifteen. Christou smiled politely, but didn't initiate any further conversation.

As Hector meditated on military humor, the President, General Flores, and Secretary Guilbert took the A Ring escalators to the second floor, immediately followed by Agents Zibart and Harrap, then Major Fielding. After waiting a minute, Hector and the major also ascended the escalator.

At the second-floor apex, the main A Ring corridor sported new floor-to-ceiling windows every fifteen feet overlooking Hector's favorite Pentagon feature, its central courtyard. The unexpected oasis was, in effect, a five-acre park in the heart of the Pentagon. In the past, Hector knew it had been a popular lunch spot and informal meeting place for all but the coldest months. Now, because of its protected location, the Courtyard was also the preferred site of formal ceremonies that earlier were held on the River Entrance's Parade Grounds.

Evidently intrigued by something he saw outside those windows, the President, hands informally jammed in his trouser pockets, had stopped to look down on the Courtyard. General Flores and Secretary Guilbert stood to either side of him. Waiting discreetly by the corridor's other wall were the Secret Service agents and Major Fielding with the CAT.

Hector slowed his pace to match Christou's. When it was clear the President was in no hurry to move on, they stopped, as well.

Hector hated silence. And he hated any missed opportunity to learn something more about the people he met.

"Are you taking part in the ceremony?" he asked the major.

"This is a political event."

Hector was finding Christou's continued stiffness in his presence curious, especially for someone who had seemed so affected by personally meeting the President. "This *is* the Pentagon. How much more military can anything get?"

"This is the United States. Unlike some countries, our military serves the political branches."

"I thought the military served the people."

"Sometimes, politicians get in the way." Hector sensed the major was suppressing either anger or frustration, but wasn't sure which, or why. An instant later, her expression told him that she realized she had said the wrong thing to the wrong person.

Hector knew an advantageous situation when he saw it. "It's all right, Major. Everyone's entitled to an opinion. And privacy."

Christou's guarded gaze flicked over Hector, acknowledging his unspoken promise not to pass on what she had unadvisedly shared with him. "I appreciate that, sir."

Hector didn't need to respond. Power in Washington was most often measured in number of favors owing. Christou now owed him for his silence, and the unspoken contract between them was that someday he might ask a favor in return. Hector's power base had just grown, ever so slightly, and he and the major both knew it.

Suddenly, the President called out from ahead. "Hec, take a look at this."

Hector obediently jogged over to the President at his second-floor window lookout, leaving Christou behind.

The President gestured toward something in the center court. "General Flores, tell Hec what you just told me."

The Chairman of the Joint Chiefs of Staff cleared his throat, signaling to Hector his discomfort with his new assignment as tour guide. "Have you ever been down there, young man?"

"Never." Hector had only seen the Courtyard in passing, the few times he had walked past the windows of the A Ring corridor.

"Do you see the building in the center?"

The building the general referred to was a colonial-style structure, whose black peaked roof was crowned by a cupola. It was the only permanent structure in the Courtyard, situated dead center in the pentagonal yard, at the intersection of six broad pathways cutting through the vivid green lawn. Each of the eight outer walls of the small building had two large, dark-tinted picture windows, bordered below by a panel of bright red. The scarlet bands stood out in stark relief against the lush vegetation of the park and the soft beige limestone walls of the encircling interior walls of the Pentagon.

The usual scattering of park benches and bright red Adirondack chairs lining the pathways were not in evidence today. Instead, the northern half of the Courtyard, to Hector's left, was filled with round, wooden dining tables that each could comfortably hold eight place settings. The rather battered tables had been arranged in curved semicircles, with their focus the center court's main entrance on the north wall. That entrance, however, was now hidden by an enormous, blue fabric backdrop framing an elevated, portable stage. Extending the length of the stage was a long banquet table backed by a forest of tightly spaced, eight-foot-tall flagstaffs. Without counting, Hector knew there would be exactly twenty-one flagstaffs—like everyone else, he watched NET-CNN. At the moment, two young soldiers in green service uniforms were taking great care in attaching the American flag to one of the center staffs.

Hector turned his attention back to the central structure and the general's question. "It's a restaurant, right?"

"Well, 'restaurant' is the formal designation. Most people call it 'the hot dog stand.' "

The President was like a little kid who could barely contain the punch line to a joke. "Tell him what else it's called."

"Ground Zero."

Hector could guess why, but was not about to ruin the President's setup.

The President prompted Flores with a conspiratorial smile. "Because . . . ?"

The heavyset general plunged into his story, as if eager to end the conversation. "During the Cold War, the Soviets were convinced we had a top-secret command post buried directly beneath the Pentagon, and the center court became their DGZ-1—Desired Ground Zero, One. If they had ever launched their missiles, the first warhead was aimed directly at the hot dog stand down there."

The President smiled broadly. And because he was the President, his Joint Chiefs Chairman and Secretary of Defense smiled, too.

"So do we?" Hector asked.

General Flores raised his eyebrows questioningly.

"Have a secret command post under the Pentagon?"

General Flores regarded Hector as if he had just asked the world's stupidest question. "Mr. MacGregor, why on God's green earth would we build a facility of critical importance under a building that, at minimum, would've been hit five times over in the first half-hour of a nuclear exchange? The only secret being kept out in that building is what they use to make the Pentagon's hamburgers."

The President chuckled, and slapped a hand on Hector's back, as if telling Flores and Guilbert they should forgive his assistant's naive questions because Hector was just a kid, after all. While Hector shrugged good-naturedly for the President's benefit, he also considered the Chairman's use of the past tense in talking about nuclear war. Maybe General Flores didn't share Christou's skepticism about what was happening here today.

Secretary Guilbert took the opportunity to intervene. "Mr. President, there're still a few final details to go over." The Secretary took a half-step away from the window, to urge the President on.

"Of course." The President gave every appearance of leaving, then hesitated. "Al . . . ?"

"Yes, sir?" General Flores had not followed Secretary Guilbert's lead in moving away from the window.

The President looked down again, into the Courtyard, but to Hector it was as if he were contemplating something much more distant. "What was *our* DGZ-1? In Russia. The Kremlin?"

"The northeast wall of the Kremlin, sir. Lenin's Tomb. A psychological target."

The President sighed deeply, as if imagining the missiles flying, Moscow and Washington both vaporized from the face of the Earth. "Sometimes, I wonder how we survived those years."

It was perfectly apparent to Hector that General Jaime Alvarez Flores shared none of the President's morose sentiment about the past.

"We survived by not backing down, sir."

The President seemed to hear something in the general's tone that Hector missed. The mood between the two men became discernibly cooler. Secretary Guilbert filled the awkward silence. "We are not backing down now, General."

"Of course not," Flores answered.

But Hector had heard the hesitation in the answer, suggesting that the general did hold the same reservations as his aide, Major Christou. Now Hector found himself wondering if everyone in the Pentagon was of like mind. And if they were, if it mattered.

Nicholas Guilbert was becoming increasingly agitated. "Mr. President, we really should . . ."

The President looked sternly at General Flores, as if to let him know the conversation would be continued later. Then he turned away from the window, to continue along the A Ring corridor through the bright rectangles of morning sun that punctuated the floor every fifteen feet.

Major Fielding, still carrying his undistinguished black case, quietly walked past Hector and Christou where they remained at the window. Fielding took up his usual position behind the President, staying well to the side, avoiding the light altogether. In less than a minute, Hector and Christou were the only ones left in the corridor. Hector shifted the President's brown-leather briefcase under his arm and turned to the major. He had to know.

"Why do all of you think this is such a bad idea?"

Hector could see that the major was judging him, asking herself if she should stay with the Department of Defense's official position, or if she could dare speak her mind again.

She made her decision. "We can't trust them."

But Hector had heard that argument before. It didn't hold up. "People said the same thing about Germany and Japan after World War II."

The major was equally familiar with the counterargument. "We occupied those countries, sir. We rebuilt their economic base. Restructured their political systems. And only then did . . ." Her voice broke off as she turned, distracted—no, angered—by something she saw outside.

Hector looked past her. On the stage, he saw more young soldiers in green, attaching additional national flags to the row of twenty-one staffs behind the banquet table.

Then he realized what was disturbing the major. Center stage, the American flag had been hung immediately beside the utilitarian blue-and-white flag of the North Atlantic Treaty Organization. But on the next staff, framing the NATO banner and so close to the Stars and Stripes that the fabric of all three flags had twisted together, hung the newest flag to become part of NATO's colors—the white, blue, and red bars of Russia.

"Russia's changed, you know," Hector said.

"You mean . . . it used to be totalitarian and corrupt. Then it was bankrupt and corrupt. Then it collapsed, and had the Sixty-Day Civil War, when no one had the time or money to be corrupt. And now there's a coalition between the crime lords and the old hard-liners, it's back to a one-party 'democratic' system with institutionalized corruption. That's some change."

"At least the ruble is worth something again and they're

not shooting each other. By allowing them to join NATO, we help them reorganize their military, and we clear the way for them to join the European Union in a few years. And *that* will force them to adopt the serious market changes that will cement their new economy."

The major did not respond.

"That's exactly what you just said we did for Germany and Japan," Hector reminded her.

"We achieved a decisive military victory over those regimes. We never beat Russia. Not militarily."

"What difference does that make?" Hector really wanted to know what the major's reasoning was, because it would reflect another insider view, this time of the military mind.

"They're still the enemy, sir. On the ropes but undefeated. And when we've fattened them up and healed their wounds, they're going to be in bed with us, buying our weapons, benefiting from our training, and familiar with all our strategies."

Hector was finding it difficult to conceal his consternation. The major was spinning a story that was a staple of the right-wing press, and completely unfounded. "After that civil war, do you *know* how long it'll take for Russia to regain anywhere near the economic power she had a generation ago?"

"With our help, ten to fifteen years."

"Exactly. A lot can happen in all that time."

"I agree. That's about how long it took Germany to rearm between wars."

"Why are you so pessimistic about the future?"

"Not pessimistic. Realistic. There's a difference."

Hector wondered if Christou had heard a single speech the President had given on the subject in the past year. "What's real, Major Christou, is that the two biggest enemies of the last century, who could have brought the world to an end if they had gone to war, are now at peace. Haven't you been listening to the President? War is over."

"If you're going to quote the President, allow me to quote Plato. 'Only the dead have seen the end of war.' If you'll follow me . . ."

She turned and walked off in the same direction the President's party had taken.

No comment Hector thought of seemed worth wasting on the major's back. So, automatically making the most of this latest trip to the Pentagon, he glanced out each of the windows he passed by.

Now, almost all the flags of NATO's current, twenty member nations were on display on the stage, along with the flags of NATO and the Russian Federation. White-uniformed naval officers had arrived in the Courtyard to cover the round, wooden tables with white linen cloths. Another few windows along, Hector corrected his first assumption. Since he'd begun working with the military, he'd been studying their insignia. The serious figures in white setting up the tables didn't have standard rank markings on their cuffs and shoulder boards. All but one of them wore thin diagonal stripes of gold, not wide bands. Except for the single lieutenant who was directing them, Hector decided the sailors must be the students from the Naval Academy who had been invited to assist at the official proceedings.

At least they *look like they know the importance of today's ceremony,* he thought. The fact that the hardworking midshipmen represented the next generation of America's military personnel helped him ignore the negative attitude of Christou, and everyone else at the Pentagon who shared her view.

As part of the next generation himself, Hector felt proud that he was with the President today. The Man had made the right choice in tirelessly pushing NATO to accept Russia. The Cold War was finally over. It was time for the *Pax Americana* to begin.

Confident in his own ability to perceive the true situation, Hector followed Major Christou deeper into the Pentagon's maze.

A maze whose center was now held by the enemy.

NINE

THIRD FLOOR, E RING

"You want to know what I've done?" Vanovich said. "Okay. This afternoon, after the festivities, I'm going to give a briefing."

"A briefing on what?" Despite the powerful air-conditioning in the sealed Red Level office, Tom felt overheated. His uncomfortably tight chest made it hard for him to breathe.

"You know how many civilians have your level of security clearance in as many areas as you do, Tommy?"

Tom didn't.

"Twenty-two," Vanovich said. "And three of them are former Presidents."

"I'm not following you."

"It's simple, Tommy Boy. You're still not high enough. I can't even tell you what we have until you've signed on."

Tom worked out the logic of that statement. "You're saying not even the President knows about . . . whatever it is . . . you've got?"

General Milo Vanovich put a shaky hand on a high-backed swivel chair in front of the workstation's four main display screens. "I've got to sit down." Tom took the chair beside him. At the side of the workstation, he noticed where a section of the console cover had been swung open. Inside he could see a laser printer unit with a dislodged circuit board. Maybe there were repairs to be made to the photocopier after all.

Shoulders rounded, Vanovich settled into his chair, sighing deeply. "Geez, remember when we'd work all night?"

"Seven nights a week," Tom said. Ten years ago, the general had been a brigadier general at Hanscom Air Force Base in Massachusetts, one of the few bases with no acknowledged flying mission. It was, instead, headquarters for the Electronic Systems Center of the Air Force Materiel Command and home to several research labs that ostensibly belonged to private industry. Hanscom was committed exclusively to cutting-edge research and development of Air Force C^4 systems—those necessary for command, control, communications, and computers.

When Tom had been there, Hanscom had had almost as many civilian employees as Air Force personnel. He'd been one of those civilians, an electronics engineer and systems designer shuttling between Vanovich's advanced concept lab on the base and Hughes Electronics in California—his actual employer.

"We did some great things together," Vanovich said.

Tom nodded. Hanscom had been the rare military-industrial complex that both acknowledged and understood the future. There'd been no twentieth-century dinosaurs at that base who felt it was their mission to fight World War II all over again, only this time with the weapons of the twenty-first century. Hanscom was aware the world had changed.

To Tom, the future of warfare wasn't the use of over-whelming force *after* war broke out, it was the use of over-whelming surveillance *before* a situation led to war. He increasingly believed the key to a world without misunder-standing had to be a world without secrets. The United States had proved that innumerable times when it had pro-vided intelligence to both sides in potential regional con-flicts. More than once, India and Pakistan both had scaled back their rhetoric when American satellite photos had been able to show that neither side was massing armies or preparing missiles for launch against the other. Many con-frontations in the Middle East, in Africa, and in Eastern Europe had been similarly defused. And every time the United States took the step of pulling back the curtain of suspicion and deception, she had delivered another, more subtle message: If a country had no secrets from the United States, it was a country the United States could attack with devastating precision.

Tom and Vanovich, in their time at Hanscom, had both come to believe that surveillance—visual or electronic—was the ultimate big stick. But, while Tom had been proud of their work to help develop the technology currently in use, he'd done his part. Five years ago, he'd moved on. He didn't want to rethink that decision now.

He stated that fact as bluntly as he could for his friend. "I got out of the game, Milo."

Vanovich's answer was to spin around in his chair to face the workstation and slip a keyboard and trackball out from a hidden shelf in the workstation's counter. "Just take a look at this for me, will you?"

The center screen directly in front of the general carried

a real-time feed from a surveillance satellite, showing about one square mile of terrain. In the middle of the image was the unmistakable shape of the Pentagon. At the bottom of the screen, Tom could detect individual cars moving on Interstate 395. "One of the new Keyholes?" he asked, not surprised by the image's acuity. During high-profile events involving international cooperation, it was usual practice for the National Reconnaissance Office to retask its satellites to observe American soil. The image did, however, seem somehow different from similar views Tom had seen in the past. He pulled his chair closer to the station.

"Something better, Tommy. You've never seen one of these in action."

As Vanovich proceeded to show off his multibillion-dollar toy as if it were a new stereo system, his earlier mood of despair disappeared. Tom welcomed the change.

"Fully digitized product," the general began. "Constant multispectral and hyperspectral datastream from the target coordinates. We can make all the adjustments to the data on the ground, on the fly, without sending commands back up. This is coming from the same feed that's going to the FBI and the boys in the basement. They can manipulate it any way they want, and at the same time we can do this. . . ."

Vanovich's stubby fingers swept over the keyboard, and the trackball disappeared beneath his hand. Suddenly, the Pentagon zoomed up until the center courtyard filled the screen. Round tables in the court looked like checkers arranged on a free-form board. Leaning closer, Tom could see uniformed figures moving among the tables, spreading out tablecloths. Then he realized what was wrong with the image.

"It's hot out there. How come I'm not seeing atmospheric turbulence?"

Vanovich held up a finger like a lawyer delivering a summation. "Look more closely! What you should be asking is, How come you're not seeing any pixels?"

The general was right. At this extreme level of magnification, they should have been seeing the image break up into flickering squares of pixels—the smallest imaging element of the charge-coupled device in the satellite that served as electronic film. The image on-screen now should have resembled a photo blown up from a newspaper—an image composed of dots.

Certainly, Tom was aware, imaging computers could manipulate those dots, build up variations over time, even enhance contrast and edge sharpness so that ever-more-detailed views could be produced. But Tom knew even the NRO's most sophisticated computers couldn't yet operate fast enough to handle that task on live, moving images.

"This is coming from an observation aircraft, right?" It was the only explanation that made sense to Tom. Something like the Darkstar UAV model on the general's desk. Something designed to circle over target sites for days, transmitting surveillance data from only a few miles overhead, without the expense of a satellite launch.

"No, sir. This is coming from three hundred miles straight up."

Tom stared at the screen. A satellite at that altitude would be moving at almost 18,000 miles an hour. "But I'm not even seeing image drift." At this level of magnification, the angle of the image should have been visibly changing as the satellite passed by.

"It's there, Tommy. Angle drift. Atmospheric turbulence. Even pixel breakup."

"Okay, Milo. You got me. I'm confused."

"Watch this." The general typed in a series of commands. Instantly the image of the Pentagon twisted on an extreme angle, degraded to a smear of rippling gray blotches, and broke up into pixel smears. The five-sided shape was still discernible, but other than that, no other details were present. It's what Tom would have expected to have seen coming from a small, twenty-year-old, low-resolution satellite straining for maximum magnification.

"And now, this," Vanovich said. He hit a key. Before Tom's eyes, the image began to subtly change. The Pentagon's shape straightened slightly and became a bit more pronounced. "And this." Another improvement. The sequence reminded Tom of the stages of an eye exam, each new lens bringing the letters into better focus. "And this . . . this . . . and this . . ."

Vanovich shot a side glance at Tom. "You understand now?"

Tom nodded slowly. "Multiple imaging sources."

"Bingo." In a voice in which Tom could hear no trace of Vanovich's previous exhaustion, the general rapidly outlined for him the specs of the latest space-surveillance platform in America's intelligence-gathering arsenal—MAJIC. According to Vanovich, Multiple Aperture, Joint Imaging Capability was a classified implementation of advances in multi-mirror telescope technology and distributed-array satellite design.

On Earth, the size of mirror that could be constructed for astronomical telescopes was limited by manufacturing techniques. The largest, one-piece, light-collecting mirror yet built was the 324-inch mirror in the Subaru Telescope, built on Mauna Kea, Hawaii, for the National Astronomical Observatory of Japan.

Mirrors of that size were extraordinarily difficult to cast and polish to the required tolerances. And even assuming a perfect mirror could be reliably made, at those larger dimensions the dynamic distortions in the mirror's base material, caused by temperature changes and sagging due to gravity, were also more pronounced. The mirror in the Subaru Telescope required 261 sensitive pistons to constantly apply changing amounts of pressure to different points beneath its reflective surface in order to achieve distortion-free viewing.

However, the general continued, advances in high-speed computing had now made possible a new approach to optical-telescope design. Many small, easier-to-manufacture mirrors could be networked together to act as a single, giant, impossible-to-manufacture mirror. Each of the thirty-six mirrors in the Keck Telescope, also on Mauna Kea, had been only seventy-two inches across. But linked together by a computer-controlled actuator system that kept each mirror focused with a precision matching the width of a single wavelength of light, those thirty-six mirrors had been able to function with the same light-gathering capability as a 386-inch mirror.

With a familiar edge of excitement returning to his voice, Vanovich rambled on about how the challenge of building individual mirrors for use in space-based telescopes had nothing to do with size. How the largest mirrors ever placed in orbit were the 94.5-inch mirrors used in the civilian Hubble Space Telescope, and the classified Keyhole surveillance satellites. And how the limiting factor on the size of space mirrors was not one of manufacturing technique, but of transportation—larger mirrors would not fit within the cargo holds of the Space Shuttle or the Air Force's expendable launch vehicles.

But just as the military breakthroughs of the Keyhole satellites had given birth to the Hubble Space Telescope, the multiple-mirror technology of civilian telescopes had given birth to MAJIC.

As Vanovich described it for Tom, each fully deployed MAJIC platform consisted of sixteen identical imaging cells orbiting in a square formation as a distributed-array satellite. The cells were kept in perfect alignment with each other through the use of solid-state, silicon microrockets—in principle, each cell was covered in computer chips with special circuits containing microgram-sized pockets of explosive propellant. Whenever orbital perturbations upset the formation's alignment, selected propellant pockets were electronically ignited to microscopically adjust the cell's position with the same lightwave-accuracy achieved in ground-based installations. And, because each cell contained a thirty-six-inch mirror, the combined power of the array was equal to a twenty-foot mirror, more than two and a half times more powerful than the Hubble.

The solar-power requirements, apparently, were minimal. Each cell only had to communicate with the others, and with any currently available satellite within the MIL-STAR system. Furthermore, if antisatellite weapons were used, during a time of hostilities, to disrupt U.S. surveillance capability, the distributed cells of the MAJIC array were small enough to be almost impossible to target individually. And, because there were no physical connections between them, even if two-thirds of the cells in each array were destroyed, the remaining cells would still provide the same observational capability as a traditional, single-mirror Keyhole satellite, at a quarter the price.

Thus, Vanovich concluded enthusiastically, because of

the low-implementation cost of each array that resulted from its ability to mass-produce identical cells, six MAJIC platforms were already on orbit, with two more to be added each fiscal year until a full constellation of twenty-four platforms was deployed.

The fact that six MAJIC arrays were already operational explained to Tom why he had noticed no image drift on the surveillance shot of the Pentagon, despite the speed with which the arrays were moving. The NRO's imaging computers had been able to build a three-dimensional model of all the fixed elements in the landscape from previous observations of the Pentagon terrain over the past few hours or days.

Tom studied the image again. The buildings, grounds, roads, and vegetation that he was looking at, as if from directly overhead, were an extrapolated virtual image composed of hundreds, if not thousands, of previous images from all angles. Since the unchanging part of the landscape was fixed in the imaging computers' memories, all the imaging computers had to process were any visual elements within the observational area that changed rapidly over time. That list would most often be moving vehicles and people. When the imaging computers analyzed the moving elements and combined the results coming from two or more orbiting arrays, no matter what the angle of observation was, they then mapped the moving elements onto the existing virtual model. All the computers had to do then was correct for the constantly changing angle caused by the arrays' movement. The advanced technology was all the general said it would be.

"Can you imagine what it will be like when all the MAJIC arrays are operational?" Vanovich asked. "We will have complete, real-time coverage of every square inch of the globe, on demand." He typed another instruction into his keyboard.

The screen image of the Pentagon's Courtyard once again expanded until it was as if Tom were ten feet directly above five people in white uniforms standing together, obviously engaged in a conversation. At this level of magnification, the resolution was soft and the movements of the people were jerky, but Tom had no doubt that an hour or two of computer image-enhancement could produce photos detailed enough to allow specific individuals to be recognized.

"Too bad they weren't using this on downtown Washington last night," Vanovich said, shaking his head. "Could've seen the bastards who hit the Archives. I mean, look at the detail, Tommy." The general tapped the screen, indicating a shoulder on the one figure to whom the other four appeared to be listening. "He's an officer, see?" Sure enough, there was a slight discoloration on each of the speaker's shoulders, exactly where officer's shoulder boards would be. "And these others," Vanovich indicated the other four people whose shoulders carried no discernible markings, "ah, . . . I can't tell what they're supposed to be."

Tom had an idea. "A busload of way-too-serious midshipmen pulled in when I got here. They were in white uniforms with narrow stripes that wouldn't show up on this."

"Well, there they are, then," General Vanovich said with a satisfaction that Tom didn't share. "And think of what comes after this, Tommy. The next generation of MAJIC arrays will have twice the number of cells *and* incorporate laser holography so we can image air turbulence at a microscopic level."

Tom was truly startled by the implications of that technology, and he knew his expression showed it.

Vanovich understood. "That's right, we're going to be able to reconstruct *sounds* from orbital observations. Another ten years and we'll be able to *listen* to what those guys are saying. Ten years past that, we'll be doing it with micro-imaging radar and there won't be a window, wall, or roof we can't hear through. Hey, the President wants a Brave New World? We're going to give it to him. And I do mean *we*," Vanovich said. "Tommy, your chips are on board in each cell."

Tom wasn't all that surprised. "That must explain the fortune in royalty checks I've been getting." When he'd worked on Vanovich's projects at the Hanscom base, all of his designs had been so classified that none could be submitted for patents by Hughes. The company hadn't even been able to resort to the common technique of fragmenting classified breakthroughs among hundreds of innocuous patents covering minor modifications to unclassified products. As a result, when Tom had left Hughes, he'd had no body of work to show for ten years' work, no published papers, and no income from his share of patents.

Other than money, he'd gotten what he wanted, though. The last five years, he'd been there for Tyler, and their time together was more centered, less disrupted. Money had been a problem at first, so he'd accepted Vanovich's offer to keep him on retainer as a Department of Defense consultant. Until today, the deal had worked out for the most part, even if the general's definition of consulting included making repairs on office equipment within high-security facilities.

Vanovich patted his arm. "Someday, Tommy. People will know what you did."

Tom wasn't sure if that was good or bad.

"Huh," the general said. "That's odd."

Tom looked at the screen, but saw nothing out of the ordinary.

"They're saluting."

Tom watched as four midshipmen saluted the officer, and then, with a blurred, jerky movement, the officer returned the salute. "So?"

"You don't salute in the Pentagon. Including the Courtyard."

Tom didn't see the importance of the action or inaction. To him, saluting was an arcane art to anyone but those in the military.

"Ah, whadda they know," Vanovich sighed. "They're just kids. You know the old saying about saluting."

Tom didn't know any sayings about saluting.

"When in doubt, whip it out," Vanovich said. Then he entered another command and the extreme close-up on the Courtyard slowly shrank to a wider view in which the Pentagon took up only the middle third.

The image changed. The four midshipmen moved toward a stairway against one of the Building's walls encircling the center court.

Tom thought again about the midshipmen he had seen get off the bus. Actually, they *had* seemed more like reservists of some kind than kids to him. Of course, anybody under fifty was a kid to Milo Vanovich.

He watched as the general continued to work his keyboard and check the screen. Maybe the old guy's body was failing, but his mind was still one of the best. And it was time Tom found out just what had his old friend so worried. He began gently. "So, if you can tell me all about MAJIC, what is it that you *can't* show me?"

Vanovich stopped typing and slowly spun his chair around. "Come to the briefing, Tommy."

"Not if it means I have to sign up again."

The two friends studied each other, and Tom knew each was thinking how far they could push this dance of offer and rejection.

"I like teaching. I like being home for my son. If you want me to consult on a classified project, I'll start work today. But I've done my Paul Revere ride. I'm not leaving Quantico."

Vanovich leaned over to pat Tom's knee. "You will. I saw your eyes light up at MAJIC. You won't be able to sleep tonight wondering what else it is we've got up there."

"You've already told me," Tom said. "Something you've made has turned into a weapon you haven't even told the President about. I'm not leaving Quantico. And I'll sleep just fine."

Vanovich slowly shook his head. Tom just as slowly nodded his own, until both men laughed.

Tom stood up. The meeting was over. "I've got Tyler for the summer. Come down for a weekend." Tom left the last part of that invitation unsaid. *Before you die . . .*

Vanovich remained seated. "You can't go."

"Milo, I won't go to the briefing."

Vanovich pointed behind Tom. "The printer. Broken."

"That wasn't a ploy?"

"Tommy, do I really need a ploy to get you to come see me?"

Tom laughed again. The old guy was shameless. "No."

"Good. You bring your tool kit?"

"Right here." Tom reached into the back pocket of his jeans and pulled out his Maxxum-model Swiss Army knife.

Like that of many actual repair technicians, it was Tom's experience that if any electronic device could not be fixed by using some combination of the eighteen tools in this particular model, then the problem was in the circuitry itself, and the only practical solution was then to replace the faulty components, not repair them.

Vanovich smiled nostalgically. Tom knew the general was remembering all the times he'd seen that knife in action before.

To begin, Tom selected the small, flathead screwdriver and asked Vanovich to try to print something from his Red Level terminal.

As the general turned back to face his keyboard, Tom glanced at the surveillance screen again. White dots randomly milled around the luncheon tables like characters in a videogame. Then the workstation's photocopier/printer/scanner began to hum as it responded to Vanovich's print command, and Tom turned his attention to something more important than watching midshipmen.

On the screen, another four white dots clustered around a single one for a few seconds, then moved toward another of the Courtyard's stairways.

Within direct sight of the world's most powerful surveillance system, Team Two was being deployed.

And no one noticed.

CENTER COURTYARD

As Team Two executed its menial work in the Pentagon's Courtyard, Ranger thought again about his unexpected meeting with Tom Chase. Though he was confident the civilian would have no way of recognizing him, that unexpected random event held the possibility of jeopardizing one of the mission's crucial objectives—to keep its sponsors hidden.

But on reflection, Ranger ultimately dismissed Chase as unimportant. Team Two had penetrated the heart of the enemy's stronghold, without suspicion and almost without effort. Successfully seizing control of that stronghold must be the only focus of his attention now. Since Chase hadn't recognized him, he did not pose a threat. Ranger moved on.

So far, the only other deviation from plan had come from the enemy. One of the original midshipmen, a female, had not arrived in time for the bus's scheduled departure.

Ranger had discovered the absence as the security passes had been distributed to his forty-one commandos. He'd based Team Two's composition on the list of Academy volunteers from 12th Company—the same number of males and females, the same skin color.

Racial characteristics and faces could not be matched identically, of course, and the members of Team Two were somewhat older than the callow midshipmen they replaced. But when Ranger had led his troops through the limousine garage to the entrance of the mezzanine-level Tricare health facility, careless security officers had merely glanced at his commandos' passes, without closely inspecting their photographs. Thus, the Pentagon's security guards had waved an enemy force inside, even allowing Team Two to bypass the metal and micro-imaging radar detectors, since who would even imagine the possibility that an entire company of midshipmen could be so easily replaced?

However, since Ranger could not be certain that some form of security screen might be in operation, none of his troops had carried traditional weapons. Instead, other arrangements had been made to ensure that what they would need would already be in place.

As for the missing female, Ranger and the mission planners had anticipated that few Americans would possess their sense of duty and commitment. From the beginning, the plan had accounted for the possibility that one or more of the midshipmen might not show for the company's assignment. Consequently, four miles from the Pentagon, Ranger had stopped the bus at a scheduled staging corner by the railroad tracks on New York Avenue. The young soldier matched to the missing female, Amy Leanne Bethune, had left the bus and entered the waiting support van. After the mission was complete, she would rejoin her squad at the primary extraction point.

Her absence would not degrade Ranger's force, though. Casualties were expected, and redundancy was part of the mission plan. In each team within each squad of four, the same task had been assigned to two soldiers of each specialty. The female soldier had merely been the first to be lost. She would not be the last.

Now, with the mission's penetration phase completed, Ranger had little to do except appear to be directing his team as they spread out linen tablecloths according to the wishes of a condescending major in charge of the NATO luncheon. So Ranger used the time to walk the pathways of the Courtyard, surreptitiously counting the Special-Forces snipers on the roof, verifying there had been no change in the number he had been informed would be on duty: ten on the inner walls in five teams of two, with two Secret Service agents for support. The number outside, which he couldn't verify visually, was reported to be twenty sharpshooters in ten teams of two, with two Secret Service agents as liaison.

However, the outside sharpshooters could be discounted at first. They would take a minimum of two minutes to respond to Team Two's attack in the Courtyard, even longer if the three planned diversions were successful. And though Ranger had no reason to believe that the diversions would not be successful, those two minutes would be more than enough for Team Two to secure its position and gather its hostages.

As he strolled the pathways in the morning sun, secure and focused, Ranger compared the Courtyard's current condition—the size of the trees, denseness of foliage—to the most recent SPOT satellite photos he had openly purchased from the French government less than a month ago, and to his own memories. He had been in this courtyard before, years ago. He had sat beneath an umbrella at an outdoor table. He had heard the story of the hot dog stand called Ground Zero. He had even eaten a hot dog here, washed down with Coca-Cola. It had seemed the patriotic thing to do, and it was a new experience for him.

But the war he would begin here today would not break new ground, because the war against tyranny and injustice was as old as humanity. Instead, Ranger and his troops would merely—and proudly—take their place as the latest in a line of heroic warriors who fought for all that was most noble in humankind.

This was a day when right would triumph over might. When the weak would persevere over the strong. When the United States would be forced to remember the ideals with which it had been born, and by doing so restore true freedom to the rest of the world.

Ranger regretted only one requirement of the plan: to go

into battle without honor, disguised, in false colors. But the enemy no longer understood even the concept of honor. It would take today's actions to redeem it.

Ranger stood in the heart of the enemy, in the center of the Pentagon, surveying Ground Zero.

Only one element was missing before the battle could begin.

The President.

TEN

"THE TANK," SECOND FLOOR, E RING

In his time on the President's staff, Hector MacGregor had heard the Man raise his voice once, to cut off the Secretary of Commerce as she tried to explain that a rise in unemployment was actually a good thing because it increased the enrollment in job-skills upgrading courses.

But Hector had never seen the President explode in outright fury until today in the Gold Room—the Joint Chiefs' exclusive conference room unofficially known as the Tank, with its imposing environment of thick gold carpeting, gold drapes, and heroic military paintings. To make the event even more memorable, the object of the President's anger was the Chief of Naval Operations, and the confrontation was being witnessed by four other four-star officers—more gold stars than Hector had ever seen massed together in one place before.

But the President wasn't behaving as if he were intimidated by his surroundings or his audience. He sat at the head of the spit-polished conference table and actually thumped a fist on its shining wood-grained surface. "This action is a wake-up call, Admiral! Something those people have been needing for the past ten years!"

Hector and Major Christou were sitting well away from the action at the table, along the Gold Room's north wall. But Hector had a good view of both the President and Admiral Hugh Paulsen. The four-star admiral was just as furious as his commander in chief, though he was not allowing himself to express his emotions at the same volume. Paulsen's soft, rounded face was white with anger, but his voice was firm, with no hint of indecision. "With respect, sir, it is a provocation. Needless. Senseless. And if you want my resignation—"

The Secretary of Defense, on the President's left, interrupted sharply. "That's enough, Admiral."

Nicholas Guilbert stared witheringly at Admiral Paulsen. Then he turned to give the same hard look to the Chairman of the Joint Chiefs, seated directly across from him. But General Flores, who had remained silent throughout the protracted and unexpectedly emotional argument, showing no sign of support for either the President or the admiral, made no move to participate now, either.

The President didn't wait for anyone else to join in. "No," he said emphatically. "That is not enough." Hector's eyebrows lifted in surprise as he observed the President's cheeks flush red. Another first. "For the first time in modern history, the world is on the brink of global political peace. There will always be terrorists. I do not argue that point."

The President looked down at the other end of the long table, and Hector saw him make deliberate eye contact with the short, intense Commandant of the Marine Corps, General Oliver Kline. "But their actions will not be the state-sponsored campaigns of the past." Then the President looked to his right, at the Chief of Staff of the Air Force, General Philip Janukatys, a former fighter pilot, still whippet-thin and fit. *"And* I concede that China is on the horizon, though it will be at least ten years before she can threaten our shores, and I remain convinced that when that day comes, she will see no need to do so.

"There will also be regional conflicts in Africa and South America. But your own reports tell me they will remain localized, and should continue to drop in number and severity the more we tie our climate-relief efforts to a firm requirement that those regions find diplomatic solutions to the problems they face.

"Make no mistake, those climate-relief efforts, those 'operations other than war' you people dislike so much, are going to be our country's mission for the next fifty years. We've all seen the studies. We know what's coming as this world continues to grow warmer. The greatest movement of refugees in human history, eclipsing that of *World War II*. The transformation of equatorial regions into parched dead zones. Our maps will be redrawn by the rising sea level. We're going to *lose* our major coastal cities."

His entire body conveying the conviction of one who has discovered absolutely what his mission in life is to be, the President continued without pausing for response from his audience. "We aren't facing the apocalypse. America will survive this new century. But for us to *prosper* in it, for us to prevent mass starvation, rampant disease, rioting, and war from engulfing half the nations in the world and dragging us down, it is our duty—America's duty—to ensure that order is maintained in the face of chaos. To do that, we have to establish that order *now,* while there is still time."

The President took a moment to fold his hands before him, and slow the tempo of his impassioned address. "Maybe it's not in human nature for us to ever arrive at an age when there will be absolutely no conflict between nations. But one thing is certain, gentlemen, and Major"— the President suddenly nodded at Major Christou and Hector across the room—"for the first time in more than half a century, the next generation in this world is no longer threatened by conflict that could end in global destruction . . . *except* in Europe. So Europe must be our *first* priority."

Hector had heard the President express these views before, but always among small and select groups who would not repeat his warnings to the press. Just as Franklin Delano Roosevelt had never publicly lobbied for America to enter World War II before Pearl Harbor, this President understood the political realities of alarming voters about events that seemed to have no immediate connection to them. Thus, he had not forced the issue of global warming on the American people. Instead, he had signed a series of secret executive orders authorizing additional funds for climate-relief planning operations which were never detailed in the published budget.

In fact, Hector knew that the initial global-warming studies to which the President had just referred had been commissioned by Presidents George Bush and Bill Clinton, also by secret executive order. Both Presidents had read those reports while still in office, but neither they nor their predecessors had ever dared reveal the reports' sobering conclusions to the public. But give that same public another decade of worsening winter storms and record-breaking floods and hurricanes, and Hector believed as the President did, that they would be grateful that their leaders had begun to secretly plan for surviving the coming climactic chaos as far back as the 1990s.

But Admiral Paulsen was not a believer of the President's dire predictions.

"As far as Europe goes," the admiral said through clenched teeth, "Russia is contained, sir."

Hector glanced sideways at Christou. The Army major had used the same words to describe Russia. Somewhat uneasily, he found himself wondering whether General Flores's chief aide had been present for similar discussions among the Joint Chiefs.

The President held his ground. "Russia is *dying,* Admiral Paulsen. The peace that embraces it now is the peace of paralysis." Hector heard the Man's voice deepen. *Here it comes,* thought Hector. *The four-score-and-twenty speech.*

"Two hundred and thirty years ago," the President said gravely, "our forefathers fought for democracy, built a unique form of government, and each generation since has learned from the past and made refinements for the future. But democracy and free markets have been thrust upon the Russians. Literally overnight, they were expected to accept what took us centuries to achieve. It is not enough that they are contained, Admiral Paulsen. Continued isolation will only lead them to another round of self-destruction that will make their Sixty-Day Civil War look like a minor family spat."

"Good," the admiral said.

The President would not accept that attitude. "And when they are gone, Admiral, who divides the spoils? Do we let Ukraine march in? They're rich. They could do it. Do we let Russia become the battlefield in a resource war among the other independent states as the crops begin to fail? There are still nuclear weapons over there. Do you honestly think some Russian general is beyond lobbing one into Germany to expand the conflict?"

The admiral lurched to his feet at that. "Jesus Christ, Mr. President, that's exactly the scenario you're putting into play. By bringing Russia into NATO, it's covered by Article Five—'the Parties agree that an armed attack on *any* of them in Europe or North America shall be considered an attack against them *all.*' What'll you do when some goddamn Russian general 'lobs' a nuke onto Beijing just to drag us into a shooting war?"

"Admiral Paulsen, war is waged when one side or another decides it has something to gain and nothing to lose. It is the goal of my administration—no, it is my *personal* intention to see to it that Russia *has* something to lose. To see that her military forces are brought up to NATO standards, to see that her remaining nuclear-force structure is made more secure under NATO command-and-control guidelines, and that by bringing this internal stability to her, the way will be paved for her eventual entry into the European Union. Because once her people are secure, once they have prosperity, they will not want to give that up. And when that day comes, they and their generals will no longer be a threat to us, to Europe, or to themselves. They will be our level allies in coping with the climatic disruption to come."

"Mr. President," the admiral said, "in this room there is a tradition of being forthright and blunt. And in that tradition, I say to you that *you* are wrong, and your actions here today threaten the security of this country not fifty years from now, but *today.*"

The tension in the room was palpable. If the President and Admiral Paulsen had not been separated by the conference table, Hector was certain they'd be settling their differences physically.

All eyes were on the President now. He spoke slowly and clearly. "Admiral Paulsen, I accept your resignation, as Chief of Naval Operations, and from the Navy, effective now."

It seemed to Hector that the admiral almost reflexively began to draw himself to attention, then stopped, as if such a formal response wasn't worth the effort. Then Hector saw an odd expression slide over the admiral's face as he looked across the table to the Chief of Staff of the Air Force.

As if a private signal had been sent, Air Force General Janukatys got heavily to his feet and stood at attention. "Mr. President, I share the views of Admiral Paulsen. Our concern must be for our country today, and not undermined by implausible scenarios of what might or might not happen half a century from now. Therefore, I also tender my resignation as Chief of Staff, and from the Air Force."

Hector saw the President look sharply from one man to the other in disbelief.

"What the hell is going on here!" The Secretary of Defense had reached his limit. "Russia has been in the works for a year! It's been debated here in this room. You all testified before the Senate NATO Observer Group. The President is not making a capricious move! But for you two to pull this crap now—it's verging on treason!"

Hector half-turned to Christou. Her dark eyes revealed the same startled shock he felt. She was staring apprehensively at the Chairman of the Joint Chiefs of Staff—her boss, General Flores—as if worried about the action that he might take in the heat of the moment.

The President was staring at the Chairman, as well. "Anyone else?"

Admiral Paulsen and General Janukatys remained standing, both men silent.

That was when General Flores pushed back his chair and stood to face the President. "Sir, I will work to the best of my abilities to support NATO's decision to extend membership to the Russian Federation."

The Chief of Staff of the Army and the Commandant of the Marine Corps also stood, and both stated their intention to do the same.

After an interminable, to Hector, moment of profound silence, the President turned back to Admiral Paulsen and General Janukatys. The betrayal he felt was obvious. "The Senate voted six months ago to amend the Washington Treaty for Russia's entry. Why do this now?"

The admiral and the general did not respond.

Nicholas Guilbert's voice was like ice. "You will consider that an order."

With a glance at the Air Force general, Admiral Paulsen spoke for both men. "If we had done this six months ago, we'd be forgotten today. No one would listen."

The President shook his head. "I do not accept that."

"That's your prerogative . . . sir."

Hector heard a gasp. He wasn't sure who had made it or if, in fact, it had come from him.

"You sons of . . ." The President bit his lip. Hector wondered if he even knew how to finish the phrase.

Secretary Guilbert took over now. He rose smoothly to his feet and spoke formally, all emotion banished. "Mr. President, with your permission." The President gave his assent. "Admiral Paulsen, General Janukatys, as of this moment your resignations have been accepted and you are relieved of duty on the Joint Staff. Until such time as your retirements can be processed, as Secretary of Defense, I order you to refrain from speaking with *anyone* about your opposition to Russia's membership in NATO. Failure to abide by this order will make you subject to immediate arrest, general court-martial, and possible forfeiture of all retirement rights and benefits. Is that understood?"

The two men replied in unison, "Yes, sir." Though Hector sensed they doubted the Secretary would be able to follow through on any of his threats.

Guilbert sat down again. "You are dismissed."

The two former Chiefs gathered their papers and left the Gold Room.

The President, the Chairman, and the two remaining Chiefs still stood in position around the table. Fascinated spectators, Hector and Christou kept their seats against the wall. The cold controlled rage Hector heard in the President's voice almost frightened him as the Man glared at General Flores. "Why was I not told?"

The Chairman held up his empty hands in a gesture of helplessness. "Sir, I didn't know."

"How could you not?!"

"I mean, I knew they were opposed to Russia's entry. I presented their views to you last year. They spoke against it at the Senate. But . . . after the vote, their objections meant nothing. Our job is to carry out the policies of the people."

The President placed his hands on the table and leaned forward. "You're against this, too, aren't you?"

"Sir, I am *not* against it. That would be a violation of my orders. I admit I have misgivings, which I have shared with you at your request. With regard to your understandable concerns about climatic challenges we might face in the long term, I believe that by jumping over the nations of Central Europe, boxing them in with NATO on their east and west borders, we are risking destabilization of the region in the short-term. In five years, I'd hate to be seeing the equivalent of a new Warsaw Pact spring up between Ukraine and the central disaffected nations. If that happens, all the studies show that new pact would look south, to Iran, to Iraq. By moving so quickly, I believe we may heighten tensions, not ease them. But I see the mission of our armed forces as doing everything we can to help NATO make this new transition as orderly and as nonthreatening as possible."

The President remained silent for a few moments, as if analyzing the General's statement for any undercurrents. Then he slowly sat down in his gold-upholstered chair. "I appreciate your candor, and your support." And then the President's rare anger was suddenly gone, replaced by his usual calm focus. He checked his watch. "How are we doing for time, Hec?"

"Twenty minutes till your opening remarks, Mr. President. The First Lady and the Vice President are already in the reception area."

The President accepted Hector's information without comment. He waved to the others to take their seats at the table again, then turned to Secretary Guilbert. "All right. Nick, you get Bobby started on a press statement to cover us on this." To General Flores: "General, I'll want my press secretary to work with the Pentagon spokesman on a joint statement. Make sure we're on the same page. I want new chiefs announced right away. Should we consider their operations deputies?"

"I wouldn't recommend it," the Chairman answered

dryly. "When the king dies around here, it's usually better to bury the retainers, too."

Hector saw the President raise an eyebrow at the Secretary of Defense. "Maybe *you'd* better watch your back come the next election."

Hector then admiringly watched the Man show why he was the Man. To General Flores, the President said, "I want your recommendations to be on Nick's desk first thing tomorrow." To Secretary Guilbert: "Nick, we'll meet tomorrow at noon to go over whatever names you work out with the general. I want to be able to talk to the candidates by tomorrow night and make announcements on Tuesday." And then back to the Chairman: "Does that work for you, Al?"

"I'll make it work, sir. Most of the people who'd be on my short list are in the Building today, anyway. I can introduce you after the ceremonies and before the NIA briefing."

"We'll do that, then." The President used his index fingers to play an impromptu short drum roll on the edge of the table. Hector knew the gesture meant he had just made a decision.

As if reading his mind, the President looked across the room at him. "Hec, I need to make some changes to my speech."

Hector leapt out of his chair at once, with the President's brown-leather briefcase in his hand. "Eighteen minutes, sir."

The President reached into his jacket for his reading glasses. Hector placed the briefcase on the table beside the President, snapped it open, and without being asked, handed the President a pen. Hector kept at least five in his own jacket at all times, as did most of the other people on the President's staff. The Man was always giving them away, or else people took them.

Secretary Guilbert had regained his usual intense demeanor. He was almost dancing with impatience as the President began sorting through the stacks of papers in his briefcase. "Sir, we should be at the reception area by now. You have to meet the ambassadors before your speech. And the generals. And the—"

Instead of responding to the Secretary, the President cut him off by speaking to Hector as he held up a stapled sheaf of pages. "This isn't the copy I was working on in the helicopter."

Hector blinked in surprise, berating himself for not paying closer attention. "Sir, weren't you doing the crossword?"

"I was using the newspaper for support, Hec. For writing. I need the copy of the speech I made notes on."

"In the helicopter, right, sir?"

"You haven't got much time."

Hector wheeled and sprinted for the main doors, frantically trying to remember the fastest route connecting the Tank to the heliport entrance.

General Flores called after him. "Just a minute, son."

"Me?" Hector stopped and looked back from the doors.

"Do you have the slightest idea where the heliport is?"

Hector knew when not to bluff. "None at all, sir."

General Flores hefted himself to his feet. "I'll call for one of the guards at the Corridor Four entrance to bring the speech."

"Won't work," the President said. "No entry to Marine One. By the time we go through Secret Service channels for clearance . . ."

General Flores turned to his aide. She was still sitting against the north wall. "Major Christou."

Christou was on her feet and at attention at once. "Yes, sir."

"Escort this young man to the heliport, then bring him back here."

Christou immediately turned in Hector's direction. "Yes, sir."

But Secretary Guilbert countermanded the general. "No, Major, take him to the reception area. That's first floor, A Ring, between Corridors Six and Seven. Mr. President, we really do have to be going."

Hector held the door open for Christou.

"Can I trust them?" the President's voice said.

Hector exchanged glances with Christou. He kept his hand on the open door.

"Trust who?" Hector heard the uncertainty in General Flores's voice.

"Admiral Paulsen. General Janukatys."

Hector felt a flash of relief as he realized the President hadn't been talking about him.

Flores answered, "In what way, sir?"

"Are they dangerous?"

Christou tried to continue through the door, but Hector put a hand out to slow her down. The implications of the President's question were chilling.

The general's response was untroubled. "They're not in the operational chain of command, if that's what you mean."

Hector didn't hear any more of whatever conversation was about to take place, because Secretary Guilbert noticed the still-open door. "Mr. MacGregor, we're all running late."

Hector followed Christou through the door. Then he and

Christou walked quickly past the two Marine guards in the entrance foyer, and through another set of glass doors to E Ring. Clearly knowing her way, the Army major led the way toward Corridor Nine.

Hector lengthened his stride and easily kept up. He wanted to ask Christou what she thought of the President's last question. He wanted to know what Paulsen and Janukatys might have said to Flores during meetings in her presence. He wanted to know if it was at all possible that in this day and age the United States military might represent a threat to the United States President.

But Hector asked no questions of Christou as they began their race to A Ring.

He wasn't sure he wanted to know which side the major was on.

THE PENTAGON/ "G" PARKING LOT/CHECKPOINT ROMEO

Amy revved the Harley into a one-eighty turn and shot into the parking lot. It was one of the smallest at the Pentagon, other than the VIP and dignitary lots at the River and Mall entrances. At the far east end was a cluster of utilitarian, limestone-faced buildings resembling a small but modern factory—the Pentagon's new heating and refrigeration plant. At the far west end was a short footpath leading to the lower level of the River Entrance Parade Grounds, right at the edge of the Boundary Channel Lagoon. A tall flagpole there carried a large Stars and Stripes, undulating slowly in the slight breeze.

Now that Amy had achieved her goal, and was no longer in motion, she suddenly became aware of the moisture trickling down her back. The day was even hotter and more humid than the weather reports had warned it might be.

As she walked back to the sergeant, she was doubly glad she had packed her uniform instead of wearing it. Her gray Navy sweatshirt was already a mess.

A HUMVEE rolled to a stop by the sergeant. It was a basic Scout version of the High Mobility Multipurpose Wheeled Vehicle, flat Army green, stripped of its plasticized canvas doors and roof.

"Yo, Navy," the driver called out, a cute corporal whose cocky grin let Amy know he knew how cute he looked. She didn't like the way his eyes dropped to take in her damp sweatshirt and tight jeans. "Someone call a taxi?" he asked, then winked. Amy hoped she wouldn't have to hurt him if he tried to act up.

Fortunately, the sergeant didn't appear to appreciate the corporal's flip attitude any more than she did. "Corporal, you will drive Midshipman Bethune directly to the Corridor Three entrance. You will not speak to the midshipman during transit, and the midshipman will use your vehicle's radio to contact me when she arrives, to tell me that her trip was uneventful. Is that understood?"

The corporal's smile vanished at once and he sat up stiffly, as if trying to come to attention. "Yes, Sergeant."

Amy threw her bag into the passenger footwell, then pulled herself up through the open door. She saw the corporal react to the sudden sight of her bare, muscled midriff as her sweatshirt rode up, but an instant later he snapped his eyes front, knowing the sergeant was still watching.

"Good luck, Midshipman," the sergeant said. "Don't spill any soup on the President. And don't swear at any more cops."

"Not today, sir!" Then the HUMVEE pulled out and drove *away* from the Pentagon.

Amy immediately turned in her seat, looked back at the checkpoint. The sergeant was talking to another soldier, paying no attention to the unexpected direction the corporal had taken. Amy prepared for the worst. She slipped her right hand to the back of her waist, getting ready to unsnap the leather sheath she wore on her belt. "This isn't the way to the Pentagon."

She saw the corporal grip the HUMVEE's hard, black steering wheel even tighter as he heard the steel edge in her voice. He opened his mouth, hesitated, repeated the odd, choking display, then: "Uh, permission to speak?"

"Make it good."

The corporal responded as if he had been jump-started, words flying out of him. "The River Entrance roads are all closed down. We have to loop around the heating plant. See? We're just doubling back."

Amy checked the road ahead. It did continue around the buildings ahead.

"On the level, ma'am," the corporal hurried on. "See? We turn in again . . ."

The HUMVEE bore to the right, went under an overpass, then entered a curving ramp that was directly across the G parking lot from Checkpoint Romeo.

Amy said nothing for the rest of the ride. The HUMVEE crossed the overpass, then looped down again by the bus terminal, finally hitting a road that curved around to the pedestrian bridges.

When the corporal brought the HUMVEE to a full stop by the Corridor Three entrance, Amy pulled the microphone from the dashboard radio and looked at him. The corporal immediately selected a frequency and told her to check in with the sergeant, which she did.

Then she jumped down from the HUMVEE's high seat and grabbed her sports bag from the floor. But she didn't walk away at once. "Look, I'm . . . not having a good day, so . . . I didn't mean to get the sergeant all over you." She gave the corporal a half-smile. It was the closest she'd come to a real apology in almost three years.

The smile came right back at her. "Bitch."

Amy instantly knew why he did it. She'd already reported to the sergeant. What was she going to do now? Complain that the corporal had used a bad word? With *her* record?

She made her smile even sweeter. Then she made a fist with her thumb sticking out between her first and index fingers and flipped it at him once as she spat out, *"Ëb tvoju mat, zalupa."*

For a moment, the corporal's sudden look of shock almost made Amy think he'd understood what she'd said she'd done to his mother. Without wasting time to find out, she spun around and headed for the staircase running up to the pedestrian walkway. She thought she heard the corporal mutter "Bitch" one more time, showing a pathetic lack of imagination and vocabulary; then the HUMVEE roared off, gears grinding between first and second.

The Defense Protective Service officers at the entrance were expecting her and let her through the security turnstile after manually checking her pass. They told her that all she had to do to catch up with her company on catering duty was to stay on this floor and follow the corridor all the way to where it ended at A Ring, then turn right. When she reached the main cafeteria between Corridors One and Ten, she'd be able to check in with food-service personnel or servers. They could tell her where to change.

The renovated corridor seemed dark after the sunshine. A double row of perfectly aligned, recessed fluorescent-light panels ran along the middle of its wide ceiling, but perhaps because of weekend power-conservation rules, only one in every pair was switched on. At the very end of the corridor, about four hundred feet or so, Amy saw a bluish glare of what had to be outdoor light coming in through a window.

The light at the end of the tunnel, she thought. The only person in the corridor, she picked up her pace, her Reeboks squeaking on the smooth terrazzo floor. She thought about what she might say to Annika Marsh when they crossed paths. After a few choice statements came to mind, she gave herself the challenge of coming up with curses that did not actually use swear words.

Just as she sprinted through the D Ring intersection, Amy saw that her long chase was finally over. Up ahead, at the next intersection, four midshipmen rushed by, their white uniforms unmistakable to her.

"Yo, guys!" she shouted, waving to get their attention. "I made it!"

The mids looked at her but didn't slow.

Amy turned her sprint into a run, at the same time trying to figure out who she was chasing. One of the four looked something like Joey Fisher, but she was pretty sure it wasn't him.

The midshipmen passed through the intersection and out of sight. Amy began to run even faster. Was it possible a second company had been brought in from the Academy? Without telling 12th Company? That didn't seem right.

"Guys! Wait up!" Amy skidded around the intersection corner expecting to see the four midshipmen still racing away, at least a hundred feet ahead of her.

Three of them were.

But the fourth was ten feet away, and he stood facing her.

He was no one she knew.

Amy stumbled to a stop, gasping for breath. "Hey, thanks . . . I'm in Twelfth Company . . . what company are you guys with?"

The midshipman's answer was not one she expected.

With a swift move he reached behind his back, drew a gun—

—and fired.

ELEVEN

FOURTH FLOOR, D RING, CORRIDOR SIX

There were 7,754 exterior windows in the Pentagon, more than seven acres of glass in all.

For the first diversion, it was necessary to break only one.

The task had been assigned to Bird Dog Four. She was twenty-eight years old, but with her blond hair dyed auburn and cut short she had easily passed for the ID photo pass of Midshipman Annika Marsh that hung from the chain around her neck.

At 1045 hours, fifteen minutes before the President was scheduled to address the crowd in the Courtyard, Bird Dog Four exited the women's rest room just off the intersection of Corridor Six and D Ring. Some areas of the Pentagon were more critical to the security of the United States than others, and this recently renovated section was one of the least—a bureaucratic no-man's-land of support offices dedicated to the management of the military, not its operation.

On this floor, Washington Headquarter Services gave out windshield decals for more than nine thousand Pentagon parking spaces. The biggest storeroom of blank forms for the Department of Defense was also located here. Thus, exactly as planned, the corridor was empty when Bird Dog Four reached A Ring and the selected window overlooking the Mall Terrace Entrance.

The three-foot-by-four-foot window, too, was exactly as shown in the exterior confirmation photographs taken last month. Before the renovations, almost every exterior window in the Pentagon could be opened—at least, those that hadn't been sealed by decades of crusted paint and screwed shut—and more than thirty percent of the Building's heat had been lost through the uninsulated glass. But this window was one of the new ones—a permanently sealed sheet of blastproof, dual-layer thermopane. Still, it would not be a problem.

Bird Dog Four had prepared her equipment in the rest room. Except for one metal device, the materials she required for her diversion had been easily concealed beneath the white skirt of her midshipman's uniform and in her white jacket. She had practiced deploying the materials so often that the action no longer required conscious thought. She had been timed at thirty-two seconds. The schedule allowed her a full minute. More than enough.

First there was the insulated glove. It had been sewn into the lining of her uniform jacket, and she had pulled it free in the rest room. Its multilayered Mylar construction was similar to the thermal-insulation blankets used in the construction of space suits. Bird Dog Four pulled the glove onto her right hand, then slipped the modified cutting torch from her jacket pocket. The torch consisted of two small gas cylinders, three inches long by three-quarters of an inch diameter, topped by a thin metal nozzle. Normally, the gas cylinders held pressurized butane, and could create a flame with a temperature of 1,200 degrees for eight minutes.

Ranger had carried that one piece of equipment into the Pentagon in his soft-sided attaché case. If the torch had been detected by an X-ray scan, the guards would have found it packed inside a small, blue-plastic tool case with the crest of the Naval Academy embossed on the side—a common gift item sold in the Academy store.

The glass in the Pentagon's windows was also heat resistant. It could be penetrated by a torch, but not in the time required, and not with equipment that could be smuggled through in a tool kit. But heat wasn't the only useful force at Team Two's disposal.

Bird Dog Four turned the safety valve on the torch's small nozzle, stood sideways, held her gloved hand out straight so it was six inches from the lower-left corner of the window, then pressed the flow-valve switch.

Instantly, a steaming jet of liquid nitrogen sprayed from the nozzle and Bird Dog Four moved her hand in a small circle. After five seconds of spraying, she released the valve and waved away the thick white vapor swirling from the base of the window. Then she tapped the bottom of the miniature cylinders against the small target area on the glass which was now cooled to a temperature of −320°F.

That circle of glass, manufactured to resist an explosive overpressure of 800 pounds per square inch, cracked like a thin layer of ice, then disintegrated silently, fragments falling free like grains of sand.

Bird Dog Four could feel a chill through her insulated

glove, but repeated the process for the second layer of thermopane. Another five seconds of liquid-nitrogen spray, another gentle tap, and there was a five-inch-wide hole through the Pentagon's blastproof window.

She placed the modified gas torch on the windowsill, tugged off her ice-frosted glove, then looked down through the window. Two HUMVEEs and a DPS patrol car were the only vehicles parked in the North Mall lot. Two soldiers in jungle-camouflage battle dress talked beside one of the HUMVEEs. Neither soldier was looking toward the Pentagon.

Bird Dog Four felt a gust of hot outside air blow in through the hole she had made. She reached under her jacket and pulled the diversion device from her waistband. It looked exactly like a pipe bomb—a foot-long piece of black, two-inch pipe, capped at both ends, with a small digital clock timer and set of batteries taped to its midsection.

But all the pieces of the device had been molded from plastic to be invisible to metal detectors. They had been hidden in the shoulder padding of Bird Dog Four's uniform jacket, and angled to disappear in the edge-thickness effect of any micro-impulse radar scanner that Pentagon security might have used.

Bird Dog Four had snapped the pieces of the fake pipe bomb together in the rest room, like assembling a model kit. Now she flipped open its end cap, inserted two fingers to find the sealed plastic bag inside, and checked her watch.

At precisely 1047 hours, she pressed her fingers against the outer bag in the pipe to burst the smaller bag inside it.

Instantly, she felt the outer bag begin to expand as the vinegar she had released reacted with the baking soda. It was a simple trick of childhood, but one which no chemical sniffer looking for explosives would ever detect.

Bird Dog Four snapped the end cap back into position and shoved the simulated pipe bomb through the hole in the window as if she were loading a miniature torpedo tube. Then she stepped back and waited until she heard a sudden loud pop from outside, like a small-caliber gunshot. The plastic bag inside the pipe bomb had filled with enough carbon dioxide to burst like an overinflated balloon.

As Bird Dog Four stepped away from the window, she saw the two soldiers crouched down by their vehicle, quickly scanning the surrounding area, guns drawn. Clearly, the bursting plastic bag had sounded like a gunshot to them as well. One of them was urgently speaking into a collar microphone.

Bird Dog Four retreated the way she had come, avoiding the escalators and elevators and entering the first stairwell on the right, to report to her staging area. She checked her watch as she jogged down the stairs.

The President was due to speak in eleven minutes.

But Bird Dog Four and forty-two others already in the Pentagon knew what none of the President's guests did.

He'd never have the chance to say a single word.

SECOND FLOOR, C RING, CORRIDOR FOUR

"So, why's the Gold Room called the Tank?" Hector asked.

It was the only question he dared ask Major Christou on their errand run to the heliport. He was reluctant to begin any further discussion of politics until he knew more about where Christou stood.

The major answered promptly, as if she, too, were relieved to talk about something other than the high-level confrontation they'd both witnessed. "Goes back to World War II. The Joint Chiefs—they were called the Combined Chiefs back then—they used to meet in the basement of the old U.S. Public Health Building over on Constitution Avenue. They had to duck under some kind of archway and one of them said it reminded him of getting into a tank. The name stuck."

"You know a lot about this place."

"It's a historic building. A lot of good stories in it."

They came to a side stairwell but just as they were about to enter it, Christou stepped aside as four midshipmen— two men and two women—rushed noisily up the stairs. As they charged by, the one in the lead nodded at Christou to thank her, presumably for giving way. Then they were gone and Hector watched Christou step into the staircase to stare after them.

"Something wrong?"

"They smelled like they just came from the shooting range. Did you catch that?"

Hector had no idea what a shooting range might smell like. "I think they're the guys helping out in the Courtyard. Maybe someone burned something in the kitchen." He started down the stairs.

When he realized the major was not behind him, he turned and put his hand on the railing. "Major, we've got to get moving here."

On the steps above him, Christou paused in thought for just a moment longer, then started down the stairs.

The stairway ended on the first floor, where the major set a fast pace to the Heliport Entrance in E Ring.

"Any ghost stories?" Hector asked breathlessly, almost on the verge of wheezing. This enforced exercise of getting around in the Pentagon clearly required military stamina.

Christou didn't break stride as she glanced at him, puzzled.

"In the Pentagon," he said. "You know, haunted meeting rooms, the spirit of Patton wandering the halls? Off the record, of course."

"You like ghost stories?"

Hector decided to come clean. "The President really goes for oddball stories. Like the hot dog stand at Ground Zero. He'd love to hear there were ghosts in the Pentagon."

For the briefest of moments, Hector saw a wry smile tug at the corners of Christou's mouth. "So, all of this interest in what I know about the Building is all about helping you butter up your boss."

"I like my job. And anyone can give him the stuff in the manuals."

"Okay, there are ghosts."

"Really?"

"I've never seen them, but I've heard the stories." Christou smiled again, as if she couldn't quite believe the topic of conversation. This time Hector found her expression warmer, more natural. The major's attitude to him was definitely changing, as so many people's did when they found out that his interest in what they knew was genuine. Even her voice sounded different—younger, more animated. Maybe the major wasn't as old as her reserved attitude had suggested.

"Okay, this whole place was built at warp speed. Back at the beginning of World War II, the War Department was spread out over twenty different office buildings, so they needed to be consolidated. Plus, we weren't in the war, but the writing was on the wall and everyone knew they'd have to expand drastically, and soon.

"Basically, a team of engineers and architects came up with the overall concept in a single weekend in July 1941. One of them, incidentally, was the fellow who designed the Hollywood Bowl. The five sides were because they had to fit it in between some existing roads on the original site. But President Roosevelt had them relocate the Building so it wouldn't block the view from Arlington Cemetery, and the shape never changed.

"Anyway, a month after that weekend, Congress approved the funds for construction. Less than thirty days later, September 1, the groundbreaking ceremony took place. Sixteen months later, that's January 15, 1943, they had the dedication ceremony. But since they built it in wedges, there were people already working here as early as April of '42."

Hector was impressed, and said so. Both with the information and Christou's easy delivery of it. As they cut across the D Ring intersection, Hector saw up ahead the interior glass doors leading to the Heliport Entrance. He checked his watch: It had taken the major six minutes to get him here. They only had ten minutes to make it back.

"So," the major continued as she pushed one of the glass doors open, "you do anything that quickly, you make mistakes. The accident rate was something like four times higher than the standard for Army construction at the time."

Hector followed her through the doors, and read between the lines. "How many people died?"

"Eight on site."

"They're the ghosts?"

"Down in the basement, especially. Just the place for that kind of thing. To speed up making the foundation, they poured concrete right onto the soil, so after fifty years, before the renovation, there were holes in the basement floor, concrete slabs heaved up. Really damp, dark, smelled like a swamp now and then. That's what this whole area was when they started construction. A swamp."

As they hurried to the exterior doors that would lead out to the heliport, Hector saw the major glance around, but he didn't know what she was looking for.

"So that's where the ghosts are, even after the renovations?"

"That's what they say. Especially at night and on weekends . . . when there's no one here to see them. Which, of course, begs the question: How does anyone know they're there?"

Hector and the major had reached the set of doors leading outside and Hector opened them this time. The torpid outdoor air was once again heavy with the scent of newly mown grass manicured for the President's brief walkthrough.

"And it's not just the basement," the major added as she and Hector almost ran along the path leading to the heliport support buildings. "I've heard stories of something up on the fifth floor, in what used to be attic storerooms. And I haven't even started on the ancient Indian burial ground."

Hector couldn't help himself. He broke out laughing. "Get out of town."

Christou's matching laugh was almost a giggle, startling Hector with its infectious quality. He and the major were getting on better than he'd ever anticipated. It seemed lots of people besides the President needed a different point of view to loosen them up. He wondered if his continued contact with Christou could get her to similarly open up her thoughts on world politics. "Seriously?"

"Seriously. Captain John Smith, early 1600s, he wrote

about visiting an Indian village here. They used to be all up and down the Potomac. Fishing villages." And then the major reverted sharply to her earlier, tight attitude. She halted abruptly. "No guards."

That was what the major had been looking for. Hector suddenly recalled there had been no Air Force guards at the security desk inside.

He and the major were right in front of the helipad now, where the presidential helicopter waited for the return flight to the White House. There were no Marine guards at either side of the stairs leading into Marine One.

"It's really hot," Hector said hesitantly, not even convincing himself. "Maybe they're inside with the air-conditioning?"

Christou motioned Hector to retreat with her, to the shade of the helipad's two-story control tower. "The helo engines aren't idling. No air-conditioning in there." She looked up at the tower. "Oh, shit."

Hector followed her gaze. One of the green-tinted, outward-slanting windows was cracked. No personnel were visible through it. His sense of unease escalating, Hector looked past the tower. He could no longer see the black-clad riflemen or the Secret Service agent stationed on the roof.

Christou grabbed him by the shoulder. Her voice cut through Hector's confusion like a laser. "Go inside, go to the security desk, call 5555. Tell them there is a Cloudy Office scenario at the Heliport Entrance." As if expecting his immediate response to her order, the major turned her attention back to the helicopter. But Hector had no idea what a Cloudy Office scenario was supposed to be. He had, however, been briefed often enough about what to do if he ever noticed suspicious activity around the President. "No—you call. You know what to tell them. I know how to use the Secret Service radio in the helo."

The major nodded, accepting his suggestion without question. She whirled around without saying anything else and ran for the Heliport Entrance to Corridor Four.

Hector sprinted across the grass toward Marine One. In five seconds the metal stairs clattered noisily as he rushed up them and to the left to the cockpit.

The two pilots' bodies lay slumped in their flight chairs, still buckled in. Dark blood dripping from their heads onto the cockpit floor.

The dashboard instruments had been smashed. Behind the two dead pilots, on the cockpit rear bulkhead, dangled what was left of the Secret Service ECOM link. The handset was on the deck, crushed. Its wires had been severed.

Fearing what he would find, Hector turned and looked into the passenger cabin.

Two dead Marine guards. Their blood staining the thick, beige, soundproofing carpet beneath them.

Between the two Marines was a cardboard carton whose label marked it as containing twenty-four cans of tomato soup. Its top flaps were open. Without even thinking of how foolish he was being, Hector found himself walking slowly forward to look into the carton. Something wrapped in a gray plastic bag filled the bottom of the box. Set into the middle of the bag was a digital time display, black numbers against a pale green background. Wires from the display disappeared into the gray plastic bag.

The time on the display was 10:52.

The President was scheduled to speak at 11:00.

Hector knew what he was looking at without even voicing the word. He just didn't believe it.

He focused on the time display. *I'm going to be late,* the only conscious thought in his mind. Something more instinctual made him turn and run.

But he *was* late.

The display ticked over. 10:53.

The bomb in the President's helicopter exploded on schedule.

It was the second diversion.

RIVER ENTRANCE PARADE GROUNDS

The third diversion weighed forty-seven pounds. Except for its electronics package, the device had been built in a small machine shop in New York at a cost of $2,300. That did not include the $5,000 promised to the American undergraduate who had constructed the device over the course of a week. When Ranger's operatives took delivery of the device, they killed its maker, but not to save the money. In principle, Ranger's funds for the mission were unlimited. Rather, it was critical to the success of the mission that the enemy have no means of determining who was responsible for today's actions. Ranger, like the mission planners, was convinced that true world stability depended on secrets.

The device was called a Flux Compression Generator. The basic technology it was based on dated back to the forties. The effect it produced had first been described in the sixties. The Semtex explosive that powered it had been developed in the seventies. And a surplus Pentium II computer chip from the nineties and the series of off-the-shelf, rechargeable batteries originally designed for use in portable medical equipment enabled the FCG to be made small enough for concealment in a thirty-cup, brushed-aluminum coffeemaker.

The coffeemaker had been installed in a white, television transmission van rented to an Italian news bureau. For the past five days, the white van had been parked on the Pentagon's River Entrance Parade Grounds. Throughout that time, it had been subjected to daily examinations by the Defense Protective Service's K-9 unit, using German shepherds trained to detect the volatile solvents given off by virtually every known type of explosive, even Semtex. But the FCG was still in place.

Encased in a fiberglass shell that had been molded around it without seams, and that contained no openings, the concealed FCG released no molecules of Semtex volatiles. Ranger's engineers had methodically eliminated any which had come in contact with the exterior surface of the shell with a decontamination procedure involving repeated acid washes followed by storage in a vacuum chamber. Semtex was already one of the hardest explosives to detect, and after the acid-vacuum treatments, neither dogs nor chemical detectors carried by the other security personnel who constantly patrolled the parade grounds had a chance of detecting the device.

Thirty minutes before the President was due to speak, a Baltimore-based, freelance television technician hired by the Italian agency when it rented the white van took the aluminum coffeemaker outside and placed it on a small folding table. Beside the coffeemaker, he placed a stack of Styrofoam cups and a plastic bag. The plastic bag was filled with packets of Equal and white-plastic stir sticks. An orange extension cord ran from the coffeemaker into the back of the van.

Twenty minutes before the President was due to speak, two Defense Protective Service officers walked past the van, not even glancing at the coffee table.

Seven minutes before the President was due to speak, the DPS and Secret Service radio channels filled with messages reporting the discovery of an apparently amateur pipe bomb in the bushes along the wall containing the Pentagon's Mall Entrance. Army personnel had cleared the area and were waiting for delivery of an Explosive Ordnance Disposal robot.

Outside the Pentagon, roof-positioned Special-Forces snipers and Secret Service personnel moved rapidly to the Mall Entrance side to sweep the area in case additional devices had also been deployed. Inside the Pentagon, the Secret Service agents accompanying the President in the reception area remained at heightened level of readiness. With three hundred guests already in attendance, including diplomats and high-ranking military officials from all the NATO countries, the ceremony was not an event that could easily be canceled.

Immediately upon the withdrawal of the snipers and agents from the roof overlooking the heliport, four of Ranger's commandos emerged from Corridor Four to eliminate the two Air Force guards at the heliport security desk. Thirty seconds later, at the heliport control tower, one of the commandos tossed a flash-bang grenade up the short staircase. Simultaneously, at the heliport's fire and first-aid station building, a second commando did the same. The other two commandos dropped the guards outside the President's helicopter and threw a second flash-bang grenade into its cockpit. At each of their target sites, Ranger's commandos neutralized the unconscious personnel with single shots to the head.

Then the two commandos in Marine One activated one of ten Semtex time bombs, which had been delivered to the Pentagon's main kitchen in a cardboard carton of soup cans. The bomb's timer began a three-minute countdown.

One minute later, five minutes before he was due to speak, the President of the United States decided not to delay his appearance until Hector MacGregor and Major Christou returned with his annotated script. Instead, with the First Lady's blessing, the President decided to speak extemporaneously, a decision anxiously questioned by the President's press secretary. But this President was known for always being on time. He would not make an exception today.

That was what Ranger had counted on. All was still unfolding as it should.

The Secret Service agents in the Pentagon's Courtyard reported that all three hundred invited guests were in position, seated at the forty round tables set up before the stage. There was no indication of trouble within the safety of the Pentagon's inner walls.

The Marine Band was given a five-minute warning. They would open with "Hail to the Chief," then the national anthem. Following the President's opening remarks, they would then play the Russian National Anthem as General Yuri Kerensky joined the President's party on the stage.

In the reception area, the President, the Vice President, the Secretary of Defense, and the Chairman of the Joint Chiefs of Staff were assembling in position, before the glass door leading to the stage entrance. The President and General Flores took the opportunity to shake hands again with Russia's General Kerensky.

Four minutes before the President was to speak, the bomb in Marine One exploded.

In the Courtyard, the blast's concussion was magnified by the hard surrounding walls. Fully half those invited were military veterans. They knew the sound of an explosion when they heard it.

At the River Entrance, the blast was almost as loud. But most of the media could not identify what they had heard.

Except for one technician, in a small white van rented to an Italian news agency.

Holding his watch in his left hand, the technician counted off thirty seconds, waiting for the security radio channels to become overloaded. Waiting for the smoke from the destroyed helicopter to be noticeable for miles. And for the President's Secret Service to realize that evacuation by Marine One was no longer an option, forcing them to fall back to one of their contingency plans. Not that the mission would allow any of those plans to succeed.

Twenty-five seconds after the Marine One bomb detonation, after ongoing radio updates announcing that both the Heliport and the Mall Terrace Entrances had been compromised, two Secret Service agents raced down Corridor Six to B Ring, each with an arm hooked around one of the President's, dragging him forward despite his protests. The President was shielded by the beige raincoat lined with Kevlar and ceramic armor that a third agent had thrown over him. A fourth agent led the way, his SIG-Sauer semi-automatic pistol already drawn.

A second team of four agents dragged the Vice President down Corridor Five, following a second planned evacuation route.

Two additional agents, sandwiching the First Lady between them, propelled her along the A Ring corridor to the kitchen and her own evacuation-path exit.

Of the three backup extraction points still available, Special Agent Zibart chose the roof option. He called for an Air Force Special Ops Pave Low III to descend to the extraction point on the C Ring roof in the Mall Terrace wedge. The helicopter would hover forty feet above the roof to drop two hostage-retrieval operators on rappelling ropes. As soon as the operatives reached the roof, they were to snap a Fulton harness around the President and two Secret Service agents, and the helicopter would immediately ascend and move off. The Secret Service Agents and the Special Ops soldiers would be human shields around the President until the five could be winched aboard.

Thirty seconds after the Marine One bomb detonation, the pilot of Black Angel One began to radio his confirmation of the Secret Service's emergency extraction request and banked over the Potomac, as he began his descent to the roof of C Ring.

At the same time, in the Italian news van at the River Entrance, the technician pressed the black switch he held in his right hand. The black switch was connected to the orange extension cord, which was connected in turn to the brushed-aluminum coffeemaker on the table outside the van.

In the coffeemaker, a compressed CO_2 gas cartridge suddenly fired, turning the cylindrical container into a mortar tube that launched the FCG. The only sound it made was the sudden whump of the gas release and the clatter of the coffeemaker lid as it landed on the roof of the news van.

The forty-seven-pound Flux Compression Generator capsule reached its operational altitude of 110 feet in less than two seconds. At that point, a timer started by the impact of the launch ignited one end of the capsule's Semtex core so that an explosion began to propagate along the length of the device.

The Semtex core was wrapped in a helical coil of copper wire through which traveled a battery-supplied current. In the hundreds of microseconds the explosion took to consume all the Semtex, the magnetic field produced by that current was violently compressed by both the explosion and the resulting short circuit that progressed through the coil.

The instant before the Semtex disintegrated the FCG and its fiberglass shell, the strength of the compressed magnetic field in the capsule approached that generated by a small nuclear bomb. The electromagnetic pulse that resulted radiated outward at the speed of light over an area with a diameter of 1,500 feet.

Instantly, every television light on the parade ground blew out in smoking, sparking explosions. Instantly, every cell phone, every radio, every electronic device from the ignition systems of the parked limousines to the PalmPilot organizers in the pockets of the reporters and the radio mikes clipped to soldiers' shirts burned out as their circuits and power supplies—designed to operate at currents of only a few tens of volts at most—were subjected to a blitzkrieg surge of thousands of volts.

The antennae and satellite dishes of the news trailers and vans absorbed that pulse, amplified it, then drove it down into the equipment that was wired to them. Simultaneous explosions resounded across the parade grounds as gouts of smoke and streaks of flame shot out of every camera and monitor. Miniature lightning displays shot from antenna to antenna and snaked along the power cables that had been laid out across the parade grounds' grass.

A hundred small fires broke out at once across the

makeshift television city. More serious explosions erupted to the side of the River Entrance, where the power-generator trailers blew out with enough force to ignite their diesel fuel supplies.

And even before the reverberations of these explosions, large and small, had faded, they were replaced by the screams of the reporters and technicians and security personnel caught in the path of exploding equipment, or those more fortunate who struggled to pull smoldering and flaming electronic devices from their pockets before their clothing and hair could ignite.

The confusion and panic were so great at the River Entrance that no one witnessed the spectacular death spirals of the circling black helicopters, whose engines had failed with the sudden death of all onboard electronics.

In less than five seconds, the detonation of one forty-seven-pound bomb costing $2,300 destroyed more than five million dollars' worth of government and private equipment. It killed ten people at once, seriously injured fifty-two others, and, true to its nature, disrupted absolutely the complex systems that guarded the safety of the President, the leaders of NATO, and the headquarters of the Department of Defense—the most secure building in America.

The third diversion had served its purpose.

The siege of the Pentagon had begun.

GROUND ZERO

ONE

SECOND FLOOR, D RING, CORRIDOR THREE

If Amy Bethune had stopped to think about what she had to do to survive, she would have been dead in less than a second.

But Amy had been trained to operate in an environment in which thought was not required. Her instincts had been honed. The reflexes of youth had been refined. And in that split second as her attacker raised his pistol to aim and fire at her, Amy found out just how good her training had been.

Even before she consciously recognized the gun in her enemy's hand, she began to pivot sideways to decrease the target area she presented. At the same time, she used her momentum to swing up her dark blue sports bag and make it *her* weapon, launching it on a fast, straight trajectory toward the gun.

The sports bag absorbed the first silenced shot, and the impact deflected it in a puff of haze and dark-blue fibers.

Amy lunged forward, below the enemy's sightline, making use of the tumbling bag's cover and distraction.

The second shot hissed through the space her body had occupied only an instant before. By now she was airborne.

Her left hand struck the gun broadside as it fired a third time, while her right-hand knuckles punched the enemy's throat.

They fell together, Amy's hand clutching the gun and twisting it back against her enemy's thumb so that as they hit the floor, the weapon was out of his grasp and in hers.

She landed on her side beside him as he swept his open left hand up to her jaw with such force her vision was mottled by explosions of color.

She felt him start to roll away. She grabbed his jacket to slow his motion, to keep him close. She felt him twist, sensed him as a shadow in her clearing sight, rising above her to strike.

She drove the gun forward from her shoulder, directly into his groin.

He groaned. She swept her empty hand against his head, driving him back to the floor, then swung the gun into his face and heard the crack of bone.

That sound brought her an intense moment of clarity. She recalled Marine Sergeant Major Gilden and her hand-to-hand combat training: *Once they're down,* the sergeant major had told her, *make sure they're never getting up.*

Amy rolled to her knees beside her enemy as he shriveled into a fetal curl. It didn't matter. Mercy had never been an option. The gun went into her right hand and became a club she used to crush his exposed temple.

His body jerked once, then lay still as blood welled up and escaped his smashed skull like a drain overflowing. Amy looked down at the first person she had ever killed. Possessed by a strange sense of calm, she wiped the bloody gun on his white trousers.

Then a silenced shot spit past her and she slapped both hands around the gun, rolled over her enemy's body, and fired up from the floor at the three hostiles in midshipman white who were almost upon her.

The weapon kicked in her hands again and again. She heard one shot scream as it etched a furrow in the corridor's terrazzo floor. A ceiling light exploded. The three hostiles flattened against one wall, then disappeared. Into an alcove or a corridor—Amy couldn't be sure which. But she was sure that, as good as her hand-to-hand skills were, she sucked as a marksman. She hadn't hit one of them.

Amy scanned the empty corridor. She had no picture of how this deserted ring section connected to the rest of the Pentagon or where she could find reinforcements quickly. And she had to be ready for the three hostiles to double back on her.

She looked at the man who'd tried to kill her, at his uniform. His single stripe said he was a Youngster, but the remains of his face said he was ten years too old to be in second year at the Academy. Then she saw the Pentagon security pass on the chain around his neck. She bent down to yank it from him, snapping the chain. The blood-spattered photograph showed Midshipman Joseph Fisher. There was only one way this man could have taken Joey's pass.

She rapidly calculated her odds of setting an effective ambush if the three hostiles tried to double back. The odds weren't good. Especially since there could be up to forty more enemy in her murdered classmates' uniforms.

Amy ransacked the dead man's pockets for spare magazines and found one, fully loaded with fifteen 9mm rounds. She shoved the spare clip into the front pocket of her jeans. That was when she checked the manufacturer's stamp on the grip of the pistol. It was a Beretta. But it wasn't like the standard M9 model she had trained with at the Academy. This one was jet black and had no cut marks or lines on the sides of its frame. It was more a smoothly curving sculpture than a lethal machine. And there was no silencer, though the pistol had barely made a sound when it had fired. She examined the clip still inside the Beretta. Four cartridges left. She tried not to think who'd been the targets of the eleven expended rounds.

Right now, she needed those reinforcements. That meant finding a phone—in a defensible position. She saw a stairwell just a few yards down the corridor.

In the same instant—the lights flickered, then a muffled echo. *An explosion,* Amy knew. *Something big.*

Again, training dictated choice of strategy. Her heart pounding madly, Amy ran for higher ground.

HELIPORT, CORRIDOR FOUR ENTRANCE

Hector MacGregor was inside Marine One again. Washington spun crazily past the windows. Rotors scattered the pages of the President's speech, curling them into a vortex of lost paperwork. The President was furious with him. And it was all Hector's fault. Because he went in—because he opened the—because he—

Hector fell onto the helipad, gagging, head throbbing, each scrape and cut stinging as he was dragged by—

"Major . . . ?" He coughed, then almost threw up as Christou rolled him roughly onto his back, onto soft grass. He saw a swirl of black smoke rising behind her, into unmarked blue sky. He felt small shocks of pain in his back, down his legs, in one foot. "What—?"

"The helicopter went up. You almost went with it." She threw herself on his body, her arms flailing at him. Then Hector realized that some of the black smoke came from him.

He sat up as if spring-loaded, throwing her back to her knees. Then both their hands flew as they patted down the burning embers still igniting his once-white shirt and gray trousers. Hector groaned as he saw the gray wad the major was using to extinguish the worst of the flames: his favorite cashmere, hand-tailored jacket. He had no idea when she had taken it off him. He looked down at his new tie. The slate-gray silk now had holes. Hector loosened the tie, tugged it off, threw it away. He looked up at the major, who, incredibly, was now standing up, reflexively straightening her uniform and brushing off soot.

"When?" he asked. All he could remember was going into Marine One for the President's speech. Then . . . nothing. He looked over at the helipad. At what was left of Marine One, listing to one side, its middle fuselage bulging, buckled, every window blown out. Oily black smoke poured from its engines, despoiling the glossy white paint just above them.

Then Hector remembered . . . the bomb in the soup carton . . . the . . . He lurched to his feet. "The President!" He wobbled as he struggled to lift and move his feet in the direction of the Heliport Entrance.

But Christou easily restrained him. "There was a second explosion. The phones aren't working. You don't belong in there."

Hector pushed her away, shook his head, almost fainted. "The hell I don't." He forced his legs to obey him but his left foot hurt like hell with every step. This time the major stopped him by twisting one of his arms, hard, as she spun him around.

"*Sir*—the President is already gone. He has to be. The Secret Service would extract him at the first sign of trouble."

Hector didn't believe her, and for good reason. He swayed but stayed standing, wondering what he'd done to his left foot. It felt more sprained than broken, but his black Italian loafer was getting tighter by the second. "You're going back in. Why can't I?"

He read the answer in her eyes. "There is a hostile force inside. You—"

"What hostile force?" A wave of nausea nearly overwhelmed him but he managed to suppress it.

"Those midshipmen we passed on the stairs. They smelled like gunsmoke."

Hector suddenly forgot all about himself. *Midshipmen! The Courtyard was filled with them!* Adrenaline surged through his body and he turned and broke into a half-running, hopping lope.

Christou charged after him. "You're a civilian!"

"So you can't give me orders!" He pushed open the glass doors, but Christou rushed through before him.

Then they both ran for Corridor Four and the President.

THIRD FLOOR, E RING

"Here's the culprit," Tom said.

Vanovich glanced over from his high-backed swivel chair in front of the Red Level workstation monitors. "Something expensive, I hope."

Tom straightened up from the exposed print engine and

clicked his Swiss Army knife closed. "The charging wire snapped, so the paper won't pick up any toner."

Vanovich eased out of his chair, his movements slow and careful. "That never happens."

Tom crossed his arms, trying not to show the distress he felt seeing his old friend's lack of mobility. "It does if someone snaps it on purpose to get a repair guy up here when he could be at a ball game." He still wasn't certain if Vanovich had actually sabotaged his own printer or not.

"Tommy boy, that's a terrible thing to say." Vanovich's soft brown eyes were guileless. "Can you fix it?"

"I can replace the charging assembly if you have a spare."

"Since they never break, I doubt building services has them in stock." Vanovich rubbed at the back of his solid neck. "Could you take one from another printer?"

"If you can get me into another Red Level . . ." Tom stopped. "Did you feel that?" There had been a tremor in the floor.

"Goddamn helicopters. They've been flying all over the place. When the President comes in—all five of those big green monsters going over at once—it feels like the roof's about to blow off."

Tom relaxed. "Right. He was landing just when I got here. Felt like Dorsey's car was going to blow off the road. Anyway . . . from what I remember of the paperwork for secure printer parts, you might as well wait for—"

The ceiling lights flickered once, in time with another small tremor.

"Okay, Milo. Now, what the hell was *that?*"

General Vanovich looked up at the ceiling of his sealed Red Level office with a thoughtful expression. "That was a power outage. We've switched over to storage batteries and in about ninety seconds the backup generators will take over."

"This whole section's been renovated. How can you have a—"

"Will you look at that?" Vanovich pushed his swivel chair aside to reach for his keyboard.

On the center screen above the general's keyboard, Tom saw the MAJIC space-surveillance image of the exterior grounds of the Pentagon. There appeared to be a cloud distortion over the helipad and an even larger one over the parade grounds.

"What's that? Rain clouds?" *That might make some sense,* Tom thought. A good old Washington thunderstorm. A nearby lightning strike could have affected the power stations. The tremors might have been caused by thunder.

But Vanovich was a more experienced image analyst than Tom was. "That's smoke. Get Dorsey in here." The general started typing very rapidly. The monitors began winking out as Tom watched. "Get him!"

Tom had just entered Vanovich's outer office when he heard the unmistakable but improbable popping of gunfire from the corridor beyond.

For a timeless, confused moment, Tom stared at the closed door to the corridor.

Then came the splintering of wood . . . more gunfire. And a strangled gasp just beyond the outer door. Tom knew it had to be Dorsey.

He turned back to the green door. It had already shut. Now the outer door was rattling. Someone was trying to open it. Dorsey must have locked it somehow, before he was shot.

Tom quickly leaned into the retina scanner and jammed

his proxcard against the metal plate, as behind him, someone began pounding on the outer door. It took all the self-control Tom possessed to keep his eye to the scanner and his back to the door. But he couldn't run and hide. He couldn't leave the general.

Another burst of gunfire. He heard the metal doorknob crash to the floor in pieces.

Just then the green door clicked.

Tom rushed through just as the outer door began to open.

In the Red Level office he whirled around and pushed at the door to swing it almost but not quite shut. Then he forced himself to slowly close the door that last inch. Whoever was about to enter Vanovich's office must not hear the click of the green door's lock.

Vanovich was still on his feet, holding a phone receiver in one hand. He held a finger to his lips in warning. "The outside lines are gone," he whispered. "We've still got internal lines on the fiber-optic system, but security isn't answering. Where's Dorsey?"

Tom mouthed his bad news more than voicing it. "They're in your office. They shot down the door."

The general nodded, not even bothering to ask who Tom meant by "they." He kept his voice low. "We're going to be okay, Tommy. Whatever this is, it can't last long."

Tom heard a crash in the outer office and felt the first touch of panic. Vanovich was a desk soldier. His old friend didn't understand. "Dorsey may be dead. I think I heard him get shot."

The general put down the receiver, put his hands on Tom's shoulders. His voice was calm, controlled. "The Pentagon knows how to deal with this kind of thing."

"What?" Tom felt sweat drip into his eyes, and shook it

away. The small, sealed room was feeling hotter despite his short-sleeved polo shirt. The air-conditioning was no longer working.

"They call it Cloudy Office. It's a training scenario. Every two years—" Vanovich paused, listened as the sound of another crash penetrated the door, then resumed whispering. "Every two years, they've been running it. Invite the press. Get the local police in. Then they simulate this kind of stuff."

The green door shook violently as if the intruder were trying to jar it off its hinges, but Vanovich kept talking. Tom felt his heartbeat steadying. He concentrated on slowing down his breathing, to conserve oxygen.

"They have soldiers act like terrorists, you know. Sometimes they take over the Secretary of Defense's office downstairs. One time they released fake nerve gas in the Tricare facility. Did you see all the little dental offices they have down there? They double as decontamination rooms." Vanovich pointed to the ceiling just above the green door. "You see that slot?"

In more control of his reactions now, Tom looked up, saw a broad, squat, U-shaped opening as wide as the door.

"This is also a *safe* room," Vanovich said. "If they try to force that door, bang, a composite-armor blast shield shoots down and the air vents are sealed. We've even got emergency rations. Tommy, trust me. They'd need a tactical nuke to get us outta here. Everything's going to be fine. We're going to be okay."

Tom didn't enjoy the thought of being sealed in with no air supply, but it was better than being shot. "They've trained for this?"

Vanovich nodded, reassuring. "We got the operational

centers of the Army, the Navy, the Air Force, and the fucking Marines in this building. Maybe those assholes out there can get into *my* office. But they sure as hell can't get anywhere near those other ones. All those Cloudy Office exercises, there're just a cover so the press doesn't start wondering what all the helicopters and troop activity is about. The real deal is Operation Cloudburst. It's part of Atlantis Rising. And . . . look, Tommy, everything I'm telling you, this is classified beyond even your need to know, okay?"

Tom had recognized the last code name. "Atlantis Rising . . . as in PROJECT ATLANTIS? You've got it in here?"

General Vanovich nodded and leaned forward, conspiratorially, as if about to tell Tom even more. But then, from the other side of the green door, a voice called out, the words muffled, but discernible.

"Major General Milo Vanovich!"

Vanovich looked warily at the door, one hand warning Tom to let him handle this, as if it was Tom who needed protection, and not the other way around.

"General. We have control of the Building. We know exactly where you are. And we know what will happen if we force the door to your Red Level facility."

The general's bushy eyebrows lifted in surprise, in response to the intruders' revelation. Tom no longer found the movement humorous.

"Speak to us, General. We have accessed the security logs. We know you signed into your office at 6:07 this morning."

"Ah, shit," Vanovich muttered. Tom wondered if the simulation scenarios had included this stage.

"General, no one needs to get hurt. If you do as we say,

no one *will* get hurt. But if you remain in there, we will start executing hostages. From today's guest list."

The answer to Tom's question about the completeness of the Cloudy Office simulations was in the expression on Vanovich's face.

"General, I'm going to make this easy for you."

Tom heard the sound of scuffling outside the green door, heavy footsteps, harsh voices.

"My men have just brought me the President of the United States. He is not the person I'm interested in today. He is expendable to me. Do you understand?"

Tom stared at Vanovich. The President *was* here today. Was it really possible that he could have been taken hostage? In the Pentagon? But then, how had anyone managed to smuggle weapons into the Building and get as far as Vanovich's office?

"They're lying . . ." Vanovich said.

Then Tom's questions became moot as a very familiar voice called out hoarsely: *"General! This is your commander in chief! Do not open that—"*

The shout was interrupted by a loud thud, then a groan.

Vanovich took a step forward, but Tom caught him by the arm. "Milo, no! The President said no!"

"This won't last long, Tommy. All we need to do is buy some time. I'll be okay." The general pushed Tom's hand away and shouted at the green door. "I need guarantees."

"I will give you five seconds to open the door. Then I will kill the President and go looking for another officer with Red Level clearance."

Vanovich turned to Tom and whispered urgently. "You have to think of Tyler! Hide behind the workstation! I'll be okay. All they want is me and my Red Level access. It won't do them any good."

Before Tom could stop him, the general was opening the green door, shouting, "I'm coming out."

With no other option, Tom ran for the Red Level workstation and squeezed himself into the space between the console and the wall. The space was just big enough for a technician to work in. All the renovated sections of the Pentagon included design features like the console workspace to facilitate upgrade and repair.

The green door clicked open, brightening the light in the sealed inner office.

Crouched in his hiding place, Tom tried to convince himself that the general was right. That the Pentagon knew what to do. That in just a few minutes, the Marines would come to the rescue.

Through the open door, he heard Vanovich's indignant voice clearly. "Where's the President?"

"Tango?" the intruder replied. "A demonstration for the general."

"My fellow Americans," a second voice said, "welcome to the Brave New World of the Brave New Century." Tom realized how they had been tricked. Every standup comic in the country could do the President. So, it seemed, could at least one terrorist.

Vanovich's voice trembled, but Tom recognized the underlying emotion was anger, not fear. "Who are you?"

"I am a patriot, General. You can call me Ranger. Who else is in that room?"

"Why don't you go in and look?"

Tom tensed. The general was trying a trick of his own—to provoke the intruder into triggering the Red Level room's automatic security measures. But the tactic was not successful.

"That won't be necessary," Ranger said. "Grenade."

Just for an instant, Tom heard the beginning of Vanovich's

cry of protest. Then the green door slammed shut and something hit the inner-office carpet.

Tom stopped breathing. He heard a faint hissing, like a large fireplace match igniting.

He thought of Tyler.

The grenade went off.

TWO

E RING

Five minutes after the third diversion, Ranger had no idea where the President was and didn't care. He never had.

General Milo Vanovich was the mission's prime target: a two-star general who had never faced combat; who would disobey a direct order from his commander in chief; and who, as director of the NIA, enjoyed absolute Red Level access to every asset owned and operated by the National Security Agency *and* the National Reconnaissance Office. So much power in such ineffectual hands. Only in America.

Ranger quick-marched General Vanovich along the newly wood-paneled corridor of E Ring, twenty-five feet beyond the River Entrance Parade Grounds, where panicked confusion still reigned. Close beside Ranger were the other three members of his squad, Tango, Hotel, and Bird Dog One, all three men still in midshipmen white, all toting

Heckler & Koch 9mm MP5 submachine guns with integral silencers, and wearing web harnesses loaded with flash-bang grenades and extra clips. With long, bulky barrels and no stocks, the silenced H&Ks were easier to use in close-quarters combat than basic-combat versions and, because of their compact size, had been much simpler to smuggle into the Pentagon's special-events kitchen.

Seconds after the grenade detonated in the general's inner office, Ranger had heard the pulsating shriek of an alarm giving the signal to evacuate the Building. That the Building's automatic alarm system continued to function despite the second diversion on the outside parade grounds was no surprise to Ranger. Most of the Pentagon's critical aboveground power and communications systems were hardened against electromagnetic pulse. It was the dozens of antennae clustered on the roof of the River Entrance wedge of the Pentagon that would most certainly have been knocked out by the EM pulse generated by the FCG device. Ranger knew the only EMP shielding at the Pentagon was where those antennae's wire leads entered the Building through electromagnetic traps. The traps were designed to dissipate the pulse and protect the equipment inside. Yet, for all that the Pentagon's designers had tried to keep the interior layout of the Building obscure, even a casual inspection of aerial photos of its exterior confirmed the rel-ative importance of a section. The roof of the most impor-tant section held the greatest number of satellite dishes and transmission antennae. And it was above that roof that the FCG had been detonated.

The Pentagon had many other meticulously detailed options for self-defense and security of significant sections and, during his tour here, Ranger had been allowed to review most of them. He had been particularly interested in the classified reports analyzing the effectiveness of all the Cloudy Office and Cloudburst security-training scenarios that were run every two years. That was when Ranger had detected a weak point in the Pentagon's defense exercises: the unquestioned assumption that local area forces would have access to instant communications, by phone or radio. Yet, today, merely by detonating a simple, garage-built EMP bomb over the parade grounds, Ranger had been able to completely isolate the Pentagon from outside help.

When he had returned from that tour and was back at his regular duty station, Ranger had even managed to obtain, illegally, an abstract of the Above-Top-Secret Atlantis Rising scenario. Since then he had learned that the Pentagon had classified all the implementations of PROJECT ATLANTIS at such a high level that fewer than one hundred people in the Building even suspected the existence of the defense forces they had at their disposal.

For now, however, it was enough that he and his team had cut the Pentagon off from the outside world. Most of the internal systems would only have to function for the next twelve hours, after which time the operational ability of any interior or exterior systems would cease to be important. Twelve hours from now, the Pentagon itself would cease to exist, along with half of Arlington County.

In fact, based on his study of the Cloudy Office and Cloudburst documents, Ranger knew it would be at least thirteen more minutes before sufficient working communications nodes could be brought in from outside the affected area. Until then, the Defense Protective Service could not even set up an Incident Command Post, let alone begin to put together an overview of what had happened to their

Building. And without that overview, the DPS could not begin to make choices from its extensive menu of countermeasures.

The weak point in the Atlantis Rising scenario had been its assumption that its existence was unknown outside a chosen, select circle. A circle that now included Ranger. And he had deliberately sized the scope of this attack to force the initiation of the Atlantis Rising scenario.

Ranger, his three commandos, and one prisoner moved quickly toward the E Ring stairwell. Tango kicked the stairwell door open, checking to make certain the first wide and brightly lit landing was clear.

Then Ranger led the descent to the two levels and two rings that had never appeared on any map of the Pentagon. He did so secure in the knowledge that Team Two, in the Courtyard, would complete their part of the mission without him.

Because Team One was standing by.

And it was almost time for them to strike.

C RING, ROOF

For the Team Two commandos in the top five floors and five rings, their first stage had been diversion. Their second was distraction.

Thus, where General Milo Vanovich was the plan's prime target, the President was the prime victim. And, as his protectors rushed to get him out of the Pentagon, their choice of path was inevitable, predetermined.

The fake pipe bomb had denied Presidential escape via the Mall Terrace—other bombs could be present in the area.

The destruction of Marine One had denied Presidential escape via the heliport. And the planned, backup roof extractions had been rendered impossible the instant the circling Air Force helicopters were exposed to the electromagnetic pulse generated over the River Entrance Parade Grounds.

As it was, all electrical systems on board the circling Air Force helicopters had burned out at once, from the fly-by-wire flight controls to the fuel pumps and engine-ignition systems. One Pave Low III had been in the midst of a sharp banking turn when the E-bomb had exploded, and had crashed in the Potomac, nosing in so forcefully that no one aboard had a chance to ditch. Another impacted spectacularly with the North Parking Lot, also with no survivors.

Only moments after that explosion, Secret Service Agents Zibart and Harrap, who had reached the roof of C Ring just before the President, saw the crashed helo burning in the parking lot. Both agents were unable to report their next move because their radios were no longer functional. The main Secret Service retransmission van had been parked outside the River Entrance, on station, in order to overcome the radio-dampening effects of the Pentagon's dense, concrete walls. The van's equipment had not been able to withstand the pulse.

Like doors slamming in a maze, Ranger's actions were progressively narrowing the agents' options for extracting the President.

From the only two remaining routes, Agent Zibart selected his next option: escape through the South Terrace pedestrian entrances. Only after reaching the second-floor, Corridor Three entrance would he decide whether to go forward into the South Parking Lot or retreat into the safe room by the security desk, the protective facility disguised as a power-switching utility room just off the escorted-visitor waiting area.

Though the First Lady's agents had their orders to take her to a River Side safe room in the event of danger, the President's agents knew using a safe room to protect the President was a decision of last resort. At a time when the Chief Executive's leadership was crucial to the country, there was no acceptable excuse for keeping the President contained and incommunicado in a high-risk environment. Still, given the severity of the attack upon the Pentagon, Agent Zibart's final decision hinged on whether he felt he could risk the President's life in a run across an open parking lot.

The two on-point agents charged down the C Ring roof-access stairway to intercept the other two secret agents who were rushing the President upward, along with Air Force Major Fielding. In one hand, the major carried the black CAT case, in the other, a collapsible Uzi submachine gun that had been concealed in the case's false bottom and withdrawn the moment the President's agents had pulled out their guns. The President was gasping for breath, but still showed no signs of fear or hesitation. The new plan was to take the President back to the fifth floor and to Corridor Six. They would then run him along the B Ring corridor, well away from all windows, until they reached the Corridor Three stairway, which led to the way down, and out.

The four Secret Service agents, Major Fielding, and the President hurtled on.

Like rats in a maze that was anything but random.

Following an exact route worked out months ago.

A route whose path and conclusion had been chosen by Ranger.

FIRST FLOOR, A RING, CORRIDOR FOUR

For the first time in his life, Hector MacGregor heard the sound of real gunfire, live and in person. It was coming from the Courtyard, and so was all the screaming.

Major Christou grabbed his arm to pull him down to his knees. Crouching down beside him, she fiercely gestured to him to stay where he was. Then she pulled off her black pumps and elbowed forward on her stomach across the A Ring floor, heading for the short flight of stairs that led up to the Courtyard doors.

Unable to do much more than catch his breath, Hector sat back against the wall, trying unsuccessfully to ignore the stabbing pains in his left foot, not to mention the mass of small, oozing burns on his back and his legs. He cringed as he heard more gunfire and the high-pitched screaming that accompanied each burst.

Christou crawled up the half-flight of stairs until she reached the Courtyard doors on the landing. Sitting with her back to one of the doors, she edged upward until her head was next to the small window in its center. Hector could see where dust from the floor had streaked the front of the major's dark-blue jacket and trousers.

Then, holding position for only a second before she pulled back, Christou jerked her head sideways to get a quick glance through the Courtyard-door window. Hector counted to five before she repeated the maneuver, as if she were waiting to confirm she had not been seen. The second time, it seemed to him she was able to hold her position a few seconds longer.

Then there was more gunfire. More desperate cries. And, suddenly, Christou was in full flight down the short staircase, yelling at him to make a run for the escalator, and not stop for anything. As the major leapt from the stairs to the highly polished terrazzo floor, her stockinged feet skidded as she landed.

This time, Hector did as he was told immediately. Heaving himself to his feet, he hopped over to the out-of-order escalator, then placed his hands on the escalator's black-rubber railings and half-jumped up each unmoving step. Light-footed, Christou raced up behind him, pushing at his back to hurry him along.

Just as they were almost at the top, a sudden metallic bang from below rang out, followed quickly by garbled shouts and cries and much louder gunfire.

Still doing just as the major had ordered, Hector did not turn around. But he had a good idea what must have happened. People fleeing the Courtyard must have flung open the doors through which the major had been looking and were now attempting to make their escape.

On the third floor of A Ring, the major stopped for a moment, to listen. Hector could still hear the sounds of people running, but the cries seemed more distant now. No one had chosen to escape up the escalator.

"The midshipmen . . . they were only shooting the *civilians.*" The major's voice was perplexed. But Hector was beyond even trying to make sense of what was happening. He asked the only question that still seemed to matter. "Did you see the President?"

Christou shook her head. Her cap of straight black hair swung forward with the motion. "I didn't have time."

The abrupt clanging of an alarm like a fire alert followed quickly by the thump of heavy footsteps on the metal stairs of the escalator spurred the major into action again. She pointed ahead toward Corridor Four and set off at a run. Hector did his best to match her fleet stride but his increasingly taxed left foot began to throb with almost unbearable intensity.

At the B Ring intersection, Christou slid to a stop, looked both ways, then ran off to the right, toward a stairwell. This time, Hector followed her up the stairs, doing what he could to support some of his weight on the stairs' metal railing. The major had pulled considerably ahead of him by the time they were two levels higher.

Hector caught up to her on the fifth-floor landing. The major had already flattened herself against the wall beside the door that opened onto the B Ring corridor. Though the shrilling of the alarm on this floor was loud enough to mask almost any other noise, the major still held up a hand, clearly advising him to keep quiet and stay where he was on the landing. Grateful to comply, Hector concentrated on breathing slowly and quietly through his open mouth.

He watched as the major placed a hand on the door's metal push bar and silently moved it forward. Only a faint metallic snap announced the opening of the door.

Then she edged slowly to the side to peer through the opening crack.

Hector watched her adjust the door a fraction of an inch at a time, every movement without sound.

There could be no doubt that Christou was no longer the restrained aide he'd been with earlier this morning. Her entire being was now charged with energy. Her eyes, her ears, and likely all her senses seemed alert to dangers that Hector knew he did not have the training or even the instincts to perceive. There was no trace of the quiet assistant to General Flores or of the accommodating guide who had helped him negotiate the Pentagon. *This is who she really is,* Hector realized. *What her training has helped her become.* He wondered if all the other military personnel he'd encountered in Washington had another face like this, another radically different persona concealed beneath the mask they adopted for civilians.

Hector fervently hoped so. If he was going to get out of the Pentagon alive, he wanted a warrior at his side, not a bureaucrat.

Suddenly, Christou stood up, with no concern for stealth, as if she had seen something unexpected through the door. Then she pushed it open, with no concern for noise.

Hector didn't understand why until he saw the hand that emerged through the doorway, holding a pistol pointed at her head.

With no glance in his direction, the major raised her hands in the air. And Hector understood that she was giving him his chance to escape.

But the door to the B Ring corridor was open wide now. Hector knew he could not escape. With his foot, he'd never make it down the stairs in time.

The major started moving backward as someone Hector could not see advanced through the doorway.

And then Hector heard a familiar voice say, "Major Christou?"

He and Christou responded simultaneously. "Mr. President!"

Joyfully, Hector dragged himself forward as the President's senior Secret Service agent came fully through the doorway and lowered his weapon.

Behind Zibart were the President, Agent Harrap, two more agents unknown to Hector, and then Major Fielding and his black case. For just a moment, the President's bulky beige raincoat puzzled Hector until he remembered the armor plates it contained.

"Do either of you know what's going on?" the President asked.

"They're midshipmen, sir," Christou said. "At least, they're in midshipmen uniforms." Her dark-blue uniform was no longer pristine, and she had no shoes, but her erect bearing, to Hector, was still that of an officer.

"You and I saw them in the Courtyard, sir, when we came in," Hector added. "They were just setting up the tables."

The President nodded, grim. "I remember."

"Major, do you know where they are now?" Hector didn't recognize the cold-eyed agent asking the question. That meant he had to be one of the advance agents stationed inside the Pentagon before the President had arrived. For all the good that had done.

"I saw some of them in the Courtyard, about two minutes ago, firing into the civilians. They had the NATO officers up on the stage."

"Sweet Lord," the President said. "My wife . . ."

"I didn't see her, sir. I'm sorry. But some of the civilians did make an escape."

Then Hector saw the President look over at him, where he leaned heavily against the railing, in his scorched and grass-stained clothing. "Hec, are you all right? I know they got my helicopter."

"They killed everyone on board, sir."

A dark shadow passed over the President's drawn face. "So I heard."

Agent Zibart interrupted the subsequent somber silence. "Major, is there an open way out?"

"Not down there," Christou said. "The River Entrance is the best chance for cover on the way out."

Zibart shook his head. "Something went off at the River Entrance. We have no communications. No contact there. What's the second choice?"

Hector was just now realizing that, in an emergency, even the President of the United States was second to the Secret Service. The hard-faced senior agent was the leader now, not the President, and everyone would be looking to Zibart to make the next decision.

"That would have to be the Metro Entrance and concourse. We stay on the B Ring corridor, follow it past Corridor One, then get down to the first floor. The far half of the Metro wedge is still under construction. The office walls have been torn out."

"More room for an ambush." Hector heard the reservation in Zibart's tense voice.

"But no blind alleys," the major countered. "And more ways through if we need them."

Hector noticed then that, during this entire time, Zibart's steel-gray eyes were in constant motion, scanning the B Ring corridor from one end to the other. "What's past the construction?"

"The medevac wagons. Far end of the bus terminal."

"Those are big targets," Zibart said.

"Or good cover."

"Either of you have a cell phone?"

Hector immediately thought of his ruined cashmere jacket out on the lawn by the helipad. His cell phone had been in its pocket.

Christou shook her head. "They won't work in here. Security jams them in the critical areas, and there's too much concrete in the rest of the Building."

"Okay, let's move out." Zibart had made his decision. The group entered the B Ring hallway, turning to the left, toward Corridor One. The President, the three other agents, and Major Fielding formed in a line behind Zibart—Harrap first, then an agent on either side of the President, and Major Fielding in the rear.

"The bus terminal, Major," Zibart prompted. "Which exit?"

"The subway security gate's closed, so there's only one exit we can get to on that side. It's right in the middle, on the ground floor."

Zibart frowned. "A single exit. That's a pinch point. It's like they want us to go there."

Once again, the major countered his concerns. "We have other options when we get there. I'll take point."

Zibart hesitated for only a moment before reaching under and behind his gray suit jacket to pull out a small pistol, which he handed to Christou. Hector watched as she immediately held the pistol sideways, flipped two small levers on its side, then slid the top part of the gun back and forth with a practiced motion. Her familiarity with the weapon was reassuring. Hector felt relief that he and the President were surrounded by people who knew what they were doing.

In Hector's opinion, the major was behaving magnificently. Despite her decidedly negative views of the President's military-policy decisions, which she had shared so frankly this morning, she was trying to do everything she could to get the President out of the Building safely. The combination of her professionalism with her political views, though, was still unsettling.

A new, unwelcome, thought struck him. What if this terrible attack wasn't about the President after all? What if it was some sort of protest about Russia joining NATO? What if Pentagon officers hostile to the President's policies were involved? Hector pushed the disturbing scenario from his mind. It was inconceivable that patriotism could become so twisted.

"I suggest two groups," the major said to Zibart. "If we stay to the sides, we can drop into offices and alcoves if we have to. There are stairwells at every intersection. We'll have to check each one before we pass."

"We've been briefed," Zibart said. Then Hector saw the agent give the President a sharp look. "Mr. President, stay between Agents Buhl and Redmer. And keep your coat buttoned up."

Obediently, the President pulled the collar of his beige raincoat tight around his throat. Then Zibart gave Christou the sign to move out and she crossed the corridor quickly, proceeding at once to edge along the wall. Zibart pointed for Fielding, then Hector to follow her. Hector understood why he'd been put last: He was injured and could slow the group down. There was only one person who had to make it out of the Pentagon. Everyone else was expendable.

Remaining on the other side of the hall, Zibart started forward, Agent Buhl close behind, then the President and Agents Redmer and Harrap. Zibart's look of intense concentration was repeated in all three agents' faces.

Even taking the time to check the stairwell doors, it took the eight of them—three on one side, five on the other—less than five minutes to cross over the intersections with Corridors Three and Two, and into the under-construction Metro wedge where the B Ring corridor ended. Various room signs indicated that the extra space where the B Ring corridor should have continued was taken up by theaters and briefing rooms. Jogging now, Christou led them along

Corridor One to C Ring, then turned left into the C Ring hallway.

Less than a hundred feet up ahead, Hector saw a temporary wall blocking the middle of the corridor. A sign beside the small, wood-framed doorway in the center of the wall warned: AUTHORIZED PERSONNEL ONLY. HARD HATS MUST BE WORN.

Zibart ducked through the small door first, disappeared for a few seconds, then waved in the others. Somewhat behind the others, Hector was the last to go through.

On the other side of the temporary wall, Hector could see what the Pentagon had looked like before its renovation. Here, the outdated linoleum floor was worn through every few feet, still highly polished nonetheless. In places, one, sometimes two, layers of linoleum tiles had been installed right over older tiles.

The light was also dimmer in this section. Only a single line of narrow fluorescent fixtures running down the center of the ceiling. Out of alignment, like a badly painted center line on a bumpy road, the line of lights appeared to weave back and forth.

On either side of this section of the C Ring hallway, the dingy brown walls were marred by lighter, rectangular or square splotches revealing cracked-plaster spaces where paintings had hung. The walls' mottled-wood wainscoting had been repaired with different colors of wood, and most of the offices along this section of corridor were missing doors. Through some of the open doorways, Hector saw bare, concrete-floored rooms, some with piles of rubble inside, others with large, plastic-wrapped cardboard boxes on wooden skids.

At least this section was quieter. The Building's alarm

system seemed to be disconnected here and the still-active sirens and bells from the other sections were more muted.

Then Christou held up her hand and the group stopped to rest. Making the most of the respite, Hector leaned against one wall, carefully keeping the weight off his left foot. He no longer had any sense of where his dress loafer left off and his grossly swollen foot and ankle began.

As the major conferred with Zibart, her words caused some of Hector's newfound sense of security to start slipping away.

"Corridor Ten is the next main intersection. If they're waiting for us, they're going to be there, one level down, on the first floor, covering the entrance from the security station. We won't have a chance."

"You said we'd have other options."

"We can go to the second floor, move into the center of the Metro Side, then go through a window onto the roof of the covered walkway. It's ten, maybe twelve feet high. Trees on either side. We can use them to get down from there. The President can follow. If they're inside waiting for us, we'll bypass them completely."

"How do we get through the window? It's blastproof."

"This is one of the old sections. It'll be a single pane of glass and a rusted frame."

Zibart's response was to lift the small earphone that dangled from the collar of his shirt and slip it into his ear. Then he flipped up his collar to expose the microphone pinned there. "Top Hat to Rainbow Base, do you copy?" After a moment, the lead agent tugged the earphone out.

"Mr. President, you ever do any parachute jumping?"

"No. But since you're asking me that question, I surely wish I had."

"You'll do fine, sir. Listen up, everyone, we're going to keep following the major."

Trying not to think how two broken legs would feel, Hector waited with the rest of the group while Christou and Zibart scouted the upcoming intersection of C Ring with Corridor Ten before waving the group on into the corridor—the major looking ahead toward E Ring, Zibart looking back toward the Courtyard.

The farther down the corridor they proceeded toward the outside wall of the Pentagon, the louder the incessant shriek of the Building alarm became. But Hector was almost getting used to the sound.

As they passed signs pointing to RAMPS, Hector remembered more from his first visit to the Pentagon. With so few elevators installed in the original version of the Building, long, sloping corridors running between the floors had been considered a more efficient way to travel through the Building. In the new version of the Building, all the Ramps were being removed. *Too bad,* he thought. With his bad foot, he'd much rather slide down to the first floor than risk jumping.

The stairwell to the second floor was clear. As soon as they reached E Ring, via Corridor One, the major urged both groups to move as fast as they could. This time, both groups were on the same side of the E Ring hallway, away from the outside-wall windows, Hector only ten feet behind.

Just before reaching their goal—the midpoint of the Metro Side of the Building—they passed two boarded-up windows. The midpoint was marked by another temporary wall that cut across the corridor. When they reached it, Christou waved everyone to a stop.

Hunched over, the major ran across the hall to the windows on the outside wall. Rising up slightly, she looked outside, then back across the corridor at Zibart as she jammed her gun into the waistband of her dark-blue trousers. Next, she pulled off her matching jacket and wrapped it tightly around her right fist. Her newly revealed long-sleeved white dress shirt with its black neck tabs was still startlingly clean.

Now Zibart, also hunched over, ran across the corridor, to look out through the window himself. A moment later, he motioned to Agent Harrap to join him. As soon as Harrap crossed over, Zibart nodded once at Christou, who then swung her protected fist at the window.

As glass shards clattered down from the window's metal frame, the wailing alarm rose to deafening volume. Hector guessed it was being broadcast from the Building's exterior now as well as from its interior.

For a count of at least five seconds, Zibart, Harrap, and Christou remained flat against the E Ring wall beneath the shattered window. A warm, moisture-laden breeze touched Hector's cheek teasingly. He stared across the hall at the bright, blue sky of freedom. *Almost there.*

Then Zibart sprang up in front of the window, gun held ready, roughly elbowed a few last shards from the frame, and leaned over the sill to look down.

Whatever he saw must have been acceptable, because he next pointed at Agents Harrap and Buhl, who instantly leapt out the window. At once, Hector realized that the two agents must have dropped no more than four feet—not ten or twelve—to the roof of the covered walkway below. The windowsill only came up to their chests.

That I can make, Hector thought with upwelling relief.

Then Zibart waved the President over and had him

glance quickly out the window and to the side. "Sir, Agent Buhl is going to drop over the side by that tree. As soon as he's down, you follow. Just jump into the branches. The raincoat will protect you, and Buhl will break your fall."

"Then what?"

"Then, sir, we're going to transition to the medical evacuation buses at the Metro terminal. And then we're going to get the hell out of Dodge."

Hector saw the President take a deep breath. "Let's do it." The President stepped in front of the window.

Just as Harrap and Buhl fell back in a double explosion of blood.

Just as the thunder of gunfire struck the President down.

Too late, Hector realized he'd had it all wrong.

This *was* about the President. And now the President was gone.

THREE

FIFTH FLOOR, D RING

Amy moved swiftly along the empty D Ring hallway, listening to the sirens and the gunfire and the screams. Continuing without hesitation, she kept close to one wall, the Beretta held ready. She was one person against at least forty. She still needed those reinforcements.

But not a phone in the Pentagon was letting her make outside calls. She had tried three offices already.

The door to the first office had said NAVY. Inside she had found a service counter and behind it a cluster of desks and low office partitions. A standup poster on the service counter had explained how to fill out a request for the Navy to move household goods. Beside the poster had been a gray, four-line phone set. Amy had immediately dialed 911, but only one line could give her a dial tone, and that line wouldn't accept a 911 call. A sticker on the base of the phone set gave an internal extension—5555—to call in the event of emergency. So she'd tried it, learning that the inter-

nal phone system, at least, was working. The call had rung
for more than a minute, though no one had picked up.

Past the next intersection, she'd tried a second office. Its
door label had proclaimed it to be a joint-procurement-fil-
ing office and she still had no idea what that meant. There
had only been two desks inside, each with a phone, but
she'd had the same results as in the Navy office. She'd even
tried dialing out on the second office's fax machine, but she
still couldn't get a dial tone.

The third office had been unlocked and cryptically identified only as JSUBMILCOMFLTSPEC/NAVDEVCON. Here, Amy
had found a desktop computer with an external modem.
When the phone on the desk hadn't worked—big surprise—she'd disconnected it and reattached it to the modem
line. Still no results.

Amy was no fool, and, despite what her fellow mids
might have thought of her, she knew she was no grand-
stander. She needed help, and there was still another place
she might find it—the parade grounds near the River
Entrance, where the reporters' television trailers and broadcast equipment had been set up. She'd seen them there
when she'd driven up on her Harley. Even if someone had
sabotaged the Pentagon's entire phone system, wherever
there were reporters there had to be cell phones. She'd even
settle for a direct microwave uplink to a news studio.

In the Metro wedge, Amy came to a temporary wall in
the middle of the D Ring hallway. The important thing
about reaching the Metro wedge was that the signs she'd
seen just before the temporary wall confirmed she was
going in the right direction for the River Entrance. Cautiously looking through the doorway in the center of the
wall, she saw stripped concrete walls, floor, and ceiling

beyond. The sirens weren't working in this section yet. She recalled Lieutenant Roth's Saturday briefing—just yesterday—in which he had joked that by the time the Pentagon construction crews were finished renovating the fifth wedge, it'd be time to start renovating the other four again.

The lieutenant had been on the bus with her company. No matter what had happened, Amy was sure he wouldn't have been easy to kill.

She returned her attention to her mission.

Focus, she told herself as she jogged through the bare concrete hallway, as she heard the echoes of more gunfire, another high scream. *There is nothing but the mission.* Amy's jogging became sprinting.

Coming to another temporary wall, this time she ran through its open, center doorway and emerged into a wide and freshly painted beige-walled hallway where the sirens were clearly operational. She'd reached the River Side. Pausing for only a fraction of a second, Amy realized that that meant she'd missed a staircase somewhere behind her—one that could have taken her down to Corridor One. Without slowing, she decided against returning to the under-construction Metro wedge. The well-lit corridors of the renovated sections felt safer.

She ran faster toward the next intersection—Corridor Two. There'd be a staircase there. She'd take the stairs to the third floor, rather than go down to the first. She'd look for a window on its exterior ring where she'd be able to observe the situation on the parade grounds. Surely, even forty enemy hostiles couldn't have cleared *all* the news personnel she'd seen there when she'd arrived.

But she would still have to assess the terrain before she ventured out into it. In combat, even assumptions that seemed as reasonable as the one she'd just made could be deadly.

She reached the third-floor landing in less than a minute. The door that led onto the corridor was much more solidly constructed than the other stairwell doors she'd passed. Opening it only wide enough to check the corridor beyond, she glimpsed the intermittent flaring of what appeared to be warning-light signals coming from the ceiling.

Looking up, she saw embedded in the ceiling tiles a device she might not have noticed if it had not been activated—a two-foot-long plastic tube flashing with yellow pulses, each as brilliant as a photographer's flash. The warning signals were intense enough to be seen through thick smoke.

She could see more of the flashing yellow lights at regular intervals along the corridor ceiling. Most of them seemed to be positioned above doors.

The alarms told Amy that she would be unlikely to find any Pentagon employees still in the River Side section. They'd already have been evacuated by now. Only the enemy would remain.

Counting on the flashing lights and fluctuating wail of the siren to provide sufficient cover, she pushed the heavy door open and entered Corridor Two. After visually checking up and down its length, she headed in the direction of E Ring, the outermost ring of the Pentagon, in search of a window overlooking the parade grounds, where the communications vans had been.

But at the intersection of Corridor Two and D Ring, the alarm sound changed abruptly from a fluctuating warble to a series of sharp, earsplitting squeals. Twenty feet beyond the intersection, Amy paused as, after five squeals, a calm female voice on the same speaker system announced pleasantly, "Ten seconds to ThreatCon Echo."

Amy didn't know what ThreatCon Echo meant, but she did recognize the voice. She'd heard it in the flight simulator she'd flamed out on last summer. Those same reassuring tones had informed her she would impact the ocean in twenty seconds, nineteen . . . "Five seconds," intoned the voice. Amy jerked her attention back to the present. "Three . . . two . . . ThreatCon Echo has been established."

Typically, the bases Amy had been on had had five levels of threat condition, from Normal to Delta, the last of which meant an attack had occurred or was imminent. *So what could be worse than ThreatCon Delta?* Amy thought. Then the alarm changed again.

Now it was as if she had been trapped abovedecks beside a gun battery—the booming noise that assaulted her was bone-jarring in its rhythmic staccato pulse and intensity.

Only at the last second did she realize what was happening.

From each section of the ceiling where a yellow light flashed, an explosive charge now drove down a black-armor blast door. On either side of her, a line of black armor plates shot toward her, dropping over every door in the corridor almost like cards being shuffled in a deck, each explosion rocking the floor beneath her feet. Sharply twisting around to visually follow the line, she was just in time to see a giant blast door slam down across the intersection of Corridor Two and D Ring, where she'd just been.

And then the yellow ceiling lights stopped flashing, and the floor no longer shook.

"Section One is secure," the female voice announced.

The trapped air in Corridor Two went flat, somehow

dead. In complete silence now, Amy could hear nothing but her own rapid breathing. No sirens, no alarms, no gunfire, no screams.

Amy knew she'd been sealed inside the Pentagon.

What she didn't know was how many of the enemy were sealed inside with her.

THIRD FLOOR, E RING

Tom didn't know how long he'd been waiting for the grenade to go off, but slowly it began to make sense to him that it already had gone off, and he just didn't remember.

There was a sharp, smoky scent to the air. His ears itched with a buzzing hum that ebbed and flowed around him as if he were being circled by bees.

And he couldn't move.

With that realization he became fully conscious.

He focused on remaining as still as possible. If his spinal cord had been damaged . . .

He concentrated on his hands. He moved his fingers a fraction of an inch; all fingers responded. He took a deep breath and felt his chest expand. Felt the sensation of pressure in both of his legs. He could feel all his limbs, so what was holding him down?

That was when he sheepishly realized the back-access panel of the Red Level workstation had toppled over on him. It must have weighed all of . . . he shrugged out from under the panel . . . ten pounds.

Tom emerged from the small niche he'd taken refuge in between the workstation and the wall, to view the destruction of Vanovich's Red Level office.

But the Red Level room was intact.

A yard-wide scorch mark blackened the beige carpet. A blue haze swirled in spirals in the air. Tiny shreds of what might be paper or cardboard were spread evenly throughout the room, on every surface. Three of the four ceiling-light panels were out, explaining the low level of room light. The lone remaining panel, flickering erratically, was the source of the crazily shifting shadows that danced from wall to wall.

And a black and gray blast door was in position in front of the room's only exit. Just as Vanovich had said it would be. It was cool to the touch. Tom studied the texture beneath its thin, clear coating. Carbon-composite fiber, woven into sheets, like an artist's canvas. He had seen similar material used for the skin of aircraft and satellites. He had no idea how many layers there would be in the door, or what other materials those layers would be made from. Likely everything from blast-absorbing aluminum honeycomb to unbreakable layers of Vectram cloth supported by steel plate. Vanovich's assessment had been that it would take a tactical nuke to blast into this room. Tom decided he wasn't far off.

Either the terrorists' grenade had been a dud or they'd only intended to stun him. In any case, Tom thought, he'd been snugly sealed in, secure and protected in a Pentagon safe room, complete with emergency rations, waiting only for the rescue operation his old friend had been so certain would arrive. While the general had been taken by unknown intruders to some unknown location for some unknown purpose.

Tom took a moment to review what he did know. Dorsey's killers had come for Vanovich, specifically. They'd known both his name and his clearance level. And by not stepping into this room, they'd revealed that they were familiar with the Pentagon's security systems.

What if they also knew about . . . Tom struggled to remember the superclassified program the general had been so anxious to talk to him about. Not Cloudy Office. Not Cloudburst. But . . . Atlantis Rising.

Vanovich had said something about it being here in the Pentagon.

That last hurried conversation all came back to Tom, now. Atlantis Rising . . . it was most likely some Pentagon-specific implementation of the larger ATLANTIS project Tom had worked on years ago, at Hughes. One of his first big contracts. But he'd only been cleared to work on a few portions of ATLANTIS, so his view of it had been heavily compartmentalized. All he really knew was that it was one of the biggest, if not *the* biggest, civil defense projects in the country, begun in the 1960s. By the time he'd joined the project, ATLANTIS was being redesigned, to focus less on nuclear war and more on environmental catastrophe. Reading between the lines at the time, Tom had had suspicions, though they were never confirmed, that the U.S. government had learned something about the global environment that it wasn't telling the rest of the country, let alone the world. His team's assignment had been the upgrading of all the communications links in the entire ATLANTIS system. At the time, no one in authority had been willing to tell him exactly where all those links would be installed.

Tom checked his watch. 11:22. The power outage he'd noticed, just before the attack, had occurred about 10:56. The terrorists took Vanovich by 11:05, maybe 11:10. He'd already lost more than ten minutes. He wasn't going to lose any more.

Tom looked for the phone. It was on the Red Level console, beside Vanovich's keyboard. As he picked up the receiver to place a call for help, Tom felt an aching in every muscle in his body, as if he were coming down with the flu. For a moment, as he held the receiver to his ear, he was sure he heard a dial tone. But the ache in his muscles and the buzzing in his ears were just the residual echo of the grenade.

The phone was dead, just as it had been for Vanovich.

It was time to leave the safe room.

Tom returned to the blast door. Fortunately, blasting wasn't required for what he had to do. Nor was a retina scan required for exit. He pulled his proxcard from his jeans' front pocket and touched it to the ID terminal beside the door.

After a five-second delay, a motor in the ceiling hummed and the blast door obligingly rose back into the ceiling.

When it came to the Pentagon, Tom Chase had complete access.

To save Milo Vanovich, he intended to use it.

THIRD FLOOR, E RING

As more bullets sprayed up through the open window, Agent-in-Charge Zibart instantly threw his body over the President's and forced the President to the floor. Still beneath the window, Major Christou pulled out her weapon and stayed flat against the wall. The remaining Secret Service agent, Redmer, charged across the E-Ring hallway and threw himself on Zibart. Major Fielding was already there, Uzi in hand.

Hector stayed where he was, against the other wall, without moving. Not because of fear, but because he had absolutely no concept of what to do.

Christou leapt up in front of the open window and fired

down and to the left, then jumped back as a burst of return gunfire smacked into the limestone-facing outside the window. "We've got to move!" she shouted. "They're running back inside!"

Now Zibart had the President sitting up against the wall of the hallway. Hector was relieved to see only black burn marks on the President's beige, Kevlar-lined raincoat, no blood. But only luck had kept the Man from being shot in the head.

Zibart took a fast, hard look to the right, toward the temporary wall and the doorway leading to the renovated half of the South Terrace wedge, then left, along the unfinished half of the E Ring hallway. "They'll come at us from both sides. We have to pull back into the offices."

But Christou disagreed strongly. "Then we'll be trapped." Hector saw inspiration light her face. She pointed left. "We go that way!" Next, she jerked her head at Hector. "You, too! Move!" Then she ran so fast she almost flew along the unfinished concrete floor, toward one of the two large, boarded-up windows they had passed only minutes ago. There, she clawed frantically at a twisted loop of yellow wire holding one side of a large plywood sheet to the window.

Major Fielding covered Agents Zibart and Redmer as they dragged the President down the hall.

By the time Hector caught up to them, the major had jerked the yellow wire free and swung the plywood sheet open like a door to reveal the opening to a wooden chute. Hector knew at once what it was—a garbage slide to one of the waste bins outside, used for hauling away construction debris. The slide would be a rough ride, but it would be better than jumping. And even more important, the major had found a way out.

Christou reached out for the President, to shove him down the chute. "Go!" she urged him.

But Zibart pulled the President back. "We don't know what's at the bottom of that! There could be glass! Or spikes of rebar!"

"Who the hell cares?" the major shouted.

Then they heard the sound of running footsteps. The sound came from both ends of the hallway. Zibart had been right and the major had been wrong.

All but Hector and the President moved into defensive position against the outside wall, guns ready. The major was on Hector's right and Major Fielding on his left. The two Secret Service agents beyond Fielding formed a protective shield around the President. Hector backed up against the wall, beneath the opening to the chute, knowing he was the only one without a purpose. He had no training and no weapon. And at this moment, he was the only one who was expendable. Then Hector had his inspiration. But there was no time to explain it, just to do it.

"I'll go!" he said and turned toward the opening to the chute. To the President he shouted, "Whatever you do, sir, land on me!" Holding onto the edge of the opening, Hector began to pull himself up into the chute.

Then the plywood sheet beside the chute disintegrated in a rattling burst of gunfire.

Fielding went down on one knee and sprayed his Uzi toward the temporary wall. Half in, half out of the chute, Hector saw Fielding fall forward, groaning, shot from behind, the Uzi skittering out of his grasp, the black CAT case under him. As Zibart had predicted, the attackers had taken positions on both sides of them. The President would be caught in the crossfire. Hector hesitated, unsure, then began lowering himself from the chute.

The major and Redmer were firing in opposite directions down the hallway. Zibart reached over to push Hector back up inside the chute. "Go!"

Then a blossom of blood flowered at the agent's shoulder and he wheeled to return fire.

As if watching a replay of old news footage of a well-known event on television, Hector saw at once what was going to happen next.

The President was all alone. Unprotected. Out of reach. A target even Hector couldn't miss.

The rest happened all at once.

He heard Christou's primal cry at the same time he saw her lunge for the President as dark shadows sprayed red as they stitched across her back, and then he felt her hand grab his leg as she shoved him up and backward, side by side with the President, through the opening of the chute, her eyes black-pupiled with pain, blood flowing from her mouth as she screamed something he couldn't hear in the waterfall roar of the gunfire as he and the President tumbled back and down the chute.

He landed on his back and struck his head on something sharp and hard. But he had time to snap out his arm so the President fell on that and not on whatever was in the bin of rubble.

Gunfire from the hallway above echoed down the plywood chute.

The bin was dark, steamy, hot.

Hector struggled to right himself, coughing on the choking dust of their impact, even as his feet refused to keep their footing. Beside him, the President coughed uncontrollably and fell sideways as he, too, tried to stand.

Balanced on his one good foot, Hector called on his extra six inches of height to punch and flail at the thick plastic tarpaulin overhead that glowed blue from the bright daylight outside.

The gunfire above them stopped suddenly just as Hector finally snagged an edge of the tarp, and tugged it to the side. He squinted in the sudden blast of light.

He pulled himself just high enough to peer over the wide rough edge of the bin to see the bus terminal past the construction fence, the four dark green Army medevac buses still in place. He looked back at the President. "Over here!"

The President pushed forward, reached up and placed his hands on the lip of the bin, then hauled himself up until his waist rested on the edge. Pivoting his body, he sat on the edge and reached a hand down for Hector.

Hector tried to jump up to match the President's move, but it was as if his left leg was jelly.

"Go!" Hector shouted, like Zibart before him.

But the President just crooked his arm and held it out for Hector to grab. The look in his eyes told Hector that the Man had no intention of leaving until Hector was with him.

The President hoisted Hector up and over the edge of the bin. Then he threw an arm around Hector's waist and dragged him away from the bin toward the construction fence twenty feet away.

They fell into an expedient pace, with Hector using the President's shoulder as a crutch. At the chain-link fence, covered on the other side by green plastic sheeting, the President climbed up without hesitation, his hands soon bleeding openly from the rough metal links.

At the top, he again reached down, and Hector took his arm and scrambled to the top as best he could with one free hand and foot.

Then the President leapt off the top of the fence. But his

beige raincoat caught on an exposed twist of wire, throwing him off balance, making him swing back, momentarily off his feet. He slid out of his raincoat like Houdini escaping from a straitjacket, then reached up both bloody hands to Hector. "Roll and I'll catch you!" the President ordered. "Don't land on that foot."

Hector jumped and rolled as the President commanded.

Then he was up again at the President's side, a three-legged race to end all three-legged races, running and hopping toward the shelter of the Army buses, both he and the President wheezing, panting, swimming in sweat.

As the first fusillade of bullets sought them out, the pavement to Hector's side erupted with clouds of dust and stone chips. The gunmen had found them. They wouldn't make it after all.

Hector felt a sharp stinging in his eye from a flying fragment. The pain threw him offstride. The President stumbled as they lost their rhythm and Hector was thrown onto his left foot. A loud crack sent a lightning bolt of pain up into his knee and his hip. His stomach churned. He couldn't stay upright. He fell against the President and felt the President fall with him just as the pavement blew apart, right before them.

For an instant, as the bullets flashed over their heads, Hector realized his fall had saved the President's life.

But now they were both sprawled out in the open. And the President no longer had his bulletproof raincoat. They were going to die. Like Zibart and Fielding and Christou . . .

Hector pressed his face into the pavement as he waited for what he knew must come. But then he saw the President, beside him, turn to look back at the Pentagon with such elated defiance that Hector had to look, too.

To the second-floor windows, where the bullets had come from.

To where a sudden straight line of violent explosions now sprayed across those windows, hurling stone and dust and glass shards and wood and twisted metal frames spinning into the air—even the twitching body of someone who one second wore white and the next split in two in a fountain of red.

Someone's firing back. . . .

And then a giant hand shoved him to the ground and a black shadow cut off the sun, and Hector looked up to see a dark angel come to rescue him—a black angel, sixty feet long, smoke pouring from its cannon ports, spitting fumes and screaming as its rotors tore the sky.

And then he realized what their angel was.

The major had already told him its name.

That's a Pave Low III. One of ours.

The huge, ungainly Air Force Special Forces helicopter touched down between them and the Pentagon, an impenetrable shield against whatever danger dared threaten the President.

The side of the helo slid open and six figures in black flew out before the machine had even settled.

Two went to one side, two to the other, all four crouching with weapons ready to fire.

And two more ran for Hector and the President and swept them into their arms as if they weighed nothing and, before Hector even accepted that somehow he was going to live, he was on his back in the Pave Low's cabin, feeling the force of the helo's engines drive him down as the machine kicked off from the ground to the safety of the skies.

And then he realized just who it was who was squeezing his hand.

"You look after this boy first," Hector heard the President of the United States shout over the roar of the engines to the Special Ops medic who knelt beside him. "This boy saved my life."

Hector heard Christou's voice one more time: *It's our job.*

He only wished he could tell her she'd done it.

FOUR

THIRD FLOOR, E RING

Tom had never heard of ThreatCon Echo.

When the automated voice recording began its ten-second countdown, he was in the E Ring corridor, just down from Vanovich's trashed office, about to choose an appropriate site where he could safely work on the Pentagon's phone lines. So he could try to summon help.

From his vantage point, he was able to see yellow ceiling lights flashing at both ends of the glassed-in sections of the wood-paneled corridor. That was right where security desks and checkpoints marked the Joint Staff section of the Pentagon. He was well aware that each ceiling light identified the site of a blast door that would be activated at the end of the countdown. He'd suffered through enough drills at Hanscom Air Force Base's high-security labs to know he risked being crushed if he strayed into one of those yellow-light areas.

But Tom also knew he was in no danger of being trapped, thanks to his proxcard and Milo Vanovich. There probably wasn't a door in the Pentagon that his card couldn't open. Vanovich himself had arranged the encoded security in the card's chip so Tom could work in any of the dozens of classified departments and projects in which the general was involved.

But just to be certain, by the time the countdown had advanced to the five-second warning stage, he chose an unlocked office on the inside of the ring—which meant it had no windows—and which had a proxcard reader by the door. Tom could tell by their absence of flashing yellow ceiling lights that none of the outside-ring offices were rigged with blast-door protection. For those offices to be made secure, their windows would need fast-deployment blast shutters, and not even the Pentagon had pockets that deep. Though it was likely that at least a few of those outer offices would have self-contained safe rooms like the general's.

It seemed odd to Tom that this office, and all the others along Vanovich's section of the E Ring corridor, was unlocked. And even though he understood that there would be few Pentagon staffers in the Building today, he wondered where those few might be. Almost 26,000 people worked in the Building on a weekday, and ten to twenty percent of them could be counted on to show up during any weekend. To be sure, the security arrangements for today's NATO ceremony would have cut that number back to the bare minimum required to staff the National Military Command Center and the service operations centers. But, still, in addition to the guests and workers at the ceremony, plus the Building's security personnel, there should be at least a thousand people in the Pentagon today. It was a mystery why some of them had apparently abandoned their workplaces without following the Pentagon's strict rules for keeping all doors secured. Unless the evacuation had been so rapid, SOP protocol had been set aside.

Fortunately, Tom thought, what he planned to do now did not require the assistance of another person. Even if the entire Pentagon was deserted, the complex networks left behind were like the enormous nervous system of some great, mindless beast, capable of impressive actions if only prodded in the right direction. And he had yet to find a communications system he couldn't bring to its knees. For ten years, his job had been to design them.

At least, in the inner office he had chosen, the protective blast door meant he'd be able to work on the phones without worrying about one of the bad guys coming back.

Bad guys. Now he was thinking like Tyler. But what else could he call them? They hadn't acted as terrorists. Terrorists would have blown up the Pentagon by now, or spread engineered anthrax through the Courtyard the day before the ceremony.

Maybe they're mercenaries working for the Chinese, Tom thought, as he waited inside the office for the countdown to conclude. *Or even industrial spies.* That couldn't be ruled out either. The technologies developed by the Department of Defense represented billions of dollars of research expenditures and the possibility of billions more in revenues when it came time to make key breakthroughs public. With incidents of industrial spying on the increase at military research labs across the country, even the Pentagon was finally realizing that its future enemies wouldn't just be nations at cross-purposes with America or the usual madmen intent on destruction. The U.S. military had already become the target of pan-national corporations who were simply after proprietary information—and simple profit.

After all, Ranger or whoever it was who had killed Dorsey and taken away the general was after something supposedly requiring Red Level clearance.

Maybe that's it, Tom thought, as the countdown reached its end. *The guys who got Milo are working for General Motors.*

Then the blast door slid across the office door, and Tom sat down at what he took to be a secretary's desk. In layout and furnishings, the room was similar to Vanovich's office, though it had no windows and no green door to one side. Two large dry-erase boards stood on easels against one wall. The boards were covered with color-coded flowcharts, dates, and indecipherable military acronyms. Tom guessed he was in some kind of scheduling department.

Among the items on the desk was a small photograph of a smiling woman in uniform behind a birthday cake, all candles lit. The photograph's frame was decorated on one side by a saluting teddy bear in a camouflage battle-dress uniform, and on the other by red, white, and blue balloons. Another incomprehensible memento of the sentimental war culture common to the Pentagon.

Tom opened the desk drawers to look for a Pentagon phone book and found it in the top left drawer. It was a small, ten-ring binder stuffed with punched pages and ruffled with Post-It notes. He placed the phone book in front of the desk's phone, just beside the bizarrely framed photograph.

The gray phone itself was standard for unclassified use in the Pentagon—it had no secure line function. But it could access seven basic lines, four buttons on one side, three on the other. Tom knew without even trying that the four outside lines would be dead. However the "bad guys" had done it, the Pentagon was cut off from normal communications.

But the red LEDs beside the three other buttons lit up as Tom tried those lines and got a dial tone for each. Those were the internal lines operating over the Pentagon's fiber-optic data system. Since they continued to work, Tom made the assumption that Ranger and his friends had used some kind of electronic jamming technique, maybe even an electromagnetic pulse generator, to blow out the wire leads emerging from the Building. However, there was still hope, he thought. If the attack had been concentrated only on the Pentagon itself, then some exterior lines must still be up and running at other locations. It was just a question of patching into them.

From Tom's engineering perspective, the Pentagon consisted of four main buildings, not one. The first was the Building itself; the second was the Remote-Loading Facility in the North Parking Lot, where trucks made deliveries without penetrating the Building's security envelope; the third was the Heating and Refrigeration Plant; and the fourth was Federal Building #2, also known as the Navy Annex. He'd been near the Navy Annex earlier in the morning when he and Dorsey had been stopped at one of the Pentagon's security checkpoints.

Poor Dorsey. Tom genuinely regretted having baited the captain. The guy had given his life for Milo Vanovich.

All four of the buildings were connected by underground passageways, through which ran the wiring, water, waste, and heating and cooling pipes, all exposed for easy repair and replacement. Of most importance to Tom now was the fact that that wiring included the fiber-optic cable supporting the Pentagon's internal communications and data network. And while he couldn't be certain of the phone setup in the RLF or the H&R Plant, which were relatively small support buildings, he was confident that the Navy Annex would have its own outgoing phone service.

Despite the military's strong commitment to joint capability since the Goldwater-Nichols Amendment, Tom knew that each military service still maintained a parochial outlook that made some top officers believe that combining operations with the others would lead to a degradation of capability. From the Navy's perspective, the Air Force just didn't strive for the same level of perfection that the Navy required as a matter of course. The Air Force felt the same way about the Army; and the Army about the Navy. The Marines graciously conceded that the other services aimed for and achieved 100 percent in everything they did. But the Marines themselves aimed for and achieved *110* percent, which left the other services lacking from their perspective, as well. Thus, the Navy Annex, or Federal Building #2, which had begun service as a critical Naval operations center in the 1940s, still maintained its own communications system. And even if it were still based on copper wires, because it was more than half a mile away, Tom doubted the Navy system had been exposed to whatever had happened to the Pentagon's phone system.

The challenge he faced now was to connect the Pentagon's internal phone system with the Naval Annex's external system. Normally, Tom knew, the task would be impossible for someone who only had the equivalent of a screwdriver to work with. However, for the Pentagon's computers, it would be simple—they did it thousands of times every day.

The key to Tom's tapping into that capability would be in the JSAMS—the Joint Staff Automated Message System, one of the most flexible and capable messaging systems in use. The new JSAMS could accept a message intended for anyone on the Joint Staff and, following the look-up tables in its computer-driven operating system, automatically forward that message in any format to virtually any communications system in the world.

Tom studied his challenge. The secretary's phone could make no outside calls, and it only had access to the Pentagon's internal phone lines. However, that internal phone system could take messages for members of the Joint Staff and use JSAMS to forward the message outside.

He had found a way to send a message out for help—as long as the person he called was a member of the Joint Staff.

Feeling better than he had all day, Tom got ready to call his J-6 contact.

The newest member of the Joint Chiefs of Staff.

COURTYARD UTILITY CORRIDOR, BASEMENT LEVEL

Ranger checked his watch. Twenty-eight minutes since the third diversion—the electromagnetic pulse over the parade grounds. The blast-door lights were exactly on schedule. Somewhere, at this precise moment, in a command post hurriedly established outside the Pentagon office building, a panicked junior officer would be recommending a total escalation to Atlantis Rising.

The junior's decision would be considered proper and would not be countermanded. And the first step in the Atlantis Rising defense of the Pentagon would be to establish ThreatCon Echo—sealing the Building off in sections to contain both the enemy and any potential damage.

But the first step would do neither. The areas being sealed

off held nothing Ranger needed. And by the time Atlantis
Rising reached the full-implementation stage, the Pentagon
defense strategy would be halted in a way its designers had
never thought possible.

But that event was at least another forty to sixty minutes
away, and responsibility for that action rested with Team
One. For now, all Ranger and his three soldiers had to do
was wait in the basement-level utility corridor that circled
beneath the Pentagon's central courtyard, and keep Major
General Vanovich in line.

Ranger encouraged Vanovich to rest on the three-foot-
wide green pipe that ran along the base of the utility corridor
wall. On the back wall, above the pipe, snaked brightly colored conduits of red and blue and orange, in great contrast to
the neutral, drab tones of the walls, floor, and ceiling tiles.

The older man's color was not good, and he had lost
considerable weight since Ranger had seen him last. But in
little more than an hour there would be access to first-aid
facilities, and the plan only required that the general remain
alive for half a day. Whatever happened after that was of no
concern to Ranger.

As he waited to be sealed into the Pentagon's basement,
Ranger watched the flashing-yellow ceiling light above the
entrance alcove that contained the freight elevators.

Originally, he knew, the basement of the Pentagon had
been a no-man's-land intended for light storage, building
support, and little else. It was dark, cramped, often wet, and
frequently smelled of the swamp it had once been. The
basement had been one of the first areas of the Pentagon to
show its age as the Building's hurriedly built infrastructure
had begun to decay.

During his tour of duty at the Pentagon, Ranger had

been told that at the time of the Desert Shield and Desert Storm operations, a fire had started in the Joint Staff area of the Pentagon, the same area in which General Vanovich had his office. When the firefighters who had responded to the emergency had pressurized a standpipe to deliver water to their hoses, the fifty-year-old, blocked, and corroded pipe blew out with such force that four feet of it disintegrated.

The resulting torrent had flooded 350,000 square feet of the basement, severely compromising the operation centers of both the Army and the Air Force at a time when they were functioning in wartime mode. And when the water had entered a broken steam pipe and shot through the 1,190-foot service tunnel running from the Pentagon to the old Heating & Refrigeration Plant, the basement of that building had been flooded to a depth of seven feet.

For that reason alone, Ranger had been told, the basement of the Pentagon had usually been considered the office location of last resort.

Slowly, though, those in charge of the Pentagon's security had realized that, failing pipes aside, the basement was also the most secure section of the Building and covert changes began to be made.

Though the work beneath the Pentagon had been ongoing for years, the first obvious reconfiguration of its lower levels was the closing down of the bus and taxi tunnels that ran beneath the Building which served the Metro concourse. At the time, Pentagon spokesmen had cited standard security concerns such as removing tempting locations for potential truck bombs. But in reality, as valid as those security concerns had been, the area reclaimed from the closed underground roadways had been about to become the office complex for President Reagan's Strategic Defense Initiative Organization.

The advantages of the basement location were not missed by the Building's other tenants, and the underground levels of the Pentagon became the first to be renovated. By their completion in 1999, more than 2 million additional square feet of usable area had been added to the Pentagon's original floor plan of 6.5 million. Ranger, however, knew that those figures, like all the Pentagon's published figures, were meaningless, because they referred only to the portions of the Pentagon that the Department of Defense had been required to make public.

In stark contrast to the professed belief of America's political leaders—that a world without secrets would invariably lead to peace—in the government's military stronghold, duplicity was the rule, not the exception. Ranger knew there were more secrets in this Building than anywhere else in the country. After all, the Pentagon was the ultimate command post to which every American military project and operation eventually had to report.

At last the ThreatCon Echo countdown reached zero. A foot-thick blast door marked with diagonal stripes of yellow and black rolled swiftly across the opening between the Pentagon's basement and the utility corridor, thudding into contact with the mechanical locks that grabbed and secured it.

Somewhere outside, Ranger knew, that panicked junior officer now believed that the Pentagon and all its secrets were secure.

And in one sense, that was true. In only twelve hours, all the Pentagon's secrets would be secure.

Because they *would* all belong to Ranger.

THIRD FLOOR, E RING

Midshipman Amy Bethune stared out at the ruins of the River Entrance Parade Grounds and saw a battlefield.

Open fires were everywhere among the television trailers and stages. Curls of smoke rose up from a dozen other places, fires that were dying out or were about to ignite. Off to the side on the ramp, two limousines blazed, and there were visible soot marks around the engine compartments of a handful of other vehicles, including a HUMVEE.

She also saw bodies. Scattered, not just in one area. Smoke rose from some of those, too, while others seemed untouched.

Her classmates had been casualties of some undeclared war. And now more lives had been taken by the enemy.

A mile away, over the Potomac, where the spire of the Washington Monument soared into the blue, unmarked sky to the north, and in the air around the great white dome of the Capitol Building almost directly in front of her, she saw another sign of war: helicopters.

The most distant were small and white, most likely belonging to television and radio stations. Amy knew the only reason civilian air traffic would hang back was because someone in authority had established control of the Pentagon's airspace.

The helos in the foreground were huge, some gray, some green, some Special Ops black. Amy recognized those as MH-60Ks and 53Js. She also saw two 47Ds, both of them capable of transporting more than forty troops, heading for the Washington Navy Yard.

A counterattack was being assembled.

But a counterattack against what?

Amy pressed against the E Ring window and strained to look past the limestone pillars to the side, checking for any sign of enemy movement. She saw nothing. She thought of smashing the glass and making a run for the stairways beside the parade grounds that led down to the closed highway. But when she tapped the grip of her Beretta against the window, the dull sound it made let her know there wasn't much she could do to break it. The window was a blast-proof laminate. She could empty a full clip at it without scratching the exterior bonding surface.

But the fact that one strategy couldn't be developed did not mean she could give up the mission. "Survival, evasion, resistance, escape," she recited to herself. SERE training. She hadn't been through it herself, but some of the Marines she had trained with last summer had taken the nineteen-day course and described it for her, when she'd pestered them to. They'd told her the ordeal had been brutal. Nine days of nonstop lectures and field exercises, then what was euphemistically called a "practical test."

In the "test," SERE students, mostly soldiers or airmen in special forces units, or pilots, male and female, were set loose in the woods around the training camp, then hunted, captured, imprisoned, and interrogated. Some students lost as many as twelve pounds during their few days of imprisonment, the conditions of which were based on what American POWs had endured in Vietnam.

Like most military training, SERE school was designed to permit participants the chance to make mistakes in a non-lethal environment so the mistakes could be corrected, theoretically increasing the odds of a student surviving similar events in the real world. However, one of the Marines Amy had spoken with told her the "test" had convinced him his best response was to make certain the enemy never captured him alive.

Amy knew she wasn't even close to making such a radical decision. Finding a safe place to hide was not one of her priorities. Her survival situation was in an office building, not a tropical jungle. She had survived the enemy attack, and she had evaded capture, for now, at least. And since it seemed unlikely she could escape, that left her with only one option: resistance.

The first thing she knew she had to do was provide behind-the-lines intelligence to the soldiers outside who were gathering for the counterattack. She looked around for suitable materials. The wood-paneled room she was in had seen some action. Its outer door into the corridor had been shot open and a few upended chairs gave evidence of a struggle. Most likely from the gray-suited man whose body lay just inside the door. She hadn't been able to find a security pass or a weapon, not even dog tags on the man, but it looked as if he had died defending this office. She'd chosen it for that reason.

As soon as she had entered, Amy had smelled the unmistakable, sharp scent of an expended explosive, but she'd been unable to find any sign of blood or gunfire other than the body and the damaged outer door. Knowing she couldn't solve the mystery with the information she had, she had wasted no more time thinking about it and had proceeded to the window overlooking the parade grounds.

Now, in the massive, dark-wood desk that dominated the office, she found what she needed: writing paper, a pen, and some adhesive tape.

She carefully printed a message in thick block letters. MSG FRM MID A. L. BETHUNE, '06. ENEMY FORCE:

? 40 DISGUISED AS MIDS, 12TH COMPANY. PISTOLS
SEEN. AUTO GUNFIRE HEARD. EXPLOSIVE USED.
THIS SECTION SEALED. "THREATCON ECHO ESTAB-
LISHED." NO PHONE COMM. She checked her watch,
then added the time. AS OF 1155 ZULU.

Then she chose the window with the least of its field of
view blocked by the pillars outside and taped her note to it.
Above it, she used more sheets of paper and the tape to
fashion a large arrowhead marker pointing at the note.

The commanders planning the counterattack would be
sure to have the entire building under surveillance, and the
arrowhead would be easily noticed by anyone with binoculars, though to read the note would probably take a telescope, or a camera with an extreme telephoto lens. Neither
of those items, however, would be difficult to come by,
given the density of military establishments within five
miles of the Building.

With her first responsibility to her fellow service members discharged, Amy decided on her next course of action.

She would reconnoiter the sealed area, looking for any
sign of enemy presence, as well as any other method to
make contact with friendly forces outside the Pentagon. If
she looked in enough drawers and cabinets, she was certain
to find a forgotten cell phone or walkie-talkie. But most
important, she had to do *something*. She had not enrolled at
the Academy in order to watch life pass by. She had
enrolled in order to take command and make a difference.
That was exactly what she planned to do now.

She switched the clips on her gun so she would start with
a full fifteen rounds, keeping the clip with only four shots in
her pocket as a backup. Carefully looking out into the corridor, she saw it was still clear, then stepped out. Quickly

assessing her options, she decided to go down two floors, to the entrance level. It would likely be sealed, but there'd be a security station there. With any luck, there'd also be an equipment locker nearby with radios and additional firearms. Perhaps even some kind of emergency communications equipment, like a ship's sound-powered telephone, something which did not depend on external electricity to operate.

But as Amy approached the end of the E Ring corridor, she saw she might again have to revise strategy. The stairway she needed was on the wrong side of the blast door that sealed off the corridor. She looked behind her, at the other end of the hall. There was a blast door there, too, but it was on the far side of a stairwell alcove.

She turned and jogged for the stairwell.

But halfway there, she heard the sound of an office blast door begin to slide open, just as she passed it.

Once again, Amy's reflexes took over—before she even saw the figure that stood in the doorway, the Beretta swung up and around as if under its own guidance.

And Midshipman Amy Bethune faced the enemy it was her mission to kill.

FIVE

THIRD FLOOR, E RING

Tom Chase threw up his hands and yelled, *"Don't shoot!"*

But the woman with the gun had gone into a half crouch and Tom saw her hands thrust the gun forward and—

—he heard the gun's report and—

—he was still on his feet, untouched, the neck chain from the proxcard he was holding dangling in front of his face.

The shooter was looking at the gun in her hand in disbelief, as if it hadn't gone off.

Tom couldn't believe it. "You missed me?" he said. "You're five feet away and you *missed* me?"

The woman raised her gun again. *"On the floor! Get on the floor now! Hands behind your back!"*

Woman? Tom thought. *Not even close.* She was just a kid in jeans, and sneakers and a ratty-looking gray sweatshirt. A nice-looking kid. The kind of kid he'd hire to baby-sit Tyler.

"Down on the floor!" the kid shouted. *"NOW! NOW! NOW!"*

Tom lowered his hands. "Or what?" he said. "You'll miss me again?"

The kid was probably a college student, working weekends on the cleaning staff or something. "How about giving me the gun?" Tom asked. He held out his hand.

All at once, the kid pointed the gun straight up and fired again, this time showering Tom with shattered fragments of dusty ceiling tile.

"LAST CHANCE!" she screamed, leveling the gun at his chest. *"GET YOUR SORRY ASS DOWN ON THAT FLOOR BEFORE I KICK YOUR BALLS FROM HERE TO NEXT WEEK YOU MOTHERFUCKING ASSHOLE!"*

Tom promptly dropped to the floor, stretched out, eye-level with her sneakers. They were spattered with blood. Not a good sign.

"That your ID?" she asked loudly.

Tom raised his hand very slowly up. "Won't do you any good. It's keyed to my retina." But the kid snatched his proxcard anyway.

"Thomas Paine Chase," she read out. "What are you doing here?" Tom sensed a slight toning down of the false belligerence the kid had used—successfully—to intimidate him.

Maybe she was ready to respond to reason. "I'm *Tom* Chase. I work as a consultant for Major General Milo Vanovich, United States Air Force. His office is down the hall. Whoever attacked the Pentagon came for him and took him away. Now can I please get up?" Tom risked turning his face to the side to see if his answers were having any effect on the kid.

She glared at him suspiciously. "Why didn't they kill you?"

Tom didn't like the implication of her question. It sounded as if she knew of others, besides Dorsey, who hadn't been so fortunate. "They didn't know I was with him, in the safe room. They threw a grenade in, but . . . looks like it was a dud. I'm still here."

She looked at his proxcard again, and Tom could see she was comparing his photo with his face.

"I was in an office down the hall," she said. "I could smell an expended explosive."

Tom grimaced. He was familiar with the term. Professionals used it.

"So it wasn't a dud," she continued. "It was probably a concussion grenade. A flash-bang."

Hell, the kid's face still has baby fat, thought Tom, *and they've already taught her to talk like that.* "You're a soldier, right?"

"I'm a sailor."

"Like there's a difference. May I get up now?"

She took a step back, lowered her weapon, and nodded.

Tom got to his feet. "That the new camouflage uniform?"

"Did you open that blast door?"

"Unh-uh, that's not how it works, kid. You're suspicious of me and now I'm suspicious of you." He held out his hand. "Where's *your* ID?"

She stared at him, making no effort to comply.

"Look, no one got in here today without a pass. Except maybe the bad guys."

That did it. She stuffed her gun into the waistband of her jeans. Then she reached into her jeans pocket, pulled out a laminated security pass, looked at it, then pulled out a second and gave that one to him instead.

Tom took it, read it, and all became clear. "Oh, shit . . . You're a midshipman."

"Yes, sir."

"Your crew was assigned to the center courtyard."

"Yes, sir."

"But whoever it was turned up there, they weren't midshipmen, were they?"

The kid's face went blank. Tom knew the look well. The kid had a mission and nothing but nothing was going to get in her way. "You saw them?" she asked.

"I arrived the same time they did. A big Annapolis bus, right? They looked kind of old for students . . . they didn't . . ." Despite her best efforts, Tom saw a sudden shimmer in the kid's clear blue eyes. "You missed that bus, didn't you?" he asked her.

He saw her unconsciously snap to attention as if reporting her failings to a superior officer. "Yes, sir. I did, sir."

"I'm really sorry"—Tom checked the pass again—"Midshipman Bethune."

He held out her pass. She looked down at the second one she still had in her hand.

"One of them had my friend's pass."

Tom knew what had happened to her friend. And to whoever had taken that pass.

"Bethune—they've got my friend, now," Tom said. "And I'm on my way to find him." He gestured toward the down staircase, offering her an invitation to join him.

The midshipman hefted the gun in her hand, then nodded once. Now side by side, they headed off together for the stairwell at the end of the corridor.

"Have you seen any more of them?" Tom asked. "I mean, besides . . ."

"Four," she said. "I dropped one. The other three withdrew."

"The one you 'dropped,' I take it, you didn't shoot him."

"No, sir. I'm . . . I'm working on that." She looked at the gun in her right hand, then at Tom. "Are you a marksman?"

"Never fired a weapon in my life."

In the puzzled silence that followed, Tom could almost hear her thinking, Why is someone with no military training working for an Air Force general?

He answered her unspoken question just as they reached the stairwell. "I'm in electronics. Circuitry design. Communications. I do consulting work on some of the general's projects."

The midshipman held back for an instant before entering the stairwell. "What do you know about ThreatCon Echo?"

"Never heard of it before," Tom said as he reached for the polished wood railing. The staircase had an open, more formal design than that common to the more utilitarian stairs scattered throughout the Building.

"Neither have I, sir."

"—but it looks like part of it involves sectioning off the threatened structure." He started down the stairs. After a moment's hesitation, the midshipman followed.

"Like watertight doors on a ship."

"Right. I think part of the idea might be to isolate the bad guys, keep them contained until they're attacked." Tom noticed the midshipman automatically move to the opposite side of the stairway, scanning ahead with every step, ready to react to whatever might be beyond the landing half a floor below them.

As they reached the first landing, the midshipman and Tom both stared down at the next set of stairs that ended on the second floor. Then Tom saw that blank look settle on the kid's face again.

"I saw a lot of helicopter traffic outside, sir. Troop transports. Attack helos. You think our side'll be coming in soon?"

"Not from outside." Tom tried a long shot. "At Annapolis, did they ever tell you about PROJECT ATLANTIS?"

The midshipman paused before answering, as if her brain had just sent a search request into the Internet. "Not in the classes I've had, sir."

"It's . . . part of the civil defense plan for what they call the National Capital Region. Washington, Arlington, all around here. From what I've been told, years ago, when they realized they could never evacuate politicians and military leaders from the area fast enough to beat Soviet submarine-launched missiles, they started going underground."

"Bomb shelters?"

"That's part of it. It's a whole shelter and evacuation system. There's an Atlantis facility under the White House. Another under the Capitol Building. And from what Milo—General Vanovich told me, I'm guessing there's one under the Pentagon, too. Makes sense if you think about it. Anyway, the general seemed to think that that's where a counterattack would come from. And that it would come pretty fast."

Midshipman Bethune was frowning. "Why would anyone keep an armed force under the Pentagon? It's not a good use of people and equipment."

Inwardly, Tom sighed. The kid was already trying to think like a general. Or in her case, an admiral. "I don't think the general was telling me they have an *army* down there, Bethune. But when you think about it, this place is riddled with tunnels going from here to the Navy Annex, and the Heating and Refrigeration Plant, and . . . you do know the operation centers for each branch of the military are down there, too? That's pretty valuable property, so it's a certainty they've got contingency plans for getting troops in here fast if there's a hostile takeover."

The kid checked her watch, still frowning. "Sir—it's been almost an hour since the takeover began. The longer the enemy is unopposed, the better he's able to dig in and the stronger his position becomes. If there were a counter-force on standby in some shelter or tunnel under the Penta-gon . . . why haven't they attacked by now?"

A good point, Tom thought. But quarterbacking the mili-tary wasn't something he had time for, now or ever. Milo Vanovich was still being held somewhere in the Building and Tom's first priority was to find him. What happened after that was after that.

"Bethune, I don't know why the military does half the things it does. All I can say is, if they haven't done anything yet, it's because some four-star thinks it's a good idea to not do anything yet. Why that would be, I haven't a clue. Nor do I care to look for one." Tom started down the stairs again.

But the midshipman didn't follow him. "There's another possibility, sir. It could be that the situation isn't considered serious enough to reveal the presence of a hidden force."

That stopped Tom. He turned around to look at her. "Bethune—what the hell is more serious than a hostile takeover of the Pentagon?"

"I don't know, sir. But if you're right about there being a counterforce on site that hasn't been activated yet, there could be a worse situation still to come."

Tom didn't like that idea one bit. What had already happened was bad enough without the kid thinking up even worse things to scare them.

For a moment, unbidden, he remembered what Vanovich had said about the briefing he was supposed to hold later today. Something that had scared the general so much he hadn't even told the President about it.

But the connection wasn't obvious and Tom put it out of his mind.

All that mattered now was finding Vanovich so he had the location ready for whoever answered his phone message.

Tom didn't want to know what could be worse than ThreatCon Echo.

SIX

WEST POTOMAC PARK, OHIO DRIVE

By the time UPN Associate Program Director Danny Assad screeched his WDCA *Uplink Live!* news van to a shimmying stop on the short spit of land that jutted out into the Potomac, a third of the distance between the Washington Monument and the Pentagon, the mystery of what had happened had escalated into a full-blown morass of confusion.

At 11:58 A.M., all live news broadcasts from the Pentagon had cut off at once. For the first minute, news directors around the world, from CNN in Atlanta to NHK broadcast studios in Tokyo, had thought it was just their own crews who had been affected. Perhaps a satellite had gone down, or an on-site generator had blown a relay.

But every news organization monitored every other news organization, and when the baffled news directors had looked up from their own blank screens to see what the competition was reporting, all those other blank screens told the story.

Something had happened at the Pentagon.

First confirmation had come within three minutes from SkyFox 1, the Bell JetRanger helicopter used by Channel 5 in D.C. to cover morning traffic jams and late-night police chases.

Since official helicopter traffic had closed the Pentagon's airspace to news helicopters, no civilian helos had been affected by the electromagnetic pulse that had brought down the Air Force's MH-53Js. The first news team to turn its camera on the Pentagon had been the crew of SkyFox 1, which had been dividing its duties between covering the Sunday-morning traffic snarl caused by the closure of so many roads near the Pentagon, and the ongoing police activity outside the National Archives.

The SkyFox cameras had revealed smoke—twenty or more columns rising like bleeding ink around the Building to stain the summer-blue sky. One enormous black cloud pulsed upward in billows from the Heliport Side, behind the Pentagon. And an even larger cloud swirled from the North Parking Lot, where flame shot up from a large but unidentifiable burning object. The rest of the columns, some black, some sooty gray, stabbed the parade grounds like a thicket of diabolic stakes. As the helicopter's camera had zoomed to maximum telephoto, the fires that burned at the base of each column had become readily visible.

Urgent calls summoning additional news crews and reporters had gone out at once, multiplying geometrically as intended recipients could not be found. It was Sunday morning. All first-string news teams were already at the Pentagon. Most second-string teams had the day off.

So many local beepers and cell phones had been accessed at once that D.C.'s cellular networks had shut down as relay circuits timed out in the onslaught. The increased communications traffic was not just from news desks. By this time, security support teams, both civilian police and military units, who were posted around the Pentagon had begun filling their own radio channels and the local phone system with frantic situation reports and calls for assistance.

Those personnel who had been stationed at checkpoints around the Pentagon, who had heard the explosions, seen the fireballs, and watched helplessly as the helicopters began falling from the sky, now started to receive the panicked groups of escapees fleeing the Building. There were many witnesses to different pieces of the nightmare, but no one with any clear idea of the entire situation.

The President was dead. The Pentagon had been nuked. A plane had crashed into the Building. Enemy paratroopers had landed. Each television and radio station had its own set of stories to choose from, and the absence of fact, combined with the need to fill air time, had led to the indiscriminate reporting of rampant speculation and rumor.

Danny Assad had listened to all of it on the radio during his high-speed drive from the Channel 20 UPN affiliate's new studio in Bethesda to the edge of the southernmost shore of the Potomac. He was the fourth of four program directors at the station, which meant he usually did what the other three directors told him to do, including getting their coffee. Danny had been too junior to be assigned to the parade grounds today. But, at twenty-five, he was also hungry enough to have been working—without pay—at the studio on a Sunday, completing his edit of a spec news feature he had put together on the honesty of local car washes.

At the time all broadcasts from the Pentagon had been cut off, he had been intercutting hours of hidden-camera footage showing car-wash employees either ignoring or sometimes stealing the money he had left openly in the cup holder of his battered Saturn. While almost everyone had passed up one-dollar and five-dollar bills, and appeared to suspect something was amiss when they discovered twenties or hundreds, Danny had lucked out using tens. Dishonest employees, it seemed, regarded a ten-dollar bill as just large enough to be useful, but not so large that its loss would cause a driver to notice and complain about its theft.

It wasn't an inspired piece, Danny admitted to himself. Truth be told, it wasn't even news. But he was in a business with such intense competition that he'd learned it was no longer enough to wait for newsworthy events to occur— enterprising reporters had to go out and find the news, or failing that, they had to make it.

But *DISASTER AT THE PENTAGON!*—the title his art director had already slapped into a graphic—was good, old-fashioned, ready-made news. And because Danny had been the only news department director ready to roll when the story broke, he'd gotten the assignment. And his shot at the big leagues.

Five minutes after Station Manager Eric Waller had slammed open the door to the editing bay to get him, Danny had been on his way out of the parking lot with the affiliate's oldest news van. His hastily drafted Channel 20 *Uplink Live!* News Team consisted of Arthur Tranh, an excitable, nineteen-year-old, summer-intern camera assistant from Washburn University, and Trish Mankin, a thirty-year-old floor director getting her first break at on-air reporting.

With the three of them in it, the creaky old van was running on pure adrenaline, not gasoline. Danny knew his team understood as well as he that this was exactly the kind of unpredictable situation that could catapult unknowns to public prominence overnight.

Danny parked the van on the side of Ohio Drive facing the Pentagon, and Arthur hurriedly extended the microwave antenna to establish a sound-and-signal link back to the studio. At the same time, Trish broke out the Betacam camera and snapped it onto its tripod, while Danny scanned the Pentagon with his boss's golf binoculars.

Neither Danny nor his crew had done this kind of work before, and everything took twice as long as it should. And when Trish left the quick-release lever in the wrong position, the camera almost fell off the tripod. By the time the camera was operational and transmitting back to the studio, military helicopters were thrumming by overhead every few seconds, and the consensus on the radio reports was that the Pentagon had been taken over by terrorists.

Danny, for one, could believe it. The parade grounds looked like a battlefield. He was just under a mile from the Pentagon's River Entrance, and he could see burning broadcast vans and generator trucks, and bodies.

Now, as Trish got ready to give her first segment, Danny, as unit director, instructed her to say "Live from *near* the Pentagon," but Mr. Waller overruled him. As Arthur used their longest telephoto lens to show the parade grounds carnage, Trish reported "Live *from* the Pentagon."

Trish's minute of glory lasted ninety seconds, as Mr. Waller informed Danny that the station was cutting to a CNN pool feed, and would return to them only if they noticed any change in conditions. The station manager also told Danny to keep checking the windows for any desperate, trapped hostages. All the other stations were using the angle that the headquarters of the most powerful military force in history might have fallen to a terrorist attack. What the competition had forgotten, Mr. Waller said, was the *human* dimension. So, if anyone tried to jump to safety from a fifth-story window, UFN Channel 20 would be the first to carry it live.

A minute later, Danny saw the big white arrow in a window on the Pentagon's third floor.

A few seconds later, Arthur found it with the camera, and Danny climbed into the back of the van to watch one of the monitors as Arthur zoomed in.

The arrow was pointing to what seemed to be a sheet of paper.

Danny shouted to Arthur to go to full telephoto, then he digitally expanded the frame on the monitor, rapidly adjusted the contrast to high, and had a graphic subroutine smooth the final jagged image.

It was a hand-printed message from someone named Mid A. L. Bethune, and it had been written less than ten minutes earlier.

Trish was breathing down his back as she read the message on the screen. "Jesus Christ," she said, "that's an honest-to-God scoop! Call Waller!"

Danny reached for his cell phone as Trish stored still frames of the message, then shouted to Arthur to switch back to his regular lens so he could get her in the shot. Trish was ecstatic. None of the other news feeds on the smaller monitors showed the message in the window. Channel 20's fourth-string team had found it first.

Then Trish noticed that Danny hadn't made the call.

"I think we should let someone else know first," Danny explained. "You know, the police."

Trish tried to take the phone from Danny but he held it behind his chair. "That's the *Pentagon!*" she said. "The police don't have any jurisdiction there! Give me the phone!"

"Trish—that message has inside information about the terrorists. If they cut the phone lines, that means they don't want any information to get out, but there it is: pistols, auto gunfire, explosives . . . even ThreatCon Echo, whatever the hell that is. I mean . . . that message could be military intelligence. Maybe it shouldn't go out to the public."

Trish made another grab for the phone. "The public has the right to know, Danny. This is news. And once it's on the air, the police and everyone else will know about it, too. That's our job."

It's also what troubled Danny. "What if the terrorists have a TV set in there? Then they'll know that the police know."

"Know what?!"

Danny felt trapped in a bad dream. This was supposed to have been his chance, but he didn't feel right about taking it. "I don't know. That there's some guy named Bethune running around on the second floor? That ThreatCon Echo has been established. I mean, that sounds like a military code word, don't you think? Maybe Bethune's some officer. Maybe that message is important."

"It *is* important. It's *news,* and we're putting it on the air." Trish imperiously held out her hand for the phone as if willing him to give it to her.

Instead, Danny reached to the control console and shut off the feed to the studio.

Trish stared at him in condemnation. "We're reporters, you asshole. We can't censor the news. We have to be neutral."

Danny knew she was right. A democracy could not stand without a free and independent press. And yet . . .

Trish had had enough. "Screw you. Arthur has a phone. I'm calling Waller."

"Go ahead! But *I'm* calling . . ." Danny didn't have the slightest idea who he should call. But from the triumphant look on Trish's face as she turned and jumped from the van, Danny knew he had to come up with one fast.

He was probably making the biggest mistake of his life. But up there, trapped in the Pentagon, was some guy named Bethune risking everything to tape a message to a window.

And Danny could help him.

Terrorists had declared war on the Pentagon.

Danny didn't feel like being neutral.

THE WHITE HOUSE

Like a knight returning from the Crusades, not someone who had just been extracted by Special Ops from the Pentagon parking lot, the President strode into the Situation Room beneath the White House, not too far from the White House Mess.

America's Chief Executive's face was streaked with dirt, his dark-blue, pinstriped suit was rumpled and torn, and the palms of his hands were white with bandages the medic on the Pave Low had applied. But his shoulders were square and each step was sure. It was exactly what the people waiting for him needed to see, Hector MacGregor knew.

Hector stumped awkwardly after the President, leaning heavily on a metal crutch to spare his thoroughly immobilized left foot, which was also mercifully numb, thanks to whatever the medic on board the rescue helicopter had injected into his ankle. The President's only visible injuries were the scrapes on his hands from the chain-link fence. The medic, however, had made the President promise to have a full set of X-rays as soon as possible. For Hector, who felt his injury was considerably more serious, the medic had suggested he get an X-ray of his foot whenever he could get around to it.

Though the Pave Low's pilot had been under orders to take his passengers straight to the Walter Reed Hospital for medical attention, the President had exercised his authority as commander in chief to directly countermand those orders. Hector and the President had been flown immediately to the White House.

The President's second order had been for the commander to report the loss of Major Ron Fielding and the CAT to the White House Military Office. Hector had been present for two National Command Authority drills. Following notification of the loss of a CAT, it took less than sixty seconds to begin the process of changing nuclear authorization codes, and less than eight minutes to complete it. Hector knew that as long as an alert status did not already exist, nothing in the U.S. arsenal could be prepped and launched in that short a time, so at least thermonuclear war would be the least of the President's worries today.

Five minutes after their heart-stopping rescue, Hector and the President had exited the Pave Low helicopter on the South Lawn of the White House. When the rotors had stopped and the side door had clanged open, Hector realized that the South Lawn was cluttered with helicopters. There was another VH-3D in VIP green and white. There were also three other military helos, all in flat green or gray combat colors. Hector couldn't identify them precisely, but they were all impressively large, blistered with curved equipment pods, and studded with gunports.

In addition to the Marine honor guards that were usually present to receive the President when he traveled via Marine One, Hector noted at least ten uniformed Treasury officers and the same number of soldiers in green service uniforms. But instead of ceremonial swords and polished sidearms, everyone was carrying small, black submachine guns. *The President has guests,* Hector had concluded, after taking a moment to consider just who might have arrived on those helos. *And those guests are worried.*

Despite the waiting crowd, which had included the President's anxious personal physician, it had taken the President and Hector only another minute to walk to the West Wing. From there, they took the stairs down to the Situation Room, which was a secure, austere, and windowless meeting room. One wall featured multiple, angled display screens that reminded Hector of the flat computer monitors mounted high overhead the floor of the New York Stock Exchange. Built into the opposite end of the room's expansive, black-surfaced conference table, and angled up from its surface, were control boards covered with glowing buttons and switches. The control boards provided secure communications links to foreign governments, U.S. embassies, and military command centers around the world.

Now, as the President entered the Situation Room, he was engulfed by aides and plunged into four and five conversations at a time as eyewitnesses and advisors all competed to deliver their accounts. It seemed as if all the world's leaders were on hold at the same time, all expecting to speak to the President personally. The State Department was overwhelmed. From what he could overhear, Hector was finally able to put together a picture of what had happened at the Pentagon—at least, a picture of what the President's staff had been able to put together, and what they'd deduced had happened. Most of the details were incomplete and some were contradictory.

First, and most personally distressing for the President, there was no word yet on his wife's fate. Some civilians who had been in the Pentagon's Courtyard when the terrorists had attacked had managed to escape in a pack. But none in the group remembered seeing the First Lady in the Courtyard. Two others, however, who had been in the reception area with the Presidential party recalled seeing her being dragged down the A Ring corridor by her Secret Service agents.

Drew Simons, the Treasury agent responsible for White House security, then told the President that the threat-response plan for the day's visit to the Pentagon had directed the First Lady's agents to immediately escort her to a safe room in the Building, in the event no clear evacuation route existed. In the absence of any additional information, the agent advised the worried President that it was best to assume all had gone as planned and that the First Lady was safe.

Hector could see that the President wasn't reassured by the assessment, but that he also wasn't going to allow his personal concern to divert his attention from the immediate crisis. And, since the Man had specifically told the Special Ops medics that he wanted Hector with him at the White House, Hector was determined to stay by his side, whatever it was the President had in mind. But at the same time, all he really wanted to do was sit down someplace and stare into space and try to come to grips with what they'd just been through.

Hector still saw Christou's wide-eyed expression as she

shoved him and the President to safety, a cloud of her own blood expanding behind her back. This afternoon, the thrill of being around the Chief Executive was not quite what it had been before eleven o'clock this morning, before he'd been directly exposed to the type of physical danger a President and a President's keepers had to be ready for.

The President's next thought was for the Vice President. That assessment report was less positive still. Two witnesses from the reception area had seen the Vice President pulled away by his protective agents. But three others had seen him a few minutes later on the stage in the center courtyard, shirt covered with blood, looking dazed as he was herded off with the captured military representatives from NATO. The President's advisors now considered the Vice President to be in the hands of the terrorists, and since his condition and whereabouts could not be known, he was, effective now, no longer in the line of succession to the Presidency.

All the activity, all the multiple conversations in the crowded Situation Room, did not disguise the absence of many who would normally be in this room in a time of crisis, but were instead, like Secretary of Defense Nicholas Guilbert, still in the Pentagon. Five witnesses had seen the Secretary's body in the Courtyard. Bullet-ridden and lifeless.

As radio contact was made with the soldiers rounding up all those who had managed to escape from the Building, more and more reports poured into the Situation Room. But the big questions remained unanswered. Finally, even the President had had enough.

"Everybody *shut up!*" the Chief Executive shouted.

Hector knew it wasn't what the President had just said, but how he had said it that created instant silence in the Situation Room. Just the fact that the President had raised his voice was enough to make everyone stop talking. It wasn't something many of them had ever heard. But then, they hadn't been with him in the Gold Room this morning when he'd faced down two of his Joint Chiefs of Staff.

"We will not allow ourselves to be consumed by panic or confusion," the President declared to the hushed group around him. "*I* will ask questions, and whoever has the answer will answer me, and everyone else will be quiet." He looked around to make sure he had everyone's attention, then came the first question. "Have the terrorists made any attempt to communicate with us?"

At once a raspy voice declared, "No, sir." Hector saw it was Lee Fogarty, a Special Assistant to the Secretary of Defense, and the most senior member of the SECDEF office present. He was a short, stocky figure in a torn Madras shirt and mismatched plaid Bermuda shorts that exposed hairy, scratched legs. "And we don't expect them to."

With a half-smile, the President eyed the obviously unsettled assistant. "Did we get you out of your rose garden, Lee?"

"Yes, sir. I had a day off."

That was enough small talk for the President. "Why don't we expect to hear from them?"

A man in uniform pushed through the crowd, an Army colonel. Hector did not recognize him. "If I may, sir?"

The President read the soldier's nameplate. "Colonel Tobin?"

"Yes, sir. I'm General Brower's chief of staff." Hector knew who General Elias X. Brower was—the commander in chief of the U.S. Continental Defense Command. The controversial CONDEFCOM was America's response to

increasing acts of terrorism at home, an expansion of an earlier, purely defensive force which had operated under the
direction of the Federal Emergency Management Agency
and the Department of Military Services. But CONDEF-
COM was the first combatant command established specifically to operate on U.S. soil, overturning more than two
centuries of legal restrictions on domestic military operations.
CONDEFCOM's functional responsibility was to defend the
United States from direct attack, whether that attack was
launched from outside or inside the country's borders. While
the Joint Chiefs merely managed their branches of the military, General Brower was one of a handful of CINCs with
the authority to command forces into battle.

"The general is in transit," Colonel Tobin said. "ETA is
forty minutes."

"Mr. President, I must protest the involvement of General Brower in these events." Hector did recognize the man
who broke in now: James Gibb, director of the FBI. As
always, Gibb was wearing a meticulous, wrinkle-free suit,
whose color and pattern were indistinguishable from all the
other suits the man wore seven days a week.

But the President was firm about there being no interruptions. "Not now, Gibb. I'll talk with you later. And we'll
deal with General Brower when he arrives." He turned his
attention back to the SECDEF special assistant. "Okay,
Lee, why no communication with the terrorists?"

"Sir, based on reports from the security personnel on
site, the terrorists used something that generated an electromagnetic pulse. We believe all standard communication
links with the Pentagon have been severed."

"What about nonstandard links?"

"We're doing okay with those. We're in contact with the

Pentagon's operations centers through secure fiber-optic networks. We've got confirmation that ThreatCon Echo has been implemented. The Building has been closed off and sectioned."

Hector saw the President pause before asking his next question, choosing the precise words he needed to use. "Colonel Tobin, keeping in mind that we are in a room full of people who have varying degrees of clearance, not all of them appropriate, am I right in assuming *all* operation centers at the Pentagon are unaffected by terrorist activity?"

Interesting, Hector thought. It sounded as if the President were referring to some kind of Pentagon operations site that was classified.

The colonel answered with the same circumspect hesitation. "Yes, sir, we are in direct contact with all such centers."

"And am I correct in assuming that at least one of those centers has the ability to launch a counteroffensive against the terrorists?"

"Yes, sir." Colonel Tobin directed a sharp look at the FBI director. "That is why General Brower is on his way here."

The President looked around the room. "All right, people, I want this room cleared of everyone except . . . whatever assistants are the senior person present for the National Security Council." The President sighed, then pointed at Congresswoman Dorothy Marlens, the astoundingly ineffectual Speaker of the House, a compromise candidate for the position, chosen more by default than by design. "Speaker Marlens, you should stay." Hector knew why. If the Vice President was captive, incapacitated, or dead, House Speaker Marlens was next in line for the Presidency, and as such, she would fill the Vice President's place as one of the four members of the NSC.

The President resumed scanning the room, as, in addition to a junior assistant to the Secretary of State whom Hector had never met, and Lee Fogarty as the highest-ranking member of the Secretary of Defense's office, he picked out FBI Director Gibb; Archie Fortis, assistant Director of the Central Intelligence Agency; Colonel Tobin; and . . . everyone in the room, including Hector, murmured in surprise as the President pointed to him and called out his name. "Everyone else into the Cabinet Room. I want an operational command center set up in there. Call in *everyone* from intelligence. I want every agency at the table. I want . . . oh, geez, is there *anyone* here from the Press Office?"

Mrs. Petty, the President's secretary answered. She had always seemed to Hector to be at least a hundred years old, but her flame-red, pixie haircut and her cord-hung, cat's-eye eyeglasses had made her an icon to the American people. It was like knowing a favorite grandmother was taking care of the President. "Sir, Nestor's on his way."

"Nestor? That's it?"

"Everyone else managed to get passes to the Courtyard."

The President made a face. Again, Hector knew why. Nestor Tallman was a junior speechwriter with only two months' experience on the Presidential staff. "Steal me somebody else's press secretary," the President said plaintively. "See if anyone from State is available. How're we doing with the media?"

Mrs. Petty looked over at the bank of television screens at the far end of the Situation Room. CNN, MSNBC, AOLCBS, the five networks . . . all except one of which were showing live helicopter shots of the Pentagon. The local Fox affiliate had gone back to running tape of shrouded bodies being wheeled out of the National Archives earlier that morning.

"What about the Archives mess?" the President suddenly asked.

Director Gibb delivered the bad news. "They did steal the Charters on display. The Declaration of Independence, the Bill of Rights, and the first and fourth pages of the Constitution. The second and third pages are still in the vault, untouched."

"Any connection to what's going on at the Pentagon?"

"Nothing's apparent. But the Bureau is actively pursuing the possibility."

"All right. Keep me informed." The President looked back at his secretary. "Mrs. Petty, you are now the official White House press liaison until someone else gets here other than Nestor. Take this down for immediate release: The White House confirms that a terrorist attack has occurred at the Pentagon. The President is unharmed and has returned to the White House, where a security briefing is under way. There will be a statement for the press at the conclusion of the briefing, expected to be in . . . thirty minutes."

"Really?" Mrs. Petty asked as she jotted the statement in her steno pad. It had a red, white, and blue crocheted cover that looked to be as historic as she was.

"It's sure as heck better than admitting we don't know when we'll have something to tell them. That would only encourage them to speculate, and we don't want that." The President clapped his hands like a grade-school teacher breaking up recess. The sound was muffled because of the bandages on his palms. "Okay, people, everyone out."

A minute later, Hector found himself at the center table with only seven others. The President was dismayed by the number of missing senior advisors.

"If the Vice President and I can't ride on the same plane

at the same time," he complained, "then how is it possible that so many other senior members of government were allowed to be at the Pentagon today?"

"We weren't expecting any trouble," the assistant director of the CIA said.

"That's baloney, Archie, and you know it," the President retorted. "The airport's shut down. The highways are closed. I saw the checkpoints from the helicopter. Why go to all that trouble if you're not expecting any?"

Colonel Tobin cleared his throat. "Mr. President, though I can't speak for the people who planned security today, it's SOP to go to all that trouble as a way of ensuring there won't be any."

Hector watched the President rubbing the bandages on his palms together. "Never mind. We'll leave it to a Senate investigation, because I'm sure there're going to be at least ten. Right now . . . Colonel Tobin, when can we initiate the Atlantis Rising defense to move against the terrorists?"

James Gibb interrupted before the colonel could answer. Hector leaned forward, to better hear why the FBI director would object to the presence of General Brower's chief aide in a crisis in which the military had already been involved. Then he leaned back, having caught the sharp look Gibb was giving him, that suggested that he was next on the director's complaint list. The director's next complaint confirmed that suspicion.

"Mr. President, please. I have to object to MacGregor's presence on national security grounds. He's not cleared for any of this."

"He is now," the President said.

"May I ask why, sir?"

Hector wanted to know the answer to that, too.

The President actually glowered at the FBI director. "Did

you hear what they were saying when I came in?" he asked. "The Secretary of Defense has been murdered. The Vice President has been wounded, at least. No one knows where General Flores is. Our helicopter flybys are showing us at least fifty bodies in the Pentagon's Courtyard, and when you add those to the seventy to a hundred people who've escaped, we're looking at at least one hundred hostages still in there. And not just any hostages, Mr. Gibb—foreign nationals. Top-ranking military officials. Diplomats. NATO command staff. All who came to this country, to the headquarters of the world's only superpower, and trusted in our might and our resolve to keep them from harm."

The President's outrage was affecting all in the room, even though he was technically addressing James Gibb. "I am not inclined to consider this an act of terrorism, Mr. Director. This is an act of war!"

Gibb tried to object. "Mr. President—"

"Don't you interrupt me! Senior government officials are dead or captured. They tried to kill me. Not kidnap me to hold me for ransom. But *kill* me. Six good, fine, brave Americans are dead because they put their lives on the line for me." The President gestured dramatically down the table at Hector. "And that young man came too close to being number seven."

As all eyes turned to Hector, and many resentfully shifted his ranking upward a notch, Hector himself felt only relief when the FBI director continued his attack.

"Surely there are other ways to reward him, sir."

"This has nothing to do with reward or gratitude. Hec was there. He went through what I went through. But I know from experience that he won't draw the same conclusions from that experience as I will."

"Sir, with respect, how can that possibly be relevant?"

"Good grief, man, do you not know how bloody this is going to get?! Sometime in the next few minutes I'm going to have to give the orders for our troops to go in there and take those SOBs out. More people will die. Count on it." The President paused to collect himself. But his upper lip trembled. "And in case you've forgotten, the First Lady is in there. My wife. And, God help me, as President, I cannot allow myself to put her safety above the security of this country and our obligation to those who came here today trusting in us."

The room became so quiet, Hector could hear the hum from the television screens behind him. The assistant from the State Department got up to turn them off.

The President cleared his voice before he spoke again. "That young man down there . . . Hector MacGregor . . . I'm trusting in him to keep me honest in what I have to do. I may be the President, but he's the people I serve. In this room the American people come first. And that means that young man comes first."

Holy shit, Mr. President, Hector thought. *Now everyone at this table is going to want to kill me if they didn't before.*

"And," the President concluded with a glare around the room, "I don't want anyone else to question me on this. Hector MacGregor has Presidential clearance. End of discussion."

But FBI Director Gibb was unwilling to yield the floor just yet.

"Very well, Mr. President, moving forward . . . I feel obligated to tell you that there is no regulation requiring you to call in the armed forces at this time. The criminals—"

"Don't you mean terrorists, Gibb?"

"No, sir," Gibb said testily, reacting badly himself to

interruption. "There is no political component in this situation. We have kidnappers holding people hostage. This entire incident falls under the authority of the FBI."

Hector thought Colonel Tobin was going to choke. "What?!"

It was Archie Fortis, the soft-spoken assistant director of the CIA, who raised his hand next, thus sparing the President from having to respond at once to James Gibb's outburst. "Uh, I probably shouldn't get into the middle of this, Mr. President, but from hostage situations we, uh, that is, the Agency, has handled, uh, I have to say that this isn't playing out like any other one I've seen."

"Hear me out, Fortis," Gibb said hurriedly, clearly aware he might have gone too far. "The remnants of whatever security forces were on site this morning have established a perimeter around the Building. Correct, Colonel Tobin?"

Tobin's response was confined to a curt nod of his head. Hector admired the colonel's self-control.

Gibb continued. "And, since ThreatCon Echo is established, all underground passages and connecting corridors between all the structures on the Pentagon reservation have been sealed. Is that also correct, Colonel?"

"SOP," Tobin said.

"Which means, the criminals are contained."

Where have I heard that before? Hector thought.

The FBI Director sat back in his chair, his delivery continuing to slow as it became apparent the President was going to allow him to finish his statement. "The Bureau will take over maintenance of the perimeter as quickly as possible. Our negotiators will attempt to initiate contact with the perpetrators. And our Hostage Rescue Team is already being assembled to move in when necessary." Gibb permitted himself a small smile of satisfaction. "Mr. President, the situation is under control."

The President turned to Archie Fortis. "Now, Archie. Why do you say this is different?"

"Well, they killed so many people right, uh, off the bat. That's unusual before a ransom is requested or demands have been made."

Gibb snorted as he leaned forward so he could look up the table at Fortis. "Oh, for . . . that's because they're outnumbered. From the uniforms they're in, we can safely assume they replaced those students from the Naval Academy, which means there're no more than forty of them. They couldn't manage three hundred hostages in a five-acre setting, so they . . . pared the list. Look at their tactics. They kept the military people, they got rid of the civilians. It's obvious that they've concentrated their efforts on capturing the most valuable hostages to trade for their demands, which we expect to be made momentarily."

Hector turned to the President. The FBI director wouldn't like it, but Hector couldn't let Gibb's false reasoning go unchallenged. "That's wrong, Mr. President."

The director turned to Hector like a wolf about to attack, but Hector's defender was still on the job.

"I want to hear this, Gibb," the President warned.

"If they wanted the most valuable hostages, why try to kill the President of the United States? Mr. Gibb, they *had* us. Agent Zibart . . . he believed they were forcing us to run in one particular direction. To the one place where there was going to be an ambush. And he was right. They knew exactly where we were going to go. And there were a lot more of them than us. They didn't say, 'You're surrounded, throw down your guns.' They just started shooting."

"Uh, MacGregor's got a point," Fortis said to Gibb. "Why kill your . . . most valuable hostage first?"

Gibb waved a dismissive hand, seeing nothing in Hector's objection that contradicted his theory. "Because they were afraid he was going to get away. Or maybe they were shooting to wound. The fact remains, they kept the NATO officers. They *are* going to contact us. They *are* going to make demands. And they will threaten those officers if we don't meet those demands. Maybe they figure we'll cave in faster with pressure from the countries the hostages are from." Gibb looked pointedly at the President. "Sir, the Bureau has profilers who will deal with these questions. We have trained negotiators. We can handle this."

That was enough for Colonel Tobin. "So can the United States military, sir."

Gibb rolled his eyes. "What are *you* thinking of doing? Calling in Delta Force?"

To Hector, that actually seemed the most appropriate strategy of all. The Army's Delta Force was specially trained to combat terrorists and to rescue hostages. He wondered why they weren't already on the way. Unless, of course, the mysterious Pentagon operations center could somehow launch a counterattack from inside.

The colonel ignored the FBI director's sarcastic delivery. "Regarding Delta Force, General Brower has been in contact with Fort Bragg."

"That means nothing," Gibb said. "You're not on-site."

Tobin's shoulders pulled back as he straightened in his chair. "General Brower is CINC of the Continental Defense Command. Delta Force *has* been placed on alert, as has SEAL Team Six." The colonel looked at the President. "They can be here within two hours, sir."

The FBI director also looked at the President. "And they have absolutely no authority to take action on American soil in a nonmilitary situation. This is the FBI's jurisdiction."

The President rubbed at his face. "My Lord, gentlemen . . . lives are at stake. *Lives* are at stake. And the two of you are squabbling about jurisdiction!"

Gibb refused to be deflected. "Sir, the military was in charge of security this morning. As a result of that security, we are now facing the worst hostage incident in American history. Now it's time for the professionals to—"

Tobin interrupted, seething. "My sentiments, exactly!"

The President tapped a finger on the edge of the table. "No offense, people, but this is getting us nowhere. I want an end to this. I want an end to it now. I am going to send troops in. I don't care if it's the Site J team, Delta Force, the FBI, or the . . . the darned Girl Scouts. If you people can't tell me what my options are, then I'm going to pick one myself and you can spend the next ten years in front of the Supreme Court trying to figure out if I was right."

The director of the FBI shook his head. "Mr. President, you are making a mistake."

"I've heard that be—" The President stopped abruptly. He looked at the Assistant Secretary of Defense. "Lee, from the reports, are there many American officers among the hostages?"

Lee Fogarty didn't understand the question or the President's obvious excitement. "Sir? What are you getting at?"

But Hector did and said so. "That makes sense, sir."

"You think so, Hec?"

Hector nodded. "It explains why they tried to kill you, but took all the military people hostage."

"Would you two care to tell the rest of us what you're talking about?" the FBI director demanded.

"There's a possibility the attackers don't intend to trade those hostages," the President said, his voice increasingly animated as he developed his idea further. "What if they took all of the military personnel hostage to disguise the fact that some of them were already working *with* the attackers."

Director Gibb made a face, to indicate he did not believe in such a possibility.

But Colonel Tobin supported the theory. "For what it's worth, sir, both General Brower and myself believe the *only* way the Pentagon could have been compromised this way is through the use of inside operatives."

Gibb slapped the table. "Which is even more reason to keep the military out of this! Mr. President, in light of what Colonel Tobin has said, how can you trust *any* of your troops until we know what happened today?"

If Gibb's question struck a nerve, Hector could not tell. Though, just this morning in the Gold Room, he had heard the Man himself ask if he could trust the Chief of Naval Operations and the Air Force Chief of Staff.

The President stood, letting everyone know he had come to his decision and the meeting was over. "Director Gibb, you will prepare your negotiators and the Hostage Rescue Team for action—"

Colonel Tobin got to his feet to protest. "Mr. President, you can't—"

The President continued, "—but you will *not* commit them to action without a direct order from me."

"Technically, Mr. President, that order should come to me from the Attorney General," the FBI director said pedantically.

"Well, Gibb, since the Attorney General is in that court-yard, if you prefer, I'll appoint Hec as Acting Attorney General and you can take your orders from him."

"No, sir. That won't be necessary."

"The second thing you will do," the President said, "is find Admiral Hugh Paulsen and General Philip Janukatys. They left the Pentagon about half an hour before the attack began."

Gibb's eyes widened, as did Tobin's, and those of everyone else at the table, including Hector. He automatically recalled his earlier fears about the military's leaders threatening the President's political control of the country.

"Sir," Director Gibb said, "do you really think they had something to do with this?"

"Find them. Bring them to me. Then I'll answer your question." The President turned to Colonel Tobin. "As for the Army, I want Delta Force brought to the closest forward base possible and standing by to go in. They are to have whatever support they need from whatever branch of the services they need it. Get that ball rolling now. I want to see you and General Brower the instant he arrives."

To Hector, the smile Colonel Tobin wore was definitely one of relief. "Yes, sir."

"I also want a direct line to Site J."

"We can connect through this room."

Then the President addressed everyone once again, before he dismissed them. "I don't know what we're facing here, people. But I assure you, I will not allow it to continue."

FBI Director Gibb had to get in the last word. "But remember, sir, it *is* a standard hostage incident, no matter how important the site is or how important the hostages are. They're going to contact us. They're going to make demands."

The CIA assistant director still looked troubled. "I, uh, I disagree. I think the President's right, it's . . . something else. They won't contact us. Because they're after, uh, something other than hostages."

"Mr. Fortis—" Hector heard a distinct tone of condescension in Gibb's voice. "The operations centers are completely sealed off, and other than those facilities, the Pentagon is just one big office building. What else is there to get?"

Hector immediately wondered if there were a connection between Site J and the sealed-off operations centers.

Then everyone's attention was diverted by urgent knocking on the closed door to the Situation Room. Colonel Tobin was closest and went to open it.

An Air Force lieutenant stood there, extremely agitated.

"What is it?" Tobin asked.

"Sir, the terrorists are threatening to start executing hostages unless their demands are met."

The room fell silent. The director of the FBI was almost gloating.

Contact had been made.

SEVEN

FIRST FLOOR, E RING, RIVER ENTRANCE SIDE

Soundlessly, slowly, Amy Bethune and Tom Chase edged down the stairs to the first floor of the Pentagon's River Entrance. Amy took the lead, pistol held ready, as Chase hung back, having told her she was better trained than he for what they might find. The guy either had no ego, or he had more sense than most civilians. Either way, it made her job easier.

Amy was well aware that the armed forces were supported by a great many civilians. Half her instructors at the Academy weren't in the military. But even though they could never match the same standards of physical fitness as a soldier or sailor or those of regimental appearance, those instructors still conducted themselves with what Amy liked to think of as a certain air of crispness and dedication, the trademark of the proper military attitude of precision, professionalism, and pride.

None of those hallmarks of personal achievement and

self-worth were apparent in Tom Chase. The fact that he wasn't bad-looking didn't make up for his sloppiness or his smart-aleck attitude, which wouldn't be tolerated for a second at the Academy. Clearly, the only reason the Air Force employed him was because he was some kind of genius. Not that she'd actually seen any signs of that, yet.

At least he doesn't seem to be a coward, Amy told herself again. Chase's commitment to finding and trying to help General Vanovich was commendable, and was really the only reason she had decided to team up with him. Not that she'd blame him if he were afraid of the enemy. She was afraid, herself. However, since fear was a part of the job she had signed up for, she had learned how to keep it from interfering with what she had to do. At the Academy, each mid was periodically required to jump from a sixty-foot platform into a pool to practice evacuating from a ship. As far as she'd been concerned, taking that first step into nothingness had been even worse than jumping out of an airplane for the first time. Worse because her brain could comprehend being sixty feet off the ground. Worse because everything was immediate, recognizable, and dangerous. At fifteen hundred feet, in the open door of the airplane, nothing had looked real, so her fear of jumping out had been intellectual, not instinctual.

Amy's first time off the platform had been her first lesson in successfully working through fear. The Academy had provided many more such lessons since.

Still, if Chase's attitude interfered in her attempts to gather on-site intelligence for the forces outside, she was prepared to knock him flat, tie him up, and leave him locked in a closet somewhere. Amy doubted he could even put up much of a struggle. Chase might look to be in good shape, for a civilian, but up against her training, he'd be a pushover.

She turned from thoughts of Tom Chase to the mission ahead. *Focus, Amy. Focus.* The stairway they were now moving down was wider than most of the others she'd encountered in the Pentagon. The others had been narrow, utilitarian passages hidden behind doors and squeezed into alcoves, existing merely to provide functional links between floors. Amy decided this one had been built for show, and for large numbers of users.

She stopped on the final stair, and looked ahead into the renovated River Entrance foyer, through the glass wall that divided the foyer into the immediate entrance area and the area in which Amy stood. Between the exterior doors and the glass wall was the security desk where incoming visitors and staff stopped first before moving through the doorway that led to the stairs and ground-level hallways. But, now, where Amy should have been able to see the doors that led outside to the VIP parking lot, there was only a giant wall of black armor, at least thirty feet across and ten feet high. It was impossible to tell if the massive blast door had risen from the floor, dropped from the ceiling, or rolled into place from either side.

"Where the f— . . . where'd that come from?" Amy made the effort to rein in her language, remembering she wasn't with her classmates now but an outsider.

She glanced sideways at Chase, who was now standing beside her. But he wasn't looking at the huge black wall, he was looking at her, eyebrows knit. "How old are you, sailor?"

"Twenty-five."

"You don't look it."

Amy shrugged and took the last step down, looked

around the foyer, noting all the places a potential enemy could be hiding. "Older or younger?" she asked, in spite of herself.

"Younger."

She looked back at him. Her matching question unspoken.

"Too old."

Amy felt insulted, didn't know why, and didn't want to waste time figuring it out. To the left of the stairs, she could see a set of glass doors that were not blocked by a ThreatCon Echo blast shield. The doors led into a spacious, wood-paneled hallway. Several enemy could be hiding in that hallway. It was the kind of location where she would plan an ambush.

"Isn't twenty-five kind of old to be at Annapolis?"

"The Academy," Amy corrected him, surprised by how annoyed she was beginning to feel. She selected a path to the hallway doors that would avoid putting her in line with any blind spots where a sniper might be hiding. Where she would hide if she were a sniper. "Annapolis is a town. The Naval Academy is the Naval Academy. The Academy is in Annapolis. They're two different things."

"Okay, the Academy. But doesn't everyone go there out of high school?"

Amy ceased working out strategy. She couldn't believe she was even taking part in this conversation, in the midst of a battle situation. "Sir, some midshipmen are accepted into the Academy upon graduation from high school. Others are accepted after serving in the Navy, or one of the other services. Some are accepted from other universities. The cut-off age for enrollment is twenty-four, meaning a graduate can be twenty-eight. I will be twenty-six when I graduate. Now be quiet. Please!"

Amy turned away from Chase and began to slide forward, against the wall, heading for the glass hallway doors. She had gone five feet when she heard rubber soles squeaking on the terrazzo and turned to see Tom walking across the foyer, completely exposed to enemy action.

"Chase! Get back under cover!"

The civilian didn't stop as ordered. He spoke loudly, voice echoing. "Midshipman Bethune, if they didn't kill us when we were making the same racket coming down the stairs, they aren't going to kill us now." He gave her a mock salute. "I'm going to check out the security desk."

Amy stared after him for a few moments as he went to a security turnstile, swiped his card through it, then walked through the doorway in the wall of glass panels that divided the stair and hallway area from the River Entrance area.

She took a last look at the glass doors leading off to the left, then followed him to the security desk.

Two guards were on the floor on the other side of the desk, both dead, both with two shots to the head. Chase was gazing down at the two men with a look of distress on his face. As she approached, he shook his head, then kneeled down beside one of the guards and removed the small radio mike clipped to the guard's shirt. A tightly coiled wire ran from the microphone to a battery pack clipped to the guard's belt.

"See this?" Chase said. He held up the two parts of the radio. The black plastic casing around the battery pack had partially melted. "Electromagnetic pulse. The power surge melted the circuits, then burst the batteries. Poor devils couldn't even call for help." Chase dropped the useless radio onto the floor.

Amy had studied EMP in her weapons courses. Most

Naval warships were protected from the effect by "hardening" their circuits—making them strong enough to absorb and dissipate momentary surges, or by surrounding critical electronic equipment with nets of copper mesh. The nets were called Faraday cages and they prevented an EM pulse from reaching the equipment in the first place. While she understood how an EM pulse was generated, it was not clear to her how one occurring just outside the Pentagon wouldn't leave evidence of much more drastic side effects than melted circuits and burst batteries. "I thought you could only get a pulse from a nuclear weapon."

Chase stood up with a sigh, brushed his hands on the sides of his jeans. "You don't need gamma rays to create EMP. Just shoot a current through a copper coil. That'll create a magnetic field, which you can then explosively compress with a shaped charge. Or, if you use an ordinary explosive to drive a high-current electron beam through a foil anode, and you shape the output mouth properly, you can aim the pulse almost like a laser. Right now, the U.S. Army's making pulse bombs that'll be small enough to fit in a Stinger missile. Their blast effect is negligible, but they'll knock out anything electronic within half a mile."

"So that's why the phones don't work?"

"Looks like."

Amy checked the foyer ceiling. "Then why are the lights still working?" The lighting level was low, only one out of two fixtures was working, but they were operational. The emergency-battery lights on the walls hadn't switched on.

Chase shrugged. "The phones got it because they have cables running outside where the blast must've been set off. The cables would have absorbed the pulse and directed it into the Building—and the phone system. But the lights, they might not have any connection to the outside. If they're strictly inside, their wires were shielded against the pulse by all the limestone and concrete in the Building.

"However, don't believe everything you see—the electricity to the Building *is* off. If you noticed a while back, the lights flickered? That's when they cycled over to battery backup for a good minute and a half. After that, apparently, the Pentagon's own generators take over."

Amy looked at the giant blast door sealing the River Entrance doors from the outside grounds. "And those worked because they were hardened against pulse effects. Because they have to work in a lethal environment."

Chase nodded. "Twenty-five, huh? I guess you just look young. Sorry if I seemed out of line, Midshipman Bethune."

"That's all right, sir." *This is not the time or the place,* Amy told herself.

"Tom. You have to call me Tom because I can't keep calling you Midshipman Bethune. It was 'Amy,' right?"

Amy chewed her lip. Who knew how much longer they'd have to work together? Better to make it simple. "You can call me 'Nuke.' "

"Nuke?"

"That's what my friends call me."

"Because you . . . want to fly bombers and rain nuclear destruction across the globe to protect the American way of life?"

What an asshole, Amy thought. "No, sir. Because I'm going to be the captain of a nuclear sub."

Amy didn't appreciate the way Chase raised his eyebrows. "I wasn't aware the Navy allowed women on subs for any kind of duty."

If Amy had a dollar from everyone who had said those

words to her, she could have bought her own sub by now. Maybe an entire fleet. "No, sir, not yet, they don't."

"But they're going to?"

"I'll be first in line."

Chase's crooked smile of what seemed to her genuine approval was unexpectedly gratifying.

"Go Navy."

Amy immediately assessed that response, ready to retaliate if necessary, but she'd heard no sarcasm. So she kept her response simple, again. "Thank you, sir."

"Tom."

"Tom."

Then he surprised her again by sticking out his hand. "Good to have you on my side, Nuke."

She shook hands with him, an oddly formal moment considering how they'd met. Unlike the people she'd met at the Academy, this civilian wasn't easily categorized in black or white absolutes. In her experience, specific mids, administrators, and instructors were friends or enemies. They would do anything for you, or they would do nothing. That was one of the reasons why she took personal responsibility for every aspect of her life, rather than take a chance depending on the loyalties of others. But she wasn't sure where Chase's loyalties lay. He was a confusing mixture of black *and* white, and it was surprising how off balance he was managing to keep her.

"Okay, Nuke." Chase turned away from the two bodies. "I was hoping these guys would have something we could use, but their radios are shot and someone beat us to their guns."

He was right. The guards' holsters were empty.

"So," he continued, "I'm guessing that the people who did this worked the whole thing out in detail."

"They're commandos, sir—Tom."

"Why do you say that?"

Now Amy knelt by the bodies. "Two shots to the head. A double tap. That's what they teach us in close-quarters combat. You can't spray an area with gunfire 'cause you might hit your own. But one shot might not hit anything vital. So you fire twice. Some of the guys say that's a waste 'cause their first shot is always good so . . ."

She looked up to see Chase studying her with a measuring look.

"Were you really going to shoot me when that door opened?"

If there was something worse than not telling the truth, Amy didn't know what it was. "No, sir—Tom. I did not intend to shoot you."

"So you missed . . . on purpose?"

In their first year at the Academy, all midshipmen were allowed five answers to questions that were put to them by their squad or company leaders. Either they could provide the information that was requested, or they could say, "Yes, sir," "No, sir," "I'll find out, sir," or, most important, "No excuse, sir." Midshipmen did not make excuses. They took responsibility. There was only one way Amy could answer Chase's question.

"It was not my intention to fire the gun at that time."

"It just . . . went off?" Chase sounded unconvinced by her admission.

"No, sir. I applied too much force to the trigger." She couldn't help herself. She had to add, "It's not my usual weapon."

"Right. That would be a . . . what? Trident nuclear missile?" Chase's wry, offhand manner puzzled Amy. She had almost killed him by accident and he didn't even seem upset.

Chase noticed her reaction. "Don't worry about it, Nuke. I understand. You are what you are. Just my good luck you're also a real lousy shot." He pointed to the security desk behind her. "You check out those drawers, I'll check these."

Still as much surprised by her own talkativeness as Chase's unpredictability, Amy was only too glad to return to pure, simple action. Going behind the desk, she located and opened the top drawer, found a box of pens and a bag of red-and-white striped peppermints. She took one of the mints and popped it in her mouth. "What are we looking for?"

"Whatever might help us. Cell phone. Guns. Walkie-talkie. Anything. . . . Now what?"

He had caught her look of surprise. "It's just . . . well, when I was upstairs, that's what I thought I should be coming down here to look for, too."

Chase didn't get it. "So . . . we're doing the right thing."

"Yeah. . . ." Amy added for herself, *It's just that I can't believe that you and I came up with the same strategy.* "We're in sync."

She saw the half-smile that briefly touched Chase's face as he went back to searching his half of the desk.

After a few seconds, neither of them had found anything useful. "Okay," Chase said, "so we just keep going down."

"Why down, s—Tom?"

"When they came for the general, I was able to overhear what they said. They were looking for someone with Red Level clearance."

"I don't know what that is."

"What if someone in the Navy has Top Secret clearance for pulse weapons that can be fired from naval guns—that same clearance wouldn't hold for the same stuff developed by the Air Force, right?"

Amy nodded.

"Red Level clearance cuts clear across the board. General Vanovich has it because he's conducting oversight on . . . well, I'd say every classified project under way in the Department of Defense, the National Security Agency, and the National Reconnaissance Office."

"Wow."

"I think I like 'wow' a lot better than f—" Chase stopped as if he'd been about to comment on her earlier language, but thought better of it. Amy was glad he had. She knew all about the double standard for swearing, one for females, and one for males. The number of appropriate occasions for females was decidedly limited. She didn't really want to get into that now.

"Don't mind me," Chase said. "My eight-year-old puts a quarter in a jar every time he swears. Problem is I think he's saving up just to do it now."

"You're married?"

"Yeah, well, I got time off for good behavior."

Amy didn't understand.

"We're divorced."

For an instant, Amy was on the verge of asking Chase if he was seeing anyone, as if they were both mids flirting over beers at Riordan's, back in Annapolis. But she caught herself just in time. What would he have thought? And what was she thinking?

She ignored the quizzical look Chase gave her as she said, "So we were talking about Red Level clearance."

"Right. Well, they took the general specifically because they knew he had Red Level clearance. But there're only a few places in the Pentagon where it'd do them any good."

"What places?"

Chase pointed at the floor. "The Star Trek rooms. That's what they call the basement operation centers. Army, Navy, Air Force, Marines. The whole lot. That's where they have their primary C^3I facilities. All with interlinked computer networks. Vanovich's clearance could get them into just about anything they wanted down there."

Amy frowned as she looked down at the two dead guards. "They'd do all this . . . just to access the Pentagon's computers?"

"It's probably the only way they could. You can't hack in through the Internet. And there's no outside phone access. The DOD's put their most critical computers on a completely separate and isolated network—fiber-optic cables running through pressurized gas conduits. You can only hack in using a DOD terminal. And the only way you get to one of those is by shooting your way through a whole lot of soldiers."

"So you think the 'bad guys' are trying to get into one of the ops centers in the basement?"

"They got into the Pentagon, Nuke. Anything's possible."

"Can you get into the basement?"

Chase held up his proxcard. "This pretty much opens anything."

Amy looked back at the huge blast door sealing the River Entrance off from the outside world.

"Except that. That's part of the Building's defense system. I can't override it. Just the interior doors."

"How *does* anyone reopen the exterior doors, after the system's activated?"

"Probably from the ops centers, once they know the Building is secure. Or from the ATLANTIS facility the general seemed to think was down there."

"How will the 'bad guys' know when the Building's secure?"

Chase held up his hands in surrender. "Hey, I don't know everything. I was just here to fix the photocopier."

"Do you know how to get to the ops centers?"

"That I do."

"All right, then let's go find your friend."

Amy had made her decision. Wherever General Vanovich was, the enemy was with him.

Before Chase could use his proxcard to go back through the security turnstile, Amy vaulted over the turnstile beside it, without using her pass. Chase froze for a moment, as if expecting alarms to sound. "Guess no system's perfect," he said when nothing happened. He swiped his card through the turnstile. As soon as they'd passed through the doorway in the glass wall, Chase turned right, toward the wood-paneled hallway she'd originally wanted to check out.

Amy held up her gun. "I'll go first." She had to be sure there was no ambush waiting beyond the hallway's glass doors.

Chase shook his head. He pointed to a wall-mounted card reader to one side of the doors. "Try running your pass through that."

Amy hesitated, then pulled out Joey Fisher's pass. "My magnetic stripe is screwed up." She ran Fisher's card through the reader. Nothing happened.

"Now, watch," Chase said. He touched his proxcard to a

metal square on the reader and Amy heard a click from the glass doors. He pushed the doors open. "If they only have the midshipmen's passes, there are some places they won't be able to get into."

"But if this is the way to the ops centers, and they couldn't get through . . ."

"Nuke, they were in here *before* the place was sealed up." Amy felt a flush heat her cheeks. The civilian was right. She'd forgotten.

He went on, "There were lots of ways down to the basement, then. But now . . . this is the best way down for us."

Once again Amy found herself following Chase as they passed through the glass doors into an elegantly appointed corridor. Anything but plain, as most of the halls in the Building were, this corridor also had recessed lighting that ran along a molded plaster ledge between its pale-blue walls and patterned ceiling. Ornately framed paintings of battle scenes hung every few feet. The white colonnades that framed the office doors reminded Amy of the front of the White House.

"This is all Joint Staff territory, like upstairs," Chase said before she could ask as he walked down the middle of the corridor, paying no attention to the office doors he passed.

Amy did, at least, convince him to slow his pace as they came to a turn in the corridor. He might be right about the enemy not being able to get in here, but if not, they would not be caught completely unaware.

She motioned to him to wait while she moved ahead, to take a quick look around the corner. Her concern relaxed somewhat as she saw another blast shield cutting through the corridor, ten feet past the turn. The blast door had a security-card reader beside it. "Okay, Tom, do your stuff."

He did, and more. As he stood by the card reader, Chase made an odd gesture with his hand, turning it back and forth rapidly. One instant, his hand was empty—both sides—and the next, Amy saw that he was holding his prox-card up between two fingers and its chain was swinging down his arm. The guy was doing magic tricks. He even gave her a wink as he touched his proxcard to the reader.

A second later, the blast door began to roll to the left and Amy looked into the first few feet of the corridor beyond. Chase's general would have to wait.

Five hostages, bound and gagged, sat on the floor of the corridor.

Behind them stood three midshipmen, all in summer-white uniforms. Two men and one woman, each holding a weapon.

One submachine gun was aimed at Chase, and two were aimed at Amy.

EIGHT

CABINET ROOM, THE WHITE HOUSE

The Cabinet Room was a mess. Styrofoam coffee cups were scattered over the entire length of the dark-wood conference table that was the focus of the formal, pale-yellow conference room for the President and his senior advisors. Half of the room's eighteen dark-brown, leather-upholstered chairs, which usually surrounded the table, had been pushed haphazardly to the side, many of them blocking the dramatic, Palladian, floor-to-ceiling windows that looked out into the Rose Garden. At the end of the table nearest the Cabinet Room's fireplace, stacks of maps and blueprints were spread out so that the people clustered around them could view them from every angle. The marble busts of George Washington and Benjamin Franklin set into the alcoves on either side of the elegant fireplace appeared to Hector to be looking over the shoulders of the map readers, like silent witnesses to history.

Entering behind the last of the President's new junior

advisors, Hector had immediately become aware of the confusion in the Cabinet Room. Other than FBI Director Gibb, who was seated at the conference table, directly opposite the President, there were no senior officials in the room. Hector saw only a gathering of nervous and tense men and women, civilian and military, not one of whom he recognized, all with White House VISITOR passes hanging around their necks. *Incredible,* he thought. *What if the President hadn't gotten out of the Pentagon? These people would need a week just to figure out who was in charge.*

James Gibb, who had hurried ahead of the others to arrive first, was adding to the atmosphere of desperation by loudly berating someone from the White House technical staff who stood at his elbow.

"What do you mean there's no phone in here?"

The technician, wearing a khaki vest festooned with protruding pockets, was cringing, as if he expected to be hit with a rolled-up newspaper. "Of course, there are, but . . . they're not calling on the phone."

"Then what are they doing? Sending e-mail?"

The President himself leaned across the table to intercede on the technician's behalf. "Mr. Director, give this young man a chance to explain. You can explain, can't you, son?"

Now seated on the President's right, Hector suddenly noticed for the first time that, even in this room, the President's place was marked symbolically. His chair back was a good four inches higher than any of the others.

The technician began to try, but after only two words, he just pointed back at the entrance to the Cabinet Room, where Hector saw another of the uniformed Air Force majors from the White House Military Office just coming in, carrying a distinctive black briefcase—the Command Authority Terminal.

The major moved directly to the President. "Sir, you'll be able to reply directly to them with this."

"The terrorists have activated it?" The President looked as bewildered as Hector felt.

"Sir, for communications purposes, they don't have to activate it. It's always on." The major placed the CAT on the Cabinet Room conference table in front of the President.

"Do I have this right?" The interruption came from FBI Director Gibb. "The terrorists have contacted us on the most secure communications link this country has?"

The major shook his head. He pointed to nine, wide-screen, high-definition television displays arranged three across and three deep in a section of the wall opposite the Cabinet Room's fireplace. Each screen had a different network or station logo in the bottom-right corner, but all were carrying the same image.

In the foreground, side by side, in ordinary office chairs, were three men, each in a different uniform, but all with conspicuous rows of colored service ribbons. All three were tied and gagged. Behind them stood two men wearing green fatigues, green caps pulled down low, and red bandanas pulled up over their mouths. The surface of the bandanas looked distorted, as if they concealed small gas masks underneath. One of the two men held a stopwatch. Both were holding pistols. The pistols were aimed at the heads of the uniformed captives.

Hector recognized two of the hostages. So did the President.

"Dear God, that's Al Flores, General Kerensky, and . . . who?"

An advisor Hector didn't recognize said, "General John Hull, British Army."

"How are they managing this?" Gibb asked the major.

But it was the Air Force lieutenant who had summoned them from the Situation Room who answered. "They have a CNN crew in there with them. One of the ones from the Courtyard. Soundman, cameraman, and Mary Askwith."

"The reporter," the FBI director said with disgust. "Terrorist massacre live on CNN, hear their demands at the top of the hour. Welcome to the twenty-first century."

The lieutenant addressed the President. "They have the previous CAT, sir. They've asked to speak to . . . someone in authority over the secure comm link by . . ." He checked his watch. "Twelve-thirty hours, sir. That's three minutes."

The President tugged down on his sober black suit jacket. "Very well."

Between the Situation Room meeting and this one, Presidential aides had provided the President with a fresh suit, shirt, and tie. He'd also washed his face and shaved. Hector was still wearing his dirt-smudged and smoke-scorched white shirt and gray trousers, but it wasn't Hector who was going to go on national television.

Nor was the President, it seemed.

"Mr. President, you can't go on national—on *inter*national television and negotiate with terrorists!"

It only took a moment's thought before Hector found himself agreeing for once with James Gibb. "He's right, sir."

The President hesitated, then nodded as he stood up. "Director Gibb, please."

The director walked around the table and sat down in the President's chair. The major with the CAT stood behind him.

The President took a chair on the director's left, then nodded to the major, who leaned forward and flipped open the CAT.

Fascinated to finally see just what was inside the President's "football," Hector stared into the open case.

Inside, in its bottom section, was a small keyboard, a panel of blue buttons that looked like a large calculator pad, and an indentation holding stacks of transparent plastic containers. The containers held the nuclear-authorization-code envelopes.

Hector watched closely as, from the inside lid, the major twisted out a thick black rubber cylinder about two inches across and five inches tall, then snapped it into position on the edge of the CAT, like a satellite telephone antenna.

The inside lid also contained a large, color video screen and two telephone handsets. Directly below the screen was a wide and shiny camera lens. At the moment, all that Hector could see on that screen was a colorful, official-looking seal against a vivid blue background. Though the seal was unfamiliar, he could see it had an eagle grasping a thunderbolt in one claw and, in the other, a symbol showing electrons orbiting a nucleus.

Gibb held his hands over the CAT like a concert pianist uncertain how to begin. "What do I do now?"

At least five people, including the President, spoke at the same time. "Pick up the phone."

The director picked up one of the handsets. It didn't have a connecting wire. "This is James Gibb, director of the FBI."

All eyes then shifted to the nine wall-mounted television screens where one of the gunmen glanced to the side as if someone had called for his attention. The gunman nodded, then pulled a matching cordless handset from his back pocket.

Now Hector understood why the shape of the gunmen's red bandanas had looked somehow distorted—they were covering some device that electronically altered the human voice.

To Hector, the gunman's altered voice sounded eerily like the voice of a crazed computer from an old science-fiction movie.

"Listen carefully, Director. The Pentagon has been reclaimed for the American people by the Sons of Liberty." With those first words from the gunman, Hector heard the sounds of rapid typing begin somewhere in the Cabinet Room. He turned to see a woman at the far end of the table, her blond head bent over the keyboard of a slim laptop computer which also had a stubby, black rubber antenna. There was something odd about the woman's appearance. She was wearing an Army green uniform that showed her rank was major, but she looked too young for the rank, and her china-doll features and sleek pulled-back hair gave her the look of a model in costume, rather than a uniformed officer on duty.

Hector turned back to the wall monitors as the gunman continued speaking.

"This is our first step in reclaiming Washington and America from the traitors who control them today," the gunman warbled in a voice in which all normal intonation had been erased. *"Do you understand?"*

Gibb's manner was cool now, unhurried, in distinct contrast to his earlier demeanor in the Situation Room. "Yes, I can hear you."

"The question was: 'Do you understand?'"

"I understand you have a great many people in there with you, and I want to work with you to make sure no one else gets hurt."

On the television screens, the gunman with the handset nodded at the other gunman, who, in response, instantly jammed his pistol against the back of the British general's neck and—

A chorus of moans went up from the onlookers in the pale-yellow Cabinet Room. Hector felt his stomach twist as General Hull jerked forward in his chair, streams of blood squirting through his gag. As the British general's head lolled to one side and his legs and arms jerked uncontrollably, half the wall-mounted television feeds flickered over to show shaken news anchors. The AOLCBS feed simply showed an empty news desk.

Other networks stayed with the CNN broadcast from the Pentagon, but digitally enlarged the shot to concentrate on the two gunmen and keep the general's body out of the picture.

Hector heard fragments of the overlapping reactions surfacing in the Cabinet Room. "Does anyone recognize that room?" "What kind of gun was that?" "Can we cut off the CNN feed?"

Then Hector heard the blond major at the other end of the table announce clearly, "J-34 has no record of the Sons of Liberty."

"Quiet!" Gibb ordered. Then he addressed the gunman again. "That was unnecessary!"

At that moment, Hector realized that nothing the FBI director was saying or that was being said in the Cabinet Room was being broadcast by CNN. Only the gunman's voice was being delivered live to the world.

"We will be the judge of what is necessary," the gunman said. *"Do you understand?"*

Gibb showed that he had learned his lesson. "I understand."

On the wall monitor, the other gunman lowered his weapon, and the first gunman began to speak again. *"The false government in Washington no longer represents the will of the American people. Our country was once strong and free because our military forces were the best in the world."*

Gibb pressed a control on the handset he held. Hector guessed it was a MUTE button because the FBI Director then shouted out, "Where the hell are my profilers?!"

"But the traitorous President," the gunman continued, *"has betrayed our military and the American people by selling us out to the Russians, as part of a worldwide conspiracy involving NATO, the United Nations, and the Federal Emergency Management Agency."*

"Sweet Jesus," someone behind Hector said in anguish, "these guys are homegrown lunatics."

"The Sons of Liberty are patriots. We are prepared to lay down our lives in defense of our country and our flag. If you wish the remaining hostages to be set free, unharmed, all of the following conditions must be met. Do you understand?"

"I understand," Gibb said calmly.

"These are the conditions. Number One: Within the hour, the President will appear on national television and confess that his efforts to admit Russia into NATO are part of a larger conspiracy to render the United States incapable of resisting a military takeover by United Nations Security Forces."

Hector heard nervous laughter from some of the advisors in the Cabinet Room, groans from others. His own reaction was one of dismay. The tabloid media would be all over this one.

The gunman continued. *"Number Two: All persons who are in the current line of succession to the Presidency, from the Speaker of the House to the Secretary of Veterans Affairs, will sign confessions admitting their complicity in this conspiracy to subject the United States to takeover by the United Nations, and these traitors will also resign.*

"Number Three: The House of Representatives and the Senate will be dissolved, in order for full and free elections to be held within thirty days. No person who has previously held a political office, or who has run for a political office, will be allowed to run in the new elections. The government will give each candidate one thousand dollars for expenses, and no candidate will spend more than that amount. These elections will be based on public appearances and debate, not television commercials."

"What *I* want to know is how the hell did headcases get into the Pentagon?" another voice said behind Hector.

"And Number Four: Until the new elections are held and a new President is chosen by the people, the Acting President of the United States will be General Elias Xavier Brower."

At that, the room went wild. General Brower was the CINC who had just been ordered to bring Delta Force to the closest forward base in preparation for an assault on the Pentagon. Hector was stunned. How could someone like General Brower be involved in this?

"To let the country know that a true and decent patriot is in charge and the threat of invasion is over," the gunman said, *"we will expect to see General Brower appear on television to accept his new responsibility within an hour of the current President's resignation speech.*

"Director Gibb, do you understand these demands?"

"Yes, I understand them," the director replied at once. Hector didn't envy the man his job. Failure as a negotiator had terrible consequences. Millions of people would soon be second-guessing Gibb and judging him harshly if he made a misstep. "May I ask if you might release some of the hostages now as a show of good faith?"

"This is how the hostages will be released," the gunman replied in his mechanical voice. *"When we see the President resign on television, we will release twenty-five hostages. When we see news reports of the traitors within the government resigning, we will release twenty-five more. And when we see General Brower accept his position as Acting President, we will release another twenty-five.*

"At that time, we will provide detailed instructions for the helicopter transport we will require from the Pentagon to a nearby airfield, and the aircraft we require to fly to safety. At each stage along the way, we will release additional hostages. Do you understand?"

"I understand," Gibb said. "May I—"

"There is nothing more for you to say." The gunman looked at his stopwatch. *"We will see the President on television within sixty minutes. For each minute he is late, we will kill one hostage on camera. Each time a helicopter or other aircraft flies overhead to spy on us, for each minute that aircraft is in range, we will kill a hostage on camera. Any attempt to launch an attack on our position will result in our shooting fifty hostages. Any attempt to end the news helicopters' coverage of the Pentagon Building will result in our shooting fifty hostages. Do you understand?"*

Even Hector understood that last condition. The Sons of Liberty were using the news helicopters to keep track of the area around the Pentagon. He recalled the broad expanse of lawn that surrounded the helipad. The terrain all around the Pentagon was the same. There was no way any rescue force could approach it unseen.

"I understand," the FBI director said. "Is there anything

else we can do for you? Do you need medical attention or supplies? Food or—"

The gunman held up his stopwatch and made a show of pressing a control at its side. *"We will see the President on all television feeds within sixty minutes, starting now."* Then he returned the handset to his back pocket. That was the end of negotiations.

Everyone started talking at once, but the President's voice rose above all the others. Silence descended on the room. "I want all air traffic within five miles of the Pentagon withdrawn. I want *our* helicopters to replace the news helos that are up there now. Stick cameras on them to continue the broadcasts. Do whatever you have to do. And does anyone know who the Sam Hill those maniacs are?"

The blond Army major at the far end of the table stood up. "Sir, there is no record of a current domestic militia or terrorist group called the Sons of Liberty."

"And you are . . . ?" the President said. Hector realized the major was too far away for the President's usual trick of reading from a name badge.

"Major Sinclair, sir." Hector detected a slight hesitation before she went on to say, "I work with General Vanovich. I was going to help with the briefing later today."

Apparently that meant something to the President, because he nodded in understanding. "Of course, Major Sinclair. I've read your reports on. . . ." The President looked at his group of unfamiliar advisors and then at Colonel Tobin, who was standing talking to the major who'd brought in the CAT. "So . . . you've been able to access all possible sources for any records on these people."

Everyone was listening to the Army major now. Hector tried to place her name. He was sure the President had never mentioned a Major Sinclair to him, and he couldn't recall ever reading one of her reports. That meant either the major worked on projects that were extremely tedious, or extremely classified. Given all the unexpected events of the day, Hector decided he'd go for classified.

"Sir, I don't believe any records could exist on them. I believe everything they've just told us is a lie."

"But they murdered General Hull," someone called out over the surprised and confused reactions to the major's statement.

"And they will murder again," Sinclair said. Hector noted the major was still standing, as if at attention. "But not for the reasons they stated."

"And why do you believe that, Major?" the President asked.

"Their demands are delusional, sir. No rational person could believe that the mechanisms of the United States government could be bypassed with the ease they're demanding."

"That's precisely what makes them dangerous," Gibb said to the President.

"With respect, sir, I disagree," said the major. "I've heard some of the firsthand witness accounts of what happened at the Pentagon today. I've watched the satellite footage we have of the attack in the Courtyard. These people acted swiftly, professionally, and with military precision and timing. Those are not attributes of a delusional mind."

"Look who their leader is," the FBI director argued, again addressing himself to the President, not the major. "General Brower. He practically invented Special Forces."

The major's response was swift. "Sir, I have served under General Brower. It is impossible for him to have had anything at all to do with this."

"Then why name him, Major?" the President asked

"To discredit the one person they fear. Those are trained soldiers in there. You can see that from the satellite footage. I say they know the greatest risk to their operation is an attack by Delta Force. That suggests they named General Brower in the way they did in order to discredit him, or at the very least, make you question his decisions."

The President looked thoughtful, as if seriously considering the major's reasoning.

Gibb, however, had thought it over long enough. "Mr. President, I don't think this warrants further discussion. It's not important who these people are. What is important is that we have less than an hour to rescue the hostages. And given what I recall of the debate that surrounded your efforts to have Russia join NATO, and given the timing of this event—and the fact that Major Sinclair believes these people are soldiers—I believe you can't discount the possibility that General Brower or other members of the military are involved."

The FBI director leaned forward, placing his hands on the table for emphasis. "Mr. President, give me the order."

"The order to do what?" Sinclair's voice asked sharply.

The director answered without looking in her direction. "To send in my people."

"The FBI Hostage Rescue Team?! Against that group?" Sinclair appealed directly to the President. "Sir, the HRT's trained for civilian incidents. They won't last five seconds in there."

"They won't have to," the President said. He turned to General Brower's chief of staff. "Colonel Tobin, I'm going to activate Site J."

NINE

FIRST FLOOR, E RING, RIVER WEDGE

Tom raised his hands and, remembering who he was with, said, "Drop it, Nuke! It's not worth it!"

The response of all three of the figures in white was to aim their submachine guns at Bethune. Tom looked at the midshipman and saw the all-too-familiar and senseless determination that tightened her young face.

But then, finally, Bethune held her right hand up and slowly crouched to place her pistol on the floor with her left.

Tom blew out the deep breath he'd unconsciously been holding.

The stocky, black-haired man in white motioned to Bethune to lie down on the floor. As soon as she was down, he went to her and kicked her gun away. The second man, a well-muscled, freckled towhead, forced Tom's hands behind his back, then spun him around, suddenly shoving him forward, bashing his face into the wall. Before he could protest,

Tom felt rough hands pull his arms and, with a plastic ripping sound, his hands were tied. Then he was spun around again until he felt dizzy. The fair-haired man who had tied his hands now held his proxcard.

Tom fell back against the wall, disoriented, feeling his tightly bound hands already begin to throb. The circulation in his wrists wouldn't last long. He saw Bethune's hands also being expertly and rapidly bound together by a thin cord of stiff plastic, like the bundling ties used to hold wires together. Her burly captor yanked the cord tight, then pulled up on the shoulder of her gray sweatshirt, forcing her hands down to her knees, then her sneakers.

Tom saw the midshipman glaring at him, as if she blamed him for their being captured. But for all he didn't want to know about guns, Tom knew that three submachine guns beat a hand pistol every time.

His captor started frisking him, patting him professionally under his arms, around his belt, then down the back of his legs and up the front. Just as Tom resigned himself to the likely discovery of his Swiss Army knife, he heard Bethune yell out an obscenity and both Tom and his captor looked up to see the midshipman's knee in her captor's groin. The black-haired man grunted, then jerked forward, head down far enough that Bethune was able to give him a sideways head butt that sent a mist of spit flying from his mouth. Before he could recover, she had hooked her foot behind his calf, checked him with her shoulder, and thrown him back onto the floor where his head struck the hard terrazzo and he gasped at the blow.

The speed and the violence of the maneuver stunned Tom. *But she dropped that bastard beautifully,* he marveled.

Bethune was just about to kick the man she had dropped

when Tom's captor took the three steps he needed to reach her and swung the butt of his submachine gun against her jaw, knocking her to the floor beside her fallen captor. Then he spit on her.

Tom jerked forward, but the six-foot brunette with the submachine gun clubbed him.

A string of crimson blood ran from Bethune's mouth as Tom staggered back. Then as Tom's captor helped the black-haired man to his feet, Tom thought he heard something that didn't sound like English. But his ears still rang from the blow to his head and he couldn't be precisely sure what he had heard.

Bethune groaned and rolled over on her side. The man she'd struck pulled back his foot as if to kick her in the ribs.

"No!" the woman with the submachine gun ordered. It was the first intelligible word any of the three had spoken. As the powerfully built man stepped back, still scowling at Bethune, Tom wondered if the woman was the leader.

Tom's freckled captor now grabbed Bethune's arm and hauled her roughly to her feet, pushing her toward the other hostages who were still sitting on the floor in the center of the corridor.

Tom counted five hostages. Four men, one woman, in bedraggled summer finery chosen for the President's NATO luncheon. One man's suit-jacket sleeve was badly torn and stained with blood. The thin, pretty woman, about fifty, wore a delicate, flowered summer dress, but no shoes. All had the same, wide-eyed, fearful expression.

Tom doubted they were any less apprehensive than he was. But his years of being a father had taught him how to hide his fears. He remembered few things more vividly than the Christmas Eve his Cherokee had spun across an icy road into the glare of an oncoming tractor-trailer's head-lights. He'd been taking Tyler to his mother.

It had been Tom's sudden cry that had burned its way into Tyler's four-year-old consciousness. The speeding semi had just missed the Cherokee, and they'd careened to a stop on the far shoulder of the road. If Tom had been cool, Tyler might have slept through the encounter. Instead, Tom had let his mask slip, and his son had awoken suddenly to the terrifying knowledge that his father was only human, that one of the two most important people in his life might not be able to keep him safe from everything bad.

Two years later, when he'd taken Tyler to Walt Disney World, their plane had hit a huge thunderstorm over Florida and was so severely shaken that the oxygen bags dropped down. Tom turned that near-disaster into a laugh-riot adventure for Tyler even though he'd been terrified Tyler's life was in danger. Tyler still talked about the time his dad surprised him with the special airplane-sneak preview of the new rides for Space Mountain and Journey to the Center of the Earth.

The towheaded man who took Tom's proxcard now used it to repeatedly raise and lower the blast shield. After the third opening of the door, the six-foot brunette came over to Tom, and pried his wallet from the back pocket of his jeans.

As the woman turned away from him, Tom whispered to Bethune, propped up against him, "Good job back there."

The midshipman didn't answer—no surprise. The right side of Bethune's jaw was already bruised purple-red and her lower lip had swollen up on that side, too, but Tom saw a flash of connection in her eyes, as she lowered one eyelid in a wink. *At least the kid can take it as well as she can give it,* Tom thought.

"FBI," a female voice said.

Tom twisted around to look up at her. The six-foot woman had a halo of frizzy brown hair, and was broad-shouldered with strong-looking arms. Tom estimated her to be about his age, and he had a vague recollection of having seen her among the midshipmen who got off the bus right in front of him.

"FBI?" the woman said again, making it a question. She held out Tom's FBI Academy instructor's pass. It had his photo and a large FBI logo.

Tom looked up at the woman and suddenly wondered if she actually knew any English. "Teacher," he said, speaking slowly. "I'm a teacher at the FBI Academy."

The woman frowned. "Teacher," she said. Then she walked back to the other two men and the three of them began another whispered conversation.

"Can you catch the language?" Tom muttered to Bethune.

"Russian," Bethune said promptly, confirming Tom's suspicion.

Tom wasn't sure which was more remarkable, that there were Russians with submachine guns in the Pentagon, or that he happened to be with someone who could understand them. "And . . . ?" he asked.

Bethune shrugged, then winced at the movement. "And I've no idea what they're talking about. I only swear in Russian." She grimaced and spit up more blood.

The midshipman caught his look of concern and mumbled. "Jerk broke a tooth. The nerve's exposed."

Distraction was the only painkiller Tom could offer. He looked over at the three still in their huddle. "So why are they here?"

"Maybe they don't want their country joining NATO."

"Then what's the connection to Milo and his clearance?"

Before Bethune could answer, the huddle broke up. The freckled Russian used Tom's proxcard to shut the blast door. At the same time, Tom watched the woman who could be the group's leader walk twenty feet down the corridor, then pull out what had to be a small radio, about the size of a cigarette lighter, with a short antenna. Tom didn't know how it had escaped the electromagnetic pulse, or, given its size, how it could send a signal more than twenty feet through the Pentagon's concrete walls and floors, but the female Russian appeared to be having a conversation over it. Her two colleagues kept glancing in her direction as they guarded the hostages in the hall.

Rationally, Tom reasoned, there was no way these three could get out of the Pentagon without entering into negotiations with someone in authority. The way these things worked, hostages were always traded for freedom. *Then again,* he thought, *hostages are often shot when deadlines pass. Or they're killed during the rescue attempt.*

And rescue had to be coming soon, he knew. Vanovich had been definite about that. Right now, probably in some deep civil-defense shelter under the Pentagon, a rescue team was already forming. What Tom needed to figure out now was if he should wait for the hostages' freedom to be negotiated. Or for a rescue attempt to take place.

But time was not on Vanovich's side. The general was not in good shape and who knew what the killers were trying to make him do for them. Tom had to find out where Vanovich was, so he'd know where to direct rescue when his phone message was received. He couldn't afford to wait for negotiations or rescue attempts.

The first break he'd already been given. The freckled

Russian hadn't finished frisking him after Bethune caused her diversion. And now, the two men's attention was focused more on their commander and her radio than on their prisoners. While this wasn't the time to attempt an escape, it *was* the time to start getting ready for one. And at least Bethune was in no condition to grandstand. There was only one way out of this situation, Tom concluded, and it would take careful planning and preparation, not hot-blooded physical stunts.

He would have to take control of what happened next. He leaned closer to Bethune, trying to make it look as if he were tired and wanted to rest his head on her shoulder. Then, as softly as he could, he murmured, "I have a Swiss Army knife in my front left pocket."

For an instant, he thought he saw a glint of humor in her eyes. "With a plastic toothpick and everything?" she whispered back. But then she sighed and shifted position, as if she, too, were tired and needed to lean back against him. Tom pushed closer against her so she could reach his jeans pocket, and though they then appeared to be sitting still, he felt Bethune find the knife and slowly begin pushing it up toward the pocket's edge.

Down the corridor, the woman put the small radio away, then started walking back toward her two colleagues. When she reached them, the three turned their backs on the hostages, well out of earshot.

Tom felt the knife about to fall out of his pocket. "I think you've got it," he said in a very low voice, without moving his lips.

"It'd better be your knife," Amy said in a matching low voice.

Tom felt his cheeks redden. Sure they were pushed up

close to each other, sure her fingers were moving up along his hip, but that kind of a comment from a kid made him uncomfortable.

Then he felt the knife begin to slip. If it hit the floor, there was no way the three Russians wouldn't hear it. He pushed harder against Amy, felt her crossed hands dig into him as she squeezed, and . . . caught the knife.

"Got it. Now don't move."

Tom ground his teeth. "Don't try anything now," he hissed urgently. "Wait till they're distracted."

The midshipman didn't answer. He could feel her move her hands. He thought he heard the snap of one of the knife blades opening. "Nuke . . . they have guns . . ."

"Tom . . . they have Heckler & Koch MP5s. I know what they are. Keep still, and keep quiet."

Then Tom couldn't say anything else because the three Russians had turned around and were walking straight toward them, all eyes on Tom.

"Tom Chase," the woman said.

Tom rapidly assessed the situation. They had his wallet. They knew who he was. "That's right."

"You. With us," the woman said. She nodded her head at the black-haired man and he swung his H&K to the side and came to haul Tom up by his arm.

"Fall down," Bethune hissed.

Tom stiffened, alarmed. This wasn't the right place or the right time.

The black-haired Russian grabbed on to Tom's arm, in the bend of his elbow, then started to pull. Tom rocked up on his feet, balanced only by the man's grip. Then, just before he could straighten out his legs, Amy whispered, *"Now!"*

Tom knew if he stood up, whatever crazy stunt she'd

planned would fail. Would she be smart enough to abort? But if she'd already committed—and he didn't cooperate— she'd be shot.

In that timeless instant of indecision, one thought rose above all the others. *The kid already got one of them. . . .*

Tom rocked up on his feet and . . . stumbled forward, crying out in surprise as he started to fall and the Russian hung on and lost balance and—

—the midshipman leapt up, swiped the submachine gun hanging from the stocky man's shoulder, and fired point blank at the other two Russians, over Tom's head.

In the wave of explosive heat from Bethune's gun barrel, Tom heard the muffled cries of the hostages mixed with those of the two Russians whose bodies now danced in the sweep of bullets from the submachine gun.

With a roar, the black-haired Russian holding Tom twisted away to face Bethune. In the exact same moment that Tom realized that there was no way Bethune could swing the H&K on its short shoulder strap in to fire at the man, and that he would seize her gun, the midshipman's hand flew up with a knife. And in the same heartbeat it took for Tom to think, *That's not my knife,* the gleaming blade sank into the man's neck and he stumbled back, his scream changing to gurgles as he clutched his throat and turned around slowly in a circle, rising up, then collapsing, motionless.

Tom, his hands still tied with plastic cord behind his back, rolled over on his knees. The three Russians were dead. Glistening slicks of blood spread out from beneath their bodies on the highly polished floor.

Tom threw up. There was nothing in his stomach. He hadn't eaten since last night's pizza with Tyler. He gagged on the bile burning his throat.

Only when he leaned forward on both hands did he realize Bethune had cut the plastic ties binding his wrists. Gasping ragged gulps of air, Tom used a numb hand to wipe the foul liquid from his lips.

Bethune was wiping a long steel blade on her jeans.

There was only one thing to say. "That's . . . that's not my knife. . . ."

She shrugged and held out the knife for his inspection. It looked to Tom about the same size as his Maxxum, but the handle was metal as well as the blade. Using only one hand, Bethune snapped the blade into the handle, then with a sharp flick of her wrist, split the handle in two and turned the knife into a pair of needle-nose pliers.

They both turned as the hostages, still in gags, thumped their feet against the floor and cried out as best they could to get Tom's and Bethune's attention.

The Russian commander was struggling to get up, her uniform and gun dripped with her own blood as she slowly raised her hand.

Tom's vision seemed to contract until all he saw was the barrel of her weapon. But just as he expected to see the bullets explode out at them, he heard, instead, a quick series of metallic clicks and then something silver flashed past his eyes, and with a strangled gasp the frizzy-haired Russian fell back and her gun slid to the floor beside her, unfired.

Tom saw a cross of silver dead center in her throat.

Bethune walked past Tom and the man whose throat she had cut, to halt beside the bodies of the man and woman she had shot.

Reaching down, she pulled her knife from the Russian woman's throat. The tool was now in the shape of an X, with the top of the X formed by the knife blade pointing out one side and the pliers' head to the other. The two ends of the open handle formed the bottom of the **X**.

Bethune straightened up, again cleaning the tool on her jeans. Then she snapped its appendages closed with one hand, until the tool became a compact metal lozenge.

"You can't do that with a plastic toothpick," she said, turning back to Tom and the hostages.

Tom took a good look at her. The kid had four notches on her belt now. But she was only getting started. The longer he stayed with Midshipman Bethune, the shorter his life would be.

And he still had to find Vanovich.

TEN

SITUATION ROOM, THE WHITE HOUSE

Once he returned to the Situation Room, Hector didn't have to check his watch. There were three digital time readouts just above the cluster of flat-panel display screens covering the far wall. One readout had already been converted into a countdown timer. In forty-eight minutes, the terrorists would begin killing hostages. Unless the President publicly resigned, along with every member of his cabinet, and every member of the House and Senate. And there was no way that was going to happen.

The windowless room felt better to Hector than the room he'd just left. There were many fewer people and the activity was not at all chaotic. Though the mood was still grim and tense, the handful of new people who had arrived in response to the President's summons to the intelligence community seemed more assured than the hastily assembled junior advisors in the Cabinet Room. Like Margaret Sinclair, who had also followed the President here. Also like the Army major, most of the new people in the Situation Room were wearing uniforms. Hector wondered if it was just their clothing that made them seem more competent, or if they really were.

Hector himself was feeling slightly more pulled together. A White House valet, on instructions from Mrs. Petty, had brought Hector a brand-new tracksuit, one of a constant stream presented to the President by visitors. Hector appreciated the thoughtful if not stylish choice of garment. He'd been able to easily stretch the dark blue, drawstring pants over his bulky foot brace. He wasn't quite as pleased about the large emblem for the *Minnesota Meat Packers Professional Development Association—50th Anniversary Meeting* that adorned his chest, but to have clean, whole clothes again felt wonderful.

The President, for his part, had managed to slip away for what could only have been a minute, to reappear in another fresh suit, shirt, and tie. The only evidence of what he had been through today was the bandages on his hands and the shadows under his eyes.

Because of his crutch, Hector had, once again, been the last to file into the Situation Room, but this time he wasn't even sure the Man realized he was still around. Hector knew that his role in less critical situations was to provide an outsider's viewpoint to the President during the decision-making process, but the President had already made his decision in this crisis: He was going to activate the mysterious Site J.

Believing his time here to be limited, given that he was probably the only person in the room who did not already know exactly what Site J was, Hector decided to make the most of it. As soon as he had entered the room, he located

Major Sinclair and limped in her direction, finding a chair at the table that was only two over from hers, with no one in between.

Sinclair seemed to be someone who knew about everything that was going on. She had also held her own against James Gibb, the director of the FBI, who noticeably had not been invited to the Situation Room for this next step. Hector had a great many questions for the major. But mostly, he knew, when the time was right, he wanted to talk to her about Major Christou.

For his first few minutes in the Situation Room, though, Hector avoided doing anything that would draw attention to himself. This was the one time he would agree with his critics: He was an impostor, with nothing to add to the current discussion. He would learn more by just listening.

Milton Meyer, an anorexically thin young assistant director from the National Security Agency, had just suggested a plan of deception. He said it would be possible for the President to make a false resignation speech and have it transmitted on every television channel the terrorists might be monitoring from the Pentagon. During the critical debate that suggestion caused, Hector noticed that no one was referring to the terrorists as the Sons of Liberty. This group, unlike director Gibb, seemed to have accepted Major Sinclair's earlier assessment that whoever the terrorists were, they had lied about their identity.

Assistant Director Meyer now was adding that the NSA had selective jamming and rebroadcasting equipment that could target the square mile around the Pentagon, blocking out all legitimate television signals and replacing them with the NSA's own. Once the President had recorded his speech, the NSA could handle the rest from a single E-4B airplane. Anticipating its possible use, the NSA had already scrambled the aircraft from Andrews Air Force Base, and Meyer said it could be within range of the Pentagon within ten minutes.

The first question that came into Hector's mind was why the NSA even had an aircraft that could selectively jam and replace television broadcasts on alert within the United States.

But even as the President sat down at the head of the black conference table, Sinclair began arguing against the NSA strategy. She was basing some of her objections on the first break that had come to the White House—a surprise phone call from a UPN news director who had discovered a message taped to a window in the Pentagon.

The Air Force's 78th Communications Squadron, which was rapidly establishing a communications network around the Pentagon to coordinate further actions, whatever they might be, had quickly confirmed the news director's find and provided photos of the message. Analysts had decided that it appeared the terrorists had gained access to the Pentagon by replacing a busload of forty midshipmen from the Naval Academy. That corresponded to eyewitness reports of the shootings in the Courtyard and Hector's own experience. However, one mid who was supposed to have been on the bus, an Amy Leanne Bethune, according to Naval Intelligence, was listed in the morning's security logs as having arrived at the Pentagon after the others. Now, if her message was to be believed, she was loose in the Pentagon, reporting on what had happened.

What was encouraging about the message was twofold. One, there was a potential spy behind enemy lines, if only a means could be found to communicate with her. Second, the UPN news director had made the unexpected decision to keep his discovery off the air. Hector knew that in time of war, intelligence was even more valuable if the one side didn't know what the other side had discovered.

"Think of what that midshipman's message implies," Major Sinclair urged the President and Milton Meyer. "The terrorists managed to get themselves and significant weaponry through the Pentagon's security envelope. To accomplish that, there have to be more of them outside the Pentagon, and we can't know where. Given their capabilities and organization, I think it's more than reasonable to conclude they've also anticipated the possibility that we might make a false television broadcast, and have taken steps to ensure the authenticity of anything they see. And that could be as simple as having an accomplice on the West Coast watching television, ready to make a call to them on a satellite phone."

The young NSA assistant director offered a countermove. "We can shut down the satellite phone systems very easily."

But the major was not convinced. "And what will you do when the terrorists tell us they'll start killing one hostage every minute until service is restored?" She turned to the head of the table. "Mr. President, we have to go in there, and we have to kill those people before they kill anyone else. It's as simple as that."

The President looked at Colonel Tobin, who was now seated at his right. "Colonel, open the line to Site J."

Tobin adjusted some of the glowing controls on the built-in console, then handed the President a telephone handset. The President looked down the table to the display screens, and Hector also turned in that direction. The move also gave him a chance to get a better look at Major Sinclair, as well.

The main display on the far wall to the left was only three feet wide and two feet high. It showed what to Hector was an unnaturally perfect overhead shot of the Pentagon. The picture was crisp and rock-steady, suggesting that it was a still photograph taken during one of the earlier reconnaissance flybys. But here and there Hector began to notice the small square shapes of moving vehicles on the nearby highways. He knew the image wouldn't be coming from a surveillance satellite, like the footage the major had referred to in the Cabinet Room, because even he knew that satellites capable of recording such detail couldn't hover in place. And the fact that the image didn't have the slightest amount of drift made him rule out an observation aircraft, as well. Hector's best guess was that this image was coming from some kind of spy balloon that could be held in position directly over the Pentagon without being noticed by the terrorists.

Then his attention shifted to one of the secondary screens to the right of the Pentagon display. One screen, about half the size of the main one, showed an unusual mission crest he had never seen before—a shield that held a stylized globe diagonally crossed by a lightning bolt. The letters across the top of the shield were USASC.

Hector was about to lean forward and ask Sinclair what the letters stood for when the mission-crest image was replaced by the word SWITCHING in the center of the screen and, looking very mundane, an AT&T logo in the bottom right-hand corner. After a second or so, that screen was replaced, in turn, by another stylized drawing showing a large satellite dish against a backdrop of stars which included the Big Dipper. Tilted letters, like those Hector had seen in the *Star Wars* films, spelled out PANMCC SITE J. And in much smaller, undistorted type below that, the phrase LIKE NO PLACE ON EARTH. Hector sat up straighter. He felt like a kid watching late-night TV, who was hoping that his parents wouldn't notice that he was staying up past his bedtime and send him packing.

Seeing the stars and reading that mission slogan immediately placed in Hector's mind the preposterous notion that Site J was some kind of *orbiting* military operations center. But he didn't see how that was possible. He had learned from his time in the White House that the United States Air Force, which had abandoned its own military astronaut programs, PROJECT HORIZON, BLUE GEMINI, and the Manned Orbiting Laboratory, in the 1960s, had, indeed, begun a highly classified, crewed spaceflight program in the 1990s, partly in response to the Space Shuttle *Challenger* disaster, which had delayed a series of military satellite launches. But the Air Force crewed vehicles were small, aerodynamic, two-person capsules designed to convey repair teams to complex military satellites. Their missions were to last no longer than six days at a time. Hector had seen a photo of one of the capsules landing by parachute at Edwards Air Force Base. The event had been publicly identified as part of an ongoing series of uncrewed lifting-body test flights. The life-support volume of the tiny crew capsule had been roughly equivalent to the inside of a small station wagon. An Air Force vehicle that small couldn't possibly support an entire operations center. Which meant, to Hector, that there were only two other possibilities. One, the U.S. military was somehow managing to run an operations center from the half-built international space station. Or, two, the mission crest and slogan were deliberate misdirection. Perhaps another question Sinclair could answer.

The final screen was replaced by an image of an intent young African-American man holding a phone like the

President's. From his close-cropped hair, lean face, and taut bearing, the man was unmistakably a soldier. But he was dressed in black, with no evidence of military rank or service ribbons that Hector could see. He had heard that type of dress referred to as a "sterile" uniform.

The President, evidently, didn't need those clues.

"Captain Kagan, this is the President."

"I've been expecting your call, sir."

"You are aware of the situation in the Pentagon?"

"Our communications have been unaffected, sir. We're in continuous contact with the NMCC and the primary ops centers. They are secure and we are confident they will remain so."

"Are you aware of the threats the terrorists have made against the hostages?"

On the screen, the captain's terrible smile bared his teeth like a predator. "We get CNN, yes, sir." He looked off to the side. "The terrorists intend to begin killing hostages in forty-four minutes."

"That is not going to happen, Captain."

"No, sir, it is not."

Hector could feel the mood of the people in the Situation Room change again. The focused intensity of the President and the almost incandescent confidence of the captain were replacing tension with a growing sense of expectation, almost excitement. A feeling that, perhaps, this crisis would finally be ending, and soon.

"I understand that you are familiar with this particular scenario."

"Yes, sir. This is a by-the-book Cloudburst exercise. It's the mission my men and I have trained for. And, sir, in the exercises . . . we *always* win."

"I am counting on you to win today, Captain."

To Hector, with those words Kagan looked like a man whose greatest dream in life had just been fulfilled. He threw the President a salute executed with such speed and precision that Hector was certain Kagan could have split concrete blocks with the edge of his hand.

"Yes, sir!"

The President returned the salute with great pride. "You may proceed when ready, Captain. God bless you."

Hector had no doubt that in Kagan he was seeing an American hero being born. *Pull this off,* Hector thought, *and in six months you'll have a book deal and five offers to be a net-work-news war consultant.* Then, as Kagan was replaced by the mysterious USASC shield, Hector found himself wishing for more details, wishing he knew how many men Kagan had on his team, and exactly where they were, and what a Cloudburst exercise entailed.

More questions for the major, Hector thought. But even as a dozen conversations broke out in the Situation Room and he wondered how he should address her, Sinclair turned to him, looking at his shirt as if counting the dozens of tiny ember burns in it, then smiled. "You look like you've seen some action."

Hector MacGregor, twenty-eight years of age, advisor to the President of the United States, and almost a self-made millionaire, actually stammered as he replied.

"I . . . I was in the P-Pentagon with th-the President."

Her smile grew, full of warmth. "I heard. You're Hector MacGregor. I'm Margaret Sinclair."

She held out her hand. For a moment, Hector didn't even have the presence of mind to reach out and take it. All he could think was, *How and why does a woman like this become a soldier?*

She smiled again, nodding her head expectantly, until

Hector suddenly broke through his mental logjam and reached out to shake. Firm grip, smooth skin. Hector felt like a huge hulking brute as his hand swallowed the Major's small hand.

"I hear you saved the President's life," the major said.

Again, Hector was without the power of speech.

Hearing this woman repeat what the President had already stated for everyone to hear in the Cabinet Room, Hector realized for the first time that these words were going to be part of his life from now on. He would always be the man who saved the President's life.

But it didn't seem right.

"The truth is," he said, "I was saved, too." He shivered in the aftermath of the strongest emotions he had ever experienced in his life. "A lot of good people died getting the two of us out of there. A . . . did you ever meet a Major Elena Christou?"

Sinclair's smile vanished. "General Flores's aide. Yes. I knew her. I heard what happened."

"She saved us. That's when . . . she got shot. The bullets that hit her . . ."

The major didn't say anything, only looked at him as if she knew and understood every thought in his mind.

"I can still see her clearly," Hector said. "The look on her face when . . . And . . . she didn't even know me. She didn't even like the President."

The major touched his hand. "She didn't have to know you. And, I think she'd argue with you about not liking the President. I don't think she *agreed* with him. But that would be private. As an officer . . . well, it doesn't even have anything to do with like or dislike. Just love."

Hector looked at her with absolutely no comprehension of what she meant.

Her expression was one of guilt-absolving understanding. "It doesn't matter what Major Christou thought of the President as a man, or as a politician. She didn't give her life for *him*. She gave her life for what he represented. You know, what they say is true, old-fashioned as it sounds: She gave her life for her country."

That was when Hector understood that, for once, words alone were not going to bring him closer to an acceptance of what had happened. He shook his head. "No," he said slowly. "I think she gave her life for me. But I'm not sure why."

Then Hector abruptly shifted the conversation back to less personal ground. "So, Major, what happens now?"

Sinclair nodded toward the head of the table. "I think that's his job for now."

The President had just finished a private conversation with Colonel Tobin and Lee Fogarty from the office of the Secretary of Defense. Now the President addressed the room. "Ladies and gentlemen, I don't want any of us to think that what happens next is easy. Even if the planned operation goes perfectly, this country will still be in a state of crisis. An attack such as this, even if it ends within the next half-hour, will have repercussions for months, if not years to come, in our relationship with NATO, in our foreign policy, and in this nation's trust in our military.

"We are all going to be called upon to recount these events from our different viewpoints. History will demand it of us. As will the American people. As commander in chief, I do wish to go on record as accepting responsibility for any flaws or shortcomings in the security arrangements at the Pentagon today. And I accept full responsibility for ordering Captain Kagan and his men into action."

From the side of the room, someone broke into applause. Others joined in until everyone had to.

But the President waved a hand to quell them. This wasn't the time. "Colonel Tobin, could you brief us, please, on what is about to transpire at the Pentagon. What Captain Kagan and his men are about to attempt."

Tobin replied at once. "Certainly, sir." But then he leaned forward to whisper something just to the President.

The President shook his head, discounting whatever objection Tobin might have raised, and spoke in a voice meant to be heard. "They all have clearance, Colonel. I guarantee you, a week from now, this will all be in the *New York Times*. The American people will not accept secrecy at a time like this, and neither will I."

Tobin accepted that pronouncement without comment. He sat back and folded his hands on the black tabletop before him. "Very well, sir. Ladies and gentlemen, Captain Franklin Kagan commands an on-site security team of ten Army Rangers. They are one of four teams who are assigned to Site J on a rotating basis."

"Why?" The question had come from a civilian at the side of the room. Hector didn't recognize him.

"For exactly this reason. To combat enemy occupation of the Pentagon reservation."

The civilian stepped forward from the side of the room. His White House pass had no name or photograph, just the word VISITOR. Though he didn't have a personalized pass as did Hector and the President's usual staff, Hector knew the man was not just another unprepared second-string official who had been called in without warning. The civilian was wearing a blue-nylon windbreaker, with the letters FEMA on the back of it. Hector decided he was most likely one of the emergency-response agency's dozens of department heads.

"Forgive me, but I'm confused," the FEMA staffer said. "Where, exactly, is Site J?"

At least I'm not the only one, Hector thought. And from the way Colonel Tobin immediately leaned back to the President to whisper to him again, Hector was very relieved that he had not been the one to ask the question.

But again the President told Tobin to continue.

"Very well," the colonel said. This time, Hector could detect a few cracks in Tobin's almost preternatural composure, though the colonel could no more argue with the President in public than he could stop breathing oxygen. "As you may know, one of the fundamental principles underlying the structure of this country's National Command Authority is the absolute ability to survive a sudden, overwhelming nuclear attack.

"To that end, key facilities of the NCA exist in multiple locations which are maintained, twenty-four hours a day, to respond instantly to a surprise attack on the United States, and to ensure unbroken continuity of government and command authority. This distributed, redundant network was, of course, much more extensive during the time of the Cold War, but it still exists today. Though the chance of a sudden nuclear attack from Russia is considered to be minimal, the system exists to protect the country in the event of a limited nuclear strike against Washington. A strike caused by a systems malfunction in the Russian command-and-control network, or by order of a rogue military leader, or in the event of limited terrorist use of weapons of mass destruction, or even catastrophic natural disaster.

"These alternate command centers exist in a variety of locations around the country. Some are a matter of public record, like the NORAD Combat Operations Center in

Cheyenne Mountain, or the National Airborne Operations Center, or the E-4B aircraft on constant standby at Offatt. The nature and location of others, as I'm sure you'll appreciate, remain among the government's most highly classified information."

The colonel paused a moment, and glanced at the President before continuing. "Site J is one of those most highly classified command facilities. It is located . . . at a considerable depth beneath the Pentagon reservation."

From the reaction of those in the room, Hector decided that he and the FEMA department head were not the only ones who hadn't known about Site J. He glanced back at Sinclair. "Ground Zero?" he asked, making a wild guess.

"That's what the people who work there call it."

With that, Hector decided General Flores was a pretty good liar. He had actually seemed insulted this morning when Hector had asked if such a facility really existed under the Pentagon.

"That's ridiculous," the FEMA staffer said. "Wouldn't the Russians have bombed the Pentagon a dozen times over at the start of any nuclear war?"

Hector quite liked the unknown federal civil servant, because he was asking all the questions Hector knew better than to ask.

The colonel folded his hands together, tightly, on the table in front of him, but he still answered the question. "Yes, sir. In the exchange of information we've had with the Russians since the end of the Cold War, we have learned that three twenty-five-megaton SS-18 warheads were targeted on the Pentagon, all scheduled to arrive within the first thirty minutes of a nuclear exchange. In fact, the Pentagon was designated as the first command-and-control facility to be hit."

"Then what good would a command center be *under* the Pentagon?"

The colonel was suddenly given the unexpected chance to change the, to him, unwelcome subject when the video communications link to Site J was abruptly reestablished, this time from their end.

A young Asian woman was on the screen. She wore a small earphone/microphone headset, and, instead of a black outfit like Kagan's, she was in a regular Army service uniform. From the head-on angle, Hector wasn't able to make out how many stripes she had on her shoulder.

"Mr. President, this is Sergeant Hanawa, Site J. I'll be the SOA link for Captain Kagan's operation. That is scheduled to commence in five minutes."

The President picked up the phone he had used before. "Thank you, Sergeant. We're standing by."

On the screen, the sergeant busied herself with setting controls that were out of sight of the video lens. It was impossible to tell exactly where she was in Site J. Directly behind her was a solid blue background. *Some kind of fabric screen,* Hector guessed. He took it as more evidence of security.

The persistent FEMA staffer broke the expectant silence. "Can you answer my question, Colonel? Why build a command center beneath a building that was guaranteed to receive an overwhelming attack?"

"Because it was the only logical place to build it, sir. First of all," the colonel said, still keeping an eye on the screen link to Site J, "as early as 1962, defense planners knew they could not evacuate key government facilities in the National Capital Region in the few minutes we'd have between detecting incoming Soviet missiles and their detonation on our soil. That's what the Cuban Missile Crisis taught us.

Given the then-current yields of Soviet warheads and even allowing for the minimal accuracy of their ICBMs and TU-4 long-range bombers, Washington's defense preparations were criminally inadequate in terms of preserving the continuity of the government in nuclear war."

Hector knew what the phrase "criminally inadequate" actually meant. The entire elaborate infrastructure of underground government bunkers and military joint command centers developed under Truman and Eisenhower had become obsolete, some installations useless before their construction had even been completed.

"And second of all," the colonel continued, his tone becoming more heated as he progressed, and his irritation grew, "even if we did have faith that some of our bunkers and shelters had gone undetected and wouldn't be targeted, if for some reason we *anticipated* a Soviet attack and ordered an evacuation of government officials, how do you think the Soviet Command would have interpreted *that* move? I'll tell you. They would have considered it as preparation for a U.S. first strike, which would, I guarantee you, have resulted in them launching their own preemptive strike.

"My God, man, every member of the National Command Authority in Washington was a pawn back then. They had to remain in position, in public, to avoid triggering a war. But once war began, they were unprotected. It was an intolerable situation, and it led to . . ." The colonel looked at his watch.

The President relented. "Thank you, Colonel. I can take it from here." He began with what Hector knew was one of his favorite layups, a brief historical note.

"The report on the need to establish a coordinated plan for civil defense and continuity of government in Washington," the President said, "was presented to President Kennedy just before his assassination. It led to a proposal called ECoG, I believe. Enhanced Continuity of Government. About a year after he took office, President Johnson signed the secret executive order authorizing funding for what the proposal called for: a two-stage Enhanced Continuity of Government Defense Initiative called PROJECT JERICHO. That's when they began planning the command site under the Pentagon. Site J for Jericho."

But then the President's history lesson was cut short by the reappearance of Sergeant Hanawa on the communications screen.

"Mr. President, we're on a two-minute countdown. The civilian personnel have gathered in the evacuation chamber." The lighting around the sergeant had changed intensity, Hector noticed, as if the facility she spoke from had gone to a low-light, nighttime mode. *Maybe to help Kagan and his men adapt their eyes to darkness,* he reasoned.

"Civilians? Where do they evacuate to?" someone asked.

"Exactly how far down are they?" another voice called out.

At a gesture from the President, Colonel Tobin attempted to answer everyone at once. "There are approximately one hundred and fifty civilian technicians and specialists assigned to Site J. SOP calls for them to evacuate the facility prior to any counterterrorist activity through a system of tunnels designated RUSH HOUR. That's another part of JERICHO. As soon as the civilians are out of harm's way, Captain Kagan will lead his men through the main connecting tunnels to a staging area in one of the lower levels of the Pentagon. From there his men will be deployed into the sectioned-off areas of the Building proper."

"Then what?" The question again came from the FEMA department head. "They just shoot everybody they see? Terrorists *and* hostages?"

Colonel Tobin clearly had no patience left for his unfamiliar questioner. "Sir, those Rangers run this exercise every two years on site. They practice it every quarter at their training facilities. The Pentagon is now under ThreatCon Echo. That is the sixth of seven threat conditions and exists when a military facility has been captured by an enemy force. Trust me, sir, the Pentagon has been reconfigured for what Kagan and his team will do next. They will have complete control of all power and communications distribution to the segmented sections. They have access to a spectrum of non-lethal weaponry, including sonic disruptors, immobilizing gases, and antimovement chemicals. These weapons will neutralize the terrorists but will not harm hostages."

"One minute," Sergeant Hanawa announced on screen.

There was a knock on the main door of the Situation Room; then it opened to show two uniformed Secret Service guards and white-haired Anthony Granville, an assistant to the President's chief of staff, recognizable at fifty feet because of the elaborately waxed handlebar mustache he affected. Hector was surprised to see the President's personal secretary behind Granville, talking to someone Hector could not see. Mrs. Petty's improbably red hair was unmistakable.

But the President waved Granville away. "Not now," he said.

Granville reluctantly allowed the Secret Service guards to close the door on him. No one argued with the President when others were present.

"Captain Kagan will deploy in thirty seconds," Sergeant Hanawa's businesslike voice stated. From the direction the sergeant was looking, Hector imagined she was facing a console containing additional video screens showing various areas of Site J.

That's when they heard the first screams.

Hanawa responded instantly, hands working quickly on unseen controls.

"Sergeant . . . ?" the President said.

Other crackling sounds came from the room speakers now. To Hector, they sounded like static.

"Sergeant, report!" Colonel Tobin demanded.

Hanawa did not look up from her controls. She spoke rapidly, but with no hint of panic. "They've broken in—"

And in that next instant, the blue screen behind the sergeant flew at her as the speakers rumbled and her black hair bounced in the air around her head and she slammed forward toward the camera lens, then disappeared from sight.

The video signal smeared into flashing dots of color, then snapped back into focus. The new image revealed more of the station's background. Tatters of blue cloth, which apparently had been intended to block any visual image of the rest of Site J behind Sergeant Hanawa, now swung slowly from an overhead rod. Beyond them, a red-painted metal railing, then an open expanse that gave view to part of a level at least one story below the sergeant's station. Directly across from Hanawa's station was a walkway, again bounded by a red-metal railing. The camera angle made Hector think of the view looking into the multi-floor atrium of a modern office building. Except that on the first-level floor, he could see the unmoving silhouette of a sprawled body, and the constant passage of dark figures running with guns.

Colonel Tobin worked at high speed at the communications controls on the tabletop between the President and himself. As he did so, other secondary display screens at the end of the room flickered with new USASC shields. But whatever attempts the colonel was making to establish a new line of communications, they weren't having any success.

The image from the fixed camera in Site J flashed with multiple bursts of light, as if fireworks were going off inside the huge room. The static from the speakers became a constant drone.

Then a new image on the Site J screen captured everyone's attention, and the President stood and gestured for silence in the Situation Room.

A figure like Kagan, all in black and wearing a backpack, and a belt and harness covered with equipment pouches, was approaching the camera. But unlike Kagan, he also carried a small submachine gun. Just like the ones Hector remembered seeing on the Pentagon terrorists. And the figure was masked. His black head covering left only a narrow slit open across his eyes.

The terrorist stopped by Sergeant Hanawa's console, then looked down into the camera. Reception from the speakers cleared then, and Hector could no longer see dark figures running in the background. Barely thirty seconds had passed since the blue-fabric screen had been destroyed and Sergeant Hanawa had violently disappeared from view.

The masked figure in black pulled an object the size and shape of a hockey puck from one of the pouches on his chest, then attached it to the mouthpiece of the telephone handset he picked up from somewhere off camera. When he spoke, he had the same rasping, mechanical tone as the self-proclaimed Sons of Liberty gunmen on CNN.

Hector could think of only one reason why the terrorists were going to such trouble to disguise their voices. They had to be worried that someone would recognize them. Which, to Hector, implied that whoever the terrorists were, they were known to those they were attacking.

"To whom am I speaking?" the figure asked.

Colonel Tobin took the handset from the President before the President could answer. "This is Colonel Tobin, United States Continental Defense Command. Who the hell are you?"

"General Brower is the CINC of CONDEFCOM," the figure said. *"Where is he?"*

"You're talking to me," Tobin snapped. "Take it or leave it."

The masked figure in black braced the handset between his shoulder and the side of his head, the familiar, innocuous action somehow appalling in a ruthless killer. Then the figure pushed back the edge of his black sleeve to check the watch he wore.

"Colonel Tobin, inform the President that he has twenty-one minutes left to go on air and resign, before we begin killing hostages."

Then the masked figure reached out to the console before him and the picture winked out, leaving another USASC shield in its place.

Tobin slowly replaced the handset on the communications console.

"Mr. President," the colonel said, "Site J is in enemy hands."

Like a man in a dream, the President said, ". . . What do we do now . . . ?"

Like every other person in the room, Hector waited for the answer, hoping someone else would have it.

ELEVEN

E RING, RIVER WEDGE

Amy flexed her hands. They felt steady, betraying not the slightest visible sign of motion.

She thought again of seeing the enemy in the uniforms of her murdered company, of being forced to surrender her weapon, of being bound, pawed, kicked, and clubbed . . . all of it.

Once again she grabbed the gun, fired at the enemy, saw them fall because of *her*. Once again she felt the easy resistance of the enemy's flesh as she drew the blade of her Leatherman under his jaw.

The last moment, when the Russian commander had dared raise her weapon again, in defiance of her defeat. When, without thinking, Amy had snapped her Leatherman into a throwing X, just as her father had taught her, and had *willed* it into the enemy's throat. With no conscious recollection of having taken time to aim.

Then Tom Chase said, "Almost got it," and she was back

with him, in a small conference room, decorated with framed front pages of newspapers from the First Gulf War. The room was close to the turn in the ground-level corridor where they had found the blast door and the hostages and the Russians. Chase had used his proxcard to seal the corridor before he, Amy, and the five civilian hostages they had untied and ungagged pulled the three slain Russians into an office and locked them inside. If more of the enemy came looking for their comrades, they would find the blood in the E Ring hallway. But without the bodies, it would be impossible to know what had happened. Or so Amy knew Chase hoped.

Once untied, the five hostages did as they were told. Two of them, the oldest man and the thin woman in the flowered dress, were married, Polish, and spoke only halting English. The other three hostages, all men, in their early to late forties, were Americans. One of them described to her, incredulously, how he had been standing right beside Secretary of Defense Nicholas Guilbert when someone dressed as a midshipman had stepped up to the Secretary and shot him in the chest at point-blank range. Some of the assassin's bullets had ricocheted off the wall behind, piercing the man's arm. The other two men had avoided even looking at Amy, preferring to address any questions to Chase. Their attitude had made it easier for her to command their attention when she'd needed it.

Amy had immediately tended to some crude first aid to clean up the hostages' minor scrapes, mostly using strips of cloth from the upholstered chair-seats as bandages. Only the man with the bullet creases on his arm was in need of serious medical attention, but he could probably hold out for a few days before infection became a real worry. Her tooth was another matter. However, trial and error quickly told her that as long as she didn't move her jaw too much, the pain retreated to a dismal nuisance, not a dangerous distraction. Eventually she'd find aspirin somewhere in the Pentagon, even if she had to search every drawer in every office they passed.

Next, Amy had turned her attention to the new equipment they had collected as the spoils of war: three H&K submachine guns, five full clips of 9mm ammunition, one flash-bang grenade, and, most important as far as Chase was concerned, the Russian commander's miniature radio, although it was broken.

Chase was working on that radio now, using the Swiss Army knife that Amy had mocked. He hadn't objected to what she'd accomplished with her Leatherman, though. As far as she could tell, after what had gone down in the corridor, Chase seemed a bit wary of her, too. And though she didn't dwell on the feeling of power that gave her, she knew she didn't object to the feeling, either. Power was precisely what she would need to complete her mission.

And her mission, now, was simple. She had killed four of the terrorists. That left thirty-six to go.

"Almost . . ." Chase said.

Amy sat at one end of the conference table, taking rounds from the partially used H&K clips to make up a sixth full one. She ended with five cartridges left over and put them into the almost exhausted backup clip for her Beretta. All the weapons used standard 9mm rounds, and as she compared the cartridges from her Beretta with those from the H&Ks, she realized why she had thought the Beretta had been silenced. The rounds were subsonic. They carried a partial load of powder intended to reduce the sound they made, and to keep them from penetrating walls in close-quarters firefights. Even more professional was the enemy's differentiation of their ammo for the different stages of their takeover plan.

"Got it," Chase announced. Before him, the Russian commander's radio was now split in two, and Amy saw that he had managed to extract an inch-square circuit board from the miniaturized device. He was holding the tiny component with minute tweezers and examining it with the extremely small magnifying glass he had folded out from his knife. Amy saw threadlike wires stretching from the circuit board to the rest of the radio on the conference table.

She got up to take a closer look. Radios were not her strong point. She preferred handling mechanical pieces, to see how they actually fit together. Just picturing how they worked wasn't the same for her.

Amy reminded herself not to say anything about Chase's beloved knife. She had put away her own Swiss Army knife about the same time she gave up playing with dolls. The beginner's blade had been good for deconstructing toys to figure out how they worked, but that was about it. Her Leatherman was folded up and back in the belt sheath she wore in the small of her back. She'd rather trust her life to that than to something with a red plastic handle.

"If it doesn't work, what good is it?" she asked.

"I've got the manufacturer and frequency," Chase said.

Amy didn't understand the significance.

"If we can get the frequency to the people outside, they can listen in to everything these guys are saying to each other."

"You don't think our side's already scanning every frequency?"

"Of course they are, but it won't be doing them much good. This is a single-sideband transmitter. Low power, very directional. The NSA would have to ring the Building with ten-meter dishes to pick up even half of what's carried on this."

"Then what good will knowing the frequency do?"

"Tells our guys where to concentrate their efforts. And once they get people in here, as long as the Russians leave their radios switched on, our side will have detectors that can track a radio's location to within a couple of feet, even if the Russians don't transmit."

"One problem, genius. If the radio's broken, how are we going to tell our guys what frequency to listen to?"

Chase looked past her at the hostages clustered on the beige, slipcovered couch up against the far wall. They weren't speaking to each other, only watching their rescuers.

"Just before you tried to kill me, I think I got a message out."

"What? How?" Chase hadn't even mentioned this action until now. And it was an important one.

"In ten words or less—the Pentagon's internal phone messaging system is still working. Better yet, it seems to have an automatic way of calling outside the Building that wasn't affected by the pulse."

"How much time if it works?"

Chase shrugged. "No way to know."

Amy didn't want to leave this capability solely in Chase's hands. A civilian might not be able to exploit it properly. "Who'd you send the message to? I know the numbers for Naval command posts, for the Academy, even for—"

"It's a dedicated Pentagon system. It only works for members of the Joint Staff."

"You called someone on the Joint Staff?"

Chase glanced over at the hostages again. "That's who I sent a message to."

Amy dropped her voice. "You don't trust the hostages?"

"I don't know them."

Amy could see where Chase was going. He hadn't bothered to volunteer who he'd sent the message to. Not that she hadn't been ready to commandeer his message capability. "And you don't trust me?"

"I don't trust the military. Don't take it personally."

Amy was unsettled to discover that while hand-to-hand combat in a life-and-death situation hadn't elevated her blood pressure, a five-minute conversation with Tom Chase could enrage her. *What is it about this guy?*

"How can I not take it personally?" she demanded.

Chase looked her in the eyes and, for the moment at least, there was no trace of the smart aleck in him. "Nuke, I'm sorry to tell you, but as an institution, the modern military is an oxymoron. There's really no excuse anymore for armed conflict."

"Excuse me?"

"Armies, navies, air forces . . . I mean, even you have to admit they're dinosaurs in the information age."

Amy opened her mouth to protest but the movement awoke her cracked tooth. She pressed her hand to her jaw.

Chase took advantage of her inability to speak. "Look, I'm not saying the forces should pack up and go home. I know we can't disarm unilaterally."

" . . . *fuggin rye* . . ." Amy managed to gasp.

"But in a civilized world—"

"Civilized?!"

"—there is no room for . . . for bayonet charges and carpet bombing and napalm and—"

"Tell that to the other guys!" she exclaimed. Then she had to grip her jaw again.

Tom held up his hands in surrender. "Maybe this isn't a good time."

All the muscles on the entire right side of Amy's face tightened as the red-hot needle of pain drilled into her tooth. She felt hot tears sting her eyes. *No!* she ordered herself. The one thing no female mid could ever do at the Academy was cry. Not if she broke her leg, not if she got her first choice of duty assignment, not even if her father died. Amy would be damned to hell before she'd cry now just because of a lousy cracked tooth.

But then, before she knew what had happened, Chase had an arm around her and was patting her back, telling her everything was going to be okay.

And for just one moment, one terrible second of escape, Amy was in her father's arms again, laughing into that much-too-big helmet, safe and secure as the Harley rolled out, knowing that nothing bad could ever happen to her, not ever, as long as she was in those arms.

That was when she just lost it.

And for the first time in four years, Midshipman Amy Bethune gave up all self-control. And finally wept for the loss of her father.

Tom Chase didn't let go.

TWELVE

SITUATION ROOM, THE WHITE HOUSE

"Contact them, Colonel," the President said. "I don't care if you have to flash mirrors at them in the Courtyard, you contact them and you buy us more time!"

Tobin said "Yes, sir!" on his way out the main door.

The President looked around the room like a drowning man.

"Does *anyone* in here have the ETA for General Brower?"

Before the door closed behind Tobin, Anthony Granville poked his head through again. "Mr. President, please, there's someone here you have to see."

The President grimaced as if he were a teenager told to clean up his room for the thousandth time. Hector sat up. This he could handle. He often screened people who wanted to meet with the President or key members of his staff.

"Sir," Hector said as he grabbed for his metal crutch, "why don't I check it out for you?"

The President nodded, then went back to a heated discussion he had just started with Milton Meyer of the NSA.

As Hector pushed back against his chair, he was suddenly aware of two things. The first was that, whatever shot the medic on the rescue helicopter had given him, it was wearing off. His foot was beginning to remind him, strongly, it was not pleased with his treatment of it today. The second realization was much pleasanter. Sinclair was beside him, one surprisingly strong hand under his arm, bracing him as she put his crutch into position.

"There you go," she said as Hector found his balance, and towered over the major. He hadn't realized how short she was. How could anyone so small have endured military training? Then he remembered the strength of her arm as she'd supported him.

"Thanks," Hector said. "I . . . guess I'll see you . . . ?" He stopped there, wondering how he could have said something so inane at the height of this crisis.

"I think we're all here for the duration," the major replied, as if what he said was entirely appropriate and welcome. "Good luck with . . . whatever."

Hector hobbled toward the door, lifting his injured foot well off the floor. As he passed the head of the conference table, he overheard an Air Force colonel calmly explaining the challenges of dropping immobilizing gas bombs on a target like the Pentagon—a strategy that Meyer of the NSA strongly objected to—and then Hector was out the door.

He waved at the assistant chief of staff who was waiting for him, along with the President's personal secretary. "Hey, Anthony, Mrs. Petty. You've got to make do with me for now."

Granville's sigh was at least two seconds longer than any sigh should take, but he took Hector firmly by the arm and said, "Oh, very well. But I know *he'll* regret not getting on to this at once."

Hector grimaced as Granville pulled him along more quickly than he could manage the crutch. He actually had to hop as he told Granville to slow down.

After a disapproving look at Hector's bandaged and braced foot, Granville veered briskly toward the small elevator that ran up to the West Wing's ground floor.

"So what've you got?" Hector asked as the narrow door closed and the hydraulic elevator began to rise.

"You'll see," Granville said cryptically.

Mrs. Petty added, "And perhaps it's just as well you're looking into it first." Hector pretended he didn't notice the sharp look of mutual suspicion that Granville and Mrs. Petty exchanged. "Mr. President is certainly busy enough without—"

"Here we are," Granville announced as the elevator hummed to a stop.

He turned left as he exited ahead of Hector, toward the executive offices.

"Down there?" Hector asked.

"Everywhere else has people who shouldn't even be here. We thought it best to keep this under wraps."

"Mr. Granville thought it best," Mrs. Petty corrected as she looked at Hector with concern. "And may I say it was a splendid thing you did, Mr. MacGregor, saving the President's life as you did."

"I had a lot of help. And the President saved my life, too."

The President's secretary beamed, the color of her overly pink cheeks deepening into little balls of color that almost matched her red hair. "Isn't that just what you'd expect?"

"He's a great man," Hector said in a kindly way to the Man's number-one fan. Then to Granville he said, "We're going to the Oval Office?"

"The only one not being used right now." Granville offered no other explanation.

The door to the Oval Office was closed, and Hector felt the weight of the almost physical force denying all entrance when the President wasn't there. But the on-duty uniformed Secret Service guard readily opened the door as Granville and Mrs. Petty ushered Hector inside.

Well, this should be interesting, Hector thought. He'd spent two years in the White House and had been in the Oval Office enough times that he'd stopped counting the visits. But that still didn't lessen the experience of actually setting foot on its rich blue carpet, especially this time, when he was here without the President and the hyperactivity that always surrounded the Chief Executive.

Like the distinctive shape of the Pentagon, the shape of this room with its colors and associations was burned into his consciousness. This room was familiar not only to him, but to millions of Americans, from its constant exposure in newscasts and newspapers, magazines and movies, and on television. The Presidential setting had become part of the collective consciousness of the country, and of the world.

And the first thing that was wrong with it today, other than the President's absence, was the fact that House Speaker Marlens was seated on the red-and-white-striped sofa to the left of the door. A man who looked very much like the prototypical, taciturn Secret Service agent, complete with slightly rumpled gray suit, was standing to one side of the Speaker, his hands behind his back.

But the biggest thing wrong with the Oval Office today

was the third visitor who sat on the opposite, red-striped sofa, banging the heels of his black hi-tops against its base, noisily swigging from a can of Coca-Cola. He was wearing black surf shorts, a hugely oversize Orioles T-shirt, and a White House pass around his skinny little neck.

It was a kid.

Hector looked at Granville. Granville nodded.

The man in the gray suit directed his impatience at Hector. "Where's the President?"

And since it wasn't Hector's job to alienate the President's guests, he immediately limped over to the man and stuck out his hand. "Hector MacGregor. The President's caught up in a security briefing and asked me to be his front man." Only then did Hector nod his head to acknowledge Speaker Marlens, whom nearly everyone in Washington knew they could safely ignore.

Slightly mollified, the man reached into his jacket and with one fluid motion extracted a black badge case, flipped it open for a two-count, then returned it to his jacket. "Captain Lassiter, DIA. Defense Intelligence Agency." He added the definition as if someone as junior as Hector might be unfamiliar with the institution.

People who expected the President and got Hector instead were most often disappointed, sometimes insulted. Hector had dealt with it before and he could deal with it now.

He turned to the boy on the opposite sofa. Eight, maybe nine, Hector guessed. He offered his hand just the same. "Hi, I'm Hector. Who are you?"

The boy held his Coke can closer to his chest, eyeing Hector's scorched and dirty shirt, and his crutch and bandaged foot. "What happened to you?"

"I fell out of a helicopter."

"While it was flying?!"

"Only Superman can do that. My helicopter was on the ground. Are you going to tell me your name?"

The boy looked over at Captain Lassiter. So did Hector when the silence stretched out.

"Tyler Chase, eight years old."

"Actually," Granville added, "he's Brigadier General Chase, the youngest appointee to the Joint Staff in history."

"Okay," Hector said, looking at the four adults in the room, "somebody better start at the beginning."

"The boy's father is in the Pentagon."

Lassiter's blunt statement hit Hector with the force of a slap.

The captain handed Hector a small, orange plastic box. "As near as anyone can tell, the . . . incident . . . at the Pentagon began at eleven hundred hours. At eleven-fifty hours, the boy received this message."

The orange box was a pager with a transparent case. Lassiter reached over and pressed a switch at its side. Hector read the narrow, single-line display: 7 0 3 - 5 0 5.

Hector looked at Lassiter. "Part of a phone number?"

"It's from my Dad," Tyler Chase suddenly said, in a way that made Hector think the kid had had to say it a number of times this morning. "It's an SOS."

"SOS?" Hector said, feeling thick and wishing someone would hurry this up and enlighten him. At least, he'd been right to spare the President this unusual interrogation.

"Yeah!" Tyler rocked himself up and out of the sofa opposite Lassiter, stopped, looked around with the Coke can in his hand, then moved as if to balance it on the sofa cushion. Before the can could make contact with the cushion,

Granville swept it out of Tyler's hand. Unperturbed, Tyler walked up to Hector and reached up for the pager, twisting it upside-down so the message now read 5O5-EOL.

"See?" the boy said as if it were the most obvious fact in the world. "S. O. S. That's five-oh-five upside down. It's a special code my dad made up."

"What about the . . . eol?" Hector asked.

"I dunno," Tyler said. "But that's what Uncle Milo sent to my dad this morning on his pager."

Before Hector could get the first word of his next question out, Lassiter answered it for him.

"General Milo Vanovich. Do you know him?"

"Only that the President was scheduled to have a briefing with the general this afternoon."

Hector watched Lassiter process that information like a machine. "All right. Then all you need to know is that the general is responsible for some advanced technology projects. Tom Chase—this boy's father—is a civilian consultant on some of those projects. This morning, I, and another DIA agent, were dispatched by General Vanovich to contact Mr. Chase. My partner drove Chase to the Pentagon. I was assigned to . . ." He looked at the boy.

"Dad said he's my baby-sitter," Tyler announced, holding his hands out in a karate pose. "I'm a yellow belt." Then he tugged Hector's left hand from his crutch. "Here . . . wanna shake?"

"Tyler—that's not a good idea." Lassiter snapped the words out like an order. "He's been wounded."

"Oh, yeah," Tyler said. Still, he shook Hector's hand formally with both hands, then stepped back.

"Captain Lassiter," Hector said, now fairly certain he knew the point of this meeting, "I realize we might be intruding on classified matters here, but does this boy's father work in communications?"

"In a way."

"So, I take it that it's significant that, forty minutes after all open lines of communication to the Pentagon were shut down, Mr. Chase somehow managed to get this message out to his son?"

"I'd say that's very significant."

"Do we know where Mr. Chase was in the Pentagon?"

"Is that important?" Lassiter asked.

"Is my dad okay?" Tyler asked.

"I'm sure he is," Hector said. "He sent you that message, didn't he?"

Tyler stared at him in eight-year-old indignation. "It's an *SOS!* He needs my help."

"And we're going to make sure he gets it."

"When?"

"Right away, Tyler."

"Can I see him?"

"As soon as we help him get out of the Pentagon."

"When?"

"Soon, Tyler."

"My mom's coming to pick me up at eight, you know."

"Everything's going to be fine. Now just let me talk to Captain Lassiter for a minute."

Tyler folded his arms so he could check his watch.

Fancy watch for an eight-year-old, Hector thought. He paused. *A Breitling?* He looked at his own wrist.

The boy grinned broadly as he slipped the $8,000 watch off his narrow wrist and placed it in Hector's outstretched hand.

Mrs. Petty clapped her hands as Tyler Chase took a bow, saying, "Thank you, ladies and gentlemen."

I'm never having any kids ever, Hector thought. "Look, about where Mr. Chase is, we've got full communications with the Pentagon ops centers, so if he's down there, it's no big deal. They're cut off and can't really tell us what's going on in the rest of the Building."

But the captain was not convinced. "The general's office is on the second floor of the River Entrance Side. If Chase had made it down to the ops centers, they'd have let you know he was safe. He wouldn't have had to pull this stunt with the Joint Staff messaging system."

"And how is this a stunt?"

"Chase is pretty smart. Somehow, he got the computer to think the boy had just been assigned to the Joint Staff, then he set up a message account, and sent him the SOS message."

"Can we use that system in reverse?"

"We might not have to. He has—"

"That's a minute," Tyler announced. "Is my dad in trouble again?"

Hector turned to the boy. "Tyler, what does your dad do for General Vanovich?"

Tyler pressed his lips together tightly and shook his head from side to side. He looked at Lassiter.

So did Hector. He needed something to be able to tell the President. Maybe the kid's father was some kind of under-cover specialist. The President would love to hear he had a man inside who could do some damage to the terrorists.

Lassiter shrugged. "A consultant. That's all I know."

"That could cover a lot of ground," Hector said. Maybe it was just a matter of asking the right question. "Tyler, do you *know* what your father does for General Vanovich?"

This time, Tyler nodded his head up and down, emphatically.

"Then why won't you tell me?"

Tyler looked over again at Lassiter.

"Captain, could you please leave us?"

"He's my responsibility."

"He's in the Oval Office."

Lassiter conceded the point and left the room. Now it was just Hector, Granville, Mrs. Petty, and Speaker Marlens, all in thrall to an eight-year-old boy.

"Okay, Tyler, it's just us here now. What does your dad do?"

Tyler leaned forward and whispered. "If I tell you . . . the captain will kill me."

Hector felt the beginnings of a terrible tension headache. "Who told you that?"

"My dad."

"Tyler, you know how important the President is, right?"

Tyler nodded.

"And you know how everybody has to do what he says, right?"

Tyler nodded. "Except Congress and the do-nothing Senate. That's what my dad says."

Behind him, Granville stifled a laugh, but Hector pressed on. "Tyler, the President is my boss and I will tell him to tell—to *order*—Captain Lassiter not to kill you. I will even get you a lifetime Presidential Pardon so nothing bad can ever happen to you because of anything you tell me today. Okay?"

Tyler narrowed his eyes. "Even if I don't do my homework?"

"You will never have to do homework again. The President will make it a law. Now will you tell me what your father does?"

Tyler shrugged. "He fixes things."

"What kind of things?"

Tyler sucked in his lower lip, looked toward the closed door.

"Captain Lassiter is afraid of the President. What sort of things does your father fix?"

"The space station."

"Your dad's an astronaut?"

Tyler nodded.

"And he's worked on the space station?"

Tyler nodded again.

Hector's spirits soared. There was an astronaut in the Pentagon. A trained specialist experienced in high-risk situations. Who had already worked out some ingenious way to communicate with the outside world, like some kind of James Bond astronaut. That could mean the kid's father was in the military. Even better.

"Granville," Hector said quickly, "go get the President to come up here. And bring . . . bring some communications people, see if Colonel Tobin can spare anyone, a Special Ops guy. Tell them we've got a secret weapon behind the lines. Take Speaker Marlens with you."

As soon as they'd gone, leaving only himself, Mrs. Petty, and Tyler Chase, Hector smiled down at the boy, the business with the watch all forgotten.

Mrs. Petty got up and walked over behind the President's desk and slipped open one of the drawers. Hector heard a rustling sound, then saw the President's secretary wave a white-fudge Oreo invitingly at Tyler. "So, dear, when was the last time your father flew into space?"

Tyler bounced off the sofa and crossed the room to claim the cookie. "He doesn't go on the shuttles."

"You mean he flies with the Air Force, then, right?" Hector asked.

Tyler shook his head.

Hector rubbed the back of his neck.

"What Mr. MacGregor means, dear, is then how does your father get up to the space station?"

"He beams up." Tyler popped the whole cookie into his mouth.

Hector felt the migraine coming down the track like an approaching freight train. "Beams? Like in, Beam me up, Scotty?"

Tyler nodded, mouth full.

"Fuck me," Hector said.

"Mr. *MacGregor!*" Mrs. Petty was actually shaking a finger at him.

Tyler's mouth opened in a huge grin revealing a glutinous mass of half-masticated cookie. "You said the f-word! That costs two quarters!"

Hector knew exactly what had happened. "Kid, your father was joking. What he told you isn't true."

"My dad's not a liar! He does so fix things! Like the space station . . . and the phones . . . and the television station . . . and the—" Tyler almost choked on the rest of his cookie, then recovered as Mrs. Petty helpfully thumped his back.

Hector opened his mouth to tell Mrs. Petty to rush down and head off the President.

But it was already too late.

The door to the Oval Office was swinging open and the President was in the doorway, not looking pleased. Right behind him were Colonel Tobin and Major Margaret Sinclair.

". . . and the photocopiers . . . and the—" Tyler's listing cut off abruptly as he looked where Hector and Mrs. Petty were looking.

"Tyler?" Major Sinclair said.

Tyler hurled himself at the major, and the greeting he shouted, to Hector's utter shock and confusion, was *"Mom!"*

THIRTEEN

SITE J

"How do you know about Site J?" Vanovich demanded shakily.

As the enormous, armored freight elevator descended, Ranger regarded Vanovich, unaffected by his prisoner's outrage. The general was merely an intelligence asset. He had belonged to the enemy. Now he belonged to Ranger. And Ranger owed him nothing. Despite the uniform the old man wore, he was no warrior. He wasn't worthy of the name.

"Answer me, you bastard."

Ranger's three commandos immediately looked at their leader, unable, he knew, to tolerate him being addressed in that manner. But like good soldiers, they waited for orders.

There would be none. Vanovich was entitled to the pathetic anger of defeat, even though the insults to the old man's honor had only begun.

"Site J," Ranger began, deciding to answer part of the general's question, if only to show him that he had no secrets left worth protecting, and that further resistance would accomplish nothing. "It derives its name from PROJECT JERICHO. Construction began 1966. The project consisted of two separate components. The first—survival. The construction of deep shelters, code-named ATLANTIS. Intended to permit the evacuation of key personnel from selected buildings in the National Capital Region within minutes, by descent in elevators similar to this one.

Ranger smiled. "Of course, that survival depended upon the Soviets being considerate enough to attack on a weekday. During business hours."

"The second stage of JERICHO was escape." Ranger noted approvingly the high color that now stained the general's sunken cheeks. There was life in the old man still. He would last the few more hours he was needed. "The need for escape routes required the construction of interconnected tunnels linking the ATLANTIS facilities with underground rail-transport routes out of the region. The code name for the tunnels was RUSH HOUR."

Vanovich's complexion was approaching deep purple. Ranger interrupted the lesson. "General, I assure you, for years, the media reported on these identical types of facilities in Moscow. Exceptionally deep shelters for the leadership, vast underground transport routes for the rest of the population. There is no great breach of security here.

"Do you think it's a coincidence that the two cities most responsible for the Cold War both have such exceptional subway systems of unusual depth and extent? Both are far deeper and larger than they need be for ordinary mass transit. Any civil engineer could tell you their range and capacity is in no way justified by the populations they serve."

Ranger paused to make his point. *"But* . . . for civil defense and continuity of government, they are suddenly completely reasonable. And, in your case, what a convenient explanation all that subway construction provided for all the earth removed in the excavation of the ATLANTIS shelters. Not to mention Site J."

"This country's had traitors before," Vanovich said stiffly. "That's the only way you got this information."

The old man was still refusing to see what was so obvious. But Ranger knew he would soon understand. "General, I'm not here because you've been betrayed by one of your own. I'm here because not even the best of America's intelligence agencies could hide the obvious, and the logical. Did you truly expect the rest of us to believe you would do nothing to protect your leaders and your way of life in the event of nuclear holocaust?"

"Go to hell," the general snapped.

The elevator stopped and an arrival tone chimed.

"Three hundred twenty feet down," Ranger said. "Close enough."

The elevator door opened into a large chamber with curved, stainless-steel walls and harsh overhead lights. In the center of that chamber stood eight commandos, in black Nomex coveralls and balaclavas, training their weapons on the elevator's passengers—the four commandos in white and their prisoner in blue.

But no challenges or recognition codes were necessary.

As Ranger stepped off the elevator, the soldiers of Team One laid down their weapons, from submachine guns to pinpoint flamethrowers, and cheered their leader.

Disappointingly, General Vanovich limited his response to one word. "How?" he asked.

"American military SOP, General." Ranger decided it would do no harm to elaborate further, considering that Vanovich was one of the few who would appreciate the simple genius of the plan. "Before commencing any military operation, you always withdraw your civilians. The civilian exit from the Pentagon was through the Site J doors to the RUSH HOUR tunnels. When your people opened the doors, my soldiers were already there, waiting for them.

"The real elegance of the strategy, General, is that after months of study, we actually concluded that you were too good for us. There was no possible way we could force our way into this site. But then we realized, if we could give you a reason to open the doors for us. . . ." Ranger shrugged, the rest of his explanation unnecessary.

Then one figure in black marched up to Ranger, saluted, and pulled off his balaclava to reveal a helmet of short red bristle, virtually no line of demarcation between the hair on his face and his scalp. It was Kilo, commander of Team One.

"No casualties," he reported.

Ranger brightened with the unexpectedly good news. *"Ausgezeichnet!"* That result was beyond the planners' best estimates. "Did they not put up *any* fight?"

Kilo pulled on sections of his coveralls to display ragged bullet holes. His broad smile revealed large, brilliant white teeth. "Their fight was good. Our armor was better."

Ranger looked beyond Kilo and his men, to the open, round blast door that led to the heart of Site J—the command center known to its staff as Ground Zero. There was only one crucial question still to be asked. The answer would determine if all that had happened to this point had been worthwhile.

"Damage?"

Kilo's smile grew even wider. "None. We moved in so quickly, we were able to maintain full communications throughout the entire command network."

Ranger inhaled deeply, ignoring the strange plastic scent that filled the air here, concentrating only on the immediate sensations of being alive, and being victorious. The American military prided themselves on the redundancy and survivability of their command-and-control network. But their arrogance had blinded them to a key flaw. Believing their Site J to be impregnable, they could not conceive of its being penetrated, only destroyed. There were no scenarios for a Site J takeover, because capturing Site J was considered impossible. Yet Ranger had just done so.

Heightening, if possible, the moment of triumph, Kilo reached under his armored vest and withdrew a thick, transparent plastic envelope. Altogether, it was at least eight inches by ten inches, and three inches thick. Inside Ranger could see a tightly folded mass of stiff and yellowed parchment.

Ranger accepted the package as a king would accept his crown.

"All of them?" Ranger asked.

Kilo nodded.

Ranger placed the package securely under his arm, and with Kilo at his side, he crossed the entrance chamber and entered Ground Zero. With America's past in his possession, it was now time to take possession of America's future.

The command center itself was like some strange confluence of past and future. The pale blue walls, the red railings and exposed staircases, the surrounding rooms and offices whose angled windows overlooked the central atrium, these were all remnants of another time—architectural designs conceived in the naive, hopeful sixties to evoke a future that would never come.

The circular floor plan of the facility added to the sense of a vision of the future. But in this case, Ranger knew, the overall dimensions had been determined not by artistic principles, but by the digging methods used. The cavern in which Site J was built, more than three hundred feet below ground level, had been blasted out by explosives. The access shaft through which the twin freight elevators and emergency stairways now ran had been lined with reinforced concrete, becoming a pipe that could be pressurized to hold some of the seeping swamp water at bay. The concrete shell that formed that pipe, with walls up to four feet thick in places, had been extended and then expanded to line the water-filled cavity created by the blasting.

After a year of construction, some of which was carried out by Navy divers, the shaft and liner had been completed and the pumps had begun to drain the artificial cavern. Over the next three years, a steel dome had been built within it, resting not on solid foundations, but on more than two hundred and thirty pads of rubber, each eight inches thick, braced by steel springs. The wire forming the springs was eight inches in diameter. Engineering stress simulations of nuclear destruction raining down on the Pentagon three hundred feet overhead had suggested that, with two hundred and thirty springs, the personnel in the Site J steel dome wouldn't even feel the vibrations.

There were four levels to the underground command center, with elevator access to two: Level Two—where Ranger and Vanovich had arrived; and Level Four—the bottommost level, where the storage batteries, generators, air scrubbers, and water pumps operated. Level Three was the action floor, where Ground Zero's communications consoles and monitoring equipment were staffed round the clock. Level Two was the command floor. It consisted of a ring of offices overlooking the action floor below. On the side opposite the elevator-entrance chamber was the cafeteria/theater/chapel and food-preparation facilities. Level One held the barracks, a cramped warren of bunks, with a handful of private quarters for officers and government officials, along with backup power generators and food and water enough for three months.

All this information, though classified to such an extent that Ranger's informants had never been able to unearth a single written reference to Ground Zero's configuration, had been remarkably easy to assemble, merely by accessing those documents which were available. The engineers and architects who designed such facilities were proud of their work, and often made reference to classified projects, thinking they were obeying secrecy restrictions simply by being vague as to locations, dates, and components.

Ranger could understand why General Vanovich believed that Ranger's knowledge of Site J could only have come from a traitor within. It was true that each single article or collection of specifications or modified drawings gathered by Ranger's researchers had provided almost no useful information. However, in these days of computer-aided research, when hundreds of articles could be sifted and compared, the patterns that led to that hidden information had been simple to detect. Ranger doubted if the hypothetical Site J diagrams his planners had painstakingly created varied from the actual facility by more than a few feet or a handful of details.

Ranger descended the red metal stairs to the Level Three action floor, where four more of Kilo's black-garbed commandos kept watch over five of their captives. As planned, the remainder of Site J's 180 civilian and military personnel who had not been killed in the initial attack were being tied up in preparation for being transferred to the upper levels.

He walked across the action floor toward the main-control consoles and the five captives whom Kilo had specifically held back from the holding areas, at Ranger's request.

Ranger was pleased with the selection: three women, two men, all military, all young. Their hands tied behind their backs with plastic security strips. The five captives had been forced to stand in a line by a secondary control station. Its beige metal console was part of the original equipment which had been installed when Site J had first been activated in the early seventies—metal panels, sharp edges, curved television screens.

But Ranger's destination was the main console, a new one, dove-gray, cloaked in molded, round-cornered, plastic panels and flat computer displays, as if military designers had finally succumbed to the fanciful depictions Hollywood had presented as military reality for years.

Ranger headed for an empty chair before the center command station. The chair was comfortably padded, high-backed, and outfitted with chest straps to hold its occupant securely in position, in case the command center's vibration-dampening springs weren't as effective as its designers hoped. As his commandos led Vanovich toward him, Ranger placed the bulky plastic envelope on the top of the gray console, then turned the padded chair facing out and motioned to the general to take his seat.

"I don't know where you got your information, but I don't have any authority here," Vanovich warned. The general's statement indicated to Ranger, gratifyingly, that the old man was familiar with its purpose. It was time to proceed.

Ranger pressed a flat switch on the gray console and a small section of it popped up. He then unfolded the mechanism beneath, angling it so a black-rubber eyepiece now appeared above the main keyboard. "Look into the scanner, General. I'll trust the computer to tell us what authority you have."

Vanovich shook his head and pushed back against the commandos who held his arms.

In a way, Ranger thought, the old man's stubbornness now, so early in the process, offered the opportunity of presenting him with another valuable lesson, which would prevent resistance later, when timing was more critical.

"We both know how it goes from here, General," Ranger said. "I ask you to do something, you refuse. I threaten you, you ignore my threats. Eventually, you force me to take drastic action. I prefer not to waste your time or mine."

Ranger nodded once at the black-clad commandos guarding the five captives. Responding instantly, two of them forced the first captive, a young Asian woman, to come forward and stand in front of General Vanovich.

Ranger read her rank and her name badge. "Sergeant Hanawa, is it?"

The woman stared at him with wide-eyed hatred and defiance. There was dried blood under one nostril and a large bruise on her forehead.

"Sergeant, look at the general, please."

She refused.

How predictable, Ranger thought.

He held out his hand and one of his commandos placed a

Beretta in it. Without looking, Ranger expertly flicked off the safety. "You know where this is going, General."

Ranger could see Vanovich's mouth tremble. It wouldn't take long. It never did.

"I know you're not a violent man," Ranger said as he aimed the Beretta at the sergeant's temple. "I know your responsibilities are for surveillance and defensive measures only."

The woman tried to pull back, but the two commandos pushed her forward so that Ranger would have a clean shot.

"And I know you've never been in combat," Ranger continued. "Never seen what a soldier sees in every battle."

Vanovich's voice shook but his gaze was unwavering. "I won't betray my country."

"I'm not asking you to," Ranger said. "All I will ask you to do is to save this young woman's life." He extended a hand toward the other four captives. "And their lives. And the lives of all the others we have on the upper levels."

Now the sergeant's eyes were tightly closed, as if she wouldn't add to the pressure on Vanovich, wouldn't beg for her life.

But she didn't have to.

"Don't make me kill her," Ranger said. "Not when it is so simple for you to prevent this."

"For the love of . . ." Vanovich entreated. "I'm not the . . ."

"Yes . . . you are." Ranger fired the gun and half of Sergeant Hanawa's head exploded.

Scraps of bloody scalp and brain tissue sprayed across Vanovich and he shuddered and tried to twist away but the commandos at his side forced him to watch as the sergeant's body crumpled to the floor, at his feet.

"The next one," Ranger said. It rarely took more than two to ensure cooperation.

The general was hyperventilating now. If the commandos had not been supporting the old man, Ranger was certain he would have collapsed, too.

The two commandos selected a second woman, an Air Force captain this time, who was more difficult to subdue than the sergeant before her. But her resistance ended when a commando twisted her arm so sharply that it audibly cracked and she all but passed out.

The commandos positioned the semiconscious captain so that her body would fall on top of the sergeant's.

Ranger saw the general swallow several times, saw the sweat on his forehead, the look of anguish in his eyes. "These are your people, General. Under your command. How can you allow this to continue, when you could stop it so easily?"

Ranger placed the barrel of his gun against the captain's head.

"Yes," Vanovich said, " . . . no . . ."

Ranger paused, finger on the trigger, as he heard the words that he had been expecting.

"What do you want me to do?"

Ranger lowered his gun. It was time to give General Vanovich his orders.

FOURTEEN

SECOND FLOOR, C RING, CORRIDOR NINE

Amy Bethune's eyes were still swollen from crying. From time to time, Tom saw her swipe at her reddened nose with the sleeve of her gray sweatshirt. But as the midshipman moved along the corridor now, one H&K submachine gun in her hands, another strapped to her back, a pistol and a grenade shoved into the waistband of her jeans, it was as if she were someone who had never shed a tear in her life.

Tom followed behind her, holding the H&K she had insisted he take and that he had reluctantly accepted. He was unwilling to add to the impossible burden the kid herself carried, the one now borne by every soldier in the country.

He knew Bethune had not enrolled in the Naval Academy so someday she could kill vast numbers of people with nuclear missiles on the submarine she hoped to command. She had enrolled for the challenge, the promise of adventure, the thrill of working with cutting-edge technology.

Sometime, over just the last decade, the five branches of

the American military had decided they no longer wished to be seen as war-fighting organizations—their advertisements portrayed them, instead, as benign institutions where America's youth could learn job skills and still party on weekends. And Bethune had bought into that new perception of the armed forces.

Tom knew how and why that change in perception had come about. Americans didn't want their sons and daughters facing death in armed conflicts anymore. Most Americans didn't even want the country's enemies to face death. Confronted with what even Tom thought was a baffling, near-schizophrenic attitude, how could any young soldier cope when the inevitable happened and they were forced to confront the brutal realities of combat?

Tom had seen Bethune in action against the three Russian terrorists. She had been a perfect soldier—she had killed the enemy expertly and efficiently, saving her life and the lives of those who were depending on her.

Sixty years ago, he knew, she would have been a hero, and her nation's admiration would have made her feel like a hero.

But today, in a society that no longer wanted war, in a country that no longer wanted to believe that violence could ever be necessary, even the hostages she'd saved were not sure what to think of her. Tom's question was: Now that Bethune knew what she was capable of, how could she not feel like a killer?

To Tom, the solution was simple. Either return to the past, when warriors were a separate elevated caste, honored but living apart from ordinary citizens. Or, make it impossible for war to exist. Finding the second option more reasonable, Tom had chosen to help Vanovich and the Air Force, because he believed that the work they did together would eventually eliminate war.

Few shared his optimism. But just as the American people had grown tired of war, Tom, like the President, believed that the rest of the world was on the same path. And when that day came, kids like Tyler would never have to experience the conflict Midshipman Bethune was feeling now.

But Tom knew he couldn't share his convictions, beliefs, or optimism with Bethune. He wasn't her father; he hadn't even known her long enough to be her friend. Right now, he was just one more American who didn't want anyone else to die. And just as Tom couldn't think like a soldier, he knew from sad experience that no soldier could be expected to think as he did.

Bethune slowed as she came to the intersection of Corridor Nine and C Ring. The blast door that sealed this access point was on the other side of the intersection, permitting full entry to C Ring to the left and the right. She held up her hand and Tom stopped, waiting for her to scout ahead.

While Bethune checked ahead, Tom looked back over his shoulder to see if anyone was following them. Four of the hostages they had saved—*Bethune* had saved—had reacted with relief when she'd told them they were better off staying in the first-floor conference room and waiting for rescue. The fifth hostage, the man with the wounded arm, was the only one who had wanted to go with his rescuers. *More to the point,* Tom thought, *he wanted to go with the guns.*

But the more the wounded man had objected to staying behind, the more agitated Bethune had become, especially when he had demanded she at least leave a weapon with him. At that point she had raised her voice, then reacted even more angrily when her agitation disturbed her cracked tooth. The wounded man had immediately capitulated and made no further protest.

Tom didn't blame him. They had all seen what she could do.

"Clear," Bethune said.

Tom nodded, not surprised. Whatever the terrorists were after in the Pentagon, it had nothing to do with the River Side.

"So, can we open that door?" Bethune mumbled in a muffled voice, referring to the blast door that sealed off the continuation of Corridor Nine past C Ring. She was trying to talk without moving her jaw.

"No card reader," Tom said. "That door's part of the main defense perimeter. Can't touch it."

It was the fourth perimeter blast door they had encountered in their efforts to find an open stairway to the basement and the ops centers—and Bethune was still having trouble understanding the logic behind the perimeter's asymmetrical layout. "Why defend only one-fifth of the Building?" she now asked.

"Not even that much," Tom pointed out. "Looks like security only enclosed the most important parts of the River Side."

"Isn't the rest of the Building important?"

"A lot of the offices are strictly for paper-pushing. No one's going to spend good money protecting sixty years' worth of office-supply reqs. Not even the military."

Bethune looked down C Ring, toward Corridor Eight. "That intersection's not blocked off till the other side. Could be stairs down there."

"After you," Tom said.

Bethune took the lead again, staying close to the outer wall of the corridor, cautiously testing each door that she came to, to see if it was locked. As she had instructed, Tom stayed a few feet back on the corridor's inner wall, stopping when she stopped, checking the doors on his side, as she covered him. The unfamiliar feel of the H&K was still disturbing.

Halfway along the corridor, Tom reached for the doorknob of a room identified only by its number. The door had three additional locks, so he didn't expect the knob would move. But the instant he touched it, he stiffened in surprise.

At once, Bethune dropped to one knee, her H&K up to her shoulder as she sighted along its barrel.

"No!" Tom said, feeling almost euphoric. He held up his left hand. His watch. It was vibrating. "My pager!" Tyler had managed to convince that bullheaded Lassiter that his dad's SOS was real.

As Bethune ran across the hall to him, Tom looked at his watch face. The alert line beneath the time display read: 1 NEW PAGE. He pushed in the bottom-right button. There it was.

MSG RECD. SEND ALPHANUMERICS. WHAT IS YOUR STATUS? USCONDEFCOM.

Bethune was reading over his shoulder. *"That's* your contact on the Joint Staff?"

"Who?" Tom asked, trying to puzzle out the acronym.

Bethune's swollen jaw made her half-grin a silly lopsided leer. "U.S. Continental Defense Command. You know what that means?" she exclaimed, one hand to her jaw, the other pumping the submachine gun in the air. "Delta Force!"

Those two words were like a sobering punch in the gut

to Tom. "We need a phone." He scanned the C Ring corridor, up and down, ignoring her puzzled reaction to his lack of enthusiasm.

Bethune pointed back the way they had come. "That third door, on your side."

She was right. That door was unlocked. Beyond it, they had already checked out a large open-plan office filled with desks and low partitions. One of its walls had windows overlooking the interior-access road that circled the Pentagon between the C and B Rings. All the windows looking onto the narrow roadway were blastproof, not that he and Bethune would have wanted to break them to climb down. Above-ground the only passageway that connected with the access road led into the Courtyard. A place neither of them wished to enter.

They were back in the large, unlocked office within ten seconds. Tom chose the first desk in the open area, but Bethune made him pick another, twenty feet from the door and well away from the windows. "Just in case," she said.

The office appeared to be some sort of data-processing center, and every desk had a computer. Since none of the computers had secure connections, whatever was done here, Tom knew it had nothing to do with any classified military activity.

The second desk displayed several family snapshots under a clear plastic desk blotter. A collection of sentimental photos of cats and cat cartoons had been pinned to the bulletin board that was part of the desk's office partition. More important, the desk had a phone. As Tom expected, its external lines were out, but its internal lines were good.

"I can get through to JSAMS," he assured Bethune. "This'll be perfect."

While she kept watch, Tom dialed into the Joint Staff Automated Message Service, then accessed Brigadier General Tyler Chase's message center, and selected the page function. Since Tom's message had told him to send alphanumerics, it appeared that Tyler's elementary pager service had been switched over to a more sophisticated receiving system. *Most likely courtesy of the NSA*, Tom thought.

He selected Keypad Messaging from the JSAMS voice menu, then began the laborious process of typing his reply, selecting letters by their position on each number button. A as 2,1. B as 2,2. All the way to Y as 9,3—the third letter on the #9 button.

The message he chose to send was simple, but urgent. IM#SAFE##WITH#AMY#BETHUNE#MID#USNA##4# RUSSIAN#TRRSTS#DEAD##VANOVICH#TAKEN#FOR #REDLVL#CLEARANCE##RESCUE#HIM#ASAP##TC.

Then he pressed the * key to send the message and hung up.

Bethune sat down on the edge of the desk. "How long will it take?"

"If the system's still working, it should go out within a minute or two. If this Special Ops group is the hot stuff you think they are, they'll have it about a second later."

"Your Jay-sixer contact wasn't in CONDEFCOM?"

Tom shook his head. "I added a new name to the Joint Staff roster. It's not a very secure system if you know the password."

"Then who did you send the message to?"

"My eight-year-old."

"You put our lives in the hands of a kid?"

"Only person I knew with a pager. At least, with a number I know."

"And he knew enough to run it up through the chain of command? That's some smart kid."

"Yeah," Tom said, "he takes after his mother."

THE WHITE HOUSE, SITUATION ROOM

The hour had passed. It had not been uneventful.

Less than ten minutes after Site J had fallen, the President had ordered the security teams in the Pentagon's sealed operations centers to probe the enemy's position and recover what hostages they could without undue risk. The important goal of their mission was to provide information the White House could use to plan a counterattack in force.

The commanders of each of the five centers deep within the Pentagon had confirmed their orders. Six-man, ops-center security teams from the Army, Navy, Air Force, and Marines, backed by four additional Marine guards from the National Military Command Center, would go out on a reconnaissance patrol.

That confirmation of orders had been the last communications the White House had received from any station in the Pentagon.

All five operation centers had fallen at once, in silence, without explanation.

And now, in the midst of that confusion, CNN returned live to the Pentagon.

Without a word spoken, the gunman in the red bandana put his gun to the neck of General Jaime Alvarez Flores, Chairman of the Joint Chiefs of Staff, and pulled the trigger.

General Flores died instantly.

Sobbing broke out among several civilians in one corner

of the Situation Room. Major Margaret Sinclair remained rigidly silent, though she, as much as they, deplored the sudden, tragic, death.

Her *Shiloh* nightmares had faded since last December, especially since General Vanovich's decision to finally open up the NIA files on the disaster. But all the terrible memories had reawakened as she'd worked on the briefing that the general was to have given to the President today. She had hoped the preparation stage would serve as Vanovich's penance and the briefing as his confession. That today would bring peace to the general, and that the President would find a way to end the QUICKSILVER dilemma.

Instead, this morning had begun with the first news bulletin about the massacre at the National Archives. Followed almost immediately by the terrorist attack on the Pentagon. And then the emergency summons from the White House because she was the most senior NIA officer who was not dead, missing, or held hostage.

As this madness had unfolded, she had drawn increasing comfort from the fact that no matter what new evil had been released into this world, her child was at a ball game with his father, safe, and unknowing. He deserved that from his parents. All children did. The normalcy of children's lives was what she was fighting to secure, for their chance to grow up in a world that would not harm them.

But then she'd discovered Tyler in the Oval Office, without Tom, who was now somewhere in the Pentagon, where he had reached out for their son. And the comfort she'd drawn strength from had vanished in an instant, with the threat so close to her family.

Ten years ago, before Tom, before Tyler, she couldn't wait to join the Army and be all that she could be, and she'd been thrilled to be a part of Colonel Brower's special project.

That's why the army wants them young, she now knew. *When you'll risk everything, before you realize what you have to lose.*

Now that she knew exactly how much she had to lose and how she never, ever wanted to lose it, the Army, ironically, seemed one of the few power centers in the world that could protect her child, his father, and secure her child's future.

From nothing to lose, to everything, Margaret thought. And now, once again, she was watching others face losing all.

On a secondary screen at the end of the Situation Room, beside the crisp MAJIC surveillance image of the Pentagon, the gunman wiped the barrel of his pistol along the gold-embroidered epaulets on the uniform of Russian General Kerensky, the only one of the first three hostages tied to the chairs who was still alive. Then the gunman pulled the Command Authority phone handset from his pocket.

The sound modulator he wore beneath his red bandana was still working. His voice was flat and mechanical. The voice of a compassionless, killing machine.

"We have waited one hour. The President has not resigned. General Flores has paid the price for that cowardly act. Each minute that follows, another will pay. The Sons of Liberty are men of our word."

The green-fatigue-clad gunman waved his gun at the camera. The viewing angle changed as the camera shifted. There were quick, choppy flashes of light and shadow, then the camera angled down through a window, into the Courtyard of the Pentagon.

"Please, God," Lee Fogarty, the assistant Secretary of

Defense, said as the camera focused and the nature of the scene became apparent.

There were twenty NATO officers on their knees, each in the uniform of whichever branch of their country's military they served, all in a line along one of the Courtyard's six radial pathways. Terrorists in white naval uniforms stood behind them. One terrorist held a pistol pointed at the back of the head of the first officer in the line. The terrorist looked up at the camera, shielding his eyes from the sun with his hand.

From off the screen, the mechanical voice said, *"Fifty seconds."*

Margaret had had enough. Ten minutes ago, after she had made certain that Tyler was safe upstairs in Mrs. Petty's care, General Brower's helicopter had finally arrived on the South Lawn. Margaret, and half the people in this room, had then tried to convince the President that Brower should have a place at this table.

But the President had been unsure. Personally, Margaret understood his hesitation, to a point. America's Chief Executive was a man who governed by consensus, perhaps the only political strategy that had a hope of uniting such a fractured and fractious country. But, today, without the advisors he knew and trusted, and without any means of judging the competency of the advice with which his new advisors deluged him, consensus and the President were far apart.

Professionally, the President's refusal to acknowledge the limits of his ability under these conditions had caused Margaret to almost lose all patience with the man. This was the reason why countries had armies. So that when the time for deliberation had passed—or had been taken away—the ability to take swift and decisive action still remained.

That time had come. The President must accept his duty.

Margaret rose to her feet, knowing her action could cause her to be ejected from the room, just as FBI Director James Gibb had been cut out of the loop much earlier. But there was no more time for diplomacy. "Mr. President, end this."

"Delta Force will end this, Major," the President said.

That decision had been the last the President had been able to make, and it was a flawed one. If the President cut her from the team now, then at least she'd know she went down fighting.

"They're still an *hour* away, sir. Are you willing to see sixty people die on CNN? Are you willing to let the American people see sixty NATO personnel under *our* protection die like this? In the heart of our defense headquarters?"

"We have been over this, Major. Are you questioning my decision?"

Margaret heard Hector MacGregor shift uneasily in his chair beside her. She had a sudden, somehow inspiring memory of how she had felt when she had touched his hand as he told her of Christou's brave action.

"No, sir, I want *you* to question it! I want you to question everything these people have said to us because it's all been *lies!*"

"Thirty seconds."

The President's eyes flicked between her and the CNN screen.

"You must get General Brower in here, sir."

"He's the man those . . . creatures specifically asked to be put in charge! Do you *want* me to play into their hands?" Margaret knew she had just been handed the opportunity she'd been looking for. The President had specifically requested her opinion. Now she could finally assist him in making the informed decision the crisis required.

"Sir, ask yourself *why* they did that! We all know that General Brower has nothing to do with these people. They named him as a smokescreen. To make us afraid of him so that when he got here you'd shunt him off to the Cabinet Room instead of letting him do his job. Asking you to resign is the same kind of smokescreen. To divert us from what they're doing in Site J!"

But the President was still having difficulty focusing on her reasoning, as she was sure he would not, in a less time-driven crisis. "Site J is closed down, Major. Every other alternate command center in the country has been alerted. Site J's even been cut off from the defense net! Whatever they planned to do down there, it's too late."

"For God's sake, sir—" Margaret knew she had to disturb him enough that he would listen and, more than that, *understand.* "They know everything else about our capabilities, why do you not believe they knew we'd shut down Site J as soon as it was compromised? If they're after information, being shut down doesn't matter. Even without having authorized access codes, they can make physical connections to our computers there and download all the encrypted data they want. And if they get away, they'll have months to decrypt everything while we spend billions rewriting every line of defense software we have."

"Fifteen seconds."

"Mr. President, they aren't who they say they are! They're not after what they say they want! And if everything they've been telling us is a lie, then the truth must be that the one man they're afraid of is General Brower! Bring him in here—"

The gunman in the Courtyard fired and the first kneeling officer pitched forward, his body convulsing in post-mortem spasms. The gunman methodically pulled the trigger twice more until the officer's body lay still, then looked back up at the camera, shielding his eyes once again.

"We begin again," the voice stated. *"Sixty seconds."*

Margaret was ready to physically wrest the President's frozen attention away from the screen and the inexorable deaths. In twelve years in the Army, she'd seen too many good people die because politicians had hesitated at the precise moment it became time to use force.

She struck the surface of the conference table with her fist to startle him back to reality. "Mr. President, bring General Brower in here and let him do his job or you explain to the American people why it is that Elena Christou and six other people had to die so you could sit in here and do nothing!"

The only sound in the room was that of the President's chair shoving back as he stood up to face Margaret.

His face had drained of all color.

In the long silence that followed, Margaret knew that of the two choices the President could make right now, one of them would not be to eject her from the room. It would be to have her court-martialed.

But he chose the other option.

"Colonel Tobin, get General Brower in here."

Tobin rushed to the door. Then the President slowly sat down, not taking his eyes off Margaret.

Margaret sat down, too. As she did so, Hector MacGregor gave her a thumbs-up in full view of the President. It was the kind of reckless, career-destroying gesture Tom would have made.

"Fifteen seconds."

Then General Brower entered the room, Colonel Tobin behind him, and it was as if a second sun had entered a solar system, changing the orbits of all other planets. The general was six feet of solid muscle, completely bald, with a severely clipped moustache that gave him a perpetual scowl.

The general's dark eyes flashed over everyone in the room, and Margaret felt certain that simply by seeing her determined face and the President's tense regard of her, he'd correctly deduce the true situation.

"Have you been following this upstairs?" the President asked after a moment's hesitation.

"Yes, sir." The general's voice was a deeply resonant baritone. Margaret knew not even constant gunfire could drown out that voice.

"Can you stop it?"

"How far are you willing to go?"

The second uniformed hostage in the Courtyard fell forward. The gunman moved down the line.

"We begin again. Sixty seconds."

"Just stop it," the President said despairingly. "For the love of God, make it end."

Brower reacted so quickly that Margaret knew he had already worked out his strategy. At once he barked to Colonel Tobin, "Get a White House video crew in here ASAP! Go! Go! Go!"

Tobin ran from the room as Brower leaned past the President and picked up a handset from the Command Authority Terminal.

"Sons of Liberty, this is General Elias X. Brower."

"Fifty seconds."

"The killing of hostages is no longer necessary."

"Will the President resign?"

General Brower put his hand on the President's shoulder, and Margaret saw that hand flex. She couldn't tell if he were squeezing the President's shoulder for reassurance or to make sure the President couldn't move. "No. But he will be removed from office within the hour."

"Continue."

"First stop the countdown. If you don't like what I'm going to lay out for you, you can always start it up again. But if you do, I'm going to come in there and personally help you make the transition to the next plane of existence."

Margaret had never been briefed on this particular style of negotiation with hostage-takers, but on the screen, the gunman in the red bandana reappeared as the camera changed angles to look inside again.

"The countdown has been put on hold. For now. How will the President be removed?"

Brower took his hand from the President's shoulder and started to pace, keeping his eyes on the gunman on the screen at all times. Margaret knew he was watching the gunman's body language, assessing the effect of each word as he said it. The gunman might have a voice like a machine, but General Brower, Margaret thought, had a mind like the finest computer.

"Okay, son, you listen good. This is how it's going to play out." Margaret smiled for the first time since morning as she heard the general fall into the rapid cadence of a drill instructor. He was going to make these bastards march to his beat. "What you wanted to do, the way you said to do it, none of that would legally last a second once you were out of the Pentagon and on your way to wherever the hell you think you're going to. If you want this to stick, we gotta do it by the books. You following me?"

"Continue."

"Listen up. We're doing this under Article Twenty-Five,

Section Four of the Constitution of the Yew-nited States. The President's cowardice in dealing with the situation today is evidence of his inability to discharge the powers and the duties of his office. Do you concur?"

The gunman shifted his stance, his attention clearly riveted on the general. At that moment, Margaret became certain the gunman was window dressing, not the leader of the terrorist group. No one naive enough to believe the general's story could have gone this far.

"I . . . We concur."

"All right, then. This makes it legal. A written declaration of the President's inability is being signed by a majority of the principal officers of the executive departments and will be transmitted to the Speaker of the House of Representatives and the President *pro tempore* of the Senate. You staying with me here?"

Margaret could see the aghast President using every bit of his self-control not to rip the phone from General Brower's hand. At least, she knew, everything the general said was going out only over the CAT, and was not being rebroadcast by CNN.

"Who becomes the President then?"

"My intel is that the Vice President has been killed."

"That is correct."

General Brower looked to the side as the door opened and Colonel Tobin returned with a young woman carrying a large video camera with an attached floodlight. Without breaking the rhythm of the conversation, Brower gestured for the camera operator to begin recording, and to include both him and the President in the shot.

"In that case, Speaker of the House Dorothy Marlens becomes the President."

"That is unacceptable."

"Don't I know it. But I've already taken care of that. President Marlen's first and only act in office will be to appoint me as Acting Secretary of State. She will then resign, as will the President *pro tempore* of the Senate. That makes me next in line as President. Sound good?"

It was several moments before the gunman replied, and Margaret knew his bluff had been called. Every instinct she had told her that the next thing he would say would be something designed to keep General Brower in negotiations for hours. The terrorists had tried to keep the general out of action by implying that he might be a co-conspirator in their plot, someone the President might not be able to trust. But because that strategy had failed, they had another in the wings. Now, they would attempt to keep him out of any planning of the counteroffensive they must know was already being planned. And the way to do that was to be sure he'd be too busy to be involved.

"That is an acceptable beginning. You must announce these facts at a press conference so the world will know."

"I've already called for one. I've got five teams driving through Washington picking up the signatures I need. Speaker Marlens is standing by to be sworn in. In two hours, this will be a goddam done deal."

Nice try, Margaret thought, but she knew the general's attempt to buy a two-hour extension wouldn't work.

"Two hours is unacceptable. You will hold a press conference in thirty minutes, or we will begin shooting hostages."

"Let me put it to you this way, son. Those hostages are the only thing keeping me from going in on your position with napalm right now. You understand? I don't give a rat's ass about you. Half the guys I know would cheer if the Pentagon went up in a fireball. And I like the idea of helping to straighten this country out as Acting President, even if it's your idea."

Margaret focused on the general more closely. He was starting to convince her that he meant what he was saying.

"I can handle the politicians out here. I think you know that and that's why you chose me. But for this to work, you gotta have the American people on your side. And that's not going to happen if you keep on killing. On the other hand, you give me some of those hostages now as a sign of good faith, it'll make me look like a hero for doing what the old President couldn't, and I'll get that press conference going in the next ninety minutes. Son, ya gotta work with me here."

On the screen, the gunman kept looking to the side. Finally he said, "*Wait*," and put the handset back in his pocket, then walked out of camera range.

General Brower took advantage of the moment to switch off his own handset and address the White House camera that was trained on him. "I'm General Elias Brower. We are in the Situation Room at the White House on Sunday, June 19, 1327 hours. I am here at the President's request to mislead and divert the terrorists who are in current control of the Pentagon.

"To fulfill the President's orders, I am required to lie to the terrorists about my willingness to cooperate with them. At the President's suggestion, we are making this video recording in order to confirm that the President has given orders for the United States Army counterterrorist Delta Force to retake the Pentagon and save the hostages. It will take approximately one hour for Delta Force to begin their attack. What we are doing here is buying time by saying whatever it is the terrorists want to hear."

That's one smooth guy, Margaret thought. She looked at Hector and he gave her a thumbs-up sign, letting her know that he realized what the general was doing. *Hector's okay, too,* Margaret added to herself. And, she guessed, there was even hope for the President, since he'd appointed Hector.

General Brower turned back to the screen. All it showed was Russian General Kerensky still tied to the office chair. Then the gunman returned, the CAT phone in his hand.

"General Brower, you will place yourself under CNN surveillance so we may confirm your location and your actions. You have one hour to appear in a press conference to announce your position as Acting President. However, if you do not appear on CNN within five minutes, we will execute one hostage for each minute you are late."

"I agree to the press conference in one hour. Give me at least thirty minutes to find a CNN crew. They're all out covering the Pentagon and we'll need to transport one back to the White House."

"Very well. Thirty minutes, beginning now."

The CNN feed from the Pentagon went dead.

The people in the Situation Room broke into fervent applause.

The President stood up to shake General Brower's hand for the benefit of the camera. "Thank you, General. You have just saved the lives of many of those hostages."

As Brower immediately began issuing a stream of rapid orders to Tobin, the President's young assistant leaned close to Margaret. "I know who saved those hostages' lives."

Margaret frowned, it was too early for congratulations. "They're not out of danger yet. When Delta goes in, it's going to be messy."

"How can you be sure? I've heard those guys are good."

Margaret stood up again, smoothing her jacket, resisting the temptation to say, *And they're not just guys.*

"One very bad sign, Mr. MacGregor, is that the terrorists aren't releasing any hostages to show good faith. That means they're keeping them as shields. Everything we've just seen here, all that supposed negotiation, both sides know it's a lie. We're each trying to keep the other side busy while we do something else behind each other's backs.

"Their advantage is that they know we have to be planning a rescue mission and that it will include Delta Force. Our disadvantage is that we still don't know what the hell they're after or how long they've given themselves to get it." Margaret picked up her briefcase. "Now, I'm going to check on Tyler and see if Tom has sent anything back to us."

MacGregor stood up beside her, so close that she had to angle her neck back to be able to look up into his eyes. The young assistant was a giant.

"Your husband will be okay," he told her.

Margaret automatically corrected him. "Ex-husband," she said. She saw a flash of something in his eyes at that. Margaret had been in high-stress situations too many times not to know how they heightened sexual tension. This young assistant, it seemed, had a few lessons still to learn about wartime romances.

But just after congratulating herself on her mature assessment of a possible situation, Margaret found MacGregor's dark eyes maintaining contact with hers well beyond what was acceptable. The contact was finally broken by someone shouting from the door, "Major Sinclair!"

Milton Meyer, the assistant director of the NSA, was waving a sheet of paper at her. "We have a reply from your husband. He's safe. . . ."

Meyer rushed up to her, to hand her the printout. His gaunt face showed that he had read it, but didn't understand its meaning.

As Margaret read its simple message, her pulse fluttered the way it did when she leapt in free fall into enemy territory.

The advantage was no longer with the terrorists.

Now she knew why they had gone to Site J.

And she alone knew what they really wanted.

QUICKSILVER

ONE

WEST POTOMAC PARK, OHIO DRIVE

To Danny Assad, from a mile away, the Pentagon almost looked peaceful. If he ignored the waning spirals of smoke from the parade grounds and the heliport, the Building was a straight line of dusky beige drawn against the gray curves and green patches of its surrounding roads and grasslands. The ordered center of a random world.

And because Danny had made a decision to respect that order, his own world had been thrown into chaos.

Cellular phone service was still sporadic, and connections rarely held for more than a few minutes. But even as Trish Mankin had used Arthur Tranh's phone to detail Danny's treason for their station manager, Danny had been able to put a call through to the White House. Several calls, actually. He had heard busy signals on six attempts before getting through to a messaging system. He had left his name, his cellular number, and a quick description of what he had found taped to a window on the Pentagon. He didn't know who else to turn to.

Ten minutes later, after Trish had smugly finished explaining to Danny that Eric Waller had just made her the team's new director, and that the story about the message in the window was going to run as soon as Arthur could reestablish the microwave link to the station, Danny's phone had chirped.

He had been leaning against the WDCA news team van at the time, because Trish had told him he wasn't allowed inside with the equipment anymore. He'd also been surprised he had a call coming in, because Trish had been trying for an open cellular channel for at least five minutes after her call to Waller cut off.

Danny had answered while Trish held out her hand and demanded to be put on, if the call were from Waller.

But it was, instead, a call from a man who called himself Colonel Ken Tobin.

"Are you the reporter who left a message about finding something in a Pentagon window?"

Danny had quickly confirmed his identity, and then had suggested they talk even more quickly because they might lose the call at any moment.

Tobin didn't seem to be in any hurry, though. "This call won't get dropped," he said. Then he asked Danny if he had a cellular fax or a way to upload a digital image of the window's message. Trish was reluctant to let him back in the van to upload the image by cellular modem, until the colonel had a word with her. When the file was ready, Tobin arranged a call to the modem's line. And despite the fact that Trish still couldn't get through to anyone on Arthur's phone, the van's modem had connected within seconds and transmitted the full image file without interruption.

Thirty seconds later, Colonel Tobin said he was looking at the picture, and that Danny had been right. This was valuable information, and if it were reported, it might endanger the life of whoever had left it.

Then Tobin had asked Danny why he hadn't reported it.

"I just thought it might be important."

"A lot of reporters would call that justification for making it public," Tobin said.

"Not if it was going to get somebody killed." That was when Danny had told Tobin that he was no longer the person making decisions. His station manager was determined to get the story on the air.

Tobin took down the details: Waller's name, the station, and the network. Then he told Danny not to worry. He also promised that he would give Danny whatever updates he could, first.

Danny had appreciated the offer, but told the colonel he didn't really need updates since he wasn't posting the story.

"It's going to be a long day," Tobin had told him. "No telling how things will turn out."

And that had been the end of the call.

For the next ten minutes, Danny had half-expected that Trish would get a call back from Waller, telling her to drop the story because someone from the White House had pressured him into not running it. But eventually it became apparent that the difficulty in getting a cellular connection or establishing a microwave link was now an impossibility.

Arthur checked some equipment in the back of the van and announced, with frustration, that almost all radio communications were being jammed.

The three would-be news giants had stared across the Potomac then. There was no question as to why communications were being jammed. Trish and Arthur talked about going home, but Danny convinced them to stay. At least they could still record pieces and take the tape back to the station to air later.

So Arthur and Trish had spent the next twenty minutes arguing over camera placement and Trish's delivery, and Danny had kept watching the Pentagon.

There were helicopters everywhere. One flew so low overhead that the whole van shook and Danny had to cover his ears until it was gone. It was something huge and military, gray and more than vaguely threatening. And it stopped a hundred feet above the Potomac, flattening the water and sending up a spray at the same time. Then it rotated 180 degrees and came back toward the news van.

As soon as the helicopter reversed its direction, Danny realized what it was doing here.

Arthur used the camera to record the huge craft landing on Ohio Drive, 100 feet behind the van. A crowd started to gather, most of them plain old gawkers. Since there was no way to make a phone call or upload a story, the other news vans that had staked out the park had quickly left. The crowd in the park murmured, impressed, as the helicopter settled onto the road and the side door slid open.

Danny knew it was Colonel Tobin before his black shoe hit the ground.

The tall, imposing soldier in his simple green uniform headed straight for Danny, as if he had somehow seen a recent photo of him.

He probably has, Danny thought. It wouldn't be too difficult for the White House to get a copy of his passport or driver's license photo.

Tobin shook hands with Danny. "You did your country a fine service today," he said.

He introduced himself to Arthur and Trish when they

came up behind Danny. Danny noticed that Tobin also knew their names. He had probably seen whatever photos they had on file with government agencies, too.

"I understand you're having some difficulties with your comm lines," Tobin said.

"All the radio frequencies are being jammed," Arthur told him.

"Not all of them." Tobin smiled. "I was just telling Mr. Assad that you helped us today. Now we're wondering if you'd like to help us again, and get exclusive access to a big story."

Danny marveled at how short a time it took for Arthur and Trish to become the military's best friend.

"Get your gear into the helo," Tobin said. "We're going to the White House."

Arthur and Trish nearly tripped over each other as they raced back to the van. Danny had all the gear he needed in his pockets.

"What's it look like over there?" Danny asked with a nod to the Pentagon.

"Off the record," Tobin said, "it's bad."

"And we can help you?"

Tobin watched Danny carefully. "Are you comfortable with that? What we've got planned involves some deceit. There'll be a story for you at the end, but not till this is over."

"Kind of inevitable, isn't it?" Danny said. "This is the information age. You fight information wars. Now, even information's become a weapon."

"In this case, we'll be asking you to broadcast the wrong information."

Danny grinned. "I'm a television reporter. People figure I do that anyway."

THE WHITE HOUSE, SITUATION ROOM

QUICKSILVER was intended to be a weapon of mass disruption," Major Sinclair said, "not destruction."

Behind the major, the Situation Room's large display screen showed the unnaturally crisp, high-altitude image of the Pentagon for which Hector MacGregor had still not identified a source. Smaller screens beside it kept up with news broadcasts from around the world, all covering one story, the only story. But Hector knew that the terrorist invasion of the Pentagon and CONDEFCOM's impending response were nothing compared to what the major had just described in her condensed version of the briefing that General Vanovich was to have delivered today to the President.

Destruction was localized. A building might collapse but the subways could still run, and television stations still broadcast. The downtown core of an entire city could vanish in the blast of a terrorist nuclear bomb, and the country would still persist.

But electromagnetic *disruption* on the scale that the major outlined was not localized. It affected everyone, everywhere. What good was an office building without electricity for elevators and lights? How long could a city last without a transportation system to bring in food, a sewage system to eliminate waste, or a phone system to direct emergency operations?

Hector felt certain that he, more than anyone else in the major's audience of eight, understood that America's infrastructure had become digitized. Every system necessary for the smooth continuance of society and commerce had become dependent on integrated circuits. Individual buildings and cities no longer had to be targeted by an enemy force. An attack on the circuits of America's infrastructure could cause the entire nation to fall.

But what frightened Hector even more was knowing that he, the youngest person in the room, seemed to be the only one who realized what General Vanovich's hitherto-secret project really meant, not for the present, but for the future.

And fear was something that Hector MacGregor had rarely felt.

He was a child of late-twentieth-century America. The Cold War was over before he was old enough to know there had been such a thing and the prospect of global nuclear armageddon had not consumed his teenage years as it had the generations before his. True, the environment was endangered, but it appeared to be reparable, at least in North America. And terrorism, though disturbingly more common, seemed most often to happen to someone else, somewhere else. The world inherited by Hector and his generation was not one that could end at any moment. It was, instead, one in which serious challenges were matched by promises of boundless opportunity. Difficult choices still had to be made, but there was no reason to believe those choices would not eventually be successful.

Admiral Hugh Paulsen, in contrast, was unable to grasp the implications of Sinclair's briefing, just as the admiral hadn't accepted the President's long-term concern about climatic catastrophe. The newly reinstated Chief of Naval Operations was rooted in a present that had been shaped by the past. "I don't care how you characterize the device," he said angrily to Sinclair. "Three hundred and sixty-four sailors *died*."

Following the televised execution of the Chairman of the Joint Chiefs of Staff, the President had directed that Admi-

ral Paulsen and General Philip Janukatys be located immediately and brought to the White House. When they had
arrived, the President had declined to formally accept their
resignations as Chiefs of the Navy and Air Force, respec-
tively. Whatever misgivings he might have had about their
lack of support for his foreign-policy decisions, they were
the two most senior military officers left alive, uncaptured,
and available to him, and he was unwilling to deny himself
benefit of their counsel.

Paulsen's and Janukatys's arrival in the Situation Room
coincided with the departure of General Elias X. Brower,
the commander in chief of CONDEFCOM, who less than
thirty minutes ago had successfully negotiated with the terrorists to stop killing hostages. A condition established in
those negotiations now required Brower to be under constant television surveillance. At the moment, he could be
seen on one of the smaller screens, in the Map Room of the
White House, just upstairs.

Because the terrorists, and the world, could now hear
General Brower's half of any phone conversation he initiated or received, the requirement to be on camera had
severely undercut his ability to plan the Delta Force assault
that was scheduled to begin within the hour. During the
negotiations, it had been Major Sinclair who had correctly
predicted that the terrorists would try to find some way in
which to obstruct the general's planning and direction of
the attack.

Fortunately, the terrorists had believed the general when
he told them that CNN coverage would not be possible—
because of the terrorists' actions, there were, he said, too
few news teams available in the region. He convinced them,
instead, to accept a UPN news team. Hector had overheard

the hurried preparations just before Sinclair had begun her briefing. The same news crew who had discovered, and then kept secret, the message taped to the window by the midshipman still loose in the Pentagon was cooperating with the White House to once again deceive the terrorists. General Brower was in the Map Room, but being taped on a ten-minute delay. The terrorists might think they were watching live coverage, but ten minutes before the Delta Force assault began, General Brower would be able to leave the White House and direct his troops from a command post near the Pentagon without the terrorists realizing he had left.

In the meantime, General Brower's absence made Paulsen and Janukatys the President's principal military advisors by default, and they were chairing Sinclair's QUICKSILVER briefing. So far Sinclair did not seem intimidated by Admiral Paulsen's rank or ill-temper. "I am aware of what happened to the *Shiloh*," she told him.

"I don't think you are. I think Vanovich set up his own little kingdom at the NIA, was captivated by his toys, and didn't give a damn about his responsibility to the country!"

"I *know* that is not true," the major said firmly. Paulsen had now made his critique more personal by disparaging the absent Vanovich. "It was the general's concerns about his country that led to his establishing the high level of secrecy that surrounded the Arctic Shade disaster."

Paulsen was about to continue his attack, but the President stopped him simply by raising a hand.

"Admiral, a moment, please. This is where I have trouble following General Vanovich's reasoning, Major. Exactly how did not revealing the existence of this QUICKSILVER weapon serve the country?"

"Orbital weapons are illegal, sir." The major's response now provoked the other Joint Chief into action.

"Labeling QUICKSILVER an orbital weapon is a technicality," General Janukatys protested.

It had been evident to everyone in the briefing that both Janukatys and Paulsen had been noticeably cool toward the President as they were escorted into the Situation Room. Both seemed well aware that at some point they had been suspected of direct involvement with the Pentagon terrorists. Each had made it apparent that he was willing to do his duty for the country in a time of crisis, but neither man was doing much to conceal his dislike of his commander in chief.

"Anything on orbit can be used as a weapon, just by putting it on a collision course with anything else that's up there."

But Sinclair held her own. "Sir, you're referring to a space-based weapons system intended for use *in* space. In that case, the International Space Station could be attacked by an enemy astronaut throwing a . . . a handful of gravel at it. But QUICKSILVER falls into the category of a space-based platform that can successfully attack *ground*-based targets. There is no question that that is illegal under international treaty. If the existence of QUICKSILVER were made known, how could we protest if China decided to orbit nuclear warheads in response?"

"I take the point, Major," the President said. "But, simply from a practical basis, my understanding until now was that the kind of technology you've described was impossible, for the next two or three decades at least." He glanced at Janukatys.

"The Air Force briefings I've been given say the Airborne Laser is our most sophisticated and advanced beamed-energy weapon. And that thing takes up a whole 747, needs a crew of, what is it, eighteen? Can only carry enough fuel for the laser to get off twenty shots. And those shots are just powerful enough, *just,* to bring down a single SCUD missile in its boost phase. And that's mostly because the missile's skin is extremely thin and it's loaded with rocket fuel, so all we need is a single spark to set it off.

"But now you're saying General Vanovich's device can stay in space without a crew, fire almost indefinitely, with each shot capable of destroying something the size of the *Shiloh?*"

"Basically . . . yes, sir, though I would qualify the 'indefinitely.' Actually, we have several different ways of measuring the platform's lifetime," the major said, turning to an easel fitted with a dry-erase board and picking up a red marker pen. Hector watched as she jotted figures on the board as she proceeded, almost like a teacher in a remedial class.

"Overall, we estimate its lasing medium to have an operational discharge lifetime of one thousand hours. Each discharge takes thirty seconds. That works out to approximately thirty thousand shots. The solar panels can collect enough energy in one daylight pass to fire twice in forty-five minutes. That's, say, twenty-eight shots in a twenty-four-hour period. If QUICKSILVER were to be used in an all-out war capacity, and assuming that its stealth characteristics made it impossible to target, the platform could continue to strike the enemy almost thirty times a day, for just over two and a half years. If used on a more selective basis, it could remain useful for as long as its propellant supply lasts, perhaps five to seven years."

General Janukatys stared skeptically at the summary equation that Sinclair had written on the easel-mounted board. "Major, that kind of space-based firepower *is* impossible. There is not enough launch capability in the entire world to supply fuel for an orbiting energy weapon with that kind of output. It's not even science fiction, it's fantasy."

Hector was as surprised by General Janukatys's objection as Sinclair appeared to be. Though QUICKSILVER did fire a laser beam, the destructive energy it unleashed did not come from the spacecraft. To him, what was most devastating about QUICKSILVER was not that its technology was so powerful, but that it was so simple.

"General Janukatys," the major said, "the key to QUICKSILVER's effectiveness is the fact that it does *not* generate the energy that reaches the ground. All it has to do is fire an extremely narrow, relatively low-power ultraviolet laser beam at the ground, three hundred pulses per second for a period of thirty seconds."

"Thirty seconds," Janukatys repeated with disdain. "And you're telling me that a laser beam that isn't energetic enough to give me a sunburn can somehow destroy a guided-missile cruiser?"

"No, sir, I am not. All the QUICKSILVER beam does is create an ionization trail in the atmosphere, and that . . . well, it creates a short circuit in the Earth's electromagnetic field. It's *artificial* lightning."

"Our ships get hit by lightning all the time, Major. So do our planes. And they survive."

"They do now, sir," Sinclair agreed. "The last plane to get knocked out of the air by a lightning strike was back in 1963, just over in Maryland. And, in 1983, NASA lost an

Atlas-Centaur rocket to lightning as it was launching. So the destructive power is still there. We've just been forced to learn how to shield our technology from it.

"But, until now, what we've been protecting ourselves from is *natural* lightning. And that's generated by the potential difference in electric charge between the ground and a cloud that at maximum is a few miles in altitude. In most circumstances, that difference isn't even strong enough to cause lightning. We need a thunderstorm, with negatively-charged rain falling down and positively-charged ice crystals rising up to rapidly increase the difference in charge between two regions. And then we need a trigger to release that charge."

The major continued, without pause, as she further developed her science lesson for Janukatys. In Hector's opinion, the general had asked for it. "In the case of natural lightning, General, it's what we call stepped leaders. Barely luminous electrical feelers that propagate out, zigzagging, bifurcating, looking for the path of least resistance between two areas of electrical charge. They carry a current somewhere between one hundred to a thousand amps, and they start ionizing the air along their path. When the negatively-charged leader from a cloud makes contact with a positively-charged leader rising from the ground, it's like a circuit is connected and all the excess electrons in the cloud are discharged into the ground, and the current strength jumps to anything between ten thousand to two hundred thousand amps.

"In the case of QUICKSILVER, the low-power laser beam acts like an artificial stepped leader that unleashes the full potential charge difference between the ground and a point almost two hundred miles up, where the magnetic field is even stronger than it is in a storm cloud. Especially since that laser beam is moving through the magnetic field at almost 18,000 miles an hour."

Hector was curious to see Sinclair glance quickly at her watch. The President had already committed Delta Force to action and there was little to be done until the attack began, so, as far as Hector knew, the briefing had not been given any additional time constraint beyond one hour.

"Let's go back to the beginning," she said, picking up a white cloth to wipe the previous figures from the dry-erase board. This time, the major used her red marker to draw simple diagrams to illustrate her examples. "The first time this type of electrodynamic effect was noticed was in 1996. The Space Shuttle ran an experiment with TSS-1R—a Tethered Satellite System. It was a half-ton, scientific instrument package on the end of a twelve-and-a-half-mile cable that was supposed to unwind from the Shuttle's cargo bay. Now, at the time, they knew that having the satellite and the Shuttle orbiting at two different altitudes, and yet remaining connected to one another by conductive cable would generate an electrical current. That's simple physics. You did it in grade school when you made a magnet out of a nail, some wire, and a battery. Electricity moving through a wire creates a magnetic field. The reverse is equally true: Move a wire through a magnetic field, and electricity will flow through that wire. It's how electrical generators and motors work.

"But what the tether scientists didn't count on was how much current would actually be generated. The Shuttle and the satellite were moving at more than 17,000 miles per hour through a magnetic field millions of times stronger than anything we can generate. The power-coupling predictions were off so badly that it was clear there was a new phenomenon at work. That cable vaporized like an overloaded fuse when the satellite was only seven miles out. Think of the power output if that wire had been two hundred miles long, moving at that speed."

"So the laser acts like a wire?" the President asked.

Like any good teacher, Sinclair reinforced student insight. "Yes, sir. That's precisely what it is. For decades, lightning researchers have coaxed lightning to strike specific targets by launching small rockets trailing thin copper wires into storm clouds. The charge shoots along the wire because that's the easiest conductive path to follow. The wire vaporizes, and creates a column of ionized air. And that's the path the lightning follows a millionth of a second later.

"About ten years ago, the University of New Mexico perfected an ultraviolet laser that had the same effect. Remember, the lightning isn't drawn to the copper wire as a physical object, it's drawn to the free electrons in that wire. By using a laser beam to ionize a thin channel of air, the laser creates a column of free electrons. To the lightning, there's no difference. Free electrons are free electrons."

Hector studied the dynamics of the room. Meyer of the NSA and Fortis of the CIA hadn't asked a single question yet. And neither had the room's newest participant, Douglas Casson, director of the National Reconnaissance Office. To Hector, that could only mean that the three men already knew all about the project. Likely even before the major's announcement that she believed she knew what the terrorists were after in the Pentagon's Site J, and that she had to take what she knew to the President.

But if no one else had a question, General Janukatys did. "If the scientific principles of artificial lightning are so obvious, Major, why did it take this long to develop? Why are we seeing it first in a space platform instead of a ground weapon? In our experience, the ground-based Tactical High Energy Laser defense system was much simpler and less expensive to develop than the airborne version."

"General, if you create an ionized channel through the air by shooting a laser up into a stormcloud, it's the same as shining radar onto an F-16. The F-16 fires a HARM missile straight back along the radar beam, and the lightning comes straight down and hits the laser. That does not make for an effective weapon.

"But, by shooting the laser from space, the almost nonexistent atmosphere that the satellite flies through then acts as an insulating barrier. At its normal orbit altitude, there's at least a thirty-mile gap between the beginning of the ionization trail and the satellite itself. If QUICKSILVER fired longer than thirty seconds, then there's a chance there could be feedback all the way back to the platform, destroying it. But thirty seconds is enough to trigger the discharge on the ground."

Janukatys frowned, unconvinced. "You can't shoot a laser through two hundred miles of atmospheric dust and turbulence and have it remain coherent."

Again, just like a teacher, Sinclair turned a student's negative response into a vote of support for what she was saying. "Sir, you've hit on one of the reasons we thought the power output of the QUICKSILVER strike on the *Shiloh* would be lower by a factor of at least ten. On the engineering side, QUICKSILVER actually sends out three laser beams."

The major quickly diagrammed the three QUICKSILVER laser beams on the dry-erase board, first sketching in the main strike beam, and then the two focusing beams. "In addition to the main ultraviolet strike beam, it uses two, low-power infrared beams. Those are used as reference markers to measure atmospheric turbulence. The atmospheric distortion those beams are subjected to is measured, and the results are used to adjust the flexible surface of the aiming mirror that transmits the main beam. The main beam is distorted in such a way that the turbulence of the atmosphere helps refocus it, instead of scattering it. It's adaptive optics, exactly the same proven technology we developed for the Keyhole surveillance satellites, and what civilian astronomers are using now in their observatories. Also," the major said, "for the first five seconds of the QUICKSILVER firing cycle, the ultraviolet beam is not even intended to reach the ground. It's spread slightly by the mirror so it ionizes a large but shallow pocket of air. As the beam continues to fire and the platform continues to move, the mirror also continues to adjust until the beam is perfectly coherent."

Hector watched with fascinated interest as the major continued adding to her diagram to show what General Vanovich had expected would happen during the tragic Arctic Shade exercise.

"By now," Sinclair went on, "about fifteen seconds into the cycle, the ionized channel will have reached the ground and the first electromagnetic discharge should be initiated. And all our estimates and ground tests showed us that the instant the electromagnetic discharge began, the beam's path would be disrupted."

The major turned away from her diagram. Her face was grave and Hector knew she was reliving something few had ever seen. "That's what happens to natural lightning. Most of the time, the stroke exhausts the electrons in its path anywhere from a thousandth of a second to a full second, and the current is shut off. That's why we expected QUICKSIL-VER to create only a momentary electromagnetic pulse, like that produced by an E-bomb when an explosive creates the pulse and destroys the mechanism that generated it at the same time."

The major turned back to the board and used the red marker to indicate how the ionized channel had become distorted. And lethal. "But in the follow-on Arctic Shade test firings we ran on decommissioned ships after the *Shiloh* disaster, we discovered that the intense power of the initial lightning actually *reinforces* the ionized channel, making it smear out to follow the path of the beam slicing down from the moving satellite. At that point, it becomes self-sustaining, like a nuclear reaction."

"But it *does* shut down?" the President asked, staring at the major's red diagram of disaster.

"Certainly. Depending on atmospheric conditions, after between thirty and forty-five seconds, the channel becomes so superheated, not even electrons can remain in it, and as they migrate out, the short circuit is, in effect, repaired and the discharge ends."

General Janukatys had only one other question, more specific than the President's. "How superheated?" The speculative look on the general's face as he stared at Sinclair's diagram brought distinct unease to Hector.

"A regular lightning bolt heats the air to about fifty thousand degrees," the major answered. "A QUICKSILVER strike reaches about fifteen *million* degrees. That's fifteen hundred times hotter than the surface of the sun. And that's what's responsible for the incredible explosive energy that's coupled into a target. Heat stress instantly fractures metals, and wildly fluctuating magnetic fields force the separated metal segments apart. Even explosives which have been rad-hardened against EMP ignite."

The major's statement, based on firsthand experience, brought a moment of reflective silence as all thought of the *Shiloh*.

"The Shuttle's not flying any more of those tethered satellites?" the President suddenly asked.

"No, sir," the major answered. "The Department of Defense put an end to that in 1996. As soon as we realized what caused the Shuttle's tether to burn out, all tethered-satellite experiments were shifted from NASA to the Naval Research Lab and the National Reconnaissance Office for re-evaluation. Both those agencies still work with civilian groups on studies of the stability of tethered satellites, but everything substantive having to do with electrodynamic effects went black."

Hector recognized that closing phrase as the Pentagon's code words for describing what happened when public research was suddenly discovered to have military value and became classified overnight. Sometimes, even the scientist who created a particular line of research was forbidden to work on it any longer if he was unable to qualify for the appropriate security clearance.

Sinclair checked her watch again.

In that moment, Douglas Casson, the director of the National Reconnaissance Office, finally spoke, and Hector's suspicions of Casson's prior knowledge of QUICKSILVER were confirmed.

"Major Sinclair, as I'm certain General Vanovich has told you, I have been aware of the QUICKSILVER project for several years."

Hector quickly glanced at the major for her reaction. She hadn't been aware.

"No, sir. The general informed me that some of the President's national security advisors knew of the project, but he did not reveal their names."

Casson nodded as if that were of no importance, but from the reactions of the others in the room, Hector saw that the slight man in the circular-framed glasses had made an important point. Since Casson was also Assistant Secretary of the Air Force for Space, he was outranked in this room only by the President. But as far as QUICKSILVER was concerned, he had been in a loop that had not even included the President, nor anyone else who was present. Though Hector still wasn't sure how much Fortis of the CIA and Meyer of the NSA actually knew or when they had learned it.

"Regardless," Casson said, "though I remain skeptical of the extent of the extraordinary powers you attribute to General Vanovich's platform, I can confirm that the surveillance photographs taken of the *Shiloh* disaster did have their time codes altered."

Everyone but Hector and the major immediately demanded an explanation, including the President.

Casson was unperturbed by the onslaught. "You all know the public hearings were run to establish that the *Shiloh* was sunk by a misfired cruise missile. The secret hearings, in turn, produced evidence that the *Shiloh* was actually sunk by an improper test of a classified directed-radiation weapon. Which was closer to the truth. In fact, however, I can confirm that, based on the surveillance product of NRO satellites which observed the test at the request of the NIA, the *Shiloh* was destroyed by a radiation pulse directed at it by the QUICKSILVER platform. This event happened two days earlier than was reported in either the public or secret hearings."

Hector thought Admiral Paulsen was going to start frothing. Even Fortis and Meyer were apoplectic. Hector could only assume that they had been taken in by the secret hearings just as the rest of the country had been fooled by the public ones.

"Mr. Casson," the admiral said heatedly, "I understand the need to keep certain information from the public in the name of national security. But there is no excuse for keeping that information hidden from the Chief of Naval Operations! Especially when it concerns the destruction of one of my ships!"

Again Casson nodded. "I suggest you take that up with General Vanovich."

To Hector, it was almost as if Casson were revealing things only to provoke strong reactions in the others. From his limited perspective, he didn't understand what the director of the NRO was trying to accomplish. Apparently, neither did the President.

"Doug, is there a point to any of this?" the President asked.

"A simple one, Mr. President," Casson answered. "QUICK-SILVER is a project that until today was unknown to the CIA, the NSA, the Joint Chiefs of Staff, and even you, sir. In the NRO, I am one of two people who know of it. At least, in its totality. I imagine there are more than that in the NIA?" Casson looked questioningly at Sinclair.

"There are fewer than fifty people with complete access to the project," she confirmed. "It was totally compartmentalized."

"So, my point, my question, is this," Casson said, as he looked around the table. "If so few people in our own government know about QUICKSILVER, how is it possible that the Russians who have taken over the Pentagon know about it? And if its capabilities were only demonstrated in the past five months, how could they have possibly had time to plan and prepare for such an elaborate takeover action?"

"Sir, we don't know that they are Russians," Sinclair pointed out.

But Casson kept to his argument. "On the contrary, Major. Your own husband—ex-husband—identified them as Russian terrorists in his ingenious message to us. The one hostage the terrorists have gone out of their way *not* to shoot is General Kerensky. Whatever accent their spokesman might have is effectively masked by the voice modulation device he's employing. And"—he looked meaningfully at Paulsen and Janukatys—"there was just as much dissent in the Russian military over their joining NATO as there was within ours."

Before Admiral Paulsen could respond, the President assumed full leadership for the first time in the briefing session. "Doug, that question will be moot in a few hours. Archie's got NIMA working on enhancing the satellite images we have of the attack in the Courtyard, and they tell me we should be able to resolve faces we can feed into the national registries. Failing that, we'll have a pretty clear picture of who they are when we start identifying the bodies after Delta Force gets through with them. So forget arguing over who they are—Major, that goes for you, too. We'll know, and we'll know soon."

"Then I suggest, sir," Sinclair replied, "that we also don't worry about how they found out about QUICKSILVER, either. The fact is, they know. The fact is, General Vanovich so thoroughly restricted access to the project that the only command site it can be controlled from is Site J."

Now Archie Fortis of the CIA joined in. "Uh, . . . there is

no such thing as a . . . um . . . single command post for any operation of the National Command Authority. As soon as . . . as soon as Site J was identified as being at . . . uh . . . risk, all the command functions for which it was . . . responsible automatically switched over to Site R."

Even Hector had heard of Site R. He had just never connected its letter designation with the Pentagon's unique mapping labels. Site R was one of the first secret Alternate National Military Command Centers to be built outside Washington during the Cold War, and it was large enough to house three thousand personnel and evacuees, including special quarters for the President. Hector had become aware of the facility directly as a result of his involvement in the President's calendar. Every three months the President went through the motions of being evacuated from wherever he happened to be as part of a Joint Emergency Evacuation Program. Though, after going there once, the Man now firmly resisted actually flying off to Site R with members of the White House Military Office.

Though Site R's location in a hollowed-out mountain in Pennsylvania was no longer secret, which meant it could be easily targeted in a missile attack, Hector had heard enough discussions about it to understand it still had a mission to perform. So much communications gear had been built into the site over the years that it now served as a key, day-to-day communications hub for the military. Site R's more public existence allowed newer and more secret command centers to stay off-line so that their locations wouldn't be inadvertently revealed.

Thus, as far as he knew, what Archie Fortis had just said was correct. Hector wouldn't have been surprised to learn that there were at least a dozen other secret, hidden sites that could take command of the country's military assets in the event key command centers were destroyed.

But Sinclair had an observation of her own to share. "The assets of the National Infrastructure Agency are as tightly controlled as those of the NRO, Mr. Casson. You do not permit command and control of your satellites to be automatically transferred from one command post to another, except in the event of planned exercises or catastrophic events. Neither do we."

"Excuse me," the President said, "but am I the only one who would classify the occupation of Site J as a catastrophic event?"

That was when Sinclair unleashed her own weapon of disruption. "Mr. President, no one questions that we have a wealth of redundant systems, backup strategies, and disaster scenarios for defending the Pentagon. But they're all for events we are *prepared* to deal with. There is, however, one event we never anticipated, and for which we have no scenario. This means our National Command Authority has a fatal flaw."

And by accident or design, the major informed her audience, the terrorists had found it.

TWO

SECOND FLOOR, C RING, JOINT PROCUREMENT
DATA-PROCESSING FACILITY

Amy Bethune was exhausted, in pain, frightened, and had never felt more alive in her life. She found no contradiction in that confusion of sensation and emotion. On the contrary, she believed herself to be lucky.

Every mid she knew had asked herself or himself the same question. And probably so had everyone who ever joined a branch of the military. When the moment came, when the new soldier or airman or sailor faced combat for the first time, what would she do?

Training could only take a new recruit so far. No matter how realistic the scenario, no matter if live ammunition was being used, no matter if there was a parachute jump from an airplane or a fast-rope descent from a helicopter. In training, one fact could not be escaped—no one was actively trying to kill you.

The risks faced in training were, in truth, little different from those faced every day by civilian police forces or firefighters. Equipment might fail, accidents might happen, but such mishaps had always existed outside combat. Even for those on leave, a commercial jet might crash on takeoff, or a tire might blow out on the freeway.

But combat was different. No one could know how he or she would react to that first stunning revelation that someone else whom you had never met was attempting to end your life.

No person in any branch of the military truly belonged until he or she had faced that moment, and gone beyond it.

But now, for Amy Bethune, still one year away from graduation, that moment had already come. And gone. She had faced the beast, she had stared it down. She had used her training, lived up to her oath as a sailor, and done her duty for her country.

Exhaustion, pain, and fear had a way of evaporating in the comforting light of accomplishment and self-knowledge.

Her only regret was that she had no one with whom to share her experience. Because Tom Chase couldn't or wouldn't understand.

She and Chase had remained in the large office bay off C Ring, waiting for a reply to the new JSAMS message they had sent. Amy had used the time to search the desks for aspirin for her cracked tooth. Three desks later, she found a treasure trove of over-the-counter medications and candy bars. She'd chewed four aspirin at once and given half of the three Snickers bars she'd found to Chase.

While Chase toiled at a computer keyboard on the desk she had selected for him, inhaling his bar and a half of candy in well under a minute, she'd crashed in a tilt-back chair to wait for her tooth to respond to the aspirin. She tried to break her half of the Snickers bars into small pieces but discovered it couldn't be done. She ended up with a handful of smooshed and unappetizing chunks which she let dissolve in her mouth.

Now she watched him typing intermittently as he attempted to open a new line of communication to the outside. Chase looked as exhausted as she felt.

She had no trouble admitting to herself that in some small part of her brain, the simple, basic, straightforward idea of throwing Chase to the floor and ripping off all his clothes was becoming immensely appealing. Fortunately, even if she were to lose all sense of reason, the rest of her had no strength or inclination to follow through on the completely unacceptable impulse. Whatever else might happen between them in the future, for now, she and Chase were soldiers behind enemy lines, and the no-fraternization rule made the situation much simpler.

Chase stopped typing.

"What is it?" Amy asked.

He held up his watch. "New message."

Amy left her chair—the aspirin were doing a fine job—and leaned over his shoulder to read the text as it scrolled across his pager watch. *Hell, Chase even smells good. That's a first.*

TELL BETHUNE WINDOW MSG RECEIVD. FIND SAFE PLACE. KEEP HEADS DOWN. MJR SINCLAIR.

Chase snorted, not quite, but almost laughing.

"What's the joke?" Amy asked.

"Sinclair's my wife. My ex-wife."

"She's a *major?*"

"Army. DIA."

"But . . . you hate the military."

Chase looked at her curiously. "No, I don't. I've spent most of my life working for the military."

"Then . . . let's just say you have an *unusual* attitude toward us."

Chase frowned at his pager. "Maybe toward some individuals. But only the dinosaurs who still think you win wars with rocks and pointy sticks."

He was either the most complex person she had met, or the most confused. "Basically," Amy said, "you win wars when your rocks and pointy sticks are better than the enemy's."

"Maybe in the old days. Today you can win before the war even starts so long as your information's better than the enemy's."

Amy was ready to argue that point. But Chase wasn't. "When this is over, we'll have lots of time for a debate. For now, let's figure out what we do next."

What are you thinking, she scolded herself, as she automatically began analyzing that "lots of time when this is over" reference for all possibilities. *The mission. The mission. That's all that matters.*

Unfortunately, there didn't seem to be much of the mission left. Amy wondered if the message she had taped to the window had been of any help.

"Well," Amy said, "the major says we should find a safe place and stay there. That sounds as if they're going to launch a counterattack."

"That's a given. You said yourself, Delta Force has to get involved." Chase gave her another quizzical look. "But you don't want to stay put, do you?"

Amy was tired of analyzing him and being analyzed herself. "What I want doesn't matter. A major has told us to stay put. That's an order."

"My ex-wife is not your commanding officer. And she sure isn't mine."

Chase had a point. Because they were isolated in the Pentagon, Amy couldn't be certain what new operational chain of command she had fallen into, especially since the people outside knew she was inside.

But then she thought of something that might mean the major's message wasn't necessarily an order. "Tom, why would a major in the DIA be sending us this message?"

"It's got to be Tyler," Chase said. "He managed to convince the captain he was with to get my first message to someone in charge, and then they called in Margaret when they realized she was his mother."

Amy felt relieved. Under that scenario, the major *wasn't* her commanding officer. She didn't have to sit out the rest of the action after all.

Then Chase spoiled it for her. "On second thought, better we stay put."

"But what about your friend? The general."

"My wife works for Milo," Chase said flatly.

"The same general you work for?"

Chase nodded. "We were both working for him ten years ago. He introduced us. Milo fancies himself a matchmaker."

Something still wasn't making sense to Amy. "So . . . *you* work for the Defense Intelligence Agency, too?"

Chase shook his head. "Unh-uh. Let's not go there."

Amy had had enough exposure to military affairs to realize that when conversations ended as abruptly as this one had, she had stumbled into something classified above her need to know. General Vanovich, Chase, *and* his ex-wife were involved in some secret operation at the Pentagon.

"Whatever you say," she reluctantly agreed. But her need to know was working overtime now.

Chase turned around in his chair to face the desk's phone. "I'll send back a confirmation message, let them know we'll stay where we are. Maybe they can let us know when they expect to attack."

He picked up the receiver, pressed an inside line, and started to dial into JSAMS.

Amy's frustration made her voice sharper than she'd intended. "They won't reveal intel like that on an unsecure line."

"Oh, Margaret and I are pretty good at reading between the lines. She'll figure out a way." Chase started punching numbers, creating his message.

Amy hated leaving a job half-finished. But orders were orders. At least she'd taken four of the enemy out, and her window sign might have prepared the reinforcements who'd come in to mop up the remainder. She sighed as she headed back for her chair. It was over.

Then gunfire boomed up from the C Ring roadway and outside the office windows, the screaming began.

THE WHITE HOUSE, SITUATION ROOM

"This is the flaw in our system," Margaret said, knowing both that she had the full attention of everyone in the room, and that her career could depend on what she said next.

"As long as everything is functioning normally," she emphasized, "no crises, no international military threats, no equipment malfunction, our National Command Authority remains monolithic, as it should. There is one location and one location only from which all command-and-control authority originates—the National Military Command Center in the Pentagon. That authority cannot be *taken* from the Pentagon. It can only be given *by* the Pentagon. That safeguard is specifically built into our system in order to prevent rogue elements within our own military from unilaterally usurping command of a squadron of bombers or a field of missiles."

Margaret met the eyes of everyone in turn, except Hector. As far as she could tell, the President had kept his young assistant here as a witness, not as a player. "But, the terrorists—the *soldiers*—who have taken over the Pentagon and Site J have accomplished their mission so quickly, and with so little damage, that our command-and-control system has not been disrupted. That means that command authority still rests with the Pentagon. In fact, *because* of our doctrine of predelegated launch authority, one of the actions those people can now undertake is to communicate directly with the commanders of any of our nuclear forces and transmit authorization codes for the preparation and launch of nuclear missiles."

"No, they can't," the President said indignantly.

Margaret fought the urge to raise her voice at America's Chief Executive. "Sir, I don't mean to suggest that those codes would be accepted, but the enemy has control of that specialized contact equipment. They have the encryption codes in the software and those codes directly burned into the master computer chips. And all lines of communication remain open. What prevents them from succeeding is that we were able to contact our nuclear-ready commanders and order them to ignore any authorization directives from Site J."

"Exactly," the President said. "The system works."

Margaret didn't want to believe the President was being deliberately obtuse. Vanovich must have realized what was happening the moment the enemy soldiers captured him. She herself had known the instant she had read Tom's message and learned that the general had been captured specifically for his Red Level clearance. Somehow, her explanation was not doing its job. She forced herself to slow down, to go over her argument step by step.

"Mr. President, our nuclear command system works, as you say, only because we have flesh-and-blood commanders for our nuclear forces. But there are no commanders on the QUICKSILVER platform. Just like the NRO's imaging satellites and the NSA's communications-monitoring satellites, QUICKSILVER responds only to computer-coded signals transmitted from one centralized command post. Site J. And as long as that site is active and undamaged and maintains regular contact with those satellites, it is impossible for any other alternate command post to access them."

The President looked directly at the director of the National Reconnaissance Office. "Is that true, Doug?"

Margaret was heartened to see Casson lose some of his equanimity. She disliked the smug little man intensely. "Well, of course, all DOD satellites are controlled through Schriever Air Force Base in Colorado."

Margaret wouldn't allow that simplification to stand. "That base is only a switchboard, sir. They can contact all of our satellites around the globe, but the messages they send have to come from an authorized source with the proper encryption codes. And in the event of war, when Schriever would be a target every bit as valuable—and as long-lived— as the Pentagon, the NRO, the NSA, the NIA, we all have dozens, if not hundreds of backup sites hidden around the country which allow us to directly transmit line-of-sight signals to our assets. With what we're facing, Schriever doesn't enter into it."

Casson did not acknowledge Margaret's interruption. "If, and I stress *if,* the Russians allow Site J to remain in contact with our key space assets, the major is correct."

The President sat back in his chair. "We have how many hundreds of billions of dollars invested in satellites and you're telling me that if something happened to Site J we'd lose them all?"

"No, sir," Margaret said. "That's the point. If something happens to Site J, if it goes off-line—because the Pentagon gets nuked, or if there's a complete power failure, then as the critical satellites pass over alternate command posts, we *can* upload reacquisition codes to them and regain control by their next orbital pass. But as a safeguard to prevent someone else from hijacking our satellites, they're programmed to ignore any reacquisition signals as long as their primary command post—Site J—continues to contact them each orbit."

"So the Russians—" The President shook his head to stop Margaret from arguing with him about the identity of the terrorists. "—whoever is down there, they have complete access to our satellites, and we can't do anything to stop them?"

Here goes, Margaret thought. "Sir, my point is, we *can* do something, but we have to do it right away. When Delta Force goes in, they can't slow down to rescue the hostages."

"What?!"

"Delta Force has to go in, go down, hit Site J, and *only* Site J. And then they either have to retake it, or destroy it."

Margaret could feel the President's eyes bore into her. "Major Sinclair, you were the one who demanded I do whatever it took to stop the terrorists from killing the hostages."

"Yes, sir. When I thought the point of the terrorists' actions was the hostages, that was my recommendation."

"But now you're convinced that what the terrorists are really after is QUICKSILVER? Why not the NRO's satellites? The NSA's?"

"Those assets are well known to our enemies. Their technical specifications are secret; their orbits change occasionally, but their existence is known. But QUICKSILVER is classified *above* Top Secret, at HALO level. There's only one way to control it, even from Site J, and that's by someone with Red Level clearance that cuts across all compartmentalization."

Margaret held up the sheet of paper Milton Meyer of the NSA had given her. "Tom's message to us said General Vanovich had been taken for his Red Level clearance. When you combine that with the fact that they have taken over Site J without damaging it, there is only one conclusion that we *can* reach."

The President tapped a finger on the table, but didn't turn it into a drum roll. Throughout this day, she had noticed that he did that whenever he was about to announce a decision. The fact that there was no drum roll meant, to her, that he was still considering all his options.

The President turned to Casson. "Keeping everything the major said in mind, what's your analysis?"

Casson didn't even pause to think about his answer, he was that certain of his assessment. "Too complicated, sir. Not for an instant am I willing to concede that in the time between QUICKSILVER's test firing last December and today, that anyone could have conceived of a way to attack the Pentagon in the manner these Russians have."

"Maybe they've had these plans for a long time," Margaret said. "Maybe they just needed a good enough excuse to put them to use."

Casson flashed a cold smile at her. "So, you do acknowledge that the terrorists are Russian?"

Margaret wasn't going to play games. "Mr. Casson, I agree with the President. We'll know who the terrorists are when we see their satellite images or identify their bodies. What concerns me is that by the time we get around to doing that, this country will have lost a critical weapons system that can easily be used against us. For years. We all know what happened to the *Shiloh*. Imagine a QUICKSILVER strike on the Capitol Dome, on the New York Stock Exchange, Hoover Dam, nuclear generating plants." She stared at the President. "The White House." At Fortis. "Your headquarters at Langley." At Meyer. "Yours at Fort Meade." At Casson. "Or yours at the Pentagon."

Margaret didn't have to ask for anyone else's opinion. She could read it in their eyes. Not one of these men believed her.

The President's tapping became a drum roll. "Thank you, Major. You can be sure we will be following up on the QUICKSILVER project. But for now, I will leave my instructions to General Brower unchanged. Delta Force is to rescue the hostages and reestablish control of the Pentagon. And then we'll have more than enough time to deal with Site J."

Margaret looked at her watch. "Sir, QUICKSILVER comes within communications range of Site J approximately every one hundred minutes. Two orbits is all it will take for someone else to gain control of it."

"If they know where it is," the President said, "and what it is. And I accept Doug's analysis that that is most unlikely."

Margaret knew this was the time to sit down. She didn't want to give up the fight, but all her powers of persuasion were useless against someone who refused to listen. She wondered how Tyler was doing with Mrs. Petty. She wondered if it was time to take him home.

No, not home, Margaret told herself. If QUICKSILVER was going to fall into enemy hands, it might be a good idea to stay out of D.C. for a while.

Margaret caught sight of the President's young assistant staring at her with a bit too much interest. *I really will have to speak to him,* she thought as she slowly sat down. *Or else he could become a . . .*

She realized MacGregor wasn't staring at her at all. He was looking at something behind her.

"There's something going wrong," he said.

Margaret turned to face the wall of display screens, bracing herself for another view of hostages being murdered.

But instead she saw proof of everything she had just said.

The satellite image of the Pentagon was no longer crisp and perfect. The edges of the building had blurred. There was atmospheric churning in the lower-left side.

To Margaret, that particular type of image degradation could only mean one thing. One of the arrays that contributed to the image of the Pentagon had been taken off-line.

And that could only be accomplished from one site. *The* site. Site J.

"There's your proof, Mr. President," Margaret said. "Whoever they are, they're stealing MAJIC."

THREE

SECOND FLOOR, C RING, JOINT PROCUREMENT
DATA-PROCESSING FACILITY

The gunfire and screams were coming from the window side of the office. Tom knew better than to run up to the windows and look. Besides, Bethune beat him to it. She grabbed one of the H&Ks from a desktop, ran halfway across the office in a hunched-over crouch, then dove down to the beige carpet to belly-crawl the rest of the way, wriggling around desks and between low office partitions.

By the time Bethune had her back to a four-foot-wide section of wall between two large windows, there had been a second round of gunfire and the cries outside had ceased. She waved a hand at Tom, telling him to stay down on his side of the office.

Then Bethune braced one hand on the barrel of her H&K, and pushed with her legs so she slowly slid up the wall, keeping flat against it as she peered to the side through the venetian blinds that covered the window. Tom could see that from her angle there was a two-inch gap between the plane of the blinds and the edge of the window. "Shit," Bethune whispered. Tom took that to mean she could see something and he crawled over to join her.

As soon as he was up against the wall beside her, his shoulders pressed against hers, he heard the sounds of people talking outside. People on the service road between the B and C Rings. He edged up the wall to look for himself.

The body of a man lay facedown in a pool of blood in the center of the black asphalt roadway, hands tied behind his back with plastic cord, his green uniform torn apart by bullets. *A hostage,* Tom thought. Someone who had tried to make a run for it.

Four men stood over the body. They were not Delta Force soldiers. Two in white Naval uniforms were clearly from the group that had replaced Bethune's classmates. The other two were completely in black—black jumpsuits, black belts and harnesses, black backpacks, black helmets and hoods, and small black machine guns.

"D'you see the new guys?" Bethune whispered.

"They didn't get in here with a pass," Tom whispered back.

Bethune turned her head in his direction, her face only inches from his. Her hair felt soft against his cheek. He felt her breath on his face. "Is there another way in?"

The same question had already been troubling Tom. "Never heard of an underground connection going beyond the grounds. But if there is one, it should be under our control."

"Maybe it is," she said in a low voice. "That stuff they're wearing? Nomex BDUs. Gore-Tex assault boots. Kevlar ballistic helmet and armor. That's all standard U.S. issue. It's for Special-Ops counterterrorism."

"Americans? Working *with* the terrorists?"

"Could explain a lot."

The sound of more voices on the roadway sent Tom and Bethune back to the gap in the blinds again. Two more men in black joined the group already in the roadway, pushing ahead of them three hostages, still alive, their hands also tied behind their backs. Two men, one woman, in U.S. Air Force uniforms, but not dress uniforms. *Not NATO guests then,* Tom thought, *maybe just unlucky enough to be working in the Building today.*

The group of terrorists, four in black, two in white, now moved on with their prisoners, leaving the dead hostage behind. As they moved out of sight, Bethune slipped down and crawled to beneath the second office window. Tom followed suit.

But the terrorists did not come into view again, and Tom heard no more voices from outside. He did hear the distant, muffled sound of a metal door closing, though. So did Bethune.

She slid up the wall to look out the second window. "There's a door down there without a blast shield," she said. "And it opens into C Ring. That gets us closer to the ops centers."

To Tom, it also explained how the men in black could have gotten into the Pentagon after the blast doors went down. Inwardly, he sighed at the complication. Margaret's message had told them to stay put and stay safe. But Tom knew that when Delta Force finally arrived, they'd be expecting fewer than forty adversaries in white Naval uniforms. "We have to get a message out to Margaret about the guys in black," he said. *That part was okay, but the next definitely wasn't.* "We also need to count bad guys—black and white—so Delta Force will know what they're up against."

Bethune's quick smile of approval reminded Tom of Margaret again, what she'd been like at Bethune's age. The feeling of familiarity was unnerving. He opened his mouth to tell that to Bethune, then changed his mind.

"Need some help?" Bethune asked, puzzled, as Tom edged away from her.

"No, you stay here and keep watch. I'll send the message, then we can look for a way down to the road."

Bethune turned back to her lookout.

Back at his desk, Tom found composing the JSAMS message unexpectedly difficult. The first message he'd sent said the enemy in white were Russians. And now his second would say the enemy in black could be Americans.

In the end, though, he passed Margaret the new information.

Because, when he gave it more thought, there really *was* only one way an enemy force could invade the Pentagon.

They had to have had help from someone on the inside.

There was no other way.

SITE J

Standing at the center of Ground Zero, in the heart of the Pentagon, Ranger surveyed his domain and felt the force of true power.

From this one underground facility, America's leaders had been ready to turn the Cold War hot. Here they could map and target the entire world, commanding missiles and bombers to any spot on the globe to wipe it out of existence. And all without leaving the comforts of home. One floor up, not fifty feet from the Red Level console, was a cafeteria with an espresso machine, Starbuck's coffee, and five different flavors of ice cream.

The power wielded in American hands was both criminal and corrupt.

That's what Ranger was putting an end to.

He checked his watch. So far, the deliberately harsh diversionary tactics up top in the Courtyard had worked as planned. There had been no signs that the American negotiators had any doubts that their military fortress was in the hands of domestic terrorists. As long as they believed more lives could be saved by negotiation than direct action, Ranger knew they'd keep their forces of counterattack on standby.

"Oh, they'll be here."

Ranger glanced back at the futuristic Red Level console and the old man seated before it. "Who will be here, General?"

"Whoever you're worried about. Delta Force, probably." Vanovich was still strapped into the chest harness of his high-backed chair, in front of the command center's main workstation, awaiting Ranger's next order. The general's chair harness was securely locked in place by a plastic security tie. Ranger had attached the tie himself. Vanovich's near-collapse after the female sergeant's death, coupled with his recent loss of weight, no doubt due to some major wasting illness, had given the old man the air of someone with nothing to lose. A dangerous state of mind for a prisoner who was worth more alive to Ranger than dead. At least until the mission was over.

A display screen to Vanovich's right showed a list of the remaining thirty-one key orbital assets controlled by the Department of Defense—in all, thirty-two assets that would be destroyed or in Ranger's control by the end of the day—if he could persuade Vanovich to continue to do as instructed. If not, he would secure what he could within the thirty-minute window he would have after Vanovich's death. In any event, the general would die—sooner or later. When was up to the general.

"You must mean Operation Cloudburst," Ranger said. "Are you familiar with this Delta Force response?"

"I know they always win."

Ranger placed a hand on the back of the general's chair as he studied the screens, waiting for the next satellite to come into position. "They'll win today, as well. Even your Rambo couldn't hold the Pentagon or this facility against the might of your army."

Ranger marveled at Vanovich's quizzical look. The man was beaten, but still possessed an insatiable need to know, even if there was no more time to make use of new knowledge. He had been peppering Ranger with questions from the time they had taken him, though he had not reciprocated without the explicit demonstration of consequences if he refused.

Ranger was willing to oblige the old man, to a point. If only to distract him from questioning Ranger's directives. "In fact, we anticipate up to three hundred of your overequipped and overtrained soldiers to storm our positions within the next three hours. We're even prepared for an assault to begin in the next thirty minutes. That is as early as your Delta Force could be deployed here. Perhaps with SEAL Team Six for company."

"They'll kill you." Vanovich said it as if that would be a good thing.

"Some things are worth dying for, don't you think?"

Ranger looked up to the top of the console where he had placed the package Kilo had given him. Vanovich stared at the package, but Ranger doubted the old man could even guess what was inside.

"You're not doing this for money," Vanovich said. His observation a statement, not a question. "This is a military operation, not a hijacking for ransom."

Ranger could see that the general no longer accepted the cover story that had convinced him to access the first satellite, MAJIC 3. *What a pity.* Ranger had told Vanovich that Team One was reprogramming the thirty-two satellites to take them out of American control, and that for a fee of one hundred million dollars per satellite, Ranger would supply to the U.S. government the new orbit information and access codes for each satellite.

From his preparatory study of the general, Ranger had become aware that Vanovich would rather die than allow his technology to be destroyed or stolen by a foreign power. Hence the hijacking cover story. It had been crafted to allow the general to believe his actions would not be irreversible, that there was a chance his satellites could be recovered, eventually. Even the *illusion* of hope had an oddly powerful effect on Americans.

A line on the display screen began to flash and Ranger heard a chime. "EKH-22?" he asked, even though he had the list memorized. The next satellite to come into range was an Enhanced Keyhole optical surveillance platform, eight years old and nearing the end of its service life. It was also going to be an example.

Vanovich was silent, no doubt mentally reviewing the same specifications as Ranger.

"Access it, General," Ranger said.

Despite his stated distrust of Ranger's real motives, the general sensibly decided not to risk his life for the aging satellite. He pulled himself closer to the workstation, then angled the black-rubber retina scanner downward and looked into it. After a few moments, another chime sounded and Vanovich typed in his personal access code. Ranger was discouraged, but not surprised to see that Vanovich's code changed each time he entered it. It was another level of security which, like the encrypted digitization of retina images, Ranger's technical support team had not had time to overcome. Unless his specialists on-site could determine the pattern by which the code changed, the general would have to live. As long as he was still cooperating.

The main screen directly in front of Vanovich responded to the scan and the code by displaying a satellite-tasking menu. The menu provided full access to all platform functions, from setting ground coordinates to be photographed, to firing engines for changes in orbit.

Ranger called out to his specialist at the far end of the Red Level console. "India, this is the first EKH."

The young woman in midshipman white was already typing on her keyboard. Pleased, Ranger checked his watch again. There could be no slippage in the schedule now, no estimates. Everything was driven by the celestial precision of the orbiting satellites. Within five hours, all thirty remaining platforms would have passed over Site J. Then Site J would have served its purpose and could be left to the Americans, who would likely still be trying to remove the hostages Ranger's teams had scattered throughout the Pentagon.

Ranger glanced up at the red-railed catwalk that circled the main floor of the command-and-control center. The black-clad commandos of Team One continued to escort the captive Site J personnel, five at a time, to the freight elevators, to take them up to the Pentagon. As they tried to shoot their way into the Building, Delta Force would discover considerably more hostages than expected, inconveniently and prominently secured in harm's way.

"New firing instructions programmed," India called out.

"Execute," Ranger said.

The young satellite specialist touched a single key and the tasking menu closed. "That's two, so far," Ranger told Vanovich. The first, whose orbit and command codes he had altered, had been MAJIC 3, a much more valuable surveillance asset. Ranger leaned forward to read the screen list and confirm that the next satellite to come into range would be VEGA 4, a space-surveillance platform operated by the NRO. Following that, the next in line was MAJIC 7, in spite of the fact that only six MAJIC arrays had been launched to date. It was time for Ranger to take his web of deception to the final stage.

He read that entry from the list aloud, as if its inclusion was unexpected. "MAJIC Seven? When was that launched?"

"Last September," the general said without hesitation. "There were problems with its orbit. It's not on-line yet."

"But only six MAJIC platforms were scheduled to be on orbit at this time."

"The full constellation calls for twelve first-generation arrays," Vanovich said, impressively convincing. "By the time the third one was operational and the community saw how powerful they were, the rest were put on fast-track development."

How reasonable, Ranger thought.

"Call up the tasking menu for MAJIC Seven."

"You'll miss the next satellite window," Vanovich observed.

Ranger feigned unconcern, as if merely curious. "We have time. Call up the menu, please."

Vanovich shrugged, as if to comply to that request would only waste Ranger's time, then leaned into the retina scanner again. After the chime, he typed in the next iteration of his always-changing access code.

The MAJIC 7 menu opened. Its CHANGE SPECIFICATIONS functions were dimmed out. For security purposes, the Americans had made it impossible for anyone to store commands for upload to this satellite at a later time. All contact had to be carried out in real time, only within preset orbital windows, and only through the encryption patterns hardwired into Site J's custom control chips.

But there was enough information on the screen for Ranger to know this satellite was distinctly unlike any of the other MAJIC arrays. In fact, since there were no separation data, it wasn't an array at all. It was a single platform. The difference was so apparent, Ranger knew the general might become suspicious if he didn't comment on it.

"General, why is this one different?"

"Like I said, problems. The array hasn't deployed from its launch shroud yet. Probably never will."

Ranger accepted the general's dismissive evaluation at face value. "Very well, we'll use it to set an example. India, when we access MAJIC Seven, set it for a terminal orbit. I want them to see it burn up over the Atlantic."

India confirmed the order. "We'll have a thirty-minute access window in two minutes," she said.

Ranger pointed to the eye scanner. "Don't think of it as giving us a satellite, General. Think of it as giving yourself a chance to erase one of your mistakes."

Without comment, Vanovich put his eye to the scanner, waited for the chime, typed in a command code.

A new window opened on the screen: a satellite-tasking menu for MAJIC 7.

Two minutes later, India announced that they had acquired the satellite and that it was awaiting commands.

Ranger felt a moment of intense calm descend upon him.

He thought of Zeus, throwing lightning bolts from Olympus.

"Change orbit and upload the first set of target coordinates," he said.

He saw the general react with a sudden bunching of all his muscles as he began to lunge forward, hands reaching out for the keyboard in front of him.

But Ranger effortlessly caught the old man's wrists.

Appalled, enraged, helpless with frustration, Vanovich stared up at him.

"That's enough, General," Ranger said. "QUICKSILVER is ours now."

The final objective had been achieved.

Whatever happened next was up to Ranger.

THE WHITE HOUSE, SITUATION ROOM

Like everyone else who was present, Hector stared in horror at the image on the main screen in the Situation Room.

It was an outline map of the world, the kind Hector would always associate with NASA's mission control. Crossing it was a yellow line, curved like the path of a roller coaster, dipping down over the Pacific then rising up over Alaska, only to curve down again and end with a flashing red dot just off the coast of Florida.

And if Major Wilhemina Bailey of the United States Space Command was correct, the line wasn't the only thing that had come to an end there. So had America's dominance in space.

"Mr. President, I am able to confirm that the bird was an Enhanced Keyhole Twenty-Two," Major Bailey said. Her image was carried on a screen to the side of the main one, and showed an African-American woman of some substance whose hands never stopped moving across the controls on the console before her. Hector had recognized her insignia as Air Force, but he had found it more difficult to identify the odd uniform she was wearing. At first, it had appeared to be a tailored, sleeveless blue tunic of some kind, worn over a long-sleeved white blouse. But when, during the course of her report from Cheyenne Mountain, the major had reached back for a binder on the table behind her, Hector had realized she was wearing a maternity jumper.

The Keyhole satellites were under the control of the NRO, and Douglas Casson was taking the loss of the platform as a personal insult. "Any idea what brought it out of orbit, Major?"

Bailey shook her head. "Sir, from the telemetry we were able to pick up, it appeared to be a deliberate deorbit burn, single vector, no sign of a misfiring or any attempt at course correction or recovery."

Casson actually seemed to shrink lower in his chair as he looked over at Sinclair. "How many satellites can they access from Site J?"

Hector saw the major check a list she had quickly written out by hand in a small, black notebook she had taken from her briefcase. "In addition to QUICKSILVER and the six MAJIC arrays, there are potentially twenty-six others, all NRO or NSA."

"Major Bailey," the President called out. "Are you picking up any sign of the MAJIC Three array reentering?"

Bailey's dark eyes flashed like the constellation of status lights that flickered on and off, slightly out of focus behind her. She was looking up at something beyond the video camera on her desk. "No, sir. MAJIC Three is off the board, so all we know is that its orbit *has* been changed. Whether it's still up there, it could take a few hours to confirm—that kind of an array is a hard little sucker to reacquire. But if it did reenter like the Keyhole, it most likely would have been over the Gulf of Mexico in full daylight. That means there might not have been a lot to see from the ground."

The President got to his feet, started to pace. "What's the status on Delta Force?"

Hector had become the group of eight's unofficial timekeeper. He checked his notes from his last quick phone call to Colonel Tobin. "C Squadron has linked with the 4th in Virginia. They'll be brought in by air when the ground assault begins. A, B, and E Squadrons are en route and will be in position in one hour. General Brower will be leaving to join them in fifty minutes."

The President looked up at the wall of display screens and Hector could tell he was watching the one showing the UPN feed of General Brower in the Map Room. "Forty-five minutes," the President repeated. He leaned down to switch on a speakerphone connection. "General Brower, once your men go into action, how long will it take them to go directly to Site J, without stopping to rescue hostages?"

It was odd to hear General Brower reply, while on the television feed he did nothing. Because of the tape delay which Colonel Tobin had set up through the UPN news crew, the viewers were seeing Brower as he was ten minutes ago. In ten more minutes, they'd see him pick up his phone and have this conversation again. Fortunately, only his half of the conversation would be broadcast.

"Could take hours, sir. The doors are designed to withstand heavy explosives."

"Hours," the President repeated. Hector thought he was familiar with most of the President's moods but he had never seen the Man like this. "General, listen carefully. Whoever's down there is using Site J to access and destroy our most vital space-based assets. In a few hours, we're going to be out a couple of hundred billion dollars of taxpayer money, and we're going to be blind and deaf to what the rest of the world is doing. Do you understand, General? We will no longer be a superpower.

"Now, I ask you again. If your men bypass the hostages, if they have whatever equipment they need, how long will it take them to recapture Site J?"

There was a long pause. Hector knew the general had to be circumspect, because whatever he said next would be heard by the terrorists ten minutes later. "Sir, in that case, I believe you'd be looking at the seventh threat condition for that facility. That would be my recommendation."

The President looked around the table. "What the heck is the seventh threat condition?"

Sinclair answered. "That would be ThreatCon X-ray, sir."

Earlier, Hector had been thrown by all the discussion about ThreatCon Echo as a classified, sixth-level threat condition. At the Pentagon, Major Christou had been very convincing as she described there being only five Threat-Cons from Normal to Delta. But going from the fifth and sixth letters of the alphabet directly to the third from last sounded extremely ominous.

"Brower can't be serious," Casson said.

"Somebody better tell me what ThreatCon X-ray is," the President warned.

That duty once again fell to Sinclair. "Threat Condition X-ray acknowledges that the enemy has attacked and holds a location, such that the only way to deny them that location is to destroy it."

The President stared at her in disbelief. "Destroy it? As in . . . what? Am I to understand that . . ." He flicked on the speakerphone to Brower again. "General Brower, am I correct in thinking you've suggested I order an *airstrike* on the *Pentagon?*"

"That would . . . seem to fulfill your needs, sir."

"Sweet Jesus." The President turned the speakerphone off.

The room was silent. Hector had to take a chance on the obvious. "Uh, sir, instead of destroying Site J, couldn't you just shut down whatever they're using to contact the satellites?"

The President pursed his lips, spoke to the display screen. "What about it, Major Bailey? You seem to be the one who knows about shutting down the Pentagon's lines of communication."

Bailey stopped adjusting controls to answer the President. "We can do a lot from here, sir. I could take out all the site-to-site traffic between J and R. I can lock them out of MILSTAR and all the SATCOMs. But they're pumping out a lot of signals through landlines in their immediate area. Those would have to be physically cut to completely isolate the facility."

The President looked to Milton Meyer. "You're the NSA. Can we cut or block or blow up all the physical lines linking Site J to the outside?"

Meyer was glum. "In theory."

"I'm not interested in theory. Can it be done?"

"It might take fifteen, twenty hours. We'd need blue-prints, network diagrams, twenty to thirty construction crews. You have to remember, sir, the system was designed to withstand nuclear war. It's robust and highly redundant."

The President turned to General Janukatys. "What does the Air Force say? Is it even possible to bomb Site J? It's what, three hundred feet down?"

"Three hundred and twenty," Sinclair confirmed.

General Janukatys pointedly ignored her. "We have the B61-11, sir. It's basically the old B53, but with significant earth-penetrating characteristics."

The President was almost vibrating. "B? We're talking 'bomb,' right? A *nuclear* bomb? Is that right?"

Janukatys nodded, completely neutral in the face of the President's agitation. Hector got no sense the general was playing any games with his commander in chief now. He was committed to serving his country, nothing more, nothing less. He recalled Christou's words. *It's our job.* "The B61-11 was designed to deliver warheads to hardened, underground facilities in North Korea and Iraq. If dropped at altitude from a B-2, it will penetrate two hundred feet of typical soil."

"That's a hundred and twenty feet short," the President said.

"And then it detonates a twenty-megaton nuclear explosive," Janukatys added. "Whatever's left of Site J after that won't be functioning."

Hector watched as the President continued to walk from one side of the room to the other.

"A nuclear bomb on American soil," he muttered, almost

to himself. "What does that do to Arlington, General? Do we have to evacuate D.C. to avoid fallout?"

"My BDA people will need to see soil reports for the Pentagon reservation to make accurate predictions," the general said. "But as I recall from our plans for using the penetrators on other facilities—at a depth of two hundred feet, the blast chamber is self-sealing. There will be minimal radioactive leakage to the atmosphere, though I'm not prepared to discuss the long-term effect on the water table."

The President nodded his head nervously. "And what happens to the hostages in the Pentagon if the bomb goes off two hundred feet beneath them?"

Janukatys spoke to his folded hands on the table before him. "I would anticipate that the shock of the initial blast wave coming up from the ground would be enough to kill them instantly. At the very least, it will render them unconscious, and then . . . it will be like a sinkhole, Mr. President. The Pentagon building will essentially be pulverized by the blast, and then collapse inward, into the depression made by the sudden vaporization of the soil beneath it."

After the brief moment of silence Janukatys's description provoked, the President looked over at the assistant director of the CIA. "What did you estimate, Archie? A hundred hostages?"

Fortis was as low-key as Janukatys. "With the, uh . . . personnel at Site J, it's more like . . . more like two hundred and eighty, sir. About a third of them civilian."

The President stared at the bandages on his palms. "So I can order the deaths of two hundred and eighty American citizens and allies. Including my wife . . . Or I can risk losing our greatest military . . . no, let's call it our greatest *technological* asset. Our ability to monitor our world. To look behind our backs. To make certain our enemies aren't working against us. To defuse wars. Prove crimes. Defend not just our country, but the world." Hector watched as the President's shoulders sagged. "What's that worth? A million lives? A billion? . . . Two hundred and eighty . . . ? Can two hundred and eighty lives measure up to what QUICKSILVER might do to us? *If* the terrorists know about it? *If* they can control it?"

Then Sinclair stood up. "Mr. President, there might be another way."

The President regarded her with intense skepticism. "Dear God, I hope so."

"What we want is a surgical strike against one target in the Pentagon. We don't have to use a nuke. And we don't have to send in two hundred and twenty-five troops."

General Janukatys rose to his feet at that. "That's insane, Major."

Hector didn't know what he meant.

But Sinclair did. She walked around the table to approach the President. "One Delta team from one Delta squadron. Six men . . . even four men. With explosives. They enter the Building, go down the elevator shafts, target the generators and the backups. Contact with the enemy is minimal. If General Brower puts the right people in, the enemy won't even know they're there."

"Who the hell are the right people?" Janukatys asked. "A mission like that, soldiers train for it, at least for days. I would hope for weeks."

Sinclair held her ground. "Delta Force is trained to respond in hours, sir. Three squadrons of them are good to go in—" She looked at her watch.

"Fifty-five minutes," Hector said.

"Fifty-five minutes. You could have more than two hundred of them fighting for hours to go through the Pentagon, ring by ring, floor by floor, or you could send a smaller force in to go straight to Site J."

"Still going to take time," Janukatys said.

"Much less time," Sinclair countered.

The President had watched each of his officers speak. Now he asked a question of his own. "How long would it take to bomb the Building, General? With the penetrator nuke?"

Janukatys looked off to the side for a moment. "We have B61-11s with the 28th at Ellsworth, South Dakota. That's about ninety minutes flying time for a B-1B Lancer . . . maybe a half-hour, forty-five minutes to prep."

"You're saying two hours," the President concluded. "And I'm going to guess that you're being optimistic."

Janukatys didn't argue. "We are no longer on instant, standby alert for our bombers, that's correct. But we can get half our bombers off the ground, loaded, within an hour. We'll do it in forty-five minutes, guaranteed."

The President rubbed his bandaged palms together, but before he could say anything else, Major Bailey broke in from SPACECOM.

"Excuse me, sir. We're putting through a download from the National Imagery and Mapping Agency. Do you want the images at your location?"

"Uh, those will be the . . . the enhanced frames from . . . from the morning's satellite imagery," Fortis said. "Send them through, Major." Fortis looked at the President. "At least we, uh, . . . will see the face of the enemy."

A screen beneath Bailey flickered once, changing from an AOL/CBS network feed to a satellite picture frame. Technical data which Hector didn't understand formed a smeared pattern to the left, reminding him of a seismograph record of a major earthquake. Then a black-and-white picture of the Pentagon's Courtyard flashed into the frame, and a moment later, it became full-color. Hector checked the time code at the bottom right of the screen. The image had been captured at 10:05 A.M., just about the time the President's party had arrived. He looked at the gray roof over the innermost A Ring. When that picture had been taken, he had been beneath it, standing at a window with the President, talking about Ground Zero. And Major Christou had been alive.

Hector stared at the insignificant white figures in the Courtyard's center. He wondered which of them had killed the major.

"Here's enhancement number one," Bailey said.

Two yellow boxes flashed, side by side, above a round white circle that Hector realized must be one of the luncheon tables. Suddenly, the boxes zoomed up as the picture was enlarged. It became an image of two midshipmen, flipping a linen tablecloth up over the table, both of them looking skyward, one more than another.

"What altitude was that taken from?" the President asked.

"It's a composite image, sir," Bailey answered. "And it's been enhanced by NIMA. So, there's no absolute answer. Figure an average altitude of three to four hundred miles."

Hector knew why the President had asked. The face of the one midshipman who was looking directly up was clear, almost sharp, easily seen.

The face of the other midshipman was at more of an angle, but Hector thought he could be recognized by anyone who might be familiar with his face.

"No identification on these two, yet," Bailey said. "But

they're running them through the FBI photo files." She adjusted a control. "Here's enhancement number two."

A second photo of the Courtyard appeared, first in black and white, then in color. This time, only a single yellow box flashed over one figure in white who was on a path some distance from the other midshipmen. Hector could see the oblong blob that was an upturned face at the center of the box.

Then the box enlarged, dragging the pixels inside with it. Blocks of them smoothed as he watched. The oblong blob acquired depth and shadows, eyes, nose, and mouth, and white-blond hair.

And a name.

"Erich . . ."

All eyes turned to Sinclair as she stood absolutely still, eyes riveted to the screen.

"Do you know him?" Casson asked.

The major started to speak, had to clear her throat to continue. "Yes, sir. *Hauptmann* Erich Kronig."

She turned to the President, and to Hector it seemed she no longer was able to believe in what she said next. "Sir, he's a captain in the German KSK." She held a hand to her forehead, trying to recall something. *"Kommando Spezialkräfte.* They're the German Delta Force." Despite everything that had happened today, it was the first time Hector had seen the Army major look rattled.

"And how do you happen to know him?" Casson demanded.

"Sir . . . I trained him." Sinclair looked around the room. "We all trained him. Two years ago, he worked at the Pentagon."

For a moment, no one spoke.

The President continued to stare at the screen, his set and grim expression that of someone whose mind was made up.

"General Janukatys," the President said. "I want that bomb in the air in thirty minutes. And God help me, your target is the Pentagon."

FOUR

FIRST FLOOR, B RING

There was only one thought in Amy Bethune's mind as she and Tom Chase silently emerged from the utility staircase off Corridor Eight: *I remind him of his* wife.

She was positive that's what he'd been about to say when they were tight up against each other beside the window upstairs. *It wasn't too shabby being compared to a major,* she admitted to herself. *But how could I be like anyone who'd marry someone like him?* General Vanovich had to be a real joker to have put Chase together with someone in the service. It took more than looks to make a relationship. Amy could guess why it hadn't worked out.

But this was not the time to think about Mr. and Mrs. Tom Chase. The doors she and her reluctant civilian partner had just come to marked the end of the B Ring corridor on the ground floor. On the other floors above, the corridor continued unbroken. But just outside these doors was the ground-level access road connecting the Courtyard to the

AE service road which ran between B Ring, where they were, and C Ring, where they wanted to go. To get to C Ring, she and Chase would have to exit the Building, go up the access road to its intersection with the service road, and then take the AE road to the doors into C Ring. All without being seen or neutralized by the enemy.

"You're sure this is a good idea?" Chase asked.

It was just the kind of question she'd come to expect from him. He knew nothing about tactics. She explained the situation to him slowly, as if he were a plebe and this was his induction week. "No one is watching the Courtyard access road. If there were, the guys we saw from the window wouldn't have had to shoot the hostage who tried to escape. Because they did shoot him, that means there's no one else on guard duty out there who could have stopped him. We just have to be careful when we reach the corner. Okay?"

"As long as they think the way you do."

Of course they do, Amy thought, without bothering to say anything more to him. *They're professionals.* She remained silent as she checked Chase's H&K to make sure his safety was still off and that the weapon was set to fire single shots. The last thing she needed was for Chase to pull the trigger once and then expend all thirty rounds in one wild burst. She had already warned him about staying aware of his barrel—if he had to start firing, she didn't want him to sweep across her from behind. But from the tentative way he was holding the weapon, she wasn't convinced he'd actually pull the trigger, even if someone were about to fire at him first.

Amy checked her own weapon, thinking about how good it was going to be to finally get to the ops centers. Then Chase would be their responsibility, and she could join the Pentagon's own security personnel for the rest of the mission.

She composed herself by refocusing on that mission now. The terrorists who killed her classmates were going to die. Missions didn't come any simpler than that.

She held her finger to her lips to remind Chase to be silent, then slowly pushed on the pressure bar until she felt the mechanism click and the door to the access road begin to move.

She held the door open, motionless, at six inches, counted to five, feeling the hot, humid air rush over her. Then she opened the door another foot, followed by another five count. When no hail of bullets responded, she crouched down to quickly check to the left, toward the Courtyard. She saw nothing. She looked right toward the intersection with the service road. Clear again.

Amy held the door for Tom as she motioned him through, then slowly, and silently let the door close.

For the moment, they were in a protected shelter. The underside of the overhead second-floor B Ring corridor ran above them like a bridge. But when they moved out from its shelter, they would be completely exposed on the narrow roadway, which, to Amy, had all the disadvantages of the floor of a deep canyon or a constricted urban alley. On either side of them, the Pentagon rose up its full five stories. On both sides, the exterior wall of the first floor was solid brick. The exterior wall of the next four floors was concrete, but at a distance it resembled limestone slabs. The concrete had been set in wooden forms deliberately constructed to create that appearance.

On either side of the roadway, the upper floors of the Building all had regular rows of windows, any one of which could have a terrorist shooter behind it. The only possible cover along the road that Amy could see was provided by two bright blue garbage Dumpsters, one to the left about halfway to the service road, the other to the right, just at the intersection. But neither Dumpster would provide protection from shooters on the upper stories or the roof.

Though Amy would not tell Chase—she still couldn't be sure of his reaction—she knew this was their moment of highest risk. They had to move swiftly to the right, reach the intersection, then turn right again to reach the C Ring doors they had seen from the second-floor window. If they met another group of terrorists moving hostages, things were going to get very messy, very quickly.

If they didn't meet the enemy, then they would soon be safely in C Ring, behind the perimeter doors that in B Ring had prevented them from reaching the below-ground operations centers.

There was no advantage in delaying the inevitable, so Amy eased forward along the brick wall to scan the roofline on both sides. Seeing nothing and no one, she motioned to Chase to keep close to her, and then she ran across to the other side of the access road. As she advanced toward the service-road intersection, she kept her eyes moving from the windows above to the intersection ahead and back again. Behind her, she heard Chase's footfalls, keeping pace.

The access road met the AE service road at a corner of the Pentagon, so the two roads formed an arrowhead. The access road was the shaft, with the service road forming the sharply angled downstrokes to the right and to the left.

Amy hugged the brick wall until she came to the second blue Dumpster at the intersection. The bin was half-filled with chunks of old plaster, stained wood, and other renovation debris. She moved quickly around it. There was another five feet of wall between the end of the Dumpster and the beginning of the intersection. As Chase joined her now, breathing audibly, Amy made a solemn promise to herself to still be in shape when she hit her mid-thirties.

Slowly, she moved forward to within inches of the end of the wall, then rapidly angled her head around the corner to look to the right, down the service road, just for an instant.

The instant was enough. Thirty feet away were two gunmen in midshipman white, guarding the C Ring doors that she and Chase needed to reach.

A torrent of appropriate words for their situation sprang into her mind in Russian, English, French, and Spanish. But she knew better than to say them aloud. Instead, she turned back to Chase and whispered, "Two, by the doors."

She saw his face tighten. "What's the plan?" he whispered back.

Amy raised her H&K.

Chase's eyes narrowed with concern. "How far are they?"

Amy frowned. She didn't like being reminded of her failing, but his point was valid. With her marksmanship, if she emptied an entire clip at both terrorists at thirty feet, she'd be lucky to hit one of them.

"Just means we have to get them closer," he said softly.

"Yeah? How?"

Chase stretched out his left hand and wiggled his fingers. She stared at them, baffled. Was he suggesting they *wave* the terrorists over? But then, in a move too fast to anticipate, he reached up to her ear with his right hand. Jerking her head away, she was just in time to see the fingers of his right hand roll to reveal his folded-up Swiss Army knife, as if he had pulled it from the air.

He waved his left hand in front of her. "Misdirection," he whispered, and then he asked her for the flash-bang grenade.

Suddenly, his behavior made a lot more sense.

Amy slipped the cylindrical explosive from her jeans pocket. It was the size and shape of a small aerosol spray can.

"Set it off around the other corner," he told her. "They'll come to check it out. We'll hide behind the Dumpster. And when they go past us, we'll take off for the doors."

Amy only had to think that one over for a second. How could someone be so smart and so absolutely clueless at the same time? Yes, she'd roll the flash-bang down the other branch of the service road. And, yes, they'd hide behind the Dumpster as the gunmen ran to investigate the explosion.

But she wasn't about to take a chance on herself and Chase outrunning a bullet.

She had a better idea, though she didn't share it. She didn't think he could handle it.

"Get behind the Dumpster," she told him. "And cover your ears."

When he was safely on the Dumpster's far end, Amy twisted off the flash-bang's no-snag cap, keeping the release tab in place. Then she sprinted to the opposite side of the road, and carefully rolled the grenade down the service road, to the left. The cardboard canister was specially designed to roll flat and straight, but she didn't waste time watching it as she ran to rejoin Chase behind the Dumpster.

At the same instant, the brick and concrete canyon rang with the reverberation of a startlingly loud thunderclap. So did her ears.

Chase took his hands from his own ears, getting ready to run. Then his eyes widened. "I hear them," he whispered. "Get down!"

But Amy was already at the edge of the Dumpster, waiting for the enemy to round the corner, her submachine gun a comforting weight in her hands.

Chase might not know what to do next.

But she did.

SITE J

" 'We hold these truths to be self-evident . . . that whenever any form of government becomes destructive of these ends, it is the *right* of the people to alter or abolish it, and to institute *new* government.' " Ranger read from the creased and cracked sheet of yellowed parchment he held in both hands. The words were faint, the ink badly faded, but he had memorized the words. It was essential to know the enemy. "You recognize this, General?"

"The Declaration of Independence, you son of a bitch. You killed all those people at the Archives."

Ranger crushed the antique document in his hands. "What we do here today is an act of self-preservation. But what you do, every day, is insidious. Your country's stated, published, strategic goals are to recast the world order in its own image. One type of democracy. One type of 'free' market. One currency. One goal—the dominance of America. And to enforce that agenda, look what you've created here—a network of satellites that watch our every move, listen to our every conversation . . . how is what you're doing to the world any different from what Stalin's secret police did to Russia? Or the *Stasi* did to East Germany? I'll tell you what's different—those were only *state* police. You're applying their tactics to the world!"

"Are you Russian?" the general asked. "Is that what this is about?"

Ranger opened his hands, heard the parchment crackle as it slowly unfolded from the new creases he had given it. "General Vanovich, sixty years ago, most of the nations of the world united to stop a single madman who had dreams of global domination. It was a just cause. And now, the cause is just again. Except this time, instead of a single madman, we are faced with more than three hundred million of you, each one determined to reshape the world in America's image. That will not happen. Today, you will find out that all men—all players on the world stage—*are* created equal and have equal right to a level playing field."

"Whoever you people are, you don't understand my country."

"Better than you, General. That's why we'll keep these until your country remembers what they mean again." Ranger refolded the Declaration and stuffed it into the envelope that held the rest of the Charters from the Archives— the Bill of Rights, and the first and last pages of the Constitution. All priceless and worthless at the same time.

"Ranger!" India called out from her station on the console. "The QUICKSILVER platform is approaching the target coordinates. It will be in range in three minutes."

"Stand by to fire." Ranger tossed the thick envelope back on top of the console. "Don't look so shocked, General. Why did you build it, if not to use it?"

"It was supposed to be a nonlethal 'off switch,' " Vanovich answered wearily. "To shut down a radar site. Turn off engines of tanks and trucks and ships. Erase computers at chemical weapons factories . . . I wanted it to end wars before they could start."

"Then you got what you wanted," Ranger said. "After today, America won't be able to go to war with anyone. You should be very proud."

THE WHITE HOUSE, WEST WING

Margaret Sinclair barreled through the crowds in the West Wing hallway, shoved two colonels and a general out of her way with hurried apologies, and pushed through a cluster of staffers from the State Department talking urgently in whispers. Though she knew four of them, she'd almost not recognized them because they were all wearing jeans.

Every hallway she entered was packed so full the White House visitor-control office had evidently run out of passes. Some of the people she saw were reduced to wearing their driver's licenses on index cards signed by a Secret Service agent.

When Margaret finally reached the door to the Cabinet Room and its uniformed Treasury guards, she paused for just a moment and looked down the hallway in the direction of the Oval Office, thinking of Tyler. She always thought of Tyler. But no matter how much she needed to see him right now, to hug him, to let him know that everything would be all right, there was something else more important that she had to see to first.

More important than Tyler. Just to think those words seemed wrong to her. Though she had long ago realized that everything she did for her country, she did for her child. She was insuring both their futures.

The Cabinet Room was standing room only. Some people were shouting. Some people were whispering. Phones rang unceasingly, landlines and cellular chirps. Ignoring them all, Margaret pushed her way through to the end of the lustrous, dark-wood conference table, stacked almost a foot high with maps of Arlington, the Capital Region, and . . . she dug through the pile until she came to what she remembered seeing there earlier—the blueprints.

She didn't even bother to wait for the elevator on her way back. She ran down the short staircase to the lower Mess level. The physical activity was helping tone down the shock she'd felt seeing Erich's face on the display screen.

The guards outside the Situation Room made no attempt to stop her as she quick-marched past them, straight-arming the door to re-enter the inner circle.

Ignoring everyone but the President, Margaret headed straight for the black conference table and unfurled the loose roll of blueprints like carpets before him. "*This* is what I was talking about, *sir*."

"I am *not* accustomed to having someone walk out while I am talking to them, Major." The President was livid.

And what if I'd stopped to tell you all the truth, Mr. President, Margaret thought. *That one of the Pentagon terrorists who had the Chairman of the Joint Chiefs of Staff and the Vice President and the Secretary of Defense and maybe even your wife shot made me remember what it's like to make love in the afternoon, smell tropical flowers in the moonlight, have a man's hands in my hair again?*

Instead, she had abruptly left the Situation Room and run up to the West Wing hallway. Now there were six large sheets, dark blue lines on pale blue paper, on the table before the President. And what was on them was more important than her brief affair with Captain Kronig.

Two years ago, Erich Kronig had arrived at the Pentagon as part of an ongoing officer-exchange program conducted between NATO partners. As a captain in Germany's newest special forces group, *Kommando Spezialkräfte,* he'd already cross-trained with Britain's SAS and America's Delta Force. Like Delta, the KSK's mandate in Germany was a combination of missions. Where Germany's GSG-9 police force operated domestically in counterterrorist and hostage-rescue situations, the KSK was set up to perform the same activities as part of military missions outside of Germany, in defense of German territory and that of its NATO allies.

As part of the National Infrastructure Agency, Margaret had prepared a training course on Infrastructure Counterterrorist Operations. It was a crash course covering everything from protecting the C^3I network of a counterterrorist force in the field, to wireless uploading of computer viruses into the enemy's C^3I network. Portions of the course were conducted at the Army's Special Warfare Center at Fort Bragg where Erich, and others like him in the exchange program, were taught how to take down or take over phone-switching systems, bank computers, and local law-enforcement radio networks.

And sometime in the course of that program, she and Erich had become discreet lovers, neither of them wishing to extend the magic of their time together into their everyday lives. She'd had no contact with him since that one week in Hawaii at the end of his tour. They had known their careers would allow them no future together. That had been part of the magic.

"And as I said then, sir, he's a dedicated professional. In the field exercises, Captain Kronig was as good as our own special forces. On the theory of infrastructure counterterrorism, he was brilliant."

Margaret turned to cut off Douglas Casson before he could

even begin to speak. "And he was here, being taught by us, as part of an ongoing, long-established NATO exchange program designed to foster familiarity with our allies. NATO officers attend West Point and the Naval Academy. They fly in our fighter squadrons. Our officers train with their officers overseas. Our Special Ops forces train with the SAS and the KSK. There was no breach of security. It was all SOP!"

Casson smiled one of his tight little smiles as he pushed up on his ridiculous circular glasses. "It's just that you seemed to react to his presence here a bit . . . shall we say, personally."

"How do you expect me to take it, Mr. Casson? There's a damn good chance he defeated Pentagon security today because of information my agency gave to him." She returned to the President. "Sir, I believe these blueprints show a way we can still save the hostages, unless you are determined to kill them all with General Janukatys's bomb."

Margaret heard the President's sharp intake of breath and knew at that moment that he wasn't going to listen to another word she had to say. *His wife is one of those hostages! Why did I say that?* But she knew the reason she had. It was seeing Erich on the screen. And feeling personally guilty, no matter what she'd just said to Casson.

Hector MacGregor spoke up to save her from herself. "Mr. President, sir, I think we're all understandably a bit overheated about this. And . . . and if you just take a moment to think about it, the situation is as under control as you can make it right now."

Margaret watched the President glare at his assistant the way he had glared at her. *Hector's about to get his butt kicked out of here, too,* Margaret thought. She had a picture of them both in some bar, buying each other a beer as satellites fell from the sky and a mushroom cloud grew over the Pentagon because she'd slept with the enemy and insulted the President.

"This is how it stands, sir," MacGregor said quickly. "The penetrator is being loaded onto the bomber in South Dakota right now. Do I have that right, General?"

Janukatys nodded without speaking, obviously having no wish to appear on the President's radar.

"Okay, so the bombing option is a little over two hours away. And Colonel Tobin reports that the Delta Force squadrons are about thirty minutes from full deployment around the Pentagon. So we've got that option covered, too. So . . . if we look at it from another perspective, why not listen to what the major has to say as a third option? You've already set in motion everything you can set in motion."

You're losing him, Margaret thought. She could see the President's anger at her reckless comment building, not dissipating.

But then MacGregor trumped it.

"That way, when this is over," he added, "no matter how it turns out, you'll be able to tell the American people that you really did consider every possibility."

As she saw the President pause to consider his assistant's argument, she tried not to think that the President's mind could be swayed not because it was the right thing to do, but because he cared about how he'd go down in history, or on the six o'clock news. Though all that really mattered was whether or not he would hear her idea.

The President picked up one of the six blueprints Margaret had spread out on the table. "Five minutes, Major. Show me what you've got."

Margaret gave MacGregor a significant look, telling him

as plainly as she could: *I owe you, kid.* Then she reached for a blueprint from the Pentagon Renovation Program. It showed the work done on Wedge #4—the section of the Pentagon whose renovation had just been completed. Wedge #4 spanned from halfway through the Metro Side to halfway through the River Side, taking in Corridors Nine and Ten.

"This is the wedge they've just renovated, Mr. President," she began. "It's where part of the Joint Staff and the SECDEF offices are located."

"I am quite familiar with it," the President said.

"All right, are you familiar with this, sir: The old Pentagon had too many bathrooms."

It was only a matter of time before they connected her uncharacteristic emotionalism of a moment before not to her passion for the mission, but to her shock over Erich. Margaret pressed on without waiting for an answer.

"Before the renovation, the Pentagon had twice as many bathrooms as any office building its size should have had. So many that when President Roosevelt toured it, just before it was finished, he asked what the hell was going on. Why so many bathrooms?"

The incredulous looks on the faces of Casson, Fortis, Meyer, Paulsen, and Janukatys were almost comical. Each of them was likely already fashioning a joke-by-joke accounting for replay later of how she'd lost both her job and her reputation this afternoon, with no help from them.

"The reason, sir, was segregation. Roosevelt had signed an executive order forbidding discrimination based on race in the government. So, the engineers building the Pentagon interpreted that as meaning they had to have the same number of toilet facilities labeled 'Colored Men' and 'Colored

Women' as for 'White Men' and 'White Women.' That's how they saw equality."

"Three and a half minutes, Major," the President said. Margaret picked up the pace of her delivery.

"Roosevelt was furious. Refused to allow it. The signs were never painted on the doors. The bathrooms were never segregated. And because the use pattern of the toilet facilities was going to change, become more evenly distributed throughout the building, the contractors changed the plumbing specifications to speed up construction."

Now Margaret placed a second blueprint over the first one, this one showing underground pipes and conduits on the north half of the Building. With her hand, she circled an area to the north of the completed Wedge #4, just skirting the edge of the River Side Parade Grounds. "Here's where those main sewage lines connect, then run out to the sewage lift stations by the North Parking Lot."

The President stared at her. "Are you suggesting someone should crawl up a sewage pipe to get into the Building?"

"Yes and no, sir," Margaret said. "After Roosevelt gave the order to stop segregating the bathrooms, to save time and money the plumbing contractors joined together groups of sewage branch pipes under the basement of the Pentagon. Here"—quickly pulling up a third blueprint, she pointed to a web of pipes coming together at the center of the wedge, merging into one larger pipe—"rather than running all the separate lines out to be joined here, at the main outflow pipes. Sir, what it comes down to is that there are five concrete conduits leading through the foundation at this point. And those five conduits have *never* been sealed."

"That's absolutely impossible," Casson said. He pushed his chair back, stood up, and walked around the table for a closer look at the blueprint. Then he took off his glasses to peer more closely at the detailed drawing. "The NRO is a tenant of the Pentagon, and I guarantee you there are no unobstructed water lines, or steam pipes, or gas pipes into or out of the Building. And no one can crawl through the Pentagon's air ducts, either."

"Mr. Casson, what I'm referring to are raw concrete conduits, not working pipes. They were all put in place when the concrete slab was poured. But by the time the plumbers got there, these five conduits were no longer needed."

Casson scornfully jabbed the blueprint with a finger. "Then where are they, Major? They're not on this blueprint." Casson looked at the President as if his, and the Chief Executive's, time were being wasted by an unstable lunatic.

"That's the point! They're not on this blueprint. They're not on *any* of the original blueprints. The Pentagon was built so fast, its engineers couldn't keep up with the architectural drawings. A lot of the underlying structure was made up on-site as the contractors went along."

"Preposterous." Casson was already on his way back to his chair.

"You can call the Army Corps of Engineers to confirm what I'm saying," Margaret said to his retreating back. "They had to make a study of the Pentagon the way it really was before they let the vendors draw up their renovation plans."

"How do you know so much about this?" the President asked, almost suspiciously.

Margaret knew she was on dangerous ground. If her idea for saving the hostages was rejected, all that she might accomplish could be to make an investigation of her connection to *Hauptmann* Erich Kronig more serious. She might well be suspected of being his inside contact, with her undue interest in the layout of the Pentagon added to their romantic entanglement. "I had a friend who—"

Once again, MacGregor came to her rescue. "That's right, sir. Major Christou even told me stories about the ghosts in the Pentagon's basement."

"Sir, because these five conduits aren't on the blueprints, Kronig doesn't know about them. They're our way in. We've got a little over two hours before the bomber gets here. We could lose half our satellites by then, *plus* QUICKSILVER. But if you send in a surgical strike, sir, you could shut down the power to Site J. Then you could call off the bomber *and* send Delta Force in for the hostages."

MacGregor added the last word. "It does keep all your options open. No restrictions."

The President nodded at his assistant, then turned to her. "And just where do you access these conduits, Major?"

Margaret felt the tide of battle turning. She reached for another blueprint, one showing the road system around the Building. She spread it out and the President followed the path of her finger as she spoke. "With a couple of jackhammers, we could get to them here—in the parade-ground overpass tunnel. An MIR scanner could see through the concrete and find them in a second."

"And where would the team come out?"

Knowing she was going to have to set him straight about a team soon, Margaret indicated the edge of the sub-basement apron, underneath the River Side parking lot and the Tricare health facility beneath that. "Right at this wall, sir. They've had so much trouble with groundwater, there's a gap surrounding the exterior basement wall that's outfitted with pumps to keep it dry. There are access hatches every twenty feet for pump maintenance. Here. And here."

The President nodded, sighing deeply. "If there's really a chance . . . All right, I'll talk to General Brower, and tell him to get a team ready."

This is it, Margaret thought. *Time to make the last sale.*

But Douglas Casson beat her to it.

The director of the NRO was unexpectedly at her elbow, his glasses in his hand, bending forward to more closely examine the blueprint showing the plumbing connections beneath the basement floor. "Excuse me, Major, but are these the kind of pipes you've been talking about?"

She saw exactly where Casson was pointing, knew what he had noticed. "Yes, sir."

"The ones that are designed to go through the five conduits you want a Delta team to use."

"That's correct, sir."

Even the President could tell there was a problem. "What is it, Doug?"

Casson straightened up and replaced his glasses. "According to the blueprint specs, this kind of liner pipe is only sixteen inches across. Which means those unsealed conduits couldn't be more than eighteen to twenty inches in diameter."

"We can't put a man through something that narrow," the President said with a frown.

"No, sir," Margaret agreed, "not a man. But—"

"You?" Casson interrupted. Margaret knew that in the NRO director's mind, she had just handed him the punch line to the story of her defeat.

"You can't be serious, Major."

"I can fit through that opening, sir. And ten years ago, I was with the First Special Forces Operational Detachment under Colonel Brower."

"Delta Force?" Casson said. "So, you were in intelligence?" He turned to the President. "They do let women in that unit, sir. It has a special name as I recall . . . the Funny Platoon? Something like that."

The President pushed the blueprints away from him. "Major, I will not send a desk soldier behind enemy lines."

But Margaret had not gone this far to give up now. She spoke more forcefully to regain his attention. "I was an operator, sir. There were five of us. All women. We were the fourth group taken through Delta Force selection and training since the eighties. Our involvement was classified. Because of the politics. I was in operations in Iraq, Liberia, and Vancouver."

Casson was dismissive. "Doing recon, no doubt. Spotting for snipers. That sort of thing."

"Call General Brower, sir. He'll tell you." Margaret's voice rose with her urgency. Her idea was being lost in the confrontation over her personal involvement in the operation.

The President looked at his watch. "General Brower will be joining his forces in five minutes. I'm not going to disturb him for—"

Margaret used her combat voice on the President, the deafening sound startling everyone in the small, windowless room, including her. "SIR, WHAT CAN I SAY TO GET YOU TO DO THE RIGHT THING? SIR?"

The President looked aghast. "You are dismissed, Major!"

Everyone at the table was standing now, but Margaret wasn't finished. Too many lives were at stake. For the first time in her military career, she did not obey an order instantly. "Sir, I apologize for my conduct. But you agreed the mission was good. You know the conduits are there. And I am the only soldier for the mission."

The President's chin quivered slightly. Margaret recognized the telltale movement as a sign of someone under great strain. She knew she was facing court-martial. Hector MacGregor could not save her this time. But the President surprised her.

"Major, I know we are all emotionally stretched right now. My wife . . . your husband—"

"Ex-husband, sir."

"—so I suggest that you leave the room now, so none of us does anything we will all regret. That is an order!"

A display screen flickered to life on the far wall.

Along with everyone else, Margaret looked up to see Major Bailey at SPACECOM in Cheyenne Mountain.

"Mr. President," the major said, "you asked for an update when I had one."

"Go ahead, Major."

"We are confirming loss of the automatic tracking signal from the QUICKSILVER platform, sir. Everything checks out on the ground, so we are assuming that it was turned off at source."

That's it, Margaret thought. *They've got what they were after.* She began rolling up her blueprints. MacGregor sympathetically moved to assist her.

"Major Bailey, do you have *any* way of tracking the platform?" the President asked.

On the screen, Bailey shook her head. "Based on the specs I've been given, I'd say that thing is pretty much invisible. I have an active search running on all likely orbital paths it might have taken after the signal stopped, but every minute that goes by increases the search space. It's your needle in a haystack, sir."

"Do you have an update on the other satellites you've been tracking?"

Bailey held up a sheet of paper. "Yes, sir. As of—"

The screen went blank.

Beside it, the seriously degraded MAJIC image of the Pentagon winked out, too.

Casson, Janukatys, and Paulsen immediately went to the controls on the table's raised consoles and turned dials and pressed contact switches. The television feeds on the other screens were intact. But the two screens that had carried information transmitted by U.S. military satellites had gone dead.

"Something to think about, gentlemen," Margaret said as she wedged the rolled-up blueprints under her arm.

"So far, everything I've told you has turned out to be right. So I'll tell you this. Whoever hijacked QUICKSILVER just used it. And you can bet he's going to keep on using it. I would. Now all you have to ask yourself is: *What's* he going to use it on?"

She was halfway out the door before she heard the President calling her name.

FIVE

50TH SPACE WING, SCHRIEVER AIR FORCE BASE, COLORADO

It began as nothing. At first, the brief flicker of an unfocused beam of infrared light, so weak it would not have registered on a soldier's infrared scope.

The beam found a spot of barren soil and locked on to it. It had been guided to that location by signals received from three NAVSTAR satellites making up part of the Global Positioning System. Beside the beam, a twisted tuft of prairie grass was still. Beside the grass, a white concrete pylon, four feet square, formed a structural support for a seventy-five-foot radio dish that looked blankly to the deep blue Colorado sky.

There were ten other dishes within half a mile of the large one. Some were covered by radomes, protective shelters that hid the orientation of the dishes within and shielded them from the sun and rain. Nearby, there were arrays of smaller dishes, arranged in rows as if mechanical aliens had planted fields of robotic flowers.

Underground wires united the dishes, combining them into the most complex and expensive satellite-tracking facility in the world, transmitting vast amounts of data through that network into space, and from space to the computers and technicians and specialists who worked at the Jack Swigert Space Operations Facility.

The infrared beam had found its target within three feet of the operational center of the Schriever Air Force Base. From this one location, once known as Falcon AFB, each Department of Defense satellite was subject to ultimate control. Communications. Electro-optical surveillance. Everything. From this base, Cheyenne Mountain received the radar scans that would either keep the country at peace, or trigger a massive launch of Minuteman missiles and plunge the world into war. Schriever even controlled the navigation system that had allowed its own position to be targeted so easily.

It was Sunday afternoon. Eight hundred and fifty-two personnel worked in the Swigert SOF. Another two hundred were active across the more than three thousand acres of the base, most either on security patrol or conducting maintenance work. Many of those indoors were keeping track of the staggering events at the Pentagon via the radio or via the ceiling-mounted televisions in the cafeterias.

Outside, by the grass, by the seventy-five-foot dish, the weak infrared beam was joined by a second, slightly stronger beam. This second one was ultraviolet, again invisible to the eye. After traveling five hundred miles through the atmosphere, it wasn't even strong enough to cause a sunburn.

But it was strong enough for its purpose.

The sky was torn by a silver blade of liquid fire.

The silver flame flowed down from the deep blue above as if being poured into a flattened funnel, the two sides of it forming straight lines that converged on the one spot of soil the laser beams had marked.

Miles above, its topmost portion kept widening, stretched by the movement of the rushing satellite that fired the beam. Though after a few more seconds, the beam itself was no longer necessary. The effect of a superheated plasma gas propagating through the atmosphere, fueled by the force of the planet's electromagnetic field, had become self-sustaining.

The burning gas, bound by the lines of magnetic force that moved through it, created an interface with the untouched atmosphere that reflected light like a mirage, shimmering like a sheet of molten silver.

Summoning the lightning.

For just an instant, the seventy-five-foot radio dish glowed as if it were sculpted from light. And then it was transformed into an expanding ball of crackling blue fire, wild tendrils spinning out from it to touch every other dish.

One by one, the other dishes were cocooned in electrical fire, and if that fire made noise, it could not be heard over the thunder. Thick blue bolts of lightning blazed in random patterns from one structure to another. Some dishes exploded. Some metal-walled maintenance sheds melted. Some antennae lifted into the air from their pylons only to shatter like crockery.

The ground itself fused in angry veins, as the lightning found the underground wires and raced along their pathways, vaporizing them within their tunnels and conduits, forming sealed channels of ionized air that even more efficiently drew the lightning directly to the Swigert Space Operations Facility.

The entire bottom floor of the building blew out in one conflagration as every computer, every backup generator, and every storage battery vaporized simultaneously.

Then the top floors dropped straight down into the void formed by the demolished bottom floor. Everyone inside became weightless for that instant between falling and ignition in the uprush of fire. Their only warning was the sudden loss of power three seconds before the end. A moment just long enough for all to wonder how the outside *and* the backup power could fail at the same time, in a place where the power *never* went off.

After thirty seconds, the entire Swigert building was ablaze, along with all who had been in it, or even nearby. Then, from those flames came a final flurry of electrical tendrils that whipped out to dance over cars that had been parked around the building. The tendrils jumped to each vehicle in turn, igniting each gas tank, until the burning building was encircled by smaller infernos, as if watched by an audience.

By now, the superheated plasma gas had consumed its fuel and lost the energy that had bound it. Released, it melted away into the cool air, creating a gentle swirl of ice crystals that quickly sublimated in the bright sunshine, and dissipated like mist.

The silver blade evaporated as it was drawn back to the sky.

In less than one minute, Schriever Air Force Base was no more than a boundary drawn on a map. All that remained standing were three older dishes on the outskirts of the Air Force base, though their circuits and wiring had melted.

Five hundred miles downrange, its function fulfilled, QUICKSILVER traveled on, patiently waiting for orders.

THE WHITE HOUSE, SITUATION ROOM

America was blind. Literally. Hector could hear the disbelief and even the fear in the voices of Fortis and Meyer and Casson as they each shouted into their telephones, with General Janukatys and Admiral Paulsen adding to the chorus.

The Chief of Staff of the Air Force was trying to work through a White House operator to get a direct-dial line to Ellsworth AFB and check on the status of the penetrator bomb and B1-B bomber that would carry it.

The Chief of Naval Operations was still waiting to be put through to any Naval base that could tell him the status of the Navy's satellites.

Feeling more useless than ever, Hector MacGregor pushed himself up from his chair, then used his crutch to hop over to the President and Major Sinclair. As he approached, he studied Sinclair as if he might see some detail he had missed earlier. All he could think was *Delta Force.* He tried to picture her in a red bandana, bare arms, muscles glistening as she sprayed a machine gun into a room full of terrorists. But the image was ludicrous. She was so small . . . so blond . . . so . . . *beautiful.*

"He used QUICKSILVER to take out Schriever," Sinclair was saying as Hector stopped beside her. "It's the perfect move."

"Explain," the President said. The Man was listening as intently as if the Army major were his most trusted advisor. *And she should be,* Hector thought. *She's been right about everything. From the beginning.*

"He's after our satellites, sir. That's why he's in the Pentagon. That's why he's in Site J. He forced the EKH to burn up. He might have done the same to MAJIC Three. Or maybe he just changed its orbit and uploaded a new command set. The point is, whatever he's doing, the end result is that he's denying us access to our satellites. And by using QUICKSILVER against our key tracking and command station, he's just made it more difficult for us to figure out exactly what he's doing."

"You know him so well, where's he going to strike next?"

"Depends where QUICKSILVER goes. Obviously, it was just over Colorado. It still has to be in some sort of polar or near-polar orbit. It doesn't carry enough fuel to change orbits too drastically and still maneuver. If it's preceding easterly . . . if I were him, I'd go after Fort Meade on the next orbit, shut down the NSA. Then we'd be blind *and* deaf."

"How long?"

"At its operational orbit, its period is one hundred minutes."

"And the bomber won't be here for one hundred and twenty."

Hector couldn't stand it when the answer was so obvious. "Sir, let her go in."

The President locked eyes with the major. "Have you ever killed anyone?"

Sinclair's expression became unreadable. "Yes, sir."

"Up close?"

"Do you want me to describe what they were wearing?"

"All right. You're going in. And I advise you to get out before that bomber arrives."

Hector was surprised that Sinclair's demeanor changed so little at that. She had just been given the opportunity she had demanded. It was her chance to play the hero. Captain Kagan, in Site J, had been almost joyful when the President had ordered him into action. Why wasn't Sinclair the same?

She turned to Hector. "You have to promise me something."

Hector was startled. "Anything."

"You stay with Tyler."

Oh, shit, Hector thought. *Her kid. Her kid could lose* both *his parents in there.*

Sinclair touched his arm. "Don't look so nervous. I mean, just for today. Tonight. Maybe for a couple of days, but that's all. Tom and I have our wills made out. We have friends in Sacramento . . . everything's arranged. That's all you have to know. Can you do that?"

"Of course," Hector said. *She's preparing to die.* "But you're coming back."

"Roger that." And then it was as if he no longer existed as she turned her full attention back to the President. "I need you to tell General Brower what your orders are."

"You tell him," the President said. "He's on his way in two minutes. His helicopter's waiting."

Margaret drew herself up, saluted. "Thank you, sir."

The President self-consciously returned the salute. "Good luck, Major."

"You're letting her go?" Casson said from across the room.

"You're darn right I am," the President answered.

"Mistake, sir."

"Only if it doesn't work," Hector said, earning a smile from the major.

She rushed to the door, then backed up just in time to avoid being hit as it burst open.

Four Secret Service agents crashed in; one elbowed Sinclair aside as two others grabbed the President's arms.

"What is this?!" he protested.

One agent bellowed like a foghorn. "We are evacuating the White House. Move! Now! NOW!"

The two agents began pushing the President toward the door.

Hector's first reaction was to try to stop them. "What's going on!?"

All four agents were shouting now and there were loud cries from the hall outside. Then James Gibb, director of the FBI, appeared in the doorway. "Mr. President, you have to get out! All of you! Now!"

Hector hobbled toward the door as the President was propelled through it. Fortis, Meyer, and Casson pushed through ahead of Sinclair, who held back, and reached out for Hector.

"Tyler," she said.

Hector nodded. He hadn't forgotten. "Oval Office, I know."

"That's two I owe you." Sinclair pulled him down for an instant to give him a swift kiss on the cheek, and she was gone, into the stampede in the hallway.

Hector hesitated, unsure if he could manage his crutch in the crowd. Then Paulsen and Janukatys were behind him.

"Move it or lose it, son," the admiral said.

"You first," Hector told him. He held up his crutch. "This is going to slow me—"

That was the end of the discussion. The admiral grabbed one arm, the general the other, and they both dragged Hector out the door just as the agents had dragged out the President.

The wave of fleeing people in the hallway tore the crutch from Hector's hand. A pulsing alarm began to sound—

something that Hector had never heard in all his time at the White House.

The admiral and the general began to haul him up the short flight of stairs to the ground level, just as twelve soldiers rushed down, in full combat gear, carrying rifles.

Seconds later, Hector and his escorts were in the main hallway of the West Wing and Hector was able to tell them about Tyler. Instantly, the two men turned against the tide of evacuating personnel, in the direction of the Oval Office.

Hector saw Tyler coming toward them, his head bobbing up and down above the crowd. He was being carried by Captain Lassiter. As the throng parted, he also saw Mrs. Petty and Anthony Granville beside Lassiter. Tyler looked scared and confused, his small face pale beneath his freckles.

Hector stopped in front of Lassiter. "His mom said he was to stay with me." He looked up at Tyler. "Your mom's okay! You're going to be okay, too!"

Lassiter looked to the two officers. General Janukatys nodded and reached out for Tyler. "C'mon, soldier." A second siren blasted. Flinching, Tyler pressed his hands over his ears and clung to Janukatys without squirming.

As they were swept along to the exit to the Rose Garden and down the steps outside, Tyler in the general's arms, Hector with his arm around the admiral's shoulders, the harsh blasts of the sirens gave way to the buffeting rumble of massing helicopters.

A green-and-white VH-3D rose into the air, banking crazily as two others identical to it lifted upward to cover each flank. Another gunship bucked into the air only seconds later. Looking upward, Hector counted at least four other military helos blanking out the sun as they circled overhead. All had guns. Some had missile launchers.

The rush was on to the South Lawn.

As Hector hopped mightily to keep up the pace, he wasn't sure anything would ever be okay again, no matter what he'd told Tyler.

In two hours, the Pentagon was going to be consumed by a nuclear fireball.

And Tyler's parents would be at Ground Zero.

AE DRIVE

Pressed against the brick wall, behind the cover of the Dumpster, Tom saw Bethune turn and move into position. *"No!"* he hissed at her. The two trained killers would be round the corner any moment. But it was too late. She was ignoring him, and he'd risk giving away their position if he protested any louder.

Tom felt his hands begin to sweat around his weapon's grip and barrel. He forced himself to think about firing the submachine gun. He really didn't know if he could.

He peered over the edge of the Dumpster and saw the first terrorist enter the intersection and move cautiously to the other side. There he stopped to look ahead to where Bethune had thrown the grenade. The man was in midshipman white.

Tom braced himself for Bethune to begin blasting. But, instead, she held her fire.

He gripped the H&K even tighter, hoping Bethune was at least waiting for both terrorists to come into range.

The first terrorist held his position, sniffed the air. Then he dropped down out of sight, as if bending to pick up something.

Tom shot a glance at Bethune. But she was absolutely motionless, crouched down at the edge of the Dumpster, her gun barrel still in a raised position.

Then the terrorist rose into view again, just as a harsh voice called out, *"Qu'est-ce que c'est?"*

Tom paused, perplexed. *French?* The first terrorists in white had spoken Russian. Their partners in black were dressed like Americans. Mercenaries? But working for whom?

The first terrorist turned, holding up a small piece of something, maybe shredded paper. Tom thought of the scattered fragments he'd seen in Vanovich's inner office after the grenade had exploded.

The first terrorist shouted back something, again in French, about what, Tom couldn't hear. He looked again at Bethune, but she still hadn't moved.

The second terrorist stepped into the intersection. He held a small sideband radio in one hand. Tom stiffened. *They're going to report this.*

There was only one thing he could do. He whispered to Bethune, "They're both in sight." Tom's stomach twisted as he said the words because he knew what Bethune would do. Or, at least, *attempt* to do.

And she did it.

In a move almost too quick to follow, Bethune lunged forward, still in a crouch, bringing her H&K down, firing a full burst.

Tom's body vibrated in time to the staccato explosions of her gun.

The silence had barely begun before Bethune charged forward, away from the Dumpster, so quickly it was as if she'd been yanked out by a rope.

All in one moment, Tom took a breath, clutched his weapon, darted out after her, not knowing which of two options was worse—to have death come to him, or to rush off to meet it. But he wouldn't let Bethune face it on her own.

Tom charged around the Dumpster and saw the midshipman down by the body of the first terrorist, ripping his neck pass from the chain around his neck. Then she swiftly patted his pockets, pulled out two clips, and picked up his submachine gun. Tom caught up to her at the second body. This terrorist was still alive. Every few seconds, the man's body shuddered as his chest rose in a long, wheezing breath.

Each breath was followed by a frothing of blood from the huge holes torn in the man's chest. *Air leaking out,* Tom thought in a daze. It was one thing to see a dead man, it was another to see someone die before one's eyes. And to see someone suffer, without making any move to help them. Because of something he himself had done.

As if gathering a trophy, Bethune ripped a bloody pass from the dying man's neck, then pulled a spare clip from his trousers.

"The radio," Tom said. He could barely breathe or talk. His ears still rang with gunfire.

Amy looked up at him, emotionless. "You get it," she said. "I'll handle the weapons."

Tom made himself bend down to take the small radio from the second terrorist's tight grip. Avoiding the man's gaze, Tom began to pry his fingers from the radio. Then he heard a final, awful bubbling sputter from the man's torn chest and throat as the man's grip relaxed.

Tom stood up, holding the radio. The man's eyes were still open. A small trickle of blood ran from the corner of his slack mouth. Tom saw the tip of the man's tongue lying on the asphalt beside him.

Tom stumbled backward.

"Let's move," Bethune said. Then she ran for the C Ring doors without looking back. So did Tom.

Bethune was holding the door open for him as he burst through, back to the cool air and subdued light of the Pentagon. At once, Tom saw that the blast door that was supposed to have covered this entrance to the Pentagon's most secure area had been jammed open by metal shims. The terrorists had kept a path to the interior sections open.

Which meant they knew more about the Pentagon's layout than even he did.

Bethune had removed the clips from the two terrorists' guns, and pulled small pieces from the firing mechanisms. She left the guns on the floor, then handed Tom four clips. "You carry these." He nodded as he took them, not wanting yet to talk.

"Misdirection," she said. "Worked out great."

Tom nodded again.

"So—which way to the ops centers?"

Tom looked around, got his bearings, realized there would be a passage to the Mezzanine Level at the next corridor. He pointed.

"You okay?" she asked. Tom got the feeling her question wasn't asked out of concern for his mental health, but more to ascertain if he were going to become a liability. The thought pushed him into speech.

"Do you feel *anything* about what you just did?"

The midshipman's reply was that of a schoolgirl reciting a lesson. "Take no pleasure, feel no regret. Do the job and move on."

Tom shuddered inwardly, half-expecting her to change shape before him. Whatever else she was, how could he ever have thought of her as a kid?

"They would have killed us the same way," Bethune added.

For Tom, that was the worst part.

He knew she was right.

SIX

SITE J

Hauptmann Erich Kronig of the *Kommando Spezialkräfte,* code name Ranger, felt liberated at last. He had divested himself of the deceitful American Naval uniform. He was no longer in the enemy's colors. Instead he was dressed as his soldiers were, in the black coveralls, boots, and belt of a commando.

He stood in that garb, in the center of Site J's main floor, knowing he had accomplished the impossible. His total force, including the four workers he had placed three months ago in the Pentagon's privately run main kitchen, had numbered only ninety-two, with twelve of those already dispersed after the attack on the Naval Academy bus. Thirteen, if he included the soldier who had been dropped from the team because her midshipman counterpart had missed the bus.

Just under a thousand others had contributed to the overall operation, though. That larger number took account of everyone from the American engineering student who had assembled the FCG in New York, to the foreign construction teams who had built the wooden replicas of Pentagon interiors in Spain. There, the actual assault had been painstakingly rehearsed in enormous warehouses leased from owners who thought their vacant buildings were being used to make movies.

Ten months it had taken to perfect the plans Kronig had followed today. The work had begun immediately after the momentous week in which the Joint Chiefs had testified before the Senate NATO Observer Group, and QUICKSILVER had been placed in orbit as MAJIC 7. The combination of those two actions had been disturbing. The negative response to the Joint Chiefs' testimony made it obvious the President was determined to push through his insane invitation for Russia to join NATO. And the cynicism with which a weapon like QUICKSILVER had been simultaneously *and* illegally moved closer to operational status only underscored how duplicitous the American government was in its foreign policy—preaching peace to hide its preparations for war.

Even before the devastating QUICKSILVER test that had destroyed the USS *Shiloh,* the true nature of the weapon was clearly to destabilize what little was left of the balance of power in the world.

At the time, Kronig had been dismayed that, in Moscow, the subsequent protest marches against NATO membership had attracted so few students. As an officer in the German army, he was all too familiar with how modern warfare assigned spoils to the victor. Countries were not so much occupied as they were absorbed. His deepest fear had been that the Russian students who had not protested, who didn't even realize their country was being stolen from them, had stayed home because their secret wish was to be Americans.

Kronig had felt the outrage the Russian students had been too compromised to be able to feel themselves. The disease of Americanism had infected more than half the world. Even China would not be able to resist it once she joined the twenty-first century and the satellite Internet wormed its way into her people's minds.

Now he looked up to follow the curved steel beams of the Site J dome arching two stories overhead, and once again he acknowledged the astonishing audacity it had taken to build this facility, so far underground, so secretly, putting it in the one place no one would suspect because it was the first place everyone would suspect. Ground Zero.

Americans, he thought. *There is so much that is exemplary about them.* Yet he still wondered if some of what made them unique could also exist without the evil that had blossomed within their culture in the last half-century. Kronig hoped so. His war was not with the American people. Only its leadership. It was his sincere desire that in the aftermath of this day's events, Americans would finally get a government that was worthy of them.

The silent alarm on his watch vibrated, alerting him that the next satellite to reach his horizon would appear in ten minutes. Reflexively, Kronig straightened his belt and his Kevlar-lined jacket, and aligned the center of his coveralls, as if they were a formal dress uniform. Then he went to join his people at their stations.

Two specialists now worked at an electronics test bed table to the side of the floor. It had been intended for fast repairs and troubleshooting operations when time was critical. But today his technicians were using it for another purpose, to rework specific components of Site J into a transportable configuration. Their work was proceeding on schedule.

Then he went to the Red Level workstation. India was still at her station at the end of the console. She was drinking from a can of Coca-Cola from the cafeteria upstairs, as she monitored four different network news feeds on the console's smaller monitors. One of them still showed General Brower in the Map Room of the White House, apparently doing little except conducting brief phone conversations in which everything he said was broadcast for the world to hear.

Kronig had been truly surprised by how quickly the President had been persuaded to capitulate to the outrageous demand that General Brower be given his position. Even more surprising had been how easily the general had accepted the demand that he be continuously shown on television—telecaptivity, as it was sometimes called, was a form of imprisonment which controlled the prisoner by taking away his privacy, and thus his ability to cause harm.

And Kronig knew the general could cause harm to his operation. He had no illusions about being able to resist an assault from the assembled forces of CONDEFCOM for any length of time, whether General Brower was involved or not. Though preventing Brower from taking an active role in the planning of the counterattack would certainly decrease its eventual effectiveness and efficiency.

From the moment Kronig's commandos took the Pentagon, it was a given that they were holding an impossible position. Their only purpose was to give their commander and his satellite specialists enough time to complete their work in Site J, then make their foolproof escape. Every communication and every demand they had made as supposed terrorists had been designed to sow confusion and reap delay.

But by this point in the mission plan, Kronig had fully expected his teams in the Pentagon to be engaged in firefights with an invading force. He had anticipated that the Americans might delay any attack until they could be certain of the motives of the Sons of Liberty. But once the first satellite had been lost—burning up on reentry because of commands sent from Site J—Kronig would have thought those motives would have become exceptionally obvious. Even to Americans trained since birth to hope for the best.

And then, once QUICKSILVER had been taken over and Schriever AFB attacked, Kronig had been prepared for an almost instant response. But none had come.

Still, whenever the Americans finally did decide to make their move, Kronig's commandos would be ready for them. All the key paths through the Pentagon to Site J were now blocked in some manner, either by explosives or hostages, or both.

On the small screens, India flipped through more television stations. Every one of them was carrying live coverage of the Pentagon. "They still don't know what happened to their tracking center in Colorado," India said. "No one's mentioned anything about it."

"They know," Kronig assured her. "But it's not anything the government will announce on television." He leaned in closer to check the screens himself. "Which stations are carrying the helicopter views?"

India touched a control and the screen on the left switched to Fox. It was one of the stations the government had charged with fulfilling the Sons of Liberty's demand for live television surveillance of the Pentagon's grounds.

From the helicopter's point of view on this channel, Kronig was able to see the entire Building from the southwest, and about a quarter mile extent of the grounds around it. A thread of black smoke still rose from the blackened hull of the President's helicopter on the scorched landing pad. There were clouds building to the north, but other than that, it was still a perfect summer afternoon.

Other helicopter surveillance coverage was carried on MSNBC and SONY, and India brought those channels to her screens as well. With curiosity, Kronig noted the crowds that were building in the park areas around the Jefferson Memorial across the Potomac. The apartment and office building roofs of Pentagon City to the south also seemed to be covered with onlookers.

Kronig unclipped the small sideband radio from his belt. "Ranger to Kilo."

Kilo answered at once. He was on the next level up, directing the defense of their position. Now that the Site J personnel had all joined the other hostages in the upper levels, Kilo's responsibility was to monitor the television surveillance, to look for the first sign of impending attack.

"Status?" Kronig asked. He was certain that first sign would be the surveillance "inexplicably" shutting down. Though Kilo would be watching for any unusual movement of vehicles and personnel which might indicate from which direction the attack might be launched.

But so far, Kilo had seen no signs of a counterattack. "No threatening movements against our position," he reported. "Significant helicopter traffic over Washington. Seven helicopters left the White House a few minutes ago, all within a minute of each other. Some television stations are saying the White House has been evacuated but they're not saying why, and there's been no official confirmation."

"What about the crowds across the river?" Kronig asked.

"Combination of news teams and civilians. They've been gathering at the security perimeters that were established this morning. There's been no police or military action to move them back. If the troops come in, that's as close as they can get and still be hidden by the crowds. They'll have to cross an open mile to get to the Building. That'll give us the warning we need."

"Road traffic?"

"A few HUMVEEs speeding back and forth on the perimeter roads, but no apparent pattern. Two of them are ambulances. My guess—they're carrying receivers, trying to pick up our transmissions."

Kronig puzzled over the Americans' inactivity. He could almost accept the fact that they hadn't launched a counter-attack yet. They were cautious. But what was troubling him most was that they didn't appear to be making any *preparations* for one. Was it possible his teams had killed *all* the top U.S. military leaders in the Courtyard?

"Thank you. Ranger out." Kronig switched the radio to standby and checked his watch again. He still had five minutes before the next satellite came within communications range. Not that satellites had ever been his primary interest. By acquiring QUICKSILVER, the mission was already a total victory. The capture or destruction of any other American space asset would merely lengthen the time it would take this country to crawl out of a pit of its own making.

Kronig told India to stand by, then returned to Vanovich. The old man was slumped in his chair in the Red Level console's center position, held up only by the locked chest straps of his padded chair. Half an hour ago, the general had been tricked into passing over control of QUICKSILVER. Kronig knew the old man could not be manipulated or threatened in the·same way again. Vanovich was no longer a man who was merely unafraid of death, he was a man who would willingly embrace it.

But Kronig was determined to put the general at his ease for as long as possible. They were both officers, after all. "It is a remarkable device," he said. "As far as we can tell from down here, when the Schriever Air Force Base was shut down, your people lost contact with every satellite they own. I'll be interested to see how long it takes for your backup sites to reclaim them."

Vanovich said nothing. From the expression he wore, the sullen grief and self-recrimination in his eyes, Kronig could see that the general knew exactly what would happen the next time QUICKSILVER returned. Still, Kronig couldn't resist one final attempt.

"In five minutes," he said, "an NSA Trumpet satellite will pass by. Are you going to let me access it?"

Vanovich looked away.

"I rather thought not," Kronig said.

"Kill me now," Vanovich growled, but his voice was weak. "Kill me in five minutes. It doesn't matter."

"I could kill more hostages."

Vanovich's grunt conveyed his disgust. "I know what you're doing. You've been taking them up to the Pentagon. You're going to let Delta Force kill them all, anyway."

"A few will die, at first. Enough to slow your soldiers down." Kronig looked at his watch. "For one hundred minutes. Just long enough to reactivate QUICKSILVER and instruct it to accept command and control from another station."

"Reactivate?" Vanovich asked.

"I shut it down, of course. Put it into its safe mode." Kronig wondered why QUICKSILVER's operational status was of interest to Vanovich. "Why so puzzled, General? Now that I have QUICKSILVER, why would I allow one of your backup stations to take it back from me?"

Vanovich looked away again, but a fraction too late. "QUICKSILVER *has* no backup station?" Kronig was astounded. He had considered the planners' inability to locate a backup command-and-control station for the weapon to be a failure of intelligence, not a foolish omission on the Americans' part. "Were you that frightened of it, to keep all control here?"

"Any sane man would."

"You are fortunate that QUICKSILVER is in the right hands now. We shall not make the same mistake."

Vanovich closed his eyes for a moment, sighing deeply as if all he wanted to do was sleep forever. "D'you know what you did to that tracking station, you goddamn bastard?"

"I have a good idea. I've read your report about what really happened to the *Shiloh*."

"That was on *water,* you . . . cretin. *Salt* water. We tested QUICKSILVER at sea because we knew the salt water would draw off the current—restrict the expansion of the EM field through the air, just in case there were any . . . unexpected results." The general's eyes blazed in sudden anger. "I was on a ship *five* miles away, and *we* got hit. On land, the effect could cover triple the area, maybe more. You say you wanted to short-circuit some radio dishes. *I* say you killed every soul on that base. And that's what you call in the 'right hands.' "

Kronig barely heard the old man's accusation. QUICK-SILVER was an even *greater* prize. With his creation, Vanovich had established a completely new paradigm of warfare. Unlimited energy delivered with pinpoint accuracy at the speed of light. From an invisible, untouchable platform in space. No missile flight time. No warning. No defense. The general was right. In the wrong hands, QUICKSILVER would have become an instrument of world domination. And how could America have been entrusted with that?

"General, I understand your concerns. Your gift will not be misused. I work for honorable men."

"Do you? Who?"

"You still don't know?"

Vanovich stared at him, waiting.

"Then ask yourself: Who does your satellite network threaten most?"

"China."

Kronig shook his head. "How can you use satellites to spy on a country where most of the people have no phones or computers? And where the people who *are* worth spying on already have full schematics of your satellites and know precisely what countermeasures to take? I know Americans are obsessed with China, but you're wrong."

"Russia."

"Another good guess, but wrong."

"India."

"They certainly don't like your satellites, the way you meddle in their affairs with Pakistan. Try again."

"Iraq? Iran? Oh hell, I don't know." Vanovich pushed against the straps to sit up straight.

The conversation was reawakening some of the old man's fighting spirit. "Don't forget Libya—and most of the

Middle East, in fact. But the kind of people you're thinking of are fortunate if they can set off a bomb near one of your embassies every few years. Do you honestly think they could accomplish what my soldiers and I achieved today? Try again, General."

"I won't play your game."

"Game," Kronig repeated, suddenly feeling provoked. "That's another of your people's problems. Everything's a game to you. There must always be a winner *and* a loser. Black or white. No give and take, no compromise. A most urealistic philosophy. You're always dividing the world into US and THEM, allies and enemies. No room for partners or equals or independent thought. That's what makes your country so dangerous. A worldview like yours can only have two outcomes: Either the entire world becomes America, or, inevitably, there will be war."

Vanovich spoke through clenched teeth. "My country has always fought for peace."

"Listen to yourself—to *fight* for *peace*." Kronig paused, to let the passion of the moment flow from him, restoring his focus. He was allowing himself to become distracted. The general was too old, too set in his ways to understand the truth about his country. "Forgive me, General. It doesn't matter. What's important is that after today, America will have to *work* for peace, in partnership with every other nation on Earth, because you will no longer have the advantage over them."

"Because you will."

"One minute to acquisition of Trumpet Fifteen," India said.

Kronig shook his head at her. This one he would allow to pass.

"What's wrong? You don't want another satellite for your collection?" Vanovich asked. "Why don't you kill me and hold my eye up to the scanner?"

Kronig stepped back from the vanquished general. "Soon enough," he said. "In ninety-five minutes. When QUICKSILVER comes by."

What Vanovich suggested had always been an option. The general's retina would continue to be useful for identification, up to thirty minutes after his death. But Kronig's technical team had not been able to guarantee that the computers wouldn't also require Vanovich to confirm his identity by inputting a personal-access code before QUICKSILVER would obey him again. Without knowing how that code changed, the general had to be kept alive, for insurance.

Vanovich looked away, in equal parts despair and disgust.

How ineffective their generals are, Kronig thought. *Vanovich so willing to give up his life. Brower so easily placed under—*

The discrepancy suddenly hit him. Kronig strode back to India's station. On the middle screen he saw it—General Brower in the Map Room of the White House.

And the White House had been evacuated.

Erich Kronig felt almost relieved by his discovery of the deception. The Americans were predictable after all.

He switched on his radio. "Ranger to all stations. We are now at general quarters. The counterattack will come at any moment, and it will be commanded by General Elias Brower."

Kilo radioed back at once that Brower was still under surveillance at the White House.

Kronig only smiled, savoring the victory he had already achieved.

And hungered for the even greater victory to come.

JEFFERSON DAVIS HIGHWAY, ARLINGTON, VIRGINIA

"Get ready, Major!" the driver shouted.

Leaning forward in the right-front passenger seat, Margaret braced her gloved hand on the edge of the speeding HUMVEE's open door. The warm wind whistled through her Army-green flight helmet. The memory of Tyler, age three, puffed out in his first snowsuit, an immobile Pillsbury Doughboy, perfectly fit the way she felt now as the HUMVEE roared north toward the parade-ground underpass directly in front of the Pentagon's River Entrance. On one of the hottest days of the summer, she was in four layers of clothing: an oversize green flight suit over a cold-weather camouflage jacket and lined pants, which in turn covered the black Nomex coveralls she wore over her jungle-camouflage shirt, pants, and tan T-shirt. Between the heat and the protective padding, she was finding it difficult to breathe.

The HUMVEE flashed into the shadow of the underpass and in a split second the driver jammed on the brakes, squealing from fifty miles an hour to ten, throwing Margaret forward. Directing her momentum out the door, she tucked and hit the pavement rolling, even as she heard the HUMVEE's engine growl as the driver floored the accelerator. The vehicle would be coming out the other side of the underpass, only one hundred feet away, at the same speed with which it had entered. And a second soldier, outfitted in the same Army-green helmet and flight suit as Margaret, would be in her seat, after springing up from his hidden position in the back of the HUMVEE.

As Margaret rolled to a stop on her side, already checking if she had any unusual pain or numbness, she felt herself hauled to her feet by two sets of powerful hands.

She pulled off her flight helmet to find two Delta Force commandos saluting her. The larger of the two said, "Welcome to Grand Central, Major."

Margaret snapped back the salute, then looked past the two commandos to find sixty more standing at the sides of the underpass tunnel, all in black assault gear, even their faces covered in greasepaint. They were the men of Delta's Assault Squadron E, the cutting edge of CONDEFCOM, experts in domestic, close-quarters urban combat and hostage rescue. Each one had arrived as she had, jumping from a speeding HUMVEE at the covered assembly point closest to their target, only two hundred feet from the River Entrance.

Some of the commandos gathered by small equipment pallets designed to be dropped from helicopters. For this operation, the pallets had been pushed from the backs of speeding ambulances. Margaret saw specialists unpacking explosives, weapons, ammunition, and rapid-ascent gear from the open crates. She knew that the ascent gear—grappling hooks, fast ropes, and winches—was for scaling the Pentagon's walls, getting to and through the windows. That was the core of Brower's planned assault.

The CONDEFCOM CINC had advised the President that using the kind of heavy artillery they'd need to get through the blast doors would absolutely rule out a surprise attack, which is what Delta Force trained for and relied upon—moving so quickly the enemy was unprepared to resist. A conventional artillery attack would take several minutes to set up within line of sight of the Pentagon, and would likely require several rounds to be fired as well. Brower made it clear that there was only one option for penetrating the Pentagon quickly enough to both rescue the hostages and get out before the bomb literally dropped. That option required bypassing the blast doors.

No matter which route Delta took into the Pentagon, Brower told the President, eventually they would have to enter the River Entrance side to gain access to Site J. So the general had decided to start there from the beginning: Delta was going to enter the Pentagon through the second- and third-floor windows of the River Entrance side. That section of the Building, housing the ops centers and the National Military Command Center, also gave direct access to the Site J elevator shaft, through the utility corridor beneath the central Courtyard.

When the time came, eighteen commandos armed with Stinger-RMP single-shot firing systems would lead the attack. Nine would rise up on scaffolds from behind the south embankment wall flanking the parade-grounds over-pass. Nine would rise up from behind the north embankment wall. Each commando would aim at a specific window on the second and third floors, in the two sections of wall that were to either side of the pillars of the main entrance. Specialists from the Army Corps of Engineers had confirmed that the blastproof laminate in the Pentagon's exterior windows could not survive the double impact of the supersonic Stinger and the resultant detonation of its 2.2-pound warhead of penetrating high explosive.

The instant the small Stinger missiles were launched, a second tier of riflemen would launch smoke grenades at the base of the River Side Entrance façade. As soon as the smoke began billowing, the rest of Assault Squadron E would race across the two-hundred-foot open area between the embankment wall and the Pentagon, fire their grappling hooks into the open window frames, and enter the Building.

While the ground attack was under way, the next phase would begin: the arrival of the Night Stalkers, also known as SOAR—the 160th Special Operations Aviation Regiment.

Six AH-6 Little Bird helicopters would form the first airborne assault, sweeping the Pentagon's roofs to prevent any terrorists from taking the high ground. As hostages were found, they would either be rushed to the open windows and lowered with ropes and harnesses, or taken to the roof and extracted ten at a time by SOAR's MH-60 Black Hawk helicopters.

Execution of Brower's ambitious plan could take no more than forty minutes. But Margaret knew that even if everything went perfectly, *all* two hundred hostages and three hundred soldiers would not be able to escape the Pentagon before the Lancer bomber arrived with its payload. As the only one who had any chance of reaching Site J and ending the terrorists' control of QUICKSILVER, Margaret was fully aware that the lives of the hostages, and of Assault Squadron E, had become her responsibility.

She rid herself of the clothing she had worn for padding until she reached her black Nomex coveralls. Then she and her two escorts double-timed across the three lanes of highway, jumped the guardrails of the center divider, and crossed three more lanes to reach a small utility-access opening in the concrete wall of the underpass, about five feet above the shoulder of the road.

The opening's cover, a plate of steel, four feet by four

feet, was off to the side, eight lug nuts lying on top of it. To the other side, a compact, 2-kW Military Tactical Generator, about half the size of a standard office desk and painted in green-brown camouflage, unobtrusively rumbled like an idling car. A thick cable ran from the MTG into the access opening. In the space beyond, Margaret heard voices and saw flashlight beams moving quickly.

"Your gear's inside, ma'am," the first commando said.

"Any trouble finding the conduits?"

The second commando cupped his hands to give Margaret a boost. "No, ma'am. They found two of the five in the first minute. They say it looks mighty cramped in there."

"Good thing I skipped lunch." Margaret put her hand on the monstrous shoulder of one commando, her boot in the cupped hands of the second, then pushed up and suddenly found herself flying through the opening to land on her knees in the access chamber. They had launched her like a missile.

At once, three flashlight beams converged on her and she shielded her eyes with her hand as she squinted to the right. She could smell something damp and rotting mixed with concrete dust. Her sinuses started to swell almost instantly. In the rush of getting away from the White House on General Brower's helicopter, she had forgotten to take decongestants.

"Major Sinclair?" a deep voice called out.

"Yes, sir," Margaret answered. She got to her feet. There was just enough clearance for her to stand upright in the chamber. It was little more than a squared-off concrete tunnel, just over five feet high and five feet wide. Along the gray concrete floor, power lines ran, thick black cables three and four inches across, marked by yellow bands every two feet.

Twenty feet along the tunnel, three soldiers from the Army Corps of Engineers were gathered by a pile of concrete rubble. Margaret jogged toward the light from the flashlights, shivering as the cool air in the tunnel began evaporating the sweat she'd worked up in all the protective gear for the HUMVEE jump.

An electric chisel and three sets of dynamic noise earphones lay beside the rubble, directly beneath a hole punched into the side of the tunnel. The soldiers' green utility uniforms were covered in concrete dust and they wore white filter masks around their necks. Two of the soldiers were crouched beside the wall, their flashlights now on the ground beside them. The third soldier, too tall to fully stand, remained partially bent over. He pointed his flashlight into the hole, but Margaret could not see any light reflect back from inside.

"You sure about this, ma'am?" he asked.

Margaret made out sergeant stripes in the backscatter from the other two flashlights. "What's it look like, Sergeant?"

"Pretty much like a garden hose, I'd say." Then the sergeant gave her his flashlight and she looked inside the old, unused sewer pipe conduit for herself. She felt the chill of failure.

The conduit looked considerably smaller than she'd expected. And its surface was unfinished concrete, roughly textured by gravel that hadn't been troweled into place. She reached in to feel the surface she'd be crawling along—it was pebbled with sharp bits of stone and concrete. Some of them flaked off as she pressed her fingers against them, but others held firm. At the very centerline of the conduit, she could also feel a layer of fine silt. That told her the conduit had cracked over the years, allowing groundwater to seep in. It wasn't a promising development. Since the conduit appeared to be sloping down, that meant sixty years' worth of run-off could have collected down there, possibly plugging it with dirt.

"How wide is that?" Margaret asked.

"It checks out at twenty inches, ma'am." The look on the sergeant's face clearly showed he thought her mission was impossible.

Margaret knew if she stopped to think about what she was planning to do, she'd never be able to get into the conduit, let alone crawl through two hundred feet of it. "Let's do it," she said.

The sergeant dragged a narrow, plastic-impregnated canvas bag forward. It held the equipment Margaret and General Brower had requested while still in the helo, before they'd landed at the Navy Annex. The general had remained there. His command post for the assault was on top of the roof overlooking the heliport and South Terrace sides of the Pentagon, half a mile away.

The first thing Margaret took from the equipment bag was a black balaclava to keep her twisted-back hair from catching on any obstructions in the conduit. Next, she pulled out a roll of duct tape and had the other two soldiers tape slender, Maglite flashlights to her wrists. Finally, she had them tie the end of a 300-foot long nylon cord to the back of her belt. If she made it through to the other end, she'd use that cord to pull through a stronger rope, and then use that to haul in her equipment.

Her preparations took less than five minutes. Margaret checked the time, and for a moment recalled waking up this morning, worrying only about being ready for General

Vanovich's QUICKSILVER briefing to the President in the Pentagon. Now, at the time scheduled for the briefing, she was in an underground tunnel, attempting to outrace an in-flight nuclear weapon, launched by the President, that was only ninety minutes from its target—her.

"Okay, good to go," she told the soldiers.

But the three were also engineers. One of them had cut open the armored vest from her equipment bag to remove a single plate of dull-gray, ceramic armor. He suggested she slide that along to give her something to protect her elbows from the rough-finished concrete. Another soldier handed her a Beretta with its clip removed, just in case the cord broke or got hung up and she ended up without her equipment.

"In that case," Margaret said, "give me the MSE link, too." If the engineers thought there was the slightest possibility she might lose the nylon cord, she at least wanted a radio that would let her transmit directly through the conduit, though she knew it would have little chance of working once she moved away from the opening. The portable Mobile Subscriber Equipment terminal, now in her equipment bag, was what she would use as a relay station at the end of the tunnel. Wire leads running back through the conduit would connect to another terminal at this end. Margaret would then be able to transmit, from within the concrete-shielded Pentagon, using a small MSE digital radiophone. Her messages would be relayed via the two connected terminals to the MSE network already established by the Army's 1111th Signal Battalion.

The digital radio was the size of a deck of playing cards and she slipped it into the front of her black coveralls along with the gun. She put the clip in a side pocket on her leg.

The soldiers wished her luck, and said they'd stand by to feed out the cord, transfer the equipment, and monitor for her radio, in case anything went wrong.

As Margaret thanked them, she added, "But in seventy minutes, if the order comes for Delta to withdraw from the area, you go with them. That's a direct order."

"Yes, ma'am," the tall soldier said, his gray eyes serious.

Margaret pulled on a pair of black Nomex gloves and switched on one of her wrist flashlights. Then she turned to face the conduit opening, stretched her arms straight ahead, holding the gray ceramic armor like a swimmer's kickboard, and told the three soldiers to lift her in.

Very carefully, they did, feeding her into the conduit as if she were a torpedo being loaded.

They got her in as far as her knees; then she wriggled forward on her forearms and knees until she was completely within the conduit.

A thousand thoughts flooded through her at once. The age of the stale-smelling, crumbling concrete. The dense presence of the earth pressing on all sides of the conduit. The bomber streaking through the sky with a nuclear payload. Fear engulfed her. How could it not?

But her secret weapon saved her.

She thought of Tyler, the babe she'd cradled in her arms, the boy she'd see become a man.

How could any fear withstand the determined courage of a mother?

Margaret pointed her flashlight ahead and saw its beam disappear into the darkness that pressed down on her, threatening to suffocate her, ready to crush her.

But it hadn't crushed her yet.

She crawled forward, into the Pentagon.

SEVEN

FBI HEADQUARTERS, WASHINGTON, D.C.

Hector still wasn't sure what had happened. He and Tyler had been swiftly loaded onto a green and white VH-3D helicopter, the kind used to transport the President, and had been lifted away with the same sort of sudden acceleration he'd felt in the special-forces rescue helicopter.

After the helo stopped climbing, the pilot's voice had come over the cabin PA saying they weren't in danger, the President was safe, and that everyone on board was being taken to a safe landing area. The pilot hadn't been able to say where that landing area would be, because he was still waiting for instructions.

They'd circled D.C. for the next twenty minutes, and then, with no explanation, made their landing just over half a mile from the White House, on the roof of the FBI Headquarters building.

The fifteen other passengers on the helo were all as confused as Hector. They were White House staffers, a few

State Department aides, and two junior liaison officers from the Defense Intelligence Agency. None of them could tell him why the White House had been evacuated, nor why so many soldiers had rushed in.

From the conversations he overheard, it appeared that most of them had no real idea about what was going on in the Pentagon, either. Hector realized that he himself had been so caught up in the intensity of the decisions facing the President that, for the first time in his two years at the White House, he had forgotten to do his job. Right now, he had no insight to share with the Man about what ordinary Americans felt or thought about the day's events. He only knew the *inside* story. The moment was humbling.

When the rear helo door swung open and the metal stairs unfolded, the passengers exited quickly, but without panic. Hector waited to the end. Still strapped into the seat beside him, Tyler was swiping his nose with the hem of his over-size Orioles T-shirt. His eyes were red-tinged, deeply shadowed.

I know what's going on and I'm *confused,* Hector thought. *What must this kid be going through? Both his parents are out there, somewhere.*

Hector experienced a rush of protectiveness. Whatever happened in the next two hours, his mission had to be to make Tyler's world as easy as he could.

His first challenge arrived with a large man in a blue FBI baseball cap and nylon windbreaker who came into the cabin from the forward door. "You MacGregor?"

"That's me," Hector confirmed as he leaned over to unfasten Tyler's seat belt.

"The President's been screaming for you." He saw Hector's bandaged and braced foot. "You need a hand or anything?"

Hector thanked the agent, but said he thought he could manage as long as he didn't have to carry Tyler. He meant that as a joke. But the agent wasn't smiling.

"You just get movin'. I'll take the kid."

Hector saw the boy shrink back in his seat.

"Tyler's with me."

"No kids allowed in the SIOC. We got a day-care room downstairs."

"One more time," Hector said. "Where I go, Tyler goes. That's it."

The FBI agent stood face-to-face with Hector. He was Hector's height but a good fifty pounds heavier. "I said the President wants you ASAP."

Even a day ago, Hector might have given way. But now, a loud voice and obnoxious manner just didn't seem all that troublesome.

"Then I suggest," Hector said calmly, "you go tell him the reason I'm not joining him is because *you* are being an asshole and causing trouble for the son of Major Sinclair."

The agent leaned forward, unpleasantly close. "What'd you call me?"

"Don't even *think* of fucking with me," Hector said, surprising even himself with the forcefulness of his voice.

Now the helo's Marine pilot and copilot had come to the forward door, obviously wondering if they should intercede.

But the agent backed off first, as if he were the one who'd been intimidated. "Your problem then," he said with a shrug. "I don't make the rules. I'll take you down to the SIOC entrance, and you can work it out with Security. Bring the kid with you." He turned, and shouldered his way past the pilot and copilot.

Hector looked at Tyler. "How much did that cost me?"

"Three quarters."

"Two for the f-word, and one for what?"

"You said . . ."—Tyler dropped his voice—". . . asshole."

Hector dropped his own voice, "So did you."

He could tell Tyler found that funny, even if he didn't exactly smile. "Let's see what a SIOC is, okay?" Hector asked, as they headed for the hatch.

Hector hobbled down the small metal stairway ahead of Tyler. The warm wind whipped at him, helping ease the day's heat. He saw clouds building on the horizon.

"Where'd my mom go?" Tyler said, jumping down the stairs two at a time.

"She went to get your dad."

"In the Pentagon?"

Hector turned toward Tyler and put an arm around his narrow shoulder, as if the fifty-pound eight-year-old could now help him by being his crutch. He could feel Tyler straighten up to offer him more support. The large FBI agent was waiting up ahead for them by an entrance door at the side of the helipad. The gusting breeze was making the agent's nylon jacket flutter against him and he kept a hand on his baseball cap.

"In the Pentagon," Hector said as he and Tyler started walking toward the agent.

"Are they coming back?"

That question tore at Hector. He didn't want to lie to Tyler, but how could he tell the truth? He took the coward's way out, regretting the words even as he said them. "Of course they are."

But Hector could see that Tyler had caught the slight delay in his answer. His shoulders tensed and he ducked his head down.

The waiting FBI agent took them through to an elevator and down to the fifth floor. When they stepped from the elevator, they faced a security desk, and beyond it a low-ceilinged, dark hallway with two sets of doors. The individual white letters attached to the gray wall above the bland, gray desk said: STRATEGIC INFORMATION AND OPERATIONS CENTER. *At least that explains SIOC,* Hector thought. He and Tyler waited by the desk while the agent went inside to talk to whoever would give dispensation to Tyler.

It took less than a minute. A familiar, long-legged figure, Drew Simons, the Treasury agent responsible for White House security, pushed quickly through the hallway doors to speak to the security guards. Hector and Tyler were to be allowed in, at once.

The guards hung an FBI VISITOR pass around Tyler's neck, alongside his White House pass. Hector took it as a good sign that as he and Tyler followed Simons through the doors and into the dark hallway, the boy held his two passes together in one hand, as if they might be talismans against evil.

As they headed toward a set of metal-covered doors, Hector asked Simons what had caused the evacuation from the White House.

"It's related to what actually happened at the Archives," the Treasury agent said. "You know there's a high-security vault beneath them?"

Hector nodded. For preservation, until the renovation of the Archives' Exhibition Hall was completed the Declaration of Independence, the first and fourth pages of the Constitution, and the Bill of Rights were kept in individual glass-display cases filled with inert helium and sealed in bronze frames. Every night when the Archives closed, the Charters' display cases descended twenty-two feet into a reinforced concrete-and-steel vault. The vault beneath the Charters' display pedestal in the rotunda of the Archives Exhibition Hall dated from 1952, and had been designed to protect the fragile documents in the event of nuclear war.

"But it's not the *only* vault beneath the Archives," Simons said. "Remember PROJECT JERICHO?"

Hector nodded again. PROJECT JERICHO had been covered in Colonel Tobin's briefing, just before Site J had been taken over. The evacuation-system project had been built in two stages. First, the deep underground evacuation centers—the ATLANTIS facilities. Second, the evacuation network of RUSH HOUR tunnels.

"It turns out there's a second ATLANTIS vault *another* one hundred and thirty feet below the original vault."

Hector thought that actually made sense. The '52 vault was only twenty-two feet deep and it wouldn't have offered much protection against the nuclear weapons of the sixties and seventies. He remembered that that was the reason Tobin had said PROJECT JERICHO was undertaken in the first place.

"So that's why the terrorists broke into the Archives," Simons continued. "Not to steal the Charters, but to access the RUSH HOUR tunnels. And Gibb and General Brower are really having a fight about that. But you'll find out."

Then Hector, Tyler, and Simons entered the FBI's largest and most advanced crisis-management operations center— forty thousand square feet of giant video screens, time readouts, and a staggering number of computer displays. FBI agents, men and women, sat at desks or consoles, or hurried between glassed-in offices and computer stations with files and printouts. Hector sensed that the surface order was only an illusion. The situation was far from resolved.

Every screen in the vast area seemed to involve the Pentagon crisis in some form or another. The SIOC wall screens, five feet by fifteen, carried multiple windows in which dozens of different television news feeds appeared. On many of the screens, there were identical photo portraits of a very attractive and very serious young woman in a Naval uniform. She had the same clear-eyed, focused look as Major Sinclair. The captions on the photos identified her as Midshipman Amy Bethune. Hector realized the photos meant that, despite the efforts of the UPN news director, other news teams covering the story had discovered Bethune's message taped to the Pentagon window. He felt sorry for the kid. If the terrorists hadn't known she was hiding in the Building, they did now. How did broadcasting that story serve the public good?

A few screens were carrying his photograph, too, along with a wide variety of captions, ranging from MILLIONAIRE STAFFER RISKS LIFE FOR PRESIDENT, to PRESIDENT RISKS LIFE FOR PLAYBOY STAFFER, and TEMPORARY STAFFER ENDANGERS PRESIDENT IN DARING ESCAPE. Hector wasn't bothered by the misrepresentation of what had happened. He had been marginally in the public spotlight long enough to know that no quote was ever accurate, no story ever complete.

The computer displays offered more crisis-related images —Pentagon schematics, along with what Hector recognized as street plans of D.C., and a large number of subway maps. The connection was not immediately apparent to him.

The tension in the huge, windowless area grew palpable as they approached the cluster of offices and workstations identified as the COUNTERTERRORISM CENTER. Simons had Hector and Tyler wait outside a large conference room which had its own wall-sized video screen. A floor-to-ceiling glass barrier served to isolate the room from the office cubicles outside.

Inside the conference room, Hector could see the President, FBI Director James Gibb, the CIA's Archibald Fortis, and Douglas Casson of the NRO. Outside the conference room, where he and Tyler stood, Hector saw several senior officers from all branches of the military rushing back and forth. That meant General Janukatys and Admiral Paulsen were most probably also somewhere nearby. But Hector saw no sign of the assistant director of the NSA, Milton Meyer.

Whatever conversation Gibb and the President were having in the glass-walled Center, it also involved General Brower. Hector could see his image quite clearly on the room's video wall. From the soldiers and the equipment in the background of the general's video link, Hector guessed the CONDEFCOM commander in chief was already on the frontlines. And that made him wonder what effect General Brower's disappearance from the White House might have had on the fate of the hostages. The Sons of Liberty had made no new demands or attempts to communicate for more than an hour. Though by now, everyone understood they had been a diversion.

Just as Tyler was reaching the end of his ability to stand still in one place, Simons returned with a mop-haired young agent in dark slacks and a white blouse, wearing FBI ID around her neck. She introduced herself to Tyler as Sophie Newman. She said she had a special desk for him, right against the wall, where he could keep an eye on Hector in the Center. But she closed the deal when she offered to bring up lunch from the FBI cafeteria and confirmed that there was *official* FBI pizza available.

Reassured, Hector followed Simons through the sliding glass door into the conference room to hear FBI Director Gibb shouting at General Brower. Gibb stood between a long conference table and the video wall. The President stood beside him. Fortis and Casson were seated at the far end of the table, in deep conversation, paying no attention to the battle of words raging in the room.

"Because *you* people have screwed this up from the beginning!" Gibb snapped at the general.

Brower's temper was easily a match for the director's. "Let me remind you, sir, that your people have full jurisdiction over the Archives massacre. And I say it is unconscionable—perhaps even criminal that you didn't realize what was going on at once! *You* are the ones who put the President at risk!"

Gibb was clearly refusing to accept responsibility for the Archives disaster. "As soon as my agents confirmed that the Charters on display had been removed from their cases and were missing, they went straight down to the original vault. The second and third pages of the Constitution were still in their storage racks. And there was no indication that *anyone* had been in the vault."

"There is no question the terrorists were in that vault," Brower thundered from the wall screen. "They had to pass through it to get down to the next one."

Gibb indignantly pointed his finger at the screen. "Which you military people kept so classified that none of my agents on the scene knew about it."

"You knew about it, sir!"

"And I was forbidden to tell my agents."

The effort and energy these two men were wasting arguing over Cold War policy decisions was appalling to Hector. Particularly when Major Sinclair was trying to break into the Pentagon while a nuclear bomb was on its way there. At the same time that an unknown madman with a superweapon was destroying the country's satellite capability.

Hector looked over at the President, wondering why he wasn't breaking this up. The Man was still standing on the far side of Gibb, his attention now on a photograph he was holding.

Hector carefully skirted behind Gibb to reach the President's side. He spoke very softly to the Man. "Mr. President, what they're fighting about, isn't this something you can deal with later?"

The President looked ten years older than he had this morning. The photograph was of the First Lady. "Hec, bottom line is that the terrorists who took the place of the midshipmen were just the first wave. A second wave took out Site J by rushing it when they got ready to evacuate their civilian workers."

Hector finally grasped the connection among the images on the computer displays he'd seen in the outside area. He forgot to keep his voice down. "Through the underground tunnels? RUSH HOUR?"

"Tom Chase and that midshipman sent us another message. They reported seeing *new* terrorists in black commando gear, like the fellow we saw on the Site J video link."

Gibb turned to the President. "They're in the same equipment worn by our own counterterrorism forces."

"And," General Brower now interrupted from the wall screen, "the counterterrorism forces of the SAS *and* Captain Kronig's KSK *and* the Russians' Black Berets and half the Hostage Rescue Teams in the world. I will not have anyone cast aspersions on the men and women of CONDEFCOM or the U.S. Army. Sir."

The President sighed. "The point is, Hec, those RUSH HOUR tunnels, they're connected to the White House, too."

"Really?"

"You know the Roosevelt tunnel?"

Hector did. He'd learned about it his first year in Washington. The idea that the ground below the city was riddled with known and unknown tunnels had been fascinating to him.

The Roosevelt tunnel was a narrow passageway under the White House built in the days immediately following Pearl Harbor to evacuate President Roosevelt in the event D.C. was also bombed. It ran under the East Lawn from the Executive Mansion, under Madison Place, and into the sub-basement of the Treasury Building. During World War II, the President's escape route from D.C. had relied on a special train car kept on standby at the Bureau of Engraving and Printing across the Mall.

Another tunnel had been built after World War II, making it possible for future Presidents to travel all the way from the White House to the evacuation train. Until he'd learned about PROJECT JERICHO, Hector had believed this second Presidential tunnel to be the longest and most elaborate of the underground network connecting to the White House. Most of the tunnels only ran a block or two and led to other Federal buildings. The most commonly used one now was the short tunnel under Pennsylvania Avenue that came up in the Treasury Annex.

"Well, the Roosevelt tunnel's just the tip of the iceberg," the President said. "When Gibb here realized the terrorists had access to the RUSH HOUR network, the Secret Service decided the White House wasn't safe and got everyone out of there."

"Doesn't the White House have vault doors and security gates?" Hector asked.

"Mr. MacGregor," Gibb said acidly. He looked at the President. "And this is my last word on the matter unless someone decides to have hearings." He returned his attention to Hector. "Those tunnels were built to increase the safety of government officials. But now, there are so many of them, that they have made D.C. one of the least defensible cities in America. Once terrorists gain access to any part of that network, they can pile up as much explosive as they can carry under the White House, the Capitol, the State Department . . . almost any key government building you can think of. And because people like General Brower, who are supposed to defend us from exactly that scenario, continue to maintain this system under Top Secret classification, the FBI and local police can do nothing to lessen the threat to this city, our government, and our way of life."

Hector was afraid to look up to see the general's reaction to that statement. He also didn't like the picture Gibb painted of D.C. being a security minefield. But this still wasn't the time for this kind of disagreement, and the President was obviously too distraught to bring an end to it himself. Hector decided to change the subject.

"Mr. President, have you been keeping up with the news reports?"

"There is no news, Hec. Only rumors." The President found a chair with arms, rolled it over to the table, and sat down heavily. "Some stations are reporting that I've already resigned and General Brower is Acting President."

"Lying to the enemy is as dangerous as using bioweapons," Gibb said sanctimoniously. "The lies can strike our own people."

"That *lie*," General Brower snapped, "saved the lives of

sixty hostages. Any misperceptions the American people have can be corrected in the morning."

"I don't think saving those lives amounted to much, do you?" Gibb asked. "Considering you're going to nuke them to death in the next two hours."

"Uh, it's . . . ninety minutes, actually," Fortis said diffidently, looking up from his discussion with Casson.

Gibb didn't even appear to hear him as he pressed on with his attack on General Brower. "If you had allowed my HRT to go in two hours ago, this would already have reached its conclusion."

"Sure would," Brower said. "With the record you people have, the Pentagon would be in flames and all the hostages would be dead. That's a conclusion we've seen before."

Hector felt helpless to stop the bickering and knew it had to stop for the President to regain his role of leadership. But the situation was unique. The Man had always been surrounded by a layer of officials who would never have permitted this to intrude into the President's inner circle.

Then General Janukatys rushed into the room, providing the interruption that changed the subject for everyone.

"Mr. President," the Air Force Chief of Staff said, "we've heard from Grand Central. Major Sinclair is in the conduit and making her way to the Pentagon."

"I'll be darned," the President said with new energy in his voice. He straightened in his chair. "They found one."

Hector realized that whatever the President and General Brower had planned to happen next, they must have been waiting for this news before proceeding. They'd just been letting Gibb hang himself in the meantime. Hector felt foolish for thinking the President could not function without his intervention.

The President looked up at the wall screen. "How long do we give her, General?"

"Ten, fifteen minutes to get through the conduit, then it depends on what sort of resistance she encounters."

"All right," the President said. He tapped his index fingers on the edge of the table. "Have your men stand by to attack. We'll give her thirty minutes to report back. We'll either go then or reconsider based on what she has to tell us."

"Yes, sir," Brower said. Hector could tell those were the orders the general had wanted to hear.

"I strongly object," Gibb said.

"Objection noted," the President said.

"You will never get Brower's men in and out of the Pentagon in time. By sending them in now, you risk losing them in the bombing at a time when we could be facing even more of these attacks across the country."

The President narrowed his eyes. "Gibb, are you suggesting we *need* CONDEFCOM now?"

"I'm suggesting that if we had done this my way, we'd be debriefing the survivors and interrogating the terrorists by now, and we'd know what was going on. Since we're completely in the dark, I think it's irresponsible to risk resources we might need in the days and weeks ahead."

"So now you're willing to let all the hostages die without making even an attempt to save some of them?" The President was as confused as Hector.

"Sir, with respect," Gibb said, "you already made that decision when you prevented me from acting at once."

The room became silent, except for a faint electronic humming that came from the video wall. Fortis and Casson stopped talking and stared in Gibb's direction. No matter how politely he had said it, the director of the FBI had just accused the President of criminal incompetence.

The President sat back in his chair, rested his elbows on its arms, and folded his hands before him. He spent several seconds in thought, then spoke in a remarkably calm tone. "Earlier today, I listened to the objections of two of the Joint Staff, and in the heat of the moment, I accepted their resignations, without knowing what I would do next. That was a mistake, but a fortunate one, as those two Chiefs survived the attack and are now able to help defend their country.

"I am not inclined to make that mistake again, so soon. So, Director Gibb, I'm going to forget you said that, until this is over. And then we will discuss what your future will be. But until that time, get out of this room, and get out of my sight."

"Sir, I must object again and—"

"Mr. Director!" the President said. "I pride myself on having a team of people who are free to object to everything I say, *when* we have the leisure to discuss policy. We have no such leisure now. This is a crisis of national importance. General Janukatys and Admiral Paulsen, despite our many disagreements, know that there is a time when we cease being politicians and policymakers, and we become *Americans,* united, and nothing more. They are doing their job for their country, not for me. And you do not belong in their company. Now get out before I have the Secret Service take you into custody."

As Hector saw the look of mixed resentment, shock, and humiliation on Gibb's face, he resisted the impulse to applaud. He was also overwhelmed, not by what the President had said, but because it was something that Sinclair might have said just as easily, and something that made sense of what Christou had done. Hector saw that whatever underlying connection bound the two women together and all the members of the military he had seen today, the tie actually connected more than just those who served in uniform.

It included the President.

Hector thought about it again and realized it also included him.

As the FBI director stormed out of the conference room, Hector looked through the glass wall to see Tyler and Special Agent Newman sharing pizza at the desk outside. The boy was earnestly explaining something to the agent, who was listening to him with her full attention.

Without ever having asked the question, Hector suddenly knew why someone like Margaret Sinclair had chosen to become a soldier, why Elena Christou had done the same, and it probably even held true for the lost midshipman, Amy Bethune. And, he was certain, that reason would hold for Brower and Paulsen and Janukatys. It would be the same for everyone.

The answer was Tyler and what he represented—America's future.

But it was one thing to know what you were fighting for, and another to win the battle.

EIGHT

BASEMENT LEVEL, F RING

Amy Bethune knew that somewhere within her, rage still burned. She carried in her pocket six pass cards, each with a photograph of a classmate, a fellow mid, a friend. And each had been taken from the body of an enemy she had killed.

Her rage had not interfered with her actions, nor did it now drive her on. But she knew it was there, carefully compartmentalized. She acknowledged it, used it, but it did not own her.

She asked herself the question Chase had asked. *What do I feel, then?*

A single word flashed into her mind. *Balance.* Right now, that was enough.

She heard Chase stop behind her on the narrow utility staircase. She stopped, too. It was just possible that he had noticed something she hadn't. He *had* been the first to think of diverting the terrorists on the service road.

She looked back at him. They were five steps away from

the Pentagon's basement, two floors beneath ground level. Chase was sniffing the air.

"It's like the grenade," he whispered.

Amy sniffed and smelled the acrid aftermath of an explosive. Then she realized she had been smelling it all the way down the stairs, but she had thought it was coming from her H&K.

A battle had been fought in the area they were approaching, and there might still be more fighting to do. Amy prepared herself for disappointment. It was entirely possible the ops centers might no longer exist.

Calm swept over her and she moved on, down the stairs.

At the bottom of the staircase was a landing and a door. The door was unlocked and unsealed. She opened it slowly. The smell of gunsmoke became stronger.

Amy led the way down the narrow hallway. On either side, the locked doors had red signs warning that electronic devices were not to be taken inside. Some doors had five different kinds of locks: doorknobs, deadbolts, number pads, card readers, and eye scanners. The door façades looked old, as if the renovation hadn't yet reached this area.

She studied the floor ahead. It sloped downward, abruptly, for about eighteen inches. That might mean that they were moving from an old section of the Pentagon to a newer one, an underground expansion of some kind. Beyond the slope, the corridor ran another twenty feet, to a T-intersection.

The light was brighter up ahead and she could see in the distance a thin tendril of blue haze hanging in the air. She looked back at Chase. His face told her he understood what the haze meant, as she did.

In less than a minute, they were at the entrance to the Army Operations Center. What was left of it.

The hallway here widened to fifteen feet across. Many

light fixtures were inset in the ceiling, but few of them were working. Most had been shattered.

Bullet holes defaced the pale green walls, battle debris littered the polished terrazzo floor. Evidence of blast damage everywhere. Pools of blood beneath twisted bodies clad in Army green. Several shot in the face or in the back of the head. There were no weapons. The attackers had taken their victims' guns.

Amy looked up and down the corridor and replayed the events that would have brought it to this condition. The holes on the left side of the entranceway to the Army ops center were like cannon balls had hit. Every surface was sprayed with blood just beyond that opening.

"It was an ambush," she told Chase. She assessed her companion's reaction. She knew she'd almost lost him in the roadway. He still wasn't talking much, but he was keeping up. Maybe he was finally getting used to it. "The attackers waited for the sealed door to open, then opened up with a fifty-caliber weapon."

"We'd better check it out," Chase said.

Amy nodded. It was the right thing to do.

She and Chase entered the Army ops center by going through a short corridor with a second set of security doors at the end, and onto the lower floor of a two-level chamber. Amy looked up to see large NEC television monitors suspended from an encircling overhang. Wall racks held groups of smaller Mitsubishi monitors in rows. A few displays rolled slowly with gray or colored bars. Some flashed like strobe lights. Most were dark. Blue smoke wreathed the chamber like morning mist.

Where it hung low to the floor, the haze almost covered the remains of the soldiers, but not quite.

Amy checked out the closer ones. A few showed no

apparent wounds. She rolled one intact body over to look for injury, but jerked back when she saw red bubbles glistening in the victim's nostrils and open mouth.

A biological agent was the first thing she thought.

Chase was at her side in an instant.

"Is that a chemical or disease weapon?" she asked.

"A disease organism wouldn't work that fast. And a chemical weapon wouldn't cause the scorch marks everywhere. See?" Chase pointed to burnt patches on the beige carpet, on the pastel-colored walls, and on the blank, wall-sized video screens.

Amy understood. "Fuel-air explosive," she said, and the rest of the scenario played out for her. "When the doors were opened, the attackers fought their way past whoever was coming out. Got to the second set of security doors. Then lobbed in an FAE and let the doors close again. It turned the whole chamber into a single bomb."

"I don't get it," Chase said, looking around the devastated room.

"An FAE's really effective. Low-risk. Good for neutralizing a large volume like—"

"No, I don't mean the weapon. They had to be taking Milo to a facility with a Red Level computer workstation. There're two over there." He pointed to what had obviously been a glassed-in alcove office off the main room. All that remained of the glass panels were slightly warped frames and a mound of shattered glass. "But the FAE destroyed them."

"There're three other operations centers and the National Military Command Center," Amy said.

"They're all gone, too," a voice said from behind them.

As if she lived in a slow-motion world, Amy became acutely aware of every detail of her surroundings. Effortlessly, gracefully, she spun around as she flipped her H&K into her hands and prepared to aim and fire.

But the target she found without thought was in Air Force blue and held no weapon, so the impulse to fire never flickered into being.

The man in Air Force blue was a technical sergeant, last name Wiley, and he was dying whether he knew it or not. Amy could see that Wiley had been caught by a burst of 9mm rounds in his lower abdomen. His pants were soaked with blood and his brown skin was ashen with shock.

Amy cleared a section of the floor and Chase helped the sergeant lie flat. Then Amy sent Chase to locate the mess room and bring back water and napkins, a first-aid kit if they had one.

"We didn't know they were out there," Wiley said shakily. He was shivering. Amy looked away from the seared bloody mess above his hip, remnants of cloth and skin and glistening intestines matted together with thick dark blood. All she could do was kneel at his side, hold his hand, and listen.

"The President called the . . . called the CO. . . ." Wiley's teeth were chattering. "He called all the COs . . . told us to get the bastards . . . but they were waiting out there . . . the shooting . . . threw in something. . . ."

"Have you seen the other ops centers?" Amy asked.

Wiley nodded weakly. "I looked everywhere . . . saw what they were doing. . . ."

"What who were doing? The enemy?"

Wiley went into a spasm that lasted only a few seconds. "Y-yes. . . . Taking everyone who wasn't injured . . . tying them up . . . gonna—gonna tie them to doors . . . put them—put them by windows in the River Side . . . so . . . so . . ."

"So when Delta Force comes in, they'll hit the hostages first?"

". . . b-bastards . . ."

Chase was back with a large medkit. It had more items in it than Amy knew how to use. There was a Ringer bag she could use to start an IV drip, maybe buy Wiley a few more minutes in case a miracle happened and a real Delta Force medic turned up. But she had never inserted a needle before. That hadn't been part of her training yet.

"Is there a manual in there?" she asked Chase, as she realized she herself was shivering. She couldn't be panicking. That was impossible. She'd killed six people today. She couldn't . . .

She felt Chase push her aside, his knife already in his hand, slicing through the sergeant's dark blue sleeve, exposing his arm. "Hang in there, Sergeant," Chase said sharply. "Concentrate on me. How many people were in here? How many people did you work with?"

Even as he spoke, Chase's hands moved swiftly and surely. He snapped the coiled-up tube free of the Ringer bag, then handed the plastic sack of rehydrating fluid to Amy and told her to hold it above the sergeant. "Come on, Sergeant. What's your name?"

"Michael . . . Mike . . ."

"Okay, Mike, this is really going to hurt, keep you awake. Here goes!"

Chase jabbed the IV needle into Wiley's arm and a weak trickle of blood spurted into the liquid-filled clear tube from the bag. He opened the valve on the tube. "How was that?"

". . . didn't feel a thing, sir, thanks . . . " Wiley said, tried to smile.

Chase determinedly dug through the medkit until he came up with a large packet of antibiotic ointment marked for use on minor burns. He ripped the bag in half and quickly squeezed the contents onto Wiley's wound. "You married, Mike? Got any kids?"

It was as if electricity had flooded through the sergeant. He grabbed Chase's shoulder as Chase ripped the wrapping off large sterile pads and placed them on the wound.

"Chrissie . . . ," the sergeant whispered, urgent, desperate to communicate. "Chrissie . . ."

Amy watched, transfixed. She had both hands on the Ringer bag to keep it steady, to keep herself steady.

Chase cracked open a small brown vial. "What, Mike? What about Chrissie? Your wife? Your little girl?"

Chase held the vial under the sergeant's nose. "C'mon, Mike, keep talking to me! What should I tell Chrissie?"

Sergeant Wiley sighed then, as if finally relaxing after a hard day at work. ". . . sorry . . ." Then his body stopped shivering.

Chase slowly straightened up. He threw the vial away like throwing a knife.

Amy was still holding the Ringer bag. She didn't know what to do with it. "I don't think there was anything else you could have done," she said.

Chase took the plastic bag from her and laid it in Wiley's lap. "Did I hear him say they were putting hostages in position to stop a counterattack?"

Amy nodded, wondering who Chrissie had been . . . was . . . and if he had a picture of her in his—

"Nuke!" Chase said loudly.

Amy rocked back, startled.

"We have to let CONDEFCOM know about the hostages. We need a phone, and we aren't going to find one working down here."

Amy forced herself to focus on what Chase was saying to her. She didn't like what it meant. They'd have to go back up. Away from the enemy and whatever basement lair they'd established. "What about General Vanovich?"

Chase picked up his H&K. "Hey, this is one of your lines: The general is just one man. If those guys cleaned the ops centers out, I'd say they have more than two hundred hostages to spread around. I think that changes things."

"Right. Let's go," Amy said, even though it meant delaying her mission.

Saving lives *was* more important than taking them.

Much as she hated to admit it, Chase was right.

STRATEGIC INFORMATION AND OPERATIONS CENTER, FBI HEADQUARTERS

Inside the conference room, there was nothing to do but watch the wall clocks count down, so Hector had taken the chance to go out and check on Tyler. The eight-year-old was in the midst of lecturing Special Agent Newman about the intricacies of the World Wrestling Federation's ongoing storyline.

"How're you guys doing out here?" Hector asked.

Tyler stopped in midsentence to show Hector his pager. "My dad's not sending me any messages."

Newman shook her head. "They don't work in here, hon. No pagers, no cell phones. We're completely shielded."

Tyler looked at Hector for confirmation.

"She's right. There's a lot of top-secret stuff around here."

"Like what?" Tyler asked.

"If I knew, it wouldn't be secret, would it?"

"Like bombs?"

Agent Newman raised her eyebrows at that. "Oh, we don't like to talk about bombs in here."

Tyler turned back to her. "Do you know how to make things blow up?"

Hector missed Newman's answer as he turned toward the sound of running footsteps and saw the NSA assistant director, Milton Meyer, charging toward the SIOC conference room. Admiral Paulsen was right behind him.

"I'll be right back," Hector said. He hopped back through the sliding glass door.

"We've got a way to track QUICKSILVER," Meyer announced breathlessly. He was holding up a sheaf of printed pages.

"Is Schriever back in action?" the President asked.

"No, sir," Paulsen answered. "We're getting firsthand reports from disaster crews dispatched from the Petersen base. It's just ten miles away. Sir, the whole facility is gone. There're only three antennae standing. The buildings are in ruins."

"Survivors?" the President asked.

"None so far."

The President turned to Meyer. "Then how do we track it?"

Meyer referred to the pages he held. "Sir, these are transcripts of the phone calls General Vanovich made and received today. He paged Tom Chase at 700 hours. Chase called back at 7:02. And at—"

"Excuse me," the President interrupted. "How is it you have this kind of information about the head of the NIA?"

Hector had been wondering the same thing. He saw

Meyer's pained expression and decided the explanation was as bad as the President probably feared.

"Sir," Meyer said, "I will provide full disclosure as to how and why this information came into my hands, but time is short today."

The Man wasn't pleased, but he was practical. "Go ahead."

"The general received a call from a Dr. Helen Shapiro. She's a physicist . . . well, she consults for the NIA on . . . the point is, she works at a company that monitors lightning strikes across North America, and one of her employees apparently had recorded the QUICKSILVER test firings earlier this year and had figured out where the tests took place. To within twenty miles, she said."

"This physicist, does she know about QUICKSILVER?"

"She has some knowledge. Her specialty is lightning and EMP."

"Do we know who the employee is?"

"I've got his personnel file here."

"And will twenty miles be close enough for us to do something about QUICKSILVER?"

"That will significantly narrow our search window."

Admiral Paulsen had something to add. "Mr. President, I've been coordinating an operation between the Air Force and the Naval Research Lab to bring down the satellite. We have Pegasus antisatellite missiles mounted on B-52s and on standby alert at Vandenburg and Cape Canaveral."

"I thought you couldn't see this thing, Admiral?"

Meyer rapidly scanned his pages. "If this . . . Stan Drewniak . . . can get us to within twenty miles of its position, we should be able to calculate an orbit and have a good shot at spreading enough flak in front of it to bring it down."

The President rubbed at the back of his neck. "And just

so I understand why you're bringing this to me: First, firing the Pegasus missiles will be a violation of the START III Treaty. Second, those transcripts of the general's calls are probably illegal. And third, Shapiro and Drewniak don't have clearances for everything you'll have to tell them."

Paulsen actually smiled. "Three out of three, sir."

The President shook his head. "Do what you have to do, gentlemen. I will want full reports, but you are now operating with the direct authority of this office."

Both men exited the conference room as quickly as they had entered.

"At least that's some good news," Hector said. He'd just checked the countdown for Major Sinclair. In about two minutes, she'd be through the conduit. Then she'd have twenty minutes to report. Meanwhile, the bomber was eighty-two minutes away. And there was no way to be certain how many satellites were being shifted in orbit or forced to reenter in the meantime. But—

"Not really, Hec. You realize that if that fellow can only detect the satellite when it fires . . ."

"Oh, shit," Hector said as he understood. "We're going to have to take another hit first."

The President nodded. "And we have no idea where."

SEWAGE CONDUIT FOUR

The silt had been accumulating for decades. Margaret Sinclair had only minutes. But the farther she crawled on through the narrow concrete conduit, the thicker the silt at its bottom became. After one hundred feet, almost halfway through, the clearance between the silt and the top of the conduit was down to fifteen inches. There was no way she could pass through it. She might actually fit in that narrow a space, but it would be so tight she'd have no way to move her arms and legs. No way to move, period.

She castigated herself for not bringing some kind of digging tool to scrape the silt away. She had her knife, but that was strapped to her calf inside her coveralls. No way to reach it. And she had abandoned the ceramic armor plate after twenty-five feet. It had just slowed her down.

She bowed her head for a moment, trying to think. Her scalp prickled under the balaclava she wore as sweat ran off in constant beads. Her vision was blurred from perspiration, but her gloves were so filthy she couldn't wipe her face.

Finally, though, that one irritation among so many—the cuts on her knees and elbows, the heat, her completely blocked sinuses—there was one thing she could do.

She brought her silt-encrusted gloves up and pulled at the balaclava until she had ripped it free of her face. For about five seconds, she felt some relief. She could even use its sodden mass to wipe her eyes.

But the air in the conduit was no cooler or drier. She was still hot and she was still sweating.

She shone her flashlight forward—at least that was working properly—but the conduit's curve kept her from seeing more than another twenty to thirty feet ahead.

Then she realized she did have a digging tool. *The second flashlight.*

She bit at the duct tape holding the spare flashlight to her left wrist, then started to unwind it until the flashlight was free. Her shoulders started to cramp with the constricted movements she was forced to make, but she wouldn't slow down.

She unscrewed the top of the Maglite, shook out the batteries, and held up the tool—a metal tube with sharp edges.

She plowed the empty metal tube into the silt and the silt broke apart easily. Four deep furrows later, she banged the flashlight barrel against the conduit wall to empty it out, and swept the silt to both sides. Her digging had gained her another three to four inches of clearance.

That was when she realized she didn't have to clear the entire surface. She crawled forward, wriggling side to side more than moving on her knees and elbows. Then she hollowed out a clear area to crawl into. She *could* just squeeze through a fifteen-inch constriction, provided she had enough space beyond it to move her arms and pull herself through.

The system worked. The silt wasn't too compacted. She started making good time again.

Until she saw the vertical shelf of soil up ahead. For a moment, frustration almost overwhelmed her. The conduit was blocked and she wasn't certain she could crawl backward through the constrictions she'd left behind her.

She forced her head down so she could watch her flashlight beam trace the full interior surface of the conduit just before her.

There was one dark gap that remained even when the light hit it.

The conduit's shifted, that's all, she told herself. *It's cracked and dropped down a few inches.*

She dug and crawled her way forward another three feet, grateful to the silt, at least, for its protection from the sharp edges of concrete that had ripped through her coveralls in just the first few feet of her journey.

She reached the break in the conduit. The section she

was in *had* settled. About eight inches. She angled her head to the side and pushed up as hard as she could against the top of the conduit, then shone her flashlight through the elevated section. No silt.

But the gap she'd have to crawl through was barely twelve inches top to bottom. Side-to-side, it was just wide enough for her shoulders to get through. And once through, the conduit was clear so she'd have enough room to pull herself up. And while twelve inches might not be a problem if this were a water slide and she were in a bathing suit, the gap was ringed by concrete splinters, and she was wearing coveralls stuffed with equipment, covered in pockets, over her BDU pants and shirt.

She *might* make it through. But then again, she might snag her coveralls, or she might just be too bulky in all her gear.

There was only one thing to do.

She had to lose her coveralls. She mentally rehearsed the steps. She'd peel them off like a banana skin down to her waist, freeing her arms at least. Then she'd pull herself through the gap and the bunched-up coveralls would jam in place on the concrete, and she'd simply pull herself out of them.

Just like pulling sleepers off Tyler when he was a baby, she told herself. It would mean losing the nylon cord and all the equipment she had planned to drag through after her. But she would still have the radio. Information was still what was most important.

She pushed her back up against the top of the conduit and tugged the coveralls' front zipper down as far as she could. Then she grabbed one sleeve and pulled her arm down, and in. Wriggling an inch at a time, she finally got one arm free. It was slightly easier to free her other arm. Then she took the radio she had stuffed into the front of the coveralls and tossed it up into the raised half of the conduit. She left the Beretta behind. It would be useless without the clip in her coveralls pocket.

Margaret took a few deep breaths, though that only made the walls of the conduit seem to close in on her more tightly, then reached up with one arm into the raised section and kicked with her feet to propel herself forward.

She turned to the side and edged one shoulder in first, in order to clear the bottom edge of the conduit, for once in her life glad her chest wasn't a single inch larger.

Now when she took a breath, she could feel the edges of the gap on her back and across her ribs at the same time. The sensation was panic-inducing. She fought back the instinctive impulse to breathe deeply and forced herself instead to empty her lungs so she could pull herself clear.

Her waist was through. Still holding her breath, she wriggled, struggled, finally felt the coveralls snag, and then she angled her elbows against the rough concrete and pulled her backside through.

Now she allowed herself the luxury of breathing again. Three deep slow breaths, and it was time to start forward. Using mostly her arms, she pulled herself along, pushing the radio ahead, until even her feet were in the new clear section of the conduit. It was still only twenty inches across, but it was almost like being outside again.

Her legs were still tangled in the trapped coveralls, but that was fine. She pulled herself along another four feet, and then the tension on her combat boots told her she had stretched the Nomex coveralls to their full length.

Now it was just a question of determination. The cuffs of

the coveralls were outside her boots. They were wide enough to be pulled on over her boots. Therefore, she told herself, they were wide enough to be pulled off.

Inch by inch she hauled herself forward, her shoulders cramping from the stress. Her boots began to strain against the coveralls. Her BDU shirt and pants began to shred, torn by the rough concrete. And then, after one mighty shove forward, her left foot jerked free of the coveralls. At once she used that boot to push against the fabric already halfway down her other boot.

She was wheezing now with every breath. Her ice-cold hands had so many small cuts and scrapes that they were raw and bleeding. But she had not come all this way to be caught by two lousy inches of ugly fabric.

And then with one last push she was free.

She lay flat in the conduit for only a moment.

It wasn't time to rest. And she'd been through worse in her training at Fort Bragg. *Yeah, right.*

She angled the flashlight to look at her watch. It felt as if she had spent hours in the conduit, but only fifteen minutes had elapsed.

Five minutes too long.

She crawled forward again, falling into a rhythm, pushing the radio ahead of her. She kept shining her flashlight ahead, certain she had progressed at least four hundred feet. But the conduit seemed endless. There was only darkness before her.

She pushed herself faster, until a merciful numbness set in to her abraded arms and legs. She shone the light forward again. Still no end. Just darkness.

For one terrifying moment, she wondered if the original plans had been wrong, and instead of this conduit ending at an exterior foundation wall, it continued on *beneath* the Pentagon.

Her breath came in gasps now as if she were running. Right elbow, left elbow, right knee, left knee. Light forward, nothing, keep crawling, keep crawling.

The end of the conduit would come soon. She had to get out soon. Two hundred feet. That was all it was supposed to be. Two hundred lousy—

And then her right elbow came down on absolutely nothing, and Margaret Sinclair fell into the void.

NINE

TUCSON, ARIZONA

Stan Drewniak floated blissfully in the hot tub overlooking his Fiji estate. His neck was stiff, but the soft hands of Gabrielle were working wonders on his tired muscles. And as for Xena, Warrior Princess, it truly was remarkable how long she could hold her breath as she—

Gabrielle punched his shoulder.

He pushed her hand away. "Gabrielle, don't—"

Then her powerfully muscled hand grabbed the sheet off Stan's chest, along with half his chest hair, and Stan was instantly and terrifyingly awake in the disaster area that was his bedroom. Gabrielle, Xena, and the Fiji estate raced back to dreamland, leaving Stan staring in slack-jawed shock at two Men in Black.

They loomed over him, both in identical dark suits, both with identical close-cropped hair. One was holding an eight-by-ten photo of Stan. The other held Stan's DiscMan. Its headphones were swinging back and forth like a noose.

"Are you Stanley N. Drewniak?" the one with the photo asked.

Stan nodded slowly. He was painfully aware that except for the dingy white sheet balled up in his lap, he was naked. He was also even more aware that whoever these two were, they had to be in law enforcement, and there was a half-smoked joint in the stolen Maria's Restaurant ashtray on the floor beside the mattress.

Stan breathed in deeply, through his nose. The room still smelled of pot. GAI was a zero-tolerance company. His job there was finished. He was busted.

"Get your clothes on, sir," the one with his DiscMan said. "You're coming with us."

"D-don't you have to read me my rights? Or something?"

"You're not under arrest."

Both men flipped open badge cases.

"Holy crap," Stan said, reading each ID card. AIR FORCE INTELLIGENCE AGENCY. They really were Men in Black.

"Why me?" he asked plaintively.

But the one with his DiscMan was not interested in a discussion. "If you do *not* get dressed *now,* we *will* take you out wearing that sheet. Have I made myself clear, *sir?*"

Stan edged off his bed, clutching the sheet, and backed up over paperback books, CD cases, and old towels and plates with pizza crusts until he found his black shorts and the least dirty T-shirt he owned. He reached down for his shorts and put them on with one hand.

"Where are we going?" Stan dropped the sheet and pulled his T-shirt over his head.

"We're taking you to work, sir."

Stan stopped in the middle of fastening one of his desert

sandals. That made no sense. "You mean, Global Atmospherics?"

"You have to hurry."

"But I'm not supposed to go back in till Tuesday."

"Change of plans," one said as he hooked his arm around Stan's and started dragging him toward the door. Stan's left sandal was half off his foot.

"What kind of plans? I don't have any plans!"

The second one was right behind him, pushing. "Sir, the United States Air Force wants you to find the Grinch."

"Ho—ly crap," Stan gasped. *If these two really are from the Air Force, then the Grinch isn't one of* ours! *It's one of . . .* theirs!

He was propelled through his living room and out the front door of his tan stucco bungalow, toward a white Chevy Suburban parked on the street.

It *all* made sense now—the one special scenario he hadn't had the nerve to suggest to Dr. Shapiro.

Suddenly, Stan was as anxious to get back to work as these two were to get him there.

"I knew it!" Stan said as he was stuffed into the backseat of the Chevy.

"Knew what, sir?"

"I found a goddamn alien spacecraft!"

Stan saw the two Men in Black exchange a glance and shake their heads. But then, what was he honestly expecting them to say? That he, Stan Drewniak, was the first to crack a decades-old government cover-up?

With a flashing orange light on its roof and a siren, the white Suburban ran all the red lights on the way to Global Atmospherics.

Deep in his own thoughts, Stan didn't notice. He was busy. Trying to decide which talk show to go on first.

BASEMENT LEVEL, AUXILIARY GROUNDWATER ABATEMENT AREA

As Margaret Sinclair pitched forward, she threw her hands out, to empty space, catching sparkling reflections from the beam of the flashlight taped to her wrist. Then, with a grunt, she stopped falling. She was halfway out of the conduit, her upper body and arms free. She'd reached the end.

She was now hanging head down from the edge of the conduit, her hands dangling five feet above a still, dark body of water. Ripples radiated across its surface from the handful of gravel and debris she'd dislodged.

Then she felt herself slip forward another inch.

At once, she braced her knees and feet against the sides and top of the conduit. She twisted up and back to place one hand on the edge of the conduit so she could direct the beam of her flashlight around the open space she was in. Four feet beyond the opening to the conduit was a rough concrete wall that ran down to the water. She swung the flashlight up. The ceiling of the wall was only a few inches above the top of the opening.

Made it, she exulted. She knew she had to be in the water abatement area built around the Pentagon's basement. She ran the beam of her flashlight along the wall. Six feet along, she located an access hatch, whose bottom lip was about three feet above the surface of the water. But there was nothing to indicate how deep the water might be.

She didn't think it was likely it would be over her head, but neither did she like the idea of sinking into another sixty years' worth of silt that could grip her boots like quicksand. And unfortunately, except for her radio and the knife strapped to her calf, which she could finally reach back for if she had to, she had nothing to test the water's depth. And with the conduit so tight, she had no way of changing her position so she could come out feet first.

There was nothing to do but go on.

She rocked back and forth in the conduit until she was certain she was securely braced by both her thighs and boots. Then arching up and back, in a form of reverse sit-up, she pulled off her camouflage shirt with its tattered long sleeves, leaving her in her standard, light-brown Army T-shirt.

Breathing hard from the exertion, she tied a knot in one sleeve of her camouflage shirt, creating a pouch for the radio. Then she did her best to snag the other sleeve on one of the sharp crusts of concrete at the edge of the conduit. Now the radio hung two feet from the surface of the water. Even if the water were ten feet deep, she'd be able to reach the radio and swim it over to the access hatch. Provided the silt didn't grab her boots.

By now, Margaret's legs were shaking with the strain she had placed on them. A check of her watch showed that it had been twenty-three minutes since she entered the conduit. She had no more time to waste.

She braced one hand on the edge of the conduit opening, then started rocking herself forward, using her other hand to push, until her knees were right at the edge. Squeezing her eyes shut and holding her breath, she gave one last push and kicked with her feet and dropped down to the water.

It was three inches deep.

Her fall had only been three feet, not enough to break the hand she used to absorb the impact of her fall, but enough to send sharp pain through her left wrist, and then her left shoulder as she hit the water-covered concrete floor and rolled.

She was on her feet a second later, half her body soaked in brackish, foul-smelling water. But, except for what felt like a minor sprain in her wrist, and raw patches of skin on her forearms and shins, she had made it unscathed.

She took the radio from her shirt pouch, and switched it on.

"Midnight Special to Grand Central," she whispered. "Do you copy? Over."

The response was instant, though garbled. "Grand Central to Midnight Special, we copy. Are you on the landing field? Over."

The reception was less than optimal. Margaret doubted she'd be able to travel very far from the tunnel and still remain in contact with the soldiers at Grand Central—the Delta Force staging point under the parade grounds.

She continued with the simple codes she and General Brower had agreed to. "Negative, Grand Central. I'm off the landing field and in the helicopter. I am about to open the hatch. Over."

But there were some things the code couldn't handle. "Midnight Special, do you have the nylon cord? Over."

"Negative, Grand Central. That got hung up and I left it behind. I'll report in five. Over."

"Midnight Special, make it faster if you can. We're ready to go home any minute. Over."

Margaret felt a new burst of urgency. In this case, "home" was the Pentagon. They were getting ready to counterattack before she even had a chance to reconnoiter.

"Copy that," she radioed back. "Back in five. Midnight Special, out."

Margaret slipped the radio into the front pocket of her camouflage service trousers, then approached the access hatch. It had two lever latches that had been recently oiled. She tried one. It moved easily. She took a breath, then turned off her flashlight.

The darkness was absolute.

Now she worked by touch, finding both latches, moving them down and then in, so the hatch opened out to the left.

No light came in from the Pentagon basement beyond, but Margaret spotted a constellation of tiny green lights. LEDs, she decided. She must be in some type of equipment room.

She listened for a moment, but heard only a faint hum. Most likely the room's air-circulation system or transformers.

She slowly eased herself through the access hatchway and pulled herself out, onto carpeted floor. On this side of the basement wall, the floor was only a foot beneath the lip of the hatch. The fetid swampy stench of the water behind her gave way to the scent of plastic, the sort of smell she'd always associated with new electronics out of the box.

Silently, she rose to her feet, feeling the chill of the room's air-conditioning on the drenched side of her body. Now she could see dozens of the tiny green lights, arranged across two sides of a corridor. The sound impression of the room suggested she was in a small enclosure, so she risked turning on the flashlight again.

She was surrounded by shelves full of storage batteries. The green lights were their charging indicators. Fifteen feet ahead of her was a large door with an IN CASE OF FIRE diagram on it. It had to be an exit.

She moved quickly to the door, tried the latch handle. It wasn't locked.

She turned the flashlight off again, opened the door just an inch.

Now there was light. Dim, distant, but enough for her to be able to tell she was in a large corridor that had been damaged, probably by something explosive.

About ten feet away, in front of and to the side of double doors which had been blown off their hinges, was a large security counter, faced in blast-damaged oak veneer. Margaret recognized the counter as one that would have been staffed by two security guards. There would be at least one computer terminal behind it, and at least one phone. It didn't matter if the phone worked or not. All she needed was to find the sticker that would be on it, identifying its location in the Building in the event of emergency.

Margaret picked up some rubble to prop open the door to the storage-battery room, to keep it from closing behind her. Then she moved toward the security counter.

But she didn't need to find the phone. On the wall, to the side of the counter, were enough large, undamaged letters to tell her she was outside the Air Force Operations Center. As she looked in through the empty doorframes, she could smell smoke from fire and explosives. Water sprinklers hissed in the distance.

She knew it was a long shot, but she switched on her radio. "Midnight Special to Grand Central, do you copy?"

But she heard only the flat, featureless hiss of digital static. The EM shielding around the Air Force ops center was going to make it even more difficult to get a message outside. She decided to return to the water abatement chamber. She had to make contact again. She had to tell Delta Force that whoever was in the Pentagon had managed to bring in major explosives. She had to warn them to be prepared for booby traps and—

She heard footsteps. Down the corridor. Coming closer.

Instantly, Margaret crouched down behind the counter. All distracting sensations from her scraped arms and legs, her sprained wrist, her bruised shoulder, passed from her consciousness. She shoved the radio into her pocket.

A splintered crack in the counter's veneer gave her a slight view of the corridor. Barely.

A figure was moving toward her. Slowly.

Margaret strained to pick out details in the dark lighting of the hall. Was it one of the terrorists in midshipman white? One of the second wave in commando black?

Without thought, she moved her right hand down to her calf and silently slipped her K-bar knife from its sheath.

She listened to the footsteps coming closer, estimating distance, watching as the figure came nearer to the counter, until its shadow fell across the splintered crack.

Her attack was fluid, precise, and until the last possible instant, silent.

She stretched up and swung around the counter to find the enemy's back directly in front of her, and she swung her left arm over the enemy's neck and shoulders as she brought her right arm up with the blade turned to slice across the carotids and trachea so there would not even be a scream and then she thought—

I know that smell—

—and did the unthinkable. She hesitated—

—and in that same moment felt a terrible stab of pain in

her left hand and in her confusion felt herself pulled up and into the air, over *those* broad shoulders she knew so well to land flat on her back on the rubble-strewn floor to look straight up into the eyes of—

"What the hell are you doing here!?" Tom Chase yelled.

He had seen the flash of the knife, felt the strength of the arm around his neck, known for one awful moment of clarity that his throat would be slashed . . . and then for an instant nothing happened.

Until, without even knowing he was doing it, *he'd* done the only thing he could. He'd grabbed his attacker's hand and squeezed it as hard as he could between thumb and forefinger, and then flipped—*Margaret.*

"You're the one carrying a submachine gun!" his ex-wife snapped at him. "You don't carry guns. I thought you were a terrorist, all right? Now let go!"

Tom released Margaret's hand, not sure which shock was stronger—being attacked by a terrorist, or encountering his ex-wife in the basement of the Pentagon. He stared dumbly at her other hand. She still held her huge, stupid knife.

"You were going to kill me," he said.

"Only during the divorce." Margaret pushed herself to her feet, shaking her left hand. "I don't believe this. The old Vulcan death grip?"

"There is no Vulcan death grip. Where's Tyler?"

"He's at the ball game with his father."

Tom didn't want to go down that path. "C'mon, Margaret. There're a lot of people getting killed in here and there's no way *both* of us should be in the same place."

"As I recall, I *told* you to find somewhere safe and keep your head—LOOK OUT!"

Margaret snapped out her arm to grab Tom's shirt and swing him around behind her as she got ready to throw her knife at—

"DROP IT!" Bethune shouted. She had her own submachine gun up to her shoulder, aimed directly at Margaret.

And at me *behind her,* Tom thought. *I'm surrounded by them.*

He waved his hands so that Bethune could see he wasn't hurt. "Midshipman Nuke Bethune, I'd like you to meet Major Margaret Sinclair-Chase."

Margaret lowered her knife. "It's just Sinclair. Are you *Amy* Bethune?"

Bethune lowered her submachine gun. "Yes, ma'am."

The major tossed her knife into her left hand and moved forward to shake hands with the midshipman.

"Look," Tom said, "we have to get to a phone so I can send out . . ." He stopped as he looked down at the floor and saw a small MSE digital radio where Margaret had been. He picked it up. "Is this yours?"

Margaret answered him by snatching it from his hand. She brushed dust and fine debris from it.

"Does that even work down here?"

Margaret pointed to a utility door that was held open by a chunk of shattered drywall. "It does in there. Let's go."

Margaret led the way into a storage-battery switching room. Tom realized it was one of the facilities that kept the Pentagon powered during interruptions in the electrical system. The fact that all the charging indicators were green meant that, somewhere, backup power generators were working.

Margaret marched straight to the back of the room. Bethune followed her, telling her everything they had learned about the disposition of the hostages. Tom paused at the door, looked to the side, hit the light switch. A bank of overhead fluorescents blazed to life, making Margaret wheel around in surprise.

"Just trying to make life easier," Tom said. But then, some of the sharpness that Margaret invariably brought out in him these days began to fade. Under the bright lights, she looked terrible. As if she'd been through a war herself.

There was black scum soaking half her T-shirt and her Army pants. The fronts of her pant legs, including both knees, were in shreds, and her arms were caked in blood. "No offense, but you look like you crawled in through a sewer."

"Ten points," Margaret said. She handed Bethune a small flashlight, then ducked through some kind of maintenance opening in the wall. Bethune followed Margaret. Tom heard water splash.

By the time he stuck his head through the opening, he could see Margaret and Bethune standing a few feet away in what almost seemed to be a storm sewer. Tom was amazed that the Pentagon had allowed any kind of pipe large enough for someone to crawl through to be connected to the Building. Then he saw what Margaret was standing in front of. A pipe opening he doubted Tyler could fit through. *But SOP for my ex-wife,* he thought.

Margaret was calling in on her radio. "Midnight Special to Grand Central." Tom sighed. The military loved their code names. "Hostages have been placed to take fire. There are hostages in the River Side offices. Do you copy?"

Tom heard the wild rise and fall of old-fashioned static. There was no connection. He wondered why they were using an analog radio.

Margaret tried again, speaking more urgently. Tom saw her hold her watch under the flashlight Bethune held. "Trouble," Margaret said.

"Is there a timetable we don't know about?" he asked.

"I'd say so," Margaret answered. "Right above us we've got three hundred Delta commandos ready to swarm all over those hostages, and in sixty-five minutes, we've got a B1-B that's going to plant a nuke right smack in the Courtyard."

Tom exploded through the access opening and splashed across the water-covered floor, startling both Margaret and Bethune. He jabbed a finger at the conduit opening the wall. "Is that how you got in here?! Because if it is, I want you to get back in there and get the hell out of here! Tyler's not losing both of his parents!"

"We've got sixty-five minutes! Midnight Special to Grand Central, do you copy?"

"Sixty-five minutes?! *It's a nuke, for God's sake!*"

"Will you calm down? It's a low-yield penetrator! It goes off underground!"

"Margaret! *We're* underground!"

"Midnight Special to Grand Central, do you copy?"

Tom fought the urge to grab that radio and throw it as far into the pipe as he could so she'd have to go after it. "How dare you," he said to her, absolutely consumed with anger. "I got caught in here by accident. But you deliberately left Tyler—"

The radio squealed with static again, rising and falling, and Margaret turned away from him to listen.

Tom was through talking. Words often failed him where his ex-wife was concerned. He grabbed her hand without warning and popped the radio from her grip. "Is this MSE?" he said. "Mobile Subscriber Equipment?"

"Yes!" Margaret lunged for him, but Tom pulled back just in time. He knew enough not to give her room for some of her fancier moves.

"Digital network?"

"Give it back or so help me—" Out of the corner of his eye Tom saw Bethune wondering whether to jump him as well. He suddenly felt as if he were caught between two raptors.

"That wasn't digital static!" Tom shouted to break through to Margaret somehow. "It should be a hiss, that's all. We should be hearing a single-tone clear signal that comes from the circuits, and *not* the reception. Okay?"

At that, Margaret finally stood back, listening to him. Maybe remembering just who it was in the family who'd repaired the VCR when Tyler had tried to play a peanut-butter sandwich in it.

He held the radio in Bethune's flashlight beam, saw what he was looking for on the radio's bottom. "Look! Here!" He showed Bethune the small Change Mode switch. "It's a dual-use radio, Margaret. You've got it set for analog."

Tom drove his thumbnail into the switch recess and felt it snap from Analog to Digital. Then he shoved the radio back into Margaret's hands.

Margaret glared at him. "It probably got knocked when it hit the floor—when you flipped me." She flicked the transmit switch. "Midnight Special to Grand Central, do you copy?"

The response came at once. "Hey, Midnight Special—get your butt off the helicopter, we're landing in sixty. Over."

Tom saw the alarm in Margaret's eyes as she called back. "No! No! There are hostages at every window and every door in the River Entrance! If you go in, they will take the fire! Repeat: The hostages will take the fire! You must abort the landing! Do you copy?"

The next few seconds were, for Tom, the longest of the day so far.

And all he could think was, *With Margaret here, the day's not over yet....*

TEN

"Abort!" the President ordered. "General Brower, you will abort the attack!"

On the wall-sized video display, General Brower turned to the side and spoke into a small, green radio. "This is Round House—all units stand down. All units stand down and hold position."

A terse voice answered, "Stand down and hold position. Copy that."

Hector finally let himself breathe again. How close had they come to killing most of the hostages? Fifteen seconds? Ten?

The President seemed equally shaken by the close call. But Brower was poised for action and still ready to go. "Mr. President, let us assume the major is correct."

"Are you doubting your own person?" the President asked. He glanced around the table in the FBI's SIOC conference room, silently polling for opinions. But by now, Hector knew, the President was unchallenged. Admiral Paulsen, General Janukatys, Archibald Fortis, Milton Meyer, even Douglas Casson, they all were firmly on his side. The President's dismissal of FBI Director James Gibb had almost been a morale booster. Hector hadn't heard a voice raised in anger since.

"I don't doubt she's reporting what Chase and Bethune told her," Brower said. "But we've had infrared viewers scanning the River Entrance windows for the past hour, specifically to see if any of those rooms were occupied. And, sir, we have seen no evidence that they are."

Hector understood the dilemma facing the President. On a side-wall display screen was an outline map of the country. A small red dot, blinking on and off, was a third of the way along a shallow curve that stretched from Ellsworth Air Force Base outside Rapid City, South Dakota, to Washington, D.C.

That little dot was code-named Red Panther Two. It was the destruction of the Pentagon and the deaths of more than two hundred hostages, including the President's wife. It was the end of a sixty-year moratorium on the use of nuclear weapons in conflict. It was a little red dot that would forever change the United States, and quite possibly the world. And the President had to balance all that against a forwarded message from one soldier who had been behind enemy lines for five minutes.

"Sir, you've given an order to release a weapon that will kill all the hostages. If you let me proceed, targeting only one quarter of the windows we had originally selected, we might lose some hostages, but by God we will be able to rescue others. If we can't save them all, let me at least try to save *some*."

The President rubbed at his temples, absolutely exhausted. "General, if this were simply a matter of mathematics, you'd be absolutely right. Getting some of them out *is* better than getting none of them. But those words you used, 'we might lose some hostages,' that's not math. That's coffins. That's mothers and fathers and sons and daughters, all losing someone. It's people with names and faces who will live or die depending on the decision *I* make. Not you."

"Sir, with respect," Brower said, "you do have to make a decision. We can't just wait it out."

"But what if Major Sinclair succeeds in reaching Site J and shutting it down?"

"Do you honestly think that's likely, sir?"

The President looked surprised by the question. "If you don't think she has a chance, then why did you allow her to go?"

Brower looked uncomfortable. "Because . . . she does have a *chance*. Maybe one in a thousand, one in a million, who knows? At the very least . . . and sir, I am sorry to put it this way, in the . . . in the math that I do in situations like this, I had to allow for the highly likely possibility that she would fail in her mission, that she would be captured, and that she would win us a few minutes of confusion and delay for the enemy."

Hector felt sick. Both because in General Brower's eyes, Margaret Sinclair's life seemed to be nothing more than a weapon to be used, and perhaps lost, in battle, and because Hector knew why it was the general had to think that way. He glanced out through the glass wall to see Tyler and Special Agent Newman at the desk outside. Newman had brought up some magazines and comics from the day-care center downstairs. Tyler was busy showing her something in a comic. Meanwhile, his mother and his father were sixty minutes from death.

Brower was not ready to give up. "Director Casson," he said. "I know this is unusual, but what isn't today? The thing is, when it comes to policy, we CINCs are usually able to air our differences with the SECDEF, without troubling the President. And as far as I can see, you're about the closest thing to the SECDEF left in one piece. So I appeal to you, if there's something more I should know about the President's reluctance, or if there is some way you might prevail upon him to see this matter from a military standpoint, I would be deeply grateful." Brower reached out for an offscreen control. "I'm going to sign off for a few minutes. But I'll be here, standing by."

The screen went blank.

Casson went to work. "Mr. President, from a purely military, and practical, point of view, I believe the general is correct. I believe the best we can hope for is a partial rescue. The more time the general has, the more successful that rescue will be."

"Point of view," the President sighed. "Perspective."

Hector felt the hair on the back of his neck bristle as the President said those words. He knew what was going to happen next.

It did.

"What do you say, Hec? What's your perspective?"

I don't belong here, Hector thought. *I never have.* But he wouldn't abandon the Man now. He couldn't. But how to answer? *I believe you should trust Major Sinclair because I'm on the verge of asking her out? I believe you should do what the general says and maybe risk losing Sinclair because she is just a soldier, after all, and a soldier's lot is to do or die? I believe that, with so many lives at stake, you can't be diverted by thoughts of one life, like your wife's, or Tyler's, or . . .*

No, that isn't it, Hector thought. *I'm the President's contrarian. How do I turn this conversation upside down? How do I change the rules?*

And then he had it. He leaned forward.

"Sir, we're talking about the wrong thing here," he said. "We're talking as if we've already lost. But we should be asking ourselves how we can win. We've got the world's best soldiers from the world's best army out there. We're fighting on our home ground."

"It's Captain Kronig's home ground, too," Casson reminded everyone. The NRO director had taken off his round-framed spectacles and was busily polishing them. "Kronig was posted at the Pentagon. He's already shown that he knows his way around. He's managed to outmaneuver us at every stage."

"He hasn't outmaneuvered us," Hector protested. He's only anticipated what the military response would be. Like General Brower said, there was only one way to get into the Pentagon quickly and that was through the River Entrance windows. So, Kronig, or whoever's in charge, that's what they figured out, too, and that's where they blocked us. So we need another strategy, another approach that he won't be expecting."

Casson put his glasses back on and gave Hector a sharp look for arguing with his elders and his betters. "Mr. MacGregor, that is why the armed forces devote tens of thousands of hours of training and hundreds of millions of dollars of their budgets on war-gaming, scenario-testing, coming up with and trying out new modes of thinking about strategy and tactics. If we had a few years, I'd say you were right." The director looked over at the time display under the map of the progress of Red Panther Two. The large red numbers cycled over to 00:59:59 as the room watched. "But we have sixty minutes. Mr. President, we have to go in."

"But not through the windows," Hector said.

Everyone looked at him.

"General Brower says there's no way through that huge blast door. If that's what he thinks, then Kronig thinks it, too. So there're no hostages behind it. So, all you have to do is go in *through* that door." Hector sat back. "That's my perspective, sir."

"Um, it sounds pretty," Fortis said, "but . . . how do you go through a door you, uh, can't go through?"

Hector reflected for a moment, then stared up at the conference-room ceiling. It was made of perfect rows of acoustic tiles, studded with pot lights that had partial spherical shields over them to redirect the light. Their rounded shape made him think of bullets in a gun, bombs in a bomber. "Too bad you can't get that bomber to drop the penetrator through the blast door without blowing up."

Hector glanced down from the ceiling to see that everyone at the table was now staring at General Janukatys. The Air Force Chief of Staff held up his hand. "Sorry, even if we don't arm the warhead, the penetrator's a gravity bomb. Its CEP—Circular Error Probable—is ten meters. That means we could miss the door by thirty-three feet on all sides, and that means we'd probably hit the roof or the wall or even the parking lot, first. And if it didn't work, we wouldn't have anything left to take out Site J. The Air Force can't help you."

Hector wasn't really surprised. It had been too much to

hope for, to think that *he* might come up with an idea the top military minds in the country had missed.

Then Admiral Paulsen said, "But the Navy *can.*"

The expectation that suddenly filled the room felt like a static charge was building, as if lightning were about to strike.

Paulsen got to his feet. "Mr. President, you give me the word, and I'll get you through that door in fifteen minutes." Then he turned to Hector and added, "God bless you, Mac-Gregor."

Hector knew he'd finally done something useful today.

He just didn't know what.

BASEMENT LEVEL, RING F

Amy still had no explanation for why Major Margaret Sinclair had married someone like Tom Chase. But she knew why Chase had married the major. Though she was covered with slime, bruised, and scraped, Chase's wife—ex-wife—was gorgeous.

She also knew how to take command. As soon as Sinclair had received confirmation that the Delta Force assault had been aborted, she had radioed back that she was proceeding to the Club Car. Then she had plunged through the access opening into the battery room, naturally assuming that Amy and Chase would follow her. And they had.

When they were back in the ruined corridor outside the Air Force ops center, Sinclair had asked Amy, "Can you handle that H&K?"

"Yes, sir—ma'am."

Sinclair had smiled at the slip. Three years at the Academy and Amy still got it wrong. The "Yes, sir!" response was so reflexive, it was hard to change it for those ten percent of officers who were female. "Any other weapons?"

Amy gave her the Beretta and Sinclair expertly checked the clip and thumbed the safety. "Clips?"

Amy passed them over.

"Good work," the major said. "You're my squad."

"And . . . ?" Chase had asked.

"You can't stay here," Sinclair told him.

"I have no intention of staying here."

"Good. Stick with us. We'll find a safe place to stow you."

"And I don't have any intention of being stowed."

"Tom, you have no idea how much it pains me to say this, but you're right. We both can't be here if that nuke hits."

At that, Amy saw Chase wave his hands at the major, as if signaling for a time-out. "That's it. Stop it right there. *Why* are they nuking the Pentagon?"

"If you keep up with us," Sinclair said, "you'll find out."

Then the three of them moved out, down the corridor, and the story the major told was incredible.

Amy knew Chase had suspected a special, classified shelter deep under the Pentagon. But she could tell that even he was surprised by Sinclair's revelation that it was a complete, alternate military command center. And by the operations details of the new weapons system—code name QUICKSILVER—that the major and General Vanovich had worked on that wasn't supposed to have been a weapons system. The major's description of that was mind-boggling. Not to mention what she told them about what really happened to the *Shiloh*.

Amy remembered gathering with her fellow mids in the

company room back at Bancroft Hall during the Dark Ages, that long, terrible stretch of winter days between Christmas and spring vacations. That's when the *Shiloh* hearings had been held in D.C. She had taken part in the heated debates that had raged about who was to blame. Now, she knew, all that expert testimony, all those charts, computer records, and even satellite photographs—they'd all been altered. The official deception was unsettling. Amy found it hard to understand how decisions like that could originate in an organization for which duty, honor, and absolute honesty were mandatory.

Some of the senior Naval officers who had testified had even been Academy graduates. *How does* that *happen?* Amy asked herself. *How do you graduate from the Academy and become an officer who can lie?* She knew it did happen. She just hoped she never found out how.

Chase, with his engineer's mind, was even more astounded by QUICKSILVER than Amy was. She took it as a matter of course that there would constantly be new and more powerful weapons added to the armory of the United States. It was one of the necessities for maintaining freedom. But Chase kept pestering the major with so many technical questions that she finally ordered him to just shut up.

Surprisingly, he did.

Amy couldn't believe these two had ever been married. Chase didn't seem to realize that Sinclair was a complete person on her own, who could function perfectly well without him. And Sinclair didn't seem to realize that Chase was someone who had to question everything. Even Amy knew that was how Chase dealt with uncertainty. He still hadn't found a place in the world in which he felt as secure as Sinclair was in the Army. At least, that was how Amy saw it.

She was aware that that was part of what had drawn her to the Navy, just as her father had been to the Air Force.

For her, there was, of course, the challenge of a demanding job only a handful of people could do, as well as the chance to serve her country. But with those responsibilities came the absolute security offered by an organization that always looked after its own. Amy knew her place in the Navy would always be as clear as the stripes on her sleeves and the ribbons on her chest. No questions. No doubts.

Chase was just looking for that kind of grounding in his own life. Obviously he was trying to provide it for their son. Amy didn't think it would be all that difficult for the right partner to calm him down. *Might even be interesting to try,* she thought.

The major led them through a series of interconnected hallways as if she had laid out the Pentagon herself. When they came to a corner where the scent of expended explosives became strong again, Sinclair moved out in front to check ahead, then waved them on.

The short hallway they were in now had once been blocked by a blast door. Amy saw no card reader on the wall, so she knew it had been a perimeter door, one of the ones which even Chase's proxcard couldn't open.

But someone had. By setting off a huge explosion.

The warped blast door had been shoved to the side of the rubble-filled hallway. "This is how they brought the hostages up," Sinclair said. She looked around at the extensive damage. Waterlines in the ceiling dripped water. Multicolored blossoms of fine wires fanned out of other broken pipes beside them. "But how the hell did they get so much firepower in here?"

Chase pointed to a jumbled pile of cardboard cartons

that had been blown down the hallway by the blast. Amy could see Campbell's Soup logos on their sides. The cartons were surrounded by some sheets of what appeared to be heavy metal foil. "Like that," he said.

Chase jogged over to the boxes, and cautiously picked up one of the scattered sheets of foil. He held them out for Amy and Sinclair to inspect. Close up, the foil screen was perforated with thousands of what seemed to be random pinpricks and slashes, incredibly fine. The irregular mesh shimmered like a moiré pattern.

"This explains how they smuggled the explosives into the Pentagon," Chase said. "Probably a lot more, too. Guns, radios, ammunition. The CIA uses these."

"What is it?" the major asked.

"An X-ray hologram." Chase handed the foil to Sinclair. "They make a 3-D X-ray of a carton of Campbell's Soup cans, scanning the carton from every angle. Then they encode that 3-D data on a 2-D sheet of lead foil, with a cutting laser. Same way they put 3-D images on a 2-D sheet of film, using visible-light lasers. Just like Tyler's dinosaur holograms.

"My guess is that the Pentagon kitchen probably brought in a couple of hundred more cartons than usual for that luncheon today. The terrorists must have packed soup cartons full of explosives and then put one of these lead-foil sheets inside each box. When security ran the cartons through the X-ray scanners at the Remote Loading dock facility, the interference pattern cut into the foil would make sure all they'd have seen would have been cans of soup. The only clue, and no one would have noticed it in a fast scan, would have been the slight increase in density of plastic explosives over soup."

As the major examined the foil, Amy couldn't help but

ask Chase, "How come the chemical sniffers didn't pick up the explosives?"

But Sinclair answered. "They're not reliable for food products. A few years ago, there was a lot of trouble at Heathrow Airport when its detectors couldn't tell the difference between plastic explosives and Christmas puddings."

Amy noticed Sinclair folding the foil into a wad, then stuffing it into a pocket on her bedraggled camouflage pants. Amy took that as a good sign. It meant the major planned to show it to someone. It meant she was planning on making it back. Then, without another word, Sinclair turned and sprinted off down the new stretch of hallway that extended past the blast-door frame.

Once again, Chase and Amy fell into line behind the major, in that order, constantly checking behind them to be sure they weren't being followed.

Fifty feet down the corridor, Amy saw a dimly lit intersecting corridor, brightened only by different-colored pipes. A large green pipe ran along the floor while orange, red, and blue ones hugged the corridor's back wall.

"Hold it," Chase said. He stopped abruptly, causing Amy to almost run into him.

"What now?" Sinclair said impatiently, though she did stop.

"We're coming up to the utility corridor that runs under the Courtyard."

"So?"

"If this is the way to Site J—and if they've put hostages in the River Entrance to slow down Delta Force—why isn't there anything in here to slow *us* down?"

Chase must have said something worth listening to, because the major turned and looked at the corridor ahead. "Maybe they didn't think anyone would get this far."

"C'mon, Margaret, think it through," Chase said. "There's no way anyone could think of holding the Pentagon indefinitely. They've got to have some sort of defense in mind."

"They also need a way out," Sinclair said. "Maybe this is it, and they needed to keep it clear."

"So they could escape into the arms of Delta Force? I don't think so."

The major checked her watch. "Fifty-five minutes, Tom. We don't have time to debate this. Best we can do is watch for booby traps."

Sinclair continued along the hallway toward the pipe-lined corridor. This time, though, she was walking quickly, rather than jogging. And she was scanning each side of the hallway for signs of wires or triggers or other traps.

At the intersection, the major headed to her left, leading them to a double-width metal staircase that rose only four feet, providing a way to cross over the large green pipe that ran along the floor. At the top of the stairs, there was a metal platform spanning the pipe that led to two large gray doors. On one door, the words UTILITY ROOM 8 were painted in dark brown. On the other door, a red sign with white letters said, AUTHORIZED PERSONNEL ONLY.

There was a card reader to the right of the doors. Pulling a proxcard out on a chain from her T-shirt, Sinclair beat Chase to the reader.

Amy heard the click of a door lock.

Then, before Sinclair could put a hand on the doors, Chase pushed them open.

Amy blinked as bright light spilled out into the gloom of the utility corridor.

"Let's move," Sinclair said as she pushed past Chase.

Shaking her head at their juvenile behavior, Amy stepped through the door. She had seen mids do this to each other at the Academy, and it never got them anywhere. All it did was distract them from the mission.

They were now in a downward-sloping, curved-ceiling tunnel in which bright light shot up from recessed panels along the tops of the walls. The walls themselves were paneled in beige-plastic material, and each wall featured dull-bronze handrails. The ambience was somehow calming and efficient at the same time.

Looking ahead, Amy could see that the tunnel corridor continued for about one hundred feet, appearing to end in a smear of light that suggested they would be stepping outdoors. But when they exited the sloping corridor, all Amy could think was that they had entered some kind of mother ship.

She was in a large, circular room, perhaps two hundred feet across, with a flattened domed ceiling almost twenty feet high at its center. Directly beneath the center was a circular, pale copper-metal-clad kiosk that held two sets of large elevator doors. Stacked beside the kiosk were five bodies, all in Marine uniforms, surrounded by a great deal of blood. There was little doubt in Amy's mind that the five soldiers were dead, but Sinclair and Chase checked each one anyway.

Amy studied the room for information about its function. Above the elevator doors, she saw individual gold letters and smaller gold script spell out:

PENTAGON BUILDING
ALTERNATE NATIONAL MILITARY COMMAND CENTER
"Like no place on Earth."

To the side of the elevator doors, she noted an oak panel with at least ten unit patches, everything from the 50th

Space Wing of the Air Force to the Army's Signal Command, as well as the National Reconnaissance Office and a circular unit patch she had never seen before. It was an American Eagle, stylized, wings spread, head turned in profile, made up of what seemed to be a pattern of printed circuits. Its unit title was the National Infrastructure Agency. Amy had never heard of it.

Beyond the kiosk, she could see room partitions jutting out from the back wall of the circular room. The partitions were made of panels of the same beige plastic facing the walls of the tunnel-corridor leading into the domed room. Various signs pointed to DECONTAMINATION SHOWERS, UNIFORMS, MEDICAL CARE, and ISOLATION UNITS.

Amy could tell that, despite his Red Level proxcard, this place was unfamiliar to Chase, too. But, interestingly enough, not to the major. Sinclair headed now through the partitioned area without hesitation, passing one partition wall punctured by a line of bullet holes.

"How long has this been here?" Chase asked the major as he and Amy followed her toward another set of gray-metal doors.

"Site J? Since the early seventies."

"You sure? We're only about thirty feet underground here," Chase said. "This wouldn't have lasted ten seconds in the seventies."

"*This* part was just added in the last five years," Sinclair said. She stopped by the second set of gray-metal doors and pulled out her proxcard. "The results of the first Cloudy Office and Cloudburst training exercises showed the Pentagon needed better ways of dealing with biological and chemical attacks. They expanded this area for scenarios in which they couldn't evacuate people to the outside of the building. Before that, it was just a Site J storage area for noncritical supplies. Now it's a full decontamination facility."

"Since when do you know so much about the Pentagon?" Chase asked.

"Since I got a higher security clearance than you," Sinclair answered.

And Chase called me *a kid,* Amy thought. She half-expected the major to add a *Nya nya* to that last response.

Beyond the second set of doors was a large platform made from closely spaced bars of metal. The lighting was dimmer here, the walls concrete, the space much more constricted. Amy looked down through the grating of the floor and saw dizzying layers of more metal platforms descending beneath her, linked by a single metal ladder that shrank to a narrow dark line much too quickly.

Chase stopped at the railing that surrounded the platform. "I'm no Schwarzkopf, but wouldn't one guy with a gun covering the last rung be enough to keep this entry clear?"

"If he knew about it," Sinclair said.

"Excuse me. But the bad guys seem to know about everything else so far. Site J? QUICKSILVER? X-ray holograms?"

Sinclair stared up at Chase with such exasperation that Amy wondered if anything had ever been easy for these two. "The emergency stairway runs beside the *elevators,* Tom. That's where the gunmen will be. *This* is a pressure relief tunnel. When an airburst goes off overhead, a pressure wave will blast down the elevator shaft and this tunnel. But this tunnel curves back to the Potomac—through baffles that'll blow easily in one direction. So the blast wave bleeds off through here, away from Site J. On the blue-prints, this is just an empty tube of concrete."

"So why does it have a ladder and a door at the bottom?"

"How about redundancy," Sinclair said. "Isn't that what you call the military's favorite word?"

Chase seemed unconvinced, but Amy was fascinated. She knew that she was hearing about—and seeing—aspects of the military she was certain she had no right to know about.

"I know who we're dealing with here," Sinclair said firmly. "And I have a good idea how he got his information about Site J. This ladder and the escape hatch at the bottom were installed for the construction crews, as a means of escape in case of emergency. They were supposed to be removed when construction was completed. So they aren't on the blueprints. Just like that sewer pipe wasn't."

"What do you mean you know who we're dealing with?"

Amy wanted to know the answer to that question, too. "Are they Russians, ma'am?" she asked.

Sinclair paused on the ladder with a sigh. "All we know is what they want. We don't know why or for whom. You might very well have come across Russians. The one person we have identified is a German special forces commando. We believe we're dealing with a group of mercenaries." She reached into her pocket, took out her MSE digital radio, and slapped it into Chase's hand. "I'm point, you're communica-tions. It doesn't get ball games." She started down the ladder rungs.

Chase slipped the radio into a pocket. "Wait a minute, how did a German commando get information about Site J?"

Sinclair halted on the ladder and looked up at him with a tight expression. "I trained him, all right? He was assigned

to the NIA through NATO. I taught him. I gave him temporary access codes. Go ahead, say it."

"Say what?" Chase asked.

"This is all my fault. Okay? We're clear? Good." She
held out her watch. "Fifty minutes, and it won't matter anymore. We have to *move!*"

She began climbing down the ladder at a double-time
clip.

"You heard the major. Let's go," Amy said.

"Great. Now I've got two of you." But Chase swung out
onto the ladder and started down, not quite as smoothly as
Sinclair, but just as quickly.

Amy slung her H&K across her back, gave Chase a ten-
foot head start, then started down above him, with only one
thought in her mind.

If Chase and Sinclair were a model for teamwork, she'd
be much better off on her own.

ELEVEN

NORTH AMERICAN LIGHTNING DETECTION NETWORK, TUCSON, ARIZONA

Stan Drewniak didn't know whether to be afraid or flattered.

Everyone else who would normally be working this Sunday afternoon in the dark, air-conditioned cavern that was the GAI monitoring room had been relieved of their duties. Except for him. In a way, this kind of treatment was cool. But in another way, the two Men in Black *could* dispose of his body without anyone ever knowing what had happened to him.

"It is *not* an alien spacecraft," Dr. Shapiro said. Stan's manager was seated in a wheeled office chair, right beside his workstation.

"I understand," Stan said. "That's what you *have* to say."

He looked over his shoulder at the unsmiling agents of the Air Force Intelligence Agency. They were standing five feet behind him. One had his hands folded behind his back.

The other was talking into a Motorola Slipstream cellular phone that was as large as a credit card, and only five times as thick.

"For God's sake, Stan, just run the numbers."

Stan nodded and set the time code reply back to 16:40 Mountain Central Time. Then he looked up at the ten-foot-wide main display screen on the far wall. He still couldn't believe it. This was the first time Shapiro had ever let him play on the big screen. *Stan Drewniak rules!*

At once he could see that lightning patterns across North America hadn't changed that much since he had left earlier this morning. The thunderstorm stretching across Louisiana into Florida had lessened substantially. Portland was still the center of major storm activity. *Like, when isn't it?* Stan thought.

The Canadian prairie storm, however, had grown down into Montana and North Dakota, with dozens of lightning flashes being recorded there every second. New storm centers had arisen over Lake Michigan and in Arkansas, and a major system was sweeping south from Philadelphia to Baltimore. By tomorrow, Stan decided, the whole North-eastern seaboard should be rained out.

But weather prediction wasn't why he was here. He watched the time code count up. Ten seconds to go.

Nine . . .

He kept his eye on Colorado. No lightning flashes at all. Calm skies.

Five . . .

He wondered if he should ask why the Air Force wasn't doing this themselves. They were the ones with the satel-lites, after all. They were supposed to be able to see every square inch of the—

"Holy crap . . ." On the big screen, the time code hit 16:41:50 and the outline of Colorado disappeared beneath the biggest lightning-flash indicator Stan had ever seen. "That was the Grinch?" he asked.

Shapiro rolled her chair closer to his. "Stan, the reason why the Grinch sightings were tied into satellite orbits is because it *is* a satellite. It's creating an electromagnetic discharge to the ground."

"Discharge?" Stan stared at the giant, shifting blob that still shimmered on the screen. "Doctor, they don't even have lightning like that on Jupiter. I'm guessing the detectors closest to the target site must have been burned out completely."

"Yes, well, as you can see, it maintained the discharge for a long time. We estimate about twenty-three seconds. What we need you to do—"

"Is call the newspapers," Stan said. "It must have hit ground. Something like that could blow out the power grid, demolish buildings."

Stan felt Shapiro's hand on his shoulder as she turned him in his chair so she could look him in the eyes.

"What we really need *you* to do, Stan, is apply the software you developed for tracking the Grinch over the Pacific. Isolate the main leader in that discharge over Colorado, and then plot the arc it followed through the sky."

"You mean you want me to find its orbit."

"Exactly."

"So . . . it *isn't* one of ours?"

Shapiro glanced at the Air Force Intelligence agents, then shrugged, as if it was finally time to tell him the truth. "It used to be one of ours. I consulted for the Pentagon when—"

"Ma'am!" One of the agents held up a hand. "He's not cleared for any additional information."

"For heaven's sake, he's already seen what this thing can do. For sure he's going to have to sign nondisclosure forms and security oaths before you can let him go, right?"

"What?!"

"Sorry, Stan," Shapiro said. "But . . . this is all Top Secret. Above Top Secret, in fact. You'll either have to swear you'll never talk about it, or . . ."

"Or what? They shoot me?"

One of the agents behind him clarified the situation. "We keep you locked up, sir. A military base. Solitary confinement. Even your trial will be closed."

Stan's mouth opened in amazement. He couldn't believe someone had actually said those words—to *him*.

"Stan, I'm sorry," Shapiro said, "but you're going to have to do this. We're the only ones with the equipment to detect this thing. And you're the only one who's figured out how to locate the coordinates where the satellite fired before."

"So it *is* a weapon?"

"I'm afraid so." Shapiro turned Stan's chair around, so he once again faced his workstation. "You have to find its orbit so the Pentagon can know where it's going to hit next."

"Right," Stan said. Here he was finally getting the chance to live out one of the best childhood—and not so childhood—fantasies he'd ever had. The government was asking him to actually *save the world,* and they didn't want him to tell anyone about it.

Stupid Pentagon, he thought to himself. But he started typing anyway.

USS *CHEYENNE*, NORFOLK NAVAL BASE COMPLEX, NORFOLK, VIRGINIA

There were many reasons why orders were not to be questioned.

One of the most important was speed.

From the Strategic Information and Operations Center in FBI Headquarters in Washington, D.C., four-star Admiral Hugh Paulsen contacted three-star Admiral Frederick Helmholtz, commander in chief of the United States Atlantic Command. Their conversation took less than a minute. Both men were aware of the capabilities of the weapons system they discussed. Any questions that might have arisen had been dealt with long ago during uncounted alerts, training scenarios, and advanced warfare experiments.

Admiral Helmholtz knew the officers under his command well enough to bypass the normal chain. Time. Speed. The tempo of operations. It was the very essence of winning.

Less than one minute after talking with Admiral Paulsen, the CINC of USACOM was speaking directly with Captain Shelby Cover, commander of the Los Angeles-class nuclear attack submarine, USS *Cheyenne.*

The *Cheyenne* was one of three submarines currently preparing for war-game maneuvers in the North Atlantic. Helmholtz had chosen her because she was on station at Norfolk, Virginia. The other two were in berths farther up the East Coast at Groton, Connecticut. Norfolk was closer. Time would be saved.

During the course of this second conversation, which lasted two minutes, thirty seconds, Helmholtz's aide ran into his office to provide the aiming coordinates for the target: North: 38°52'10"; West: 77°6'32". Unlike in the past, terrain maps were not needed. The final course corrections could be given on the fly.

On any other day, the *Cheyenne*'s commander might have paused to ask one question. Submarine captains were known for their individuality and the order Helmholtz had just passed on to Captain Cover had never been given to any Naval commander in the history of the service. But Cover had been following the news and was aware of the recent events at the Pentagon. He followed his orders at once, as did his crew. They had been drilling for just such a procedure for years. Only the target coordinates were different. And these were loaded simply by having the weapons control officer type them in on his command-and-control system in the *Cheyenne*'s control room.

Seven minutes after Captain Cover had said, "Yes, sir," to Admiral Helmholtz, the tourists who were visiting the Norfolk base, along with most of the base staff, were shocked into silence by the enormous roar bumping through the moist, summer sea air as it reverberated across Willoughby Bay.

They stared with incomprehension as an eighteen-foot-long, twenty-one-inch-wide cylindrical missile rose up in an explosion of billowing smoke and glowing red fire. The missile had been fired from the *Cheyenne*'s Vertical Launch System launch tube, midway between her conning tower and her stern. The submarine was still docked.

For twelve seconds, they heard the scream of the small rocket booster that carried the missile up, until the long tube began to angle toward the north as if toppling. Then a different sound took over as a miniature jet engine ignited and the missile accelerated away, bearing northwest across the mouth of the James River, over Hampton and Newport News, to cut inland along the Virginia coast.

With no one to witness the event, small, stubby wings now folded out to stabilize the missile in level flight. Its forward-terrain-following radar kept it five hundred feet above ground level, matching each rise and dip in the contours of the landscape below. And six times a second, the missile's onboard Global Positioning System guidance computer sought assurance from three different NAVSTAR satellites that it was on the right course.

It was. The USS *Cheyenne*'s launch had been successful. At an airspeed of 600 miles an hour, a Tomahawk Land Attack Missile, Block IV, would strike the target in eleven minutes, twenty-five seconds.

The commandos of Delta Force Assault Squadron E stood ready to launch their attack, in eleven minutes, thirty seconds.

It was time to fight back.

With an all-out assault on the Pentagon.

TWELVE

SITE J

As the photographs of the dead midshipmen flashed across the television screens, Erich Kronig was thinking of his own youth. Of riding horseback. Even of the long-ago week in Hawaii with the wife of Tom Chase. But the oasis of calm that was his center, his armor against the high-stakes risks he courted as this mission spiraled to its end, that oasis continued to elude him.

Because the enemy had not yet entered the battlefield.

There'd been nothing and no one to fight.

"Where *are* they?" he said to Kilo, looking over the commando's shoulder at the five television screens on the security-and-communications console. It was inconceivable that the Americans had not yet launched a counterattack.

He and Kilo were on the second-level command floor of the enemy's Site J. Below them was the action floor where General Vanovich had been secured to his Red Level workstation and Kronig's specialists had almost finished assembling the mechanism that would allow some Site J control functions to be relocated.

Kilo rotated all available channels across his console's five screens, mercifully keeping the sound turned off as the kaleidoscope of images flashed by. Many of the television stations were showing portraits of the midshipmen of Twelfth Company. Because there was no news footage of the tractor-trailer being discovered with the original Naval Academy bus inside, Kronig was certain no one yet knew what had happened to the missing young people. But it was clear that someone had finally determined how so many "terrorists" had managed to gain entrance to the Pentagon today.

Kronig knew exactly how events *should* be unfolding right now. As of more than an hour ago, when he'd used QUICKSILVER to knock out Schriever Air Force Base, the Americans should have realized that their key objective would be to get to Site J as quickly as possible. Since a thirty-ton blast door sealed the Site J RUSH HOUR tunnels that Kronig's Team One had used, the Americans would be forced to go through the Pentagon. And the quickest way to Site J through the Pentagon was to come in by the River Entrance side.

So Kronig had placed the hostages there. Tied up in offices, by doors, in hallways and stairwells. By now, whatever ordnance General Brower had decided to use on the blastproof windows should have killed the first fifty hostages. When the American commandos stormed in through those breached windows, they would find rivers of blood that they themselves had caused to flow.

And that would stop them cold, he knew, faster than any machine-gun barrage. Because Americans could not abide failure. Rather than risk being called before a board of inquiry to explain how they had been outmaneuvered by an enemy, the Delta Force commanders would halt the attack.

Many times while planning the mission, he had found himself pitying the enemy. Though the American soldiers were expected to do their duty and follow orders, right or wrong, the citizens they served did not honor that contract with respect or support.

Americans no longer had any real concept of war. And through their caution and aversion to risk, they were, as well, ensuring that their armies would soon lose the ability to wage war in any form. Which is why a monstrosity like QUICKSILVER even came to exist. To the Americans, it was an impersonal, remote means by which to deliver death and destruction. But if an enemy were not engaged face-to-face, soldiers would never learn that death had a personal cost, and destruction came with consequence. And this weapon of mass devastation had developed in a people who prided themselves on their morality.

Kronig idly toyed with the thick plastic envelope that contained the Americans' great charters of freedom. *How these people have fallen,* he mused as he noted the lack of activity on the television screens before him. *They won't even fight for a national symbol like their Pentagon.*

He instructed Kilo to keep switching through the channels. The commercial television signals were available to them down here because of Site J's multiply redundant, exterior-communications network: a web of deeply buried fiber-optic links connected to repeater stations throughout Virginia and Maryland. It was complex, self-correcting, and virtually untraceable. It had to be. It had been designed to survive total nuclear war.

Then, as Kilo switched from channel to channel, some aspect of the Pentagon story still on each of the five screens, there was a momentary loss of signal.

"That's another fiber-optic link down," Kilo said. "They must have crews out, digging them up and cutting them."

Kronig wasn't concerned. That had also been anticipated. But he knew it would take at least twenty crews the better part of a day to complete the task. He checked the time.

"Sixty-five minutes, my friend." That's all that was required. In one hour and five minutes, QUICKSILVER would be back in line-of-sight communication with the Site J repeater stations surrounding the Pentagon, some at a distance of fifty miles. Kronig took pleasure in knowing that one of those stations was inconspicuously located on the White House roof, a classified present from the NSA. In fact, all of the organizations that worked out of Site J had taken responsibility for their own communications lines, refusing to share the details with their partners, in order to more thoroughly compartmentalize the information. That their lack of cooperation also made them more vulnerable never appeared to have become a concern to them or their masters. To Kronig, it sometimes seemed that the American intelligence community had become so insular and self-absorbed that if the CIA thought it could gain a victory over the NSA, it would actually make no difference to the CIA if that interagency conflict led to some defeat for the United States. As in all things American, winning was everything.

The television signals returned as the communications network reconfigured itself, bypassing whatever link had just been cut. General Brower had long since disappeared from his telecaptivity in the White House. As Kronig had finally realized, the general was being broadcast on a tape delay so that he had been able to join his troops well before the initially mysterious evacuation of the White House. When that had taken place, Kilo had wondered if it was possible that Kronig had set a coup in motion. For a short time, Kronig had wondered the same.

But eventually, the mystery had been explained. There had been a bomb threat at the White House, and the President was now overseeing the response to the Sons of Liberty's takeover of the Pentagon from FBI Headquarters.

The fact that the White House press office was still reporting that the authorities remained in contact with the Sons of Liberty was more proof to Kronig of the way the American government so easily embraced lies. After the last of the hostages had been tied up in the River Entrance Side, Kronig had withdrawn all his men to Site J, closing off the elevator access and sealing even the emergency stairways that ran beside them. His commandos who had initially assumed the role of domestic U.S. terrorists had actually been out of contact with the White House for more than an hour.

Clearly, the President—or whoever was in charge—was aware of that, because the aerial surveillance shots of the Pentagon, which the Sons of Liberty had demanded, had ended along with the broadcast of General Brower. Despite what they might say to the public, the American authorities had obviously concluded that they weren't dealing with domestic terrorists and that the hostages' lives were not the true stakes of the game.

Fortunately, a female reporter named Trish Mankin was still broadcasting live from a park across the river from the Pentagon. Behind her, Kronig had a clear view of both the parade grounds and the River Entrance. The afternoon shadows were lengthening. He could see more clouds in the sky. But as yet there were no signs of any enemy action, no concentrations of troops or equipment.

"Still nothing," Kilo said as he completed his run through the stations and began again. He looked up at Kronig. "They do have to know about the satellites, don't they? Is it possible they don't?"

Kronig had wondered about that himself. He tapped Kilo's shoulder. "I'll go to the source," he said. "Keep watching."

Kronig moved past his commandos who were now grouped in Site J, ready to defend it or escape from it, depending on the Americans' next action. Tango was keeping several of them amused with his uncanny impression of the American President, the one that had so effectively fooled General Vanovich.

Kronig enjoyed hearing his soldiers' laughter. His losses had been lower than anticipated and they knew it. Eight commandos had been killed by snipers in the Courtyard in the first few minutes of the takeover. Four others had died during the attacks on the operations centers. Fourteen had been wounded, but only two required a stretcher. Six of his commandos were still missing. That was a casualty rate of more than a third, but considering the conditions they had faced and what they had achieved, Kronig considered it an acceptable level of loss. Nor was that rate likely to increase. Defending Site J no longer seemed a likely scenario, considering no attempt was being made to retake it.

Kronig decided to wait five more minutes. Even if the Americans were to attack then, there was no possibility they could gain entry to Site J in less than an hour. Which meant it was almost time to send his soldiers home.

He acknowledged the warm greetings of his troops as he

reached the red-metal staircase that led down to the action floor. He knew they could sense that the mission was almost over. That they had won. And that they would all be going home to their own peoples as heroes. What more could any soldier ask?

Kronig stepped out onto the action floor. Coming up behind Vanovich's high-backed chair, he turned it around so that the general would face him.

"I have an interesting problem for you, General," Kronig said. "No one appears to be interested in trying to get your QUICKSILVER back. A full counterattack should be under way now. We know how long it takes to deploy CONDEF-COM forces. They've had ample opportunity to arrive here and begin operations. Yet . . . nothing. No sign of them."

For a moment, Kronig saw in Vanovich's gaze a hint of victory, as if for once the general had the upper hand. "Maybe they don't need to attack the site to stop you," he said.

"Of course, they do. They might be able to cut us off from all communications within a day. But not within the next hour."

For the first time since he'd been tricked into accessing QUICKSILVER, Vanovich straightened up in his chair, as if rallying. "Let me tell you something about Americans. We like to win. And if we can't win, then the next best thing is to make sure the other guy loses, too. In the bad old days, our strategists called it Mutual Assured Destruction. It meant the Soviets could launch all their goddamn missiles at us, but we'd launch ours right back at them, so nobody would be able to win a nuclear war.

"The people I know are not going to let someone like you walk out of here a winner. If you've been stupid enough to set it up so that their only possible option is to lose, I guarantee you they'll arrange something so you lose, too."

Kronig heard no useful insight in the general's tiresome ravings, only the futile bravado of a defeated enemy. "You've forgotten one thing, General. I've already won. I have control of your weapon."

Vanovich jerked his head at the workstation behind him. "According to the time on that screen, you don't get QUICKSILVER for another sixty-two minutes."

"Which is too little time for Delta Force to reach this facility and stop me."

"You know what it takes to deploy Delta Force on American soil? A Threat Condition. ThreatCons. You know what those are?"

"Of course I know." Kronig turned away. He was learning nothing here. It was time to order his soldiers to evacuate.

"Yeah? What comes after ThreatCon Delta?"

Kronig turned back to Vanovich. The old man was becoming desperate, knowing he was going to die within an hour, as soon as his creation had been captured again. He shrugged. "That's classified, SCI, Special Compartmentalized Information. But you see, I know everything. After ThreatCon Delta comes ThreatCon Echo. The Pentagon is in it now. Blast doors have descended. No doubt there are additional personnel we missed capturing who are locked in safe rooms. The entire Building has been fragmented to make it more difficult for us to defend it. Fortunately, we have no intention of doing so."

Vanovich fixed Kronig with an unblinking stare of challenge. "So what comes after ThreatCon Echo?"

Kronig knew the answer. But it was ridiculous. "General Vanovich, be serious. This is the Pentagon."

Vanovich didn't let it go. "What comes after ThreatCon Echo?"

"ThreatCon X-ray. It would require the self-destruction of the Pentagon? But how? The Building does not have that capability."

Vanovich smiled. "ThreatCon X-ray doesn't say anything about self-destruction. It says there is no hope of recovery and so the terrorist forces will be denied the location."

Again, Kronig saw something in the general's eyes, but he refused to be drawn into the old man's revenge fantasy. "We're three hundred and twenty feet underground. They can do anything they want to the Pentagon. If they wish to. But we won't be—we simply *can't* be touched."

Vanovich smiled so broadly that Kronig knew he was being insulted. "You don't understand, do you, you dumb son of a bitch. They are *not* going to let you walk out of here with QUICKSILVER. I know these people. I'm actually afraid of them myself. They'll set off a fifty-megaton airburst twenty miles up and black out the entire East Coast just so you can't transmit a signal. If they have to, they'll use the Pentagon for a bull's-eye and keep lobbing W-80 warheads into it until they've melted their way down here. They've got penetrator bombs that can punch down two hundred feet, you fucking moron. When that goes off a hundred feet overhead, the pressure wave will turn us into jelly and the radiation will hard-boil us. Don't you get it? They don't have to come down in here to kick your ass. You're fucked!"

The back of Kronig's hand slammed against Vanovich's stupidly grinning face before Kronig was even aware he had reacted.

The general slumped back in his chair, a hand to his mouth. Blood trickled from his split lip.

Kronig was shocked by his own unconscious action. He drew himself to attention. "As an officer of the German army, I apologize for my—"

"Is *that* who sent you here? The *Germans?*" Vanovich was staring at him in amazement as if even the idea were ludicrous.

Kronig flushed. He had no more time to waste on this man, this prisoner and his feeble efforts to distract him. Yet, could it be possible that he and the planners had not anticipated everything? *Would* the Americans actually contemplate using nuclear weapons within two miles of their White House? The radiation alone would—

Then it hit him. A penetrator bomb. Such a weapon plunging two hundred feet below ground level would, in effect, seal itself off from the atmosphere. With no immediate radiation threat, there would be nothing to prevent a panicky leader from employing it. And the White House had been *evacuated* . . .

Kronig spun around and shouted, *"We are withdrawing!"*

A cheer went up from his soldiers.

Kilo leaned over the red-metal railing, looking down at Kronig in surprise. "Not you," Kronig called up to him. "You and I are staying with the technicians. The rest— you're going home!"

More cheers, the sound of thunder as the metal staircase rattled beneath the stampede of descending feet.

"They'll be waiting for you," Vanovich said. "Just like you were waiting for them."

Kronig looked down at his captive. Now the contempt was his. "And just where do you think they'll be waiting, old man?"

"The RUSH HOUR tunnels. As soon as you open the main blast door."

"Your entire army can wait in the tunnels for eternity if they wish. Maybe they'll enjoy the penetrator bomb along with you. But that's not how we're getting out."

Kronig stalked away from the general, toward the side of the action floor where an open staircase descended to Level Four of Site J.

On the stairs, the orderly, single file of departing commandos moved to the side to allow him to pass. He stepped off the stairs onto the floor of Level Four and walked quickly along the line of commandos proceeding into the storage and engineering facilities.

Site J's lowest level was darker, more constricted than the three above. Its floor was a metal grid, selected to protect against any flooding that might occur. It was also noisier, suggesting the hold of some vast ship. The hum of air circulators, generators, water pumps, and cooling and heating equipment bounced off all the hard, metal surfaces.

But Kronig could no longer be distracted. He headed toward the outermost wall of the facility. There, at the far reaches of a utility room, Tango was already opening the pressure hatch for the first group of Kronig's commandos. Despite what Vanovich had fantasized, Kronig knew there could be no enemy forces on the other side of the hatch.

This part of Site J had been the first to be checked once Kronig's troops had taken over. The escape route had already been scouted today. It was intact and ready for use. And what made it so useful, and so foolproof, was that it wasn't on any blueprint. The circular hatch had been temporarily installed only for the use of the construction crews that had built Site J. It was supposed to have been removed, the opening welded over after the facility was completed. But in every reference to similar, unclassified structures that

Kronig's researchers had unearthed, mention had been made of the cost savings and increased safety factor realized by leaving the emergency exit in place. Though no one on his teams had ever seen an actual schematic of Site J, this door was in the precise location that Kronig's researchers had predicted it would be.

Kronig watched as Tango slowly pushed the three-foot-thick metal door open. A gust of cold, damp air swept into the generator room. Light from Level Four spilled past Kronig into the darkness beyond the hatch, revealing a narrow metal ramp sloping downward. The ramp led toward a twenty-foot-in-diameter, concrete-lined air channel, whose opening was only fifteen feet away. Fifty feet farther on in the channel, a glowing green lightstick marked the beginning of the escape route. Kronig's scouts had laid out a series of the lightsticks all through the concrete-lined airway that ran from Ground Zero to a pressure door at the shore of the Potomac, just under a mile away. The inlet it opened into was called Roaches Run, a few hundred feet north of Ronald Reagan Airport and directly below the George Washington Parkway.

Tango stopped at the entrance way and saluted his commander. "It has been an honor, sir."

Kronig returned the salute, then clapped his lieutenant on the shoulders. "And for me. *Reisen mit Gott, mein Freund.*" He looked at the waiting line of expectant faces, some of the wounded resting with their arms around the shoulders of their comrades-in-arms. Kronig had never felt such pride. *"Alle von Sie."* He looked back at Tango. "I will join you in ninety minutes. But if I don't, you will proceed at 2100 hours as planned."

Once the sun set, the commandos would be able to go

through the pressure door as if it were an airlock, and swim up ten feet to the surface of the Potomac. Throughout the night, beginning at 2115 hours, a series of vans would pick up the soldiers in small groups from a road on Gravelly Point, where they could not be observed from the parkway. Kronig had told the mission planners that he would not consider undertaking the operation unless he knew his soldiers would have a reasonable chance to withdraw undetected. The undocumented exit to the air channel had been the perfect solution.

For the final stage of their withdrawal, the commandos' plane reservations had been made weeks ago. Singly and in pairs, they would all return to their homes over the next three days, from airports across North America. Within seventy-two hours, no one who had been involved in the mission would remain on American soil. Victory would be complete.

Tango nodded. "We will see you in ninety minutes." Then he started down the ramp, its metal surface clanging beneath his boots, sending echoes all through the vast concrete cavern that surrounded Site J. Then he was across the ramp, at the air channel, and the splashing of boots heralded for Kronig the beginning of his troops' trek to safety.

It took less than two minutes for all fifty-two commandos to exit Ground Zero, including the two on stretchers. Site J's infirmary had conveniently provided the stretchers.

Tango paused at the entrance to the channel, his figure outlined against the green glow of the lightstick. As the last soldier passed him, he turned to face Kronig, raised his hand in farewell.

As Kronig raised his hand in turn, Tango swung his submachine gun up, aiming it at a point just above Kronig's position.

"DON'T MOVE!" Tango shouted.

At last! The calm of a warrior came back to Kronig as he stepped out onto the sloping metal ramp, shielding his eyes from the light through the hatch. He looked up to locate Tango's target and saw a metal ladder running down the curve of the facility's exterior wall. A ladder that also had not been on any of the blueprints.

Then his eyes adjusted further to the darkness and he saw what Tango had seen. Ten feet above the hatch opening, a figure clung to the ladder. He saw the silhouette of a gun on the figure's back.

The Americans *had* launched their counterattack. But stealthily. Who could have guessed they would show such restraint?

"Don't shoot unless you have to," Kronig warned Tango. Then he shouted, "You! On the ladder! Drop your weapons and climb down slowly!"

The figure responded by cautiously sliding the gun off one shoulder, then holding the weapon to the side by its strap.

"Drop it!" Kronig commanded.

He felt the breeze of the gun's falling as it dropped to the bottom of the cavern, and heard its splash as it struck the dark, unseen groundwater, twenty feet below the ramp.

"Now down! Slowly!"

The figure descended slowly, rung by rung. Tango ran forward to stand at Kronig's side, H&K held ready for any treachery.

Two feet above the doorway, Kronig was surprised to see the figure wore sneakers and jeans. Two more rungs down, and he saw . . . a gray sweatshirt?

He reached out from the ramp and grabbed the figure's arm, hauling him—no, *her!*—onto the ramp beside him.

And then, as he twisted his captive into the light from the hatchway behind him, all his questions were answered.

He knew that face.

"Midshipman Bethune," Kronig said, almost as if he were scolding her. "You missed your bus."

THIRTEEN

NORTH AMERICAN LIGHTNING DETECTION NETWORK, TUCSON, ARIZONA

The first time Stan Drewniak had gone on a Grinch hunt, he had had too little information.

This time, he had too much.

Virtually all the lightning detectors in the western United States had been overwhelmed by the EM pulse generated by the rogue satellite. If Stan were to believe their readings, he'd have to conclude the pulse had struck with equal intensity over an area of 250,000 square miles, which was more than twice the size of Colorado. And that was ridiculous.

But Dr. Shapiro had given him the exact geographical coordinates of the strike, a location ten miles east of Colorado Springs, 6,267 feet above sea level. With that site as the point of contact, Stan had begun to work backward to trace the pulse's path through the atmosphere, so he could determine its point of origin. Keeping in mind, of course, that that point of origin had been moving at 18,000 miles an hour.

Dr. Shapiro was also able to tell him that the rogue satellite would be in some type of polar orbit. But Stan would have to determine if the satellite had been traveling north to south, or south to north. Fortunately that part of his assignment had been a snap. All he had had to do was compare the timing of the signals received from the Canadian detectors to those that had been received from the detectors in Mexico. He had his answer in less than a minute. The rogue satellite was traveling north to south.

Now, Stan was ready to refine his analysis. And once again, he was the right man for the job. When he'd been looking—on his own time—for the Grinch in the Pacific, he'd developed data-sorting equations for detectors looking westward. With the Grinch now over the west half of the country, he couldn't use the detectors directly beneath it. So he eliminated all their data. Instead, he focused on the data from the detectors in the *eastern* part of the country, that would have to look west to find the Grinch. This sweet move saved him hours of calculations. And he knew he had saved Dr. Shapiro days.

Within ten minutes, Stan was happily plotting an orbit for the Grinch that fell within a five-hundred-mile range, centered almost directly over the Colorado-Kansas border. At that point, Dr. Shapiro helpfully suggested some statistical transformations that he could apply to the data. Two minutes after that, Stan was able to replot the orbit, reducing its error to plus or minus fifty miles.

But Dr. Shapiro wanted an even higher threshold of accuracy—plus or minus ten miles. The key to that was measuring the Doppler shift of a moving radio source toward and away from the detectors. So Stan compared the readings from the detectors in Mexico that lay almost directly ahead of the satellite to those from the Canadian detectors that were directly behind it.

Then he used the differences in those readings to work out the position and heading of the Grinch for each of the twenty-three seconds it had generated the EM pulse. At 18,000 miles per hour, that gave him a track of 115 miles. And *that* was just enough information for the computer to then extrapolate the Grinch's *entire* orbit with enough certainty even to satisfy his boss.

Stan sat back in his chair, linking his fingers behind his head, thoroughly enjoying the sight of *his* brilliant achievement now being plotted on the world map of GAI's main event screen. Even if there was no one else to impress but Dr. Shapiro and the two Men in Black.

The yellow sine-wave trace of the rogue satellite's orbit moved off the right-hand side of the wall map, to the east. Then, at the left-hand side of the map, the yellow line reappeared in the west, curving down and rising up again. The path of the second orbit was offset eastward by fifteen hundred miles, bringing the Pentagon's satellite back across the United States on a line beginning halfway between Toronto and Montreal in Canada, then it moved on to pass almost directly over the middle of Jamaica in the Caribbean.

"There you go," Stan said smugly, spinning his chair around to smile at his manager. His calculation had taken just under twenty minutes. Personally, he thought, it was a work of genius, and surely genius should get some kind of reward. "So, do I get a raise or—?"

"Washington." After uttering just this one word, Shapiro pushed herself out of her chair so quickly she sent it rolling into Stan's. Then she grabbed a cell phone from the Men in Black.

Stan was confused. It wasn't as if the Grinch was going to crash into the capital city. According to the orbit on the wall screen, all it was going to do was pass directly over D.C., plus or minus ten miles.

Dr. Shapiro was actually shouting this conclusion over the phone as if he'd predicted the end of the world.

Some people really need to get a life, Stan thought.

Now that all the excitement was over, he wondered if there was anything worth eating in the GAI staff lunchroom.

STRATEGIC INFORMATION AND OPERATIONS CENTER, FBI HEADQUARTERS

It's like watching a video game, Hector thought.

The center panel of the five-by-fifteen-foot video display in the SIOC conference room showed a wide-angle, black-and-white image of rushing terrain transmitted by the video camera in the nose of the Tomahawk cruise missile that was speeding toward D.C. At the bottom of the image, there was only a smear of twisting light and shadow, the ground a mere five hundred feet below. At the top, he could see the horizon, changing slowly enough that actual details were visible: roads, houses, trees, fields.

To the side were streams of numbers swiftly altered as the missile swept along the contours of the ground it flew over. The airspeed indicator was holding fairly steady, close to 520 knots. But the TIME TO TARGET was counting down in a blur by hundredths of seconds. The GPS longitude and latitude readings were changing almost as quickly, and so were the figures for altitude.

Hector glanced down at his watch to compare its reading with that on the screen. The Tomahawk was only five minutes away. Admiral Paulsen had predicted that if they went up to the roof of the FBI building, they'd be able to hear it pass by. No one had wanted to test out that prediction.

Seated in an armchair between the conference table and the wall screen, the President was looking pensive. He turned to Paulsen, in a chair to his right. "How could you do this so quickly? When I was in the Senate, I remember we had briefings on using these things against Korean missile sites. The Navy told us it took days to plot the course for each missile—to load the terrain maps into their memory, run tests."

The admiral responded like a parent anxious to describe a prodigy's accomplishments. His earlier animosity toward the President was no longer in evidence. In partnership with General Janukatys, the three men were now working in easy concert. The message they were conveying was that they were all professionals doing their jobs, along with Casson, Fortis, and Meyer.

"These are the new Block Fours, sir. It's not necessary to do step-by-step programming of their target routes anymore. We type in the longitude and latitude, and the cruise missile's onboard computers program themselves based on contact with the Global Positioning System and their terrain-following radar. Of course, we also have the advantage that no one in Virginia is going to try to shoot us down, and all the air traffic controllers are clearing the airspace."

"Okay," the President said, "I understand you can hit the Pentagon like that. But how can you be so certain you'll hit the blast doors?"

"See the crosshairs at the center of the screen?" Paulsen said proudly. "When the missile swings around on its final, straight-in approach, it will be about three miles from the River Entrance. The onboard camera will go to telephoto, and back on the *Cheyenne* some young weapons control officer with a steady hand will use a joystick to hold those crosshairs on the blast door. In fact," the admiral added, "if for any reason he feels he can't make the target, he can use that joystick to fly the missile up and bring it around for another pass."

It is *a video game,* Hector thought. He turned in his chair to look back through the glass wall behind him, at Tyler and Special Agent Newman. The two were playing cards now, and Tyler had a noticeably larger pile of Lifesaver candies before him than Newman.

"And the hostages on the second and third floors, you're sure they won't be affected by the blast?" The President's question wasn't needed to remind any of them that the First Lady's fate was still unknown. The Man was suffering, but he was still doing his job.

Paulsen hastened to repeat his assurances. "Again, sir, the Tomahawk's carrying one of the dummy warheads it was going to use in the maneuvers. In this case, it's five hundred pounds of sand. I swear to you that blast door is going to be hit by one and a half tons of machinery traveling at six hundred miles an hour, with all its force concentrated on an impact area slightly under two square feet. There will be a minor explosion from the missile's unused fuel, but the majority of the energy coupled into the door will be mechanical. The hostages will definitely feel the bang, sir, but they won't be hurt."

"From your lips, Admiral," the President said. He looked over at Air Force General Janukatys on the other side of

Paulsen. "How much longer till you start flying your fighter planes this way?"

"Give us the funding, sir, and we'll do it in two years."

An awkward pause followed the exchange. For a moment, the two men had spoken as if they both expected their relationship to be business as usual tomorrow morning. But Hector knew that couldn't be possible. No matter how today turned out, tomorrow was going to be anything but usual.

The President turned back to the video screen. "General Brower, are you watching this?"

The CONDEFCOM CINC was in a smaller video window to the side of the Tomahawk transmission. "Yes, sir. We're standing by to go in . . . four minutes."

Then, as if sharing the same thought at the same time, Hector and everyone else in the room looked over at the stylized map showing the progress of the Lancer bomber, Red Panther Two. The penetrator nuclear bomb was forty minutes away.

The President laid down his rules of engagement. "You will have twenty minutes, General Brower. Twenty minutes after entering the Pentagon, I want all your men, and however many hostages you've found, on helicopters and on your way out. Is that understood?"

Brower wasn't pleased by the restriction, Hector could tell, but he acknowledged the order.

"Is Colonel Tobin on the circuit?" the President asked.

Tobin's voice crackled from the speakers above the video screen. "I'm here, sir. I'm with the UPN team in the park."

"What's your time delay?"

"They're running fifteen minutes behind now, sir," Tobin said. "From where we are, we can see Delta Force assembled against the embankment walls by the overpass. That started about two minutes ago. But there's no sign of them on the feed that's going out from fifteen minutes ago. If terrorists in the Pentagon are watching this, they won't suspect a thing until they hear that missile hit."

"You've got a good crew there, Colonel," the President said.

"Don't I know it, sir."

"But as soon as that Tomahawk hits in . . . three minutes now, they're going to know we're coming in, so that's when you end the broadcast and start withdrawing everyone from the security perimeter. You'll have thirty-five minutes to get the civilians out of there. Is that understood?"

"Yes, sir."

"So that's it. Now . . . we wait." Silence followed the President's deep sigh.

But at two minutes, fifty seconds from target, Drew Simons burst noisily into the room. "Mr. President, the lightning-detection people, they were able to calculate an orbit from the QUICKSILVER attack on Schriever."

"Without another strike? That's wonderful. Can knowing where it is help us out?"

"Not really, sir," Simons said. "I'm afraid this is bad news, not good news. Apparently QUICKSILVER will be passing almost directly over Washington fifty minutes from now. Based on what we've seen at Schriever . . . sir, if they fire that thing at the White House, it could take out everything in a five-mile radius, including this building."

Paulsen and Janukatys got to their feet at once. Hector prepared himself to do the same. He'd run out of painkillers for his foot and had been debating whether or not to take any more. Now he wished he'd asked for more.

Paulsen said it first. "Mr. President, there have been

news reports stating that you're here in FBI Headquarters. This could be a target. You'll have to leave."

On the video screen, the Tomahawk TIME TO TARGET counter rolled over to two minutes. Now Hector could see the silhouettes of buildings on the horizon, including, on the left of the screen, the distinctive column of the Washington Monument. He could feel the countdown beginning to have the effect of paralyzing all rational thought in him and hoped the decision makers were not having the same problem.

But then the Man made the decision for everyone and Hector forgot about trying to stand.

"Well," the President said, "I'm not going anywhere. QUICKSILVER won't get here for fifty minutes, and the bomber's here in forty. General Janukatys, will that bomb do what you say it will?"

"Yes, sir."

The President looked at each of them in turn, his gaze steady, unafraid. "My thanks to each of you. For doing your best. Forty minutes, gentlemen. Then, one way or another, this will be over."

As Washington rushed ever closer in the Tomahawk's video display, Hector visualized Major Sinclair at the center of the target.

Though this was no game, there would be winners and losers.

And the final outcome was still a toss-up.

SITE J

Margaret recognized the voice that spoke a mere five feet above her and Tom.

First someone said, "It has been an honor, sir."

And then she heard Erich, his smooth voice as assured as she remembered, as charmingly clipped, with only the slightest trace of an accent.

"And for me," she heard him say, then add, in German, "Go with God, my friend. All of you."

She remembered that voice from the long days—and nights—when its owner had helped restore her belief in herself and her future. Now, for the sake of her country's beliefs and its future, she was ready for the first chance to silence it.

Until a few moments ago, it had seemed as if that chance might come immediately.

Thirty seconds ago, she and Tom had been on the metal ramp above. They'd been waiting for Midshipman Bethune to descend the ladderlike wide Us of metal that were welded to the outer wall of the Site J facility.

But then the pressure wheel on the circular hatchway began to move. She and Tom had been startled, but not surprised. The chemical lightstick in the air channel had marked it as the enemy's probable escape route.

The wheel on the door had already begun to spin faster as Tom had leapt to the left, intending to escape detection by going back up the wall ladder. But Bethune had already moved too far down. So he had quickly climbed down beneath the ramp to the ledge five feet below.

Margaret had swung over the ramp side rail to the right, released her grip, and dropped to the ledge. She'd almost lost her footing and fallen the next ten feet to the water below, but Tom had reached out to steady her. His hand was still on her back as a brace as she held on to the studs or rivets—it was too dark to say which—that protruded from the metal-clad wall of Site J.

Now, with Tom pressed close against her on the one-foot ledge, Margaret listened as a group of soldiers—more than fifty—marched across the ramp and to the tunnel. Tom obviously wanted to tell her something. She could feel his breath near her ear, but Margaret shook her head to keep him silent.

Now it seemed only Erich was above on the ramp.

Margaret prepared herself to take him. She knew she could. It would be her way of redeeming herself.

But then, disaster.

She and Tom heard someone in the tunnel call out to Erich. Bethune had been spotted on the wall ladder to the side of the ramp.

But, instead of instantly shooting Bethune as Margaret fully expected, Erich was *greeting* the midshipman, as if he knew her. Then he and the commando from the tunnel reentered Site J with Bethune.

The solid clang of the pressure door as it was pulled shut was followed by the whisper of the spinning pressure wheel.

Tom took his hand from her back as he reached out for one of the metal ladder rungs.

"Stop!" Margaret hissed, as Tom's movement rocked her sideways. A single misstep could topple them both into the water. If that happened, she did not know of a way they could regain the ramp.

"We have to follow them! That guy took Milo," he hissed back. "I recognized his voice."

Margaret fought to keep her balance, as she pressed closer to the cold, rough surface of Site J's outer metal-clad wall. Whatever heat came from being down 320 feet was being bled off by the cavern's water and the facility's heat exchangers.

"If they've got the general in there, he's up on Level Three," she whispered as loudly as she dared. "That's where the Red Level station is. We need to give them time to get up there so they don't hear us come in."

"We don't have time," Tom said, voice still low. But he was back in position, and his hand was on her back again.

Margaret held out her right arm and Tom, without being told what to do, found the backlight button on her watch and pressed it so she could read the time.

Fifteen fifty hours. Forty minutes until the bomber arrived. If worst came to worst, they could follow the enemy troops out through the air channel.

The light on Margaret's watch face winked out before Tom could read the time for himself. As he reached for her wrist, Margaret pulled it back. "Stop it! Forty minutes!"

Then they made the transition from the ledge to the ladder rungs, and swung over the ramp's guardrail. Margaret was just about to tell Tom not to rattle the ramp when she realized that he was moving almost as quietly as she.

Back on the ramp again, outside the closed hatchway, Margaret tested the pressure wheel. "How did Erich Kronig know Bethune?" she whispered to Tom. The wheel responded to her touch, moving slowly, but easily.

"Who's Kronig?"

Margaret began to open the hatch door very slowly, keeping the rate as steady as she could. "The commando who spoke German? The one who took Bethune and the general." Sometimes talking to Tom was like talking to a box full of hammers.

"The name he gave Milo was Ranger. How do *you* know his real name?"

"He was a NATO-exchange officer. He spent six months

in my department. He's the German commando I trained, okay? Now why did he know Bethune?"

"Nuke is definitely not one of *them*," Tom said in a low voice. "So just get that out of your mind. What did you train him to do?"

"Nuke?"

"It's the kid's nickname. She wants to be a sub commander."

"You seem to know a lot about *the kid*." Margaret couldn't believe she had just said that. If she was lucky, Tom wouldn't notice. It had just slipped out without thought or intention. She concentrated on slowing the turning of the wheel. She didn't want to pop the door open.

But Tom rarely missed anything that might work out to his advantage. "You're jealous," he said. She just knew he had that infuriating grin on his face, even if she couldn't see it.

Margaret moved one hand smoothly over the other, turning the wheel infinitely slowly, in case a guard with a gun was on the other side. Even if the movement were noticed, there was a chance Erich might think one of his own soldiers was returning from the air channel.

"Why would I be jealous of you?" she asked, knowing she shouldn't.

"You're always asking how I am, who I'm seeing, whether or not we should have dinner."

Margaret's hands froze on the wheel. "I am not," she said indignantly.

"C'mon, you even wanted to go to the ball game today."

"Not with you, you idiot. With Tyler." All resistance in the wheel vanished. "Now stand back. There could be a guard inside."

The sudden alarm on Tom's face perversely pleased Margaret as she wrenched open the hatch door and thrust her Beretta through the opening.

Nothing.

Just the hum of machinery, the damp smell of air-conditioning, and the tang of electronics. There was no sign of Erich or his commando or Midshipman Bethune.

Margaret waved Tom through, then stepped in behind him, and slowly pulled the door closed. Thinking ahead, just in case, she closed the pressure wheel only by a half turn. Then she looked around to locate the path to the main generators.

She kept her whisper as soft as possible. "Anyway, I've *never* asked about who you're dating. *You're* the one who's always asking about *me*."

The light in the Site J facility was at low levels here, only a few fixtures on at key intersections and over the doors to mechanical rooms. But it was enough for her to see that the look of shock was now on Tom's face. "Who said that?"

"Tyler," Margaret told him. "Are you going to call your own son a liar?"

"Tyler's the one who says you're always asking about me."

Margaret stopped in midstep. Tyler had been playing them both. "Someone's been getting too much playtime with Uncle Milo."

Tom nodded, understanding her perfectly. "I'll have a talk with him when I get back."

"We both will," Margaret said, looking at him curiously. There had been an undertone in Tom's statement.

He was looking at her reproachfully. "Why didn't you tell me about Milo? And I don't mean his project."

This one was simple. "Because he made me promise not to," Margaret said. "Sorry, Tom. He thought the chemo was working."

She moved ahead then to lead the way down a small turn in a narrow hallway. A sign on a plastic-wood-finished door read: GENERATOR ROOM. It was locked, but that didn't concern her. "You've got your tool kit, right?" Her ex-husband always had his tool kit.

Tom did that thing with his fingers and made his Swiss Army knife materialize in midair.

Margaret sighed. "Are you ever going to grow up?"

Tom crouched down by the keyhole in the doorknob. "You first," he said. Then he began doing what he'd always done best, while Margaret stood watch with her gun.

Three hundred and twenty feet above, the bomber was thirty-six minutes away.

But the Tomahawk had already begun its final approach.

FOURTEEN

It was flying with manual guidance now.

In the control room of the USS *Cheyenne,* still berthed in Norfolk, Weapons Control Officer Lieutenant Miken Marano kept her right hand on her joystick, her left hand on her ARM, ABORT, and HOME controls, and all of her attention on the two video windows before her on the tactical display of her weapons console.

One screen showed the forward view from the TLAM's Visual Targeting Camera. The other showed the missile's position, GPS-accurate to six inches, as a small yellow triangle in the middle of a constantly scrolling map.

At twenty-five miles downrange from the target site, Lieutenant Marano began to nudge the cruise missile's altitude from 500 to 200 feet. Feedback actuators in the joystick let her feel the buffeting of the headwinds and the thermals the missile encountered. But this close to the ground at 600 miles per hour, they were only minor disturbances.

She recognized the Anacostia River up ahead, and the Washington Navy Yard on its north shore. That was her landmark. "Coming up on the dogleg," she announced to Captain Cover. But she did not take her eyes from the displays.

St. Elizabeth's Hospital flashed by to the right as Lieutenant Marano located the Capitol Dome and expertly locked the crosshairs onto it.

One hundred and forty miles north, the Tomahawk cruise missile responded at once, adjusting its wings and deflecting its jet exhaust by fractions of an inch to make the course correction.

Thirty seconds from impact, Marano was unaware of everything except the images on the screens. She *was* the missile, homing in on her target, slowly dropping her airspeed.

The Tomahawk flashed over the Navy Yard, crossed Virginia Avenue, sped north-northwest, parallel to New Jersey Avenue.

"Going wide," Marano said, and eased the crosshairs to the side of the Capitol Dome. Behind her, the control room was absolutely silent. She sensed two officers behind her were holding their breath.

Above the streets of D.C., the cruise missile gleamed in the June sunlight, glowed against the dark clouds gathering to the north, then responded to the joystick's sudden movement by banking in a graceful turn around the Capitol Building, disappearing for an instant behind the dome, then streaking off due east for the Mall.

It dropped down to 150 feet, now, its exhaust shaking the leaves of the trees with its passing. A mile and a quarter ahead was the Washington monument.

The crosshairs were locked on to it. The cruise missile blurred through the air, no longer in the sky, skimming the earth.

"Going wide . . . " Marano said, no longer conscious of how her hands and fingers responded to each feedback nudge of the joystick.

The Tomahawk twisted in the sunlight, arcing around the white marble spire, rolling from side to side as it looped back over the Tidal Basin until its ultimate target finally appeared in its sights.

The Pentagon.

Straight ahead.

Lieutenant Marano used the walkways at either side of the parade grounds as her runway approach lines.

The surface of the Potomac rippled as the Tomahawk screamed past, only fifty feet above the water.

The crosshairs locked on the River Entrance.

First Floor.

Dead Center.

Until the cruise missile was only a streak of white climbing the green slope of the parade grounds at 100 miles an hour directly—

—on target.

The central concrete pillars exploded outward in perfect symmetry as the Tomahawk's unused fuel formed a fireball that flared out behind them, then was sucked into the instant passageway punched into the blast door.

The burning fuel billowed into the Pentagon.

The River Entrance foyer became an instant inferno.

The force of the impact converted its glass doors into powder that swirled down the wood-paneled hallways of the Joint Chiefs of Staff.

And the wadded-up mass of the cruise missile and blast door ended its life in the far wall of the foyer, embedded three feet in the concrete, just above the last steps of the staircase.

Within seconds, the missile's fuel exhausted itself.

Flames licked across the exposed wires and wood of the ceiling. Wood paneling burned in the foyer and hallways.

Then the Pentagon's water sprinklers turned on.

In Norfolk, Virginia, Lieutenant Marano was still staring at the blank screens on her tactical display, oblivious to the applause and cheers rocking the control room. She had just blown a gaping hole into the headquarters of her own Department of Defense. The task had not been on her to-do list when she'd reported to her duty station this morning. It would take some getting used to.

And in Arlington, Virginia, on the echo of the Tomahawk's thunderous collision with the River Entrance blast door, 225 black-clad commandos of Delta Force, Assault Squadron E, burst up and across the parade grounds, beginning their 200-foot charge from the Jefferson Davis Highway.

The siege of the Building was over.

The Pentagon had become the battleground.

SITE J

"This is the answer," Kronig shouted triumphantly as he escorted Midshipman Amy Bethune up the stairs to the action floor. To Kilo.

The Team One leader was waiting, weapon in hand, startled by the sight of a new prisoner. "How did we miss her?" Kronig understood that Kilo saw Bethune's presence as a personal failing. Team One had secured Site J and had accounted for every member of its staff.

Across the floor, at the Red Level console, India had turned in her chair to see what Kronig had discovered. The two technicians at the electronics test-bed table had done the same. Quite correctly, all the specialists had stayed at their posts.

General Vanovich's padded chair was unable to turn. It was locked in position.

"You didn't," Kronig said. "She's been an inadvertent spy for Delta Force. On the inside. That's why they haven't attacked yet."

Kilo inspected Bethune more closely. "The midshipman on television."

"The one who missed her bus," Kronig said. "It's obvious what happened. She saw where we put the hostages, and somehow she told them." He looked at the girl, little more than a child, really. "Isn't that right?"

Bethune's answer was to spit at him, but she only hit his shoulder. Kronig wiped the spittle from his coveralls. He nodded at Tango and Kilo. "Search her."

Kilo abruptly locked his arms through Bethune's, from behind, and swung her into the air. Snarling like an animal, the girl kicked her feet out, making Tango jump back, wary, searching for a new approach. Kilo swiftly retaliated, butting the front of his own forehead into the back of her skull.

Kronig heard the crunch of the girl's teeth as her jaws slammed together. Heard the whimper as her head lolled to the side. Then Tango quickly patted her down and relieved her of two H&K clips, a folding tool from her belt, and seven Pentagon passes on chains.

Kronig's admiration for her spirit became something else as he examined those passes. One was hers. The others, some of them sticky with blood, belonged to his six missing soldiers.

He roughly pushed her head up, saw her flinch with pain. Blood trickled from the side of her mouth.

"You're no Academy student," he said. "Who are you?"

Her words were slurred as if she were drunk. "Bethune. Amy Leanne. Midshipman, United States Navy."

Kronig rapped his fist against her jaw and she reacted as if he had shocked her with a cattle prod. She stiffened in Kilo's grip, hot tears streaking her face. *This . . .* child *hadn't killed six of his commandos.* And *found her way down here.*

Unless . . .

Kronig leaned in close so that he would be all that she could see. "Who's with you?"

He could see by her wide eyes that she was terrified of him. He raised his fist and she shrank back. Kronig sighed. It would be like torturing an infant.

"She didn't kill anyone," he said. "She's with someone. Tango, go down, check the door again. Kilo, you're with him."

But Tango held back. He gave Kronig the folding tool he had taken from the girl.

Curious, Kronig turned the tool over in his hands. It had opened to form a pair of needle-nose pliers. The point its jaws made was caked with dried blood. *Six soldiers with a pair of pliers?!* He reached out and grasped the girl's shoulder, bunching her gray sweatshirt in his fist. He pulled her from Kilo's grip, twisting her body around as he checked her for wounds.

She had none. So the blood wasn't hers. But the blood

was smeared everywhere, as if she had been in hand-to-hand combat with a knife. How . . .

Her furious cry hit his ears as her elbow drove into his throat and her foot swung back to strike Kilo's stomach as she grabbed for her folding tool. Her attack was aborted only by the butt of Tango's submachine gun smashing into the side of her head, effectively dropping her to the floor.

Even then the girl kept trying to push herself up, though she no longer had the strength or the motor control to do so.

Kronig massaged his bruised throat. "I don't know what she is," he croaked. "But check to make sure she was alone."

"Should I tie her up?" Kilo asked.

Kronig shook his head, still collecting his voice. He unsnapped the flap on his holster. Kilo nodded. He and Tango went to the stairs, started down.

The girl stared up at Kronig, defiant. Now a long string of blood and saliva hung from her mouth. Her brown hair was stained dark red where Tango's weapon had hit her. Kronig kept his distance. He drew his pistol. "For what it's worth, soldier, I salute you."

The girl's hands and arms trembled terribly as she pushed herself up to a sitting position, never taking her clear blue eyes off him.

"Ranger!"

The shout came from India, still at her console.

"They've attacked! The television coverage is . . . I don't know, half of it's ended . . . but there's a news helicopter showing smoke at the River Side . . . I can see soldiers on the parade grounds . . . helicopters coming in . . ."

Kronig nodded his head, unconcerned. "They're just killing hostages by coming in the windows."

"No—they're going into the ground entrance. They got through the blast door. You can see them run in!"

"Impossible," Kronig said, looking down at the girl. But he knew he'd have to see it for himself.

She was still staring up at him. But not with fear. *She couldn't be American. Perhaps a British exchange student, or a—*

He pulled back on the slide of his gun, raised it to fire . . .

The lights went out.

SECOND FLOOR, E RING, RIVER ENTRANCE SIDE

Like ghosts the Delta Force commandos swept through the Pentagon, through the mist of spraying water and the smoke of destruction. Swift, silent, cloaked in black, in the shadows, their faces masked by thermal visors that gave them the power to see in absolute darkness.

Office by office, stairwell by stairwell, they moved forward with clockwork precision, the only sound the rustle of their equipment, the solid pad of their boots.

Floor after floor, a door was knocked down, a three-man team rushed in, weapons up, moving back and forth, seeking targets.

But all they found were hostages, two, three, sometimes four to an office. In one ground-floor conference room, they found five hostages unbound who claimed to have been rescued by the midshipman who had left the message on the window.

They also found hostages placed to draw fire. Some had even been tied to doors that Delta would normally have blasted open. But forewarned by the Army major who had personally penetrated the enemy's line, the commandos had already adjusted their tactics to match the situation.

The enemy had constructed a classic high-stress, high-risk situation. With each door opened, the commandos' nerves were stretched tauter; triggers formed grooves in tense fingers that would not, could not, relax.

But the hallmark of Delta Force training was not learning how to fire a weapon at a terrorist. It was learning how *not* to fire at a hostage.

Wherever they found NATO officers and civilians, the commandos now cut their ropes and plastic ties. Then teams of commandos rapidly escorted freed hostages to helicopters waiting on the roof or in the small VIP parking lot beside the River Entrance. From either location, the rescued were flown ten miles south to Fort Belvoir, for treatment of their injuries and, more important, discreet confirmation of their identities.

They did not find the one hostage they had been alerted to watch for. A woman whom each of them would recognize without difficulty. The President's wife was still missing.

Yet the rest of the mission proceeded without incident.

The Pentagon's hallways and corridors were swarming with soldiers carrying thousands of rounds of ammunition. But not one round was expended.

The River Side had only been a feint to slow them down.

The real battle still remained to be fought.

At Ground Zero.

FIFTEEN

SITE J, UTILITIES DECK

Since Site J was considered impregnable, the main generators had never been designed to defeat sabotage. To Tom, the master control board was laughably unsophisticated. If he'd wanted to, he could simply push on three large rocker switches and cut all the power to the above-Top-Secret installation, as easily as turning off a light.

"Can you shut it down?" Margaret asked. She was still whispering, even though the hum of the generators in this control room made it very unlikely they could be heard.

The entire bottom level of Site J reminded Tom of a cramped and crowded and noisy old factory. Not enough lights. Narrow metal doors. Open, metal-grid floors everywhere. Though not in this electrical generator room, where thick, black-rubber mats covered the floor.

"Just turning off the power won't work," Tom explained. He loved seeing the look of annoyance that crossed Margaret's face. It only happened when she was afraid he was going to be right about something. He touched one of the main power switches. "If we shut that off, batteries will kick in right away, and the backup generators will start up." He pointed to the power system status board above the circuit switches. Its small red, green, and amber dome lights revealed to Tom the basic power distribution plan for the entire facility. "It's very clear," he added, mostly because he knew Margaret wouldn't have a clue how the board actually worked.

From the tone of her voice, she knew he was baiting her. "Okay. So what do we do?"

"I'll cause a surge. That should blow out some equipment, trip some circuit breakers. The batteries and backup generators will still come on, but there might not be a lot for them to do."

"So why don't we take out the batteries and backups, too?"

Tom shook his head and tapped the status board. "According to this, they're all up on the top floor."

"We can get to them."

Right, Tom thought. *Past who knows how many killers with guns?* "Let's see what we can get away with down here, first," he said. "Then we can figure out how to get Nuke."

"Shutting down communications comes first, Tom. No point in saving your girlfriend if we can't call off the bomber."

Tom took a deep breath. After everything he had been through today, this was one discussion he absolutely didn't need to have. "She's not my girlfriend." Tom had finally gotten the chance to tell Margaret all about Bethune's lost classmates and how that explained why the terrorists knew her. How she'd missed the bus.

Margaret poked him in the ribs. The poke hurt. "You mean: She's not my girlfriend, *yet*."

"Margaret, she's a *soldier*. You know what they're like."

"Just your type."

"Don't start." He began looking around the generator room.

"What d'you need?"

Tom reached past Margaret to get it from the top of a generator control cabinet, held it up. "Duct tape. Just the thing."

He knelt down and used his knife to pop the cover from the main circuit-breaker panel. There were three main power buses, good old-fashioned 1970s vintage. Best of all, there was no indication of computer-control circuits installed to monitor the power buses' performance, or stop him from doing what he was about to attempt. "Perfect," he said.

He tore off strips of duct tape, then reached in to tightly wrap them around the circuit-breaker switches that protected each bus, until each switch was jammed in the On position, with no way of shutting off.

"What are you doing?" Margaret asked.

"Putting pennies in the fuse box," Tom told her. "Next, I overload the circuits. These switches will try to open to protect the equipment down the line, but because I've jammed them . . . meltdown."

"Less talk, more work."

"You asked me. I told you." Tom looked around the room again, trying to find something nonconductive. He saw a small, three-stair wooden stepladder folded at the side of the room. "Give me your stupid knife." Margaret pulled her K-bar from the scabbard on her leg and handed it over.

Tom put the stepladder on the floor, stepped on two of the legs and rocked them apart. Then he picked up one of the step rungs that had fallen free, a piece of wood about fourteen inches long by five inches wide and one inch thick.

"What are you going to do with that?" Margaret asked.

This time Tom ignored her. *My girlfriend. Just what I need in my life. Another ex-wife.*

He placed Margaret's knife sideways on the end of the wooden step, then taped it into position with the duct tape, fashioning a crude scythe. When he was finished, he had a highly conductive piece of metal with a long wooden handle.

"Are you going to ruin my knife?" Margaret asked, her eyes daring him to even try.

"Only if I'm lucky," Tom told her. "Stand back over there and close your eyes."

Margaret moved away, but Tom knew she couldn't help but watch.

He, on the other hand, had no choice. He knelt by the open circuit-breaker box, lined up the knife with three thick strands of copper wire above the breakers, then plunged the blade in, while holding on to the wooden step.

The instant the metal blade touched the wires, fountains of sparks sprang from the knife and from the circuit breakers Tom had taped shut.

He heard the generators growl as they stepped up their output to meet the unexpected high demand, and then give a satisfying *phhht*.

Except for the sparks, the lights went out.

The end of the wooden step was on fire now, and Tom dropped it to the floor and quickly stamped it out, taking care not to slice his sneakers on the blade.

Margaret switched on a small flashlight she pulled from her pocket. "Don't you ever teach Tyler how to do that," she said.

"You're right. It's so much better that he learns from his mother how to kill." Tom studied the status board. The small dome lights were flickering back to life on battery power. "Okay, we're halfway there. The main generators are out. I think half the batteries are off-line. But the backup generators will come on soon. Ninety seconds, two minutes."

Margaret played her flashlight over the status board. "Is there any way to tell if the communications lines are down?"

"Not from that. And if they're so important, they probably have separate circuit breakers wired into them."

"Then we have to go upstairs and take out the other generators." Margaret went to rescue her knife. The duct tape had melted, holding the blackened blade to the charred wood. "Nice going. You screwed up my knife."

"You know, Tyler's starting to sound like—"

BANG!

The door to the generator room flew open, smashing against the side wall to reveal two men in black commando gear, both with guns and flashlights pointed directly at Tom and Margaret.

The man in front was smaller, with close-cropped red hair and beard. "Move away from the generators," he ordered.

Tom felt paralyzed. As soon as there was nothing critical behind them, it was entirely possible these men might kill them.

But the hopeless situation wasn't stopping Margaret. "What if we don't?" she challenged them belligerently. "Afraid you might blow something up?"

The red-haired commando lowered his weapon. "Then we shoot your feet, and we drag you out ourselves."

Tom glared at Margaret. If she'd just kept quiet, maybe

they'd only have been taken prisoner. *But, no, she always has to go and—*

The wooden step and knife flipped through the air as Margaret shoved him to the side.

The red-haired man fired his submachine gun straight ahead but by then Margaret's charred knife was in his throat, and Tom was rolling to the side, on the floor where Margaret had pushed him, and his ex-wife was lunging for the blazing gun.

The battle Tom watched in amazement was lit only by the beam of Margaret's dropped flashlight and the flashlights attached to the guns of the two terrorists.

Margaret was already ripping the submachine gun out of the hands of the red-haired man as he fell to his knees with a gargling cry, bright-red blood spurting from his neck. The second gunman had brought his gun up, but had waited for just an instant to avoid shooting his partner. That briefest of hesitations had given Margaret all the time she needed to swing the captured gun up into his face, violently knocking him to the side.

Then they were both outside the door and in the narrow hallway where Tom couldn't see them.

He scrambled to his feet and ran forward, skidding around the body of the red-haired man who lay twitching horribly on the black-rubber floor.

And then Tom stopped dead because of what he saw in the hallway.

The tall gunman was lashing viciously out at Margaret with his hand, and though she was a foot shorter and a hundred pounds lighter, she reached up and caught that hand, and twisted it back at the wrist until Tom heard a crack and the man grunted with pain.

She got him, Tom thought in awe.

But Margaret wasn't finished.

Suddenly she was pushing up close to the man as he slipped back against the wall, her hands, her fists, her rigid fingers, striking his face with blow after blow.

The man tried to cover his face. He forced her back as he brought his knee up into her stomach, and took his chance to draw his own knife.

Tom shot forward but Margaret's hand had already deflected the knife; her other, flat and open, drove straight into the man's eye. Tom stepped back.

The man's eye burst like a lightbulb popping.

The screaming ended only when Margaret's other hand smashed the man's larynx. He choked and doubled over, hands going for his face, forgetting his knife was now in the open.

And then in a move so fast Tom didn't see it begin till it ended, Margaret had the man's knife, grabbed the hair on his crown, jerked his head back, and drew the knife across his throat so swiftly and so deeply that his death made no sound.

His body crumpled to the floor.

The battle, all twenty seconds of it, was over.

Margaret stood over her vanquished foe, chest heaving deeply, mouth open, nostrils flared. In the soft light of the fallen flashlights, she seemed something other than human to Tom.

But today, Tom had seen this before. With Bethune.

He said nothing to the woman who had once been his lover, his wife, and still was the mother of his son. Instead, he turned and reentered the generator room, and returned a moment later with her knife.

He wiped it clean on his jeans, then handed it to her, handle first. More than anything else he might have done, he hoped the gesture would say what he could not yet say aloud.

This time he understood. And he was grateful.

STRATEGIC INFORMATION AND OPERATIONS CENTER, FBI HEADQUARTERS

General Janukatys was wearing an almost nonexistent headset: an earphone with a slender microphone that reached no more than two inches along his clean-shaven jaw. But it was enough, Hector knew, for him to keep track of all the radio traffic among the rescue helicopters. The operation had been under way for ten minutes.

"We have forty-six hostages in the air," Janukatys reported. "Only one injury so far, still no sign of resistance."

"They've withdrawn into Site J," Casson said. But the NRO director's conclusion wasn't news. That was what everyone in the conference room had expected. Everything else that had happened had clearly been designed to slow CONDEFCOM's response. And that part of the terrorists' plan had worked perfectly.

Now it remained to be seen if the rest of it would, as well.

"Fifty-six hostages," Janukatys said. "They're starting to pick them up from the roof now. No contact with the enemy."

The President sat quietly in his chair, idly picking at the bandages on his hands, watching the multiple video screens showing helicopter coverage of the Pentagon. This time, though, the observation helos were all military. The last of the news helos had been restricted from the area.

Hector knew why the President remained silent.

There had been no more messages from Tom Chase.

Not one of the radio messages had been from Major Sinclair.

And not one of the hostages had been the First Lady.

Hector looked out at Tyler, still playing cards with Special Agent Newman on the other side of the glass wall. Tyler saw him looking, smiled and waved. Hector waved back. It wasn't time yet for him to talk to Tyler. There wasn't anything new he could say about his parents.

They had another thirty minutes.

Until the bomber arrived.

And the Pentagon ran out of time.

SITE J, ACTION LEVEL

Pain was no longer an issue for Amy Bethune. Hatred had erased all other sensation.

Before her, without question, was the monster who had somehow killed her classmates. All that mattered now was that she should kill him.

It was the only thought in her mind as she had spit on him, as she had been searched, as she had attacked him and been attacked in return. And it was the only thought in her now as she sat on the floor and looked up at him as he brought his gun down to end her life.

Then the lights went out.

Instinctively, she rolled away from her position, feeling the floor buck with the impact of the bullet the monster had fired.

He'll see me in the muzzle flash, Amy knew. Her effort to

escape was ultimately useless. The bullet would find her anyway.

Except it didn't come.

Instead, a wall of electronic equipment blew out in a gout of sparks and blue flames.

A female in midshipman white ran from her console to the fire, along with two other fake sailors who had been working at a diagnostic table. Even the monster with the gun was distracted. So, somehow, Amy pushed herself to her feet, and stumbled to cover. She squeezed herself into a narrow opening behind a tall cabinet of electronic equipment on the far side of the floor, away from the red-metal staircase.

She hunched there for a moment, catching her breath, shivering as the pain tried to reclaim her and couldn't. *But pain is good,* she reminded herself. *It lets you know you're still alive.* And as long as she was alive, she had a chance to kill the monster. She put a hand to her jaw and pushed, just to sharpen her instincts.

Despite the waves of fire in her jaw, or maybe because of it, she now heard a muffled burst of automatic gunfire, and knew it had to come from the levels below. She thought of Chase and Sinclair. It had been a short burst. Surely no one could get two people that easily. At least, not the major.

Of course not, she told herself. The firing was more likely the only response possible in a surprise attack. Major Sinclair had probably ambushed one of the enemy. She had a machine gun now. She would run up to this floor and spray the room . . . but even in this fantasy, Amy wanted the major to miss killing the monster. She needed to kill him herself.

She heard the whoosh of fire extinguishers as the reflections of the flashing of sparks slowly faded from the wall and overhang near her. Machinery rumbled above her, then a few lights flickered on. But the lights were much weaker than before, pale amber, like candle flames.

"Is it working?" she heard the monster shout.

A woman answered, "Yes, we're still on-line."

When the monster spoke again, his voice was calmer. Amy recognized the tone. She had felt that way herself.

"Good," she heard the monster say. "You two, take your guns, find that girl, and kill her."

Amy looked to both sides, but there was no other cover, nowhere else she could hide. She inched up the back wall, to her feet, getting ready to leap out at the first gunman she saw.

She wouldn't be captured again, and she had no intention of surrendering.

Footsteps were coming closer. Her hiding place was obvious.

Amy returned to her fantasy. *Not much longer,* she thought. *If you're going to come to my rescue, Major, this would be a good time.*

The gunfire began.

Margaret decided to take out the two men with the submachine guns first.

As soon as she had stuck her head up from the stairwell, she'd seen Erich Kronig in black at a Red Level console with a woman in white. But there was no sign of Bethune.

She quickly scanned the rest of the action floor and saw two other men in white, carrying H&Ks ready to fire as they moved toward the far side of the room.

She's slipped away from them, Margaret thought. *Probably when the power went out.*

She checked her line of sight, made certain she wouldn't be shooting into any possible hiding place beyond the two gunmen, then dropped them both in two quick bursts. The first with a perfect cluster between his shoulder blades. The second before he'd even completed turning to return fire.

Then she swung her weapon toward Erich, and was surprised to see he was not attempting to run. Instead, he stood behind a high-backed chair at one end of the console, looking in her direction, but pointing a Beretta at the occupant of the chair, someone Margaret couldn't see.

But she could guess, even before Erich turned the chair around. General Vanovich. With Erich's gun against his neck.

"Come into the open, Midshipman," Erich called out. "This is an Air Force general. The Navy would be displeased if you let him die for you."

He thinks I'm Bethune, Margaret realized. That meant the midshipman *was* loose in the facility. *If I can provide a diversion . . .*

She rose from the stairwell, stepped onto the metal floor.

Erich stared at her in the dim light. They were twenty feet apart.

"You're not . . . *Margaret?*"

"Erich." Margaret stepped to the side, the H&K she had taken from the red-haired man at her hip, keeping her eyes on Erich Kronig but watching the woman at the left of the console as well. "General."

"Kill him, Major," Vanovich said fiercely. He didn't flinch as the Beretta pushed deeper into his neck. "That's an order!"

Erich remained behind Vanovich's chair so the only way Margaret could get him was by firing through the general. There had to be another way. But in the meantime, she raised her weapon, sighted on the few square inches of Erich's face she could see behind Vanovich.

"Think, Margaret!" Erich said quickly. "Do you know about QUICKSILVER? Do you know what it can do?"

Margaret held her fire, seeking her opportunity. "Put down your weapon and step away from the general," she said. She heard the hum of an elevator beginning to move. Erich's eyes shifted to the side. He looked surprised. *Good,* Margaret thought. *The more he's kept off balance, the better.*

"You don't want to kill me," Erich warned.

"Wrong."

"Not until the general gives me access to QUICKSILVER again."

"Never!" Vanovich growled.

Erich ignored him. He focused on Margaret. "Here's the offer I—"

Margaret missed the rest of what her former lover said as she suddenly whipped her gun barrel around, toward the woman in white, and fired.

The woman was knocked back over the console, her pistol spinning from her hand, her sneak attack stopped before it could begin.

Margaret had her sights back on Erich before the body hit the ground.

"I'm not even going to count to three," she said. She heard the elevator stop on the level above.

Erich looked up to that level and frowned. He spoke more rapidly, urgent in his desire that she understand him. "I have programmed QUICKSILVER with an automatic firing sequence."

Vanovich struggled against his chair restraints. "He told me he put it in a safe mode."

"On an internal countdown!" Erich said. "If it doesn't receive my signal when it passes over again, it will fire. Directly into Washington."

Margaret didn't waver in her aim. But she had seen what had happened to the *Shiloh*. "Can he do that, General?"

"It's . . . possible. He fired it once."

"It's more than possible," Erich said. "Think, Margaret. I had to have a backup scenario if I was forced to leave Site J before the completion of my mission. Isn't that what you taught me? Have a backup scenario?"

"How do we shut it down, General?"

Erich answered Margaret before Vanovich could. *"You* can't. Only *I* know what code to send. Give me access to QUICKSILVER, I'll cancel the firing sequence, then you let me leave with my men."

"Wrong again," Margaret said.

"Then Washington burns, and either way, my mission is complete."

"What mission?"

"To restore balance to the world."

"Whose balance, Erich? Moscow's? Beijing's?"

Erich leaned forward to Vanovich. "Don't feel too badly, General. You see, she doesn't know, either." Erich checked his watch. "Thirty minutes, Margaret. Either you give me QUICKSILVER by then, or I'll make you responsible for the deaths of hundreds of thousands. Perhaps even millions."

And with that mention of time, Margaret realized that it didn't matter what might happen in thirty minutes unless she could stop what would happen in twenty.

"TOM!" she shouted. *"TOMMMM!"*

"Your husband, too?" Kronig said, his eyebrows lifting.

"I saw him, you know. I recognized his photo from the picture you had with your son."

Margaret fired a burst into the ceiling of the next floor up. *"CHASE! GET YOUR ASS OUT HERE NOW!"*

"He's an engineer, isn't he? So *he* blew out the main generators, and now he's about to do the same to the backups, upstairs. But then you'll never be able to contact QUICKSILVER. So what happens to Washington really will be your fault."

Margaret knew why Tom wasn't answering. She'd told him not to move if she was captured, being used as bait to draw him out of cover.

"Tom! If you're up there, listen to me! I'm all right! But you have to stop the bomber! Erich's set QUICKSILVER to fire on D.C. If we don't have Site J, we can't stop it!"

She endured one long moment before Tom finally answered. "What do I do?"

"Get up to the Building, get upstairs, use my radio, you'll get right to General Brower. Tell him to abort the bombing. He has the authority to recall."

"What about the generators?"

God, he can be so thick *sometimes!* *"Don't* touch them. We need to be able to contact the platform from here. Now *move!* We've only got twenty minutes."

"Eighteen, now," Erich said, amused. Then he shouted, *"Better hurry, Tom!"*

Margaret heard running footsteps. Tom was on his way upstairs.

She took close aim again. Eighteen minutes. Tom could make it. Brower was standing by for her call. They'd be okay. "It's over, Erich."

"Not for another seventeen minutes and fifty seconds," he said. "Maybe we should just wait."

But Margaret wasn't in the mood for games. "General, if you don't make it, how do I stop QUICKSILVER?"

"Use your access code to—ahhhh!"

Erich had slammed his gun into the side of the general's head.

"Next word he says, I shoot," Erich threatened. "By now, all I need are his retinas."

"And his access code. You know it changes each time he uses it."

Margaret saw Erich's lips thin, his careful façade of control crumbling.

"You need him," she said to goad him. "I don't."

"I know Americans, Margaret. And I know you. The general is godfather to your son."

"I have my orders."

"So have I."

And as simply as that, Erich Kronig shot the general.

SIXTEEN

SITE J, PRIMARY ACCESS SHAFT

Tom couldn't question what he had to do.

Margaret was on the level below him. He'd seen her holding a submachine gun, aiming it at the man who held a gun to Vanovich's head. He hadn't seen Bethune.

Tom knew he couldn't even think about what might have happened to Bethune. Nor about what might happen to Margaret or to Vanovich if those weapons were to fire. If he did, he could never leave Site J. And that would mean he could never stop the bomber.

He had his orders and his mission.

Now the sound of his racing footsteps echoed against the curved stainless-steel walls of the Level Two entrance chamber. The elevator car he had taken up from Level Four was still there, its doors open.

Tom rushed inside, swinging around to press the CLOSE control. Then he pulled his proxcard from his front jeans pocket, touched it to the security reader, and pressed the backlit plastic rectangle marked ENTRANCE LEVEL.

The elevator doors slid shut. Tom checked his watch. His best guess was eighteen minutes left. He could make it in time.

Except the elevator wasn't moving.

Tom pressed the ENTRANCE LEVEL control again. But nothing changed. Then he realized what had happened. ThreatCon Echo. Site J had been sealed behind its own secure perimeter—the one barrier in the Pentagon that his card couldn't bypass.

He punched the OPEN control, the doors parted, and Tom got out. Somewhere, he knew, Ranger or Kronig or whoever the hell was behind this attack had to have kept at least one passageway open to the surface. He remembered the blast door into C Ring that the two terrorists had propped open. The two terrorists that Bethune had killed in the AE service road.

Outside again in the elevator-entrance chamber, Tom touched his card to the CALL ELEVATOR panel on the wall and the doors of the second elevator opened. He ran in. But ten seconds later, he learned it was locked down, too. Like the first elevator, it would only run from Level Four to Level Two, no higher.

It had to be the stairs.

This time, he touched his proxcard to the emergency-exit door to the right of the two elevators. The door clicked and Tom pushed it open, and headed through to the metal-grid landing. Then he looked up at the converging lines of the elevator scaffolding and rising metal stairs.

Three hundred and twenty feet. Thirty-two stories. Sixteen minutes.

He couldn't stop to think. He couldn't stop to question. He had his mission.

Tom began to run.

RED PANTHER TWO

Pittsburgh was on the horizon, sliding past to the north, as the Rockwell B1-B Lancer began its descent from 35,000 feet.

For now, its variable wings were in their fully-swept-back position, giving the 157-foot aircraft a wingspan of only 78 feet. But to make its final approach from the northwest, the plane would come in on a low and slow vector. The usual, near-Mach-speed approach rehearsed so often by the crew was not required now since enemy fire would not be an issue. Instead, the Chief of Staff of the Air Force had personally instructed them that, for this mission, their CEP *must* be zero.

For that approach, the Lancer's wings would swing out to their full 137-foot span, as a system of internal pumps redistributed the aircraft's fuel supply to keep it in trim.

In the cabin, the four crewmen had remained silent, except for the formal procedure when they had received nuclear authorization from the National Command Authority. The copilot and Offensive Systems Operator had recited the seven-letter authenticator code which appeared on their NCA display, so that the pilot could confirm that the command was genuine. During this recitation, not one of the crew's three men and one woman had been certain who actually was the current head of the NCA.

As they were scrambled from their base, the news reports were confusing. Some stations were reporting the

President had resigned. That Speaker of the House Marlens had become the new President. Other reports claimed that General Brower was Acting President.

But the command had been confirmed as authentic, and the prearming sequence on the B61-11 nuclear weapon in Red Panther Two's bomb bay had powered up. Despite their unspoken but shared misgivings that they might be taking this unprecedented and unimaginable action on the authority of House Speaker Marlens, the crew would do their duty as a component of the country's defense.

It was with great relief that they later accepted a direct communication from General Janukatys. The Air Force Chief of Staff informed them that the President was still the President, and that the mission they were embarked upon would save the country from incalculable harm.

While that knowledge had no bearing on how well they would perform their duty, the four knew it might help them through the long nights that would follow.

As Pittsburgh passed from view, the copilot radioed on a frequency that would take the transmission directly to General Janukatys.

"This is Red Panther Two to Cannonball. We are coming up on fifteen minutes from target. Do we have confirmation of mission status? Over."

The general's response was immediate. "Roger that, Red Panther Two. Your mission is go. Repeat, your mission is go. Over."

"Copy that, Cannonball. Our mission is go. Uh, General, we would like to request additional confirmation at five minutes. Over."

"Understood, Red Panther Two. I'll expect your call. Cannonball out."

The pilot heard one of the crew sigh. The question had to be asked. "Still enjoying the ride?"

The Defensive Systems Operator answered. There were no DSO functions on this flight, and given the nature of the mission, the young captain had been given the option of not taking part. "You're my crew," the DSO had replied. "We're doing this together."

The pilot wished they weren't doing it at all. But they would. To the utmost of their abilities.

"Fourteen minutes to target," the copilot announced.

"Weapons systems," the pilot said. "Prepare for delivery."

The bomber flew on toward the Pentagon, 170 miles away.

SITE J

Vanovich cried out as the bullet shattered his kneecap. But that was exactly the response Erich had wanted.

And he had been right.

Margaret, trusting Margaret, had not returned fire, even when she believed that the only thing keeping her from killing him had just been destroyed.

"You see!" Erich called over Vanovich's gasps of pain. "You can't shoot! You're a mother! You're an American! This is not your battle!" For the first time he took his gun off Vanovich and pointed it directly at Margaret. "Drop your weapon and you can escape with me, through the air channel, then go home to your son. I owe you that much."

"You owe me nothing!"

"But Margaret, your computer codes opened the NIA to my troops. You made it possible for us to learn all your plans."

"Drop your weapon!" Margaret shouted.

Erich felt regret. Their affair hadn't been all work. But Margaret was, like him, a soldier. He knew she'd understand. He took aim.

But the impact of Midshipman Bethune spoiled his shot.

She screamed right into his ear as she landed on his back in a great leap from behind the Red Level console.

Erich staggered and fell headfirst into the back of Vanovich's chair, rebounded backward, then fell again, catching the side of his jaw on the arm of the chair.

Bethune's ineffective punches pummeled his back and his sides. Even as he struck the floor, Erich realized that meant she had no weapons. And he knew she was too weak to do much damage.

He kicked his foot against the base of the console to straighten out, then twist beneath her. But Bethune hung on grimly, grabbing his gun hand, digging her ragged nails into his flesh as she banged his hand down. Again and again, until his gun fired again toward the ceiling and the recoil tore it from his hand.

Then she reared up astride him and began punching him again, her unfocused attack fueled by anger or by rage, but not by whatever training had enabled her to defeat six of his soldiers.

Though the girl's proximity was all that kept Margaret from shooting him, Erich knew it was time to put an end to her disruption.

He reached into his pocket, found her folding tool, felt for its blade and thumbed it open. Then as Bethune raised both hands to swing doubled fists down against him, he stabbed her with her own weapon.

Bethune gasped, then doubled over when he gave the

weapon a death twist, leaving her to clutch her abdomen as
he ripped the tool from her.

But the gout of blood he expected did not spurt across
him.

Erich looked at the tool in his hand.

He had unfolded a blunt metal file.

His moment of discovery cost him his edge. The midshipman slapped the tool from his hand, then as she drew
back to renew her attack with her weapon, she suddenly
stopped.

In an instant she was off him and running away.

Erich rolled to his side and then to his feet. He looked to
see what Bethune had seen.

Margaret was down, her body curled in a ball. A slowly
expanding disk of red liquid beneath her.

SITE J, PRIMARY ACCESS SHAFT

There was no way of measuring how far he had come,
except by the change in his body.

Tom's legs were lead, heavy, autonomous appendages
aware of nothing except their own impending collapse.
Each wheezing breath he took seared and strained his overwhelmed lungs. Black stars sparkled at the edges of his
vision.

It took two hands on the metal railing now to pull him
upward, step by step.

Keep the pace steady, he kept telling himself. *Can't collapse on the second-to-last landing.* But each time he broke
his rhythm to check his watch, he knew he had to keep
climbing as fast as he could. There was no time for pacing.

He'd been climbing for eight minutes. He was certain he was almost at the top. But he wasn't there yet.

And then he fell.

Tom's aching knee did not rise high enough and his foot caught a step. He pitched forward, striking his shins, his forearms, his chin. For a moment he knew all it would take would be to close his eyes for only a second and he would be asleep or unconscious and the pain would go away.

But that wasn't going to happen.

Tyler's dad owed his son a ball game.

Tom started crawling up the stairs until he could run again. And nine minutes after he began his climb, he reached the decontamination facility beneath the center of the Pentagon's Courtyard.

He burst through the doors that led from the central elevator kiosk and ran for the sloping tunnel that led up to the utility corridor.

Tom thundered down the metal stairs bridging the large green pipe, then tore along the corridor, bouncing off the beige cinder-block walls until he found an opening to a radial corridor.

There he halted, gasping, wheezing. The opening to the corridor seemed somehow wrong. He was certain there should be a blast door covering there because it led into the River Entrance side.

But there was no time to think anything through. He had less than ten minutes.

Tom charged down the corridor until he came to a utility stairwell, then sprinted up a floor, ran out into the Courtyard, pulled out Margaret's radio, switched it on, and started transmitting with six minutes to go.

"This is Tom Chase to anyone. Abort the bombing!

Abort the bombing! We need Site J to contact QUICKSIL-VER! Contact General Brower! Is anyone there?!"

He took his thumb off the transmit button.

Digital static. No one was broadcasting.

No . . . it can't be . . . Then Tom understood.

The surrounding walls of the Pentagon. They'd been deliberately laced with copper shielding and foils. Specifically to prevent the broadcast and reception of unauthorized radio transmissions.

He looked up five stories, to the roof. They would hear him there.

He had five and a half minutes.

Tom began to run again.

STRATEGIC INFORMATION AND OPERATIONS CENTER, FBI HEADQUARTERS

The President was on his feet and Hector had never seen anyone so bereft, or so alone.

The flashing red light that was Red Panther Two was directly over D.C. on the map. Janukatys had just told them the bomber would be circling to the southeast now, avoiding the storm front that had almost reached the city. The aircraft would come in at the Pentagon on almost the same vector as the Tomahawk cruise missile had.

The countdown said the Lancer was just over five minutes from its target.

The President went to stand by Janukatys.

"They'll be calling in for their five-minute confirmation," the President said.

The Air Force general nodded.

The Man held out his hand for Janukatys's headphone. "It'll be my order," he said.

RED PANTHER TWO

"Coming up on five minutes from target," the copilot said.

The pilot opened the circuit. "This is Red Panther Two to Cannonball. Do you copy?"

The voice that replied was as unexpected as it was recognizable.

"Colonel Boone, this is the President."

"Yes, sir."

"I want to tell you personally that the authorization, *my* authorization, stands. And though . . . though it might not seem that way, you are performing an act that will save uncounted lives and prevent untold sorrow."

"Yes, sir."

"And I want you all to know, it's *important* that you know, that what you are about to do is an order directly from your commander in chief. There can be no question, no doubt, that you are doing your duty. The responsibility is completely my own. Is that clear, Colonel?"

"Yes, sir."

"Is it clear to your entire crew?"

Colonel Boone opened the circuit so that the President could hear the crew's reply.

Then the pilot spoke again. "Thank you, sir. We are commencing our final run. We have target lock, and the package is hot."

"God be with you."

"And you, sir. This is Red Panther Two. Out."

"Three minutes from target," the copilot said.

No one spoke after that. There was nothing left to say.

B RING, ROOF

Tom Chase exploded from the roof-access doorway, tripped, and sprawled across the flat, gravel roof.

But the radio didn't slip from his hand.

He was already shouting into the radio as he rolled over and on to his knees, then got up and ran toward the A Ring roof. It was slate-covered, peaked, a few feet higher. The extra height would give him better range. "This is Tom Chase to General Brower! Abort the bomb! This is a message from Major Sinclair! Abort the bomb! Abort the bomb!"

He took his thumb off the radio as he scrambled up the side of the roof.

"This is Round House Control to unidentified traffic," a voice on the radio replied. "Where is Major Sinclair?"

Tom stopped on the topmost section of the roof, one foot on either side of the slope, the Courtyard directly below him to the left, the River Entrance and parade grounds four rings over to his right.

"Major Sinclair is in Site J! She's with Vanovich. QUICK-SILVER is on an autofire sequence to strike D.C. They need Site J to stay intact so they can contact the satellite and re-program it! Abort the damn bomb!"

"Identify yourself, please."

Tom yelled full force into the radio. "Stop following fucking procedure you moron and abort the bomb! I'm Tom Chase! Major Sinclair's my wife! You got my pager message through our son Tyler! Stop the fucking bomb!"

"Stand by, unidentified traffic."

Tom looked at his watch. Two minutes. "Don't go through channels! Please, God, call that aircraft! Tell them to swing around or pull up but don't go through the whole goddamn chain of command!"

No answer.

Tom stood on the roof and looked up at the sky. Heavy gray clouds reached down to the city. He saw the smear of rain beginning beneath them. He turned his body in a circle, slowly, feeling dizzy, searching for any, for some glimmer of metal in the sky.

But he saw nothing. The sky was empty.

As if a warning had been issued.

Tom held up Margaret's radio again. "This is Tom Chase to anyone who can hear me! Don't bomb the Pentagon! This is a message from Major Sinclair! Don't drop your bomb!"

And then he saw it. From the northeast.

A single, silver glint against dark clouds.

Ten, maybe twenty miles away.

The only plane in the sky.

STRATEGIC INFORMATION AND OPERATIONS CENTER, FBI HEADQUARTERS

With a sudden start, the President pulled his headset free and looked at it for a moment. He handed it to Janukatys. "General, someone wants us to abort?"

Even Hector jumped to his feet as Janukatys lunged for the headset. He jammed it into his ear.

"This is Janukatys!"

"What? Tom Chase? Yes, we know he's in there! Jesus,

Mary, and Joseph!" Hector stopped breathing as Janukatys turned to the President. "Major Sinclair is inside Site J!"

Hector braced himself against the conference table.

"She says we need Site J intact to reach QUICKSIL-VER!"

The President looked confused. "But what about the terrorists?"

"Sir!" Janukatys shouted. "There's no time! We have to abort the bomb!"

"*Do it!*" the President commanded.

Janukatys slapped his hands over the console controls. "Red Panther Two, this is General Janukatys. Abort your run! Command authorization Alpha Alpha Zulu Tango Niner Niner X-ray! Do you copy, Red Panther Two! Do you copy!"

Janukatys twisted a control. A blare of static. Then the answer came back from Colonel Boone.

"*It's too late, General. The bomb's away.*"

SEVENTEEN

RED PANTHER TWO

The B61-11 was released at 5,000 feet, directly over Washington's Mount Olivet Cemetery. The bomb was 16 feet long and weighed 5,200 pounds. One-third of its weight was its hardened steel casing enabling the warhead to penetrate 45 feet of concrete, or 200 feet of soil, before detonation.

The B61-11 was a gravity bomb, whose airframe was designed to provide it with a five-to-one glide ratio. The bomb flew solely by the pull of gravity and the momentum imparted by the bomber that released it. A simple GPS guidance system, combined with inertial and barometric sensors, acted to adjust its tailfins and control surfaces to bring it in exactly on target, with a theoretical precision of plus or minus six inches.

Without a propulsion system of its own, the B61-11's course was set at the moment of release. Unlike a cruise missile, its target coordinates could not be changed in flight.

The bomb was released at 16:31:45.

It would reach its target in seventy-two seconds.

And nothing could stop it.

STRATEGIC INFORMATION AND OPERATIONS CENTER, FBI HEADQUARTERS

"I refuse to accept that!" the President shouted. "Turn it around!"

"We can't!" Janukatys said.

"Set it off in the air!"

"We'd flatten the city!"

"We have to do *something!*" Hector said.

Then Janukatys shouted to whatever microphone would hear him. *"Disarm the fuze! Red Panther Two, disarm the fuze!"*

RED PANTHER TWO

Colonel Boone twisted in the pilot's seat as the Lancer shuddered through a high-G-accelerating turn to leave the impact site.

"Disarm the fuze!" the colonel shouted to the Offensive Systems Operator.

The OSO flipped open the cover on the abort switch, twisted the safety latch off, pressed the red-and-white-striped button down. The light above it glowed red. The B61-11 was not responding to the signal.

"Malfunction!" the OSO cried out. "We're out of range!"

"Not for long!" Boone said.

A RING, ROOF

No one responded to Tom's urgent pleas.

And then he saw it was already too late.

There were two objects in the sky now. One a patch of bright gray against the storm clouds, rapidly curving up. There was no question it was a plane, gaining altitude, changing course. Escaping.

The other object was a single dot of black, almost invisible, continuing on course.

And Tom knew what that was and where its course would take it.

His arm fell to his side, the radio useless in his hand.

The entire day had been for nothing. Everything would be lost. Because they'd dropped the bomb.

The storm-driven wind picked up, pushing at him, as if urging him to find shelter. But that made no sense. Not in the handful of seconds that were left to him.

He looked out over the city of Washington, wondering where in it Tyler was. Praying he was safe. Hoping his boy would someday forgive his parents for what they had and hadn't done today.

Tom's momentary smile was rueful. When he had been talking so quickly on the radio, he'd called Margaret his wife. It was probably the first time in five years he hadn't said "ex-wife" a second later.

He looked back to the sky. The black dot didn't appear to be moving. But he recognized that as an optical illusion. Because it was moving toward him.

The bright gray spot that he guessed was the bomber also seemed to be motionless, frozen in the sky, as if it, too, was coming in on a direct line to the Pentagon.

But that couldn't be true. Bomber pilots were trained to pull away after releasing their payloads.

The gray dot was getting larger. So was the black dot. *Illusions,* Tom thought. *Misdirection.* What was the Building if not the greatest piece of misdirection in the world? It was much more than just a bureaucratic madhouse, a puzzle palace, the biggest office building in the world. It was exactly what everyone had always wanted to believe it was: a fortress full of secrets and conspiracies and Top-Secret command posts.

And now it was going to pay the price for its deceptions.

Tom wondered what would kill him first, the radiation blast, or the shock wave. He decided the shock wave would. The soil would absorb a lot of the gamma rays. That's probably why someone had thought this would be a good idea.

God, he hated the Pentagon.

RED PANTHER TWO

Its wings swept in like those of a hawk dropping from the sky to steal its prey.

The B61-11 had a good thirty seconds' head start before Colonel Boone brought the Lancer out of its turn and vectored it toward the target coordinates.

The colonel pushed the throttle forward—this was no time to ease anything—and was jolted back against the ejection seat as the aircraft lurched forward, propelled by 120,000 pounds of thrust coming from her four GE-102 turbofan engines.

The Lancer shuddered as its wings locked into place. The airspeed climbed. The ground-collision alert alarm began chiming and a calm recorded voice announced impact in twenty seconds.

"What's the color?" the colonel shouted.

"Red!" the OSO answered. "We're still out of range!"

The Lancer accelerated, as it raced its own bomb to Ground Zero.

A RING, ROOF

As Tom watched, the penetrator bomb grew visibly larger with each heartbeat. But that he understood.

The bomb was over the Capitol Dome now, a thousand feet up he guessed, the size of a car, and it was closing fast.

What he didn't understand was that the *bomber* was on the same path.

Tom's legs were shaking. From the wind, from exhaustion, or fear, he'd never know. But he refused to sit down. He'd face death on his feet.

He saw the bomb's shadow flash across the Jefferson Memorial.

Only seconds now.

He was sorry he wasn't with Margaret.

Then the bomber expanded so quickly Tom couldn't track it even as he wheeled around to see it flash by—no more than one hundred feet above the roof of the Pentagon. The air exploded with a sonic boom of such intensity that every blastproof window in the Courtyard blew out at once as those five flat walls acted to concentrate the sound.

And even as the pressure wave of the bomber swept over Tom on the roof, he saw a black streak shoot like a laser beam straight into the Courtyard. Right into its center. Slicing through the top of the roof of the hotdog stand. Throwing a nearby tree up into the air. Then plunge down into the grass, and—

Tom struggled to keep his footing on the pitched slate roof.

This is it, he thought.

And it was.

SITE J, ACTION FLOOR

Amy tried to be like Chase. Sinclair was down. The major was bleeding. She couldn't panic. She had to focus. She had to *try.*

She slowly rolled the major off her side. She saw the wound. A large tear on the side of the major's left biceps.

Not fatal, Amy thought. *She's only been winged.* All she had to do was stop the bleeding.

Sinclair's camouflage pants were in shreds. With shaking fingers, Amy tore a strip up one leg until she had a yard-long piece of cloth. She wrapped the cloth around the major's upper arm, used Sinclair's own knife to complete the tourniquet.

Sinclair was moaning. Amy talked to her, to get her to come around, the way she'd heard Chase talk to Sergeant Wiley.

Then Sinclair spoke. Amy listened carefully. A single word. "Kronig."

Amy was flooded by a sudden rush of adrenaline. She twisted around in confusion. The monster was gone.

But the general wasn't. She saw the blood beneath his chair.

"Oh, God," Amy whispered. Things were happening too fast. She left Sinclair. She ran over to the general, forced herself to slice into his blood-soaked, torn trousers to get cloth for a tourniquet above his shattered kneecap. "Did you see where he went?" she asked.

Vanovich's pallor was alarming, his breathing shallow, labored. He jerked his head in the direction of the electronics test bed.

Just past it, half-hidden by the table and crouched behind a duty desk, was Kronig. He was looking down, his hands were busy. He did not seem aware she still existed.

Amy needed a weapon. She saw her Leatherman on the floor where Kronig had dropped it, picked it up, folded in the metal file, and closed her hand around it. She still needed a gun.

She ran back to Sinclair. The major was trying to sit up, staring at her watch as if she couldn't read it. "What time?" she asked.

Amy checked it. "Three minutes," she said. Either Chase had succeeded, or he hadn't.

Sinclair grabbed for Amy's arm. "Don't let him escape."

"No, ma'am," Amy promised. Then she picked up Sinclair's H&K, checked the clip. Half full, not half empty. Her fingers were no longer shaking. She was ready.

"And if you have the choice," the major said, "don't kill him."

Amy looked at Sinclair in disbelief. She suddenly felt dizzy. She jammed her tongue against her cracked tooth to force herself back on high alert. *I'm not dead yet,* she told herself as the exposed nerve reawakened.

"We have to know how much he's found out, who he works for, how much . . . how much they know. . . ." The major hugged her wounded arm to her side.

Amy turned and ran toward Kronig, shouting, "Hands on

your head! Step away from—" But then Kronig raised a
Beretta and fired at her. Amy dropped behind the test bed
for cover.

Under the table, she saw his legs. Saw him begin to
move away.

She fired along the floor, sending sparks and ricochets
off the metal test-bed legs. Then she rolled as Kronig
returned fire.

Amy's heart was pounding hard again. Her alertness factor shot even higher. She knew he'd be heading for the
hatchway exit on Level Four, to join his soldiers. As if he
could outrun a nuclear explosion.

"Give it up!" she shouted.

Now Kronig abandoned the test bed. He ran for the stairs
leading down, firing back at her.

But firing from the hip while running reduced his marksmanship to Amy's level.

She rolled behind the test bed, firing again, keeping him
cornered behind electronics cabinets, still thirty feet from
the stairway.

Then she heard him running again. Out in the open.
Exposed.

She leapt up, to pursue him, running through his spray of
bullets as she fired back her own.

They were both untouched. Their guns clicked empty at
the same moment.

Kronig was only ten feet from the staircase.

With a shout of utter frustration, Amy swung her submachine gun by its strap and launched it at Kronig so it caught
him square in the back, sending him flying. Then she
charged, legs pumping.

Kronig's gun skidded off to one side. Something else

that he'd been carrying fell away to the other. It was the size of a thick book, with a large, black antenna on the side.

A radio, Amy decided. To help him escape. But he wasn't going to.

He was getting up when she jumped him, slamming him back to the floor.

He tried to heave her off, but this time she had no distractions.

She pulled out her Leatherman, flicked out the proper tool—the three-inch blade, sharpened on both sides.

As she swore at him in German, and as his eyes widened in surprise, she rammed the blade into his abdomen, just under the lip of his armored flak jacket.

Then the bomb hit and the lights went out, and the first explosion sent Amy flying with visions of nuclear hell.

RED PANTHER TWO

Just as the Lancer reached Mach One, the OSO shouted, *"Green!"*

Colonel Boone pulled back on the stick. For all its high-tech capabilities, the B1-B still flew like a World War II fighter. The Lancer missed the Navy Annex on its rise of land by mere feet, and seconds later spiraled into a victory roll.

They had come within range.

A second before impact, the B61-11 had been disarmed.

Now the bomb was only a giant steel bullet.

It would not detonate. But the Pentagon was not yet safe.

A RING, ROOF

Tom stared down into the Courtyard to see the splinters and shattered tiles of the hotdog stand's roof flutter through the air. And just when he realized that the bomb had somehow been disarmed, the first explosion ripped through the Pentagon.

The shock wave of the penetrator piercing the ground shattered the pipes that supplied natural gas to the Building. It also shattered other pipes that carried water and wires and fiber-optic cables. Their sparks found the gas. The fireball that ballooned from the interior wall of the Heliport Side rose up three hundred feet, trailing oily black smoke. But the debris falling from the sky reassured Tom mightily. It had only been an ordinary explosion. There was no mushroom cloud.

We're going to make it, he thought with hope.

Then a second explosion destroyed the center of the heliport side. Its shock wave buffeted Tom. But he heard nothing. The sonic boom of the Lancer had put him into immediate sound paralysis.

In profound silence, he now saw the flashes of more explosions in the two opposite sides of the Building. Water sprayed up from the South Terrace side. Then flaming fragments rained down as if a volcano had erupted.

Bits of burning wood struck the gray slate tiles beside him. Tom jerked back, waving his arms to keep his balance, losing the radio with the movement.

Then his feet slipped, and he tumbled down the outer slope of the roof, finally rolling to a stop on the flat tar and gravel roof stretching over the River Side section.

And then a third explosion, this time from the interior

wall of the River Side, hit him with the force that finally conquered him.

Sprawled on the roof of B Ring, Tom slipped into unconsciousness.

He did not see the Pentagon consume itself.

STRATEGIC INFORMATION AND OPERATIONS CENTER, FBI HEADQUARTERS

"IT DIDN'T GO OFF!"

Hector didn't know which was more amazing. The fact that the nuke had been disarmed, or the realization that all the screaming was coming from Milton Meyer of the NSA.

The President was on his feet, shaking General Janukatys's hand. In the main window of the video screen, General Brower was shouting orders to resume the evacuation of hostages. There were more than one hundred and twenty still unaccounted for, and radio voices were reporting fires beginning to spread through the Pentagon.

Then Hector heard tapping on the sliding-glass door to the conference room. It was Special Agent Newman. Tyler was pressing his face into its surface to make funny faces.

He wants to know what the shouting's about, Hector thought.

He hopped over to the door, stepped through. "Everything's okay," he said to Tyler. "Your dad's a hero."

"I know that," Tyler said. "Is he coming home now?"

"Soon, I think," Hector said. "You only have to stay here a little while longer."

"How about my mom?"

"As soon as we talk to her, I'll let you know."

Tyler stared up at him. "You shouldn't lie, you know."

"I know," Hector said.

Tyler turned around and walked back to his desk. Agent Newman gave Hector a questioning look but Hector just shrugged. He had nothing more to offer her. He returned to the conference room for the next crisis session.

One catastrophe had been averted, but an even larger one was almost upon them.

In ten minutes, QUICKSILVER would enter the skies over D.C.

And they still didn't know who controlled it.

EIGHTEEN

SITE J, ACTION FLOOR

Margaret heard water. She wondered if Tyler had let the tap run again. Then she was awake. Her left arm felt stiff and swollen. It flared with pain with every breath she took. But she *was* awake. Not dead. Despite the shadows that surrounded her. Their darkness lightened only by a handful of glowing computer displays.

Then she heard the whir of an elevator. She fumbled for her watch. Pressed the backlight.

The bomb had gone off just over a minute ago. *But it couldn't have,* she told herself. *Otherwise* . . .

She pulled her Maglite from her pocket, twisted it on.

Bethune was by the staircase, standing, holding on to the red-metal railing. Vanovich was still strapped in his chair, his head slumped forward on his chest.

Erich was gone.

Margaret struggled to her feet.

The elevator, she thought. But why would he go up?

Why not follow his commandos through the air channel?

She found the answer when she went to Bethune, knowing the midshipman would need help with the general.

Through the stairwell, Margaret could see in the light cast by her small flashlight that Site J's lowest level was filling with water. With the power off, the groundwater pumps had stopped. But groundwater couldn't fill up the cavern this quickly.

"The explosion must have cracked something," Margaret said.

"All those soldiers we saw go into the tunnel," Bethune replied, "they must have drowned. Maybe they're drowning now."

"Probably," Margaret said. "If the river baffles failed, it would have flooded the tunnel like a tidal bore."

Bethune nodded. "Good."

Margaret understood. "C'mon. I need your help with the general."

Bethune nodded again. "We have to get him out of here."

"No," Margaret said as she pulled Bethune from the stairway. "He has to contact QUICKSILVER."

As yet, Margaret had no plan for how they might do that without power. But she trusted that some planner must have added a backup battery system to such a critical piece of equipment. The fact that the screen behind Vanovich still functioned gave her hope.

She and Bethune approached Vanovich's chair. The general hadn't stirred.

"What if he's dead?" Bethune asked.

"We can still use his eyes." It was probably the coldest thing Margaret had ever said. But it was true.

Vanovich looked up at them. "The hell you will."

Bethune reached out and sliced the general free of his straps.

"Thank you. Now turn my chair around. Let's see what we have to work . . ."

Vanovich stared at the Red Level console. Margaret ran her flashlight's beam over it, trying to see what he saw in the soft glow of the screen.

"What is it?" she asked.

Vanovich put his broad hand over a square opening in the console. To Margaret, it looked as if something should fold out from the opening.

"He took the master control. The retina scanner." Vanovich twisted around to grab Margaret's hand. "The encryption chips."

"He had a radio," Bethune said. "When he was trying to run, just before the bomb went off."

"What kind?" the general asked.

Bethune traced the shape in the air, a box the size of a large book. "With a stubby black antenna on the side."

Margaret and Vanovich looked at each other. "Satellite phone," they both said at the same time.

"Could he do it?" Margaret asked Vanovich. "Build a remote control for it?"

"He's got the chip. He's got the scanner. All he needs is the code. And if he can get away with what he does have, it won't take more than a week or two for his people to crack it."

"Who *are* his people?" Bethune asked.

Vanovich didn't answer that question. "You have to stop him," he told Margaret.

"The elevators are working. He must have unsealed the site when he realized he couldn't get through the air channel." Margaret suddenly regretted not closing the Level Four pressure hatch securely. If she had, Erich might have been drowned the moment he opened it, instead of seeing the water swirl in. *But then what would have happened to the encryption chip?*

"Can you walk?" Margaret asked Vanovich.

"I'm sure I could, if I still had a right knee."

Margaret wanted to smile. But she didn't have the strength anymore. "C'mon, Bethune, we have to get him up to the next level and the elevator."

Margaret saw Bethune look at her arm.

"I can handle him," the midshipman said. "You hold the elevator."

Bethune came in on the general's right side, put his arm over her shoulder, lifted him out of the chair and onto his feet.

Margaret watched how his face twisted in pain.

"You be careful," he cautioned Bethune.

"I'll try to be, sir." The midshipman shifted her shoulders to take on as much of his weight as she could.

They started splashing through the water, toward the flight of stairs leading up to Level Two. The water was up to their ankles and still rising. Margaret's combat boots weren't porous, but Bethune's sneakers were soaked. The general's black oxfords weren't much drier.

"Do more than try," Vanovich said. "I'm ticklish."

Margaret did smile at that. He was such a strange person. In so many ways, he'd always reminded her of Tom. On Tom's best days.

She held her flashlight on the staircase so Bethune and the general could see where they were going; then they all began their ascent.

Margaret knew there were no guarantees for what they would find when they arrived.

QUICKSILVER was only five minutes away.

And Erich Kronig still controlled it.

A RING, ROOF

Erich limped onto the roof and into a cloud of smoke. The wind kept the smoke moving quickly, creating brief moments of clear viewing. Those moments were enough to make Erich smile through the sharp reminders of his knife wound.

The Pentagon was dying.

Across the Courtyard, two sections were ablaze, their concentric roofs pierced by a dozen different fires. And on this side of the Courtyard, there was more debris all around him, scattered across the entire River Entrance roof, some of it burning among the satellite dishes and microwave relays, the hundreds of small fires adding to the celebration of his victory.

Because it *was* a victory.

The nature of this mission was such that he had early on accepted his return would not be required for success.

Erich hoped that was true for his soldiers as well.

The moment he had seen the swirling reflections in the glow of the display screens as the water climbed the stairs from Level Four, he had known his people were lost. Heroes, every one, for all the great deeds they had accomplished.

The most important being the removal of QUICKSILVER from the enemy's arsenal. Though the American satellite network was also in disarray. And as a welcome bonus, the headquarters of the country's military operations was now in ruins.

The playing field was level again. It would be a world of partners, not adversaries.

Provided he accomplished one last task. His final backup scenario.

There were so many helicopters flying in the vicinity that Erich knew a major hostage-rescue mission was under way. The firefighters would come soon. Even water bombers for the sections of the Building that burned out of control.

He looked through the smoke to the storm clouds now filling more than half the D.C. sky. He saw erratic flashes of lightning illuminate them from within. Perhaps Nature would spare America more suffering and douse these flames with rain.

But Erich didn't intend to spare America more suffering. The young country barely knew the meaning of the word.

So in these last few minutes of freedom, he was going to offer America a lesson that might ensure its survival as a nation in this century. He would make sure that the country's greatest weapon of terror would become known to the world, so that every person on the globe could know the nature of their enemy and America would have no choice but to change its ways.

QUICKSILVER would be within range within five minutes.

Erich held in his hand the key to unlocking its awesome power.

And knowing that his life would end here, he knew exactly how he would use that key.

COURTYARD

The smoke in the hallways was too thick. Major Sinclair suggested they move into the Courtyard, rather than try to make it to an exterior exit. There was still smoke in the central oasis, but the growing wind kept it moving, even as red and gold smoldering embers sifted through the green trees and grass.

Sinclair found a folding chair from the President's luncheon lying on its side, and set it up beside a large pine, letting the tree serve as a windbreak. She helped Bethune lower Vanovich into the chair.

"He'll be on the roof," the general said, even as he stifled a moan. "He'll have better range there."

Amy looked up at the surrounding walls. All the window frames were free of glass. Smoke poured from the shattered windows of two of the sides. Smoke and flames from another. She felt as if she were in the exercise yard of a prison just claimed by a riot.

"You want him, too, don't you," Sinclair said.

Amy nodded.

"Enough to go up after him?"

More than anything, that's exactly what Amy wanted—no, needed—to do. She had made it her mission to kill all those responsible for the deaths of her friends. With his commandos drowned in the tunnel, Kronig had become the last one.

"We'll go together," Amy said. But then she saw the sudden concerned look Sinclair gave to the general, even though the major had been ready to shoot him down in Site J.

Sinclair seemed to read the question in her eyes. "If we can't get QUICKSILVER back, the general is the best chance we have to find it, and fight it again. And Kronig knows that. We can't leave him alone."

Amy knew there was only one thing she could do. "Ma'am, I'll stay with the general. You get Kronig."

"You don't strike me as someone who likes to give up the fight." But Sinclair was already checking her watch.

"I don't. But . . . you're the better soldier, ma'am." Amy took a deep breath. "I'd . . . I'd just make it personal."

She offered the major her Leatherman. "It's the only weapon I've got left."

"You keep it," Sinclair said. "I've got my knife." She rubbed her wounded left arm. Amy knew that her tourniquet had worked to stop the bleeding. Now Sinclair had wrapped the cloth strips around her biceps to keep the wound covered.

"Good luck, ma'am."

Sinclair nodded, then patted Vanovich on his shoulder. It looked as if the general were asleep. But he raised his head. "If he does have a remote, you take it from him."

"I intend to."

"And you destroy it."

"That remote could help tell us who he's working for."

"Not the remote. QUICKSILVER."

Amy could tell the major was in a hurry to get moving. "I wouldn't know how to do that, General."

"Use your access code. Adjust the firing cycle and the beam depth. You know what to do."

Amy thought it odd that Sinclair didn't acknowledge the order. "You rest now, General. You've got a lot to tell Tyler."

Sinclair turned to leave, but didn't take that first step. "Bethune, how long have you known my husband—ex-husband?"

Amy wasn't sure what she meant by that. "I just met him this morning, ma'am. We were both trapped in the River Side."

Sinclair smiled, as if thinking something over. "He's a good guy, Bethune."

Amy grinned. "For a civilian."

Sinclair returned the grin before she took off toward the stone stairs leading back inside the Pentagon.

More than anything else, Amy wanted to be at her side. She hated giving up the fight so close to the end. She hated not finishing what she had started.

But she told herself that she was only one small part of this conflict today. It wasn't important which soldier struck the final blow, only that, in the end, the right side won. She had done her job. She would have to be content with that. As for what still remained to be done, that was up to the rest of the team.

She bent down to check out her new mission, General Vanovich. His soft brown eyes fluttered open as if he was aware that she was watching him.

"So," he said, "are you seeing anyone?"

B RING, ROOF

Tom was in Captain Dorsey's white Chevy Suburban again, driving up to the Pentagon on a perfect June day. He could feel the vehicle shake with the winds kicked up by the President's fleet of helicopters. Almost as if they were landing right on top of him.

The sudden fear of being crushed woke Tom at once, to look up into the smoke-wreathed sky in time to see two helicopters rush by overhead.

Then he started to cough, his lungs full of smoke, his nostrils full of soot. He sat up on the rough gravel surface and looked at the small fires surrounding him, finally remembering where he was.

Tom checked his pockets for Margaret's radio. He didn't have it. It must have slipped from his hand when he lost his footing on the slate roof. But he had to find out what had happened to Vanovich and Margaret and Bethune. He needed to know about QUICKSILVER.

More helicopters roared past above. One was Army green with a large red cross on its side. It seemed to have taken off from in front of the River Entrance Side.

Rescue helos, Tom thought. *If I can get to one of those . . .*

He forced himself to his feet, his stiff and aching legs protesting each movement. He felt as if every muscle in his body had been pushed to its limit. He started for a roof entrance shed.

Just a few minutes more, he told himself. *I only have to last a few minutes more.*

But the shed wasn't a good idea. Smoke poured from its open door. The fire below must be spreading.

"E Ring," Tom said aloud. If he went to the E Ring on the River Side and waved his arms, one of the helicopters would see him as it took off or landed. Through the clouds of smoke, he saw a narrow catwalk running along the top of the slate roof over one of the radial corridors. He headed that way.

And then he saw there was someone already on it.

A commando in black with distinctive blond hair.

Erich Kronig.

Erich moved awkwardly along the catwalk, pressing one hand tightly against his knife wound. It had been such a small blade. But instead of a minor cut, he was beginning to think the midshipman had hit something major.

He used his other hand to help support himself as he moved along. He needed to get to the D Ring roof. There was a cluster of small, prefab sheds there, each one a simple aluminum-walled closet to protect antenna blocks and wiring terminals for the dozens of microwave relays and antennae and small satellite dishes that sprouted from the River Side roof like a plot of biomechanical mushrooms.

He'd be able to hide at the center of those sheds, Erich knew. He would have clear access to the sky, but be blocked from the sight of the rescue helicopters as they came and went. Plus, when the time came, he would have a perfect view of QUICKSILVER's might.

Erich was halfway across the AE service road, moving from the B Ring to C, when he felt the catwalk rail shake beneath his hand. He looked over his shoulder. Through a veil of smoke, he saw a figure running after him.

"No . . ." he said aloud. He had not come this far to lose now.

Erich pushed himself to walk faster. Blood seeped from his wound as his muscles cramped. He could not let any-thing—anyone—stop him. He still had a reason to live.

After five fast strides, Tom was already breathing hard, wheezing in the smoke, realizing how exhausted he was.

There was one reason that would explain why Kronig was on this roof.

He had killed Margaret.

And that would cost him.

* * *

Margaret reached the roof and quickly scanned the new terrain. Only two sections of the Building had large sections of roof that were mostly untouched: the River Side and the Metro Side.

But she knew Erich. He enjoyed setting the scene. A perfect rosebud in a flawless crystal vase. Cushions before the fireplace arranged just so, with an artist's eye for color and shape and feel.

If he had programmed QUICKSILVER to strike Washington, she knew he would go where the view would be best.

She ran for the catwalk that would take her to the River Side roof.

Distant thunder rumbled from the city. The gathering storm clouds were almost overhead. Margaret felt the first light sprinkle of rain.

Erich reached the cluster of protective sheds, coughing badly. He had purposely walked through the thickest concentrations of smoke, in order to remain hidden.

The tactic seemed to have worked. Through watering eyes stung by smoke, he could see a figure on the catwalk, still. But it was far away, as if whoever it was was no longer after him. There was no one closer.

He backed into a corner formed by two sheds at ninety degrees to each other. There was a fire burning near one of the sheds. The air was cold as the thunderstorm moved in. The heat from the fire felt good.

Erich took his hand away from his side. Blood pulsed from the open wound.

That's all right, he told himself. *Not much longer.*

He pulled the remote-control satellite transceiver from

his shirt. He switched it on, pointing the thick antenna toward the northwest.

The first small green LED flashed silently on the front of the transceiver.

QUICKSILVER was coming.

And then a hatefully familiar voice said, "Better hurry, Erich."

Tom had found Kronig. In a small alcove formed by two prefab sheds.

When Tom had realized what Kronig was doing, moving through the thickest clouds of smoke to remain hidden, Tom had done the same. Kronig had never realized he was being followed.

"Tom Chase," Kronig said as Tom stepped from the smoke and into the alcove. The sheltered space formed a square about fifteen feet across, two sides bounded by the sheds, two sides open.

Now Tom realized that Kronig was the same Naval lieutenant he had seen so much earlier that day, arriving on a Naval Academy bus with his crew of impostors. At the time, he'd had the odd feeling that the blond officer might have recognized him. He'd been right. He just didn't know why.

"How do you know me?" Tom asked. He recognized the device Kronig held as a type of satellite radio transceiver. He could guess what Kronig intended to do with it.

"I saw you in a photograph. You and Tyler—he's wearing a red baseball cap."

Tom hated even hearing this man say Tyler's name. But he knew the photograph. Tyler was five in that picture. It was one of Tom's favorite shots of his son. It was one of Margaret's, too.

"Where did you see that?" Tom stared at Kronig wondering if he had any weapons. He wondered what it would take to rush him and grab the transceiver.

"Margaret showed it to me," Kronig answered. He kept taking quick looks at the transceiver, as if expecting to see something.

Tom could see a line of green LEDs on its face. Two of the lights were flashing. It was a signal-strength meter. QUICKSILVER must be closing in.

Then he saw the blood that stained Kronig's dark uniform. "You need help," he said. "We should get a medic up here." *And have you placed in custody at the same time,* Tom thought.

"Not a good idea. It's not safe up here. Or hadn't you noticed?"

Tom took another step forward. Kronig held his ground. However bad his wound was, it didn't seem to be affecting his readiness to fight.

"Where is my wife?" Tom fought to keep his voice steady.

"Ex-wife," Kronig corrected him.

"Where is she?"

"Dead. With all my men. Drowned in Site J."

So it was true. Tom thought of Margaret, of Margaret and Tyler. He reached into his pocket for his knife. "You killed her, you . . ."

"On the contrary, Tom, I loved your ex-wife . . . for a while . . . in my way."

"She wouldn't have anything to do with you."

"Ah, but she did. Such a passionate, willing lover, if you remember."

"You're lying!"

And then Margaret was behind him. "No, Tom, he's not."

"Margaret! You're alive!" Tom said.

"More or less." Margaret felt light-headed from the run and the smoky air, but she was ready to take that transceiver. Provided Tom didn't get in the way. "Give me the radio, Erich. We can work out a deal to send you home."

"Too late." Erich held up the transceiver so Margaret could see the signal-strength meter. Every green light was flickering. "Almost here."

Margaret drew her blackened K-bar knife. But then Erich reached under his flak jacket. She tensed. If he had a gun, she would have to throw the knife at once, only one chance.

But he brought out a transparent package filled with something thick, like wads of folded yellowed paper. He held the package over the small fire that the wind had fanned into life beside him.

"Think carefully, Margaret," he said. "You could throw your knife, but for what? In one hand, a satellite transceiver you can't use. In the other, just above the fire, your country's so-called Great Charters of Freedom."

Margaret was stunned. She had known they were missing. But why did *Erich* have them? Unless . . . "The RUSH HOUR tunnels. That's how you got your commandos into Site J."

"Such a fine mind. What a shame it will be lost here."

Now all the green lights glowed across the face of the transceiver. Erich squeezed something on it, and a metal arm swung out from the side, topped by a black eyecup. He held it to his right eye.

"He's accessing QUICKSILVER," Tom warned.

"There's no way he could have broken the codes," Margaret said.

Erich lowered the transceiver. There was a small number pad in one corner, and he entered in a series of numbers with his thumb, like dialing a cellular phone.

"I didn't have to break your codes," Erich said. "All my team needed was your encryption circuits. They installed them in this transceiver. Now I can invent my own code and use my own eye. QUICKSILVER has a new master."

A red button suddenly lit up on the transceiver. Erich pressed it with his thumb.

"There, I've overridden the autofire sequence. Until now, until I reestablished contact, QUICKSILVER was programmed to fire at the Pentagon. But I think that might be overkill, today. I've chosen a new target. FBI Headquarters."

"What, you're afraid they're going to arrest you?" Tom's voice was derisive.

"Not at all. I expect to die here. But the White House has been evacuated, and the news channels reported your President has moved to the FBI's ops center."

"Tom! Tyler's with Hector MacGregor!"

Tom's eyes met Margaret's. "The *President's* Hector MacGregor?"

Margaret nodded. "Tyler's with the President."

"Throw the stupid knife!" Tom shouted.

Erich lowered the transparent package containing the Charters closer to the flames of the wood fire. "I'll destroy them!" he threatened.

"You're saying that to the wrong guy!"

And then Tom charged forward and Erich dropped the Charters into the fire and Margaret threw her knife, striking

Erich in the shoulder, the impact flinging him back against the thin metal wall of the shed.

As Margaret lunged at Kronig, Tom shut his eyes and plunged his right hand into the stack of burning wood to pull the smoking package of parchment from the flames. The melting plastic merged with the skin on his hand.

But the Charters were safe. Singed around the edges, smoke-infused. But intact.

Tom cradled the Charters in the crook of his arm. He looked over at Margaret.

Kronig was gone but Margaret had the transceiver. She was kneeling, swiftly inputting numbers on its keypad before her. She looked into the eyecup and pressed the red button, but the button didn't light up.

Tom used his left hand to stuff the Charters under his gray Polo shirt and tuck its hem into his jeans. Then he knelt down beside Margaret, who was now swearing blisteringly at the transceiver.

"What's wrong?"

"It won't accept my retina scan. My records are in the computer system, not the encryption chip!"

Tom dug out his proxcard from his jeans front pocket. "My scan's on the card's chip."

Margaret thrust the transceiver at him. "Do it!"

Tom touched his card to the induction reader on the transceiver; then he looked into the eyecup.

A moment later, the red button lit up.

"It worked!" Margaret said.

"But I don't know any codes!"

"That's *my* job!" Margaret grabbed back the transceiver

and began punching in numbers. Tom looked again for Kronig, but he was nowhere to be seen.

The sky was much darker now. The helicopters had begun flying with searchlights. And more rain was obviously coming, along with thunder and lightning. Dark sheets hung in the sky to the east.

Margaret finished her entry and pressed the red button. She rocked back on her heels, waiting.

The other LED indicators on the device shimmered as the entry was processed. Then a liquid-crystal display panel in which Tom could see a set of longitude and latitude measurements suddenly went blank.

Margaret sighed in relief. "I did it."

"You're welcome," Tom said.

"Oh, Tom, I'm sorry. *We* did it. We erased Erich's last command."

She held up her hand to give him a high five, then stopped as she saw his right palm. Badly burned, it was bright red, pebbled with blisters, and smeared with blackened strings of melted plastic.

"I . . . you saved the Charters."

"For a friend," Tom said, thinking of Dorsey. "So what happens now?"

They both looked up, but there was no chance of seeing a satellite passing. Clouds filled the sky. Thunder rumbled.

"The general wants me to destroy it."

"Good idea."

"I don't know if I can with this."

"Let me see?" Tom asked.

Margaret held the transceiver for him so he could examine its various controls.

"I can't believe you slept with that guy," Tom said as he checked the eye scanner.

"We're divorced, remember?"

"Yeah, but, I always thought you had taste. What's that?"

Tom pointed to the liquid-crystal display that had been blank a moment ago. Now there was a new set of longitude and latitude figures in it. 38°52'10"; 77°6'32".

"Oh, no," Margaret said.

Suddenly, the dark afternoon lit up as if caught in the beam of a colossal searchlight.

Tom stared past Margaret, over the parade grounds and the Potomac, to see a giant blade of molten silver stab through the raging thunderstorm clouds.

Spectacular forks of lightning branched wildly from all sides of the clouds. Strands streaked erratically along their bottom edges for miles.

Then the air became solid with a sound that was as physical as it was audible as the roar of the blade reached them.

Tom knew what had happened. He turned to Margaret.

"You erased the new command, but not the *old* one."

And he knew what he was seeing.

QUICKSILVER.

Coming for the Pentagon.

NINETEEN

GROUND ZERO

Tom and Margaret stood together on the roof of the Pentagon, pelted by rain, pushed back by the wind, transfixed by the terror and the majesty of the phenomenon before them.

For miles around, the undersides of the dark storm clouds were lit up as if a new sun were rising beneath them.

Fountains of steam sprayed out from either side of the reflective blade as the rain was vaporized in midfall.

The ground shook.

The thunder was absolute.

Then the silver blade touched down at the edge of the Boundary Channel Lagoon, at the foot of the gently sloping parade grounds.

Helicopters caught by the long whips of lightning turned into madly spinning, incandescent swirls of sparks.

"ACCESS!" Margaret shouted as she shoved the transceiver at Tom.

Tom touched his proxcard to the device, then held his eye to the scanner. The red light came on.

"WE HAVE TO GET AWAY FROM THE ANTENNAE!" he yelled, pushing Margaret ahead of him, away from the sheds, from anything metal, conductive.

Even as they scrambled across the shaking roof, Margaret was punching numbers into the transceiver.

Above them, another helicopter was swept into a fireball. Tom looked up just as it plunged to the B Ring roof of the Mall section. A moment later, a writhing web of electricity streaked from the silver blade to engulf the lightning rod of the Washington Monument.

"CAN YOU SHUT IT OFF?!" Tom shouted.

Strands of Margaret's long blond hair streamed behind her in the rain and wind. *"I HAVE! BUT IT'S SELF-SUSTAINING!"*

The blade cut closer. Tom saw swirling eddies of debris and rubble from the earlier conflagration of the television news vans lift into the air from the parade grounds. In only seconds, the blade would reach the front of the River Side. When it struck the rooftop antenna array, he knew the Building itself might not survive the impact.

Tom dragged Margaret with him as he ran along the roof in the direction of the South Terrace Side.

But that's where Erich Kronig was waiting.

Where he charged at them wielding Margaret's knife.

She sidestepped him easily, but she was a professional. Tom wasn't.

In the strobelike flashes of the now-incessant lightning, Tom was suddenly in Kronig's grip, an arm across his chest, Margaret's knife at his throat.

"GIVE ME THE TRANSCEIVER!" Kronig screamed.

Tom nodded once at Margaret. Without a single word spoken, they both knew what had to happen next.

Margaret stepped forward, holding out the transceiver, almost within Kronig's reach.

And just when Tom felt the commando's grip on him loosen, he shouted to mask the pain of his burned flesh and with all his strength squeezed Kronig's hand between the thumb and forefinger. Then he whirled around to pull that arm forward and flip him.

But Kronig didn't move.

Tyler's agonizing little trick hadn't fazed him. And now Kronig offset Tom's attempted flip by half-turning so that Tom's momentum was turned back against him, and Tom was catapulted onto his back.

But as Kronig reached down to haul Tom back to his feet, Margaret's combat boot connected with his jaw.

Kronig lost his grip on Tom, fell back, then recovered and came after Margaret.

She ducked his charge, spun him around, but froze as she saw her own knife aimed directly at her eyes.

Kronig raised that knife high, silhouetted against the silver blade. Lightning flashes seared through the hot rain. The wind rose to hurricane levels.

And then Tom's body rammed right into Kronig and the knife flew free as Tom grabbed Kronig's belt and kept him running for twenty feet until they reached a radial catwalk, completely metal, where Tom threw Kronig forward so that he crashed into the catwalk, momentarily stunned then turned to pull himself up and—

QUICKSILVER touched the Pentagon Building.

Instantly every piece of metal on the roof glowed like neon, surrounded by a nimbus of electrified air.

Antennae exploded. Metal conduits melted. The catwalks writhed as if attempting to peel themselves off the roofs.

But Kronig slipped off his catwalk in time, to the safety of the roof. Now he stumbled toward the transceiver, with no weapon but himself.

In that same instant, before Margaret could be threatened again, Tom saw her knife on the roof, at their feet. Philosophy did not enter into his next decisive action.

He picked up that knife and threw it.

The point caught in Kronig's flak jacket. Kronig grabbed the knife with both hands, unharmed. He bared his teeth in triumph as he advanced on their position, knowing neither Tom nor Margaret could call up the reserves to resist him.

And then a stream of electricity flowed along the metal catwalk and a double strand shot out to the roof to snare Kronig and the knife that he held in his hand. And with a startled scream, Kronig was jerked back against the catwalk with so much force applied to the knife that its point was driven through his armor and into his chest.

Lightning discharges wreathed Kronig's body as he was fused to the catwalk, the knife deep inside him.

Tom and Margaret threw themselves flat on the roof. Tom reached out for Margaret's hand as they waited for more sheets of QUICKSILVER lightning to spread across the soaked roof of the Pentagon.

But then, just as the blade should have engulfed the entire structure, a spinning maelstrom of electrical discharges spiraled down to the center of the Courtyard, and as if being sucked down some extradimensional drain, the gleaming silver QUICKSILVER effect shot into the ground, absorbed by the water that had flooded all of Site J, even as the blade's upper reaches evaporated back into the clouds.

And then, the lightning was over. Tom and Margaret were just two people in a soft summer rain. White smoke rose from a few of the larger fires in the Pentagon, but the little ones were gone.

There was no thunder. There was no lightning.

The suffocating heat of the day was gone at last.

Tom and Margaret stood up and embraced, but just for a moment. Because Margaret pulled away and ran across the roof to find the transceiver. She brought it back to Tom. "Access," she said.

He did, with both his card and his eye.

Margaret began entering more numbers.

Tom didn't ask what she was doing. He knew. She was killing Vanovich's creation.

Margaret sent her next set of commands to the platform. For herself, she didn't know if Vanovich's orders were right. She didn't even know if they had been orders.

But this was what she had to do.

Tom stood beside her as she pressed the red button.

Together, they looked to the south. The skies there were still clear in patches among the darkening clouds.

Then, among those clouds, a new glow began, as of something vast and reflective shimmering above them.

QUICKSILVER was firing again, Margaret told Tom.

But this time she was deliberately keeping the laser unfocused. To produce a wide but shallow pocket of ionized air high enough in the atmosphere that the discharge would never reach the ground. And this time the effect would be prolonged. More than two minutes. Time enough for a feedback charge to travel all the way back to the QUICKSILVER platform.

The feedback charge reached its target.

The heavens themselves became QUICKSILVER.

Then the heavens exploded.

QUICKSILVER was gone.

For a long time, Tom and Margaret stood on the roof and watched the clouds. Until helicopters filled the air again and they saw the soldiers of Delta Force coming for them.

But Margaret saw that Tom wasn't watching the soldiers approach. He was looking at Erich's blackened body on the catwalk.

"Are you going to be okay?" she asked.

"He would have done the same to us," Tom said.

"This doesn't have to change you," she told him. "It's not as if there's only one way to be. That one side is right and the other is wrong."

"I know," Tom said. "But because there are people like you, there can be people like me. I don't think it works the other way 'round."

"It doesn't matter," Margaret said. She poked him in the ribs. "Tyler needs us both. Just as we are."

Then Tom smiled just like Tyler. He reached out and hugged her.

They started to walk toward the soldiers. Margaret couldn't resist a final question.

"So what do you think?" she asked him. "*Can* lightning strike twice?"

This time he didn't smile. He laughed.

So did she.

They both knew the answer to that one.

TWENTY

AFTERMATH

The President's wife was found exactly where she was supposed to be, unharmed in a ground-floor safe room, along
with her two Secret Service agents. The gas explosions
resulting from the impact of the B61-11 penetrator bomb
had shaken them up, but nothing a weekend at Camp David
couldn't set right. The first-string UPN *Uplink Live!* news
team of Danny Assad, Trish Mankin, and Arthur Tranh were
given the exclusive story, as well as Presidential citations.

Hector MacGregor required four pins in his ankle. His
presence as a member of the Presidential inner circle of
senior advisory staff was never questioned again.

Hector was with the President the day after the incident,
when the Man visited General Vanovich at Walter Reed
Army Medical Center. Hector and the general hit it off at
once. At the end of the President's visit, the general asked
Hector to stay behind, then asked if he were seeing anyone.

The final death toll, including the martyred midshipmen

of 12th Company, was 337 at the Pentagon, 895 at Schriever Air Force Base, and 60 at the National Archives.

The Declaration of Independence, the Constitution, and the Bill of Rights, were back on display for the Fourth of July. The President led the nation in a ceremony to rededicate the priceless documents to the memory of the brave souls who had died to defend them. Full restoration of the charters was expected to take years.

The bodies of seventy-five terrorists were also recovered. Sixty of them were positively identified, though the findings remained classified.

Russia did not join NATO that year. There was considerable debate whether or not NATO should even continue to exist. Once the identities and allegiance of the terrorists were discovered, most of that debate took place in classified discussions.

Admiral Paulsen and Air Force General Janukatys retired with full pensions three months after the incident.

Following the recommendation of an independent damage-assessment firm, the renovation of the Pentagon continued, though with a new completion date some ten years in the future. Site J was not listed among the facilities to be renovated. It still was not mentioned in any public records.

Officially, the extensive damage endured by the Pentagon was a result of the terrorists' actions, an errant cruise missile launched as part of the Delta Force counterattack, and a freak electrical storm produced by an unprecedented confluence of *El Niño* conditions.

The Tucson-based GAI corporation was awarded a $35-million contract to study the rare phenomenon on behalf of FEMA. The project was headed by Dr. Helen Shapiro, and her newly promoted associate, Stanislaus J. Drewniak.

During the still ongoing renovation of the Pentagon, the cost to the Federal government to recover the unexploded nuclear bomb 200 feet beneath the Courtyard tallied more than $200 million.

At the end of the day of the incident, as the President was leaving the FBI's Strategic Information and Operations Center, he stopped to have a final, friendly word with Tyler Chase.

The President's Outreach Assistant, Hector MacGregor, was tired and his foot hurt and so he really didn't pay attention until he realized that Tyler had asked if the President wanted to "shake." Hector was two seconds too slow in reacting to what happened next. The Secret Service never even saw it coming.

Officially, the neck brace the President wore for the next two weeks was attributed to minor injuries obtained during his escape from the Pentagon. Unofficially, the President let Tyler keep the watch, and Hector had the unusual experience of being one of the few people ever to hear the President use the f-word. Tyler made America's Chief Executive pay two quarters for the privilege.

TWENTY-ONE

WALTER REED ARMY MEDICAL CENTER, FRIDAY, JUNE 24

Vanovich lay back in his hospital bed, his right leg raised in traction, playing with a turquoise-and-silver bolo tie. Tom Chase was convinced his old friend would never die. He had too much on his mind.

"Kronig asked me," the general said, "who did our satellite systems threaten most? I said Russia, China, Middle Eastern countries . . . all the usual suspects. And he kept telling me I was wrong."

"Misdirection," Tom said.

"If they had gotten away with it," Margaret added. "They didn't want anyone knowing who ended up with the satellites. So he would have lied about any answer you guessed."

"But he didn't lie," Vanovich said. "The CIA was in here yesterday. They showed me the identification files on thirty of the terrorists so far. They're all commandos, career soldiers, special forces, and they're from six different countries."

"Mercenaries," Tom said.

"No way, Tommy. We weren't just up against *one* other country, we were up against a bloc of them. Who do our satellites threaten the most? That's what he kept asking me. And the answer is: *Everyone*. Think about it. The CIA is putting the finishing touches on a cabal of senior officers from NATO. France, Germany, Poland, Turkey . . . they were all in on it. And we're going to face it again. The Cold War's over. Now they want us out of Europe. And they resent like hell anything we do to try to change NATO's mission."

"Kronig wanted us off the planet," Tom said.

Vanovich nodded. "That day's coming, too."

Margaret reached out to touch the bolo tie. "Is this the latest in patient attire?"

Tom was surprised to see a slight flush of color come to Vanovich's cheeks.

"Oh, that's a little get-well gift from a friend for whom I have a lot of explaining to do."

Margaret seemed to be thinking along the same lines as Tom. "What kind of explaining? Best done over candlelight and wine?"

"In this case, I think, Florida. In the rainy season. Something nice and dramatic. You know. Thunder and lightning."

Tom and Margaret passed a smile between them.

"How about you two?" the general asked, raising his wildly spiked eyebrows. "Any plans for—"

"No." They both said it at the same time.

Vanovich smiled and sighed. "Well, can't blame me for trying. You tell Tyler I said hello. I'll come see him as soon as they let me out next week."

Tom and Margaret got up. "He's got a new watch in his collection he wants to show you," Margaret said. "It's a keeper."

They said good-bye as a family. More than ever, Tom thought, that's what they were.

On the way out of the main building, Margaret asked Tom if he thought the general really would be released next week.

"That's what the doctors said. He's got some time left. We all do."

They were just going down the wide front steps when a gleaming chrome-and-black Harley Davidson 55 Panhead pulled up in front of them.

"Major Sinclair, Mr. Chase!"

The driver was Bethune. The extremely tall passenger with the heavy cast on his foot was Hector MacGregor. They shook hands all around, Tom offering his left hand. His right hand was still bandaged. He found himself listening to the way Hector spoke to Margaret. He knew Margaret was listening in the same way when he spoke to Bethune.

"I'm just letting Hec off before I park," Bethune said.

"Going to see the general?" Tom asked.

"Oh, yeah," MacGregor said. "He's quite the guy."

They all agreed and said their good-byes, as well.

Tom and Margaret paused at a pedestrian crossing leading to the parking lots. They looked back at the Harley.

MacGregor was giving Bethune his helmet. Bethune was on her tiptoes giving MacGregor a kiss that had a good chance of melting his cast.

"Good old Uncle Milo," Tom said. He smiled at his wife—ex-wife. "Think we should tell them about how this sort of thing turns out?"

"They'll find out. Besides, not every story ends the same way."

Tom looked up at the sky. It had become a bit of a habit

over this past week. But the sky was clear today, only a few white clouds scattered about.

"It wasn't enough, was it?" he asked. "Just blowing it up like that."

Margaret shook her head. "It never is. Milo said it. We're going to have to face it again."

"But not today," Tom said.

"Not today."

They gave each other a quick kiss on the cheek, then went off in their separate directions, both looking up to the same sky, both thinking the same thoughts of the future.

ARCTIC FLAG
SIX DAYS LATER

30th SPACE WING, VANDENBURG AIR FORCE BASE, CALIFORNIA, SATURDAY, JUNE 25

Four visitors arrived by limousine from Los Angeles, sixty-five miles to the south. One by private jet from Seattle. Three by an Air Force C-20 Gulfstream III from Washington, D.C. In all, there were seven men, one woman. Two of them might be recognized by regular viewers of CNN. The other six were content to keep to the shadows where the true power rested and decisions were made. Major General Milo Vanovich and Major Margaret Sinclair were not among them. None of the eight had ever held elective office.

At 2230 hours on the evening of June 25, six days after the events at the Pentagon, those eight assembled at a non-descript storage hangar located at the South Vandenburg launch facility site. More than sixty aerospace contractors maintained facilities on the base. Yet this hangar was unmarked. It was closest to the spotlit gantry tower of Space

Launch Complex 4E, the Titan IV SLC from which the country's largest payloads could be placed into low polar orbits.

The hangar was kept closed. The visitors entered by a personnel door. Overhead lights switched on, bank after bank, until the hangar interior was daylight bright.

But the object within, resting on its support cradle, remained as black as space, as dark as shadows.

It was forty-three feet long, eight feet wide. It massed ten thousand pounds. And it reflected little light because it was sheathed in faceted black carbon-fiber panels doped with metal particles to scatter and absorb radar beams as effectively as the skin of a Stealth fighter.

At one end, the opening of a large jagged bell was sealed by a red circle of insulating foam stenciled with the warning: REMOVE BEFORE FLIGHT. The object's winglike solar panels had not yet been installed. But they were there, folded carefully and wrapped in thermal blankets, resting in crates along the hangar wall.

There was nothing unusual or sinister about the platform's existence. It was standard procedure that every spacecraft, whether an interplanetary probe or the prototype of a new communications satellite, be built in triplicate. The first was called the engineering model, the second, the flight model, the third, which this was, the spare. In practice, all three were identical, no differences between them.

It was simply an exercise in that which the military deemed desirable.

Redundancy.

The engineers who had awaited the eight visitors completed their briefing in less than ten minutes. New batteries would have to be installed. Nicks on the composite skin would require the replacement of eighteen of the platform's 321 carbon tiles. And, of course, new security codes would have to be programmed into the control chips, the same ones built according to specifications developed at Hughes Electronics by Tom Chase.

But all of that was standard operating procedure. The platform in the hangar was no longer a prototype. It was a proven technology.

There was little debate among the eight visitors.

Certainly there were some legal questions to be examined concerning placing the platform into orbit, now that its full capabilities were known. For now, they agreed, it would be best if the elected members of the Administration were kept out of the loop. The President would have to be told, but the time to tell him would be carefully chosen.

In the meantime, funds were available for the necessary upgrades to the spare. Funds were also available for its cleanroom, temperature-controlled storage once the upgrades were completed and the platform was flight certified.

But none of the eight thought the storage charges would need to be paid for long. A technology as powerful as this could not be placed on a shelf any more than atomic weapons could have been abandoned after 1945.

Margaret Sinclair had been right. With the coming of QUICKSILVER the world had changed.

Except in one way.

Whatever happened next, it was still up to the Pentagon.

ACKNOWLEDGMENTS

Once again we have benefited from the knowledge and experience of many people who know the reality of the things we write about, and we trust they will be entertained by the fictional uses to which we have put their factual input.

Some of those people to whom we are most indebted can be acknowledged in these pages. In the Pentagon, we must especially thank Philip Strub and Glenn Flood for sharing their invaluable insights and expertise, and for being so generous with their time. Tom Fontana, of the Pentagon Renovation Project, also went beyond the call of duty to show us the Building not only as it is today, but as it will be after its "slab-to-ceiling" renovation is complete in 2008.

At the United States Naval Academy, we gratefully thank Lieutenant J.G. Leslie Hull-Ryde, Lieutenant Jill Clary, Lieutenant David Kayea, Commander Glenn Fogg, and last, but certainly not least, Midshipman Jamie Fleischhacker of the Class of the Century, and all the members of her company who took time from their busiest week to make us feel welcome on the Yard. Our time with you was both informative and inspirational, and we look forward to returning for new projects.

In Los Angeles, the enthusiastic staff of the Naval Office of Information, West, has again provided encouragement and guidance. In particular, we thank Petty Officer 1st Class Bill Danzig, Lieutenant Darren Morton (USNA Class of '90), and Lieutenant Mel Scheurrmann.

Our agent, Martin Shapiro, and all at Shapiro-Lichtman-Stein, provide more encouragement than they can know.

Our publishing team, as always, deserves the highest praise: our editor, John Ordover, who thought there should be something more than just satellites at Ground Zero; Scott Shannon, whose good-natured patience we regularly strained; Tony Greco, who created such a compelling cover; the managing editorial and production staff: Donna Ruvituso, Erin Galligan, Donna O'Neill, Lisa Feuer, Twisne Fan, Linda Dingler, and Carole Schwindeller; publishers Gina Centrello and Jack Romanos; and Anthony Fredrickson for his exemplary maps. We also are especially grateful to Denise and Michael Okuda of the Banzai Institute, who saw to it that New Year's arrived on schedule, and to Hazel Perry for her Harley-Davidson expertise. And special thanks must be made to Jon Povill who, without knowing it, first inspired us to write this book.

We also must thank all the members of the U.S. military who contacted us about our previous book, *Icefire,* and kindly offered diplomatic comments and necessary corrections regarding military matters. We hope you will see your much-appreciated guidance reflected in these pages, along with our respect for your accomplishments and our gratitude for your mission.

For the record, TSS-1, the first tethered satellite experiment intended to generate electrical power by moving through the Earth's magnetic field, flew on the space shuttle *Atlantis,* flight STS-46, in 1992. On that mission, the tether jammed after only 250 meters had been deployed and no data relating to power generation was obtained. However, the experiment was considered by NASA to be so important that, even in a time of severe budgetary restraint, additional funds were allocated to allow the experiment to fly again, as TSS-1R (Tethered Satellite System Reflight) on STS-75, in 1996. That flight provided the unexpected results referred to by Major Sinclair.

Despite the fact that NASA reported the experiment's results require "rewriting the laws of physics," at the time of this writing, when NASA has the next 43 shuttle flights planned up to STS-136 in 2004, not one is publicly acknowledged to conduct additional tethered satellite experiments, almost as if the scientific community has lost interest in so fundamental a challenge to their understanding of the Earth's electromagnetic field.

However, ongoing orbital experiments with tethered satellite systems are still being conducted, not by the civilian agency, NASA, but by the Naval Research Laboratory and the National Reconnaissance Office, both operating within the Department of Defense. In their public announcements, these agencies emphasize that the tethered satellites they have launched are connected by "non-conductive" tethers, indicating that there is no attempt being made to explore the phenomenon which so startled scientists in 1996.

Even without the prodding of people who know better, we find the apparent abandonment of such an intriguing field of study to be an improbable scenario.

Finally, should you ever find yourself in an emergency

situation at the Pentagon, the emergency number used in this book has been fictionalized in order to avoid having ordinary citizens "try it out." In the event of ThreatCon Echo, please check your local directory.

J&G Reeves-Stevens
Los Angeles, April 1999
arcticflag@aol.com

Also from
bestselling authors

JUDITH & GARFIELD
REEVES-STEVENS

ICEFIRE

The most destructive
natural disaster in
history *isn't* natural...

POCKET STAR
BOOKS

2805-01